The Complete Dr. Thorndyke

Volume II:
Stories From

John Thorndyke's Cases
The Singing Bone
The Great Portrait Mystery
and
Apocryphal Material

The Complete Dr. Thorndyke

Volume II:
Stories From
John Thorndyke's Cases
The Singing Bone
The Great Portrait Mystery
and
Apocryphal Material

By

R. Austin Freeman

Edited by
David Marcum

ISBN Hardback 978-1-78705-394-6
ISBN Paperback 978-1-78705-395-3
AUK ePub ISBN 978-1-78705-396-0
AUK PDF ISBN 978-1-78705-397-7

These works are in the Public Domain in Great Britain
Portrait of Dr. Thorndyke by H.M. Brock (1908)
Selected illustrations from *John Thorndyke's Cases* and *The Singing Bone*
by H.M. Brock and Henry Raleigh

Published in the UK by
MX Publishing
335 Princess Park Manor, Royal Drive,
London, N11 3GX
www.mxpublishing.co.uk

David Marcum can be reached at:
thepapersofsherlockholmes@gmail.com

Cover design by Brian Belanger
www.belangerbooks.com and *www.redbubble.com/people/zhahadun*

CONTENTS

Introductions

Adventures

John Thorndyke's Cases

The Singing Bone

The Great Portrait Mystery

Apocrypha

The Complete Dr. Thorndyke

Volume II:
Stories From
John Thorndyke's Cases
The Singing Bone
The Great Portrait Mystery
and
Apocryphal Material

Dr. John Thorndyke

5A King's Bench Walk
in the late 1890's when
Thorndyke would have moved in

5A King's Bench Walk
Photographed by the Editor
during his
Sherlock Holmes Pilgrimage No. 3
(September 8th, 2016)

Meet Dr. Thorndyke
by R. Austin Freeman

My subject is Dr. John Thorndyke, the hero or central character of most of my detective stories. So I'll give you a short account of his real origin – of the way in which he did in fact come into existence.

To discover the origin of John Thorndyke I have to reach back into the past for at least fifty years, to the time when I was a medical student preparing for my final examination. For reasons which I need not go into I gave rather special attention to the legal aspects of medicine and the medical aspects of law. And as I read my text-books, and especially the illustrative cases, I was profoundly impressed by their dramatic quality. Medical jurisprudence deals with the human body in its relation to all kinds of legal problems. Thus its subject matter includes all sorts of crime against the person and all sorts of violent death and bodily injury: Hanging, drowning, poisons and their effects, problems of suicide and homicide, of personal identity and survivorship, and a host of other problems of the highest dramatic possibilities, though not always quite presentable for the purposes of fiction. And the reported cases which were given in illustration were often crime stories of the most thrilling interest. Cases of disputed identity such as the Tichbourne Case, famous poisoning cases such as the Rugeley Case and that of Madeline Smith, cases of mysterious disappearance or the detection of long-forgotten crimes such as that of Eugene Aram. All these, described and analysed with strict scientific accuracy, formed the matter of Medical Jurisprudence which thrilled me as I read and made an indelible impression.

But it produced no immediate results. I had to pass my examinations and get my diploma, and then look out for the means of earning my living. So all this curious lore was put away for the time being in the pigeon-holes of my mind – which Dr. Freud would call the *Unconscious* – not forgotten, but ready to come to the surface when the need for it should arise. And there it reposed for some twenty years, until failing health compelled me to abandon medical practice and take to literature as a profession.

It was then that my old studies recurred to my mind. A fellow doctor, Conan Doyle, had made a brilliant and well-deserved success by the creation of the immortal Sherlock Holmes. Considering that achievement, I asked myself whether it might not be possible to devise a detective story of a slightly different kind – one based on the science of Medical Jurisprudence, in which, by the sacrifice of a certain amount of dramatic

1

effect, one could keep entirely within the facts of real life, with nothing fictitious excepting the persons and the events. I came to the conclusion that it was, and began to turn the idea over in my mind.

But I think that the influence which finally determined the character of my detective stories, and incidentally the character of John Thorndyke, operated when I was working at the Westminster Ophthalmic Hospital. There I used to take the patients into the dark room, examine their eyes with the ophthalmoscope, estimate the errors of refraction, and construct an experimental pair of spectacles to correct those errors. When a perfect correction had been arrived at, the formula for it was embodied in a prescription which was sent to the optician who made the permanent spectacles.

Now when I was writing those prescriptions it was borne in on me that in many cases, especially the more complex, the formula for the spectacles, and consequently the spectacles themselves, furnished an infallible record of personal identity. If, for instance, such a pair of spectacles should have been found in a railway carriage, and the maker of those spectacles could be found, there would be practically conclusive evidence that a particular person had travelled by that train. About that time I drafted out a story based on a pair of spectacles, which was published some years later under the title of *The Mystery of 31 New Inn*, and the construction of that story determined, as I have said, not only the general character of my future work but of the hero around whom the plots were to be woven. But that story remained for some years in cold storage. My first published detective novel was *The Red Thumb-mark*, and in that book we may consider that John Thorndyke was born. And in passing on to describe him I may as well explain how and why he came to be the kind of person that he is.

I may begin by saying that he was not modelled after any real person. He was deliberately created to play a certain part, and the idea that was in my mind was that he should be such a person as would be likely and suitable to occupy such a position in real life. As he was to be a medico-legal expert, he had to be a doctor and a fully trained lawyer. On the physical side I endowed him with every kind of natural advantage. He is exceptionally tall, strong, and athletic because those qualities are useful in his vocation. For the same reason he has acute eyesight and hearing and considerable general manual skill, as every doctor ought to have. In appearance he is handsome and of an imposing presence, with a symmetrical face of the classical type and a Grecian nose. And here I may remark that his distinguished appearance is not merely a concession to my personal taste but is also a protest against the monsters of ugliness whom some detective writers have evolved.

These are quite opposed to natural truth. In real life a first-class man of any kind usually tends to be a good-looking man.

Mentally, Thorndyke is quite normal. He has no gifts of intuition or other supernormal mental qualities. He is just a highly intellectual man of great and varied knowledge with exceptionally acute reasoning powers and endowed with that invaluable asset, a scientific imagination (by a scientific imagination I mean that special faculty which marks the born investigator, the capacity to perceive the essential nature of a problem before the detailed evidence comes into sight). But he arrives at his conclusions by ordinary reasoning, which the reader can follow when he has been supplied with the facts, though the intricacy of the train of reasoning may at times call for an exposition at the end of the investigation.

Thorndyke has no eccentricities or oddities which might detract from the dignity of an eminent professional man, unless one excepts an unnatural liking for Trichinopoly cheroots. In manner he is quiet, reserved and self-contained, and rather markedly secretive, but of a kindly nature, though not sentimental, and addicted to occasional touches of dry humour. That is how Thorndyke appears to me.

As to his age. When he made his first bow to the reading public from the doorway of Number 4 King's Bench Walk he was between thirty-five and forty. As that was thirty years ago, he should now be over sixty-five. But he isn't. If I have to let him *"grow old along with me"* I need not saddle him with the infirmities of age, and I can (in his case) put the brake on the passing years. Probably he is not more than fifty after all!

Now a few words as to how Thorndyke goes to work. His methods are rather different from those of the detectives of the Sherlock Holmes school. They are more technical and more specialized. He is an investigator of crime but he is not a detective. The technique of Scotland Yard would be neither suitable nor possible to him. He is a medico-legal expert, and his methods are those of medico-legal science. In the investigation of a crime there are two entirely different methods of approach. One consists in the careful and laborious examination of a vast mass of small and commonplace detail: Inquiring into the movements of suspected and other persons, interrogating witnesses and checking their statements particularly as to times and places, tracing missing persons, and so forth – the aim being to accumulate a great body of circumstantial evidence which will ultimately disclose the solution of the problem. It is an admirable method, as the success of our police proves, and it is used with brilliant effect by at least one of our contemporary detective writers. But it is essentially a police method.

3

The other method consists in the search for some fact of high evidential value which can be demonstrated by physical methods and which constitutes conclusive proof of some important point. This method also is used by the police in suitable cases. Finger-prints are examples of this kind of evidence, and another instance is furnished by the Gutteridge murder. Here the microscopical examination of a cartridge-case proved conclusively that the murder had been committed with a particular revolver, a fact which incriminated the owner of that revolver and led to his conviction.

This is Thorndyke's procedure. It consists in the interrogation of things rather than persons, of the ascertainment of physical facts which can be made visible to eyes other than his own. And the facts which he seeks tend to be those which are apparent only to the trained eye of the medical practitioner.

I feel that I ought to say a few words about Thorndyke's two satellites, Jervis and Polton. As to the former, he is just the traditional narrator proper to this type of story. Some of my readers have complained that Dr. Jervis is rather slow in the uptake. But that is precisely his function. He is the expert misunderstander. His job is to observe and record all the facts, and to fail completely to perceive their significance. Thereby he gives the reader all the necessary information, and he affords Thorndyke the opportunity to expound its bearing on the case.

Polton is in a slightly different category. Although he is not drawn from any real person, he is associated in my mind with two actual individuals. One is a Mr. Pollard, who was the laboratory assistant in the hospital museum when I was a student, and who gave me many a valuable tip in matters of technique, and who, I hope, is still to the good. The other was a watch- and clock-maker of the name of Parsons – familiarly known as Uncle Parsons – who had premises in a basement near the Royal Exchange, and who was a man of boundless ingenuity and technical resource. Both of these I regard as collateral relatives, so to speak, of Nathaniel Polton. But his personality is not like either. His crinkly countenance is strictly his own copyright.

To return to Thorndyke, his rather technical methods have, for the purposes of fiction, advantages and disadvantages. The advantage is that his facts are demonstrably true, and often they are intrinsically interesting. The disadvantage is that they are frequently not matters of common knowledge, so that the reader may fail to recognize them or grasp their significance until they are explained. But this is the case with all classes of fiction. There is no type of character or story that can be made sympathetic and acceptable to every kind of reader. The personal equation affects the reading as well as the writing of a story.

4

R. Austin Freeman
(1862-1943)

5A King's Bench Walk
in the early 1900's when
Thorndyke was in practice

Dr. Thorndyke: In the Footsteps
of Sherlock Holmes
by David Marcum

When Sherlock Holmes began his practice as a "Consulting Detective", his ideas of scientific criminal investigations caused the London police to look upon him as a mere "theorist". He was perceived as an amateur to be tolerated, often with amusement – until, that is, his assistance was required. Then they were more than willing to come knocking upon his door, asking for whatever help that they could receive. And usually this help took the form of brilliant solutions to bizarre and otherwise insoluble problems.

Holmes espoused methods and ideas that were considered ludicrous in the late 1800's. For instance, his frustration knew no bounds when a crime scene was disturbed. Holmes realized that so much could be determined from the physical evidence – footprints, fibers, and spatters. The police were happy to trod into and disturb the evidence as if they were herds of field beasts, with the equivalent level of intelligence.

However, Holmes's methods, and the science behind catching criminals, eventually won out and became so important that it's hard to now imagine the world without them. Many of the exact same techniques and methods that he advocated are now standard practice. From being an amateur with unusual ideas, Holmes is now recognized around the world as The Great Detective. In 2002, Holmes received a posthumous Honorary Fellowship from the British Royal Society of Chemistry, based on the fact that he was beyond his time in using chemistry and chemical sciences as a means of solving crimes.

And before that, in 1985, Scotland Yard introduced *HOLMES* (*Home Office Large Major Enquiry System*), an elaborate computer system designed to process the masses of information collected and evaluated during a criminal investigation, in order to ensure that no vital clues are overlooked. This system, providing total compatibility and consistency between all the police forces of England, Scotland, Wales, and Northern Ireland, as well as the Royal Military Police, has since been upgraded by the improved *HOLMES 2* – and like the first version, there is absolutely no doubt as to who is being honored and memorialized for his work in dragging criminology out of the dark ages.

Many famous Great Detectives followed in Holmes's footsteps – Nero Wolfe and Ellery Queen, Hercule Poirot and Solar Pons – each with their own methods and techniques, but before they began their careers, and while Holmes was still in practice in Baker Street, another London consultant – Dr. John Thorndyke – opened his doors, using the scientific methods developed and perfected by Holmes and taking them to a whole new level of brilliance.

Meet Dr. Thorndyke

Dr. John Evelyn Thorndyke was born on July 4th, 1870. We don't know about where he was raised, or if he has any family. At no point will we be introduced to a more brilliant brother who sometimes *is* the British Government. He was educated at the medical school of St. Margaret's Hospital in London, and while there, he met fellow student Christopher Jervis. They became friends but, after completing school in 1895, they lost touch with one another. Over the next six years, Thorndyke remained at St. Margaret's, taking on various jobs, hanging "about the chemical and physical laboratories, the museum and *post mortem* room," and learning what he could. He obtained his M.D. and his Doctor of Sciences, and then was called to the bar in 1896.

He'd prepared himself with the hope of obtaining a position as a coroner, but he learned of the unexpected retirement of one of St. Margaret's lecturers in medical jurisprudence. He applied for the position and, rather to his own surprise, it was awarded to him. (He would continue to maintain his association with the hospital, going on to become the Medical Registrar, Pathologist, Curator of the Museum, and then Professor of Medical Jurisprudence, all while maintaining his own private consulting practice.

It was when Thorndyke was named lecturer that he obtained his chambers at 5A King's Bench Walk, in the Inner Temple, that amazing and historic area between Fleet Street and the River. Founded over eight-hundred years ago by the Knights Templar, it is one of the four Inns of Court, (along with the Middle Temple, Lincoln's Inn, and Gray's Inn.) The buildings along King's Bench Walk, and particularly No.'s 4, 5, and 6, have a great deal of historical significance – and not just because Dr. John Thorndyke practiced at 5A for a number of years.

Thorndyke was quite fortunate to obtain a suite of rooms on multiple floors at this location, which leads to speculation about his influence and resources – a question which has no answer. In any case, it was there that he opened his practice and began to wait for clients and cases. He also made the acquaintance of elderly Nathaniel Polton, that man-of-all-work with the crinkly smile who ran the household, as well as Thorndyke's upstairs laboratory.

Like Sherlock Holmes during those early years in the 1870's when he had rooms in Montague Street next to the British Museum and spent his vast amounts of free time learning his craft, Thorndyke also found a way to make the empty hours more useful. He had the unique idea of imagining increasingly complex crimes – often a murder or series of them, for instance – and then, when he had planned every single aspect of the crime, he would turn around and work out the solution from the other side. While doing this, he made extensive notes of each of these theoretical exercises, and retained them for their later usefulness when encountering real-life crimes.

His first legal case was *Regina v Gummer* in 1897. Sadly, no further information about this affair is ever revealed to us, but we may be certain that Thorndyke used his considerable skills to bring it to a satisfactory conclusion, adding to his reputation as he did so.

In the meantime, Jervis had a more unfortunate story. As his time at school ended, his funds ran out rather unexpectedly, and after paying his various fees, he was left with earning his living as a medical assistant, or sometimes serving as a *locum tenens*, moving from one low-paying and temporary job to another, with no prospects of improvement.

Jervis is unemployed on the morning of March 22nd, 1901 when he encounters Thorndyke a few doors up from 5A King's Bench Walk. The two friends are happy to see one another, and before long, Jervis is involved in an investigation that will change his life in several ways, as recounted in *The Red Thumb Mark*.

But it should not be assumed that every Thorndyke adventure is narrated by Jervis in a typical Watsonian manner. In fact, the very next book, *The Eye of Osiris*, is instead told from the perspective of one of Thorndyke's students, Dr. Paul Berkeley. It is one of several that provide a look at Thorndyke – and Jervis – from a different perspective. But Jervis returns as narrator in the third novel, *The Mystery of 31 New Inn*, and we see Thorndyke through his eyes for a good many of both the novels and short stories.

Here a word might be mentioned about the Chronology of the Thorndyke stories. For some this is an irrelevant factor, but for others – like me – understanding the correct chronological placement of the stories is very important. Like the volumes that make up the Sherlock Holmes Canon, the Thorndyke stories aren't published in chronological order – a case set in 1907 (such as "Percival Bland's Proxy") might be collected before one that occurs in 1908, ("The Missing Mortgagee"), or it might not. For instance, *The Red Thumb Mark* (1907) is set in March and April 1901. (This chronological placement, by the way, is determined by noticing that a specific date is given three times in the book – in the British fashion of day before month – *9.3.01* – or *March 9th, 1901.* The dates for the events of the rest of the book can be carefully worked out from this fixed point.)

The next book, *The Eye of Osiris* (1911) is primarily set in the summer of 1904 (with Chapter 1, something of a prologue, taking place in late 1902.) Then, the next book to follow, *The Mystery of 31 New Inn* (1912), jumps back to the spring of 1902, about a year after the events of *The Red Thumb Mark*, and before *The Eye of Osiris.* And one of the short stories, "The Man With the Nailed Shoes" occurs in September and October 1901, between the first two books. Clearly, there is a great deal of material for the chronologicist in the Thorndyke Chronicles.

As Jervis becomes a part of Thorndyke's world, following their reacquaintance in March 1901, he meets others in Thorndyke's circle, including policemen such as Superintendent Miller and Inspector Badger, lawyers like Robert Anstey, Marchmont, and Brodribb, and other physicians like Dr. Paul Berkeley and Dr. Humphrey Jardine. He also has more opportunity to learn from his friend as he begins his own studies in order to become a similar specialist in the medico-legal practice – although he'll never be another Thorndyke.

Through Jervis's eyes – as well as others along the way – we build up our knowledge of Dr. Thorndyke. In appearance, he is tall and athletic, just under six feet in height, slender, and weighing around one-hundred-and-eighty pounds. He is exceptionally handsome – and has been called the handsomest detective in literature. He has no vices, except – perhaps – that he enjoys a Trichinopoly cigar upon occasion when he is feeling especially triumphant – although there is one time when the criminal's knowledge of this fact leads to a clever attempt at Thorndyke's murder . . . .

There are several instances where Thorndyke displays a marked resemblance to Sherlock Holmes – and not just in his scientific approach to crime. The two men sometimes say similar things – such as when Holmes says *"It is quite a pretty little problem,"* (in "A Scandal in Bohemia") or *". . . there are some pretty little problems among them"* (in "The Musgrave Ritual"). Thorndyke mimics this in *Felo de Se? ("There, Jervis," said he, "is quite a pretty little problem for you to excogitate")* or *"Ah, there is a very pretty little problem for you to consider"* (in *The Eye of Osiris*).

And who can forget the many instances when Holmes refers to *data*:

- *"It is a capital mistake to theorize before one has data. Insensibly one begins to twist facts to suit theories, instead of theories to suit facts." – "*A Scandal in Bohemia"
- *"I had,"* said he, *"come to an entirely erroneous conclusion which shows, my dear Watson, how dangerous it always is to reason from insufficient data." –* "The Speckled Band"
- *"No data yet,"* he answered. *"It is a capital mistake to theorize before you have all the evidence. It biases the judgment." – A Study in Scarlet*
- *"The temptation to form premature theories upon insufficient data is the bane of our profession." – The Valley of Fear*
- *"Still, it is an error to argue in front of your data." –* "Wisteria Lodge"

Thorndyke's version? *". . . believe me, it is a capital error to decide beforehand what data are to be sought for." –* from *The Mystery of 31 New Inn.* There are others.

Then there is Holmes's quote from "The Man With the Twisted Lip":

"You have a grand gift of silence, Watson," said he. "It makes you quite invaluable as a companion."

Here's the Thorndyke equivalent:

"It has just been borne in upon me, Jervis," said he, "that you are the most companionable fellow in the world. You have the heaven-sent gift of silence."

And then there is the time, in "The Anthropologist at Large", that a client – expecting a Holmes-like performance as based on "The Blue Carbuncle" – presents Thorndyke with an object for examination:

"I understand," said he, "that by examining a hat it is possible to deduce from it, not only the bodily characteristics of the wearer, but also his mental and moral qualities, his state of health, his pecuniary position, his past history, and even his domestic relations and the peculiarities of his place of abode. Am I right in this supposition?"

The ghost of a smile flitted across Thorndyke's face as he laid the hat upon the remains of the newspaper. "We must not expect too much," he observed. "Hats, as you know, have a way of changing owners . . . ."

11

Another area of intersection between Holmes and Thorndyke is the assembly of information. Recall Holmes's *"ponderous commonplace books in which he placed his cuttings"* as mentioned in "The Engineer's Thumb". We find, also in "The Anthropologist at Large", that Thorndyke does the same thing:

> *[H]is method of dealing with [the morning newspaper] was characteristic. The paper was laid on the table after breakfast, together with a blue pencil and a pair of office shears. A preliminary glance through the sheets enabled him to mark with the pencil those paragraphs that were to be read, and these were presently cut out and looked through, after which they were either thrown away or set aside to be pasted in an indexed book.*

No doubt and examination of Thorndyke's lodgings at 5A King's Bench Walk would reveal – in addition to a series of indexed commonplace books filled with clippings – a number of other items and aspects that would remind one of 221b Baker Street.

Like many locations where the detective's residence is almost a character in and of itself – Sherlock Holmes's London address at 221 Baker Street, and the New York homes of Ellery Queen on West 87th Street and Nero Wolfe's Brownstone on West 35th Street – Thorndyke's rooms at 5A King's Bench Walk are a living and vibrant place – from the entry way, where a heavy door known as "The Oak" leads visitors into a most comfortable wood-paneled sitting room, located on the (British) first floor, one flight up from the ground floor. On the next floor up, Polton has his laboratory and workshop, containing everything that is needed (or what might be manufactured) in order to solve the case.

On the next floor, underneath the attic, are bedrooms belonging to Thorndyke, Jervis, and Polton. Even after Jervis has married – and now you know that he does get married! – he continues to reside a good deal of the time in King's Bench Walk. As he explains in *When Rogues Fall Out* (1932, with the U.S. title of *Dr. Thorndyke's Discovery*):

> *Here, perhaps, since my records of Thorndyke's practice have contained so little reference to my own personal affairs, I should say a few words concerning my domestic habits. As the circumstances of our practice often made it desirable for me to stay late at our chambers, I had retained there the bedroom that I had occupied before my marriage; and, as these*

*circumstances could not always be foreseen, I had arranged
with my wife the simple rule that the house closed at eleven
o'clock. If I was unable to get home by that time, it was to be
understood that I was staying at the Temple. It may sound like
a rather undomestic arrangement, but it worked quite
smoothly, and it was not without its advantages. For the brief
absence gave to my homecomings a certain festive quality,
and helped to keep alive the romantic element in my married
life. It is possible for the most devoted husbands and wives to
see too much of one another.*

Thorndyke's Other Appearances

Through the years, Thorndyke's reputation continues to grow, as presented through a number of adventures. Surprisingly, in light of the tens of thousands of Post-Canonical Sherlock Holmes that have come to light over the years, as discovered by latter-day Literary Agents taking over Watson's first Literary Agent, Sir Arthur Conan Doyle, stopped literary-agenting, there have been almost no additional Thorndyke cases brought to the public's attention. The few exceptions to this statement are *Goodbye, Dr. Thorndyke* (1972) by Norman Donaldson, and *Dr. Thorndyke's Dilemma* (1974) by John H. Dirckx. Both narratives deal with Thorndyke and Jervis in their latter years, and each is written by an expert in the field of Thorndyke scholarship.

Donaldson also wrote what might be the final scholarly word on the subject, *In Search of Dr. Thorndyke* (1971). In fact, he had intended his pastiche, *Goodbye, Dr. Thorndyke*, to be published as the conclusion to this book, but it ended up appearing separately.

To my knowledge, "The Great Fathomer", as Thorndyke is sometimes known, has rarely appeared in other locations. He is mentioned in the Solar Pons tale "The Adventure of the Proper Comma" by August Derleth, which finds Dr. Parker returning "from Thorndyke & Polton with an analysis of the capsules Mrs. Buxton had carried with her . . . ."

In my own book of authorized Solar Pons stories, *The Papers of Solar Pons* (2017), Thorndyke makes two appearances. "The Adventure of the Additional Heirs" has Pons and Parker visiting King's Bench Walk:

> *At 5A, we learned that our friend Thorndyke, the medical
> juris-practitioner, was out on some investigation or other, but
> Pons handed the papers,* sans *photograph, into the care of
> Polton, his crinkly-faced laboratory technician, with a
> detailed explanation of what he wished to learn. The man*

nodded and smiled, and without any extraneous chit-chat, shut the door, freeing us to return to Fleet Street. We paused at the edge of the walk to look at the photograph, still in Pons's hand.

Later Thorndyke sends Pons a detailed report that helps toward the solution of the problem. And in "The Affair of the Distasteful Society", set in July 1921, Pons and Parker attend the first meeting of a group gathered to honor Sherlock Holmes, where the following conversation occurs:

"I see that you invited Thorndyke, and that little Belgian over on Farraway Street," said Rath.
"And Sexton Blake as well," replied Sir Amory.
"Sexton Blake is a fictional character, Sir Amory," said Pons with a smile.

In my story, "The Adventure of the Two Sisters", to be included in an upcoming Solar Pons anthology, Dr. Parker writes:

Pons was not the only detective who offered his services to the London populace, although he might have been the most well-known. We were friends with several others, including the former Belgian policeman who lived in Farraway Street, and another rather mysterious fellow in nearby Bottle Street. And of course, Pons went way back with Thorndyke, whose chambers were across town. It wasn't unusual for Pons and the others to regularly confer on investigations, or simply to sit down and share a few drinks and professional anecdotes.

Thorndyke doesn't just appear in some of my Solar Pons adventures. He's also been referenced off-stage in a couple of Sherlock Holmes adventures that I've pulled from Watson's Tin Dispatch Box – and it's more than likely that others will follow. In "The "London Wheel", contained in *The MX Book of New Sherlock Holmes Stories – Part IV: 2016 Annual* (2016), Holmes, looking through some documents, states:

"I believe," said Holmes, "that I have enough amateur legal training that I can get a sense of the implications of the clauses in question in both of these documents." He pulled the folded pages from his pocket. "I thought about sending a message to my protégé *Thorndyke in King's Bench Walk for*

14

*his opinion, as he could have been here very quickly, should
he be at home at all and not out on his own business. However,
I don't believe that will be necessary.*

Perhaps it is a point of interest that Thorndyke is referred to Holmes's
protégé. Possibly more information will be forthcoming, such as that
which is hinted in my forthcoming story, "The Coombs Contrivance". Set
in 1889, when Thorndyke was nineteen years old, Holmes and Watson are
discussing a precocious Baker Street Irregular:

> *[Holmes] pinched the bridge of his nose. "Do you trust
> Levi's judgment, Watson?"*
> *I considered. "For an eight-year-old, he's remarkable
> perceptive – as much as any of the other Irregulars who have
> assisted you. The Wiggins family, or the Peakes, or
> Thorndyke, before he went away to university."*

So was Thorndyke, perhaps, a gifted Irregular who learned from The
Master, and then went on to create his own successful practice, taking what
he learned to a next very successful level? Possibly. As Robert Downey,
Jr. succinctly stated when playing Holmes in 2009's *Sherlock Holmes*:
"Food for thought!"

Thorndyke is also mentioned in Bob Byrne's Holmes story, "The
Adventure of the Parson's Son" (*The MX Book of New Sherlock Holmes
Stories – Part III: 1896-1929*), wherein Holmes, examining a piece of
evidence, cries:

> *"Ha! I believe we have discredited the coat entirely.
> Though I wish I could get Thorndyke to examine it. Would that
> we were back in London."*

And it isn't just Thorndyke who has appeared elsewhere. His lawyer
friend Marchmont has assisted Holmes and Watson in a small way a
couple of my own forthcoming adventures, *Sherlock Holmes and The
Eye of Heka* and "The Coombs Contrivance".

Although I have encouraged these Thorndyke cameos in my own
stories or in Holmes and Pons books that I edit, his appearances elsewhere
are much more fleeting. In the 2015 BBC radio series *The Rivals*, Inspector
Lestrade, Holmes's most frequent associate at Scotland Yard, is placed
into the events of the Thorndyke short story "The Moabite Cipher". And
Thorndyke has only had a handful of other media appearances. In 1964,

the BBC produced seven episodes (now mostly lost) of *Thorndyke*, starring Peter Copley. The episodes were:

- "The Case of Oscar Brodski'
- "The Old Lag"
- "A Case of Premeditation"
- "The Mysterious Visitor"
- "The Case of Phyllis Annesley" – Adapted from "Phyllis Annesley's Peril"
- "Percival Bland's Brother" – Adapted from "Percival Bland's Proxy"
- "The Puzzle Lock"

From 1971 to 1973, Thames TV aired *The Rivals of Sherlock Holmes*, and two stories were adapted: "A Message from the Deep Sea" starring John Neville (who had also played Holmes in 1965's *A Study in Terror*), and "The Moabite Cipher" starring Barrie Ingram. Except for a 1963 BBC Radio adaption of *Mr. Pottermack's Oversight*, and a few on-air readings by a single performer, there have been no other Thorndyke adaptations – which is a terrible shame, as the stories certainly lend themselves to visual and audible interpretations. Perhaps a new generation will discover Thorndyke, Jervis, and the rest, and they will find popularity once again, as they did more than a century ago.

Copley, Neville, and Ingram as Thorndyke

A Few (Hundred) Words About R. Austin Freeman
Thorndyke's Chronicler

Richard Austin Freeman was born on April 11, 1862 in the Soho district of London. He was the son of a skilled tailor and the youngest of five children. As he grew, it was expected that he would become a tailor as well, but instead he had an interest in natural history and medicine, and

16

so he obtained employment in a pharmacist's shop. While there, he qualified as an apothecary and could have gone on to manage the shop, but instead he began to study medicine at Middlesex Hospital.

Austin Freeman qualified as a physician in 1887, and in that same year he married. Faced with the twin facts of his new marital responsibilities and his very limited resources as a young doctor, he made the unusual decision to join the Colonial Service, spending the next seven years in Africa as an Assistant Colonial Surgeon. This continued until the early 1890's, when he contracted Blackwater Fever, an illness that eventually forced him to leave the service and return permanently to England.

For several years, he served as a *locum tenens* for various physicians, a bleak time in his life as he moved from job to job, his income low, and his health never quite recovered. (These experiences were reflected in the narratives of Doctors Jervis and Berkeley.) However, he supplemented his meager income and exercised his creativity during these years by beginning to write. His early publications included *Travels and Live in Ashanti and Jaman* (1898), recounting some of his African sojourns.

In 1900, Freeman obtained work as an assistant to Dr. John James Pitcairn (1860-1936) at Holloway Prison. Although he wasn't there for very long, the association between the two men was enough to turn Freeman's attention toward writing mysteries. Over the next few years, they co-wrote several under the pseudonym *Clifford Ashdown*, including *The Adventures of Romney Pringle* (1902), *The Further Adventures of Romney Pringle* (1903), *From a Surgeon's Diary* (1904-1905), and *The Queen's Treasure* (written around 1905-1906, and published posthumously in 1975.) The specifics of the two men's writing arrangement are unknown to the present day, although much research was carried out by Freeman scholar Percival Mason ("P.M.") Stone, who was actually able to confirm Pitcairn's involvement and influence. Following this association, which apparently helped to train Freeman to be a better writer and to focus on a recurring character, his luck changed, and he was able, within just a few years, to abandon the practice of medicine, which had never been successful, and become a professional author.

In approximately 1904, Freeman began developing a mystery novella based on a short job that he had held at the Western Ophthalmic Hospital. This effort, "31 New Inn", was published in 1905, and it is the true first Dr. Thorndyke story. In it, we meet narrator Dr. Christopher Jervis, working as a *locum tenens*, moving from practice to practice in the same bleak existence that Freeman had experienced. Jervis becomes involved with a patient that may or may not be in danger. Unsure what to do, he recalls his former classmate, the brilliant Dr. John Thorndyke.

Curiously, this novella, (included in Volume II of this newly reissued collection *The Complete Dr. Thorndyke*), has numerous references to the events of the first Thorndyke novel, *The Red Thumb Mark*, which would not be published until 1907. Much of Freeman's life is obscure and unknown, including his writing processes and milestones, but clearly, with so much already clearly defined in this novella about Thorndyke and Jervis, he had firmly established not only fixed aspects of their histories, but the plot of *The Red Thumb Mark* as well, several years before the book's publication. One wonders why he chose to first publish "31 New Inn", since it occurs chronologically a whole year *after* the events of *The Red Thumb Mark*.

Interestingly – at least to a chronologicist such as myself – the original novella of "31 New Inn" is specifically set in April 1900, as indicated internally. However, when it was later revised to become the third Thorndyke novel, *The Mystery of 31 New Inn*, (1912, and included in Volume I of *The Complete Dr. Thorndyke*), the narrative's date is changed to 1902 – which fits, since the events definitely occur after *The Red Thumb Mark*, which takes place in March and April 1901.

Like Rex Stout's Nero Wolfe, who seemed to have sprung fully formed from his creator's brow, Thorndyke and his world are well-defined and immediately real. Although certain characters are added to the circle through the years, the basic layout – with Thorndyke, Jervis, and Polton (the man-of-all-work crinkly-smiled assistant) are always at 5A, ready to spring into action when Jervis – or one of the other varied narrators who show up throughout the series – arrive with a curious problem.

Freeman had found his voice with the Thorndyke books and short stories, and he was able to make use of his lifelong interest in medicine and natural science – often conducting extensive experiments to work out exactly how the solutions in his stories could be discovered. And in Thorndyke's early days, Freeman was able to turn the literary form inside out with the creation of the "Inverted Mystery Story", wherein the criminal is known from the beginning – the motive is explained, the planning and execution of the crime are observed, and the miscreant is left to believe that all is well and that he'll never be caught. And then, in the second part of the story, Thorndyke enters to inexorably follow the trail that is completely invisible to everyone else, scraping away, layer by layer and point by point, until the truth is inevitably revealed.

As Freeman explained:

> *Some years ago I devised, as an experiment, an inverted detective story in two parts. The first part was a minute and detailed description of a crime, setting forth the antecedents,*

motives, and all attendant circumstances. The reader had seen the crime committed, knew all about the criminal, and was in possession of all the facts. It would have seemed that there was nothing left to tell. But I calculated that the reader would be so occupied with the crime that he would overlook the evidence. And so it turned out. The second part, which described the investigation of the crime, had to most readers the effect of new matter.

This format went on to be used by a great many authors through the years. For example several of the Lord Peter Wimsey narratives come close to being this type of story, and television's *Columbo* used this type of story-telling as its basis.

While these volumes are an attempt to reintroduce the modern reader to Thorndyke, and are a celebration of him and his world, it must be discussed at some point that Freeman held views that are unacceptable. Unlike Sir Arthur Conan Doyle, who spent his last decades championing spiritualism but never allowed it to creep into the Sherlock Holmes stories, Freeman sometimes did let his own prejudices make their way into the Thorndyke tales. In his book *Social Decay and Regeneration* (1921), he expressed his rather nationalistic view that England had become an "homogenized, restless, unionized working class". Worse, he inexcusably and detestably supported the eugenics movement, arguing that people with "undesirable" traits should not be allowed to reproduce by means such as "segregation, marriage restriction, and sterilization". He referred to immigrants as "Sub-Man", and argued that society needed to be protected from "degenerates of the destructive type."

Some have attempted to excuse his beliefs as being a product of his times. For instance, it has been written that he had a distrust of Jews because of the competition that his father, a tailor, had faced when Freeman was a boy. Later, he served in the Colonial Service in Africa during some of the worst years in terms of treatment of natives by the British, and as an older man, he existed in the Great Britain between the two wars when great upheavals disrupted much of what he had known and expected.

Sadly, there are occasional racial stereotypes and references in the Thorndyke books. As I explain in the *Editor's Caveat*, some of these stereotypes had to be unfortunately maintained within the story in order to accurately reflect the plot and the characters of those times. However, there are some words or phrases that were used in the original stories – vile racial epithets that have no business being repeated or perpetuated anywhere – that I have cheerfully and happily removed. (There weren't many of them, but any are too many.)

These books are intended to bring Dr. Thorndyke and his adventures to a new generation – and not to be an untouchable and sacred literary artifact, with every nasty stain preserved and archived for the historical record. As I warn in the *Caveat*, if readers find that they want to experience the original versions as they were first written, with those hateful words included, then they would be advised to go and seek out the original books, because you won't find that filth here. These versions celebrate Dr. Thorndyke and Dr. Jervis – who do not use the awful stereotyped language, I'm glad to say! – and as such, I felt no need whatsoever to include and perpetuate the objectionable and offensive material

From Thorndyke's creation until 1914, Freeman wrote four novels and two volumes of short stories. Then, with the commencement of the First World War, he entered military service. In February 1915, at the age of fifty-two, he joined the Royal Army Medical Corps. Due to his health, which had never entirely recovered from his time in Africa, he spent the duration of the war involved with various aspects of the ambulance corps, having been promoted very early to the rank of Captain. He wrote nothing about Thorndyke during this period, but he did publish one book concerning the adventures of a scoundrel, *The Exploits of Danby Croker* (1916).

Following the war, he resumed his previous life, writing approximately one Thorndyke novel per year, as well as three more volumes of Thorndyke short stories and a number of other unrelated items, until his death on September 28th, 1943 – likely related to Parkinson's Disease, which had plagued him in later years.

Upon learning the news, *Chicago Tribune* columnist Vincent Starrett wrote:

> *When all the bright young things have performed their appointed task of flatting the complexes of neurotic semi-literates, and have gone their way to oblivion, the best of the Thorndyke stories will live on – minor classics on the shelf that holds the good books the world.*

Raymond Chandler wrote in his famous essay, which initially appeared in a couple of magazines and then was published in the book of the same name, *The Simple Art of Murder* (1950):

This man Austin Freeman is a wonderful performer. He has no equal in his genre, and he is also a much better writer than you might think, if you were superficially inclined, because in spite of the immense leisure of his writing, he accomplishes an even suspense which is quite unexpected . . . There is even a gaslight charm about his Victorian love affairs, and those wonderful walks across London.

In the introduction to *Great Stories of Detection, Mystery, and Horror* (1928), Dorothy L. Sayers, Chronicler of Lord Peter Wimsey, stated:

Thorndyke will cheerfully show you all the facts. You will be none the wiser . . . .

Discovering Dr. Thorndyke

I first encountered Dr. Thorndyke in a rather backwards way – in passing only – and it took several decades to correct that mistake. In approximately 1980, my dad gave me Otto Penzler's *The Private Lives of Private Eyes, Spies, Crime Fighters, and Other Good Guys* (1977). This wonderful oversized book has biographies of twenty-five well-known heroes, along with lists of the original books featuring each one.

My dad bought it for me because it had a chapter about Sherlock Holmes. There were a few others in there that I recognized or had already read about– Ellery Queen and Perry Mason – and soon I would become fanatical about a few more – Nero Wolfe and Hercule Poirot. Over the next few years I would also find the chapters on James Bond and Lew Archer indispensable, and later than that I would come to appreciate the entries about Philip Marlowe, Sam Spade, Miss Marple, Philo Vance, and Lord Peter Wimsey. But there were a few that, to this day, I've never bothered to read – such as Modesty Blaise or Mr. Moto – and a few others that I skimmed but otherwise ignored. And one of these was the biography of Dr. Thorndyke.

That fact was easily understandable, as throughout the entire time that I was growing up in eastern Tennessee – and in the years since as well – I've never come across a Thorndyke book for sale here in the wild, either in a new bookstore or in a used one. If I'd found one, I might have bought and read it, liked it, and then sought out others. Instead, I was bound to discover Thorndyke by way of Sherlock Holmes.

I've been collecting traditional Sherlock Holmes pastiches since the same time that I discovered the Sherlockian Canon, when I was ten years old in 1975. Since that time, I've collected, read, and chronologicized literally thousands of them. It never gets old, and I'm constantly looking for more – and that means checking Amazon to see what new releases are on the horizon.

In 2012, someone – and I've never determined who – began releasing a variety of Holmes stories for Kindle under the author name *Dr. John H. Watson.* This wasn't too unusual – there have been a number of pastiches that officially list Watson as the author, rather than putting the editor of Watson's papers first. Of course, after determining that these latest entries weren't going to be available as real books, I bought the e-versions, and then printed them on real paper. (I cannot stand e-books – ephemeral electronic blips that you lease instead of buy. I'll only buy those titles if they aren't going to be released as legitimate books – and in this case, it's a good thing that I did, as each of these Kindle stories that I found and paid for were soon withdrawn.)

As I read these latest "Holmes" stories, I noticed that each had a definite style that captured the writing from the late 1800's or early 1900's. (No matter how modern pasticheurs try to achieve that, they never quite pull it off.) But in one of the first two or three titles that I read, I caught a couple of mistakes. In one story, Holmes and Watson leave 221 Baker Street and are immediately in the area around The Temple and Fleet Street, rather than in Marylebone, where Baker Street is properly located. On another occasion, the story's policeman – who had been identified up to that point as Inspector Lestrade – was inexplicably named *Superintendent Miller* – but only in one instance. And in another place in one of the stories, Holmes's address was stated to be *5A King's Bench Walk*.

It was then that some vague memory triggered in my head, and I realized why these stories had captured the style of the late Victorian and early Edwardian eras: *It was because they had actually been written then.* I recalled – from reading Otto Penzler's book of biographies so long ago - that 5A King's Bench Walk belonged to Dr. Thorndyke, and not Sherlock Holmes. Someone was taking the original Thorndyke stories, which I had never before read, and simply changing names: Dr. Thorndyke, Dr. Jervis, and Superintendent Miller became Sherlock Holmes, Dr. Watson, and Inspector Lestrade, respectively.

Between 2012 and 2014, the anonymous author continued to load new Kindle editions on Amazon of Thorndyke-converted to-Holmes stories, and I continued to buy them. As soon as I had one, I would read it, and then try to figure out the original Thorndyke story from which it was taken. When I'd done so, I'd post a review, identifying what this editor was doing, from where he or she was taking the story, and urging that person, whoever it was, give credit to R. Austin Freeman instead of listing the author as Dr. John H. Watson.

Soon after each of my reviews would appear, the story would be withdrawn. I don't know if it was because the editor had made enough money from the initial sales, or if my reviews alerted him or her that they're game had been uncovered. In any case, I still have the printed copies of each of these converted stories – possibly the only copies that are still in existence.

For the record, over that two year period, this editor produced sixteen converted tales – four of the original Thorndyke novels, and twelve short stories. One of the original short stories, "The Mandarin's Pearl", was converted twice, with slight variations – initially published as "The Dragon Pearl", withdrawn, and later revised and reloaded as "The Oriental Pearl":

- "The Bloodied Thumbprint" – Originally the first Thorndyke novel, *The Red Thumb Mark*;
- "The Eye of Ra" – Originally the second Thorndyke novel, *The Eye of Osiris*;
- "The Cat's Eye Mystery" – Originally the sixth Thorndyke novel, *The Cat's Eye*;
- "The Julius Dalton Mystery" – Originally the ninth Thorndyke novel, *The D'Arblay Mystery*;
- "The Green Jacket Mystery" – Originally "The Green Check Jacket";
- "Mr. Crofton's Disappearance" – Originally "The Mysterious Visitor";
- "The Coded Lock" – Originally "The Puzzle Lock";
- "The Duplicated Letter" – Originally "The Stalking Horse";
- "The Bullion Robbery" – Originally "The Stolen Ingots";
- "The Talking Corpse" – Originally "The Contents of a Mare's Nest";
- "The Blue Diamond Mystery" – Originally "The Fisher of Men";
- "The Dragon Pearl" – Originally "The Mandarin's Pearl". (This story was also reworked and published again as a Holmes story under the title "The Oriental Pearl");
- "The Ingenious Murder" – Originally "The Aluminium Dagger";

- "The Bloodhound Superstition" – Originally "The Singing Bone"; *and*
- "The Magic Box" – Originally "The Magic Casket".

For quite a while, I was happy to have these as Holmes stories, and I even considered converting the rest of the Thorndyke adventures into additions to the extended Holmes Canon as well. (For at that time I cared nothing for Dr. Thorndyke.) It was partly with these converted stories in mind that I was motivated to go ahead and publish *Sherlock Holmes in Montague Street* (2014, 2016), which did the same thing to the Martin Hewitt stories, making them early adventures of Holmes before he met Watson and moved to Baker Street. I had long before decided to my own satisfaction that Martin Hewitt *was* a young Sherlock Holmes, with his identity changed through the preparations of a different literary agent than Sir Arthur Conan Doyle.

The taking of old public-domain stories featuring other detectives as the main protagonists and switching them so that Holmes is the main character has also been done by Alan Lance Andersen for his collection *The Affairs of Sherlock Holmes* (2015, 2016), wherein various non-series Sax Rohmer stories from nearly a hundred years ago were reworked as Holmes tales. Other non-Holmes authors have sometimes done the same thing. Raymond Chandler revised some of his early short stories so that the original characters' names were changed to Philip Marlowe. Ross MacDonald – (Kenneth Millar) also rewrote his old stories as well, making them into Lew Archer cases instead. More recently, the British ITV series *Marple* has taken non-Miss Marple Agatha Christie stories and converted them into episodes featuring that character.

So I had no problems with this type of change – and still don't. In fact, in my foreword to *Sherlock Holmes of Montague Street*, I wrote that I would rather have these converted Thorndyke stories as Holmes adventures, because I would rather read about Holmes than Thorndyke. But gradually my mind began to change, and I became more curious about Thorndyke, as presented in the proper fashion.

In 2013, I was able to go to London, as well as other places in England and Scotland, on the first (of three so far) Holmes Pilgrimages. For the most part, if a location wasn't related to Holmes, I didn't visit it. There were a few exceptions – I did intentionally visit Solar Pons's house at 7B Praed Street, Hercule Poirot's two residences, James Bond's flat in Chelsea – but everything else was pretty much pure Holmes.

One day, during my Holmesian rambles, I was making my way east down Fleet Street, and I visited both of the possible locations of "Pope's

Court" (as featured in "The Red-Headed League"), Poppin's Court and Mitre Court. (The latter is also one of the locations where Denis Nayland Smith and Dr. Petrie had quarters in some of the Fu Manchu books.) I decided that Mitre Court was certainly the original of "Pope's Court", and I passed through it to find myself unexpectedly in The Temple.

That's the amazing thing about a Holmes Pilgrimage to London – one travels to a site and finds two more very close by. I had planned to visit The Temple, but hadn't realized that I was so close. And now here I was – and more interesting was the fact that I was walking along King's Bench Walk, which runs downhill from the Miter Court passage. I recalled that Thorndyke had lived at 5A, so I made my way there – but without too much awe on that day, because I hadn't actually read any Thorndyke adventures yet – just some converted Holmes stories.

After I returned home, the thought of that side-trip to Thorndyke's front door stuck in my mind, and I sought out and read the first novel in the series, *The Red Thumb Mark.* I was so impressed that I kept going, and discovered a wonderful series of books and stories – fascinating characters and mysteries, and very evocative descriptions of both the London and the countryside of those times.

When I returned on my second Holmes Pilgrimage in 2015, I took the second Thorndyke book with me, reading it while there – while also reading Holmes stories too, of course! This one, *The Eye of Osiris*, has a great deal of London atmosphere, and I spent part of one late afternoon tracking down locations in this book – or what's now left of them – in the area around Fetter Lane to the north of Thorndyke's home in The Temple. It was truly unforgettable.

And of course I made an intentional stop at King's Bench Walk on that 2015 trip, and again on Holmes Pilgrimage No. 3 in 2016. By that point I was a Thorndyke fan, and I took the trouble to write to the current occupiers of 5A before I traveled to see if I could step inside and perhaps spend a moment in Thorndyke's old quarters. Sadly, they did not respond – either because it was simply beneath them to do so, or possibly because they get too many people like me who want to make a literary pilgrimage to what is a functioning and thriving business location.

While making photographs at Thorndyke's old doorway, I had several chances to go inside when someone else would enter or leave – My ever-present deerstalker and I could have simply been bold enough to slip in and then talk my way onward. It worked at other places on my Holmes Pilgrimages – the laboratory at Barts where Holmes and Watson met, for instance, and the site of the (former?) Diogenes Club at No. 78 Pall Mall, where they acted just oddly enough to make me think that the club is still there. But for some reason, barging into Thorndyke's old chambers without proper permission didn't feel quite right. But if or when I make Holmes Pilgrimage No. 4, I'll definitely make an even greater effort to see the doctor's former rooms.

The Editor and his deerstalker at 5A King's Bench Walk
September 2016

With many thanks . . . .

These last few years have been an amazing ride, and I've been able to play in the Sherlockian sandbox more than I'd ever imagined. (And subsequently, the Solar Pons sandbox, and now Thorndyke, too! Along the way, I've been able to meet some incredible people, both in person and in the modern electronic way, and also I've been able to read several hundred new Holmes adventures, as well as to be able to share them with others.

Still, what is most important is my amazingly wonderful wife (of over thirty years!) Rebecca, and our truly awesome son and my friend, Dan. I love you both, and you are everything to me! I am the luckiest guy in the world.

I have all the gratitude in the world for everyone that I've encountered along the way – It's an undeniable fact that Sherlock Holmes authors are the *best* people! I'd like to thank those who offer support, encouragement, and friendship, sometimes patiently waiting on me to reply as my time is directed in many other directions. Many many thanks to (in alphabetical order): Brian Belanger, Derrick Belanger, Bob Byrne, Roger Johnson, Mark Mower, Denis Smith, Tom Turley, Dan Victor, and Marcia Wilson.

In particular, I'd also like to especially thank Steve Emecz, who is always supportive of every idea that I pitch. It's been my particular good fortune that he crossed my path – it changed my life in a way that would have never happened otherwise, and I'm grateful for every opportunity!

I hope that these books will provide pleasure to those discovering Dr. Thorndyke for the first time, and to others who have known him for a long time. As always, I approach these matters from a Sherlockian perspective, so of course these stories, to me, are a peripheral extension of Holmes's world, and as such they are just more tiny threads woven into the ongoing Great Holmes Tapestry. However, they are wonderful on their own, and however one reads them, I wish great joy upon the journey.

David Marcum
October 2018

Questions, comments, and story submissions
may be addressed to David Marcum at
thepapersofsherlockholmes@gmail.com

5A King's Bench Walk
in the late 1890's when
Thorndyke was in residence

Editor's *Caveat*

These stories have been prepared using modern text-converting software, and as such, occasional deviations in punctuation have occurred. Those who absolutely must have the original version, down to each jot and dash, should understand that this version was created in order to present Dr. Thorndyke's adventures to a modern audience, and not to preserve an absolute pristine model for the historical archives.

Similarly, these stories were written in a time when racial prejudice and stereotypes were much more common than today. While some of these stereotypes must be unfortunately maintained within the story in order to accurately reflect the plot and the characters of those times, there are some words that were used in the original stories – vile racial epithets that have no business being repeated or perpetuated anywhere – that I have cheerfully removed. (There weren't many of them, but *any* are *too many*.)

If readers find that they want to experience the original versions as they were first written, with those hateful and ignorant words included, then they would be advised to seek out the original books. These versions celebrate Dr. Thorndyke and Dr. Jervis – who do *not* use the awful stereotyped language, I'm glad to say! – and as such, I felt no need whatsoever to include objectionable and offensive material simply for the sake of honoring or archiving the historical record.

David Marcum
Editor

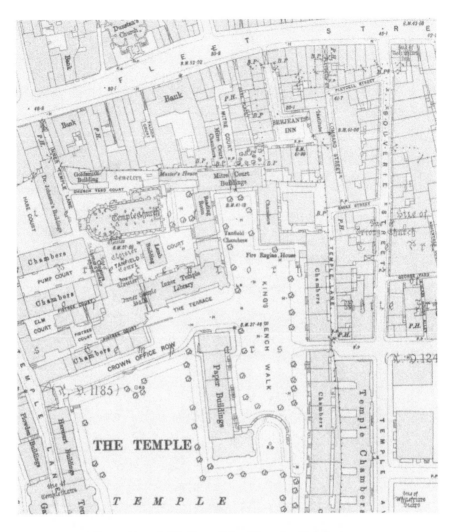

King's Bench Walk and the Temple, London
around 1900

33

JOHN THORNDYKE'S CASES

1909 Chatto and Windus Cover

Related by Christopher Jervis, M.D.

BY

R. AUSTIN FREEMAN

Preface

The stories in this collection, inasmuch as they constitute a somewhat new departure in this class of literature, require a few words of introduction. The primary function of all fiction is to furnish entertainment to the reader, and this fact has not been lost sight of. But the interest of so-called "detective" fiction is, I believe, greatly enhanced by a careful adherence to the probable, and a strict avoidance of physical impossibilities – and, in accordance with this belief, I have been scrupulous in confining myself to authentic facts and practicable methods. The stories have, for the most part, a medico-legal motive, and the methods of solution described in them are similar to those employed in actual practice by medical jurists. The stories illustrate, in fact, the application to the detection of crime of the ordinary methods of scientific research. I may add that the experiments described have in all cases been performed by me, and that the micro-photographs are, of course, from the actual specimens.

I take this opportunity of thanking those of my friends who have in various ways assisted me, and especially the friend to whom I have dedicated this book, by whom I have been relieved of the very considerable labour of making the micro-photographs, and greatly assisted in procuring and preparing specimens. I must also thank Messrs. Pearson for kindly allowing me the use of Mr. H. M. Brock's admirable and sympathetic drawings, and the artist himself for the care with which he has maintained strict fidelity to the text.

R. A. F.

Gravesend,
September 21, 1909.

To my friend
Frank Standfield
In memory of many a pleasant evening
spent with microscope and camera
this volume is dedicated

The Man With the Nailed Shoes

There are, I suppose, few places even on the East Coast of England more lonely and remote than the village of Little Sundersley and the country that surrounds it. Far from any railway, and some miles distant from any considerable town, it remains an outpost of civilization, in which primitive manners and customs and old-world tradition linger on into an age that has elsewhere forgotten them. In the summer, it is true, a small contingent of visitors, adventurous in spirit, though mostly of sedate and solitary habits, make their appearance to swell its meagre population, and impart to the wide stretches of smooth sand that fringe its shores a fleeting air of life and sober gaiety, but in late September – the season of the year in which I made its acquaintance – its pasture-lands lie desolate, the rugged paths along the cliffs are seldom trodden by human foot, and the sands are a desert waste on which, for days together, no footprint appears save that left by some passing sea-bird.

I had been assured by my medical agent, Mr. Turcival, that I should find the practice of which I was now taking charge "an exceedingly soft billet, and suitable for a studious man," and certainly he had not misled me, for the patients were, in fact, so few that I was quite concerned for my principal, and rather dull for want of work. Hence, when my friend John Thorndyke, the well-known medico-legal expert, proposed to come down and stay with me for a weekend and perhaps a few days beyond, I hailed the proposal with delight, and welcomed him with open arms.

"You certainly don't seem to be overworked, Jervis," he remarked, as we turned out of the gate after tea, on the day of his arrival, for a stroll on the shore. "Is this a new practice, or an old one in a state of senile decay?"

"Why, the fact is," I answered, "there is virtually no practice. Cooper – my principal – has been here about six years, and as he has private means he has never made any serious effort to build one up, and the other man, Dr. Burrows, being uncommonly keen, and the people very conservative, Cooper has never really got his foot in. However, it doesn't seem to trouble him."

"Well, if he is satisfied, I suppose you are," said Thorndyke, with a smile. "You are getting a seaside holiday, and being paid for it. But I didn't know you were as near to the sea as this."

We were entering, as he spoke, an artificial gap-way cut through the low cliff, forming a steep cart-track down to the shore. It was locally known as Sundersley Gap, and was used principally, when used at all, by the farmers' carts which came down to gather seaweed after a gale.

"What a magnificent stretch of sand!" continued Thorndyke, as we reached the bottom, and stood looking out seaward across the deserted beach. "There is something very majestic and solemn in a great expanse of sandy shore when the tide is out, and I know of nothing which is capable of conveying the impression of solitude so completely. The smooth, unbroken surface not only displays itself untenanted for the moment, but it offers convincing testimony that it has lain thus undisturbed through a considerable lapse of time. Here, for instance, we have clear evidence that for several days only two pairs of feet besides our own have trodden this gap."

"How do you arrive at the 'several days'?" I asked.

"In the simplest manner possible," he replied. "The moon is now in the third quarter, and the tides are consequently neap-tides. You can see quite plainly the two lines of seaweed and jetsam which indicate the high-water marks of the spring-tides and the neap-tides respectively. The strip of comparatively dry sand between them, over which the water has not risen for several days, is, as you see, marked by only two sets of footprints, and those footprints will not be completely obliterated by the sea until the next spring-tide – nearly a week from to-day."

"Yes, I see now, and the thing appears obvious enough when one has heard the explanation. But it is really rather odd that no one should have passed through this gap for days, and then that four persons should have come here within quite a short interval of one another."

"What makes you think they have done so?" Thorndyke asked.

"Well," I replied, "both of these sets of footprints appear to be quite fresh, and to have been made about the same time."

"Not at the same time, Jervis," rejoined Thorndyke. "There is certainly an interval of several hours between them, though precisely how many hours we cannot judge, since there has been so little wind lately to disturb them, but the fisherman unquestionably passed here not more than three hours ago, and I should say probably within an hour, whereas the other man – who seems to have come up from a boat to fetch something of considerable weight – returned through the gap certainly not less, and probably more, than four hours ago."

I gazed at my friend in blank astonishment, for these events befell in the days before I had joined him as his assistant, and his special knowledge and powers of inference were not then fully appreciated by me.

"It is clear, Thorndyke," I said, "that footprints have a very different meaning to you from what they have for me. I don't see in the least how you have reached any of these conclusions."

"I suppose not," was the reply, "but, you see, special knowledge of this kind is the stock-in-trade of the medical jurist, and has to be acquired by special study, though the present example is one of the greatest simplicity. But let us consider it point by point, and first we will take this set of footprints which I have inferred to be a fisherman's. Note their enormous size. They should be the footprints of a giant. But the length of the stride shows that they were made by a rather short man. Then observe the massiveness of the soles, and the fact that there are no nails in them. Note also the peculiar clumsy tread – the deep toe and heel marks, as if the walker had wooden legs, or fixed ankles and knees. From that character we can safely infer high boots of thick, rigid leather, so that we can diagnose high boots, massive and stiff, with nailless soles, and many sizes too large for the wearer. But the only boot that answers this description is the fisherman's thigh-boot – made of enormous size to enable him to wear in the winter two or three pairs of thick knitted stockings, one over the other. Now look at the other footprints, there is a double track, you see, one set coming from the sea and one going towards it. As the man (who was bow-legged and turned his toes in) has trodden in his own footprints, it is obvious that he came from the sea, and returned to it. But observe the difference in the two sets of prints, the returning ones are much deeper than the others, and the stride much shorter. Evidently he was carrying something when he returned, and that something was very heavy. Moreover, we can see, by the greater depth of the toe impressions, that he was stooping forward as he walked, and so probably carried the weight on his back. Is that quite clear?"

"Perfectly," I replied. "But how do you arrive at the interval of time between the visits of the two men?"

"That also is quite simple. The tide is now about halfway out. It is thus about three hours since high water. Now, the fisherman walked just about the neap-tide, high-water mark, sometimes above it and sometimes below. But none of his footprints have been obliterated. Therefore he passed after high water – that is, less than three hours ago, and since his footprints are all equally distinct, he could not have passed when the sand was very wet. Therefore he probably passed less than an hour ago. The other man's footprints, on the other hand, reach only to the neap-tide, high-water mark, where they end abruptly. The sea has washed over the remainder of the tracks and obliterated them. Therefore he passed not less than three hours and not more than four days ago – probably within twenty-four hours."

As Thorndyke concluded his demonstration the sound of voices was borne to us from above, mingled with the tramping of feet, and immediately afterwards a very singular party appeared at the head of the gap descending towards the shore. First came a short burly fisherman clad in oilskins and sou'-wester, clumping along awkwardly in his great sea-boots, then the local police-sergeant in company with my professional rival Dr. Burrows, while the rear of the procession was brought up by two constables carrying a stretcher. As he reached the bottom of the gap the fisherman, who was evidently acting as guide, turned along the shore, retracing his own tracks, and the procession followed in his wake.

"A surgeon, a stretcher, two constables, and a police-sergeant," observed Thorndyke. "What does that suggest to your mind, Jervis?"

"A fall from the cliff," I replied, "or a body washed up on the shore."

"Probably," he rejoined, "but we may as well walk in that direction."

We turned to follow the retreating procession, and as we strode along the smooth surface left by the retiring tide Thorndyke resumed.

"The subject of footprints has always interested me deeply for two reasons. First, the evidence furnished by footprints is constantly being brought forward, and is often of cardinal importance, and, secondly, the whole subject is capable of really systematic and scientific treatment. In the main the data are anatomical, but age, sex, occupation, health, and disease all give their various indications. Clearly, for instance, the footprints of an old man will differ from those of a young man of the same height, and I need not point out to you that those of a person suffering from *locomotor ataxia* or *paralysis agitans* would be quite unmistakable."

"Yes, I see that plainly enough," I said.

"Here, now," he continued, "is a case in point." He halted to point with his stick at a row of footprints that appeared suddenly above high-water mark, and having proceeded a short distance, crossed the line again, and vanished where the waves had washed over them. They were easily distinguished from any of the others by the clear impressions of circular rubber heels.

"Do you see anything remarkable about them?" he asked.

"I notice that they are considerably deeper than our own," I answered.

"Yes, and the boots are about the same size as ours, whereas the stride is considerably shorter – quite a short stride, in fact. Now there is a pretty constant ratio between the length of the foot and the length of the leg, between the length of leg and the height of the person, and between the stature and the length of stride. A long foot means a long leg, a tall man, and a long stride. But here we have a long foot and a short stride. What do you make of that?" He laid down his stick – a smooth partridge cane, one side of which was marked by small lines into inches and feet – beside the footprints to demonstrate the discrepancy.

"The depth of the footprints shows that he was a much heavier man than either of us," I suggested, "perhaps he was unusually fat."

"Yes," said Thorndyke, "that seems to be the explanation. The carrying of a dead weight shortens the stride, and fat is practically a dead weight. The conclusion is that he was about five feet ten inches high, and excessively fat." He picked up his cane, and we resumed our walk, keeping an eye on the procession ahead until it had disappeared round a curve in the coast-line, when we mended our pace somewhat. Presently we reached a small headland, and, turning the shoulder of cliff, came full upon the party which had preceded us. The men had halted in a narrow bay, and now stood looking down at a prostrate figure beside which the surgeon was kneeling.

"We were wrong, you see," observed Thorndyke. "He has not fallen over the cliff, nor has he been washed up by the sea. He is lying above high-water mark, and those footprints that we have been examining appear to be his."

As we approached, the sergeant turned and held up his hand.

"I'll ask you not to walk round the body just now, gentlemen," he said. "There seems to have been foul play here, and I want to be clear about the tracks before anyone crosses them."

Acknowledging this caution, we advanced to where the constables were standing, and looked down with some curiosity at the dead man. He was a tall, frail-looking man, thin to the point of emaciation, and appeared to be about thirty-five years of age. He lay in an easy posture, with half-closed eyes and a placid expression that contrasted strangely enough with the tragic circumstances of his death.

"It is a clear case of murder," said Dr. Burrows, dusting the sand from his knees as he stood up. "There is a deep knife-wound above the heart, which must have caused death almost instantaneously."

"How long should you say he has been dead, Doctor?" asked the sergeant.

"Twelve hours at least," was the reply. "He is quite cold and stiff."

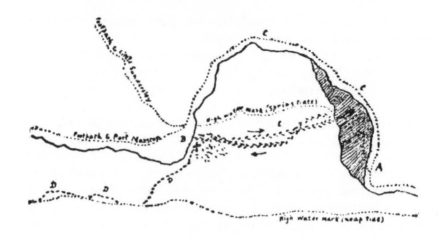

PLAN OF ST. BRIDGET'S BAY
+ Position of the Body
A: Top of Shepherd's Path
B: Overhanging Cliff
C: Footpath along Edge of Cliff
D D D: Tracks of Hearn's Shoes
E: Tracks of the Nailed Shoes
F: Shepherd's Path Ascending Shelving Cliff

"Twelve hours, eh?" repeated the officer. "That would bring it to about six o'clock this morning."

"I won't commit myself to a definite time," said Dr. Burrows hastily. "I only say not less than twelve hours. It might have been considerably more."

"Ah" said the sergeant. "Well, he made a pretty good fight for his life, to all appearances." He nodded at the sand, which for some feet around the body bore the deeply indented marks of feet, as though a furious struggle had taken place. "It's a mighty queer affair," pursued the sergeant, addressing Dr. Burrows. "There seems to have been only one man in it – there is only one set of footprints besides those of the deceased – and we've got to find out who he is, and I reckon there won't be much trouble about that, seeing the kind of trade-marks he has left behind him."

"No," agreed the surgeon, "there ought not to be much trouble in identifying those boots. He would seem to be a labourer, judging by the hob-nails."

"No, sir, not a labourer," dissented the sergeant. "The foot is too small, for one thing, and then the nails are not regular hob-nails. They're a good deal smaller, and a labourer's boots would have the nails all round the edges, and there would be iron tips on the heels, and probably on the toes too. Now these have got no tips, and the nails are arranged in a pattern on the soles and heels. They are probably shooting-boots or sporting shoes of some kind." He strode to and fro with his notebook in his hand, writing down hasty memoranda, and stooping to scrutinize the impressions in the sand. The surgeon also busied himself in noting down the facts concerning which he would have to give evidence, while Thorndyke regarded in silence and with an air of intense preoccupation the footprints around the body which remained to testify to the circumstances of the crime.

"It is pretty clear, up to a certain point," the sergeant observed, as he concluded his investigations, "how the affair happened, and it is pretty clear, too, that the murder was premeditated. You see, Doctor, the deceased gentleman, Mr. Hearn, was apparently walking home from Port Marston. We saw his footprints along the shore – those rubber heels make them easy to identify – and he didn't go down Sundersley Gap. He probably meant to climb up the cliff by that little track that you see there, which the people about here call the Shepherd's Path. Now the murderer must have known that he was coming, and waited upon the cliff to keep a lookout. When he saw Mr. Hearn enter the bay, he came down the path and attacked him, and, after a tough struggle, succeeded in stabbing him. Then he turned and went back up the path. You can see the double track between the path and the place where the struggle took place, and the footprints going to the path are on top of those coming from it."

"If you follow the tracks," said Dr. Burrows, "you ought to be able to see where the murderer went to."

"I'm afraid not," replied the sergeant. "There are no marks on the path itself – the rock is too hard, and so is the ground above, I fear. But I'll go over it carefully all the same."

The investigations being so far concluded, the body was lifted on to the stretcher, and the cortège, consisting of the bearers, the Doctor, and the fisherman, moved off towards the Gap, while the sergeant, having civilly wished us "Good-evening," scrambled up the Shepherd's Path, and vanished above.

"A very smart officer that," said Thorndyke. "I should like to know what he wrote in his notebook."

"His account of the circumstances of the murder seemed a very reasonable one," I said.

"Very. He noted the plain and essential facts, and drew the natural conclusions from them. But there are some very singular features in this case, so singular that I am disposed to make a few notes for my own information."

He stooped over the place where the body had lain, and having narrowly examined the sand there and in the place where the dead man's feet had rested, drew out his notebook and made a memorandum. He next made a rapid sketch-plan of the bay, marking the position of the body and the various impressions in the sand, and then, following the double track leading from and to the Shepherd's Path, scrutinized the footprints with the deepest attention, making copious notes and sketches in his book.

"We may as well go up by the Shepherd's Path," said Thorndyke. "I think we are equal to the climb, and there may be visible traces of the murderer after all. The rock is only a sandstone, and not a very hard one either."

We approached the foot of the little rugged track which zigzagged up the face of the cliff, and, stooping down among the stiff, dry herbage, examined the surface. Here, at the bottom of the path, where the rock was softened by the weather, there were several distinct impressions on the crumbling surface of the murderer's nailed boots, though they were somewhat confused by the tracks of the sergeant, whose boots were heavily nailed. But as we ascended the marks became rather less distinct, and at quite a short distance from the foot of the cliff we lost them altogether, though we had no difficulty in following the more recent traces of the sergeant's passage up the path.

When we reached the top of the cliff we paused to scan the path that ran along its edge, but here, too, although the sergeant's heavy boots had left quite visible impressions on the ground, there were no signs of any other feet. At a little distance the sagacious officer himself was pursuing his investigations, walking backwards and forwards with his body bent double, and his eyes fixed on the ground.

"Not a trace of him anywhere," said he, straightening himself up as we approached. "I was afraid there wouldn't be after all this dry weather. I shall have to try a different tack. This is a small place, and if those boots belong to anyone living here they'll be sure to be known."

"The deceased gentleman – Mr. Hearn, I think you called him," said Thorndyke as we turned towards the village " – is he a native of the locality?"

"Oh no, sir," replied the officer. "He is almost a stranger. He has only been here about three weeks, but, you know, in a little place like this a man soon gets to be known – and his business, too, for that matter," he added, with a smile.

"What was his business, then?" asked Thorndyke.

"Pleasure, I believe. He was down here for a holiday, though it's a good way past the season, but, then, he had a friend living here, and that makes a difference. Mr. Draper up at the Poplars was an old friend of his, I understand. I am going to call on him now."

We walked on along the footpath that led towards the village, but had only proceeded two or three hundred yards when a loud hail drew our attention to a man running across a field towards us from the direction of the cliff.

"Why, here is Mr. Draper himself," exclaimed the sergeant, stopping short and waving his hand. "I expect he has heard the news already."

Thorndyke and I also halted, and with some curiosity watched the approach of this new party to the tragedy. As the stranger drew near we saw that he was a tall, athletic-looking man of about forty, dressed in a Norfolk knickerbocker suit, and having the appearance of an ordinary country gentleman, excepting that he carried in his hand, in place of a walking-stick, the staff of a butterfly-net, the folding ring and bag of which partly projected from his pocket.

"Is it true, Sergeant?" he exclaimed as he came up to us, panting from his exertions. "About Mr. Hearn, I mean. There is a rumour that he has been found dead on the beach."

"It's quite true, sir, I am sorry to say, and, what is worse, he has been murdered."

"My God! You don't say so!"

He turned towards us a face that must ordinarily have been jovial enough, but was now white and scared and, after a brief pause, he exclaimed, "Murdered! Good God! Poor old Hearn! How did it happen, Sergeant? And when? And is there any clue to the murderer?"

"We can't say for certain when it happened," replied the sergeant, "and as to the question of clues, I was just coming up to call on you."

"On me!" exclaimed Draper, with a startled glance at the officer. "What for?"

"Well, we should like to know something about Mr. Hearn – who he was, and whether he had any enemies, and so forth – anything, in fact, that would give as a hint where to look for the murderer. And you are the only person in the place who knew him at all intimately."

Mr Draper's pallid face turned a shade paler, and he glanced about him with an obviously embarrassed air.

"I'm afraid," he began in a hesitating manner, "I'm afraid I shan't be able to help you much. I didn't know much about his affairs. You see he was – well – only a casual acquaintance – "

"Well," interrupted the sergeant, "you can tell us who and what he was, and where he lived, and so forth. We'll find out the rest if you give us the start."

"I see," said Draper. "Yes, I expect you will." His eyes glanced restlessly to and fro, and he added presently, "You must come up to-

47

morrow, and have a talk with me about him, and I'll see what I can remember."

"I'd rather come this evening," said the sergeant firmly.

"Not this evening," pleaded Draper. "I'm feeling rather – this affair, you know, has upset me. I couldn't give proper attention – "

His sentence petered out into a hesitating mumble, and the officer looked at him in evident surprise at his nervous, embarrassed manner. His own attitude, however, was perfectly firm, though polite.

"I don't like pressing you, sir," said he, "but time is precious – we'll have to go single file here. This pond is a public nuisance. They ought to bank it up at this end. After you, sir."

The pond to which the sergeant alluded had evidently extended at one time right across the path, but now, thanks to the dry weather, a narrow isthmus of half-dried mud traversed the morass, and along this Mr. Draper proceeded to pick his way. The sergeant was about to follow, when suddenly he stopped short with his eyes riveted upon the muddy track. A single glance showed me the cause of his surprise, for on the stiff, putty-like surface, standing out with the sharp distinctness of a wax mould, were the fresh footprints of the man who had just passed, each footprint displaying on its sole the impression of stud-nails arranged in a diamond-shaped pattern, and on its heel a group of similar nails arranged in a cross.

The sergeant hesitated for only a moment, in which he turned a quick startled glance upon us. Then he followed, walking gingerly along the edge of the path as if to avoid treading in his predecessor's footprints. Instinctively we did the same, following closely, and anxiously awaiting the next development of the tragedy. For a minute or two we all proceeded in silence, the sergeant being evidently at a loss how to act, and Mr. Draper busy with his own thoughts. At length the former spoke.

"You think, Mr. Draper, you would rather that I looked in on you to-morrow about this affair?"

"Much rather, if you wouldn't mind," was the eager reply.

"Then, in that case," said the sergeant, looking at his watch, "as I've got a good deal to see to this evening, I'll leave you here, and make my way to the station."

With a farewell flourish of his hand he climbed over a stile, and when, a few moments later, I caught a glimpse of him through an opening in the hedge, he was running across the meadow like a hare.

The departure of the police-officer was apparently a great relief to Mr. Draper, who at once fell back and began to talk with us.

"You are Dr. Jervis, I think," said he. "I saw you coming out of Dr. Cooper's house yesterday. We know everything that is happening in the

48

village, you see." He laughed nervously, and added, "But I don't know your friend."

I introduced Thorndyke, at the mention of whose name our new acquaintance knitted his brows, and glanced inquisitively at my friend.

"Thorndyke," he repeated, "the name seems familiar to me. Are you in the Law, sir?"

Thorndyke admitted the impeachment, and our companion, having again bestowed on him a look full of curiosity, continued, "This horrible affair will interest you, no doubt, from a professional point of view. You were present when my poor friend's body was found, I think?"

"No," replied Thorndyke, "we came up afterwards, when they were removing it."

Our companion then proceeded to question us about the murder, but received from Thorndyke only the most general and ambiguous replies. Nor was there time to go into the matter at length, for the footpath presently emerged on to the road close to Mr. Draper's house.

"You will excuse my not asking you in to-night," said he, "but you will understand that I am not in much form for visitors just now."

We assured him that we fully understood, and, having wished him "Good-evening," pursued our way towards the village.

"The sergeant is off to get a warrant, I suppose," I observed.

"Yes, and mighty anxious lest his man should be off before he can execute it. But he is fishing in deeper waters than he thinks, Jervis. This is a very singular and complicated case – one of the strangest, in fact, that I have ever met. I shall follow its development with deep interest."

"The sergeant seems pretty cocksure, all the same," I said.

"He is not to blame for that," replied Thorndyke. "He is acting on the obvious appearances, which is the proper thing to do in the first place. Perhaps his notebook contains more than I think it does. But we shall see."

When we entered the village I stopped to settle some business with the chemist, who acted as Dr. Cooper's dispenser, suggesting to Thorndyke that he should walk on to the house, but when I emerged from the shop some ten minutes later he was waiting outside, with a smallish brown-paper parcel under each arm. Of one of these parcels I insisted on relieving him, in spite of his protests, but when he at length handed it to me its weight completely took me by surprise.

"I should have let them send this home on a barrow," I remarked.

"So I should have done," he replied, "only I did not wish to draw attention to my purchase, or give my address."

Accepting this hint I refrained from making any inquiries as to the nature of the contents (although I must confess to considerable curiosity

49

on the subject), and on arriving home I assisted him to deposit the two mysterious parcels in his room.

When I came downstairs a disagreeable surprise awaited me. Hitherto the long evenings had been spent by me in solitary and undisturbed enjoyment of Dr. Cooper's excellent library, but to-night a perverse fate decreed that I must wander abroad, because, forsooth, a preposterous farmer, who resided in a hamlet five miles distant, had chosen the evening of my guest's arrival to dislocate his bucolic elbow. I half-hoped that Thorndyke would offer to accompany me, but he made no such suggestion, and in fact seemed by no means afflicted at the prospect of my absence.

"I have plenty to occupy me while you are away," he said cheerfully, and with this assurance to comfort me I mounted my bicycle and rode off somewhat sulkily along the dark road.

My visit occupied in all a trifle under two hours, and when I reached home, ravenously hungry and heated by my ride, half-past-nine had struck, and the village had begun to settle down for the night.

"Sergeant Payne is a-waiting in the surgery, sir," the housemaid announced as I entered the hall.

"Confound Sergeant Payne!" I exclaimed. "Is Dr. Thorndyke with him?"

"No, sir," replied the grinning damsel. "Dr. Thorndyke is *hout*."

"*Hout*!" I repeated (my surprise leading to unintentional mimicry).

"Yes, sir. He went *hout* soon after you, sir, on his bicycle. He had a basket strapped on to it – leastways a hamper – and he borrowed a basin and a kitchen-spoon from the cook."

I stared at the girl in astonishment. The ways of John Thorndyke were, indeed, beyond all understanding.

"Well, let me have some dinner or supper at once," I said, "and I will see what the sergeant wants."

The officer rose as I entered the surgery, and, laying his helmet on the table, approached me with an air of secrecy and importance.

"Well, sir," said he, "the fat's in the fire. I've arrested Mr. Draper, and I've got him locked up in the court-house. But I wish it had been someone else."

"So does he, I expect," I remarked.

"You see, sir," continued the sergeant, "we all like Mr. Draper. He's been among us a matter of seven years, and he's like one of ourselves. However, what I've come about is this: It seems the gentleman who was with you this evening is Dr. Thorndyke, the great expert. Now Mr. Draper seems to have heard about him, as most of us have, and he is very anxious for him to take up the defence. Do you think he would consent?"

50

"I expect so," I answered, remembering Thorndyke's keen interest in the case, "but I will ask him when he comes in."

"Thank you, sir," said the sergeant. "And perhaps you wouldn't mind stepping round to the court-house presently yourself. He looks uncommon queer, does Mr. Draper, and no wonder, so I'd like you to take a look at him, and if you could bring Dr. Thorndyke with you, he'd like it, and so should I, for, I assure you, sir, that although a conviction would mean a step up the ladder for me, I'd be glad enough to find that I'd made a mistake."

I was just showing my visitor out when a bicycle swept in through the open gate, and Thorndyke dismounted at the door, revealing a square hamper – evidently abstracted from the surgery – strapped on to a carrier at the back. I conveyed the sergeant's request to him at once, and asked if he was willing to take up the case.

"As to taking up the defence," he replied, "I will consider the matter, but in any case I will come up and see the prisoner."

With this the sergeant departed, and Thorndyke, having unstrapped the hamper with as much care as if it contained a collection of priceless porcelain, bore it tenderly up to his bedroom, whence he appeared, after a considerable interval, smilingly apologetic for the delay.

"I thought you were dressing for dinner," I grumbled as he took his seat at the table.

"No," he replied. "I have been considering this murder. Really it is a most singular case, and promises to be uncommonly complicated, too."

"Then I assume that you will undertake the defence?"

"I shall if Draper gives a reasonably straightforward account of himself."

It appeared that this condition was likely to be fulfilled, for when we arrived at the court-house (where the prisoner was accommodated in a spare office, under rather free-and-easy conditions considering the nature of the charge) we found Mr. Draper in an eminently communicative frame of mind.

"I want you, Dr. Thorndyke, to undertake my defence in this terrible affair, because I feel confident that you will be able to clear me. And I promise you that there shall be no reservation or concealment on my part of anything that you ought to know."

"Very well," said Thorndyke. "By the way, I see you have changed your shoes."

"Yes, the sergeant took possession of those I was wearing. He said something about comparing them with some footprints, but there can't be any footprints like those shoes here in Sundersley. The nails are fixed in the soles in quite a peculiar pattern. I had them made in Edinburgh."

"Have you more than one pair?"

"No. I have no other nailed boots."

"That is important," said Thorndyke. "And now I judge that you have something to tell us that bears on this crime. Am I right?"

"Yes. There is something that I am afraid it is necessary for you to know, although it is very painful to me to revive memories of my past that I had hoped were buried for ever. But perhaps, after all, it may not be necessary for these confidences to be revealed to anyone but yourself."

"I hope not," said Thorndyke, "and if it is not necessary you may rely upon me not to allow any of your secrets to leak out. But you are wise to tell me everything that may in any way bear upon the case."

At this juncture, seeing that confidential matters were about to be discussed, I rose and prepared to withdraw, but Draper waved me back into my chair.

"You need not go away, Dr. Jervis," he said. "It is through you that I have the benefit of Dr. Thorndyke's help, and I know that you doctors can be trusted to keep your own counsel and your clients' secrets. And now for some confessions of mine. In the first place, it is my painful duty to tell you that I am a discharged convict – an 'old lag,' as the cant phrase has it."

He coloured a dusky red as he made this statement, and glanced furtively at Thorndyke to observe its effect. But he might as well have looked at a wooden figure-head or a stone mask as at my friend's immovable visage, and when his communication had been acknowledged by a slight nod, he proceeded.

"The history of my wrong-doing is the history of hundreds of others. I was a clerk in a bank, and getting on as well as I could expect in that not very progressive avocation, when I had the misfortune to make four very undesirable acquaintances. They were all young men, though rather older than myself, and were close friends, forming a sort of little community or club. They were not what is usually described as 'fast.' They were quite sober and decently-behaved young follows, but they were very decidedly addicted to gambling in a small way, and they soon infected me. Before long I was the keenest gambler of them all. Cards, billiards, pool, and various forms of betting began to be the chief pleasures of my life, and not only was the bulk of my scanty salary often consumed in the inevitable losses, but presently I found myself considerably in debt, without any visible means of discharging my liabilities. It is true that my four friends were my chief – in fact, almost my only – creditors, but still, the debts existed, and had to be paid.

"Now these four friends of mine – named respectively Leach, Pitford, Hearn, and Jezzard – were uncommonly clever men, though the full extent of their cleverness was not appreciated by me until too late. And I, too, was clever in my way, and a most undesirable way it was, for I possessed the fatal gift of imitating handwriting and signatures with the most remarkable accuracy. So perfect were my copies that the writers themselves were frequently unable to distinguish their own signatures from my imitations, and many a time was my skill invoked by some of my companions to play off practical jokes upon the others. But these jests were strictly confined to our own little set, for my four friends were most careful and anxious that my dangerous accomplishment should not become known to outsiders.

"And now follows the consequence which you have no doubt foreseen. My debts, though small, were accumulating, and I saw no prospect of being able to pay them. Then, one night, Jezzard made a proposition. We had been playing bridge at his rooms, and once more my ill luck had caused me to increase my debt. I scribbled out an IOU, and pushed it across the table to Jezzard, who picked it up with a very wry face, and pocketed it.

"'Look here, Ted,' he said presently, 'this paper is all very well, but, you know, I can't pay my debts with it. My creditors demand hard cash.'

"'I'm very sorry,' I replied, 'but I can't help it.'

"'Yes, you can,' said he, 'and I'll tell you how.' He then propounded a scheme which I at first rejected with indignation, but which, when the others backed him up, I at last allowed myself to be talked into, and actually put into execution. I contrived, by taking advantage of the carelessness of some of my superiors at the bank, to get possession of some blank cheque forms, which I filled up with small amounts – not more than two or three pounds – and signed with careful imitations of the signatures of some of our clients. Jezzard got some stamps made for stamping on the account numbers, and when this had been done I handed over to him the whole collection of forged cheques in settlement of my debts to all of my four companions.

"The cheques were duly presented – by whom I do not know, and although, to my dismay, the modest sums for which I had drawn them had been skilfully altered into quite considerable amounts, they were all paid without demur excepting one. That one, which had been altered from three pounds to thirty-nine, was drawn upon an account which was already slightly overdrawn. The cashier became suspicious. The cheque was impounded, and the client communicated with. Then, of course, the mine exploded. Not only was this particular forgery detected, but inquiries were set afoot which soon brought to light the others. Presently circumstances, which I need not describe, threw some suspicion on me. I at once lost my nerve, and finally made a full confession.

"The inevitable prosecution followed. It was not conducted vindictively. Still, I had actually committed the forgeries, and though I endeavoured to cast a part of the blame on to the shoulders of my treacherous confederates, I did not succeed. Jezzard, it is true, was arrested, but was discharged for lack of evidence, and, consequently, the whole burden of the forgery fell upon me. The jury, of course, convicted me, and I was sentenced to seven years' penal servitude.

"During the time that I was in prison an uncle of mine died in Canada, and by the provisions of his will I inherited the whole of his very considerable property, so that when the time arrived for my release, I came out of prison, not only free, but comparatively rich. I at once dropped my own name, and, assuming that of Alfred Draper, began to look about for some quiet spot in which I might spend the rest of my days in peace, and with little chance of my identity being discovered. Such a place I found in Sundersley, and here I have lived for the last seven years, liked and respected, I think, by my neighbours, who have little suspected that they were harbouring in their midst a convicted felon.

"All this time I had neither seen nor heard anything of my four confederates, and I hoped and believed that they had passed completely out of my life. But they had not. Only a month ago I met them once more, to my sorrow, and from the day of that meeting all the peace and security of my quiet existence at Sundersley have vanished. Like evil spirits they have stolen into my life, changing my happiness into bitter misery, filling my days with dark forebodings and my nights with terror."

Here Mr. Draper paused, and seemed to sink into a gloomy reverie.

"Under what circumstances did you meet these men?" Thorndyke asked.

"Ah!" exclaimed Draper, arousing with sudden excitement, "the circumstances were very singular and suspicious. I had gone over to Eastwich for the day to do some shopping. About eleven o'clock in the forenoon I was making some purchases in a shop when I noticed two men looking in the window, or rather pretending to do so, whilst they conversed earnestly. They were smartly dressed, in a horsy fashion, and looked like well-to-do farmers, as they might very naturally have been since it was market-day. But it seemed to me that their faces were familiar to me. I looked at them more attentively, and then it suddenly dawned upon me, most unpleasantly, that they resembled Leach and Jezzard. And yet they were not quite like. The resemblance was there, but the differences were greater than the lapse of time would account for. Moreover, the man who resembled Jezzard had a rather large mole on the left cheek just under the eye, while the other man had an eyeglass stuck in one eye, and wore a waxed moustache, whereas Leach had always been clean-shaven, and had never used an eyeglass.

"As I was speculating upon the resemblance they looked up, and caught my intent and inquisitive eye, whereupon they moved away from the window, and when, having completed my purchases, I came out into the street, they were nowhere to be seen.

"That evening, as I was walking by the river outside the town before returning to the station, I overtook a yacht which was being towed downstream. Three men were walking ahead on the bank with a long tow-line, and one man stood in the cockpit steering. As I approached, and was reading the name *Otter* on the stern, the man at the helm looked round, and with a start of surprise I recognized my old acquaintance Hearn. The recognition, however, was not mutual, for I had grown a beard in the interval, and I passed on without appearing to notice him, but when I overtook the other three men, and recognized, as I had feared, the other three members of the gang, I must have looked rather hard at Jezzard, for he suddenly halted, and exclaimed, 'Why, it's our old friend Ted! Our long-lost and lamented brother!' He held out his hand with effusive cordiality, and began to make inquiries as to my welfare, but I cut him short with the remark that I was not proposing to renew the acquaintance, and, turning off on to a footpath that led away from the river, strode off without looking back.

"Naturally this meeting exercised my mind a good deal, and when I thought of the two men whom I had seen in the town, I could hardly believe that their likeness to my quondam friends was a mere coincidence. And yet when I had met Leach and Jezzard by the river, I had found them little altered, and had particularly noticed that Jezzard had no mole on his face, and that Leach was clean-shaven as of old.

"But a day or two later all my doubts were resolved by a paragraph in the local paper. It appeared that on the day of my visit to Eastwich a number of forged cheques had been cashed at the three banks. They had been presented by three well-dressed, horsy-looking men who looked like well-to-do farmers. One of them had a mole on the left cheek, another was distinguished by a waxed moustache and a single eyeglass, while the description of the third I did not recognize. None of the cheques had been drawn for large amounts, though the total sum obtained by the forgers was nearly four hundred pounds, but the most interesting point was that the cheque-forms had been manufactured by photographic process, and the water-mark skilfully, though not quite perfectly, imitated. Evidently the swindlers were clever and careful men, and willing to take a good deal of trouble for the sake of security, and the result of their precautions was that the police could make no guess as to their identity.

"The very next day, happening to walk over to Port Marston, I came upon the *Otter* lying moored alongside the quay in the harbour. As soon as I recognized the yacht, I turned quickly and walked away, but a minute later I ran into Leach and Jezzard, who were returning to their craft. Jezzard greeted me with an air of surprise. 'What! Still hanging about here, Ted?' he exclaimed. 'That is not discreet of you, dear boy. I should earnestly advise you to clear out.'

"'What do you mean?' I asked.

"'Tut, tut!' said he. 'We read the papers like other people, and we know now what business took you to Eastwich. But it's foolish of you to hang about the neighbourhood where you might be spotted at any moment.'

"The implied accusation took me aback so completely that I stood staring at him in speechless astonishment, and at that unlucky moment a tradesman, from whom I had ordered some house-linen, passed along the quay. Seeing me, he stopped and touched his hat.

"'Beg pardon, Mr. Draper,' said he, 'but I shall be sending my cart up to Sundersley to-morrow morning if that will do for you.'

"I said that it would, and as the man turned away, Jezzard's face broke out into a cunning smile.

"So you are Mr. Draper, of Sundersley, now, are you?' said he. 'Well, I hope you won't be too proud to come and look in on your old friends. We shall be staying here for some time.'

"That same night Hearn made his appearance at my house. He had come as an emissary from the gang, to ask me to do some work for them – to execute some forgeries, in fact. Of course I refused, and pretty bluntly, too, whereupon Hearn began to throw out vague hints as to what might happen if I made enemies of the gang, and to utter veiled, but quite intelligible, threats. You will say that I was an idiot not to send him packing, and threaten to hand over the whole gang to the police, but I was never a man of strong nerve, and I don't mind admitting that I was mortally afraid of that cunning devil, Jezzard.

"The next thing that happened was that Hearn came and took lodgings in Sundersley, and, in spite of my efforts to avoid him, he haunted me continually. The yacht, too, had evidently settled down for some time at a berth in the harbour, for I heard that a local smack-boy had been engaged as a deck-hand, and I frequently encountered Jezzard and the other members of the gang, who all professed to believe that I had committed the Eastwich forgeries. One day I was foolish enough to allow myself to be lured on to the yacht for a few minutes, and when I would have gone ashore, I found that the shore ropes had been cast off, and that the vessel was already moving out of the harbour. At first I was furious, but the three scoundrels were so jovial and good-natured, and so delighted with the joke of taking me for a sail against my will, that I presently cooled down, and having changed into a pair of rubber-soled shoes (so that I should not make dents in the smooth deck with my hobnails), bore a hand at sailing the yacht, and spent quite a pleasant day.

"From that time I found myself gradually drifting back into a state of intimacy with these agreeable scoundrels, and daily becoming more and more afraid of them. In a moment of imbecility I mentioned what I had seen from the shop-window at Eastwich, and, though they passed the matter off with a joke, I could see that they were mightily disturbed by it. Their efforts to induce me to join them were redoubled, and Hearn took to calling almost daily at my house – usually with documents and signatures which he tried to persuade me to copy.

"A few evenings ago he made a new and startling proposition. We were walking in my garden, and he had been urging me once more to rejoin the gang – unsuccessfully, I need not say. Presently he sat down on a seat against a yew-hedge at the bottom of the garden, and, after an interval of silence, said suddenly, "'Then you absolutely refuse to go in with us?'

"'Of course I do,' I replied. 'Why should I mix myself up with a gang of crooks when I have ample means and a decent position?'

"'Of course,' he agreed, 'you'd be a fool if you did. But, you see, you know all about this Eastwich job, to say nothing of our other little exploits, and you gave us away once before. Consequently, you can take it from me that, now Jezzard has run you to earth, he won't leave you in peace until you have given us some kind of a hold on you. You know too much, you see, and as long as you have a clean sheet you are a standing menace to us. That is the position. You know it, and Jezzard knows it, and he is a desperate man, and as cunning as the devil.'

"'I know that,' I said gloomily.

"'Very well,' continued Hearn. 'Now I'm going to make you an offer. Promise me a small annuity – you can easily afford it – or pay me a substantial sum down, and I will set you free for ever from Jezzard and the others.'

"'How will you do that?' I asked.

"'Very simply,' he replied. 'I am sick of them all, and sick of this risky, uncertain mode of life. Now I am ready to clean off my own slate and set you free at the same time, but I must have some means of livelihood in view.'

"'You mean that you will turn King's evidence?' I asked.

"'Yes, if you will pay me a couple of hundred a year, or, say, two thousand down on the conviction of the gang.'

"I was so taken aback that for some time I made no reply, and as I sat considering this amazing proposition, the silence was suddenly broken by a suppressed sneeze from the other side of the hedge.

"Hearn and I started to our feet. Immediately hurried footsteps were heard in the lane outside the hedge. We raced up the garden to the gate and out through a side alley, but when we reached the lane there was not a soul in sight. We made a brief and fruitless search in the immediate neighbourhood, and then turned back to the house. Hearn was deathly pale and very agitated, and I must confess that I was a good deal upset by the incident.

"'This is devilish awkward,' said Hearn.

"'It is rather,' I admitted, 'but I expect it was only some inquisitive yokel.'

"'I don't feel so sure of that,' said he. 'At any rate, we were stark lunatics to sit up against a hedge to talk secrets.'

"He paced the garden with me for some time in gloomy silence, and presently, after a brief request that I would think over his proposal, took himself off.

"I did not see him again until I met him last night on the yacht. Pitford called on me in the morning, and invited me to come and dine with them. I at first declined, for my housekeeper was going to spend the evening with her sister at Eastwich, and stay there for the night, and I did not much like leaving the house empty. However, I agreed eventually, stipulating that I should be allowed to come home early, and I accordingly went. Hearn and Pitford were waiting in the boat by the steps – for the yacht had been moved out to a buoy – and we went on board and spent a very pleasant and lively evening. Pitford put me ashore at ten o'clock, and I walked straight home, and went to bed. Hearn would have come with me, but the others insisted on his remaining, saying that they had some matters of business to discuss."

"Which way did you walk home?" asked Thorndyke.

"I came through the town, and along the main road."

"And that is all you know about this affair?"

"Absolutely all," replied Draper. "I have now admitted you to secrets of my past life that I had hoped never to have to reveal to any human creature, and I still have some faint hope that it may not be necessary for you to divulge what I have told you."

"Your secrets shall not be revealed unless it is absolutely indispensable that they should be," said Thorndyke, "but you are placing your life in my hands, and you must leave me perfectly free to act as I think best."

With this he gathered his notes together, and we took our departure.

58

"A very singular history, this, Jervis," he said, when, having wished the sergeant "Good-night," we stepped out on to the dark road. "What do you think of it?"

"I hardly know what to think," I answered, "but, on the whole, it seems rather against Draper than otherwise. He admits that he is an old criminal, and it appears that he was being persecuted and blackmailed by the man Hearn. It is true that he represents Jezzard as being the leading spirit and prime mover in the persecution, but we have only his word for that. Hearn was in lodgings near him, and was undoubtedly taking the most active part in the business, and it is quite possible, and indeed probable, that Hearn was the actual *deus ex machina*."

Thorndyke nodded. "Yes," he said, "that is certainly the line the prosecution will take if we allow the story to become known. Ha! What is this? We are going to have some rain."

"Yes, and wind too. We are in for an autumn gale, I think."

"And that," said Thorndyke, "may turn out to be an important factor in our case."

"How can the weather affect your case?" I asked in some surprise. But, as the rain suddenly descended in a pelting shower, my companion broke into a run, leaving my question unanswered.

On the following morning, which was fair and sunny after the stormy night, Dr. Burrows called for my friend. He was on his way to the extemporized mortuary to make the post-mortem examination of the murdered man's body. Thorndyke, having notified the coroner that he was watching the case on behalf of the accused, had been authorized to be present at the autopsy, but the authorization did not include me, and, as Dr. Burrows did not issue any invitation, I was not able to be present. I met them, however, as they were returning, and it seemed to me that Dr. Burrows appeared a little huffy.

"Your friend," said he, in a rather injured tone, "is really the most outrageous stickler for forms and ceremonies that I have ever met."

Thorndyke looked at him with an amused twinkle, and chuckled indulgently.

"Here was a body," Dr. Burrows continued irritably, "found under circumstances clearly indicative of murder, and bearing a knife-wound that nearly divided the arch of the aorta, in spite of which, I assure you that Dr. Thorndyke insisted on weighing the body, and examining every organ – lungs, liver, stomach, and brain – yes, actually the brain! – as if there had been no clue whatever to the cause of death. And then, as a climax, he insisted on sending the contents of the stomach in a jar, sealed with our respective seals, in charge of a special messenger, to Professor Copland, for analysis and report. I thought he was going to demand an examination

59

for the tubercle bacillus, but he didn't, which," concluded Dr. Burrows, suddenly becoming sourly facetious, "was an oversight, for, after all, the fellow may have died of consumption."

Thorndyke chuckled again, and I murmured that the precautions appeared to have been somewhat excessive.

"Not at all," was the smiling response. "You are losing sight of our function. We are the expert and impartial umpires, and it is our business to ascertain, with scientific accuracy, the cause of death. The *prima facie* appearances in this case suggest that the deceased was murdered by Draper, and that is the hypothesis advanced. But that is no concern of ours. It is not our function to confirm an hypothesis suggested by outside circumstances, but rather, on the contrary, to make certain that no other explanation is possible. And that is my invariable practice. No matter how glaringly obvious the appearances may be, I refuse to take anything for granted."

Dr. Burrows received this statement with a grunt of dissent, but the arrival of his dogcart put a stop to further discussion.

Thorndyke was not subpoenaed for the inquest. Dr. Burrows and the sergeant having been present immediately after the finding of the body, his evidence was not considered necessary, and, moreover, he was known to be watching the case in the interests of the accused. Like myself, therefore, he was present as a spectator, but as a highly interested one, for he took very complete shorthand notes of the whole of the evidence and the coroner's comments.

I shall not describe the proceedings in detail. The jury, having been taken to view the body, trooped into the room on tiptoe, looking pale and awe-stricken, and took their seats, and thereafter, from time to time, directed glances of furtive curiosity at Draper as he stood, pallid and haggard, confronting the court, with a burly rural constable on either side.

The medical evidence was taken first. Dr. Burrows, having been sworn, began, with sarcastic emphasis, to describe the condition of the lungs and liver, until he was interrupted by the coroner.

"Is all this necessary?" the latter inquired. "I mean, is it material to the subject of the inquiry?"

"I should say not," replied Dr. Burrows. "It appears to me to be quite irrelevant, but Dr. Thorndyke, who is watching the case for the defence, thought it necessary."

"I think," said the coroner, "you had better give us only the facts that are material. The jury want you to tell them what you consider to have been the cause of death. They don't want a lecture on pathology."

"The cause of death," said Dr. Burrows, "was a penetrating wound of the chest, apparently inflicted with a large knife. The weapon entered between the second and third ribs on the left side close to the sternum or breast-bone. It wounded the left lung, and partially divided both the pulmonary artery and the aorta – the two principal arteries of the body."

"Was this injury alone sufficient to cause death?" the coroner asked.

"Yes," was the reply, "and death from injury to these great vessels would be practically instantaneous."

"Could the injury have been self-inflicted?"

"So far as the position and nature of the wound are concerned," replied the witness, "self-infliction would be quite possible. But since death would follow in a few seconds at the most, the weapon would be found either in the wound, or grasped in the hand, or, at least, quite close to the body. But in this case no weapon was found at all, and the wound must therefore certainly have been homicidal."

"Did you see the body before it was moved?"

"Yes. It was lying on its back, with the arms extended and the legs nearly straight, and the sand in the neighbourhood of the body was trampled as if a furious struggle had taken place."

"Did you notice anything remarkable about the footprints in the sand?"

"I did," replied Dr. Burrows. "They were the footprints of two persons only. One of these was evidently the deceased, whose footmarks could be easily identified by the circular rubber heels. The other footprints were those of a person – apparently a man – who wore shoes, or boots, the soles of which were studded with nails, and these nails were arranged in a very peculiar and unusual manner, for those on the soles formed a lozenge or diamond shape, and those on the heel were set out in the form of a cross."

"Have you ever seen shoes or boots with the nails arranged in this manner?"

"Yes. I have seen a pair of shoes which I am informed belong to the accused, the nails in them are arranged as I have described."

"Would you say that the footprints of which you have spoken were made by those shoes?"

"No, I could not say that. I can only say that, to the best of my belief, the pattern on the shoes is similar to that in the footprints."

This was the sum of Dr. Burrows' evidence, and to all of it Thorndyke listened with an immovable countenance, though with the closest attention. Equally attentive was the accused man, though not equally impassive. Indeed, so great was his agitation that presently one of the constables asked permission to get him a chair.

The next witness was Arthur Jezzard. He testified that he had viewed the body, and identified it as that of Charles Hearn – that he had been acquainted with deceased for some years, but knew practically nothing of his affairs. At the time of his death deceased was lodging in the village.

"Why did he leave the yacht?" the coroner inquired. "Was there any kind of disagreement!"

"Not in the least," replied Jezzard. "He grew tired of the confinement of the yacht, and came to live ashore for a change. But we were the best of friends, and he intended to come with us when we sailed."

"When did you see him last?"

"On the night before the body was found – that is, last Monday. He had been dining on the yacht, and we put him ashore about midnight. He said as we were rowing him ashore that he intended to walk home along the sands as the tide was out. He went up the stone steps by the watch-house, and turned at the top to wish us good-night. That was the last time I saw him alive."

"Do you know anything of the relations between the accused and the deceased?" the coroner asked.

"Very little," replied Jezzard. "Mr. Draper was introduced to us by the deceased about a month ago. I believe they had been acquainted some years, and they appeared to be on excellent terms. There was no indication of any quarrel or disagreement between them."

"What time did the accused leave the yacht on the night of the murder?"

"About ten o'clock. He said that he wanted to get home early, as his housekeeper was away and he did not like the house to be left with no one in it."

This was the whole of Jezzard's evidence, and was confirmed by that of Leach and Pitford. Then, when the fisherman had deposed to the discovery of the body, the sergeant was called, and stepped forward, grasping a carpet-bag, and looking as uncomfortable as if he had been the accused instead of a witness. He described the circumstances under which he saw the body, giving the exact time and place with official precision.

"You have heard Dr. Burrows' description of the footprints?" the coroner inquired.

"Yes. There were two sets. One set were evidently made by deceased. They showed that he entered St. Bridget's Bay from the direction of Port Marston. He had been walking along the shore just about high-water mark, sometimes above and sometimes below. Where he had walked below high-water mark the footprints had of course been washed away by the sea."

"How far back did you trace the footprints of deceased?"

"About two-thirds of the way to Sundersley Gap. Then they disappeared below high-water mark. Later in the evening I walked from the Gap into Port Marston, but could not find any further traces of deceased. He must have walked between the tide-marks all the way from Port Marston to beyond Sundersley. When these footprints entered St. Bridget's Bay they became mixed up with the footprints of another man, and the shore was trampled for a space of a dozen yards as if a furious struggle had taken place. The strange man's tracks came down from the Shepherd's Path, and went up it again, but, owing to the hardness of the ground from the dry weather, the tracks disappeared a short distance up the path, and I could not find them again."

"What were these strange footprints like?" inquired the coroner.

"They were very peculiar," replied the sergeant. "They were made by shoes armed with smallish hob-nails, which were arranged in a diamond-shaped pattern on the holes and in a cross on the heels. I measured the footprints carefully, and made a drawing of each foot at the time." Here the sergeant produced a long notebook of funereal aspect, and, having opened it at a marked place, handed it to the coroner, who examined it attentively, and then passed it on to the jury. From the jury it was presently transferred to Thorndyke, and, looking over his shoulder, I saw a very workmanlike sketch of a pair of footprints with the principal dimensions inserted.

Thorndyke surveyed the drawing critically, jotted down a few brief notes, and returned the sergeant's notebook to the coroner, who, as he took it, turned once more to the officer.

"Have you any clue, sergeant, to the person who made these footprints?" he asked.

By way of reply the sergeant opened his carpet-bag, and, extracting therefrom a pair of smart but stoutly made shoes, laid them on the table.

"Those shoes," he said, "are the property of the accused. He was wearing them when I arrested him. They appear to correspond exactly to the footprints of the murderer. The measurements are the same, and the nails with which they are studded are arranged in a similar pattern."

"Would you swear that the footprints were made with these shoes?" asked the coroner.

"No, sir, I would not," was the decided answer. "I would only swear to the similarity of size and pattern."

"Had you ever seen these shoes before you made the drawing?"

"No, sir," replied the sergeant, and he then related the incident of the footprints in the soft earth by the pond which led him to make the arrest.

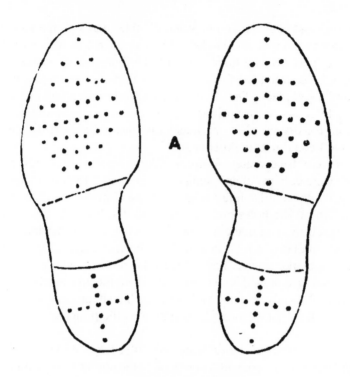

The Sergeant's Sketch

Extreme length, 11¾ inches.
Width at A, 4½ inches.
Length of heel, 3¼ inches
Width of heel at cross, 3 inches.

The coroner gazed reflectively at the shoes which he held in his hand, and from them to the drawing, then, passing them to the foreman of the jury, he remarked, "Well, gentlemen, it is not for me to tell you whether these shoes answer to the description given by Dr. Burrows and the sergeant, or whether they resemble the drawing which, as you have heard, was made by the officer on the spot and before he had seen the shoes, that is a matter for you to decide. Meanwhile, there is another question that we must consider." He turned to the sergeant and asked, "Have you made any inquiries as to the movements of the accused on the night of the murder?"

"I have," replied the sergeant, "and I find that, on that night, the accused was alone in the house, his housekeeper having gone over to Eastwich. Two men saw him in the town about ten o'clock, apparently walking in the direction of Sundersley."

This concluded the sergeant's evidence, and when one or two more witnesses had been examined without eliciting any fresh facts, the coroner briefly recapitulated the evidence, and requested the jury to consider their verdict. Thereupon a solemn hush fell upon the court, broken only by the whispers of the jurymen, as they consulted together, and the spectators gazed in awed expectancy from the accused to the whispering jury. I glanced at Draper, sitting huddled in his chair, his clammy face as pale as that of the corpse in the mortuary hard by, his hands tremulous and restless, and, scoundrel as I believed him to be, I could not but pity the abject misery that was written large all over him, from his damp hair to his incessantly shifting feet.

The jury took but a short time to consider their verdict. At the end of five minutes the foreman announced that they were agreed, and, in answer to the coroner's formal inquiry, stood up and replied, "We find that the deceased met his death by being stabbed in the chest by the accused man, Alfred Draper."

"That is a verdict of wilful murder," said the coroner, and he entered it accordingly in his notes. The Court now rose. The spectators reluctantly trooped out, the jurymen stood up and stretched themselves, and the two constables, under the guidance of the sergeant, carried the wretched Draper in a fainting condition to a closed fly that was waiting outside.

"I was not greatly impressed by the activity of the defence," I remarked maliciously as we walked home.

Thorndyke smiled. "You surely did not expect me to cast my pearls of forensic learning before a coroner's jury," said he.

"I expected that you would have something to say on behalf of your client," I replied. "As it was, his accusers had it all their own way."

"And why not?" he asked. "Of what concern to us is the verdict of the coroner's jury?"

"It would have seemed more decent to make some sort of defence," I replied.

"My dear Jervis," he rejoined, "you do not seem to appreciate the great virtue of what Lord Beaconsfield so felicitously called 'a policy of masterly inactivity', and yet that is one of the great lessons that a medical training impresses on the student."

"That may be so," said I. "But the result, up to the present, of your masterly policy is that a verdict of wilful murder stands against your client, and I don't see what other verdict the jury could have found."

"Neither do I," said Thorndyke.

I had written to my principal, Dr. Cooper, describing the stirring events that were taking place in the village, and had received a reply from him instructing me to place the house at Thorndyke's disposal, and to give him every facility for his work. In accordance with which edict my colleague took possession of a well-lighted, disused stable-loft, and announced his intention of moving his things into it. Now, as these "things" included the mysterious contents of the hamper that the housemaid had seen, I was possessed with a consuming desire to be present at the "flitting," and I do not mind confessing that I purposely lurked about the stairs in the hopes of thus picking up a few crumbs of information.

But Thorndyke was one too many for me. A misbegotten infant in the village having been seized with inopportune convulsions, I was compelled, most reluctantly, to hasten to its relief, and I returned only in time to find Thorndyke in the act of locking the door of the loft.

"A nice light, roomy place to work in," he remarked, as he descended the steps, slipping the key into his pocket.

"Yes," I replied, and added boldly, "What do you intend to do up there?"

"Work up the case for the defence," he replied, "and, as I have now heard all that the prosecution have to say, I shall be able to forge ahead."

This was vague enough, but I consoled myself with the reflection that in a very few days I should, in common with the rest of the world, be in possession of the results of his mysterious proceedings. For, in view of the approaching assizes, preparations were being made to push the case through the magistrate's court as quickly as possible in order to obtain a committal in time for the ensuing sessions. Draper had, of course, been already charged before a justice of the peace and evidence of arrest taken, and it was expected that the adjourned hearing would commence before the local magistrates on the fifth day after the inquest.

The events of these five days kept me in a positive ferment of curiosity. In the first place an inspector of the Criminal Investigation Department came down and browsed about the place in company with the sergeant. Then Mr. Bashfield, who was to conduct the prosecution, came and took up his abode at the "Cat and Chicken." But the most surprising visitor was Thorndyke's laboratory assistant, Polton, who appeared one evening with a large trunk and a sailor's hammock, and announced that he was going to take up his quarters in the loft.

As to Thorndyke himself, his proceedings were beyond speculation. From time to time he made mysterious appearances at the windows of the loft, usually arrayed in what looked suspiciously like a nightshirt. Sometimes I would see him holding a negative up to the light, at others manipulating a photographic printing-frame, and once I observed him with a paintbrush and a large gallipot, on which I turned away in despair, and nearly collided with the inspector.

"Dr. Thorndyke is staying with you, I hear," said the latter, gazing earnestly at my colleague's back, which was presented for his inspection at the window.

"Yes," I answered. "Those are his temporary premises."

"That is where he does his bedevilments, I suppose?" the officer suggested.

"He conducts his experiments there," I corrected haughtily.

"That's what I mean," said the inspector, and, as Thorndyke at this moment turned and opened the window, our visitor began to ascend the steps.

"I've just called to ask if I could have a few words with you, Doctor," said the inspector, as he reached the door.

"Certainly," Thorndyke replied blandly. "If you will go down and wait with Dr. Jervis, I will be with you in five minutes."

The officer came down the steps grinning, and I thought I heard him murmur "Sold!" But this may have been an illusion. However, Thorndyke presently emerged, and he and the officer strode away into the shrubbery. What the inspector's business was, or whether he had any business at all, I never learned, but the incident seemed to throw some light on the presence of Polton and the sailor's hammock. And this reference to Polton reminds me of a very singular change that took place about this time in the habits of this usually staid and sedate little man, who, abandoning the somewhat clerical style of dress that he ordinarily affected, broke out into a semi-nautical costume, in which he would sally forth every morning in the direction of Port Marston. And there, on more than one occasion, I saw him leaning against a post by the harbour, or lounging outside a waterside tavern in earnest and amicable conversation with sundry nautical characters.

On the afternoon of the day before the opening of the proceedings we had two new visitors. One of them, a grey-haired spectacled man, was a stranger to me, and for some reason I failed to recall his name, Copland, though I was sure I had heard it before. The other was Anstey, the barrister who usually worked with Thorndyke in cases that went into Court. I saw very little of either of them, however, for they retired almost immediately to the loft, where, with short intervals for meals, they remained for the rest of the day, and, I believe, far into the night. Thorndyke requested me not to mention the names of his visitors to anyone, and at the same time apologized for the secrecy of his proceedings.

"But you are a doctor, Jervis," he concluded, "and you know what professional confidences are, and you will understand how greatly it is in our favour that we know exactly what the prosecution can do, while they are absolutely in the dark as to our line of defence."

I assured him that I fully understood his position, and with this assurance he retired, evidently relieved, to the council chamber.

The proceedings, which opened on the following day, and at which I was present throughout, need not be described in detail. The evidence for the prosecution was, of course, mainly a repetition of that given at the inquest. Mr. Bashfield's opening statement, however, I shall give at length, inasmuch as it summarized very clearly the whole of the case against the prisoner.

"The case that is now before the Court," said the counsel, "involves a charge of wilful murder against the prisoner Alfred Draper, and the facts, in so far as they are known, are briefly these: On the night of Monday, the 27th of September, the deceased, Charles Hearn, dined with some friends on board the yacht *Otter*. About midnight he came ashore, and proceeded to walk towards Sundersley along the beach. As he entered St. Bridget's Bay, a man, who appears to have been lying in wait, and who came down the Shepherd's Path, met him, and a deadly struggle seems to have taken place. The deceased received a wound of a kind calculated to cause almost instantaneous death, and apparently fell down dead.

"And now, what was the motive of this terrible crime? It was not robbery, for nothing appears to have been taken from the corpse. Money and valuables were found, as far as is known, intact. Nor, clearly, was it a case of a casual affray. We are, consequently, driven to the conclusion that the motive was a personal one, a motive of interest or revenge, and with this view the time, the place, and the evident deliberateness of the murder are in full agreement.

"So much for the motive. The next question is, Who was the perpetrator of this shocking crime? And the answer to that question is given in a very singular and dramatic circumstance, a circumstance that illustrates once more the amazing lack of precaution shown by persons who commit such crimes. The murderer was wearing a very remarkable pair of shoes, and those shoes left very remarkable footprints in the smooth sand, and those footprints were seen and examined by a very acute and painstaking police-officer, Sergeant Payne, whose evidence you will hear presently. The sergeant not only examined the footprints, he made careful drawings of them on the spot – on the spot, mind you, not from memory – and he made very exact measurements of them, which he duly noted down. And from those drawings and those measurements, those tell-tale shoes have been identified, and are here for your inspection.

"And now, who is the owner of those very singular, those almost unique shoes? I have said that the motive of this murder must have been a personal one, and, behold! the owner of those shoes happens to be the one person in the whole of this district who could have had a motive for compassing the murdered man's death. Those shoes belong to, and were taken from the foot of, the prisoner, Alfred Draper, and the prisoner, Alfred Draper, is the only person living in this neighbourhood who was acquainted with the deceased.

"It has been stated in evidence at the inquest that the relations of these two men, the prisoner and the deceased, were entirely friendly, but I shall prove to you that they were not so friendly as has been supposed. I shall prove to you, by the evidence of the prisoner's housekeeper, that the deceased was often an unwelcome visitor at the house, that the prisoner often denied himself when he was really at home and disengaged, and, in short, that he appeared constantly to shun and avoid the deceased.

"One more question and I have finished. Where was the prisoner on the night of the murder? The answer is that he was in a house little more than half-a-mile from the scene of the crime. And who was with him in that house? Who was there to observe and testify to his going forth and his coming home? No one. He was alone in the house. On that night, of all nights, he was alone. Not a soul was there to rouse at the creak of a door or the tread of a shoe – to tell as whether he slept or whether he stole forth in the dead of the night.

"Such are the facts of this case. I believe that they are not disputed, and I assert that, taken together, they are susceptible of only one explanation, which is that the prisoner, Alfred Draper, is the man who murdered the deceased, Charles Hearn."

Immediately on the conclusion of this address, the witnesses were called, and the evidence given was identical with that at the inquest. The only new witness for the prosecution was Draper's housekeeper, and her evidence fully bore out Mr. Bashfield's statement. The sergeant's account of the footprints was listened to with breathless interest, and at its conclusion the presiding magistrate – a retired solicitor, once well known in criminal practice – put a question which interested me as showing how clearly Thorndyke had foreseen the course of events, recalling, as it did, his remark on the night when we were caught in the rain.

"Did you," the magistrate asked, "take these shoes down to the beach and compare them with the actual footprints?"

"I obtained the shoes at night," replied the sergeant, "and I took them down to the shore at daybreak the next morning. But, unfortunately, there had been a storm in the night, and the footprints were almost obliterated by the wind and rain."

When the sergeant had stepped down, Mr. Bashfield announced that that was the case for the prosecution. He then resumed his seat, turning an inquisitive eye on Anstey and Thorndyke.

The former immediately rose and opened the case for the defence with a brief statement.

"The learned counsel for the prosecution," said he, "has told us that the facts now in the possession of the Court admit of but one explanation – that of the guilt of the accused. That may or may not be, but I shall now proceed to lay before the Court certain fresh facts – facts, I may say, of the most singular and startling character, which will, I think, lead to a very different conclusion. I shall say no more, but call the witnesses forthwith, and let the evidence speak for itself."

The first witness for the defence was Thorndyke, and as he entered the box I observed Polton take up a position close behind him with a large wicker trunk. Having been sworn, and requested by Anstey to tell the Court what he knew about the case, he commenced without preamble:

"About half-past-four in the afternoon of the 28th of September I walked down Sundersley Gap with Dr. Jervis. Our attention was attracted by certain footprints in the sand, particularly those of a man who had landed from a boat, had walked up the Gap, and presently returned, apparently to the boat.

"As we were standing there Sergeant Payne and Dr. Burrows passed down the Gap with two constables carrying a stretcher. We followed at a distance, and as we walked along the shore we encountered another set of footprints – those which the sergeant has described as the footprints of the deceased. We examined these carefully, and endeavoured to frame a description of the person by whom they had been made."

"And did your description agree with the characters of the deceased?" the magistrate asked.

"Not in the least," replied Thorndyke, whereupon the magistrate, the inspector, and Mr. Bashfield laughed long and heartily.

"When we turned into St. Bridget's Bay, I saw the body of deceased lying on the sand close to the cliff. The sand all round was covered with footprints, as if a prolonged, fierce struggle had taken place. There were two sets of footprints, one set being apparently those of the deceased and the other those of a man with nailed shoes of a very peculiar and conspicuous pattern. The incredible folly that the wearing of such shoes indicated caused me to look more closely at the footprints, and then I made the surprising discovery that there had in reality been no struggle, that, in fact, the two sets of footprints had been made at different times."

"At different times!" the magistrate exclaimed in astonishment.

"Yes. The interval between them may have been one of hours or one only of seconds, but the undoubted fact is that the two sets of footprints were made, not simultaneously, but in succession."

"But how did you arrive at that fact?" the magistrate asked.

"It was very obvious when one looked," said Thorndyke. "The marks of the deceased man's shoes showed that he repeatedly trod in his own footprints, but never in a single instance did he tread in the footprints of the other man, although they covered the same area. The man with the nailed shoes, on the contrary, not only trod in his own footprints, but with equal frequency in those of the deceased. Moreover, when the body was removed, I observed that the footprints in the sand on which it was lying were exclusively those of the deceased. There was not a sign of any nail-marked footprint under the corpse, although there were many close around it. It was evident, therefore, that the footprints of the deceased were made first and those of the nailed shoes afterwards."

As Thorndyke paused the magistrate rubbed his nose thoughtfully, and the inspector gazed at the witness with a puzzled frown.

"The singularity of this fact," my colleague resumed, "made me look at the footprints yet more critically, and then I made another discovery. There was a double track of the nailed shoes, leading apparently from and back to the Shepherd's Path. But on examining these tracks more closely, I was astonished to find that the man who had made them had been walking backwards – that, in fact, he had walked backwards from the body to the Shepherd's Path, had ascended it for a short distance, had turned round, and returned, still walking backwards, to the face of the cliff near the corpse, and there the tracks vanished altogether. On the sand at this spot were some small, inconspicuous marks which might have been made by the end of a rope, and there were also a few small fragments which had fallen from the cliff above. Observing these, I examined the surface of the cliff, and at one spot, about six feet above the beach, I found a freshly rubbed spot on which were parallel scratches such as might have been made by the nailed sole of a boot. I then ascended the Shepherd's Path, and examined the cliff from above, and here I found on the extreme edge a rather deep indentation, such as would be made by a taut rope, and, on lying down and looking over, I could see, some five feet from the top, another rubbed spot with very distinct parallel scratches."

"You appear to infer," said the chairman, "that this man performed these astonishing evolutions and was then hauled up the cliff?"

"That is what the appearances suggested," replied Thorndyke.

The chairman pursed up his lips, raised his eyebrows, and glanced doubtfully at his brother magistrates. Then, with a resigned air, he bowed to the witness to indicate that he was listening.

"That same night," Thorndyke resumed, "I cycled down to the shore, through the Gap, with a supply of plaster of Paris, and proceeded to take plaster moulds of the more important of the footprints." (Here the magistrates, the inspector, and Mr. Bashfield with one accord sat up at

71

attention. Sergeant Payne swore quite audibly, and I experienced a sudden illumination respecting a certain basin and kitchen spoon which had so puzzled me on the night of Thorndyke's arrival.) "As I thought that liquid plaster might confuse or even obliterate the prints in sand, I filled up the respective footprints with dry plaster, pressed it down lightly, and then cautiously poured water on to it. The moulds, which are excellent impressions, of course show the appearance of the boots which made the footprints, and from these moulds I have prepared casts which reproduce the footprints themselves.

"The first mould that I made was that of one of the tracks from the boat up to the Gap, and of this I shall speak presently. I next made a mould of one of the footprints which have been described as those of the deceased."

"Have been described!" exclaimed the chairman. "The deceased was certainly there, and there were no other footprints, so, if they were not his, he must have flown to where he was found."

"I will call them the footprints of the deceased," replied Thorndyke imperturbably. "I took a mould of one of them, and with it, on the same mould, one of my own footprints. Here is the mould, and here is a cast from it." (He turned and took them from the triumphant Polton, who had tenderly lifted them out of the trunk in readiness.) "On looking at the cast, it will be seen that the appearances are not such as would be expected. The deceased was five feet nine inches high, but was very thin and light, weighing only nine stone six pounds, as I ascertained by weighing the body, whereas I am five feet eleven and weigh nearly thirteen stone. But yet the footprint of the deceased is nearly twice as deep as mine – that is to say, the lighter man has sunk into the sand nearly twice as deeply as the heavier man."

The magistrates were now deeply attentive. They were no longer simply listening to the despised utterances of a mere scientific expert. The cast lay before them with the two footprints side by side, the evidence appealed to their own senses and was proportionately convincing.

"This is very singular," said the chairman, "but perhaps you can explain the discrepancy?"

"I think I can," replied Thorndyke, "but I should prefer to place all the facts before you first."

"Undoubtedly that would be better," the chairman agreed. "Pray proceed."

"There was another remarkable peculiarity about these footprints," Thorndyke continued, "and that was their distance apart – the length of the stride, in fact. I measured the steps carefully from heel to heel, and found them only nineteen-and-a-half inches. But a man of Hearn's height would have an ordinary stride of about thirty-six inches – more if he was walking fast. Walking with a stride of nineteen-and-a-half inches he would look as if his legs were tied together.

"I next proceeded to the Bay, and took two moulds from the footprints of the man with the nailed shoes, a right and a left. Here is a cast from the mould, and it shows very clearly that the man was walking backwards."

"How does it show that?" asked the magistrate.

"There are several distinctive points. For instance, the absence of the usual 'kick off' at the toe, the slight drag behind the heel, showing the direction in which the foot was lifted, and the undisturbed impression of the sole."

"You have spoken of moulds and casts. What is the difference between them?"

"A mould is a direct, and therefore reversed, impression. A cast is the impression of a mould, and therefore a facsimile of the object. If I pour liquid plaster on a coin, when it sets I have a mould, a sunk impression, of the coin. If I pour melted wax into the mould I obtain a cast, a facsimile of the coin. A footprint is a mould of the foot. A mould of the footprint is a cast of the foot, and a cast from the mould reproduces the footprint."

"Thank you," said the magistrate. "Then your moulds from these two footprints are really facsimiles of the murderer's shoes, and can be compared with these shoes which have been put in evidence?"

"Yes, and when we compare them they demonstrate a very important fact."

"What is that?"

"It is that the prisoner's shoes were not the shoes that made those footprints." A buzz of astonishment ran through the court, but Thorndyke continued stolidly, "The prisoner's shoes were not in my possession, so I went on to Barker's pond, on the clay margin of which I had seen footprints actually made by the prisoner. I took moulds of those footprints, and compared them with these from the sand. There are several important differences, which you will see if you compare them. To facilitate the comparison I have made transparent photographs of both sets of moulds to the same scale. Now, if we put the photograph of the mould of the prisoner's right shoe over that of the murderer's right shoe, and hold the two superposed photographs up to the light, we cannot make the two pictures coincide. They are exactly of the same length, but the shoes are of different shape. Moreover, if we put one of the nails in one photograph over the corresponding nail in the other photograph, we cannot make the rest of the nails coincide. But the most conclusive fact of all – from which there is no possible escape – is that the number of nails in the two shoes is not the same. In the sole of the prisoner's right shoe there are forty nails, in that of the murderer there are forty-one. The murderer has one nail too many."

There was a deathly silence in the court as the magistrates and Mr. Bashfield pored over the moulds and the prisoner's shoes, and examined the photographs against the light. Then the chairman asked, "Are these all the facts, or have you something more to tell us?" He was evidently anxious to get the key to this riddle.

"There is more evidence, your Worship," said Anstey. "The witness examined the body of deceased." Then, turning to Thorndyke, he asked, "You were present at the post-mortem examination?"

"I was."

"Did you form any opinion as to the cause of death?"

"Yes. I came to the conclusion that death was occasioned by an overdose of morphia."

A universal gasp of amazement greeted this statement. Then the presiding magistrate protested breathlessly, "But there was a wound, which we have been told was capable of causing instantaneous death. Was that not the case?"

"There was undoubtedly such a wound," replied Thorndyke. "But when that wound was inflicted the deceased had already been dead from a quarter to half-an-hour."

"This is incredible!" exclaimed the magistrate. "But, no doubt, you can give us your reasons for this amazing conclusion?"

"My opinion," said Thorndyke, "was based on several facts. In the first place, a wound inflicted on a living body gapes rather widely, owing to the retraction of the living skin. The skin of a dead body does not retract, and the wound, consequently, does not gape. This wound gaped very slightly, showing that death was recent, I should say, within half-an-hour. Then a wound on the living body becomes filled with blood, and blood is shed freely on the clothing. But the wound on the deceased contained only a little blood-clot. There was hardly any blood on the clothing, and I had already noticed that there was none on the sand where the body had lain."

"And you consider this quite conclusive?" the magistrate asked doubtfully.

"I do," answered Thorndyke. "But there was other evidence which was beyond all question. The weapon had partially divided both the aorta and the pulmonary artery – the main arteries of the body. Now, during life, these great vessels are full of blood at a high internal pressure, whereas after death they become almost empty. It follows that, if this wound had been inflicted during life, the cavity in which those vessels lie would have become filled with blood. As a matter of fact, it contained practically no blood, only the merest oozing from some small veins, so that it is certain that the wound was inflicted after death. The presence and nature of the poison I ascertained by analyzing certain secretions from the body, and the analysis enabled me to judge that the quantity of the poison was large, but the contents of the stomach were sent to Professor Copland for more exact examination."

"Is the result of Professor Copland's analysis known?" the magistrate asked Anstey.

"The professor is here, your Worship," replied Anstey, "and is prepared to swear to having obtained over one grain of morphia from the contents of the stomach, and as this, which is in itself a poisonous dose, is only the unabsorbed residue of what was actually swallowed, the total quantity taken must have been very large indeed."

"Thank you," said the magistrate. "And now, Dr. Thorndyke, if you have given us all the facts, perhaps you will tell us what conclusions you have drawn from them."

"The facts which I have stated," said Thorndyke, "appear to me to indicate the following sequence of events. The deceased died about midnight on September 27, from the effects of a poisonous dose of morphia, how or by whom administered I offer no opinion. I think that his body was conveyed in a boat to Sundersley Gap. The boat probably contained three men, of whom one remained in charge of it, one walked up the Gap and along the cliff towards St. Bridget's Bay, and the third, having put on the shoes of the deceased, carried the body along the shore to the Bay. This would account for the great depth and short stride of the tracks that have been spoken of as those of the deceased. Having reached the Bay, I believe that this man laid the corpse down on his tracks, and then trampled the sand in the neighbourhood. He next took off deceased's shoes and put them on the corpse. Then he put on a pair of boots or shoes which he had been carrying – perhaps hung round his neck – and which had been prepared with nails to imitate Draper's shoes. In these shoes he again trampled over the area near the corpse. Then he walked backwards to the Shepherd's Path, and from it again, still backwards, to the face of the cliff. Here his accomplice had lowered a rope, by which he climbed up to the top. At the top he took off the nailed shoes, and the two men walked back to the Gap, where the man who had carried the rope took his confederate on his back, and carried him down to the boat to avoid leaving the tracks of stockinged feet. The tracks that I saw at the Gap certainly indicated that the man was carrying something very heavy when he returned to the boat."

"But why should the man have climbed a rope up the cliff when he could have walked up the Shepherd's Path?" the magistrate asked.

"Because," replied Thorndyke, "there would then have been a set of tracks leading out of the Bay without a corresponding set leading into it, and this would have instantly suggested to a smart police-officer – such as Sergeant Payne – a landing from a boat."

"Your explanation is highly ingenious," said the magistrate, "and appears to cover all the very remarkable facts. Have you anything more to tell us?"

"No, your Worship," was the reply, "excepting" (here he took from Polton the last pair of moulds and passed them up to the magistrate) "that you will probably find these moulds of importance presently."

As Thorndyke stepped from the box – for there was no cross-examination – the magistrates scrutinized the moulds with an air of perplexity, but they were too discreet to make any remark.

When the evidence of Professor Copland (which showed that an unquestionably lethal dose of morphia must have been swallowed) had been taken, the clerk called out the – to me – unfamiliar name of Jacob Gummer. Thereupon an enormous pair of brown dreadnought trousers, from the upper end of which a smack-boy's head and shoulders protruded, walked into the witness-box.

Jacob admitted at the outset that he was a smack-master's apprentice, and that he had been "hired out" by his master to one Mr. Jezzard as deck-hand and cabin-boy of the yacht *Otter*.

"Now, Gummer," said Anstey, "do you remember the prisoner coming on board the yacht?"

"Yes. He has been on board twice. The first time was about a month ago. He went for a sail with us then. The second time was on the night when Mr. Hearn was murdered."

"Do you remember what sort of boots the prisoner was wearing the first time he came?"

"Yes. They were shoes with a lot of nails in the soles. I remember them because Mr. Jezzard made him take them off and put on a canvas pair."

"What was done with the nailed shoes?"

"Mr. Jezzard took 'em below to the cabin."

"And did Mr. Jezzard come up on deck again directly?"

"No. He stayed down in the cabin about ten minutes."

"Do you remember a parcel being delivered on board from a London boot-maker?"

"Yes. The postman brought it about four or five days after Mr. Draper had been on board. It was labelled 'Walker Bros., Boot and Shoe Makers, London.' Mr. Jezzard took a pair of shoes from it, for I saw them on the locker in the cabin the same day."

76

"Did you ever see him wear them?"

"No. I never see 'em again."

"Have you ever heard sounds of hammering on the yacht?"

"Yes. The night after the parcel came I was on the quay alongside, and I heard someone a-hammering in the cabin."

"What did the hammering sound like?"

"It sounded like a cobbler a-hammering in nails."

"Have you over seen any boot-nails on the yacht?"

"Yes. When I was a-clearin' up the cabin the next mornin', I found a hobnail on the floor in a corner by the locker."

"Were you on board on the night when Mr. Hearn died?"

"Yes. I'd been ashore, but I came aboard about half-past-nine."

"Did you see Mr. Hearn go ashore?"

"I see him leave the yacht. I had turned into my bunk and gone to sleep, when Mr. Jezzard calls down to me, 'We're putting Mr. Hearn ashore,' says he, 'and then,' he says, 'we're a-going for an hour's fishing. You needn't sit up,' he says, and with that he shuts the scuttle. Then I got up and slid back the scuttle and put my head out, and I see Mr. Jezzard and Mr. Leach a-helpin' Mr. Hearn acrost the deck. Mr. Hearn he looked as if he was drunk. They got him into the boat – and a rare job they had – and Mr. Pitford, what was in the boat already, he pushed off. And then I popped my head in again, 'cause I didn't want them to see me."

"Did they row to the steps?"

"No. I put my head out again when they were gone, and I heard 'em row round the yacht, and then pull out towards the mouth of the harbour. I couldn't see the boat, 'cause it was a very dark night."

"Very well. Now I am going to ask you about another matter. Do you know anyone of the name of Polton?"

"Yes," replied Gummer, turning a dusky red. "I've just found out his real name. I thought he was called Simmons."

"Tell us what you know about him," said Anstey, with a mischievous smile.

"Well," said the boy, with a ferocious scowl at the bland and smiling Polton, "one day he come down to the yacht when the gentlemen had gone ashore. I believe he'd seen 'em go. And he offers me ten shillin' to let him see all the boots and shoes we'd got on board. I didn't see no harm, so I turns out the whole lot in the cabin for him to look at. While he was lookin' at 'em he asks me to fetch a pair of mine from the fo'c'sle, so I fetches 'em. When I come back he was pitchin' the boots and shoes back into the locker. Then, presently, he nips off, and when he was gone I looked over the shoes, and then I found there was a pair missing. They was an old pair of Mr. Jezzard's, and what made him nick 'em is more than I can understand."

"Would you know those shoes if you saw them!"

"Yes, I should," replied the lad.

"Are these the pair?" Anstey handed the boy a pair of dilapidated canvas shoes, which he seized eagerly.

"Yes, these is the ones what he stole!" he exclaimed.

Anstey took them back from the boy's reluctant hands, and passed them up to the magistrate's desk. "I think," said he, "that if your Worship will compare these shoes with the last pair of moulds, you will have no doubt that these are the shoes which made the footprints from the sea to Sundersley Gap and back again."

The magistrates together compared the shoes and the moulds amidst a breathless silence. At length the chairman laid them down on the desk.

"It is impossible to doubt it," said he. "The broken heel and the tear in the rubber sole, with the remains of the chequered pattern, make the identity practically certain."

As the chairman made this statement I involuntarily glanced round to the place where Jezzard was sitting. But he was not there, neither he, nor Pitford, nor Leach. Taking advantage of the preoccupation of the Court, they had quietly slipped out of the door. But I was not the only person who had noted their absence. The inspector and the sergeant were already in earnest consultation, and a minute later they, too, hurriedly departed.

The proceedings now speedily came to an end. After a brief discussion with his brother-magistrates, the chairman addressed the Court.

"The remarkable and I may say startling evidence, which has been heard in this court to-day, if it has not fixed the guilt of this crime on any individual, has, at any rate, made it clear to our satisfaction that the prisoner is not the guilty person, and he is accordingly discharged. Mr. Draper, I have great pleasure in informing you that you are at liberty to leave the court, and that you do so entirely clear of all suspicion, and I congratulate you very heartily on the skill and ingenuity of your legal advisers, but for which the decision of the Court would, I am afraid, have been very different."

That evening, lawyers, witnesses, and the jubilant and grateful client gathered round a truly festive board to dine, and fight over again the battle of the day. But we were scarcely halfway through our meal when, to the indignation of the servants, Sergeant Payne burst breathlessly into the room.

"They've gone, sir!" he exclaimed, addressing Thorndyke. "They've given us the slip for good."

"Why, how can that be?" asked Thorndyke.

78

"They're dead, sir! All three of them!"

"Dead!" we all exclaimed.

"Yes. They made a burst for the yacht when they left the court, and they got on board and put out to sea at once, hoping, no doubt, to get clear as the light was just failing. But they were in such a hurry that they did not see a steam trawler that was entering, and was hidden by the pier. Then, just at the entrance, as the yacht was creeping out, the trawler hit her amidships, and fairly cut her in two. The three men were in the water in an instant, and were swept away in the eddy behind the north pier, and before any boat could put out to them they had all gone under. Jezzard's body came up on the beach just as I was coming away."

We were all silent and a little awed, but if any of us felt regret at the catastrophe, it was at the thought that three such cold-blooded villains should have made so easy an exit, and to one of us, at least, the news came as a blessed relief.

The Stranger's Latchkey

The contrariety of human nature is a subject that has given a surprising amount of occupation to makers of proverbs and to those moral philosophers who make it their province to discover and expound the glaringly obvious, and especially have they been concerned to enlarge upon that form of perverseness which engenders dislike of things offered under compulsion, and arouses desire of them as soon as their attainment becomes difficult or impossible. They assure us that a man who has had a given thing within his reach and put it by, will, as soon as it is beyond his reach, find it the one thing necessary and desirable, even as the domestic cat which has turned disdainfully from the preferred saucer, may presently be seen with her head jammed hard in the milk-jug, or, secretly and with horrible relish, slaking her thirst at the scullery sink.

To this peculiarity of the human mind was due, no doubt, the fact that no sooner had I abandoned the clinical side of my profession in favour of the legal, and taken up my abode in the chambers of my friend Thorndyke, the famous medico-legal expert, to act as his assistant or junior, than my former mode of life – that of a locum tenens, or minder of other men's practices – which had, when I was following it, seemed intolerably irksome, now appeared to possess many desirable features, and I found myself occasionally hankering to sit once more by the bedside, to puzzle out the perplexing train of symptoms, and to wield that power – the greatest, after all, possessed by man – the power to banish suffering and ward off the approach of death itself.

Hence it was that on a certain morning of the long vacation I found myself installed at The Larches, Burling, in full charge of the practice of my old friend Dr. Hanshaw, who was taking a fishing holiday in Norway. I was not left desolate, however, for Mrs. Hanshaw remained at her post, and the roomy, old-fashioned house accommodated three visitors in addition. One of these was Dr. Hanshaw's sister, a Mrs. Haldean, the widow of a wealthy Manchester cotton factor; the second was her niece by marriage, Miss Lucy Haldean, a very handsome and charming girl of twenty-three, while the third was no less a person than Master Fred, the only child of Mrs. Haldean, and a strapping boy of six.

"It is quite like old times – and very pleasant old times, too – to see you sitting at our breakfast-table, Dr. Jervis." With these gracious words and a friendly smile, Mrs. Hanshaw handed me my tea-cup.

I bowed. "The highest pleasure of the altruist," I replied, "is in contemplating the good fortune of others."

Mrs. Haldean laughed. "Thank you," she said. "You are quite unchanged, I perceive. Still as suave and as – shall I say *oleaginous*?"

"No, please don't!" I exclaimed in a tone of alarm.

"Then I won't. But what does Dr. Thorndyke say to this backsliding on your part? How does he regard this relapse from medical jurisprudence to common general practice?"

"Thorndyke," said I, "is unmoved by any catastrophe, and he not only regards the 'Decline and Fall-off of the Medical Jurist' with philosophic calm, but he even favours the relapse, as you call it. He thinks it may be useful to me to study the application of medico-legal methods to general practice."

"That sounds rather unpleasant – for the patients, I mean," remarked Miss Haldean.

"Very," agreed her aunt. "Most cold-blooded. What sort of man is Dr. Thorndyke? I feel quite curious about him. Is he at all human, for instance?"

"He is entirely human," I replied, "the accepted tests of humanity being, as I understand, the habitual adoption of the erect posture in locomotion, and the relative position of the end of the thumb – "

"I don't mean that," interrupted Mrs. Haldean. "I mean human in things that matter."

"I think those things matter," I rejoined. "Consider, Mrs. Haldean, what would happen if my learned colleague were to be seen in wig and gown, walking towards the Law Courts in any posture other than the erect. It would be a public scandal."

"Don't talk to him, Mabel," said Mrs. Hanshaw, "he is incorrigible. What are you doing with yourself this morning, Lucy?"

Miss Haldean (who had hastily set down her cup to laugh at my imaginary picture of Dr. Thorndyke in the character of a quadruped) considered a moment.

"I think I shall sketch that group of birches at the edge of Bradham Wood," she said.

"Then, in that case," said I, "I can carry your traps for you, for I have to see a patient in Bradham."

"He is making the most of his time," remarked Mrs. Haldean maliciously to my hostess. "He knows that when Mr. Winter arrives he will retire into the extreme background."

Douglas Winter, whose arrival was expected in the course of the week, was Miss Haldean's fiancé. Their engagement had been somewhat protracted, and was likely to be more so, unless one of them received some unexpected accession of means, for Douglas was a subaltern in the Royal

Engineers, living, with great difficulty, on his pay, while Lucy Haldean subsisted on an almost invisible allowance left her by an uncle.

I was about to reply to Mrs. Haldean when a patient was announced, and, as I had finished my breakfast, I made my excuses and left the table.

Half-an-hour later, when I started along the road to the village of Bradham, I had two companions. Master Freddy had joined the party, and he disputed with me the privilege of carrying the "traps," with the result that a compromise was effected, by which he carried the camp-stool, leaving me in possession of the easel, the bag, and a large bound sketching-block.

"Where are you going to work this morning?" I asked, when we had trudged on some distance.

"Just off the road to the left there, at the edge of the wood. Not very far from the house of the mysterious stranger." She glanced at me mischievously as she made this reply, and chuckled with delight when I rose at the bait.

"What house do you mean?" I inquired.

"Ha!" she exclaimed, "the investigator of mysteries is aroused. He saith, 'Ha! ha!' amidst the trumpets, he smelleth the battle afar off."

"Explain instantly," I commanded, "or I drop your sketch-block into the very next puddle."

"You terrify me," said she. "But I will explain, only there isn't any mystery except to the bucolic mind. The house is called Lavender Cottage, and it stands alone in the fields behind the wood. A fortnight ago it was let furnished to a stranger named Whitelock, who has taken it for the purpose of studying the botany of the district, and the only really mysterious thing about him is that no one has seen him. All arrangements with the house-agent were made by letter, and, as far as I can make out, none of the local tradespeople supply him, so he must get his things from a distance – even his bread, which really is rather odd. Now say I am an inquisitive, gossiping country bumpkin."

"I was going to," I answered, "but it is no use now."

She relieved me of her sketching appliances with pretended indignation, and crossed into the meadow, leaving me to pursue my way alone, and when I presently looked back, she was setting up her easel and stool, gravely assisted by Freddy.

My "round," though not a long one, took up more time than I had anticipated, and it was already past the luncheon hour when I passed the place where I had left Miss Haldean. She was gone, as I had expected, and I hurried homewards, anxious to be as nearly punctual as possible. When I entered the dining-room, I found Mrs. Haldean and our hostess seated at the table, and both looked up at me expectantly.

"Have you seen Lucy?" the former inquired.

"No," I answered. "Hasn't she come back? I expected to find her here. She had left the wood when I passed just now."

Mrs. Haldean knitted her brows anxiously. "It is very strange," she said, "and very thoughtless of her. Freddy will be famished."

I hurried over my lunch, for two fresh messages had come in from outlying hamlets, effectually dispelling my visions of a quiet afternoon, and as the minutes passed without bringing any signs of the absentees, Mrs. Haldean became more and more restless and anxious. At length her suspense became unbearable. She rose suddenly, announcing her intention of cycling up the road to look for the defaulters, but as she was moving towards the door, it burst open, and Lucy Haldean staggered into the room.

Her appearance filled us with alarm. She was deadly pale, breathless, and wild-eyed, her dress was draggled and torn, and she trembled from head to foot.

"Good God, Lucy!" gasped Mrs. Haldean. "What has happened? And where is Freddy?" she added in a sterner tone.

"He is lost!" replied Miss Haldean in a faint voice, and with a catch in her breath. "He strayed away while I was painting. I have searched the wood through, and called to him, and looked in all the meadows. Oh! where can he have gone?" Her sketching "kit," with which she was loaded, slipped from her grasp and rattled on to the floor, and she buried her face in her hands and sobbed hysterically.

"And you have dared to come back without him?" exclaimed Mrs. Haldean.

"I was getting exhausted. I came back for help," was the faint reply.

"Of course she was exhausted," said Mrs. Hanshaw. "Come, Lucy, come, Mabel. Don't make mountains out of molehills. The little man is safe enough. We shall find him presently, or he will come home by himself. Come and have some food, Lucy."

Miss Haldean shook her head. "I can't, Mrs. Hanshaw – really I can't," she said, and, seeing that she was in a state of utter exhaustion, I poured out a glass of wine and made her drink it.

Mrs. Haldean darted from the room, and returned immediately, putting on her hat. "You have got to come with me and show me where you lost him," she said.

"She can't do that, you know," I said rather brusquely. "She will have to lie down for the present. But I know the place, and will cycle up with you."

"Very well," replied Mrs. Haldean, "that will do. What time was it," she asked, turning to her niece, "when you lost the child? and which way
– "

She paused abruptly, and I looked at her in surprise. She had suddenly turned ashen and ghastly, her face had set like a mask of stone, with parted lips and staring eyes that were fixed in horror on her niece.

There was a deathly silence for a few seconds. Then, in a terrible voice, she demanded, "What is that on your dress, Lucy?" And, after a pause, her voice rose into a shriek. "What have you done to my boy?"

I glanced in astonishment at the dazed and terrified girl, and then I saw what her aunt had seen – a good-sized blood-stain halfway down the front of her skirt, and another smaller one on her right sleeve. The girl herself looked down at the sinister patch of red and then up at her aunt. "It looks like – like blood," she stammered. "Yes, it is – I think – of course it is. He struck his nose – and it bled – "

"Come," interrupted Mrs. Haldean, "let us go," and she rushed from the room, leaving me to follow.

I lifted Miss Haldean, who was half-fainting with fatigue and agitation, on to the sofa, and, whispering a few words of encouragement into her ear, turned to Mrs. Hanshaw.

"I can't stay with Mrs. Haldean," I said. "There are two visits to be made at Rebworth. Will you send the dogcart up the road with somebody to take my place?"

"Yes," she answered. "I will send Giles, or come myself if Lucy is fit to be left."

I ran to the stables for my bicycle, and as I pedalled out into the road I could see Mrs. Haldean already far ahead, driving her machine at frantic speed. I followed at a rapid pace, but it was not until we approached the commencement of the wood, when she slowed down somewhat, that I overtook her.

"This is the place," I said, as we reached the spot where I had parted from Miss Haldean. We dismounted and wheeled our bicycles through the gate, and laying them down beside the hedge, crossed the meadow and entered the wood.

It was a terrible experience, and one that I shall never forget – the white-faced, distracted woman, tramping in her flimsy house-shoes over the rough ground, bursting through the bushes, regardless of the thorny branches that dragged at skin and hair and dainty clothing, and sending forth from time to time a tremulous cry, so dreadfully pathetic in its mingling of terror and coaxing softness, that a lump rose in my throat, and I could barely keep my self-control.

"Freddy! Freddy-boy! Mummy's here, darling!" The wailing cry sounded through the leafy solitude, but no answer came save the whirr of wings or the chatter of startled birds. But even more shocking than that terrible cry – more disturbing and eloquent with dreadful suggestion – was the way in which she peered, furtively, but with fearful expectation, among the roots of the bushes, or halted to gaze upon every molehill and hummock, every depression or disturbance of the ground.

So we stumbled on for a while, with never a word spoken, until we came to a beaten track or footpath leading across the wood. Here I paused to examine the footprints, of which several were visible in the soft earth, though none seemed very recent, but, proceeding a little way down the track, I perceived, crossing it, a set of fresh imprints, which I recognized at once as Miss Haldean's. She was wearing, as I knew, a pair of brown golf-boots, with rubber pads in the leather soles, and the prints made by them were unmistakable.

"Miss Haldean crossed the path here," I said, pointing to the footprints.

"Don't speak of her before me!" exclaimed Mrs. Haldean, but she gazed eagerly at the footprints, nevertheless, and immediately plunged into the wood to follow the tracks.

"You are very unjust to your niece, Mrs. Haldean," I ventured to protest.

She halted, and faced me with an angry frown.

"You don't understand!" she exclaimed. "You don't know, perhaps, that if my poor child is really dead, Lucy Haldean will be a rich woman, and may marry to-morrow if she chooses?"

"I did not know that," I answered, "but if I had, I should have said the same."

"Of course you would," she retorted bitterly. "A pretty face can muddle any man's judgment."

She turned away abruptly to resume her pursuit, and I followed in silence. The trail which we were following zigzagged through the thickest part of the wood, but its devious windings eventually brought us out on to an open space on the farther side. Here we at once perceived traces of another kind. A litter of dirty rags, pieces of paper, scraps of stale bread, bones and feathers, with hoof-marks, wheel ruts, and the ashes of a large wood fire, pointed clearly to a gipsy encampment recently broken up. I laid my hand on the heap of ashes, and found it still warm, and on scattering it with my foot a layer of glowing cinders appeared at the bottom.

"These people have only been gone an hour or two," I said. "It would be well to have them followed without delay."

A gleam of hope shone on the drawn, white face as the bereaved mother caught eagerly at my suggestion.

"Yes," she exclaimed breathlessly, "she may have bribed them to take him away. Let us see which way they went."

We followed the wheel tracks down to the road, and found that they turned towards London. At the same time I perceived the dogcart in the distance, with Mrs. Hanshaw standing beside it, and, as the coachman observed me, he whipped up his horse and approached.

"I shall have to go," I said, "but Mrs. Hanshaw will help you to continue the search."

"And you will make inquiries about the gipsies, won't you?" she said.

I promised to do so, and as the dogcart now came up, I climbed to the seat, and drove off briskly up the London Road.

The extent of a country doctor's round is always an unknown quantity. On the present occasion I picked up three additional patients, and as one of them was a case of incipient pleurisy, which required to have the chest strapped, and another was a neglected dislocation of the shoulder, a great deal of time was taken up. Moreover, the gipsies, whom I ran to earth on Rebworth Common, delayed me considerably, though I had to leave the rural constable to carry out the actual search, and, as a result, the clock of Burling Church was striking six as I drove through the village on my way home.

I got down at the front gate, leaving the coachman to take the dogcart round, and walked up the drive, and my astonishment may be imagined when, on turning the corner, I came suddenly upon the inspector of the local police in earnest conversation with no less a person than John Thorndyke.

"What on earth has brought you here?" I exclaimed, my surprise getting the better of my manners.

"The ultimate motive-force," he replied, "was an impulsive lady named Mrs. Haldean. She telegraphed for me – in your name."

"She oughtn't to have done that," I said.

"Perhaps not. But the ethics of an agitated woman are not worth discussing, and she has done something much worse – she has applied to the local J.P. (a retired Major-General), and our gallant and unlearned friend has issued a warrant for the arrest of Lucy Haldean on the charge of murder."

"But there has been no murder!" I exclaimed.

"That," said Thorndyke, "is a legal subtlety that he does not appreciate. He has learned his law in the orderly-room, where the qualifications to practise are an irritable temper and a loud voice. However, the practical point is, Inspector, that the warrant is irregular. You can't arrest people for hypothetical crimes."

The officer drew a deep breath of relief. He knew all about the irregularity, and now joyfully took refuge behind Thorndyke's great reputation.

When he had departed – with a brief note from my colleague to the General – Thorndyke slipped his arm through mine, and we strolled towards the house.

"This is a grim business, Jervis," said he. "That boy has got to be found for everybody's sake. Can you come with me when you have had some food?"

"Of course I can. I have been saving myself all the afternoon with a view to continuing the search."

"Good," said Thorndyke. "Then come in and feed."

A nondescript meal, half-tea and half-dinner, was already prepared, and Mrs. Hanshaw, grave but self-possessed, presided at the table.

"Mabel is still out with Giles, searching for the boy," she said. "You have heard what she has done!"

I nodded.

"It was dreadful of her," continued Mrs. Hanshaw, "but she is half-mad, poor thing. You might run up and say a few kind words to poor Lucy while I make the tea."

I went up at once and knocked at Miss Haldean's door, and, being bidden to enter, found her lying on the sofa, red-eyed and pale, the very ghost of the merry, laughing girl who had gone out with me in the morning. I drew up a chair, and sat down by her side, and as I took the hand she held out to me, she said, "It is good of you to come and see a miserable wretch like me. And Jane has been so sweet to me, Dr. Jervis, but Aunt Mabel thinks I have killed Freddy – you know she does – and it was really my fault that he was lost. I shall never forgive myself!"

She burst into a passion of sobbing, and I proceeded to chide her gently.

"You are a silly little woman," I said, "to take this nonsense to heart as you are doing. Your aunt is not responsible just now, as you must know, but when we bring the boy home she shall make you a handsome apology. I will see to that."

She pressed my hand gratefully, and as the bell now rang for tea, I bade her have courage and went downstairs.

"You need not trouble about the practice," said Mrs. Hanshaw, as I concluded my lightning repast, and Thorndyke went off to get our bicycles. "Dr. Symons has heard of our trouble, and has called to say that he will take anything that turns up, so we shall expect you when we see you."

"How do you like Thorndyke?" I asked.

"He is quite charming," she replied enthusiastically, "so tactful and kind, and so handsome, too. You didn't tell us that. But here he is. Good-bye, and good luck."

She pressed my hand, and I went out into the drive, where Thorndyke and the coachman were standing with three bicycles.

"I see you have brought your outfit," I said as we turned into the road, for Thorndyke's machine bore a large canvas-covered case strapped on to a strong bracket.

"Yes, there are many things that we may want on a quest of this kind. How did you find Miss Haldean?"

"Very miserable, poor girl. By the way, have you heard anything about her pecuniary interest in the child's death?"

"Yes," said Thorndyke. "It appears that the late Mr. Haldean used up all his brains on his business, and had none left for the making of his will – as often happens. He left almost the whole of his property – about eighty thousand pounds – to his son, the widow to have a life-interest in it. He also left to his late brother's daughter, Lucy, fifty pounds a year, and to his surviving brother Percy, who seems to have been a good-for-nothing, a hundred a year for life. But – and here is the utter folly of the thing – if the son should die, the property was to be equally divided between the brother and the niece, with the exception of five hundred a year for life to the widow. It was an insane arrangement."

"Quite," I agreed, "and a very dangerous one for Lucy Haldean, as things are at present."

"Very, especially if anything should have happened to the child."

"What are you going to do now?" I inquired, seeing that Thorndyke rode on as if with a definite purpose.

"There is a footpath through the wood," he replied. "I want to examine that. And there is a house behind the wood which I should like to see."

"The house of the mysterious stranger," I suggested.

"Precisely. Mysterious and solitary strangers invite inquiry."

We drew up at the entrance to the footpath, leaving Willett the coachman in charge of the three machines, and proceeded up the narrow track. As we went, Thorndyke looked back at the prints of our feet, and nodded approvingly.

"This soft loam," he remarked, "yields beautifully clear impressions, and yesterday's rain has made it perfect."

We had not gone far when we perceived a set of footprints which I recognized, as did Thorndyke also, for he remarked, "Miss Haldean – running, and alone." Presently we met them again, crossing in the opposite direction, together with the prints of small shoes with very high heels. "Mrs. Haldean on the track of her niece," was Thorndyke's comment, and a minute later we encountered them both again, accompanied by my own footprints.

"The boy does not seem to have crossed the path at all," I remarked as we walked on, keeping off the track itself to avoid confusing the footprints.

"We shall know when we have examined the whole length," replied Thorndyke, plodding on with his eyes on the ground. "Ha! here is something new," he added, stopping short and stooping down eagerly – "a man with a thick stick – a smallish man, rather lame. Notice the difference between the two feet, and the peculiar way in which he uses his stick. Yes, Jervis, there is a great deal to interest us in these footprints. Do you notice anything very suggestive about them?"

"Nothing but what you have mentioned," I replied. "What do you mean?"

"Well, first there is the very singular character of the prints themselves, which we will consider presently. You observe that this man came down the path, and at this point turned off into the wood, then he returned from the wood and went up the path again. The imposition of the prints makes that clear. But now look at the two sets of prints, and compare them. Do you notice any difference?"

"The returning footprints seem more distinct – better impressions."

"Yes, they are noticeably deeper. But there is something else." He produced a spring tape from his pocket, and took half-a-dozen measurements. "You see," he said, "the first set of footprints have a stride of twenty-one inches from heel to heel – a short stride, but he is a smallish man, and lame. The returning ones have a stride of only nineteen-and-a-half inches – hence the returning footprints are deeper than the others, and the steps are shorter. What do you make of that?"

"It would suggest that he was carrying a burden when he returned," I replied.

"Yes, and a heavy one, to make that difference in the depth. I think I will get you to go and fetch Willett and the bicycles."

I strode off down the path to the entrance, and, taking possession of Thorndyke's machine, with its precious case of instruments, bade Willett follow with the other two.

When I returned, my colleague was standing with his hands behind him, gazing with intense preoccupation at the footprints. He looked up sharply as we approached, and called out to us to keep off the path if possible.

"Stay here with the machines, Willett," said he. "You and I, Jervis, must go and see where our friend went to when he left the path, and what was the burden that he picked up."

We struck off into the wood, where last year's dead leaves made the footprints almost indistinguishable, and followed the faint double track for a long distance between the dense clumps of bushes. Suddenly my eye caught, beside the double trail, a third row of tracks, smaller in size and closer together. Thorndyke had seen them, too, and already his measuring-tape was in his hand.

"Eleven-and-a-half inches to the stride," said he. "That will be the boy, Jervis. But the light is getting weak. We must press on quickly, or we shall lose it."

Some fifty yards farther on, the man's tracks ceased abruptly, but the small ones continued alone, and we followed them as rapidly as we could in the fading light.

"There can be no reasonable doubt that these are the child's tracks," said Thorndyke, "but I should like to find a definite footprint to make the identification absolutely certain."

A few seconds later he halted with an exclamation, and stooped on one knee. A little heap of fresh earth from the surface-burrow of a mole had been thrown up over the dead leaves, and fairly planted on it was the clean and sharp impression of a diminutive foot, with a rubber heel showing a central star. Thorndyke drew from his pocket a tiny shoe, and pressed it on the soft earth beside the footprint, and when he raised it the second impression was identical with the first.

"The boy had two pairs of shoes exactly alike," he said, "so I borrowed one of the duplicate pair."

He turned, and began to retrace his steps rapidly, following our own fresh tracks, and stopping only once to point out the place where the unknown man had picked the child up. When we regained the path we proceeded without delay until we emerged from the wood within a hundred yards of the cottage.

"I see Mrs. Haldean has been here with Giles," remarked Thorndyke, as he pushed open the garden-gate. "I wonder if they saw anybody."

He advanced to the door, and having first rapped with his knuckles and then kicked at it vigorously, tried the handle.

"Locked," he observed, "but I see the key is in the lock, so we can get in if we want to. Let us try the back."

The back door was locked, too, but the key had been removed.

"He came out this way, evidently," said Thorndyke, "though he went in at the front, as I suppose you noticed. Let us see where he went."

The back garden was a small, fenced patch of ground, with an earth path leading down to the back gate. A little way beyond the gate was a small barn or outhouse.

"We are in luck," Thorndyke remarked, with a glance at the path. "Yesterday's rain has cleared away all old footprints, and prepared the surface for new ones. You see there are three sets of excellent impressions

– two leading away from the house, and one set towards it. Now, you notice that both of the sets leading from the house are characterized by deep impressions and short steps, while the set leading to the house has lighter impressions and longer steps. The obvious inference is that he went down the path with a heavy burden, came back empty-handed, and went down again – and finally – with another heavy burden. You observe, too, that he walked with his stick on each occasion."

By this time we had reached the bottom of the garden. Opening the gate, we followed the tracks towards the outhouse, which stood beside a cart-track, but as we came round the corner we both stopped short and looked at one another. On the soft earth were the very distinct impressions of the tyres of a motor-car leading from the wide door of the outhouse. Finding that the door was unfastened, Thorndyke opened it, and looked in, to satisfy himself that the place was empty. Then he fell to studying the tracks.

"The course of events is pretty plain," he observed. "First the fellow brought down his luggage, started the engine, and got the car out – you can see where it stood, both by the little pool of oil, and by the widening and blurring of the wheel-tracks from the vibration of the free engine. Then he went back and fetched the boy – carried him pick-a-back, I should say, judging by the depth of the toe-marks in the last set of footprints. That was a tactical mistake. He should have taken the boy straight into the shed."

He pointed as he spoke to one of the footprints beside the wheel-tracks, from the toe of which projected a small segment of the print of a little rubber heel.

We now made our way back to the house, where we found Willett pensively rapping at the front door with a cycle-spanner. Thorndyke took a last glance, with his hand in his pocket, at an open window above, and then, to the coachman's intense delight, brought forth what looked uncommonly like a small bunch of skeleton keys. One of these he inserted into the keyhole, and as he gave it a turn, the lock clicked, and the door stood open.

The little sitting-room, which we now entered, was furnished with the barest necessaries. Its centre was occupied by an oilcloth-covered table, on which I observed with surprise a dismembered "Bee" clock (the works of which had been taken apart with a tin-opener that lay beside them) and a box-wood bird-call. At these objects Thorndyke glanced and nodded, as though they fitted into some theory that he had formed, examined carefully the oilcloth around the litter of wheels and pinions, and then proceeded on a tour of inspection round the room, peering inquisitively into the kitchen and store-cupboard.

"Nothing very distinctive or personal here," he remarked. "Let us go upstairs."

There were three bedrooms on the upper floor, of which two were evidently disused, though the windows were wide open. The third bedroom showed manifest traces of occupation, though it was as bare as the others, for the water still stood in the wash-hand basin, and the bed was unmade. To the latter Thorndyke advanced, and, having turned back the bedclothes, examined the interior attentively, especially at the foot and the pillow. The latter was soiled – not to say grimy – though the rest of the bed-linen was quite clean.

"Hair-dye," remarked Thorndyke, noting my glance at it. Then he turned and looked out of the open window. "Can you see the place where Miss Haldean was sitting to sketch?" he asked.

"Yes," I replied, "there is the place well in view, and you can see right up the road. I had no idea this house stood so high. From the three upper windows you can see all over the country excepting through the wood."

"Yes," Thorndyke rejoined, "and he has probably been in the habit of keeping watch up here with a telescope or a pair of field-glasses. Well, there is not much of interest in this room. He kept his effects in a cabin trunk which stood there under the window. He shaved this morning. He has a white beard, to judge by the stubble on the shaving-paper, and that is all. Wait, though. There is a key hanging on that nail. He must have overlooked that, for it evidently does not belong to this house. It is an ordinary town latchkey."

He took the key down, and having laid a sheet of notepaper, from his pocket, on the dressing-table, produced a pin, with which he began carefully to probe the interior of the key-barrel. Presently there came forth, with much coaxing, a large ball of grey fluff, which Thorndyke folded up in the paper with infinite care.

"I suppose we mustn't take away the key," he said, "but I think we will take a wax mould of it."

He hurried downstairs, and, unstrapping the case from his bicycle, brought it in and placed it on the table. As it was now getting dark, he detached the powerful acetylene lamp from his machine, and, having lighted it, proceeded to open the mysterious case. First he took from it a small insufflator, or powder-blower, with which he blew a cloud of light yellow powder over the table around the remains of the clock. The powder settled on the table in an even coating, but when he blew at it smartly with his breath, it cleared off, leaving, however, a number of smeary impressions which stood out in strong yellow against the black oilcloth. To one of these impressions he pointed significantly. It was the print of a child's hand.

He next produced a small, portable microscope and some glass slides and cover-slips, and having opened the paper and tipped the ball of fluff from the key-barrel on to a slide, set to work with a pair of mounted needles to tease it out into its component parts. Then he turned the light of the lamp on to the microscope mirror and proceeded to examine the specimen.

"A curious and instructive assortment this, Jervis," he remarked, with his eye at the microscope, "woollen fibres – no cotton or linen. He is careful of his health to have woollen pockets – and two hairs – very curious ones, too. Just look at them, and observe the root bulbs."

I applied my eye to the microscope, and saw, among other things, two hairs – originally white, but encrusted with a black, opaque, glistening stain. The root bulbs, I noticed, were shrivelled and atrophied.

"But how on earth," I exclaimed, "did the hairs get into his pocket?"

"I think the hairs themselves answer that question," he replied, "when considered with the other curios. The stain is obviously lead sulphide. But what else do you see?"

"I see some particles of metal – a white metal apparently – and a number of fragments of woody fibre and starch granules, but I don't recognize the starch. It is not wheat-starch, nor rice, nor potato. Do you make out what it is?"

Thorndyke chuckled. "Experientia does it," said he. "You will have, Jervis, to study the minute properties of dust and dirt. Their evidential value is immense. Let us have another look at that starch. It is all alike, I suppose."

It was, and Thorndyke had just ascertained the fact when the door burst open and Mrs. Haldean entered the room, followed by Mrs. Hanshaw and the police inspector. The former lady regarded my colleague with a glance of extreme disfavour.

"We heard that you had come here, sir," said she, "and we supposed you were engaged in searching for my poor child. But it seems we were mistaken, since we find you here amusing yourselves fiddling with these nonsensical instruments."

"Perhaps, Mabel," said Mrs. Hanshaw stiffly, "it would be wiser, and infinitely more polite, to ask if Dr. Thorndyke has any news for us."

"That is undoubtedly so, madam," agreed the inspector, who had apparently suffered also from Mrs. Haldean's impulsiveness.

"Then perhaps," the latter lady suggested, "you will inform us if you have discovered anything."

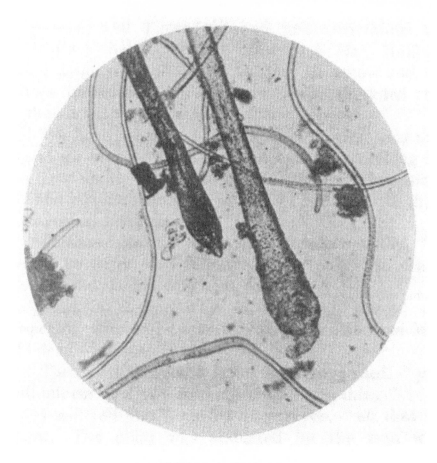

Fluff From the Key-Barrel
Magnified 77 Diameters

"I will tell you." replied Thorndyke, "all that we know. The child was abducted by the man who occupied this house, and who appears to have watched him from an upper window, probably through a glass. This man lured the child into the wood by blowing this bird-call. He met him in the wood, and induced him – by some promises, no doubt – to come with him. He picked the child up and carried him – on his back, I think – up to the house, and brought him in through the front door, which he locked after him. He gave the boy this clock and the bird-call to amuse him while he went upstairs and packed his trunk. He took the trunk out through the back door and down the garden to the shed there, in which he had a motor-car. He got the car out and came back for the boy, whom he carried down to the car, locking the back door after him. Then he drove away."

"You know he has gone," cried Mrs. Haldean, "and yet you stay here playing with these ridiculous toys. Why are you not following him?"

"We have just finished ascertaining the facts," Thorndyke replied calmly, "and should by now be on the road if you had not come."

Here the inspector interposed anxiously. "Of course, sir, you can't give any description of the man. You have no clue to his identity, I suppose?"

"We have only his footprints," Thorndyke answered, "and this fluff which I raked out of the barrel of his latchkey, and have just been examining. From these data I conclude that he is a rather short and thin man, and somewhat lame. He walks with the aid of a thick stick, which has a knob, not a crook, at the top, and which he carries in his left hand. I think that his left leg has been amputated above the knee, and that he wears an artificial limb. He is elderly, he shaves his beard, has white hair dyed a greyish black, is partly bald, and probably combs a wisp of hair over the bald place. He takes snuff, and carries a leaden comb in his pocket."

As Thorndyke's description proceeded, the inspector's mouth gradually opened wider and wider, until he appeared the very type and symbol of astonishment. But its effect on Mrs. Haldean was much more remarkable. Rising from her chair, she leaned on the table and stared at Thorndyke with an expression of awe – even of terror, and as he finished she sank back into her chair, with her hands clasped, and turned to Mrs. Hanshaw.

"Jane!" she gasped, "it is Percy – my brother-in-law! He has described him exactly, even to his stick and his pocket-comb. But I thought he was in Chicago."

"If that is so," said Thorndyke, hastily repacking his case, "we had better start at once."

"We have the dogcart in the road," said Mrs. Hanshaw.

"Thank you," replied Thorndyke. "We will ride on our bicycles, and the inspector can borrow Willett's. We go out at the back by the cart-track, which joins the road farther on."

"Then we will follow in the dogcart," said Mrs. Haldean. "Come, Jane."

The two ladies departed down the path, while we made ready our bicycles and lit our lamps.

"With your permission, Inspector," said Thorndyke, "we will take the key with us."

"It's hardly legal, sir," objected the officer. "We have no authority."

"It is quite illegal," answered Thorndyke, "but it is necessary, and necessity – like your military J.P. – knows no law."

The inspector grinned and went out, regarding me with a quivering eyelid as Thorndyke locked the door with his skeleton key. As we turned into the road, I saw the light of the dogcart behind us, and we pushed forward at a swift pace, picking up the trail easily on the soft, moist road.

"What beats me," said the inspector confidentially, as we rode along, "is how he knew the man was bald. Was it the footprints or the latchkey? And that comb, too, that was a regular knock-out."

These points were, by now, pretty clear to me. I had seen the hairs with their atrophied bulbs – such as one finds at the margin of a bald patch, and the comb was used, evidently, for the double purpose of keeping the bald patch covered and blackening the sulphur-charged hair. But the knobbed stick and the artificial limb puzzled me so completely that I presently overtook Thorndyke to demand an explanation.

"The stick," said he, "is perfectly simple. The ferrule of a knobbed stick wears evenly all round – that of a crooked stick wears on one side – the side opposite the crook. The impressions showed that the ferrule of this one was evenly convex. Therefore it had no crook. The other matter is more complicated. To begin with, an artificial foot makes a very characteristic impression, owing to its purely passive elasticity, as I will show you to-morrow. But an artificial leg fitted below the knee is quite secure, whereas one fitted above the knee – that is, with an artificial knee-joint worked by a spring – is much less reliable. Now, this man had an artificial foot, and he evidently distrusted his knee-joint, as is shown by his steadying it with his stick on the same side. If he had merely had a weak leg, he would have used the stick with his right hand – with the natural swing of the arm, in fact – unless he had been very lame, which he evidently was not. Still, it was only a question of probability, though the probability was very great. Of course, you understand that those particles of woody fibre and starch granules were disintegrated snuff-grains."

This explanation, like the others, was quite simple when one had heard it, though it gave me material for much thought as we pedalled on along the dark road, with Thorndyke's light flickering in front, and the dogcart pattering in our wake. But there was ample time for reflection, for our pace rather precluded conversation, and we rode on, mile after mile, until my legs ached with fatigue. On and on we went through village after village, now losing the trail in some frequented street, but picking it up again unfailingly as we emerged on to the country road, until at last, in the paved High Street of the little town of Horsefield, we lost it for good. We rode on through the town out on to the country road, but although there were several tracks of motors, Thorndyke shook his head at them all. "I have been studying those tyres until I know them by heart," he said. "No, either he is in the town, or he has left it by a side road."

There was nothing for it but to put up the horse and the machines at the hotel, while we walked round to reconnoiter, and this we did, tramping up one street and down another, with eyes bent on the ground, fruitlessly searching for a trace of the missing car.

Suddenly, at the door of a blacksmith's shop, Thorndyke halted. The shop had been kept open late for the shoeing of a carriage horse, which was just being led away, and the smith had come to the door for a breath of air. Thorndyke accosted him genially.

"Good-evening. You are just the man I wanted to see. I have mislaid the address of a friend of mine, who, I think, called on you this afternoon – a lame gentleman who walks with a stick. I expect he wanted you to pick a lock or make him a key."

"Oh, I remember him!" said the man. "Yes, he had lost his latchkey, and wanted the lock picked before he could get into his house. Had to leave his motor-car outside while he came here. But I took some keys round with me, and fitted one to his latch."

He then directed us to a house at the end of a street close by, and, having thanked him, we went off in high spirits.

"How did you know he had been there?" I asked.

"I didn't, but there was the mark of a stick and part of a left foot on the soft earth inside the doorway, and the thing was inherently probable, so I risked a false shot."

The house stood alone at the far end of a straggling street, and was enclosed by a high wall, in which, on the side facing the street, was a door and a wide carriage-gate. Advancing to the former, Thorndyke took from his pocket the purloined key, and tried it in the lock. It fitted perfectly, and when he had turned it and pushed open the door, we entered a small courtyard. Crossing this, we came to the front door of the house, the latch of which fortunately fitted the same key, and this having been opened by Thorndyke, we trooped into the hall. Immediately we heard the sound of an opening door above, and a reedy, nasal voice sang out, "Hello, there! Who's that below?"

The voice was followed by the appearance of a head projecting over the baluster rail.

"You are Mr. Percy Haldean, I think," said the inspector.

At the mention of this name, the head was withdrawn, and a quick tread was heard, accompanied by the tapping of a stick on the floor. We started to ascend the stairs, the inspector leading, as the authorized official, but we had only gone up a few steps, when a fierce, wiry little man danced out on to the landing, with a thick stick in one hand and a very large revolver in the other.

97

"Move another step, either of you," he shouted, pointing the weapon at the inspector, "and I let fly, and mind you, when I shoot I hit."

He looked as if he meant it, and we accordingly halted with remarkable suddenness, while the inspector proceeded to parley.

"Now, what's the good of this, Mr. Haldean?" said he. "The game's up, and you know it."

"You clear out of my house, and clear out sharp," was the inhospitable rejoinder, "or you'll give me the trouble of burying you in the garden."

I looked round to consult with Thorndyke, when, to my amazement, I found that he had vanished – apparently through the open hall-door. I was admiring his discretion when the inspector endeavoured to reopen negotiations, but was cut short abruptly.

"I am going to count fifty," said Mr. Haldean, "and if you aren't gone then, I shall shoot."

He began to count deliberately, and the inspector looked round at me in complete bewilderment. The flight of stairs was a long one, and well lighted by gas, so that to rush it was an impossibility. Suddenly my heart gave a bound and I held my breath, for out of an open door behind our quarry, a figure emerged slowly and noiselessly on to the landing. It was Thorndyke, shoeless, and in his shirt-sleeves.

Slowly and with cat-like stealthiness, he crept across the landing until he was within a yard of the unconscious fugitive, and still the nasal voice droned on, monotonously counting out the allotted seconds.

"Forty-one, forty-two, forty-three – "

There was a lightning-like movement – a shout – a flash – a bang – a shower of falling plaster, and then the revolver came clattering down the stairs. The inspector and I rushed up, and in a moment the sharp click of the handcuffs told Mr. Percy Haldean that the game was really up.

Five minutes later Freddy-boy, half-asleep, but wholly cheerful, was borne on Thorndyke's shoulders into the private sitting-room of the Black Horse Hotel. A shriek of joy saluted his entrance, and a shower of maternal kisses brought him to the verge of suffocation. Finally, the impulsive Mrs. Haldean, turning suddenly to Thorndyke, seized both his hands, and for a moment I hoped that she was going to kiss him, too. But he was spared, and I have not yet recovered from the disappointment.

The Stranger is Run to Earth

The Anthropologist at Large

Thorndyke was not a newspaper reader. He viewed with extreme disfavour all scrappy and miscellaneous forms of literature, which, by presenting a disorderly series of unrelated items of information, tended, as he considered, to destroy the habit of consecutive mental effort.

"It is most important," he once remarked to me, "habitually to pursue a definite train of thought, and to pursue it to a finish, instead of flitting indolently from one uncompleted topic to another, as the newspaper reader is so apt to do. Still, there is no harm in a daily paper – so long as you don't read it."

Accordingly, he patronized a morning paper, and his method of dealing with it was characteristic. The paper was laid on the table after breakfast, together with a blue pencil and a pair of office shears. A preliminary glance through the sheets enabled him to mark with the pencil those paragraphs that were to be read, and these were presently cut out and looked through, after which they were either thrown away or set aside to be pasted in an indexed book.

The whole proceeding occupied, on an average, a quarter-of-an-hour.

On the morning of which I am now speaking he was thus engaged. The pencil had done its work, and the snick of the shears announced the final stage. Presently he paused with a newly-excised cutting between his fingers, and, after glancing at it for a moment, he handed it to me.

"Another art robbery," he remarked. "Mysterious affairs, these – as to motive, I mean. You can't melt down a picture or an ivory carving, and you can't put them on the market as they stand. The very qualities that give them their value make them totally unnegotiable."

"Yet I suppose," said I, "the really inveterate collector – the pottery or stamp maniac, for instance – will buy these contraband goods even though he dare not show them."

"Probably. No doubt the *cupiditas habendi*, the mere desire to possess, is the motive force rather than any intelligent purpose – "

The discussion was at this point interrupted by a knock at the door, and a moment later my colleague admitted two gentlemen. One of these I recognized as a Mr. Marchmont, a solicitor, for whom we had occasionally acted, the other was a stranger – a typical Hebrew of the blonde type – good-looking, faultlessly dressed, carrying a bandbox, and obviously in a state of the most extreme agitation.

"Good-morning to you, gentlemen," said Mr. Marchmont, shaking hands cordially. "I have brought a client of mine to see you, and when I tell you that his name is Solomon Löwe, it will be unnecessary for me to say what our business is."

"Oddly enough," replied Thorndyke, "we were, at the very moment when you knocked, discussing the bearings of his case."

"It is a horrible affair!" burst in Mr. Löwe. "I am distracted! I am ruined! I am in despair!"

He banged the bandbox down on the table, and flinging himself into a chair, buried his face in his hands.

"Come, come," remonstrated Marchmont, "we must be brave, we must be composed. Tell Dr. Thorndyke your story, and let us hear what he thinks of it."

He leaned back in his chair, and looked at his client with that air of patient fortitude that comes to us all so easily when we contemplate the misfortunes of other people.

"You must help us, sir," exclaimed Löwe, starting up again. "You must, indeed, or I shall go mad. But I shall tell you what has happened, and then you must act at once. Spare no effort and no expense. Money is no object – at least, not in reason," he added, with native caution. He sat down once more, and in perfect English, though with a slight German accent, proceeded volubly, "My brother Isaac is probably known to you by name."

101

Thorndyke nodded.

"He is a great collector, and to some extent a dealer – that is to say, he makes his hobby a profitable hobby."

"What does he collect?" asked Thorndyke.

"Everything," replied our visitor, flinging his hands apart with a comprehensive gesture – "everything that is precious and beautiful – pictures, ivories, jewels, watches, objects of art and *vertu* – everything. He is a Jew, and he has that passion for things that are rich and costly that has distinguished our race from the time of my namesake Solomon onwards. His house in Howard Street, Piccadilly, is at once a museum and an art gallery. The rooms are filled with cases of gems, of antique jewellery, of coins and historic relics – some of priceless value – and the walls are covered with paintings, every one of which is a masterpiece. There is a fine collection of ancient weapons and armour, both European and Oriental, rare books, manuscripts, *papyri*, and valuable antiquities from Egypt, Assyria, Cyprus, and elsewhere. You see, his taste is quite catholic, and his knowledge of rare and curious things is probably greater than that of any other living man. He is never mistaken. No forgery deceives him, and hence the great prices that he obtains, for a work of art purchased from Isaac Löwe is a work certified as genuine beyond all cavil."

He paused to mop his face with a silk handkerchief, and then, with the same plaintive volubility, continued, "My brother is unmarried. He lives for his collection, and he lives with it. The house is not a very large one, and the collection takes up most of it, but he keeps a suite of rooms for his own occupation, and has two servants – a man and wife – to look after him. The man, who is a retired police sergeant, acts as caretaker and watchman. The woman as housekeeper and cook, if required, but my brother lives largely at his club. And now I come to this present catastrophe."

He ran his fingers through his hair, took a deep breath, and continued.

"Yesterday morning Isaac started for Florence by way of Paris, but his route was not certain, and he intended to break his journey at various points as circumstances determined. Before leaving, he put his collection in my charge, and it was arranged that I should occupy his rooms in his absence. Accordingly, I sent my things round and took possession.

"Now, Dr. Thorndyke, I am closely connected with the drama, and it is my custom to spend my evenings at my club, of which most of the members are actors. Consequently, I am rather late in my habits, but last night I was earlier than usual in leaving my club, for I started for my brother's house before half-past-twelve. I felt, as you may suppose, the responsibility of the great charge I had undertaken, and you may, therefore, imagine my horror, my consternation, my despair, when, on letting myself in with my latchkey, I found a police-inspector, a sergeant, and a constable in the hall. There had been a robbery, sir, in my brief absence, and the account that the inspector gave of the affair was briefly this:

"While taking the round of his district, he had noticed an empty hansom proceeding in leisurely fashion along Howard Street. There was nothing remarkable in this, but when, about ten minutes later, he was returning, and met a hansom, which he believed to be the same, proceeding along the same street in the same direction, and at the same easy pace, the circumstance struck him as odd, and he made a note of the number of the cab in his pocket-book. It was 72,863, and the time was 11:35.

"At 11:45 a constable coming up Howard Street noticed a hansom standing opposite the door of my brother's house, and, while he was looking at it, a man came out of the house carrying something, which he put in the cab. On this the constable quickened his pace, and when the man returned to the house and reappeared carrying what looked like a portmanteau, and closing the door softly behind him, the policeman's suspicions were aroused, and he hurried forward, hailing the cabman to stop.

"The man put his burden into the cab, and sprang in himself. The cabman lashed his horse, which started off at a gallop, and the policeman broke into a run, blowing his whistle and flashing his lantern on to the cab. He followed it round the two turnings into Albemarle Street, and was just in time to see it turn into Piccadilly, where, of course, it was lost. However, he managed to note the number of the cab, which was 72,863, and he describes the man as short and thick-set, and thinks he was not wearing any hat.

"As he was returning, he met the inspector and the sergeant, who had heard the whistle, and on his report the three officers hurried to the house, where they knocked and rang for some minutes without any result. Being now more than suspicious, they went to the back of the house, through the mews, where, with great difficulty, they managed to force a window and effect an entrance into the house.

"Here their suspicions were soon changed to certainty, for, on reaching the first-floor, they heard strange muffled groans proceeding from one of the rooms, the door of which was locked, though the key had not been removed. They opened the door, and found the caretaker and his wife sitting on the floor, with their backs against the wall. Both were bound hand and foot, and the head of each was enveloped in a green-baize bag, and when the bags were taken off, each was found to be lightly but effectively gagged.

"Each told the same story. The caretaker, fancying he heard a noise, armed himself with a truncheon, and came downstairs to the first-floor, where he found the door of one of the rooms open, and a light burning inside. He stepped on tiptoe to the open door, and was peering in, when he was seized from behind, half-suffocated by a pad held over his mouth, pinioned, gagged, and blindfolded with the bag.

"His assailant – whom he never saw – was amazingly strong and skilful, and handled him with perfect ease, although he – the caretaker – is a powerful man, and a good boxer and wrestler. The same thing happened to the wife, who had come down to look for her husband. She walked into the same trap, and was gagged, pinioned, and blindfolded without ever having seen the robber. So the only description that we have of this villain is that furnished by the constable."

"And the caretaker had no chance of using his truncheon?" said Thorndyke.

"Well, he got in one backhanded blow over his right shoulder, which he thinks caught the burglar in the face, but the fellow caught him by the elbow, and gave his arm such a twist that he dropped the truncheon on the floor."

"Is the robbery a very extensive one?"

"Ah!" exclaimed Mr. Löwe, "that is just what we cannot say. But I fear it is. It seems that my brother had quite recently drawn out of his bank four thousand pounds in notes and gold. These little transactions are often carried out in cash rather than by cheque" – here I caught a twinkle in Thorndyke's eye – "and the caretaker says that a few days ago Isaac brought home several parcels, which were put away temporarily in a strong cupboard. He seemed to be very pleased with his new acquisitions, and gave the caretaker to understand that they were of extraordinary rarity and value.

"Now, this cupboard has been cleared out. Not a vestige is left in it but the wrappings of the parcels, so, although nothing else has been touched, it is pretty clear that goods to the value of four thousand pounds have been taken, but when we consider what an excellent buyer my brother is, it becomes highly probable that the actual value of those things is two or three times that amount, or even more. It is a dreadful, dreadful business, and Isaac will hold me responsible for it all."

"Is there no further clue?" asked Thorndyke. "What about the cab, for instance?"

"Oh, the cab," groaned Löwe – "that clue failed. The police must have mistaken the number. They telephoned immediately to all the police stations, and a watch was set, with the result that number 72,863 was stopped as it was going home for the night. But it then turned out that the cab had not been off the rank since eleven o'clock, and the driver had been in the shelter all the time with several other men. But there is a clue. I have it here."

Mr. Löwe's face brightened for once as he reached out for the bandbox.

"The houses in Howard Street," he explained, as he untied the fastening, "have small balconies to the first-floor windows at the back. Now, the thief entered by one of these windows, having climbed up a rain-water pipe to the balcony. It was a gusty night, as you will remember, and this morning, as I was leaving the house, the butler next door called to me and gave me this. He had found it lying in the balcony of his house."

He opened the bandbox with a flourish, and brought forth a rather shabby billycock hat.

"I understand," said he, "that by examining a hat it is possible to deduce from it, not only the bodily characteristics of the wearer, but also his mental and moral qualities, his state of health, his pecuniary position, his past history, and even his domestic relations and the peculiarities of his place of abode. Am I right in this supposition?"

The ghost of a smile flitted across Thorndyke's face as he laid the hat upon the remains of the newspaper. "We must not expect too much," he observed. "Hats, as you know, have a way of changing owners. Your own hat, for instance" (a very spruce, hard felt), "is a new one, I think."

"Got it last week," said Mr. Löwe.

"Exactly. It is an expensive hat, by Lincoln and Bennett, and I see you have judiciously written your name in indelible marking-ink on the lining. Now, a new hat suggests a discarded predecessor. What do you do with your old hats?"

"My man has them, but they don't fit him. I suppose he sells them or gives them away."

"Very well. Now, a good hat like yours has a long life, and remains serviceable long after it has become shabby, and the probability is that many of your hats pass from owner to owner, from you to the shabby-genteel, and from them to the shabby ungenteel. And it is a fair assumption that there are, at this moment, an appreciable number of tramps and casuals wearing hats by Lincoln and Bennett, marked in indelible ink with the name S. Löwe, and anyone who should examine those hats, as you suggest, might draw some very misleading deductions as to the personal habits of S. Löwe."

Mr. Marchmont chuckled audibly, and then, remembering the gravity of the occasion, suddenly became portentously solemn.

"So you think that the hat is of no use, after all?" said Mr. Löwe, in a tone of deep disappointment.

"I won't say that," replied Thorndyke. "We may learn something from it. Leave it with me, at any rate, but you must let the police know that I have it. They will want to see it, of course."

"And you will try to get those things, won't you?" pleaded Löwe.

"I will think over the case. But you understand, or Mr. Marchmont does, that this is hardly in my province. I am a medical jurist, and this is not a medico-legal case."

"Just what I told him," said Marchmont. "But you will do me a great kindness if you will look into the matter. Make it a medico-legal case," he added persuasively.

Thorndyke repeated his promise, and the two men took their departure.

For some time after they had left, my colleague remained silent, regarding the hat with a quizzical smile. "It is like a game of forfeits," he remarked at length, "and we have to find the owner of 'this very pretty thing.'" He lifted it with a pair of forceps into a better light, and began to look at it more closely.

"Perhaps," said he, "we have done Mr. Löwe an injustice, after all. This is certainly a very remarkable hat."

"It is as round as a basin," I exclaimed. "Why, the fellow's head must have been turned in a lathe!"

Thorndyke laughed. "The point," said he, "is this. This is a hard hat, and so must have fitted fairly, or it could not have been worn, and it was a cheap hat, and so was not made to measure. But a man with a head that shape has got to come to a clear understanding with his hat. No ordinary hat would go on at all.

"Now, you see what he has done – no doubt on the advice of some friendly hatter. He has bought a hat of a suitable size, and he has made it hot – probably steamed it. Then he has jammed it, while still hot and soft, on to his head, and allowed it to cool and set before removing it. That is evident from the distortion of the brim. The important corollary is, that this hat fits his head exactly – is, in fact, a perfect mould of it, and this fact, together with the cheap quality of the hat, furnishes the further corollary that it has probably only had a single owner.

"And now let us turn it over and look at the outside. You notice at once the absence of old dust. Allowing for the circumstance that it had been out all night, it is decidedly clean. Its owner has been in the habit of brushing it, and is therefore presumably a decent, orderly man. But if you look at it in a good light, you see a kind of bloom on the felt, and through this lens you can make out particles of a fine white powder which has worked into the surface."

He handed me his lens, through which I could distinctly see the particles to which he referred.

"Then," he continued, "under the curl of the brim and in the folds of the hatband, where the brush has not been able to reach it, the powder has collected quite thickly, and we can see that it is a very fine powder, and very white, like flour. What do you make of that?"

"I should say that it is connected with some industry. He may be engaged in some factory or works, or, at any rate, may live near a factory, and have to pass it frequently."

"Yes, and I think we can distinguish between the two possibilities. For, if he only passes the factory, the dust will be on the outside of the hat only. The inside will be protected by his head. But if he is engaged in the works, the dust will be inside, too, as the hat will hang on a peg in the dust-laden atmosphere, and his head will also be powdered, and so convey the dust to the inside."

He turned the hat over once more, and as I brought the powerful lens to bear upon the dark lining, I could clearly distinguish a number of white particles in the interstices of the fabric.

"The powder is on the inside, too," I said.

He took the lens from me, and, having verified my statement, proceeded with the examination. "You notice," he said, "that the leather head-lining is stained with grease, and this staining is more pronounced at the sides and back. His hair, therefore, is naturally greasy, or he greases it artificially, for if the staining were caused by perspiration, it would be most marked opposite the forehead."

He peered anxiously into the interior of the hat, and eventually turned down the head-lining, and immediately there broke out upon his face a gleam of satisfaction.

"Ha!" he exclaimed. "This is a stroke of luck. I was afraid our neat and orderly friend had defeated us with his brush. Pass me the small dissecting forceps, Jervis."

I handed him the instrument, and he proceeded to pick out daintily from the space behind the head-lining some half-a-dozen short pieces of hair, which he laid, with infinite tenderness, on a sheet of white paper.

"There are several more on the other side," I said, pointing them out to him.

108

"Yes, but we must leave some for the police," he answered, with a smile. "They must have the same chance as ourselves, you know."

"But surely," I said, as I bent down over the paper, "these are pieces of horsehair!"

"I think not," he replied, "but the microscope will show. At any rate, this is the kind of hair I should expect to find with a head of that shape."

"Well, it is extraordinarily coarse," said I, "and two of the hairs are nearly white."

"Yes, black hairs beginning to turn grey. And now, as our preliminary survey has given such encouraging results, we will proceed to more exact methods, and we must waste no time, for we shall have the police here presently to rob us of our treasure."

He folded up carefully the paper containing the hairs, and taking the hat in both hands, as though it were some sacred vessel, ascended with me to the laboratory on the next floor.

"Now, Polton," he said to his laboratory assistant, "we have here a specimen for examination, and time is precious. First of all, we want your patent dust-extractor."

The little man bustled to a cupboard and brought forth a singular appliance, of his own manufacture, somewhat like a miniature vacuum cleaner. It had been made from a bicycle foot-pump, by reversing the piston-valve, and was fitted with a glass nozzle and a small detachable glass receiver for collecting the dust, at the end of a flexible metal tube.

"We will sample the dust from the outside first," said Thorndyke, laying the hat upon the work-bench. "Are you ready, Polton?"

The assistant slipped his foot into the stirrup of the pump and worked the handle vigorously, while Thorndyke drew the glass nozzle slowly along the hat-brim under the curled edge. And as the nozzle passed along, the white coating vanished as if by magic, leaving the felt absolutely clean and black, and simultaneously the glass receiver became clouded over with a white deposit.

"We will leave the other side for the police," said Thorndyke, and as Polton ceased pumping he detached the receiver, and laid it on a sheet of paper, on which he wrote in pencil, "Outside," and covered it with a small bell-glass. A fresh receiver having been fitted on, the nozzle was now drawn over the silk lining of the hat, and then through the space behind the leather head-lining on one side, and now the dust that collected in the receiver was much of the usual grey colour and fluffy texture, and included two more hairs.

"And now," said Thorndyke, when the second receiver had been detached and set aside, "we want a mould of the inside of the hat, and we must make it by the quickest method. There is no time to make a paper mould. It is a most astonishing head," he added, reaching down from a nail a pair of large callipers, which he applied to the inside of the hat, "six inches and nine-tenths long by six and six-tenths broad, which gives us" – he made a rapid calculation on a scrap of paper – "the extraordinarily high cephalic index of *95·6.*"

Polton now took possession of the hat, and, having stuck a band of wet tissue-paper round the inside, mixed a small bowl of plaster-of-Paris, and very dexterously ran a stream of the thick liquid on to the tissue-paper, where it quickly solidified. A second and third application resulted in a broad ring of solid plaster an inch thick, forming a perfect mould of the inside of the hat, and in a few minutes the slight contraction of the plaster in setting rendered the mould sufficiently loose to allow of its being slipped out on to a board to dry.

We were none too soon, for even as Polton was removing the mould, the electric bell, which I had switched on to the laboratory, announced a visitor, and when I went down I found a police-sergeant waiting with a note from Superintendent Miller, requesting the immediate transfer of the hat.

"The next thing to be done," said Thorndyke, when the sergeant had departed with the bandbox, "is to measure the thickness of the hairs, and make a transverse section of one, and examine the dust. The section we will leave to Polton – as time is an object, Polton, you had better imbed the hair in thick gum and freeze it hard on the microtome, and be very careful to cut the section at right angles to the length of the hair – meanwhile, we will get to work with the microscope."

The hairs proved on measurement to have the surprisingly large diameter of $1/135^{th}$ of an inch – fully double that of ordinary hairs, although they were unquestionably human. As to the white dust, it presented a problem that even Thorndyke was unable to solve. The application of reagents showed it to be carbonate of lime, but its source for a time remained a mystery.

"The larger particles," said Thorndyke, with his eye applied to the microscope, "appear to be transparent, crystalline, and distinctly laminated in structure. It is not chalk, it is not whiting, it is not any kind of cement. What can it be?"

"Could it be any kind of shell?" I suggested. "For instance – "

"Of course!" he exclaimed, starting up, "you have hit it, Jervis, as you always do. It must be mother-of-pearl. Polton, give me a pearl shirt-button out of your oddments box."

The button was duly produced by the thrifty Polton, dropped into an agate mortar, and speedily reduced to powder, a tiny pinch of which Thorndyke placed under the microscope.

"This powder," said he, "is, naturally, much coarser than our specimen, but the identity of character is unmistakable. Jervis, you are a treasure. Just look at it."

I glanced down the microscope, and then pulled out my watch. "Yes," I said, "there is no doubt about it, I think, but I must be off. Anstey urged me to be in court by 11:30 at the latest."

With infinite reluctance I collected my notes and papers and departed, leaving Thorndyke diligently copying addresses out of the Post Office Directory.

My business at the court detained me the whole of the day, and it was near upon dinner-time when I reached our chambers. Thorndyke had not yet come in, but he arrived half-an-hour later, tired and hungry, and not very communicative.

"What have I done?" he repeated, in answer to my inquiries. "I have walked miles of dirty pavement, and I have visited every pearl-shell cutter's in London, with one exception, and I have not found what I was looking for. The one mother-of-pearl factory that remains, however, is the most likely, and I propose to look in there to-morrow morning.

111

Meanwhile, we have completed our data, with Polton's assistance. Here is a tracing of our friend's skull taken from the mould. You see it is an extreme type of brachycephalic skull, and markedly unsymmetrical. Here is a transverse section of his hair, which is quite circular – unlike yours or mine, which would be oval. We have the mother-of-pearl dust from the outside of the hat, and from the inside similar dust mixed with various fibres and a few granules of rice starch. Those are our data."

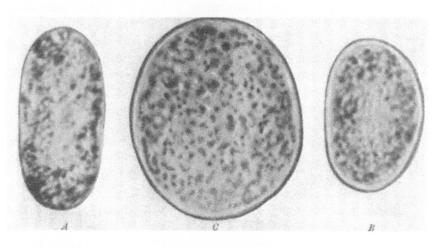

Transverse Sections of Human Hair

A – Of a Black Man
B – Of an Englishman
C – Of the Burglar

All Magnified 600 Diameters

"Supposing the hat should not be that of the burglar after all?" I suggested.

"That would be annoying. But I think it is his, and I think I can guess at the nature of the art treasures that were stolen."

"And you don't intend to enlighten me?"

"My dear fellow," he replied, "you have all the data. Enlighten yourself by the exercise of your own brilliant faculties. Don't give way to mental indolence."

I endeavoured, from the facts in my possession, to construct the personality of the mysterious burglar, and failed utterly, nor was I more successful in my endeavour to guess at the nature of the stolen property, and it was not until the following morning, when we had set out on our quest and were approaching Limehouse, that Thorndyke would revert to the subject.

"We are now," he said, "going to the factory of Badcomb and Martin, shell importers and cutters, in the West India Dock Road. If I don't find my man there, I shall hand the facts over to the police, and waste no more time over the case."

"What is your man like?" I asked.

"I am looking for an elderly Japanese, wearing a new hat or, more probably, a cap, and having a bruise on his right cheek or temple. I am also looking for a cab-yard, but here we are at the works, and as it is now close on the dinner-hour, we will wait and see the hands come out before making any inquiries."

We walked slowly past the tall, blank-faced building, and were just turning to re-pass it when a steam whistle sounded, a wicket opened in the main gate, and a stream of workmen – each powdered with white, like a miller – emerged into the street. We halted to watch the men as they came out, one by one, through the wicket, and turned to the right or left towards their homes or some adjacent coffee-shop, but none of them answered to the description that my friend had given.

The outcoming stream grew thinner, and at length ceased, the wicket was shut with a bang, and once more Thorndyke's quest appeared to have failed.

"Is that all of them, I wonder?" he said, with a shade of disappointment in his tone, but even as he spoke the wicket opened again, and a leg protruded. The leg was followed by a black and a curious globular head, covered with iron-grey hair, and surmounted by a cloth cap, the whole appertaining to a short, very thick-set man, who remained thus, evidently talking to someone inside.

Suddenly he turned his head to look across the street, and immediately I recognized, by the pallid yellow complexion and narrow eye-slits, the physiognomy of a typical Japanese. The man remained talking for nearly another minute. Then, drawing out his other leg, he turned towards us, and now I perceived that the right side of his face, over the prominent cheekbone, was discoloured as though by a severe bruise.

"Ha!" said Thorndyke, turning round sharply as the man approached, "either this is our man or it is an incredible coincidence." He walked away at a moderate pace, allowing the Japanese to overtake us slowly, and when the man had at length passed us, he increased his speed somewhat, so as to maintain the distance.

Our friend stepped along briskly, and presently turned up a side street, whither we followed at a respectful distance, Thorndyke holding open his pocket-book, and appearing to engage me in an earnest discussion, but keeping a sharp eye on his quarry.

"There he goes!" said my colleague, as the man suddenly disappeared – "the house with the green window-sashes. That will be number thirteen."

It was, and, having verified the fact, we passed on, and took the next turning that would lead us back to the main road.

Some twenty minutes later, as we were strolling past the door of a coffee-shop, a man came out, and began to fill his pipe with an air of leisurely satisfaction. His hat and clothes were powdered with white like those of the workmen whom we had seen come out of the factory. Thorndyke accosted him.

"Is that a flour-mill up the road there?"

"No, sir. Pearl-shell. I work there myself."

"Pearl-shell, eh?" said Thorndyke. "I suppose that will be an industry that will tend to attract the aliens. Do you find it so?"

"No, sir, not at all. The work's too hard. We've only got one foreigner in the place, and he ain't an alien – he's a Jap."

"Japanese!" exclaimed Thorndyke. "Really. Now, I wonder if that would chance to be our old friend Kotei – you remember Kotei?" he added, turning to me.

114

"No, sir, this man's name is Futashima. There was another fellow like him in the works, a chap named Itu, a pal of Futashima's, but he's left."

"Ah! I don't know either of them. By the way, usen't there to be a cab-yard just about here?"

"There's a yard up Rankin Street where they keep vans and one or two cabs. That chap Itu works there now. Taken to horseflesh. Drives a van sometimes. Queer start for a Japanese man."

"Very." Thorndyke thanked the man for his information, and we sauntered on towards Rankin Street. The yard was at this time nearly deserted, being occupied only by an ancient and crazy four-wheeler and a very shabby hansom.

"Curious old houses, these that back on to the yard," said Thorndyke, strolling into the enclosure. "That timber gable, now," pointing to a house, from a window of which a man was watching us suspiciously, "is quite an interesting survival."

"What's your business, mister?" demanded the man in a gruff tone.

"We are just having a look at these quaint old houses," replied Thorndyke, edging towards the back of the hansom, and opening his pocket-book, as though to make a sketch.

"Well, you can see 'em from outside," said the man.

"So we can," said Thorndyke suavely, "but not so well, you know."

At this moment the pocket-book slipped from his hand and fell, scattering a number of loose papers about the ground under the hansom, and our friend at the window laughed joyously.

"No hurry," murmured Thorndyke, as I stooped to help him to gather up the papers – which he did in the most surprisingly slow and clumsy manner. "It is fortunate that the ground is dry." He stood up with the rescued papers in his hand, and, having scribbled down a brief note, slipped the book in his pocket.

"Now you'd better mizzle," observed the man at the window.

"Thank you," replied Thorndyke, "I think we had." And, with a pleasant nod at the custodian, he proceeded to adopt the hospitable suggestion.

"Mr. Marchmont has been here, sir, with Inspector Badger and another gentleman," said Polton, as we entered our chambers. "They said they would call again about five."

"Then," replied Thorndyke, "as it is now a quarter-to-five, there is just time for us to have a wash while you get the tea ready. The particles that float in the atmosphere of Limehouse are not all mother-of-pearl."

115

Thorndyke's Strategy

Our visitors arrived punctually, the third gentleman being, as we had supposed, Mr. Solomon Löwe. Inspector Badger I had not seen before, and he now impressed me as showing a tendency to invert the significance of his own name by endeavouring to "draw" Thorndyke, in which, however, he was not brilliantly successful.

"I hope you are not going to disappoint Mr. Löwe, sir," he commenced facetiously. "You have had a good look at that hat – we saw your marks on it – and he expects that you will be able to point us out the man, name and address all complete." He grinned patronizingly at our unfortunate client, who was looking even more haggard and worn than he had been on the previous morning.

"Have you – have you made any – discovery?" Mr Löwe asked with pathetic eagerness.

"We examined the hat very carefully, and I think we have established a few facts of some interest."

"Did your examination of the hat furnish any information as to the nature of the stolen property, sir?" inquired the humorous inspector.

Thorndyke turned to the officer with a face as expressionless as a wooden mask.

"We thought it possible," said he, "that it might consist of works of Japanese art, such as netsukes, paintings, and such like."

Mr. Löwe uttered an exclamation of delighted astonishment, and the facetiousness faded rather suddenly from the inspector's countenance.

"I don't know how you can have found out," said he. "We have only known it half-an-hour ourselves, and the wire came direct from Florence to Scotland Yard."

"Perhaps you can describe the thief to us," said Mr. Löwe, in the same eager tone.

"I dare say the inspector can do that," replied Thorndyke.

"Yes, I think so," replied the officer. "He is a short strong man, with a dark complexion and hair turning grey. He has a very round head, and he is probably a workman engaged at some whiting or cement works. That is all we know, if you can tell us any more, sir, we shall be very glad to hear it."

"I can only offer a few suggestions," said Thorndyke, "but perhaps you may find them useful. For instance, at 13, Birket Street, Limehouse, there is living a Japanese gentleman named Futashima, who works at Badcomb and Martin's mother-of-pearl factory. I think that if you were to call on him, and let him try on the hat that you have, it would probably fit him."

The inspector scribbled ravenously in his notebook, and Mr. Marchmont – an old admirer of Thorndyke's – leaned back in his chair, chuckling softly and rubbing his hands.

"Then," continued my colleague, "there is in Rankin Street, Limehouse, a cab-yard, where another Japanese gentleman named Itu is employed. You might find out where Itu was the night before last, and if you should chance to see a hansom cab there – number 22,481 – have a good look at it. In the frame of the number-plate you will find six small holes. Those holes may have held brads, and the brads may have held a false number card. At any rate, you might ascertain where that cab was at 11:30 the night before last. That is all I have to suggest."

Mr. Löwe leaped from his chair. "Let us go – now – at once – there is no time to be lost. A thousand thanks to you, Doctor – a thousand-million thanks. Come!"

He seized the inspector by the arm and forcibly dragged him towards the door, and a few moments later we heard the footsteps of our visitors clattering down the stairs.

"It was not worth while to enter into explanations with them," said Thorndyke, as the footsteps died away – "nor perhaps with you?"

"On the contrary," I replied, "I am waiting to be fully enlightened."

"Well, then, my inferences in this case were perfectly simple ones, drawn from well-known anthropological facts. The human race, as you know, is roughly divided into three groups – the black, the white, and the yellow races. But apart from the variable quality of colour, these races have certain fixed characteristics associated especially with the shape of the skull, of the eye-sockets, and the hair.

"Thus in the black races the skull is long and narrow, the eye-sockets are long and narrow, and the hair is flat and ribbon-like, and usually coiled up like a watch-spring. In the white races the skull is oval, the eye-sockets are oval, and the hair is slightly flattened or oval in section, and tends to be wavy, while in the yellow or Mongol races, the skull is short and round, the eye-sockets are short and round, and the hair is straight and circular in section. So that we have, in the black races, long skull, long orbits, flat hair, in the white races, oval skull, oval orbits, oval hair, and in the yellow races, round skull, round orbits, round hair.

"Now, in this case we had to deal with a very short round skull. But you cannot argue from races to individuals, there are many short-skulled Englishmen. But when I found, associated with that skull, hairs which were circular in section, it became practically certain that the individual was a Mongol of some kind. The mother-of-pearl dust and the granules of rice starch from the inside of the hat favoured this view, for the pearl-shell

118

industry is specially connected with China and Japan, while starch granules from the hat of an Englishman would probably be wheat starch.

"Then as to the hair: It was, as I mentioned to you, circular in section, and of very large diameter. Now, I have examined many thousands of hairs, and the thickest that I have ever seen came from the heads of Japanese, but the hairs from this hat were as thick as any of them. But the hypothesis that the burglar was a Japanese received confirmation in various ways. Thus, he was short, though strong and active, and the Japanese are the shortest of the Mongol races, and very strong and active.

"Then his remarkable skill in handling the powerful caretaker – a retired police-sergeant – suggested the Japanese art of ju-jitsu, while the nature of the robbery was consistent with the value set by the Japanese on works of art. Finally, the fact that only a particular collection was taken, suggested a special, and probably national, character in the things stolen, while their portability – you will remember that goods of the value of from eight to twelve thousand pounds were taken away in two hand-packages – was much more consistent with Japanese than Chinese works, of which the latter tend rather to be bulky and ponderous. Still, it was nothing but a bare hypothesis until we had seen Futashima – and, indeed, is no more now. I may, after all, be entirely mistaken."

He was not, however, and at this moment there reposes in my drawing-room an ancient netsuke, which came as a thank-offering from Mr. Isaac Löwe on the recovery of the booty from a back room in No. 13, Birket Street, Limehouse. The treasure, of course, was given in the first place to Thorndyke, but transferred by him to my wife on the pretence that but for my suggestion of shell-dust the robber would never have been traced. Which is, on the face of it, preposterous.

The Blue Sequin

Thorndyke stood looking up and down the platform with anxiety that increased as the time drew near for the departure of the train.

"This is very unfortunate," he said, reluctantly stepping into an empty smoking compartment as the guard executed a flourish with his green flag. "I am afraid we have missed our friend." He closed the door, and, as the train began to move, thrust his head out of the window.

"Now I wonder if that will be he," he continued. "If so, he has caught the train by the skin of his teeth, and is now in one of the rear compartments."

The subject of Thorndyke's speculations was Mr. Edward Stopford, of the firm of Stopford and Myers, of Portugal Street, solicitors, and his connection with us at present arose out of a telegram that had reached our chambers on the preceding evening. It was reply-paid, and ran thus:

"Can you come here to-morrow to direct defence? Important case. All costs undertaken by us. – STOPFORD AND MYERS."

Thorndyke's reply had been in the affirmative, and early on this present morning a further telegram – evidently posted overnight – had been delivered:

"Shall leave for Woldhurst by 8:25 from Charing Cross. Will call for you if possible. – EDWARD STOPFORD."

He had not called, however, and, since he was unknown personally to us both, we could not judge whether or not he had been among the passengers on the platform.

"It is most unfortunate," Thorndyke repeated, "for it deprives us of that preliminary consideration of the case which is so invaluable." He filled his pipe thoughtfully, and, having made a fruitless inspection of the platform at London Bridge, took up the paper that he had bought at the bookstall, and began to turn over the leaves, running his eye quickly down the columns, unmindful of the journalistic baits in paragraph or article.

"It is a great disadvantage," he observed, while still glancing through the paper, "to come plump into an inquiry without preparation – to be confronted with the details before one has a chance of considering the case in general terms. For instance – "

He paused, leaving the sentence unfinished, and as I looked up inquiringly I saw that he had turned over another page, and was now reading attentively.

"This looks like our case, Jervis," he said presently, handing me the paper and indicating a paragraph at the top of the page. It was quite brief, and was headed "*Terrible Murder in Kent*," the account being as follows:

> *A shocking crime was discovered yesterday morning at the little town of Woldhurst, which lies on the branch line from Halbury Junction. The discovery was made by a porter who was inspecting the carriages of the train which had just come in. On opening the door of a first-class compartment, he was horrified to find the body of a fashionably-dressed woman stretched upon the floor. Medical aid was immediately summoned, and on the arrival of the divisional surgeon, Dr. Morton, it was ascertained that the woman had not been dead more than a few minutes.*
>
> *"The state of the corpse leaves no doubt that a murder of a most brutal kind has been perpetrated, the cause of death being a penetrating wound of the head, inflicted with some pointed implement, which must have been used with terrible violence, since it has perforated the skull and entered the brain. That robbery was not the motive of the crime is made clear by the fact that an expensively fitted dressing-bag was found on the rack, and that the dead woman's jewellery, including several valuable diamond rings, was untouched. It is rumoured that an arrest has been made by the local police.*

"A gruesome affair," I remarked, as I handed back the paper, "but the report does not give us much information."

"It does not," Thorndyke agreed, "and yet it gives us something to consider. Here is a perforating wound of the skull, inflicted with some pointed implement – that is, assuming that it is not a bullet wound. Now, what kind of implement would be capable of inflicting such an injury? How would such an implement be used in the confined space of a railway-carriage, and what sort of person would be in possession of such an implement? These are preliminary questions that are worth considering, and I commend them to you, together with the further problems of the possible motive – excluding robbery – and any circumstances other than murder which might account for the injury."

"The choice of suitable implements is not very great," I observed.

"It is very limited, and most of them, such as a plasterer's pick or a geological hammer, are associated with certain definite occupations. You have a notebook?"

121

The Discovery

122

I had, and, accepting the hint, I produced it and pursued my further reflections in silence, while my companion, with his notebook also on his knee, gazed steadily out of the window. And thus he remained, wrapped in thought, jotting down an entry now and again in his book, until the train slowed down at Halbury Junction, where we had to change on to a branch line.

As we stepped out, I noticed a well-dressed man hurrying up the platform from the rear and eagerly scanning the faces of the few passengers who had alighted. Soon he espied us, and, approaching quickly, asked, as he looked from one of us to the other, "Dr. Thorndyke?"

"Yes," replied my colleague, adding, "And you, I presume, are Mr. Edward Stopford?"

The solicitor bowed. "This is a dreadful affair," he said, in an agitated manner. "I see you have the paper. A most shocking affair. I am immensely relieved to find you here. Nearly missed the train, and feared I should miss you."

"There appears to have been an arrest," Thorndyke began.

"Yes – my brother. Terrible business. Let us walk up the platform. Our train won't start for a quarter-of-an-hour yet."

We deposited our joint Gladstone and Thorndyke's travelling-case in an empty first-class compartment, and then, with the solicitor between us, strolled up to the unfrequented end of the platform.

"My brother's position," said Mr. Stopford, "fills me with dismay – but let me give you the facts in order, and you shall judge for yourself. This poor creature who has been murdered so brutally was a Miss Edith Grant. She was formerly an artist's model, and as such was a good deal employed by my brother, who is a painter – Harold Stopford, you know, A.R.A. now – "

"I know his work very well, and charming work it is."

"I think so, too. Well, in those days he was quite a youngster – about twenty – and he became very intimate with Miss Grant, in quite an innocent way, though not very discreet, but she was a nice respectable girl, as most English models are, and no one thought any harm. However, a good many letters passed between them, and some little presents, amongst which was a beaded chain carrying a locket, and in this he was fool enough to put his portrait and the inscription, '*Edith, from Harold*'.

"Later on Miss Grant, who had a rather good voice, went on the stage, in the comic opera line, and, in consequence, her habits and associates changed somewhat, and, as Harold had meanwhile become engaged, he was naturally anxious to get his letters back, and especially to exchange the locket for some less compromising gift. The letters she eventually sent him, but refused absolutely to part with the locket.

"Now, for the last month Harold has been staying at Halbury, making sketching excursions into the surrounding country, and yesterday morning he took the train to Shinglehurst, the third station from here, and the one before Woldhurst.

"On the platform here he met Miss Grant, who had come down from London, and was going on to Worthing. They entered the branch train together, having a first-class compartment to themselves. It seems she was wearing his locket at the time, and he made another appeal to her to make an exchange, which she refused, as before. The discussion appears to have become rather heated and angry on both sides, for the guard and a porter at Munsden both noticed that they seemed to be quarrelling, but the upshot of the affair was that the lady snapped the chain, and tossed it together with the locket to my brother, and they parted quite amiably at Shinglehurst, where Harold got out. He was then carrying his full sketching kit, including a large holland umbrella, the lower joint of which is an ash staff fitted with a powerful steel spike for driving into the ground.

"It was about half-past-ten when he got out at Shinglehurst. By eleven he had reached his pitch and got to work, and he painted steadily for three hours. Then he packed up his traps, and was just starting on his way back to the station, when he was met by the police and arrested.

"And now, observe the accumulation of circumstantial evidence against him. He was the last person seen in company with the murdered woman – for no one seems to have seen her after they left Munsden. He appeared to be quarrelling with her when she was last seen alive, he had a reason for possibly wishing for her death, he was provided with an implement – a spiked staff – capable of inflicting the injury which caused her death, and, when he was searched, there was found in his possession the locket and broken chain, apparently removed from her person with violence.

"Against all this is, of course, his known character – he is the gentlest and most amiable of men – and his subsequent conduct – imbecile to the last degree if he had been guilty, but, as a lawyer, I can't help seeing that appearances are almost hopelessly against him."

"We won't say 'hopelessly,'" replied Thorndyke, as we took our places in the carriage, "though I expect the police are pretty cocksure. When does the inquest open?"

"To-day at four. I have obtained an order from the coroner for you to examine the body and be present at the post-mortem."

"Do you happen to know the exact position of the wound?"

"Yes, it is a little above and behind the left ear – a horrible round hole, with a ragged cut or tear running from it to the side of the forehead."

"And how was the body lying?"

124

"Right along the floor, with the feet close to the off-side door."

"Was the wound on the head the only one?"

"No, there was a long cut or bruise on the right cheek – a contused wound the police surgeon called it, which he believes to have been inflicted with a heavy and rather blunt weapon. I have not heard of any other wounds or bruises."

"Did anyone enter the train yesterday at Shinglehurst?" Thorndyke asked.

"No one entered the train after it left Halbury."

Thorndyke considered these statements in silence, and presently fell into a brown study, from which he roused only as the train moved out of Shinglehurst Station.

"It would be about here that the murder was committed," said Mr. Stopford, "at least, between here and Woldhurst."

Thorndyke nodded rather abstractedly, being engaged at the moment in observing with great attention the objects that were visible from the windows.

"I notice," he remarked presently, "a number of chips scattered about between the rails, and some of the chair-wedges look new. Have there been any platelayers at work lately?"

"Yes," answered Stopford, "they are on the line now, I believe – at least, I saw a gang working near Woldhurst yesterday, and they are said to have set a rick on fire. I saw it smoking when I came down."

"Indeed, and this middle line of rails is, I suppose, a sort of siding?"

"Yes, they shunt the goods trains and empty trucks on to it. There are the remains of the rick – still smouldering, you see."

Thorndyke gazed absently at the blackened heap until an empty cattle-truck on the middle track hid it from view. This was succeeded by a line of goods-waggons, and these by a passenger coach, one compartment of which – a first-class – was closed up and sealed. The train now began to slow down rather suddenly, and a couple of minutes later we brought up in Woldhurst Station.

It was evident that rumours of Thorndyke's advent had preceded us, for the entire staff – two porters, an inspector, and the station-master – were waiting expectantly on the platform, and the latter came forward, regardless of his dignity, to help us with our luggage.

"Do you think I could see the carriage?" Thorndyke asked the solicitor.

"Not the inside, sir," said the station-master, on being appealed to. "The police have sealed it up. You would have to ask the inspector."

"Well, I can have a look at the outside, I suppose?" said Thorndyke, and to this the station-master readily agreed, and offered to accompany us.

"What other first-class passengers were there?" Thorndyke asked.

"None, sir. There was only one first-class coach, and the deceased was the only person in it. It has given us all a dreadful turn, this affair has," he continued, as we set off up the line. "I was on the platform when the train came in. We were watching a rick that was burning up the line, and a rare blaze it made, too, and I was just saying that we should have to move the cattle-truck that was on the mid-track, because, you see, sir, the smoke and sparks were blowing across, and I thought it would frighten the poor beasts. And Mr. Felton he don't like his beasts handled roughly. He says it spoils the meat."

"No doubt he is right," said Thorndyke. "But now, tell me, do you think it is possible for any person to board or leave the train on the off-side unobserved? Could a man, for instance, enter a compartment on the off-side at one station and drop off as the train was slowing down at the next, without being seen?"

"I doubt it," replied the station-master. "Still, I wouldn't say it is impossible."

"Thank you. Oh, and there's another question. You have a gang of men at work on the line, I see. Now, do those men belong to the district?"

"No, sir, they are strangers, every one, and pretty rough diamonds some of 'em are. But I shouldn't say there was any real harm in 'em. If you was suspecting any of 'em of being mixed up in this – "

"I am not," interrupted Thorndyke rather shortly. "I suspect nobody, but I wish to get all the facts of the case at the outset."

"Naturally, sir," replied the abashed official, and we pursued our way in silence.

"Do you remember, by the way," said Thorndyke, as we approached the empty coach, "whether the off-side door of the compartment was closed and locked when the body was discovered?"

"It was closed, sir, but not locked. Why, sir, did you think – ?"

"Nothing, nothing. The sealed compartment is the one, of course?"

Without waiting for a reply, he commenced his survey of the coach, while I gently restrained our two companions from shadowing him, as they were disposed to do. The off-side footboard occupied his attention specially, and when he had scrutinized minutely the part opposite the fatal compartment, he walked slowly from end to end with his eyes but a few inches from its surface, as though he was searching for something.

Near what had been the rear end he stopped, and drew from his pocket a piece of paper. Then, with a moistened finger-tip he picked up from the footboard some evidently minute object, which he carefully transferred to the paper, folding the latter and placing it in his pocket-book.

He next mounted the footboard, and, having peered in through the window of the sealed compartment, produced from his pocket a small insufflator or powder-blower, with which he blew a stream of impalpable smoke-like powder on to the edges of the middle window, bestowing the closest attention on the irregular dusty patches in which it settled, and even measuring one on the jamb of the window with a pocket-rule. At length he stepped down, and, having carefully looked over the near-side footboard, announced that he had finished for the present.

As we were returning down the line, we passed a working man, who seemed to be viewing the chairs and sleepers with more than casual interest.

"That, I suppose, is one of the plate-layers?" Thorndyke suggested to the station-master.

"Yes, the foreman of the gang," was the reply.

"I'll just step back and have a word with him, if you will walk on slowly." And my colleague turned back briskly and overtook the man, with whom he remained in conversation for some minutes.

"I think I see the police inspector on the platform," remarked Thorndyke, as we approached the station.

"Yes, there he is," said our guide. "Come down to see what you are after, sir, I expect." Which was doubtless the case, although the officer professed to be there by the merest chance.

"You would like to see the weapon, sir, I suppose?" he remarked, when he had introduced himself.

"The umbrella-spike," Thorndyke corrected. "Yes, if I may. We are going to the mortuary now."

"Then you'll pass the station on the way. So, if you care to look in, I will walk up with you."

This proposition being agreed to, we all proceeded to the police-station, including the station-master, who was on the very tiptoe of curiosity.

"There you are, sir," said the inspector, unlocking his office, and ushering us in. "Don't say we haven't given every facility to the defence. There are all the effects of the accused, including the very weapon the deed was done with."

"Come, come," protested Thorndyke, "we mustn't be premature." He took the stout ash staff from the officer, and, having examined the formidable spike through a lens, drew from his pocket a steel calliper-gauge, with which he carefully measured the diameter of the spike, and the staff to which it was fixed. "And now," he said, when he had made a note of the measurements in his book, "we will look at the colour-box and the sketch. Ha! a very orderly man, your brother. Mr. Stopford. Tubes all in their places, palette-knives wiped clean, palette cleaned off and rubbed bright, brushes wiped – they ought to be washed before they stiffen – all this is very significant." He unstrapped the sketch from the blank canvas to which it was pinned, and, standing it on a chair in a good light, stepped back to look at it.

"And you tell me that that is only three hours' work!" he exclaimed, looking at the lawyer. "It is really a marvellous achievement."

"My brother is a very rapid worker," replied Stopford dejectedly.

"Yes, but this is not only amazingly rapid. It is in his very happiest vein – full of spirit and feeling. But we mustn't stay to look at it longer." He replaced the canvas on its pins, and having glanced at the locket and some other articles that lay in a drawer, thanked the inspector for his courtesy, and withdrew.

"That sketch and the colour-box appear very suggestive to me," he remarked, as we walked up the street.

"To me also," said Stopford gloomily, "for they are under lock and key, like their owner, poor old fellow."

He sighed heavily, and we walked on in silence.

The mortuary-keeper had evidently heard of our arrival, for he was waiting at the door with the key in his hand, and, on being shown the coroner's order, unlocked the door, and we entered together, but, after a momentary glance at the ghostly, shrouded figure lying upon the slate table, Stopford turned pale and retreated, saying that he would wait for us outside with the mortuary-keeper.

As soon as the door was closed and locked on the inside, Thorndyke glanced curiously round the bare, whitewashed building. A stream of sunlight poured in through the skylight, and fell upon the silent form that lay so still under its covering-sheet, and one stray beam glanced into a corner by the door, where, on a row of pegs and a deal table, the dead woman's clothing was displayed.

"There is something unspeakably sad in these poor relics, Jervis," said Thorndyke, as we stood before them. "To me they are more tragic, more full of pathetic suggestion, than the corpse itself. See the smart, jaunty hat, and the costly skirts hanging there, so desolate and forlorn, the dainty lingerie on the table, neatly folded – by the mortuary-man's wife, I hope – the little French shoes and open-work silk stockings. How pathetically eloquent they are of harmless, womanly vanity, and the gay, careless life, snapped short in the twinkling of an eye. But we must not give way to sentiment. There is another life threatened, and it is in our keeping."

He lifted the hat from its peg, and turned it over in his hand. It was, I think, what is called a "picture-hat" – a huge, flat, shapeless mass of gauze and ribbon and feather, spangled over freely with dark-blue sequins. In one part of the brim was a ragged hole, and from this the glittering sequins dropped off in little showers when the hat was moved.

"This will have been worn tilted over on the left side," said Thorndyke, "judging by the general shape and the position of the hole."

"Yes," I agreed. "Like that of the Duchess of Devonshire in Gainsborough's portrait."

"Exactly."

He shook a few of the sequins into the palm of his hand, and, replacing the hat on its peg, dropped the little discs into an envelope, on which he wrote, "From the hat," and slipped it into his pocket. Then, stepping over to the table, he drew back the sheet reverently and even tenderly from the dead woman's face, and looked down at it with grave pity. It was a comely face, white as marble, serene and peaceful in expression, with half-closed eyes, and framed with a mass of brassy, yellow hair, but its beauty was marred by a long linear wound, half-cut, half-bruise, running down the right cheek from the eye to the chin.

"A handsome girl," Thorndyke commented – "a dark-haired blonde. What a sin to have disfigured herself so with that horrible peroxide." He smoothed the hair back from her forehead, and added, "She seems to have applied the stuff last about ten days ago. There is about a quarter-of-nch of dark hair at the roots. What do you make of that wound on the cheek?"

"It looks as if she had struck some sharp angle in falling, though, as the seats are padded in first-class carriages, I don't see what she could have struck."

"No. And now let us look at the other wound. Will you note down the description?" He handed me his notebook, and I wrote down as he dictated, "A clean-punched circular hole in skull, an inch behind and above margin of left ear – diameter, an inch and seven-sixteenths, starred fracture of parietal bone, membranes perforated, and brain entered deeply, ragged scalp-wound, extending forward to margin of left orbit, fragments of gauze and sequins in edges of wound. That will do for the present. Dr. Morton will give us further details if we want them."

He pocketed his callipers and rule, drew from the bruised scalp one or two loose hairs, which he placed in the envelope with the sequins, and, having looked over the body for other wounds or bruises (of which there were none), replaced the sheet, and prepared to depart.

As we walked away from the mortuary, Thorndyke was silent and deeply thoughtful, and I gathered that he was piecing together the facts that he had acquired. At length Mr. Stopford, who had several times looked at him curiously, said, "The post-mortem will take place at three, and it is now only half-past-eleven. What would you like to do next?"

129

Thorndyke, who, in spite of his mental preoccupation, had been looking about him in his usual keen, attentive way, halted suddenly.

"Your reference to the post-mortem," said he, "reminds me that I forgot to put the ox-gall into my case."

"Ox-gall!" I exclaimed, endeavouring vainly to connect this substance with the technique of the pathologist. "What were you going to do with – "

But here I broke off, remembering my friend's dislike of any discussion of his methods before strangers.

"I suppose," he continued, "there would hardly be an artist's colourman in a place of this size?"

"I should think not," said Stopford. "But couldn't you get the stuff from a butcher? There's a shop just across the road."

"So there is," agreed Thorndyke, who had already observed the shop. "The gall ought, of course, to be prepared, but we can filter it ourselves – that is, if the butcher has any. We will try him, at any rate."

He crossed the road towards the shop, over which the name "Felton" appeared in gilt lettering, and, addressing himself to the proprietor, who stood at the door, introduced himself and explained his wants.

"Ox-gall?" said the butcher. "No, sir, I haven't any just now, but I am having a beast killed this afternoon, and I can let you have some then. In fact," he added, after a pause, "as the matter is of importance, I can have one killed at once if you wish it."

"That is very kind of you," said Thorndyke, "and it would greatly oblige me. Is the beast perfectly healthy?"

"They're in splendid condition, sir. I picked them out of the herd myself. But you shall see them – ay, and choose the one that you'd like killed."

"You are really very good," said Thorndyke warmly. "I will just run into the chemist's next door, and get a suitable bottle, and then I will avail myself of your exceedingly kind offer."

He hurried into the chemist's shop, from which he presently emerged, carrying a white paper parcel, and we then followed the butcher down a narrow lane by the side of his shop. It led to an enclosure containing a small pen, in which were confined three handsome steers, whose glossy, black coats contrasted in a very striking manner with their long, greyish-white, nearly straight horns.

"These are certainly very fine beasts, Mr. Felton," said Thorndyke, as we drew up beside the pen, "and in excellent condition, too."

He leaned over the pen and examined the beasts critically, especially as to their eyes and horns. Then, approaching the nearest one, he raised his stick and bestowed a smart tap on the under-side of the right horn, following it by a similar tap on the left one, a proceeding that the beast viewed with stolid surprise.

"The state of the horns," explained Thorndyke, as he moved on to the next steer, "enables one to judge, to some extent, of the beast's health."

"Lord bless you, sir," laughed Mr. Felton, "they haven't got no feeling in their horns, else what good 'ud their horns be to 'em?"

Apparently he was right, for the second steer was as indifferent to a sounding rap on either horn as the first. Nevertheless, when Thorndyke approached the third steer, I unconsciously drew nearer to watch, and I noticed that, as the stick struck the horn, the beast drew back in evident alarm, and that when the blow was repeated, it became manifestly uneasy.

"He don't seem to like that," said the butcher. "Seems as if – Hullo, that's queer!"

Thorndyke had just brought his stick up against the left horn, and immediately the beast had winced and started back, shaking his head and moaning. There was not, however, room for him to back out of reach, and Thorndyke, by leaning into the pen, was able to inspect the sensitive horn, which he did with the closest attention, while the butcher looked on with obvious perturbation.

"You don't think there's anything wrong with this beast, sir, I hope," said he.

"I can't say without a further examination," replied Thorndyke. "It may be the horn only that is affected. If you will have it sawn off close to the head, and sent up to me at the hotel, I will look at it and tell you. And, by way of preventing any mistakes, I will mark it and cover it up, to protect it from injury in the slaughter-house."

He opened his parcel and produced from it a wide-mouthed bottle labelled "Ox-gall," a sheet of gutta-percha tissue, a roller bandage, and a stick of sealing-wax. Handing the bottle to Mr. Felton, he encased the distal half of the horn in a covering by means of the tissue and the bandage, which he fixed securely with the sealing-wax.

"I'll saw the horn off and bring it up to the hotel myself, with the ox-gall," said Mr. Felton. "You shall have them in half-an-hour."

He was as good as his word, for in half-an-hour Thorndyke was seated at a small table by the window of our private sitting-room in the Black Bull Hotel. The table was covered with newspaper, and on it lay the long grey horn and Thorndyke's travelling-case, now open and displaying a small microscope and its accessories. The butcher was seated solidly in an armchair waiting, with a half-suspicious eye on Thorndyke for the report, and I was endeavouring by cheerful talk to keep Mr. Stopford from sinking into utter despondency, though I, too, kept a furtive watch on my colleague's rather mysterious proceedings.

I saw him unwind the bandage and apply the horn to his ear, bending it slightly to and fro. I watched him, as he scanned the surface closely through a lens, and observed him as he scraped some substance from the pointed end on to a glass slide, and, having applied a drop of some reagent, began to tease out the scraping with a pair of mounted needles. Presently he placed the slide under the microscope, and, having observed it attentively for a minute or two, turned round sharply.

"Come and look at this, Jervis," said he.

I wanted no second bidding, being on tenterhooks of curiosity, but came over and applied my eye to the instrument.

"Well, what is it?" he asked.

"A multipolar nerve corpuscle – very shrivelled, but unmistakable."

"And this?"

He moved the slide to a fresh spot.

"Two pyramidal nerve corpuscles and some portions of fibres."

"And what do you say the tissue is?"

"Cortical brain substance, I should say, without a doubt."

"I entirely agree with you. And that being so," he added, turning to Mr. Stopford, "we may say that the case for the defence is practically complete."

"What, in Heaven's name, do you mean?" exclaimed Stopford, starting up.

"I mean that we can now prove when and where and how Miss Grant met her death. Come and sit down here, and I will explain. No, you needn't go away, Mr. Felton. We shall have to subpoena you. Perhaps," he continued, "we had better go over the facts and see what they suggest. And first we note the position of the body, lying with the feet close to the off-side door, showing that, when she fell, the deceased was sitting, or more probably standing, close to that door. Next there is this." He drew from his pocket a folded paper, which he opened, displaying a tiny blue disc. "It is one of the sequins with which her hat was trimmed, and I have in this envelope several more which I took from the hat itself.

"This single sequin I picked up on the rear end of the off side footboard, and its presence there makes it nearly certain that at some time Miss Grant had put her head out of the window on that side.

"The next item of evidence I obtained by dusting the margins of the off-side window with a light powder, which made visible a greasy impression three-and-a-quarter inches long on the sharp corner of the right-hand jamb (right-hand from the inside, I mean).

"And now as to the evidence furnished by the body. The wound in the skull is behind and above the left ear, is roughly circular, and measures one inch and seven-sixteenths at most, and a ragged scalp-wound runs from it towards the left eye. On the right cheek is a linear contused wound three-and-a-quarter inches long. There are no other injuries.

"Our next facts are furnished by this." He took up the horn and tapped it with his finger, while the solicitor and Mr. Felton stared at him in speechless wonder. "You notice it is a left horn, and you remember that it was highly sensitive. If you put your ear to it while I strain it, you will hear the grating of a fracture in the bony core. Now look at the pointed end, and you will see several deep scratches running lengthwise, and where those scratches end the diameter of the horn is, as you see by this calliper-gauge, one inch and seven-sixteenths. Covering the scratches is a dry blood-stain, and at the extreme tip is a small mass of a dried substance which Dr. Jervis and I have examined with the microscope and are satisfied is brain tissue."

"Good God!" exclaimed Stopford eagerly. "Do you mean to say – "

"Let us finish with the facts, Mr. Stopford," Thorndyke interrupted. "Now, if you look closely at that blood-stain, you will see a short piece of hair stuck to the horn, and through this lens you can make out the root-bulb. It is a golden hair, you notice, but near the root it is black, and our calliper-gauge shows us that the black portion is fourteen sixty-fourths of an inch long. Now, in this envelope are some hairs that I removed from the dead woman's head. They also are golden hairs, black at the roots, and when I measure the black portion I find it to be fourteen sixty-fourths of an inch long. Then, finally, there is this."

He turned the horn over, and pointed to a small patch of dried blood. Embedded in it was a blue sequin.

Mr. Stopford and the butcher both gazed at the horn in silent amazement. Then the former drew a deep breath and looked up at Thorndyke.

"No doubt," said he, "you can explain this mystery, but for my part I am utterly bewildered, though you are filling me with hope."

"And yet the matter is quite simple," returned Thorndyke, "even with these few facts before us, which are only a selection from the body of evidence in our possession. But I will state my theory, and you shall judge." He rapidly sketched a rough plan on a sheet of paper, and continued, "These were the conditions when the train was approaching Woldhurst: Here was the passenger-coach, here was the burning rick, and here was a cattle-truck. This steer was in that truck. Now my hypothesis is that at that time Miss Grant was standing with her head out of the off-side window, watching the burning rick. Her wide hat, worn on the left side, hid from her view the cattle-truck which she was approaching, and then this is what happened." He sketched another plan to a larger scale. "One of the steers – this one – had thrust its long horn out through the bars. The point of that horn struck the deceased's head, driving her face violently

133

against the corner of the window, and then, in disengaging, ploughed its way through the scalp, and suffered a fracture of its core from the violence of the wrench. This hypothesis is inherently probable, it fits all the facts, and those facts admit of no other explanation."

The solicitor sat for a moment as though dazed. Then he rose impulsively and seized Thorndyke's hands. "I don't know what to say to you," he exclaimed huskily, "except that you have saved my brother's life, and for that may God reward you!"

The butcher rose from his chair with a slow grin.

"It seems to me," said he, "as if that ox-gall was what you might call a blind, eh, sir?"

And Thorndyke smiled an inscrutable smile.

When we returned to town on the following day we were a party of four, which included Mr. Harold Stopford. The verdict of "Death by misadventure," promptly returned by the coroner's jury, had been shortly followed by his release from custody, and he now sat with his brother and me, listening with rapt attention to Thorndyke's analysis of the case.

"So, you see," the latter concluded, "I had six possible theories of the cause of death worked out before I reached Halbury, and it only remained to select the one that fitted the facts. And when I had seen the cattle-truck, had picked up that sequin, had heard the description of the steers, and had seen the hat and the wounds, there was nothing left to do but the filling in of details."

"And you never doubted my innocence?" asked Harold Stopford.

Thorndyke smiled at his quondam client.

"Not after I had seen your colour-box and your sketch," said he, "to say nothing of the spike."

The Moabite Cipher

A large and motley crowd lined the pavements of Oxford Street as Thorndyke and I made our way leisurely eastward. Floral decorations and drooping bunting announced one of those functions inaugurated from time to time by a benevolent Government for the entertainment of fashionable loungers and the relief of distressed pickpockets. For a Russian Grand Duke, who had torn himself away, amidst valedictory explosions, from a loving if too demonstrative people, was to pass anon on his way to the Guildhall, and a British Prince, heroically indiscreet, was expected to occupy a seat in the ducal carriage.

Near Rathbone Place Thorndyke halted and drew my attention to a smart-looking man who stood lounging in a doorway, cigarette in hand.

"Our old friend Inspector Badger," said Thorndyke. "He seems mightily interested in that gentleman in the light overcoat. How d'ye do, Badger?" for at this moment the detective caught his eye and bowed. "Who is your friend?"

"That's what I want to know, sir," replied the inspector. "I've been shadowing him for the last half-hour, but I can't make him out, though I believe I've seen him somewhere. He don't look like a foreigner, but he has got something bulky in his pocket, so I must keep him in sight until the Duke is safely past. I wish," he added gloomily, "these beastly Russians would stop at home. They give us no end of trouble."

"Are you expecting any – occurrences, then?" asked Thorndyke.

"Bless you, sir," exclaimed Badger, "the whole route is lined with plain-clothes men. You see, it is known that several desperate characters followed the Duke to England, and there are a good many exiles living here who would like to have a rap at him. Hallo! What's he up to now?"

The man in the light overcoat had suddenly caught the inspector's too inquiring eye, and forthwith dived into the crowd at the edge of the pavement. In his haste he trod heavily on the foot of a big, rough-looking man, by whom he was in a moment hustled out into the road with such violence that he fell sprawling face downwards. It was an unlucky moment. A mounted constable was just then backing in upon the crowd, and before he could gather the meaning of the shout that arose from the bystanders, his horse had set down one hind-hoof firmly on the prostrate man's back.

The inspector signalled to a constable, who forthwith made a way for us through the crowd, but even as we approached the injured man, he rose stiffly and looked round with a pale, vacant face.

135

"Are you hurt?" Thorndyke asked gently, with an earnest look into the frightened, wondering eyes.

"No, sir," was the reply, "only I feel queer – sinking – just here."

He laid a trembling hand on his chest, and Thorndyke, still eyeing him anxiously, said in a low voice to the inspector, "Cab or ambulance, as quickly as you can."

A cab was led round from Newman Street, and the injured man put into it. Thorndyke, Badger, and I entered, and we drove off up Rathbone Place. As we proceeded, our patient's face grew more and more ashen, drawn, and anxious, his breathing was shallow and uneven, and his teeth chattered slightly. The cab swung round into Goodge Street, and then – suddenly, in the twinkling of an eye – there came a change. The eyelids and jaw relaxed, the eyes became filmy, and the whole form subsided into the corner in a shrunken heap, with the strange gelatinous limpness of a body that is dead as a whole, while its tissues are still alive.

"God save us! The man's dead!" exclaimed the inspector in a shocked voice – for even policemen have their feelings. He sat staring at the corpse, as it nodded gently with the jolting of the cab, until we drew up inside the courtyard of the Middlesex Hospital, when he got out briskly, with suddenly renewed cheerfulness, to help the porter to place the body on the wheeled couch.

"We shall know who he is now, at any rate," said he, as we followed the couch to the casualty-room. Thorndyke nodded unsympathetically. The medical instinct in him was for the moment stronger than the legal.

The house-surgeon leaned over the couch, and made a rapid examination as he listened to our account of the accident. Then he straightened himself up and looked at Thorndyke.

"Internal hæmorrhage, I expect," said he. "At any rate, he's dead, poor beggar! – as dead as Nebuchadnezzar. Ah! here comes a bobby. It's his affair now."

A sergeant came into the room, breathing quickly, and looked in surprise from the corpse to the inspector. But the latter, without loss of time, proceeded to turn out the dead man's pockets, commencing with the bulky object that had first attracted his attention, which proved to be a brown-paper parcel tied up with red tape.

"Pork-pie, begad!" he exclaimed with a crestfallen air as he cut the tape and opened the package. "You had better go through his other pockets, sergeant."

The small heap of odds and ends that resulted from this process tended, with a single exception, to throw little light on the man's identity, the exception being a letter, sealed, but not stamped, addressed in an exceedingly illiterate hand to Mr. Adolf Schönberg, 213, Greek Street, Soho.

"He was going to leave it by hand, I expect," observed the inspector, with a wistful glance at the sealed envelope. "I think I'll take it round myself, and you had better come with me, sergeant."

He slipped the letter into his pocket, and, leaving the sergeant to take possession of the other effects, made his way out of the building.

"I suppose, Doctor," said he, as we crossed into Berners Street, "you are not coming our way! Don't want to see Mr. Schönberg, h'm?"

Thorndyke reflected for a moment. "Well, it isn't very far, and we may as well see the end of the incident. Yes, let us go together."

No. 213, Greek Street, was one of those houses that irresistibly suggest to the observer the idea of a church organ, either jamb of the doorway being adorned with a row of brass bell-handles corresponding to the stop-knobs.

These the sergeant examined with the air of an expert musician, and having, as it were, gauged the capacity of the instrument, selected the middle knob on the right-hand side and pulled it briskly, whereupon a first-floor window was thrown up and a head protruded. But it afforded us a momentary glimpse only, for, having caught the sergeant's upturned eye, it retired with surprising precipitancy, and before we had time to speculate on the apparition, the street-door was opened and a man emerged. He was about to close the door after him when the inspector interposed.

"Does Mr. Adolf Schönberg live here?"

The new-comer, a very typical Jew of the red-haired type, surveyed us thoughtfully through his gold-rimmed spectacles as he repeated the name.

"Schönberg – Schönberg? Ah, yes! I know. He lives on the third-floor. I saw him go up a short time ago. Third-floor back." And indicating the open door with a wave of the hand, he raised his hat and passed into the street.

"I suppose we had better go up," said the inspector, with a dubious glance at the row of bell-pulls. He accordingly started up the stairs, and we all followed in his wake.

There were two doors at the back on the third-floor, but as the one was open, displaying an unoccupied bedroom, the inspector rapped smartly on the other. It flew open almost immediately, and a fierce-looking little man confronted us with a hostile stare.

"Well?" said he.

"Mr. Adolf Schönberg?" inquired the inspector.

"Well? What about him?" snapped our new acquaintance.

"I wished to have a few words with him," said Badger.

137

"Then what the deuce do you come banging at my door for?" demanded the other.

"Why, doesn't he live here?"

"No. First-floor front," replied our friend, preparing to close the door.

"Pardon me," said Thorndyke, "but what is Mr. Schönberg like? I mean – "

"Like?" interrupted the resident. "He has a carroty beard and gold gig-lamps!" and, having presented this impressionist sketch, he brought the interview to a definite close by slamming the door and turning the key.

With a wrathful exclamation, the inspector turned towards the stairs, down which the sergeant was already clattering in hot haste, and made his way back to the ground-floor, followed, as before, by Thorndyke and me. On the doorstep we found the sergeant breathlessly interrogating a smartly-dressed youth, whom I had seen alight from a hansom as we entered the house, and who now stood with a notebook tucked under his arm, sharpening a pencil with deliberate care.

"Mr. James saw him come out, sir," said the sergeant. "He turned up towards the Square."

"Did he seem to hurry?" asked the inspector.

"Rather," replied the reporter. "As soon as you were inside, he went off like a lamplighter. You won't catch him now."

"We don't want to catch him," the detective rejoined gruffly. Then, backing out of earshot of the eager pressman, he said in a lower tone, "That was Mr. Schönberg, beyond a doubt, and it is clear that he has some reason for making himself scarce, so I shall consider myself justified in opening that note."

He suited the action to the word, and, having cut the envelope open with official neatness, drew out the enclosure.

"My hat!" he exclaimed, as his eye fell upon the contents. "What in creation is this? It isn't shorthand, but what the deuce is it?"

He handed the document to Thorndyke, who, having held it up to the light and felt the paper critically, proceeded to examine it with keen interest. It consisted of a single half-sheet of thin notepaper, both sides of which were covered with strange, crabbed characters, written with a brownish-black ink in continuous lines, without any spaces to indicate the divisions into words, and, but for the modern material which bore the writing, it might have been a portion of some ancient manuscript or forgotten codex.

"What do you make of it, Doctor?" inquired the inspector anxiously, after a pause, during which Thorndyke had scrutinized the strange writing with knitted brows.

"Not a great deal," replied Thorndyke. "The character is the Moabite or Phoenician – primitive Semitic, in fact – and reads from right to left. The language I take to be Hebrew. At any rate, I can find no Greek words, and I see here a group of letters which may form one of the few Hebrew words that I know – the word *badim* – 'lies'. But you had better get it deciphered by an expert."

"If it is Hebrew," said Badger, "we can manage it all right. There are plenty of Jews at our disposal."

"You had much better take the paper to the British Museum," said Thorndyke, "and submit it to the keeper of the Phoenician antiquities for decipherment."

Inspector Badger smiled a foxy smile as he deposited the paper in his pocket-book. "We'll see what we can make of it ourselves first," he said, "but many thanks for your advice, all the same, Doctor. No, Mr. James, I can't give you any information just at present, you had better apply at the hospital."

"I suspect," said Thorndyke, as we took our way homewards, "that Mr. James has collected enough material for his purpose already. He must have followed us from the hospital, and I have no doubt that he has his report, with 'full details,' mentally arranged at this moment. And I am not sure that he didn't get a peep at the mysterious paper, in spite of the inspector's precautions."

"By the way," I said, "what do you make of the document?"

"A cipher, most probably," he replied. "It is written in the primitive Semitic alphabet, which, as you know, is practically identical with primitive Greek. It is written from right to left, like the Phoenician, Hebrew, and Moabite, as well as the earliest Greek, inscriptions. The paper is common cream-laid notepaper, and the ink is ordinary indelible Chinese ink, such as is used by draughtsmen. Those are the facts, and without further study of the document itself, they don't carry us very far."

"Why do you think it is a cipher rather than a document in straightforward Hebrew?"

"Because it is obviously a secret message of some kind. Now, every educated Jew knows more or less Hebrew, and, although he is able to read and write only the modern square Hebrew character, it is so easy to transpose one alphabet into another that the mere language would afford no security. Therefore, I expect that, when the experts translate this document, the translation or transliteration will be a mere farrago of unintelligible nonsense. But we shall see, and meanwhile the facts that we have offer several interesting suggestions which are well worth consideration."

"As, for instance – ?"

139

"Now, my dear Jervis," said Thorndyke, shaking an admonitory forefinger at me, "don't, I pray you, give way to mental indolence. You have these few facts that I have mentioned. Consider them separately and collectively, and in their relation to the circumstances. Don't attempt to suck my brain when you have an excellent brain of your own to suck."

On the following morning the papers fully justified my colleague's opinion of Mr. James. All the events which had occurred, as well as a number that had not, were given in the fullest and most vivid detail, a lengthy reference being made to the paper "found on the person of the dead anarchist," and "written in a private shorthand or cryptogram."

The report concluded with the gratifying – though untrue – statement that "in this intricate and important case, the police have wisely secured the assistance of Dr. John Thorndyke, to whose acute intellect and vast experience the portentous cryptogram will doubtless soon deliver up its secret."

"Very flattering," laughed Thorndyke, to whom I read the extract on his return from the hospital, "but a little awkward if it should induce our friends to deposit a few trifling mementoes in the form of nitro-compounds on our main staircase or in the cellars. By the way, I met Superintendent Miller on London Bridge. The 'cryptogram,' as Mr. James calls it, has set Scotland Yard in a mighty ferment."

"Naturally. What have they done in the matter?"

"They adopted my suggestion, after all, finding that they could make nothing of it themselves, and took it to the British Museum. The Museum people referred them to Professor Poppelbaum, the great palæographer, to whom they accordingly submitted it."

"Did he express any opinion about it?"

"Yes, provisionally. After a brief examination, he found it to consist of a number of Hebrew words sandwiched between apparently meaningless groups of letters. He furnished the Superintendent off-hand with a translation of the words, and Miller forthwith struck off a number of hectograph copies of it, which he has distributed among the senior officials of his department, so that at present" – here Thorndyke gave vent to a soft chuckle – "Scotland Yard is engaged in a sort of missing word – or, rather, missing sense – competition. Miller invited me to join in the sport, and to that end presented me with one of the hectograph copies on which to exercise my wits, together with a photograph of the document."

"And shall you?" I asked.

"Not I," he replied, laughing. "In the first place, I have not been formally consulted, and consequently am a passive, though interested, spectator. In the second place, I have a theory of my own which I shall test if the occasion arises. But if you would like to take part in the competition,

140

I am authorized to show you the photograph and the translation. I will pass them on to you, and I wish you joy of them."

He handed me the photograph and a sheet of paper that he had just taken from his pocket-book, and watched me with grim amusement as I read out the first few lines.

"Woe, city, lies, robbery, prey, noise, whip, rattling, wheel, horse, chariot, day, darkness, gloominess, clouds, darkness, morning, mountain, people, strong, fire, them, flame."

"It doesn't look very promising at first sight," I remarked. "What is the Professor's theory?"

"His theory – provisionally, of course – is that the words form the message, and the groups of letters represent mere filled-up spaces between the words."

"But surely," I protested, "that would be a very transparent device."

Thorndyke laughed. "There is a childlike simplicity about it," said he, "that is highly attractive – but discouraging. It is much more probable that the words are dummies, and that the letters contain the message. Or, again, the solution may lie in an entirely different direction. But listen! Is that cab coming here?"

It was. It drew up opposite our chambers, and a few moments later a brisk step ascending the stairs heralded a smart rat-tat at our door. Flinging open the latter, I found myself confronted by a well-dressed stranger, who, after a quick glance at me, peered inquisitively over my shoulder into the room.

"I am relieved, Dr. Jervis," said he, "to find you and Dr. Thorndyke at home, as I have come on somewhat urgent professional business. My name," he continued, entering in response to my invitation, "is Barton, but you don't know me, though I know you both by sight. I have come to ask you if one of you – or, better still, both – could come to-night and see my brother."

"That," said Thorndyke, "depends on the circumstances and on the whereabouts of your brother."

"The circumstances," said Mr. Barton, "are, in my opinion, highly suspicious, and I will place them before you – of course, in strict confidence."

Thorndyke nodded and indicated a chair.

The Cipher

"My brother," continued Mr. Barton, taking the proffered seat, "has recently married for the second time. His age is fifty-five, and that of his wife twenty-six, and I may say that the marriage has been – well, by no means a success. Now, within the last fortnight, my brother has been attacked by a mysterious and extremely painful affection of the stomach, to which his doctor seems unable to give a name. It has resisted all treatment hitherto. Day by day the pain and distress increase, and I feel that, unless something decisive is done, the end cannot be far off."

"Is the pain worse after taking food?" inquired Thorndyke.

"That's just it!" exclaimed our visitor. "I see what is in your mind, and it has been in mine, too, so much so that I have tried repeatedly to obtain samples of the food that he is taking. And this morning I succeeded." Here he took from his pocket a wide-mouthed bottle, which, disengaging from its paper wrappings, he laid on the table. "When I called, he was taking his breakfast of arrowroot, which he complained had a gritty taste, supposed by his wife to be due to the sugar. Now I had provided myself with this bottle, and, during the absence of his wife, I managed unobserved to convey a portion of the arrowroot that he had left into it, and I should be greatly obliged if you would examine it and tell me if this arrowroot contains anything that it should not."

He pushed the bottle across to Thorndyke, who carried it to the window, and, extracting a small quantity of the contents with a glass rod, examined the pasty mass with the aid of a lens. Then, lifting the bell-glass cover from the microscope, which stood on its table by the window, he smeared a small quantity of the suspected matter on to a glass slip, and placed it on the stage of the instrument.

"I observe a number of crystalline particles in this," he said, after a brief inspection, "which have the appearance of arsenious acid."

"Ah!" ejaculated Mr. Barton, "just what I feared. But are you certain?"

"No," replied Thorndyke, "but the matter is easily tested."

He pressed the button of the bell that communicated with the laboratory, a summons that brought the laboratory assistant from his lair with characteristic promptitude.

"Will you please prepare a Marsh's apparatus, Polton," said Thorndyke.

"I have a couple ready, sir," replied Polton.

"Then pour the acid into one and bring it to me, with a tile."

As his familiar vanished silently, Thorndyke turned to Mr. Barton.

"Supposing we find arsenic in this arrowroot, as we probably shall, what do you want us to do?"

"I want you to come and see my brother," replied our client.

143

"Why not take a note from me to his doctor?"

"No, no. I want you to come – I should like you both to come – and put a stop at once to this dreadful business. Consider! It's a matter of life and death. You won't refuse! I beg you not to refuse me your help in these terrible circumstances."

"Well," said Thorndyke, as his assistant reappeared, "let us first see what the test has to tell us."

Polton advanced to the table, on which he deposited a small flask, the contents of which were in a state of brisk effervescence, a bottle labelled "calcium hypochlorite," and a white porcelain tile. The flask was fitted with a safety-funnel and a glass tube drawn out to a fine jet, to which Polton cautiously applied a lighted match. Instantly there sprang from the jet a tiny, pale violet flame. Thorndyke now took the tile, and held it in the flame for a few seconds, when the appearance of the surface remained unchanged save for a small circle of condensed moisture. His next proceeding was to thin the arrowroot with distilled water until it was quite fluid, and then pour a small quantity into the funnel. It ran slowly down the tube into the flask, with the bubbling contents of which it became speedily mixed. Almost immediately a change began to appear in the character of the flame, which from a pale violet turned gradually to a sickly blue, while above it hung a faint cloud of white smoke. Once more Thorndyke held the tile above the jet, but this time, no sooner had the pallid flame touched the cold surface of the porcelain, than there appeared on the latter a glistening black stain.

"That is pretty conclusive," observed Thorndyke, lifting the stopper out of the reagent bottle, "but we will apply the final test." He dropped a few drops of the hypochlorite solution on to the tile, and immediately the black stain faded away and vanished. "We can now answer your question, Mr. Barton," said he, replacing the stopper as he turned to our client. "The specimen that you brought us certainly contains arsenic, and in very considerable quantities."

"Then," exclaimed Mr. Barton, starting from his chair, "you will come and help me to rescue my brother from this dreadful peril. Don't refuse me, Dr. Thorndyke, for mercy's sake, don't refuse."

Thorndyke reflected for a moment.

"Before we decide," said he, "we must see what engagements we have."

With a quick, significant glance at me, he walked into the office, whither I followed in some bewilderment, for I knew that we had no engagements for the evening.

"Now, Jervis," said Thorndyke, as he closed the office door, "what are we to do?"

144

"We must go, I suppose," I replied. "It seems a pretty urgent case."

"It does," he agreed. "Of course, the man may be telling the truth, after all."

"You don't think he is, then?"

"No. It is a plausible tale, but there is too much arsenic in that arrowroot. Still, I think I ought to go. It is an ordinary professional risk. But there is no reason why you should put your head into the noose."

"Thank you," said I, somewhat huffily. "I don't see what risk there is, but if any exists I claim the right to share it."

"Very well," he answered with a smile, "we will both go. I think we can take care of ourselves."

He re-entered the sitting-room, and announced his decision to Mr. Barton, whose relief and gratitude were quite pathetic.

"But," said Thorndyke, "you have not yet told us where your brother lives."

"Rexford," was the reply – "Rexford, in Essex. It is an out-of-the-way place, but if we catch the seven-fifteen train from Liverpool Street, we shall be there in an hour-and-a-half."

"And as to the return? You know the trains, I suppose?"

"Oh yes," replied our client. "I will see that you don't miss your train back."

"Then I will be with you in a minute," said Thorndyke, and, taking the still-bubbling flask, he retired to the laboratory, whence he returned in a few minutes carrying his hat and overcoat.

The cab which had brought our client was still waiting, and we were soon rattling through the streets towards the station, where we arrived in time to furnish ourselves with dinner-baskets and select our compartment at leisure.

During the early part of the journey our companion was in excellent spirits. He despatched the cold fowl from the basket and quaffed the rather indifferent claret with as much relish as if he had not had a single relation in the world, and after dinner he became genial to the verge of hilarity. But, as time went on, there crept into his manner a certain anxious restlessness. He became silent and preoccupied, and several times furtively consulted his watch.

"The train is confoundedly late!" he exclaimed irritably. "Seven minutes behind time already!"

"A few minutes more or less are not of much consequence," said Thorndyke.

"No, of course not, but still – Ah, thank Heaven, here we are!"

He thrust his head out of the off-side window, and gazed eagerly down the line. Then, leaping to his feet, he bustled out on to the platform while the train was still moving.

Even as we alighted a warning bell rang furiously on the up-platform, and as Mr. Barton hurried us through the empty booking-office to the outside of the station, the rumble of the approaching train could be heard above the noise made by our own train moving off.

"My carriage doesn't seem to have arrived yet," exclaimed Mr. Barton, looking anxiously up the station approach. "If you will wait here a moment, I will go and make inquiries."

He darted back into the booking-office and through it on to the platform, just as the up-train roared into the station. Thorndyke followed him with quick but stealthy steps, and, peering out of the booking-office door, watched his proceedings. Then he turned and beckoned to me.

"There he goes," said he, pointing to an iron footbridge that spanned the line, and, as I looked, I saw, clearly defined against the dim night sky, a flying figure racing towards the "up" side.

It was hardly two-thirds across when the guard's whistle sang out its shrill warning.

"Quick, Jervis," exclaimed Thorndyke, "she's off!"

He leaped down on to the line, whither I followed instantly, and, crossing the rails, we clambered up together on to the foot-board opposite an empty first-class compartment. Thorndyke's magazine knife, containing, among other implements, a railway-key, was already in his hand. The door was speedily unlocked, and, as we entered, Thorndyke ran through and looked out on to the platform.

"Just in time!" he exclaimed. "He is in one of the forward compartments."

He relocked the door, and, seating himself, proceeded to fill his pipe.

"And now," said I, as the train moved out of the station, "perhaps you will explain this little comedy."

"With pleasure," he replied, "if it needs any explanation. But you can hardly have forgotten Mr. James's flattering remarks in his report of the Greek Street incident, clearly giving the impression that the mysterious document was in my possession. When I read that, I knew I must look out for some attempt to recover it, though I hardly expected such promptness. Still, when Mr. Barton called without credentials or appointment, I viewed him with some suspicion. That suspicion deepened when he wanted us both to come. It deepened further when I found an impossible quantity of arsenic in his sample, and it gave place to certainty when, having allowed him to select the trains by which we were to travel, I went up to the laboratory and examined the time-table, for I then found that the last train

146

for London left Rexford ten minutes after we were due to arrive. Obviously this was a plan to get us both safely out of the way while he and some of his friends ransacked our chambers for the missing document."

"I see, and that accounts for his extraordinary anxiety at the lateness of the train. But why did you come, if you knew it was a 'plant'?"

"My dear fellow," said Thorndyke, "I never miss an interesting experience if I can help it. There are possibilities in this, too, don't you see?"

"But supposing his friends have broken into our chambers already?"

"That contingency has been provided for, but I think they will wait for Mr. Barton – and us."

Our train, being the last one up, stopped at every station, and crawled slothfully in the intervals, so that it was past eleven o'clock when we reached Liverpool Street. Here we got out cautiously, and, mingling with the crowd, followed the unconscious Barton up the platform, through the barrier, and out into the street. He seemed in no special hurry, for, after pausing to light a cigar, he set off at an easy pace up New Broad Street.

Thorndyke hailed a hansom, and, motioning me to enter, directed the cabman to drive to Clifford's Inn Passage.

"Sit well back," said he, as we rattled away up New Broad Street. "We shall be passing our gay deceiver presently – in fact, there he is, a living, walking illustration of the folly of underrating the intelligence of one's adversary."

At Clifford's Inn Passage we dismissed the cab, and, retiring into the shadow of the dark, narrow alley, kept an eye on the gate of Inner Temple Lane. In about twenty minutes we observed our friend approaching on the south side of Fleet Street. He halted at the gate, plied the knocker, and after a brief parley with the night-porter vanished through the wicket. We waited yet five minutes more, and then, having given him time to get clear of the entrance, we crossed the road.

The porter looked at us with some surprise.

"There's a gentleman just gone down to your chambers, sir," said he. "He told me you were expecting him."

"Quite right," said Thorndyke, with a dry smile, "I was. Good-night."

We slunk down the lane, past the church, and through the gloomy cloisters, giving a wide berth to all lamps and lighted entries, until, emerging into Paper Buildings, we crossed at the darkest part to King's Bench Walk, where Thorndyke made straight for the chambers of our friend Anstey, which were two doors above our own.

"Why are we coming here?" I asked, as we ascended the stairs.

But the question needed no answer when we reached the landing, for through the open door of our friend's chambers I could see in the darkened room Anstey himself with two uniformed constables and a couple of plain-clothes men.

"There has been no signal yet, sir," said one of the latter, whom I recognized as a detective-sergeant of our division.

"No," said Thorndyke, "but the M.C. has arrived. He came in five minutes before us."

"Then," exclaimed Anstey, "the ball will open shortly, ladies and gents. The boards are waxed, the fiddlers are tuning up, and – "

"Not quite so loud, if you please, sir," said the sergeant. "I think there is somebody coming up Crown Office Row."

The ball had, in fact, opened. As we peered cautiously out of the open window, keeping well back in the darkened room, a stealthy figure crept out of the shadow, crossed the road, and stole noiselessly into the entry of Thorndyke's chambers. It was quickly followed by a second figure, and then by a third, in which I recognized our elusive client.

"Now listen for the signal," said Thorndyke. "They won't waste time. Confound that clock!"

The soft-voiced bell of the Inner Temple clock, mingling with the harsher tones of St. Dunstan's and the Law Courts, slowly told out the hour of midnight, and as the last reverberations were dying away, some metallic object, apparently a coin, dropped with a sharp clink on to the pavement under our window.

At the sound the watchers simultaneously sprang to their feet.

"You two go first," said the sergeant, addressing the uniformed men, who thereupon stole noiselessly, in their rubber-soled boots, down the stone stairs and along the pavement. The rest of us followed, with less attention to silence, and as we ran up to Thorndyke's chambers, we were aware of quick but stealthy footsteps on the stairs above.

"They've been at work, you see," whispered one of the constables, flashing his lantern on to the iron-bound outer door of our sitting-room, on which the marks of a large jemmy were plainly visible.

The sergeant nodded grimly, and, bidding the constables to remain on the landing, led the way upwards.

As we ascended, faint rustlings continued to be audible from above, and on the second-floor landing we met a man descending briskly, but without hurry, from the third. It was Mr. Barton, and I could not but admire the composure with which he passed the two detectives. But suddenly his glance fell on Thorndyke, and his composure vanished. With a wild stare of incredulous horror, he halted as if petrified. Then he broke away and raced furiously down the stairs, and a moment later a muffled shout and the sound of a scuffle told us that he had received a check. On the next flight we met two more men, who, more hurried and less self-possessed, endeavoured to push past, but the sergeant barred the way.

"Why, bless me!" exclaimed the latter, "it's Moakey, and isn't that Tom Harris?"

"It's all right, sergeant," said Moakey plaintively, striving to escape from the officer's grip. "We've come to the wrong house, that's all."

The sergeant smiled indulgently. "I know," he replied. "But you're always coming to the wrong house, Moakey, and now you're just coming along with me to the right house."

He slipped his hand inside his captive's coat, and adroitly fished out a large, folding jimmy, whereupon the discomforted burglar abandoned all further protest.

On our return to the first-floor, we found Mr. Barton sulkily awaiting us, handcuffed to one of the constables, and watched by Polton with pensive disapproval.

"I needn't trouble you to-night, Doctor," said the sergeant, as he marshalled his little troop of captors and captives. "You'll hear from us in the morning. Good-night, sir."

The melancholy procession moved off down the stairs, and we retired into our chambers with Anstey to smoke a last pipe.

"A capable man, that Barton," observed Thorndyke – "ready, plausible, and ingenious, but spoilt by prolonged contact with fools. I wonder if the police will perceive the significance of this little affair."

"They will be more acute than I am if they do," said I.

"Naturally," interposed Anstey, who loved to "cheek" his revered senior, "because there isn't any. It's only Thorndyke's bounce. He is really in a deuce of a fog himself."

However this may have been, the police were a good deal puzzled by the incident, for, on the following morning, we received a visit from no less a person than Superintendent Miller, of Scotland Yard.

"This is a queer business," said he, coming to the point at once – "this burglary, I mean. Why should they want to crack your place, right here in the Temple, too? You've got nothing of value here, have you? No 'hard stuff,' as they call it, for instance?"

"Not so much as a silver teaspoon," replied Thorndyke, who had a conscientious objection to plate of all kinds.

"It's odd," said the superintendent, "deuced odd. When we got your note, we thought these anarchist idiots had mixed you up with the case – you saw the papers, I suppose – and wanted to go through your rooms for some reason. We thought we had our hands on the gang, instead of which we find a party of common crooks that we're sick of the sight of. I tell you, sir, it's annoying when you think you've hooked a salmon, to bring up a blooming eel."

"It must be a great disappointment," Thorndyke agreed, suppressing a smile.

"It is," said the detective. "Not but what we're glad enough to get these beggars, especially Halkett, or Barton, as he calls himself – a mighty slippery customer is Halkett, and mischievous, too – but we're not wanting any disappointments just now. There was that big jewel job in Piccadilly, Taplin and Horne's. I don't mind telling you that we've not got the ghost of a clue. Then there's this anarchist affair. We're all in the dark there, too."

"But what about the cipher?" asked Thorndyke.

"Oh, hang the cipher!" exclaimed the detective irritably. "This Professor Poppelbaum may be a very learned man, but he doesn't help us much. He says the document is in Hebrew, and he has translated it into Double Dutch. Just listen to this!" He dragged out of his pocket a bundle of papers, and, dabbing down a photograph of the document before Thorndyke, commenced to read the Professor's report. "'*The document is written in the characters of the well-known inscription of Mesha, King of Moab*'* (who the devil's he? Never heard of him. Well known, indeed!) *'The language is Hebrew, and the words are separated by groups of letters, which are meaningless, and obviously introduced to mislead and confuse the reader. The words themselves are not strictly consecutive, but, by the interpellation of certain other words, a series of intelligible sentences is obtained, the meaning of which is not very clear, but is no doubt allegorical. The method of decipherment is shown in the accompanying tables, and the full rendering suggested on the enclosed sheet. It is to be noted that the writer of this document was apparently quite unacquainted with the Hebrew language, as appears from the absence of any grammatical construction.*' That's the Professor's report, Doctor, and here are the tables showing how he worked it out. It makes my head spin to look at 'em."

He handed to Thorndyke a bundle of ruled sheets, which my colleague examined attentively for a while, and then passed on to me.

"This is very systematic and thorough," said he. "But now let us see the final result at which he arrives."

	Space	Word	Space	Word	Space	Word
Moabite	Y٦	٩٣△٩	△٦	٩٤o	٩△	٦Y٤
Hebrew		בְּרִים		עִיר		אוֹ
Translation		LIES		CITY		WOE
Moabite	ל٦	6Y٩	6 Y٤	٦٩x	H I	6I٦
Hebrew		קוֹל		טֶרֶף		גֵּזֶל
Translation		NOISE		PREY		ROBBERY
Moabite	w٩	٥٦Yצ	٩٢	wo٩	٦o≢	xYw
Hebrew		אוֹפַן		רַעַשׁ		שׁוֹט
Translation		WHEEL		RATTLING		WHIP
Moabite	Y٦	٦Yz	△٦	٣٩٦٩٣	٩٤x	≢Y≢
Hebrew		יוֹם		מֶרְכָּבָה		סוּס
Translation		DAY		CHARIOT		HORSE

The Professor's Analysis

"It may be all very systematic," growled the superintendent, sorting out his papers, "but I tell you, sir, it's all Bosh!" The latter word he jerked out viciously, as he slapped down on the table the final product of the Professor's labours. "There," he continued, "that's what he calls the *full rendering*, and I reckon it'll make your hair curl. It might be a message from Bedlam."

Thorndyke took up the first sheet, and as he compared the constructed renderings with the literal translation, the ghost of a smile stole across his usually immovable countenance.

"The meaning is certainly a little obscure," he observed, "though the reconstruction is highly ingenious, and, moreover, I think the Professor is probably right. That is to say, the words which he has supplied are probably the omitted parts of the passages from which the words of the cryptogram were taken. What do you think, Jervis?"

He handed me the two papers, of which one gave the actual words of the cryptogram, and the other a suggested reconstruction, with omitted words supplied. The first read:

> *Woe city lies robbery prey*
> *Noise whip rattling wheel horse chariot*
> *Day darkness gloominess cloud darkness*
> *Morning mountain people strong*
> *Fire them flame*

151

Turning to the second paper, I read out the suggested rendering:

"*Woe to the bloody city! It is full of lies and robbery. The prey departeth not. The noise of a whip, and the noise of the rattling of the wheels, and of the prancing horses, and of the jumping chariots.*

"*A day of darkness and of gloominess, a day of clouds, and of thick darkness, as the morning spread upon the mountains, a great people and a strong.*

"*A fire devoureth before them, and behind them a flame burneth.*'"

Here the first sheet ended, and, as I laid it down, Thorndyke looked at me inquiringly.

"There is a good deal of reconstruction in proportion to the original matter," I objected. "The Professor has 'supplied' more than three-quarters of the final rendering."

"Exactly," burst in the superintendent, "it's all Professor and no cryptogram."

"Still, I think the reading is correct," said Thorndyke. "As far as it goes, that is."

"Good Lord!" exclaimed the dismayed detective. "Do you mean to tell me, sir, that that balderdash is the real meaning of the thing?"

"I don't say that," replied Thorndyke. "I say it is correct as far as it goes, but I doubt its being the solution of the cryptogram."

"Have you been studying that photograph that I gave you?" demanded Miller, with sudden eagerness.

"I have looked at it," said Thorndyke evasively, "but I should like to examine the original if you have it with you."

"I have," said the detective. "Professor Poppelbaum sent it back with the solution. You can have a look at it, though I can't leave it with you without special authority."

He drew the document from his pocket-book and handed it to Thorndyke, who took it over to the window and scrutinized it closely. From the window he drifted into the adjacent office, closing the door after him, and presently the sound of a faint explosion told me that he had lighted the gas-fire.

"Of course," said Miller, taking up the translation again, "this gibberish is the sort of stuff you might expect from a parcel of crack-brained anarchists, but it doesn't seem to mean anything."

"Not to us," I agreed, "but the phrases may have some pre-arranged significance. And then there are the letters between the words. It is possible that they may really form a cipher."

"I suggested that to the Professor," said Miller, "but he wouldn't hear of it. He is sure they are only dummies."

"I think he is probably mistaken, and so, I fancy, does my colleague. But we shall hear what he has to say presently."

"Oh, I know what he will say," growled Miller. "He will put the thing under the microscope, and tell us who made the paper, and what the ink is composed of, and then we shall be just where we were." The superintendent was evidently deeply depressed.

We sat for some time pondering in silence on the vague sentences of the Professor's translation, until, at length, Thorndyke reappeared, holding the document in his hand. He laid it quietly on the table by the officer, and then inquired, "Is this an official consultation?"

"Certainly," replied Miller. "I was authorized to consult you respecting the translation, but nothing was said about the original. Still, if you want it for further study, I will get it for you."

"No, thank you," said Thorndyke. "I have finished with it. My theory turned out to be correct."

"Your theory!" exclaimed the superintendent, eagerly. "Do you mean to say – ?"

"And, as you are consulting me officially, I may as well give you this."

He held out a sheet of paper, which the detective took from him and began to read.

"What is this?" he asked, looking up at Thorndyke with a puzzled frown. "Where did it come from?"

"It is the solution of the cryptogram," replied Thorndyke.

The detective re-read the contents of the paper, and, with the frown of perplexity deepening, once more gazed at my colleague.

"This is a joke, sir. You are fooling me," he said sulkily.

"Nothing of the kind," answered Thorndyke. "That is the genuine solution."

"But it's impossible!" exclaimed Miller. "Just look at it, Dr. Jervis."

I took the paper from his hand, and, as I glanced at it, I had no difficulty in understanding his surprise. It bore a short inscription in printed Roman capitals, thus:

"*THE PICKERDILLEY STUF IS UP THE CHIMBLY 416 WARDOUR ST 2ND FLOUR BACK IT WAS HID BECOS OF OLD MOAKEYS JOOD MOAKEY IS A BLITER.*"

"Then that fellow wasn't an anarchist at all?" I exclaimed.

"No," said Miller. "He was one of Moakey's gang. We suspected Moakey of being mixed up with that job, but we couldn't fix it on him. By Jove!" he added, slapping his thigh, "if this is right, and I can lay my hands on the loot! Can you lend me a bag, Doctor? I'm off to Wardour Street this very moment."

We furnished him with an empty suit-case, and, from the window, watched him making for Mitre Court at a smart double.

"I wonder if he will find the booty," said Thorndyke. "It just depends on whether the hiding-place was known to more than one of the gang. Well, it has been a quaint case, and instructive, too. I suspect our friend Barton and the evasive Schönberg were the collaborators who produced that curiosity of literature."

"May I ask how you deciphered the thing?" I said. "It didn't appear to take long."

"It didn't. It was merely a matter of testing a hypothesis, and you ought not to have to ask that question," he added, with mock severity, "seeing that you had what turned out to have been all the necessary facts, two days ago. But I will prepare a document and demonstrate to you to-morrow morning."

"So Miller was successful in his quest," said Thorndyke, as we smoked our morning pipes after breakfast. "The 'entire swag,' as he calls it, was 'up the chimbly,' undisturbed."

He handed me a note which had been left, with the empty suit-case, by a messenger, shortly before, and I was about to read it when an agitated knock was heard at our door. The visitor, whom I admitted, was a rather haggard and dishevelled elderly gentleman, who, as he entered, peered inquisitively through his concave spectacles from one of us to the other.

"Allow me to introduce myself, gentlemen," said he. "I am Professor Poppelbaum."

Thorndyke bowed and offered a chair.

"I called yesterday afternoon," our visitor continued, "at Scotland Yard, where I heard of your remarkable decipherment and of the convincing proof of its correctness. Thereupon I borrowed the cryptogram, and have spent the entire night in studying it, but I cannot connect your solution with any of the characters. I wonder if you would do me the great favour of enlightening me as to your method of decipherment, and so save me further sleepless nights? You may rely on my discretion."

"Have you the document with you?" asked Thorndyke.

The Professor produced it from his pocket-book, and passed it to my colleague.

"You observe, Professor," said the latter, "that this is a laid paper, and has no water-mark?"

"Yes, I noticed that."

"And that the writing is in indelible Chinese ink?"

"Yes, yes," said the savant impatiently, "but it is the inscription that interests me, not the paper and ink."

154

"Precisely," said Thorndyke. "Now, it was the ink that interested me when I caught a glimpse of the document three days ago. 'Why,' I asked myself, 'should anyone use this troublesome medium' – for this appears to be stick ink – 'when good writing ink is to be had?' What advantages has Chinese ink over writing ink? It has several advantages as a drawing ink, but for writing purposes it has only one: It is quite unaffected by wet. The obvious inference, then, was that this document was, for some reason, likely to be exposed to wet. But this inference instantly suggested another, which I was yesterday able to put to the test – thus."

He filled a tumbler with water, and, rolling up the document, dropped it in. Immediately there began to appear on it a new set of characters of a curious grey colour. In a few seconds Thorndyke lifted out the wet paper, and held it up to the light, and now there was plainly visible an inscription in transparent lettering, like a very distinct water-mark. It was in printed Roman capitals, written across the other writing, and read:

"THE PICKERDILLEY STUF IS UP THE CHIMBLY 416 WARDOUR ST 2ND FLOUR BACK IT WAS HID BECOS OF OLD MOAKEYS JOOD MOAKEY IS A BLITER."

The Professor regarded the inscription with profound disfavour.

"How do you suppose this was done?" he asked gloomily.

"I will show you," said Thorndyke. "I have prepared a piece of paper to demonstrate the process to Dr. Jervis. It is exceedingly simple."

He fetched from the office a small plate of glass, and a photographic dish in which a piece of thin notepaper was soaking in water.

"This paper," said Thorndyke, lifting it out and laying it on the glass, "has been soaking all night, and is now quite pulpy."

He spread a dry sheet of paper over the wet one, and on the former wrote heavily with a hard pencil, "Moakey is a bliter." On lifting the upper sheet, the writing was seen to be transferred in a deep grey to the wet paper, and when the latter was held up to the light the inscription stood out clear and transparent as if written with oil.

"When this dries," said Thorndyke, "the writing will completely disappear, but it will reappear whenever the paper is again wetted."

The Professor nodded.

"Very ingenious," said he – "a sort of artificial palimpsest, in fact. But I do not understand how that illiterate man could have written in the difficult Moabite script."

"He did not," said Thorndyke. "The 'cryptogram' was probably written by one of the leaders of the gang, who, no doubt, supplied copies to the other members to use instead of blank paper for secret communications. The object of the Moabite writing was evidently to divert attention from the paper itself, in case the communication fell into the wrong hands, and I must say it seems to have answered its purpose very well."

The Professor started, stung by the sudden recollection of his labours.

"Yes," he snorted, "but I am a scholar, sir, not a policeman. Every man to his trade."

He snatched up his hat, and with a curt "Good-morning," flung out of the room in dudgeon.

Thorndyke laughed softly.

"Poor Professor!" he murmured. "Our playful friend Barton has much to answer for."

The Mandarin's Pearl

Mr. Brodribb stretched out his toes on the kerb before the blazing fire with the air of a man who is by no means insensible to physical comfort.

"You are really an extraordinarily polite fellow, Thorndyke," said he.

He was an elderly man, rosy-gilled, portly, and convivial, to whom a mass of bushy, white hair, an expansive double chin, and a certain prim sumptuousness of dress imparted an air of old-world distinction. Indeed, as he dipped an amethystine nose into his wine-glass, and gazed thoughtfully at the glowing end of his cigar, he looked the very type of the well-to-do lawyer of an older generation.

"You are really an extraordinarily polite fellow, Thorndyke," said Mr. Brodribb.

"I know," replied Thorndyke. "But why this reference to an admitted fact?"

"The truth has just dawned on me," said the solicitor. "Here am I, dropping in on you, uninvited and unannounced, sitting in your own armchair before your fire, smoking your cigars, drinking your Burgundy – and deuced good Burgundy, too, let me add – and you have not dropped a single hint of curiosity as to what has brought me here."

"I take the gifts of the gods, you see, and ask no questions," said Thorndyke.

"Devilish handsome of you, Thorndyke – unsociable beggar like you, too," rejoined Mr. Brodribb, a fan of wrinkles spreading out genially from the corners of his eyes, "but the fact is I have come, in a sense, on business – always glad of a pretext to look you up, as you know – but I want to take your opinion on a rather queer case. It is about young Calverley. You remember Horace Calverley? Well, this is his son. Horace and I were schoolmates, you know, and after his death the boy, Fred, hung on to me rather. We're near neighbours down at Weybridge, and very good friends. I like Fred. He's a good fellow, though cranky, like all his people."

"What has happened to Fred Calverley?" Thorndyke asked, as the solicitor paused.

"Why, the fact is," said Mr. Brodribb, "just lately he seems to be going a bit queer – not mad, mind you – at least, I think not – but undoubtedly queer. Now, there is a good deal of property, and a good many highly interested relatives, and, as a natural consequence, there is some talk of getting him certified. They're afraid he may do something involving the estate or develop homicidal tendencies, and they talk of

157

possible suicide – you remember his father's death – but I say that's all bunkum. The fellow is just a bit cranky, and nothing more."

"What are his symptoms?" asked Thorndyke.

"Oh, he thinks he is being followed about and watched, and he has delusions. Sees himself in the glass with the wrong face, and that sort of thing, you know."

"You are not highly circumstantial," Thorndyke remarked.

Mr. Brodribb looked at me with a genial smile.

"What a glutton for facts this fellow is, Jervis. But you're right, Thorndyke. I'm vague. However, Fred will be here presently. We travel down together, and I took the liberty of asking him to call for me. We'll get him to tell you about his delusions, if you don't mind. He's not shy about them. And meanwhile I'll give you a few preliminary facts. The trouble began about a year ago. He was in a railway accident, and that knocked him all to pieces. Then he went for a voyage to recruit, and the ship broke her propeller-shaft in a storm and became helpless. That didn't improve the state of his nerves. Then he went down the Mediterranean, and after a month or two, back he came, no better than when he started. But here he is, I expect."

He went over to the door and admitted a tall, frail young man whom Thorndyke welcomed with quiet geniality, and settled in a chair by the fire. I looked curiously at our visitor. He was a typical neurotic – slender, fragile, eager. Wide-open blue eyes with broad pupils, in which I could plainly see the characteristic "hippus" – that incessant change of size that marks the unstable nervous equilibrium – parted lips, and wandering taper fingers, were as the stigmata of his disorder. He was of the stuff out of which prophets and devotees, martyrs, reformers, and third-rate poets are made.

"I have been telling Dr. Thorndyke about these nervous troubles of yours," said Mr. Brodribb presently. "I hope you don't mind. He is an old friend, you know, and he is very much interested."

"It is very good of him," said Calverley. Then he flushed deeply, and added, "But they are not really nervous, you know. They can't be merely subjective."

"You think they can't be?" said Thorndyke.

"No, I am sure they are not." He flushed again like a girl, and looked earnestly at Thorndyke with his big, dreamy eyes. "But you doctors," he said, "are so dreadfully sceptical of all spiritual phenomena. You are such materialists."

"Yes," said Mr. Brodribb, "the doctors are not hot on the supernatural, and that's the fact."

158

"Supposing you tell us about your experiences," said Thorndyke persuasively. "Give us a chance to believe, if we can't explain away."

Calverley reflected for a few moments. Then, looking earnestly at Thorndyke, he said, "Very well. If it won't bore you, I will. It is a curious story."

"I have told Dr. Thorndyke about your voyage and your trip down the Mediterranean," said Mr. Brodribb.

"Then," said Calverley, "I will begin with the events that are actually connected with these strange visitations. The first of these occurred in Marseilles. I was in a curio-shop there, looking over some Algerian and Moorish tilings, when my attention was attracted by a sort of charm or pendant that hung in a glass case. It was not particularly beautiful, but its appearance was quaint and curious, and took my fancy. It consisted of an oblong block of ebony in which was set a single pear-shaped pearl more than three-quarters of an inch long. The sides of the ebony block were lacquered – probably to conceal a joint – and bore a number of Chinese characters, and at the top was a little gold image with a hole through it, presumably for a string to suspend it by. Excepting for the pearl, the whole thing was uncommonly like one of those ornamental tablets of Chinese ink.

"Now, I had taken a fancy to the thing, and I can afford to indulge my fancies in moderation. The man wanted five pounds for it. He assured me that the pearl was a genuine one of fine quality, and obviously did not believe it himself. To me, however, it looked like a real pearl, and I determined to take the risk, so I paid the money, and he bowed me out with a smile – I may almost say a grin – of satisfaction. He would not have been so well pleased if he had followed me to a jeweller's to whom I took it for an expert opinion, for the jeweller pronounced the pearl to be undoubtedly genuine, and worth anything up to a thousand pounds.

"A day or two later, I happened to show my new purchase to some men whom I knew, who had dropped in at Marseilles in their yacht. They were highly amused at my having bought the thing, and when I told them what I had paid for it, they positively howled with derision.

"'Why, you silly guffin,' said one of them, a man named Halliwell, 'I could have had it ten days ago for half-a-sovereign, or probably five shillings. I wish now I had bought it. Then I could have sold it to you.'

"It seemed that a sailor had been hawking the pendant round the harbour, and had been on board the yacht with it.

"'Deuced anxious the beggar was to get rid of it, too,' said Halliwell, grinning at the recollection. 'Swore it was a genuine pearl of priceless value, and was willing to deprive himself of it for the trifling sum of half-a-jimmy. But we'd heard that sort of thing before. However, the curio-man

159

seems to have speculated on the chance of meeting with a greenhorn, and he seems to have pulled it off. Lucky curio man!'

"I listened patiently to their gibes, and when they had talked themselves out I told them about the jeweller. They were most frightfully sick, and when we had taken the pendant to a dealer in gems who happened to be staying in the town, and he had offered me five hundred pounds for it, their language wasn't fit for a divinity students' debating club. Naturally the story got noised abroad, and when I left, it was the talk of the place. The general opinion was that the sailor, who was traced to a tea-ship that had put into the harbour, had stolen it from some Chinese passenger, and no less than seventeen different Chinamen came forward to claim it as their stolen property.

"Soon after this I returned to England, and, as my nerves were still in a very shaky state, I came to live with my cousin Alfred, who has a large house at Weybridge. At this time he had a friend staying with him, a certain Captain Raggerton, and the two men appeared to be on very intimate terms. I did not take to Raggerton at all. He was a good-looking man, pleasant in his manners, and remarkably plausible. But the fact is – I am speaking in strict confidence, of course – he was a bad egg. He had been in the Guards, and I don't quite know why he left, but I do know that he played bridge and baccarat pretty heavily at several clubs, and that he had a reputation for being a rather uncomfortably lucky player. He did a good deal at the race-meetings, too, and was in general such an obvious undesirable that I could never understand my cousin's intimacy with him, though I must say that Alfred's habits had changed somewhat for the worse since I had left England.

"The fame of my purchase seems to have preceded me, for when, one day, I produced the pendant to show them, I found that they knew all about it. Raggerton had heard the story from a naval man, and I gathered vaguely that he had heard something that I had not, and that he did not care to tell me, for when my cousin and he talked about the pearl, which they did pretty often, certain significant looks passed between them, and certain veiled references were made which I could not fail to notice.

"One day I happened to be telling them of a curious incident that occurred on my way home. I had travelled to England on one of Holt's big China boats, not liking the crowd and bustle of the regular passenger-lines. Now, one afternoon, when we had been at sea a couple of days, I took a book down to my berth, intending to have a quiet read till tea-time. Soon, however, I dropped off into a doze, and must have remained asleep for over an hour. I awoke suddenly, and as I opened my eyes, I perceived that the door of the state-room was half-open, and a well-dressed Chinaman, in native costume, was looking in at me. He closed the door immediately,

160

and I remained for a few moments paralyzed by the start that he had given me. Then I leaped from my bunk, opened the door, and looked out. But the alley-way was empty. The Chinaman had vanished as if by magic.

"This little occurrence made me quite nervous for a day or two, which was very foolish of me, but my nerves were all on edge – and I am afraid they are still."

"Yes," said Thorndyke. "There was nothing mysterious about the affair. These boats carry a Chinese crew, and the man you saw was probably a Serang, or whatever they call the gang-captains on these vessels. Or he may have been a native passenger who had strayed into the wrong part of the ship."

"Exactly," agreed our client. "But to return to Raggerton. He listened with quite extraordinary interest as I was telling this story, and when I had finished he looked very queerly at my cousin.

"'A deuced odd thing, this, Calverley,' said he. 'Of course, it may be only a coincidence, but it really does look as if there was something, after all, in that – '

"'Shut up, Raggerton,' said my cousin. 'We don't want any of that rot.'

"'What is he talking about?' I asked.

"'Oh, it's only a rotten, silly yarn that he has picked up somewhere. You're not to tell him, Raggerton.'

"'I don't see why I am not to be told,' I said, rather sulkily. 'I'm not a baby.'

"'No,' said Alfred, 'but you're an invalid. You don't want any horrors.'

"In effect, he refused to go into the matter any further, and I was left on tenter-hooks of curiosity.

"However, the very next day I got Raggerton alone in the smoking-room, and had a little talk with him. He had just dropped a hundred pounds on a double event that hadn't come off, and I expected to find him pliable. Nor was I disappointed, for, when we had negotiated a little loan, he was entirely at my service, and willing to tell me everything, on my promising not to give him away to Alfred.

"'Now, you understand,' he said, 'that this yarn about your pearl is nothing but a damn silly fable that's been going the round in Marseilles. I don't know where it came from, or what sort of demented rotter invented it. I had it from a Johnnie in the Mediterranean Squadron, and you can have a copy of his letter if you want it.'

"I said that I did want it. Accordingly, that same evening he handed me a copy of the narrative extracted from his friend's letter, the substance of which was this:

161

"About four months ago there was lying in Canton Harbour a large English barque. Her name is not mentioned, but that is not material to the story. She had got her cargo stowed and her crew signed on, and was only waiting for certain official formalities to be completed before putting to sea on her homeward voyage. Just ahead of her, at the same quay, was a Danish ship that had been in collision outside, and was now laid up pending the decision of the Admiralty Court. She had been unloaded, and her crew paid off, with the exception of one elderly man, who remained on board as ship-keeper. Now, a considerable part of the cargo of the English barque was the property of a certain wealthy mandarin, and this person had been about the vessel a good deal while she was taking in her lading.

"One day, when the mandarin was on board the barque, it happened that three of the seamen were sitting in the galley smoking and chatting with the cook – an elderly Chinaman named Wo-li – and the latter, pointing out the mandarin to the sailors, expatiated on his enormous wealth, assuring them that he was commonly believed to carry on his person articles of sufficient value to buy up the entire lading of a ship.

"Now, unfortunately for the mandarin, it chanced that these three sailors were about the greatest rascals on board, which is saying a good deal when one considers the ordinary moral standard that prevails in the forecastle of a sailing-ship. Nor was Wo-li himself an angel. In fact, he was a consummate villain, and seems to have been the actual originator of the plot which was presently devised to rob the mandarin.

"This plot was as remarkable for its simplicity as for its cold-blooded barbarity. On the evening before the barque sailed, the three seamen, Nilsson, Foucault, and Parratt, proceeded to the Danish ship with a supply of whisky, made the ship-keeper royally drunk, and locked him up in an empty berth. Meanwhile Wo-li made a secret communication to the mandarin to the effect that certain stolen property, believed to be his, had been secreted in the hold of the empty ship. Thereupon the mandarin came down hot-foot to the quay-side, and was received on board by the three seamen, who had got the covers off the after-hatch in readiness. Parratt now ran down the iron ladder to show the way, and the mandarin followed, but when they reached the lower deck, and looked down the hatch into the black darkness of the lower hold, he seems to have taken fright, and begun to climb up again. Meanwhile Nilsson had made a running bowline in the end of a loose halyard that was rove through a block aloft, and had been used for hoisting out the cargo. As the mandarin came up, he leaned over the coaming of the hatch, dropped the noose over the Chinaman's head, jerked it tight, and then he and Foucault hove on the fall of the rope. The unfortunate Chinaman was dragged from the ladder, and, as he swung

162

clear, the two rascals let go the rope, allowing him to drop through the hatches into the lower hold. Then they belayed the rope, and went down below. Parratt had already lighted a slush-lamp, by the glimmer of which they could see the mandarin swinging to and fro like a pendulum within a few feet of the ballast, and still quivering and twitching in his death-throes. They were now joined by Wo-li, who had watched the proceedings from the quay, and the four villains proceeded, without loss of time, to rifle the body as it hung. To their surprise and disgust, they found nothing of value excepting an ebony pendant set with a single large pearl, but Wo-li, though evidently disappointed at the nature of the booty, assured his comrades that this alone was well worth the hazard, pointing out the great size and exceptional beauty of the pearl. As to this, the seamen knew nothing about pearls, but the thing was done, and had to be made the best of, so they made the rope fast to the lower deck-beams, cut off the remainder and unrove it from the block, and went back to their ship.

"It was twenty-four hours before the ship-keeper was sufficiently sober to break out of the berth in which he had been locked, by which time the barque was well out to sea, and it was another three days before the body of the mandarin was found. An active search was then made for the murderers, but as they were strangers to the ship-keeper, no clues to their whereabouts could be discovered.

"Meanwhile, the four murderers were a good deal exercised as to the disposal of the booty. Since it could not be divided, it was evident that it must be entrusted to the keeping of one of them. The choice in the first place fell upon Wo-li, in whose chest the pendant was deposited as soon as the party came on board, it being arranged that the Chinaman should produce the jewel for inspection by his confederates whenever called upon.

"For six weeks nothing out of the common occurred, but then a very singular event befell. The four conspirators were sitting outside the galley one evening, when suddenly the cook uttered a cry of amazement and horror. The other three turned to see what it was that had so disturbed their comrade, and then they, too, were struck dumb with consternation, for, standing at the door of the companion-hatch – the barque was a flush-decked vessel – was the mandarin whom they had left for dead. He stood quietly regarding them for fully a minute, while they stared at him transfixed with terror. Then he beckoned to them, and went below.

"So petrified were they with astonishment and mortal fear that they remained for a long time motionless and dumb. At last they plucked up courage, and began to make furtive inquiries among the crew, but no one – not even the steward – knew anything of any passengers, or, indeed, of any Chinaman, on board the ship, excepting Wo-li.

"At day-break the next morning, when the cook's mate went to the galley to fill the coppers, he found Wo-li hanging from a hook in the ceiling. The cook's body was stiff and cold, and had evidently been hanging several hours. The report of the tragedy quickly spread through the ship, and the three conspirators hurried off to remove the pearl from the dead man's chest before the officers should come to examine it. The cheap lock was easily picked with a bent wire, and the jewel abstracted, but now the question arose as to who should take charge of it. The eagerness to be the actual custodian of the precious bauble, which had been at first displayed, now gave place to equally strong reluctance. But someone had to take charge of it, and after a long and angry discussion Nilsson was prevailed upon to stow it in his chest.

"A fortnight passed. The three conspirators went about their duties soberly, like men burdened with some secret anxiety, and in their leisure moments they would sit and talk with bated breath of the apparition at the companion-hatch, and the mysterious death of their late comrade.

"At last the blow fell.

"It was at the end of the second dog-watch that the hands were gathered on the forecastle, preparing to make sail after a spell of bad weather. Suddenly Nilsson gave a husky shout, and rushed at Parratt, holding out the key of his chest.

"'Here you, Parratt,' he exclaimed, 'go below and take that accursed thing out of my chest.'

"'What for?' demanded Parratt, and then he and Foucault, who was standing close by, looked aft to see what Nilsson was staring at.

"Instantly they both turned white as ghosts, and fell trembling so that they could hardly stand, for there was the mandarin, standing calmly by the companion, returning with a steady, impassive gaze their looks of horror. And even as they looked he beckoned and went below.

"'D'ye hear, Parratt?' gasped Nilsson, 'take my key and do what I say, or else – '

"But at this moment the order was given to go aloft and set all plain sail, the three men went off to their respective posts, Nilsson going up the fore-topmast rigging, and the other two to the main-top. Having finished their work aloft, Foucault and Parratt who were both in the port watch, came down on deck, and then, it being their watch below, they went and turned in.

"When they turned out with their watch at midnight, they looked about for Nilsson, who was in the starboard watch, but he was nowhere to be seen. Thinking he might have slipped below unobserved, they made no remark, though they were very uneasy about him, but when the starboard watch came on deck at four o'clock, and Nilsson did not appear with his

164

mates, the two men became alarmed, and made inquiries about him. It was now discovered that no one had seen him since eight o'clock on the previous evening, and, this being reported to the officer of the watch, the latter ordered all hands to be called. But still Nilsson did not appear. A thorough search was now instituted, both below and aloft, and as there was still no sign of the missing man, it was concluded that he had fallen overboard.

"But at eight o'clock two men were sent aloft to shake out the fore-royal. They reached the yard almost simultaneously, and were just stepping on to the foot-ropes when one of them gave a shout, then the pair came sliding down a backstay, with faces as white as tallow. As soon as they reached the deck, they took the officer of the watch forward, and, standing on the heel of the bowsprit, pointed aloft. Several of the hands, including Foucault and Parratt, had followed, and all looked up, and there they saw the body of Nilsson, hanging on the front of the fore-topgallant sail. He was dangling at the end of a gasket, and bouncing up and down on the taut belly of the sail as the ship rose and fell to the send of the sea.

"The two survivors were now in some doubt about having anything further to do with the pearl. But the great value of the jewel, and the consideration that it was now to be divided between two instead of four, tempted them. They abstracted it from Nilsson's chest, and then, as they could not come to an agreement in any other way, they decided to settle who should take charge of it by tossing a coin. The coin was accordingly spun, and the pearl went to Foucault's chest.

"From this moment Foucault lived in a state of continual apprehension. When on deck, his eyes were for ever wandering towards the companion hatch, and during his watch below, when not asleep, he would sit moodily on his chest, lost in gloomy reflection. But a fortnight passed, then three weeks, and still nothing happened. Land was sighted, the Straits of Gibraltar passed, and the end of the voyage was but a matter of days. And still the dreaded mandarin made no sign.

"At length the ship was within twenty-four hours of Marseilles, to which port a large part of the cargo was consigned. Active preparations were being made for entering the port, and among other things the shore tackle was being overhauled. A share in this latter work fell to Foucault and Parratt, and about the middle of the second dog-watch – seven o'clock in the evening – they were sitting on the deck working an eye-splice in the end of a large rope. Suddenly Foucault, who was facing forward, saw his companion turn pale and stare aft with an expression of terror. He immediately turned and looked over his shoulder to see what Parratt was staring at. It was the mandarin, standing by the companion, gravely watching them, and as Foucault turned and met his gaze, the Chinaman beckoned and went below.

"For the rest of that day Parratt kept close to his terrified comrade, and during their watch below he endeavoured to remain awake, that he might keep his friend in view. Nothing happened through the night, and the following morning, when they came on deck for the forenoon watch, their port was well in sight. The two men now separated for the first time, Parratt going aft to take his trick at the wheel, and Foucault being set to help in getting ready the ground tackle.

"Half-an-hour later Parratt saw the mate stand on the rail and lean outboard, holding on to the mizzen-shrouds while he stared along the ship's side. Then he jumped on to the deck and shouted angrily, 'Forward, there! What the deuce is that man up to under the starboard cat-head?'

"The men on the forecastle rushed to the side and looked over. Two of them leaned over the rail with the bight of a rope between them, and a third came running aft to the mate. 'It's Foucault, sir,' Parratt heard him say. 'He's hanged hisself from the cat-head.'

"As soon as he was off duty, Parratt made his way to his dead comrade's chest, and, opening it with his pick-lock, took out the pearl. It was now his sole property, and, as the ship was within an hour or two of her destination, he thought he had little to fear from its murdered owner. As soon as the vessel was alongside the wharf, he would slip ashore and get rid of the jewel, even if he sold it at a comparatively low price. The thing looked perfectly simple.

"In actual practice, however, it turned out quite otherwise. He began by accosting a well-dressed stranger and offering the pendant for fifty pounds, but the only reply that he got was a knowing smile and a shake of the head. When this experience had been repeated a dozen times or more, and he had been followed up and down the streets for nearly an hour by a suspicious gendarme, he began to grow anxious. He visited quite a number of ships and yachts in the harbour, and at each refusal the price of his treasure came down, until he was eager to sell it for a few francs. But still no one would have it. Everyone took it for granted that the pearl was a sham, and most of the persons whom he accosted assumed that it had been stolen. The position was getting desperate. Evening was approaching – the time of the dreaded dog-watches – and still the pearl was in his possession. Gladly would he now have given it away for nothing, but he dared not try, for this would lay him open to the strongest suspicion.

"At last, in a by-street, he came upon the shop of a curio-dealer. Putting on a careless and cheerful manner, he entered and offered the pendant for ten francs. The dealer looked at it, shook his head, and handed it back.

"'What will you give me for it?' demanded Parratt, breaking out into a cold sweat at the prospect of a final refusal.

"The dealer felt in his pocket, drew out a couple of francs, and held them out.

"'Very well,' said Parratt. He took the money as calmly as he could, and marched out of the shop, with a gasp of relief, leaving the pendant in the dealer's hand.

"The jewel was hung up in a glass case, and nothing more was thought about it until some ten days later, when an English tourist, who came into the shop, noticed it and took a liking to it. Thereupon the dealer offered it to him for five pounds, assuring him that it was a genuine pearl, a statement that, to his amazement, the stranger evidently believed. He was then deeply afflicted at not having asked a higher price, but the bargain had been struck, and the Englishman went off with his purchase.

"This was the story told by Captain Raggerton's friend, and I have given it to you in full detail, having read the manuscript over many times since it was given to me. No doubt you will regard it as a mere traveller's tale, and consider me a superstitious idiot for giving any credence to it."

"It certainly seems more remarkable for picturesqueness than for credibility," Thorndyke agreed. "May I ask," he continued, "whether Captain Raggerton's friend gave any explanation as to how this singular story came to his knowledge, or to that of anybody else?"

"Oh yes," replied Calverley. "I forgot to mention that the seaman, Parratt, very shortly after he had sold the pearl, fell down the hatch into the hold the ship was unloading, and was very badly injured. He was taken to the hospital, where he died on the following day, and it was while he was lying there in a dying condition that he confessed to the murder, and gave this circumstantial account of it."

"I see," said Thorndyke, "and I understand that you accept the story as literally true?"

"Undoubtedly." Calverley flushed defiantly as he returned Thorndyke's look, and continued, "You see, I am not a man of science. Therefore my beliefs are not limited to things that can be weighed and measured. There are things, Dr. Thorndyke, which are outside the range of our puny intellects, things that science, with its arrogant materialism, puts aside and ignores with close-shut eyes. I prefer to believe in things which obviously exist, even though I cannot explain them. It is the humbler and, I think, the wiser attitude."

"But, my dear Fred," protested Mr. Brodribb, "this is a rank fairy-tale."

Calverley turned upon the solicitor. "If you had seen what I have seen, you would not only believe – you would know."

167

"Tell us what you have seen, then," said Mr. Brodribb.

"I will, if you wish to hear it," said Calverley. "I will continue the strange history of the Mandarin's Pearl."

He lit a fresh cigarette and continued, "The night I came to Beechhurst – that is my cousin's house, you know – a rather absurd thing happened, which I mention on account of its connection with what has followed. I had gone to my room early, and sat for some time writing letters before getting ready for bed. When I had finished my letters, I started on a tour of inspection of my room. I was then, you must remember, in a very nervous state, and it had become my habit to examine the room in which I was to sleep before undressing, looking under the bed, and in any cupboards and closets that there happened to be. Now, on looking round my new room, I perceived that there was a second door, and I at once proceeded to open it to see where it led to. As soon as I opened the door, I got a terrible start. I found myself looking into a narrow closet or passage, lined with pegs, on which the servant had hung some of my clothes. At the farther end was another door, and, as I stood looking into the closet, I observed, with startled amazement, a man standing holding the door half-open, and silently regarding me. I stood for a moment staring at him, with my heart thumping and my limbs all of a tremble. Then I slammed the door and ran off to look for my cousin.

"He was in the billiard-room with Raggerton, and the pair looked up sharply as I entered.

"'Alfred,' I said, 'where does that passage lead to out of my room?'

"'Lead to?' said he. 'Why, it doesn't lead anywhere. It used to open into a cross corridor, but when the house was altered, the corridor was done away with, and this passage closed up. It is only a cupboard now.'

"'Well, there's a man in it – or there was just now.'

"'Nonsense!' he exclaimed. 'Impossible! Let us go and look at the place.'

"He and Raggerton rose, and we went together to my room. As we flung open the door of the closet and looked in, we all three burst into a laugh. There were three men now looking at us from the open door at the other end, and the mystery was solved. A large mirror had been placed at the end of the closet to cover the partition which cut it off from the cross corridor.

"This incident naturally exposed me to a good deal of chaff from my cousin and Captain Raggerton, but I often wished that the mirror had not been placed there, for it happened over and over again that, going to the cupboard hurriedly, and not thinking of the mirror, I got quite a bad shock on being confronted by a figure apparently coming straight at me through an open door. In fact, it annoyed me so much, in my nervous state, that I

168

even thought of asking my cousin to give me a different room, but, happening to refer to the matter when talking to Raggerton, I found the Captain so scornful of my cowardice that my pride was touched, and I let the affair drop.

"And now I come to a very strange occurrence, which I shall relate quite frankly, although I know beforehand that you will set me down as a liar or a lunatic. I had been away from home for a fortnight, and as I returned rather late at night, I went straight to my room. Having partly undressed, I took my clothes in one hand and a candle in the other, and opened the cupboard door. I stood for a moment looking nervously at my double, standing, candle in hand, looking at me through the open door at the other end of the passage. Then I entered, and, setting the candle on a shelf, proceeded to hang up my clothes. I had hung them up, and had just reached up for the candle, when my eye was caught by something strange in the mirror. It no longer reflected the candle in my hand, but instead of it, a large coloured paper lantern. I stood petrified with astonishment, and gazed into the mirror, and then I saw that my own reflection was changed, too. That, in place of my own figure, was that of an elderly Chinaman, who stood regarding me with stony calm.

"I must have stood for near upon a minute, unable to move and scarce able to breathe, face to face with that awful figure. At length I turned to escape, and, as I turned, he turned also, and I could see him, over my shoulder, hurrying away. As I reached the door, I halted for a moment, looking back with the door in my hand, holding the candle above my head, and even so he halted, looking back at me, with his hand upon the door and his lantern held above his head.

"I was so much upset that I could not go to bed for some hours, but continued to pace the room, in spite of my fatigue. Now and again I was impelled, irresistibly, to peer into the cupboard, but nothing was to be seen in the mirror save my own figure, candle in hand, peeping in at me through the half-open door. And each time that I looked into my own white, horror-stricken face, I shut the door hastily and turned away with a shudder, for the pegs, with the clothes hanging on them, seemed to call to me. I went to bed at last, and before I fell asleep I formed the resolution that, if I was spared until the next day, I would write to the British Consul at Canton, and offer to restore the pearl to the relatives of the murdered mandarin.

The Apparition in the Mirror

"On the following day I wrote and despatched the letter, after which I felt more composed, though I was haunted continually by the recollection of that stony, impassive figure, and from time to time I felt an irresistible impulse to go and look in at the door of the closet, at the mirror and the pegs with the clothes hanging from them. I told my cousin of the visitation that I had received, but he merely laughed, and was frankly incredulous, while the Captain bluntly advised me not to be a superstitious donkey.

"For some days after this I was left in peace, and began to hope that my letter had appeased the spirit of the murdered man, but on the fifth day, about six o'clock in the evening, happening to want some papers that I had left in the pocket of a coat which was hanging in the closet, I went in to get them. I took in no candle, as it was not yet dark, but left the door wide open to light me. The coat that I wanted was near the end of the closet, not more than four paces from the mirror, and as I went towards it I watched my reflection rather nervously as it advanced to meet me. I found my coat, and as I felt for the papers, I still kept a suspicious eye on my double. And, even as I looked, a most strange phenomenon appeared – the mirror seemed for an instant to darken or cloud over, and then, as it cleared again, I saw, standing dark against the light of the open door behind him, the figure of the mandarin. After a single glance, I ran out of the closet, shaking with agitation, but as I turned to shut the door, I noticed that it was my own figure that was reflected in the glass. The Chinaman had vanished in an instant.

"It now became evident that my letter had not served its purpose, and I was plunged in despair, the more so since, on this day, I felt again the dreadful impulse to go and look at the pegs on the walls of the closet. There was no mistaking the meaning of that impulse, and each time that I went, I dragged myself away reluctantly, though shivering with horror. One circumstance, indeed, encouraged me a little. The mandarin had not, on either occasion, beckoned to me as he had done to the sailors, so that perhaps some way of escape yet lay open to me.

"During the next few days I considered very earnestly what measures I could take to avert the doom that seemed to be hanging over me. The simplest plan, that of passing the pearl on to some other person, was out of the question, It would be nothing short of murder. On the other hand, I could not wait for an answer to my letter, for even if I remained alive, I felt that my reason would have given way long before the reply reached me. But while I was debating what I should do, the mandarin appeared to me again, and then, after an interval of only two days, he came to me once more. That was last night. I remained gazing at him, fascinated, with my flesh creeping, as he stood, lantern in hand, looking steadily in my face. At last he held out his hand to me, as if asking me to give him the pearl, then the mirror darkened, and he vanished in a flash. and in the place where he had stood there was my own reflection looking at me out of the glass.

"That last visitation decided me. When I left home this morning the pearl was in my pocket, and as I came over Waterloo Bridge, I leaned over the parapet and flung the thing into the water. After that I felt quite relieved for a time. I had shaken the accursed thing off without involving anyone in the curse that it carried. But presently I began to feel fresh misgivings, and the conviction has been growing upon me all day that I have done the wrong thing. I have only placed it forever beyond the reach of its owner, whereas I ought to have burnt it, after the Chinese fashion, so that its non-material essence could have joined the spiritual body of him to whom it had belonged when both were clothed with material substance.

"But it can't be altered now. For good or for evil, the thing is done, and God alone knows what the end of it will be."

As he concluded, Calverley uttered a deep sigh, and covered his face with his slender, delicate hands. For a space we were all silent and, I think, deeply moved, for, grotesquely unreal as the whole thing was, there was a pathos, and even a tragedy, in it that we all felt to be very real indeed.

Suddenly Mr. Brodribb started and looked at his watch.

"Good gracious, Calverley, we shall lose our train."

The young man pulled himself together and stood up. "We shall just do it if we go at once," said he. "Good-bye," he added, shaking Thorndyke's hand and mine. "You have been very patient, and I have been rather prosy, I am afraid. Come along, Mr. Brodribb."

Thorndyke and I followed them out on to the landing, and I heard my colleague say to the solicitor in a low tone, but very earnestly, "Get him away from that house, Brodribb, and don't let him out of your sight for a moment."

I did not catch the solicitor's reply, if he made any, but when we were back in our room I noticed that Thorndyke was more agitated than I had ever seen him.

"I ought not to have let them go," he exclaimed. "Confound me! If I had had a grain of wit, I should have made them lose their train."

He lit his pipe and fell to pacing the room with long strides, his eyes bent on the floor with an expression sternly reflective. At last, finding him hopelessly taciturn, I knocked out my pipe and went to bed.

As I was dressing on the following morning, Thorndyke entered my room. His face was grave even to sternness, and he held a telegram in his hand.

"I am going to Weybridge this morning," he said shortly, holding the "flimsy" out to me. "Shall you come?"

I took the paper from him, and read:

172

Come, for God's sake! F. C. is dead. You will understand. –
BRODRIBB

I handed him back the telegram, too much shocked for a moment to speak. The whole dreadful tragedy summed up in that curt message rose before me in an instant, and a wave of deep pity swept over me at this miserable end to the sad, empty life.

"What an awful thing, Thorndyke!" I exclaimed at length. "To be killed by a mere grotesque delusion."

"Do you think so?" he asked dryly. "Well, we shall see, but you will come?"

"Yes," I replied, and as he retired, I proceeded hurriedly to finish dressing.

Half-an-hour later, as we rose from a rapid breakfast, Polton came into the room, carrying a small roll-up case of tools and a bunch of skeleton keys.

"Will you have them in a bag, sir?" he asked.

"No," replied Thorndyke, "in my overcoat pocket. Oh, and here is a note, Polton, which I want you to take round to Scotland Yard. It is to the Assistant Commissioner, and you are to make sure that it is in the right hands before you leave. And here is a telegram to Mr. Brodribb."

He dropped the keys and the tool-case into his pocket, and we went down together to the waiting hansom.

At Weybridge Station we found Mr. Brodribb pacing the platform in a state of extreme dejection. He brightened up somewhat when he saw us, and wrung our hands with emotional heartiness.

"It was very good of you both to come at a moment's notice," he said warmly, "and I feel your kindness very much. You understood, of course, Thorndyke?"

"Yes," Thorndyke replied. "I suppose the mandarin beckoned to him."

Mr. Brodribb turned with a look of surprise. "How did you guess that?" he asked, and then, without waiting for a reply, he took from his pocket a note, which he handed to my colleague. "The poor old fellow left this for me," he said. "The servant found it on his dressing-table."

Thorndyke glanced through the note and passed it to me. It consisted of but a few words, hurriedly written in a tremulous hand.

He has beckoned to me, and I must go. Good-bye, dear old friend.

173

"How does his cousin take the matter?" asked Thorndyke.

"He doesn't know of it yet," replied the lawyer. "Alfred and Raggerton went out after an early breakfast, to cycle over to Guildford on some business or other, and they have not returned yet. The catastrophe was discovered soon after they left. The maid went to his room with a cup of tea, and was astonished to find that his bed had not been slept in. She ran down in alarm and reported to the butler, who went up at once and searched the room, but he could find no trace of the missing one, except my note, until it occurred to him to look in the cupboard. As he opened the door he got rather a start from his own reflection in the mirror, and then he saw poor Fred hanging from one of the pegs near the end of the closet, close to the glass. It's a melancholy affair – but here is the house, and here is the butler waiting for us. Mr. Alfred is not back yet, then, Stevens?"

"No, sir." The white-faced, frightened-looking man had evidently been waiting at the gate from distaste of the house, and he now walked back with manifest relief at our arrival. When we entered the house, he ushered us without remark up on to the first-floor, and, preceding us along a corridor, halted near the end. "That's the room, sir," said he, and without another word he turned and went down the stairs.

We entered the room, and Mr. Brodribb followed on tiptoe, looking about him fearfully, and casting awe-struck glances at the shrouded form on the bed. To the latter Thorndyke advanced, and gently drew back the sheet.

"You'd better not look, Brodribb," said he, as he bent over the corpse. He felt the limbs and examined the cord, which still remained round the neck, its raggedly-severed end testifying to the terror of the servants who had cut down the body. Then he replaced the sheet and looked at his watch. "It happened at about three o'clock in the morning," said he. "He must have struggled with the impulse for some time, poor fellow! Now let us look at the cupboard."

We went together to a door in the corner of the room, and, as we opened it, we were confronted by three figures, apparently looking in at us through an open door at the other end.

"It is really rather startling," said the lawyer, in a subdued voice, looking almost apprehensively at the three figures that advanced to meet us. "The poor lad ought never to have been here."

It was certainly an eerie place, and I could not but feel, as we walked down the dark, narrow passage, with those other three dimly-seen figures silently coming towards us, and mimicking our every gesture, that it was no place for a nervous, superstitious man like poor Fred Calverley. Close to the end of the long row of pegs was one from which hung an end of stout box-cord, and to this Mr. Brodribb pointed with an awe-struck gesture. But Thorndyke gave it only a brief glance, and then walked up to the mirror, which he proceeded to examine minutely. It was a very large glass, nearly seven feet high, extending the full width of the closet, and reaching to within a foot of the floor, and it seemed to have been let into the partition from behind, for, both above and below, the woodwork was in front of it. While I was making these observations, I watched Thorndyke with no little curiosity. First he rapped his knuckles on the glass. Then he lighted a wax match, and, holding it close to the mirror, carefully watched the reflection of the flame. Finally, laying his cheek on the glass, he held the match at arm's length, still close to the mirror, and looked at the reflection along the surface. Then he blew out the match and walked back into the room, shutting the cupboard door as we emerged.

"I think," said he, "that as we shall all undoubtedly be subpoenaed by the coroner, it would be well to put together a few notes of the facts. I see there is a writing-table by the window, and I would propose that you, Brodribb, just jot down a *précis* of the statement that you heard last night, while Jervis notes down the exact condition of the body. While you are doing this, I will take a look round."

"We might find a more cheerful place to write in," grumbled Mr. Brodribb. "However – "

Without finishing the sentence, he sat down at the table, and, having found some sermon paper, dipped a pen in the ink by way of encouraging his thoughts. At this moment Thorndyke quietly slipped out of the room, and I proceeded to make a detailed examination of the body, in which occupation I was interrupted at intervals by requests from the lawyer that I should refresh his memory.

We had been occupied thus for about a quarter-of-an-hour, when a quick step was heard outside, the door was opened abruptly, and a man burst into the room. Brodribb rose and held out his hand.

"This is a sad home-coming for you, Alfred," said he.

"Yes, my God!" the newcomer exclaimed. "It's awful."

He looked askance at the corpse on the bed, and wiped his forehead with his handkerchief. Alfred Calverley was not extremely prepossessing. Like his cousin, he was obviously neurotic, but there were signs of dissipation in his face, which, just now, was pale and ghastly, and wore an expression of abject fear. Moreover, his entrance was accompanied by that of a perceptible odour of brandy.

He had walked over, without noticing me, to the writing-table, and as he stood there, talking in subdued tones with the lawyer, I suddenly found Thorndyke at my side. He had stolen in noiselessly through the door that Calverley had left open.

175

"Show him Brodribb's note," he whispered, "and then make him go in and look at the peg."

With this mysterious request, he slipped out of the room as silently as he had come, unperceived either by Calverley or the lawyer.

"Has Captain Raggerton returned with you?" Brodribb was inquiring.

"No, he has gone into the town," was the reply, "but he won't be long. This will be a frightful shock to him."

At this point I stepped forward. "Have you shown Mr. Calverley the extraordinary letter that the deceased left for you?" I asked.

"What letter was that?" demanded Calverley, with a start.

Mr. Brodribb drew forth the note and handed it to him. As he read it through, Calverley turned white to the lips, and the paper trembled in his hand.

"'*He has beckoned to me, and I must go,*'" he read. Then, with a furtive glance at the lawyer, "Who had beckoned? What did he mean?"

Mr. Brodribb briefly explained the meaning of the allusion, adding, "I thought you knew all about it."

"Yes, yes," said Calverley, with some confusion. "I remember the matter now you mention it. But it's all so dreadful and bewildering."

At this point I again interposed. "There is a question," I said, "that may be of some importance. It refers to the cord with which the poor fellow hanged himself. Can you identify that cord, Mr. Calverley?"

"I!" he exclaimed, staring at me, and wiping the sweat from his white face. "How should I? Where is the cord?"

"Part of it is still hanging from the peg in the closet. Would you mind looking at it?"

"If you would very kindly fetch it – you know I – er – naturally – have a – "

"It must not be disturbed before the inquest," said I, "but surely you are not afraid – "

"I didn't say I was afraid," he retorted angrily. "Why should I be?"

With a strange, tremulous swagger, he strode across to the closet, flung open the door, and plunged in.

A moment later we heard a shout of horror, and he rushed out, livid and gasping.

"What is it, Calverley?" exclaimed Mr. Brodribb, starting up in alarm.

But Calverley was incapable of speech. Dropping limply into a chair, he gazed at us for a while in silent terror. Then he fell back uttering a wild shriek of laughter.

Mr. Brodribb looked at him in amazement. "What is it, Calverley?" he asked again.

As no answer was forthcoming, he stepped across to the open door of the closet and entered, peering curiously before him. Then he, too, uttered a startled exclamation, and backed out hurriedly, looking pale and flurried.

"Bless my soul!" he ejaculated. "Is the place bewitched?"

He sat down heavily and stared at Calverley, who was still shaking with hysteric laughter, while I, now consumed with curiosity, walked over to the closet to discover the cause of their singular behaviour. As I flung open the door, which the lawyer had closed, I must confess to being very considerably startled, for though the reflection of the open door was plain enough in the mirror, my own reflection was replaced by that of a Chinaman. After a momentary pause of astonishment, I entered the closet and walked towards the mirror, and simultaneously the figure of the Chinaman entered and walked towards me. I had advanced more than halfway down the closet when suddenly the mirror darkened, there was a whirling flash, the Chinaman vanished in an instant, and, as I reached the glass, my own reflection faced me.

I turned back into the room pretty completely enlightened, and looked at Calverley with a new-born distaste. He still sat facing the bewildered lawyer, one moment sobbing convulsively, the next yelping with hysteric laughter. He was not an agreeable spectacle, and when, a few moments later, Thorndyke entered the room, and halted by the door with a stare of disgust, I was moved to join him. But at this juncture a man pushed past Thorndyke, and, striding up to Calverley, shook him roughly by the arm.

"Stop that row!" he exclaimed furiously. "Do you hear? Stop it!"

"I can't help it, Raggerton," gasped Calverley. "He gave me such a turn – the mandarin, you know."

"What!" ejaculated Raggerton.

He dashed across to the closet, looked in, and turned upon Calverley with a snarl. Then he walked out of the room.

"Brodribb," said Thorndyke, "I should like to have a word with you and Jervis outside." Then, as we followed him out on to the landing, he continued. "I have something rather interesting to show you. It is in here."

He softly opened an adjoining door, and we looked into a small unfurnished room. A projecting closet occupied one side of it, and at the door of the closet stood Captain Raggerton, with his hand upon the key. He turned upon us fiercely, though with a look of alarm, and demanded, "What is the meaning of this intrusion? and who the deuce are you? Do you know that this is my private room?"

"I suspected that it was," Thorndyke replied quietly. "Those will be your properties in the closet, then?"

Raggerton turned pale, but continued to bluster. "Do I understand that you have dared to break into my private closet?" he demanded.

"I have inspected it," replied Thorndyke, "and I may remark that it is useless to wrench at that key, because I have hampered the lock."

"The devil you have!" shouted Raggerton.

"Yes, you see, I am expecting a police-officer with a search warrant, so I wished to keep everything intact."

Raggerton turned livid with mingled fear and rage. He stalked up to Thorndyke with a threatening air, but, suddenly altering his mind, exclaimed, "I must see to this!" and flung out of the room.

Thorndyke took a key from his pocket, and, having locked the door, turned to the closet. Having taken out the key to unhamper the lock with a stout wire, he reinserted it and unlocked the door. As we entered, we found ourselves in a narrow closet, similar to the one in the other room, but darker, owing to the absence of a mirror. A few clothes hung from the pegs, and when Thorndyke had lit a candle that stood on a shelf, we could see more of the details.

"Here are some of the properties," said Thorndyke. He pointed to a peg from which hung a long, blue silk gown of Chinese make, a mandarin's cap, with a pigtail attached to it, and a beautifully-made *papier-mâché* mask. "Observe," said Thorndyke, taking the latter down and exhibiting a label on the inside, marked, *Renouard à Paris.* "No trouble has been spared."

He took off his coat, slipped on the gown, the mask, and the cap, and was, in a moment, in that dim light, transformed into the perfect semblance of a Chinaman.

"By taking a little more time," he remarked, pointing to a pair of Chinese shoes and a large paper lantern, "the make-up could be rendered more complete, but this seems to have answered for our friend Alfred."

"But," said Mr. Brodribb, as Thorndyke shed the disguise, "still, I don't understand – "

"I will make it clear to you in a moment," said Thorndyke. He walked to the end of the closet, and, tapping the right-hand wall, said, "This is the back of the mirror. You see that it is hung on massive well-oiled hinges, and is supported on this large, rubber-tyred castor, which evidently has ball bearings. You observe three black cords running along the wall, and passing through those pulleys above. Now, when I pull this cord, notice what happens."

He pulled one cord firmly, and immediately the mirror swung noiselessly inwards on its great castor, until it stood diagonally across the closet, where it was stopped by a rubber buffer.

"Bless my soul!" exclaimed Mr. Brodribb. "What an extraordinary thing!"

The effect was certainly very strange, for, the mirror being now exactly diagonal to the two closets they appeared to be a single, continuous passage, with a door at either end. On going up to the mirror, we found that the opening which it had occupied was filled by a sheet of plain glass, evidently placed there as a precaution to prevent any person from walking through from one closet into the other, and so discovering the trick.

"It's all very puzzling," said Mr. Brodribb. "I don't clearly understand it now."

"Let us finish here," replied Thorndyke, "and then I will explain. Notice this black curtain. When I pull the second cord, it slides across the closet and cuts off the light. The mirror now reflects nothing into the other closet. It simply appears dark. And now I pull the third cord."

He did so, and the mirror swung noiselessly back into its place.

"There is only one other thing to observe before we go out," said Thorndyke, "and that is this other mirror standing with its face to the wall. This, of course, is the one that Fred Calverley originally saw at the end of the closet. It has since been removed, and the larger swinging glass put in its place. And now," he continued, when we came out into the room, "let me explain the mechanism in detail. It was obvious to me, when I heard poor Fred Calverley's story, that the mirror was 'faked,' and I drew a diagram of the probable arrangement, which turns out to be correct. Here it is." He took a sheet of paper from his pocket and handed it to the lawyer. "There are two sketches. Sketch 1 shows the mirror in its ordinary position, closing the end of the closet. A person standing at A, of course, sees his reflection facing him at, apparently, *A-1*. Sketch *2* shows the mirror swung across. Now a person standing at *A* does not see his own reflection at all, but if some other person is standing in the other closet at *B*, *A* sees the reflection of *B* apparently at *B-1* – that is, in the identical position that his own reflection occupied when the mirror was straight across."

"I see now," said Brodribb, "but who set up this apparatus, and why was it done?"

"Let me ask you a question," said Thorndyke. "Is Alfred Calverley the next-of-kin?"

"No, there is Fred's younger brother. But I may say that Fred has made a will quite recently very much in Alfred's favour."

"There is the explanation, then," said Thorndyke. "These two scoundrels have conspired to drive the poor fellow to suicide, and Raggerton was clearly the leading spirit. He was evidently concocting some story with which to work on poor Fred's superstitions when the mention of the Chinaman on the steamer gave him his cue. He then invented the very picturesque story of the murdered mandarin and the

179

stolen pearl. You remember that these 'visitations' did not begin until after that story had been told, and Fred had been absent from the house on a visit. Evidently, during his absence, Raggerton took down the original mirror, and substituted this swinging arrangement, and at the same time procured the Chinaman's dress and mask from the theatrical property dealers. No doubt he reckoned on being able quietly to remove the swinging glass and other properties and replace the original mirror before the inquest."

"By God!" exclaimed Mr. Brodribb, "it's the most infamous, cowardly plot I have ever heard of. They shall go to gaol for it, the villains, as sure as I am alive."

But in this Mr. Brodribb was mistaken, for immediately on finding themselves detected, the two conspirators had left the house, and by nightfall were safely across the Channel, and the only satisfaction that the lawyer obtained was the setting aside of the will on facts disclosed at the inquest.

As to Thorndyke, he has never to this day forgiven himself for having allowed Fred Calverley to go home to his death.

The Aluminium Dagger

The "urgent call" – the instant, peremptory summons to professional duty – is an experience that appertains to the medical rather than the legal practitioner, and I had supposed, when I abandoned the clinical side of my profession in favour of the forensic, that henceforth I should know it no more. That the interrupted meal, the broken leisure, and the jangle of the night-bell, were things of the past, but in practice it was otherwise. The medical jurist is, so to speak, on the borderland of the two professions, and exposed to the vicissitudes of each calling, and so it happened from time to time that the professional services of my colleague or myself were demanded at a moment's notice. And thus it was in the case that I am about to relate.

The sacred rite of the "tub" had been duly performed, and the freshly-dried person of the present narrator was about to be insinuated into the first instalment of clothing, when a hurried step was heard upon the stair, and the voice of our laboratory assistant, Polton, arose at my colleague's door.

"There's a gentleman downstairs, sir, who says he must see you instantly on most urgent business. He seems to be in a rare twitter, sir – "

Polton was proceeding to descriptive particulars, when a second and more hurried step became audible, and a strange voice addressed Thorndyke.

"I have come to beg your immediate assistance, sir, a most dreadful thing has happened. A horrible murder has been committed. Can you come with me now?"

"I will be with you almost immediately," said Thorndyke. "Is the victim quite dead?"

"Quite. Cold and stiff. The police think – "

"Do the police know that you have come for me?" interrupted Thorndyke.

"Yes. Nothing is to be done until you arrive."

"Very well. I will be ready in a few minutes."

"And if you would wait downstairs, sir," Polton added persuasively, "I could help the doctor to get ready."

With this crafty appeal, he lured the intruder back to the sitting-room, and shortly after stole softly up the stairs with a small breakfast tray, the contents of which he deposited firmly in our respective rooms, with a few timely words on the folly of "undertaking murders on an empty stomach." Thorndyke and I had meanwhile clothed ourselves with a celerity known only to medical practitioners and quick-change artists, and in a few minutes descended the stairs together, calling in at the laboratory for a few appliances that Thorndyke usually took with him on a visit of investigation.

As we entered the sitting-room, our visitor, who was feverishly pacing up and down, seized his hat with a gasp of relief. "You are ready to come?" he asked. "My carriage is at the door," and, without waiting for an answer, he hurried out, and rapidly preceded us down the stairs.

The carriage was a roomy brougham, which fortunately accommodated the three of us, and as soon as we had entered and shut the door, the coachman whipped up his horse and drove off at a smart trot.

"I had better give you some account of the circumstances, as we go," said our agitated friend. "In the first place, my name is Curtis, Henry Curtis. Here is my card. Ah! And here is another card, which I should have given you before. My solicitor, Mr. Marchmont, was with me when I made this dreadful discovery, and he sent me to you. He remained in the rooms to see that nothing is disturbed until you arrive."

"That was wise of him," said Thorndyke. "But now tell us exactly what has occurred."

"I will," said Mr. Curtis. "The murdered man was my brother-in-law, Alfred Hartridge, and I am sorry to say he was – well, he was a bad man. It grieves me to speak of him thus – *de mortuis*, you know – but, still, we must deal with the facts, even though they be painful."

"Undoubtedly," agreed Thorndyke.

"I have had a great deal of very unpleasant correspondence with him – Marchmont will tell you about that – and yesterday I left a note for him, asking for an interview, to settle the business, naming eight o'clock this morning as the hour, because I had to leave town before noon. He replied, in a very singular letter, that he would see me at that hour, and Mr. Marchmont very kindly consented to accompany me. Accordingly, we went to his chambers together this morning, arriving punctually at eight o'clock. We rang the bell several times, and knocked loudly at the door, but as there was no response, we went down and spoke to the hall-porter. This man, it seems, had already noticed, from the courtyard, that the electric lights were full on in Mr. Hartridge's sitting-room, as they had been all night, according to the statement of the night-porter. So now, suspecting that something was wrong, he came up with us, and rang the bell and battered at the door. Then, as there was still no sign of life within, he inserted his duplicate key and tried to open the door – unsuccessfully, however, as it proved to be bolted on the inside. Thereupon the porter fetched a constable, and, after a consultation, we decided that we were justified in breaking open the door. The porter produced a crowbar, and by our unified efforts the door was eventually burst open. We entered, and –

182

My God! Dr. Thorndyke, what a terrible sight it was that met our eyes! My brother-in-law was lying dead on the floor of the sitting-room. He had been stabbed – stabbed to death, and the dagger had not even been withdrawn. It was still sticking out of his back."

He mopped his face with his handkerchief, and was about to continue his account of the catastrophe when the carriage entered a quiet side-street between Westminster and Victoria, and drew up before a block of tall, new, red-brick buildings. A flurried hall-porter ran out to open the door, and we alighted opposite the main entrance.

"My brother-in-law's chambers are on the second-floor," said Mr. Curtis. "We can go up in the lift."

The porter had hurried before us, and already stood with his hand upon the rope. We entered the lift, and in a few seconds were discharged on to the second floor, the porter, with furtive curiosity, following us down the corridor. At the end of the passage was a half-open door, considerably battered and bruised. Above the door, painted in white lettering, was the inscription, "Mr. Hartridge", and through the doorway protruded the rather foxy countenance of Inspector Badger.

"I am glad you have come, sir," said he, as he recognized my colleague. "Mr. Marchmont is sitting inside like a watch-dog, and he growls if any of us even walks across the room."

The words formed a complaint, but there was a certain geniality in the speaker's manner which made me suspect that Inspector Badger was already navigating his craft on a lee shore.

We entered a small lobby or hall, and from thence passed into the sitting-room, where we found Mr. Marchmont keeping his vigil, in company with a constable and a uniformed inspector. The three rose softly as we entered, and greeted us in a whisper, and then, with one accord, we all looked towards the other end of the room, and so remained for a time without speaking.

There was, in the entire aspect of the room, something very grim and dreadful. An atmosphere of tragic mystery enveloped the most commonplace objects, and sinister suggestions lurked in the most familiar appearances. Especially impressive was the air of suspense – of ordinary, every-day life suddenly arrested – cut short in the twinkling of an eye. The electric lamps, still burning dim and red, though the summer sunshine streamed in through the windows. The half-emptied tumbler and open book by the empty chair, had each its whispered message of swift and sudden disaster, as had the hushed voices and stealthy movements of the waiting men, and, above all, an awesome shape that was but a few hours since a living man, and that now sprawled, prone and motionless, on the floor.

"This is a mysterious affair," observed Inspector Badger, breaking the silence at length, "though it is clear enough up to a certain point. The body tells its own story."

We stepped across and looked down at the corpse. It was that of a somewhat elderly man, and lay, on an open space of floor before the fireplace, face downwards, with the arms extended. The slender hilt of a dagger projected from the back below the left shoulder, and, with the exception of a trace of blood upon the lips, this was the only indication of the mode of death. A little way from the body a clock-key lay on the carpet, and, glancing up at the clock on the mantelpiece, I perceived that the glass front was open.

"You see," pursued the inspector, noting my glance, "he was standing in front of the fireplace, winding the clock. Then the murderer stole up behind him – the noise of the turning key must have covered his movements – and stabbed him. And you see, from the position of the dagger on the left side of the back, that the murderer must have been left-handed. That is all clear enough. What is not clear is how he got in, and how he got out again."

"The body has not been moved, I suppose," said Thorndyke.

"No. We sent for Dr. Egerton, the police-surgeon, and he certified that the man was dead. He will be back presently to see you and arrange about the post-mortem."

"Then," said Thorndyke, "we will not disturb the body till he comes, except to take the temperature and dust the dagger-hilt."

He took from his bag a long, registering chemical thermometer and an insufflator or powder-blower. The former he introduced under the dead man's clothing against the abdomen, and with the latter blew a stream of fine yellow powder on to the black leather handle of the dagger. Inspector Badger stooped eagerly to examine the handle, as Thorndyke blew away the powder that had settled evenly on the surface.

"No finger-prints," said he, in a disappointed tone. "He must have worn gloves. But that inscription gives a pretty broad hint."

He pointed, as he spoke, to the metal guard of the dagger, on which was engraved, in clumsy lettering, the single word, "*TRADITORE*".

"That's the Italian for '*traitor*", continued the inspector, "and I got some information from the porter that fits in with that suggestion. We'll have him in presently, and you shall hear."

"Meanwhile," said Thorndyke, "as the position of the body may be of importance in the inquiry, I will take one or two photographs and make a rough plan to scale. Nothing has been moved, you say? Who opened the windows?"

184

"They were open when we came in," said Mr. Marchmont. "Last night was very hot, you remember. Nothing whatever has been moved."

Thorndyke produced from his bag a small folding camera, a telescopic tripod, a surveyor's measuring-tape, a boxwood scale, and a sketch-block. He set up the camera in a corner, and exposed a plate, taking a general view of the room, and including the corpse. Then he moved to the door and made a second exposure.

"Will you stand in front of the clock, Jervis," he said, "and raise your hand as if winding it? Thanks. Keep like that while I expose a plate."

I remained thus, in the position that the dead man was assumed to have occupied at the moment of the murder, while the plate was exposed, and then, before I moved, Thorndyke marked the position of my feet with a blackboard chalk. He next set up the tripod over the chalk marks, and took two photographs from that position, and finally photographed the body itself.

The photographic operations being concluded, he next proceeded, with remarkable skill and rapidity, to lay out on the sketch-block a ground-plan of the room, showing the exact position of the various objects, on a

185

scale of a quarter-of-an-inch to the foot – a process that the inspector was inclined to view with some impatience.

"You don't spare trouble, Doctor," he remarked, "nor time either," he added, with a significant glance at his watch.

"No," answered Thorndyke, as he detached the finished sketch from the block. "I try to collect all the facts that may bear on a case. They may prove worthless, or they may turn out of vital importance. One never knows beforehand, so I collect them all. But here, I think, is Dr. Egerton."

The police-surgeon greeted Thorndyke with respectful cordiality, and we proceeded at once to the examination of the body. Drawing out the thermometer, my colleague noted the reading, and passed the instrument to Dr. Egerton.

"Dead about ten hours," remarked the latter, after a glance at it. "This was a very determined and mysterious murder."

"Very," said Thorndyke. "Feel that dagger, Jervis."

I touched the hilt, and felt the characteristic grating of bone.

"It is through the edge of a rib!" I exclaimed.

"Yes, it must have been used with extraordinary force. And you notice that the clothing is screwed up slightly, as if the blade had been rotated as it was driven in. That is a very peculiar feature, especially when taken together with the violence of the blow."

"It is singular, certainly," said Dr. Egerton, "though I don't know that it helps us much. Shall we withdraw the dagger before moving the body?"

"Certainly," replied Thorndyke, "or the movement may produce fresh injuries. But wait." He took a piece of string from his pocket, and, having drawn the dagger out a couple of inches, stretched the string in a line parallel to the flat of the blade. Then, giving me the ends to hold, he drew the weapon out completely. As the blade emerged, the twist in the clothing disappeared. "Observe," said he, "that the string gives the direction of the wound, and that the cut in the clothing no longer coincides with it. There is quite a considerable angle, which is the measure of the rotation of the blade."

"Yes, it is odd," said Dr. Egerton, "though, as I said, I doubt that it helps us."

"At present," Thorndyke rejoined dryly, "we are noting the facts."

"Quite so," agreed the other, reddening slightly, "and perhaps we had better move the body to the bedroom, and make a preliminary inspection of the wound."

We carried the corpse into the bedroom, and, having examined the wound without eliciting anything new, covered the remains with a sheet, and returned to the sitting-room.

"Well, gentlemen," said the inspector, "you have examined the body and the wound, and you have measured the floor and the furniture, and taken photographs, and made a plan, but we don't seem much more forward. Here's a man murdered in his rooms. There is only one entrance to the flat, and that was bolted on the inside at the time of the murder. The windows are some forty feet from the ground. There is no rain-pipe near any of them. They are set flush in the wall, and there isn't a foothold for a fly on any part of that wall. The grates are modern, and there isn't room for a good-sized cat to crawl up any of the chimneys. Now, the question is, How did the murderer get in, and how did he get out again?"

"Still," said Mr. Marchmont, "the fact is that he did get in, and that he is not here now, and therefore he must have got out, and therefore it must have been possible for him to get out. And, further, it must be possible to discover how he got out."

The inspector smiled sourly, but made no reply.

"The circumstances," said Thorndyke, "appear to have been these: The deceased seems to have been alone. There is no trace of a second occupant of the room, and only one half-emptied tumbler on the table. He was sitting reading when apparently he noticed that the clock had stopped – at ten minutes to twelve. He laid his book, face downwards, on the table, and rose to wind the clock, and as he was winding it he met his death."

"By a stab dealt by a left-handed man, who crept up behind him on tiptoe," added the inspector.

Thorndyke nodded. "That would seem to be so," he said. "But now let us call in the porter, and hear what he has to tell us."

The custodian was not difficult to find, being, in fact, engaged at that moment in a survey of the premises through the slit of the letter-box.

"Do you know what persons visited these rooms last night?" Thorndyke asked him, when he entered looking somewhat sheepish.

"A good many were in and out of the building," was the answer, "but I can't say if any of them came to this flat. I saw Miss Curtis pass in about nine."

"My daughter!" exclaimed Mr. Curtis, with a start. "I didn't know that."

"She left about nine-thirty," the porter added.

"Do you know what she came about?" asked the inspector.

"I can guess," replied Mr. Curtis.

"Then don't say," interrupted Mr. Marchmont. "Answer no questions."

"You're very close, Mr. Marchmont," said the inspector. "We are not suspecting the young lady. We don't ask, for instance, if she is left-handed."

187

He glanced craftily at Mr. Curtis as he made this remark, and I noticed that our client suddenly turned deathly pale, whereupon the inspector looked away again quickly, as though he had not observed the change.

"Tell us about those Italians again," he said, addressing the porter. "When did the first of them come here?"

"About a week ago," was the reply. "He was a common-looking man – looked like an organ-grinder – and he brought a note to my lodge. It was in a dirty envelope, and was addressed '*Mr. Hartridge, Esq., Brackenhurst Mansions*', in a very bad handwriting. The man gave me the note and asked me to give it to Mr. Hartridge. Then he went away, and I took the note up and dropped it into the letter-box."

"What happened next?"

"Why, the very next day an old hag of an Italian woman – one of them fortune-telling swines with a cage of birds on a stand – came and set up just by the main doorway. I soon sent her packing, but, bless you! She was back again in ten minutes, birds and all. I sent her off again – I kept on sending her off, and she kept on coming back, until I was reg'lar wore to a thread."

"You seem to have picked up a bit since then," remarked the inspector with a grin and a glance at the sufferer's very pronounced bow-window.

"Perhaps I have," the custodian replied haughtily. "Well, the next day there was a ice-cream man – a reg'lar waster, he was. Stuck outside as if he was froze to the pavement. Kept giving the errand-boys tasters, and when I tried to move him on, he told me not to obstruct his business. Business, indeed! Well, there them boys stuck, one after the other, wiping their tongues round the bottoms of them glasses, until I was fit to bust with aggravation. And he kept me going all day.

"Then, the day after that there was a barrel-organ, with a mangy-looking monkey on it. He was the worst of all. Profane, too, he was. Kept mixing up sacred tunes and comic songs: '*Rock of Ages*', '*Bill Bailey*', '*Cujus Animal*', and '*Over the Garden Wall*'. And when I tried to move him on, that little blighter of a monkey made a run at my leg, and then the man grinned and started playing, '*Wait 'til the Clouds Roll By*'' I tell you, it was fair sickening."

189

He wiped his brow at the recollection, and the inspector smiled appreciatively.

"And that was the last of them?" said the latter, and as the porter nodded sulkily, he asked, "Should you recognize the note that the Italian gave you?"

"I should," answered the porter with frosty dignity.

The inspector bustled out of the room, and returned a minute later with a letter-case in his hand.

"This was in his breast-pocket," said he, laying the bulging case on the table, and drawing up a chair. "Now, here are three letters tied together. Ah! This will be the one." He untied the tape, and held out a dirty envelope addressed in a sprawling, illiterate hand to "*Mr. Hartridge, Esq.*" "Is that the note the Italian gave you?"

The porter examined it critically. "Yes," said he, "that is the one."

The inspector drew the letter out of the envelope, and, as he opened it, his eyebrows went up.

"What do you make of that, Doctor?" he said, handing the sheet to Thorndyke.

Thorndyke regarded it for a while in silence, with deep attention. Then he carried it to the window, and, taking his lens from his pocket, examined the paper closely, first with the low power, and then with the highly magnifying Coddington attachment.

"I should have thought you could see that with the naked eye," said the inspector, with a sly grin at me. "It's a pretty bold design."

190

"Yes," replied Thorndyke, "a very interesting production. What do you say, Mr. Marchmont?"

The solicitor took the note, and I looked over his shoulder. It was certainly a curious production. Written in red ink, on the commonest notepaper, and in the same sprawling hand as the address, was the following message: *"You are given six days to do what is just. By the sign above, know what to expect if you fail."* The sign referred to was a skull and crossbones, very neatly, but rather unskilfully, drawn at the top of the paper.

"This," said Mr. Marchmont, handing the document to Mr. Curtis, "explains the singular letter that he wrote yesterday. You have it with you, I think?"

"Yes," replied Mr. Curtis, "here it is."

He produced a letter from his pocket, and read aloud:

Yes, come if you like, though it is an ungodly hour. Your threatening letters have caused me great amusement. They are worthy of Sadler's Wells in its prime.

Alfred Hartridge

"Was Mr. Hartridge ever in Italy?" asked Inspector Badger.

"Oh yes," replied Mr. Curtis. "He stayed at Capri nearly the whole of last year."

"Why, then, that gives us our clue. Look here. Here are these two other letters: E.C. postmark – Saffron Hill is E.C. And just look at that!"

He spread out the last of the mysterious letters, and we saw that, besides the *memento mori*, it contained only three words: *"Beware! Remember Capri!"*

"If you have finished, Doctor, I'll be off and have a look round Little Italy. Those four Italians oughtn't to be difficult to find, and we've got the porter here to identify them."

"Before you go," said Thorndyke, "there are two little matters that I should like to settle. One is the dagger. It is in your pocket, I think. May I have a look at it?"

The inspector rather reluctantly produced the dagger and handed it to my colleague.

"A very singular weapon, this," said Thorndyke, regarding the dagger thoughtfully, and turning it about to view its different parts. "Singular both in shape and material. I have never seen an aluminium hilt before, and bookbinder's morocco is a little unusual."

"The aluminium was for lightness," explained the inspector, "and it was made narrow to carry up the sleeve, I expect."

"Perhaps so," said Thorndyke.

He continued his examination, and presently, to the inspector's delight, brought forth his pocket lens.

"I never saw such a man!" exclaimed the jocose detective. "His motto ought to be, '*We magnify thee.*' I suppose he'll measure it next."

The inspector was not mistaken. Having made a rough sketch of the weapon on his block, Thorndyke produced from his bag a folding rule and a delicate calliper-gauge. With these instruments he proceeded, with extraordinary care and precision, to take the dimensions of the various parts of the dagger, entering each measurement in its place on the sketch, with a few brief, descriptive details.

"The other matter," said he at length, handing the dagger back to the inspector, "refers to the houses opposite."

He walked to the window, and looked out at the backs of a row of tall buildings similar to the one we were in. They were about thirty yards distant, and were separated from us by a piece of ground, planted with shrubs and intersected by gravel paths.

"If any of those rooms were occupied last night," continued Thorndyke, "we might obtain an actual eyewitness of the crime. This room was brilliantly lighted, and all the blinds were up, so that an observer at any of those windows could see right into the room, and very distinctly, too. It might be worth inquiring into."

"Yes, that's true," said the inspector, "though I expect, if any of them have seen anything, they will come forward quick enough when they read the report in the papers. But I must be off now, and I shall have to lock you out of the rooms."

As we went down the stairs, Mr. Marchmont announced his intention of calling on us in the evening, "unless," he added, "you want any information from me now."

"I do," said Thorndyke. "I want to know who is interested in this man's death."

"That," replied Marchmont, "is rather a queer story. Let us take a turn in that garden that we saw from the window. We shall be quite private there."

He beckoned to Mr. Curtis, and, when the inspector had departed with the police-surgeon, we induced the porter to let us into the garden.

"The question that you asked," Mr. Marchmont began, looking up curiously at the tall houses opposite, "is very simply answered. The only person immediately interested in the death of Alfred Hartridge is his executor and sole legatee, a man named Leonard Wolfe. He is no relation of the deceased, merely a friend, but he inherits the entire estate – about twenty-thousand pounds. The circumstances are these: Alfred Hartridge was the elder of two brothers, of whom the younger, Charles, died before his father, leaving a widow and three children. Fifteen years ago the father died, leaving the whole of his property to Alfred, with the understanding that he should support his brother's family and make the children his heirs."

"Was there no will?" asked Thorndyke.

"Under great pressure from the friends of his son's widow, the old man made a will shortly before he died, but he was then very old and rather childish, so the will was contested by Alfred, on the grounds of undue influence, and was ultimately set aside. Since then Alfred Hartridge has not paid a penny towards the support of his brother's family. If it had not been for my client, Mr. Curtis, they might have starved. The whole burden of the support of the widow and the education of the children has fallen upon him.

"Well, just lately the matter has assumed an acute form, for two reasons. The first is that Charles's eldest son, Edmund, has come of age. Mr. Curtis had him articled to a solicitor, and, as he is now fully qualified, and a most advantageous proposal for a partnership has been made, we have been putting pressure on Alfred to supply the necessary capital in accordance with his father's wishes. This he had refused to do, and it was with reference to this matter that we were calling on him this morning. The second reason involves a curious and disgraceful story. There is a certain Leonard Wolfe, who has been an intimate friend of the deceased. He is, I may say, a man of bad character, and their association has been of a kind creditable to neither. There is also a certain woman named Hester Greene, who had certain claims upon the deceased, which we need not go into at present. Now, Leonard Wolfe and the deceased, Alfred Hartridge, entered into an agreement, the terms of which were these: (1) Wolfe was to marry Hester Greene, and in consideration of this service, (2) Alfred Hartridge was to assign to Wolfe the whole of his property, absolutely, the actual transfer to take place on the death of Hartridge."

"And has this transaction been completed?" asked Thorndyke.

"Yes, it has, unfortunately. But we wished to see if anything could be done for the widow and the children during Hartridge's lifetime. No doubt, my client's daughter, Miss Curtis, called last night on a similar mission – very indiscreetly, since the matter was in our hands, but, you know, she is engaged to Edmund Hartridge – and I expect the interview was a pretty stormy one."

Thorndyke remained silent for a while, pacing slowly along the gravel path, with his eyes bent on the ground – not abstractedly, however, but with a searching, attentive glance that roved amongst the shrubs and bushes, as though he were looking for something.

"What sort of man," he asked presently, "is this Leonard Wolfe? Obviously he is a low scoundrel, but what is he like in other respects? Is he a fool, for instance?"

"Not at all, I should say," said Mr. Curtis. "He was formerly an engineer, and, I believe, a very capable mechanician. Latterly he has lived on some property that came to him, and has spent both his time and his money in gambling and dissipation. Consequently, I expect he is pretty short of funds at present."

"And in appearance?"

"I only saw him once," replied Mr. Curtis, "and all I can remember of him is that he is rather short, fair, thin, and clean-shaven, and that he has lost the middle finger of his left hand."

"And he lives at?"

"Eltham, in Kent. Morton Grange, Eltham," said Mr. Marchmont. "And now, if you have all the information that you require, I must really be off, and so must Mr. Curtis."

The two men shook our hands and hurried away, leaving Thorndyke gazing meditatively at the dingy flower-beds.

"A strange and interesting case, this, Jervis," said he, stooping to peer under a laurel-bush. "The inspector is on a hot scent – a most palpable red herring on a most obvious string, but that is his business. Ah, here comes the porter, intent, no doubt, on pumping us, whereas – " He smiled genially at the approaching custodian, and asked, "Where did you say those houses fronted?"

"Cotman Street, sir," answered the porter. "They are nearly all offices."

"And the numbers? That open second-floor window, for instance?"

"That is Number Six, but the house opposite Mr. Hartridge's rooms is Number Eight."

"Thank you."

Thorndyke was moving away, but suddenly turned again to the porter.

"By the way," said he, "I dropped something out of the window just now – a small flat piece of metal, like this." He made on the back of his visiting card a neat sketch of a circular disc, with a hexagonal hole through it, and handed the card to the porter. "I can't say where it fell," he continued. "These flat things scale about so. But you might ask the gardener to look for it. I will give him a sovereign if he brings it to my chambers, for, although it is of no value to anyone else, it is of considerable value to me."

The porter touched his hat briskly, and as we turned out at the gate, I looked back and saw him already wading among the shrubs.

The object of the porter's quest gave me considerable mental occupation. I had not seen Thorndyke drop any thing, and it was not his way to finger carelessly any object of value. I was about to question him on the subject, when, turning sharply round into Cotman Street, he drew up at the doorway of number six, and began attentively to read the names of the occupants.

"'Third-floor,'" he read out, "'Mr. Thomas Barlow, Commission Agent.' Hum! I think we will look in on Mr. Barlow."

He stepped quickly up the stone stairs, and I followed, until we arrived, somewhat out of breath, on the third-floor. Outside the Commission Agent's door he paused for a moment, and we both listened curiously to an irregular sound of shuffling feet from within. Then he softly opened the door and looked into the room. After remaining thus for nearly a minute, he looked round at me with a broad smile, and noiselessly set the door wide open. Inside, a lanky youth of fourteen was practising, with no mean skill, the manipulation of an appliance known by the appropriate name of *diabolo*, and so absorbed was he in his occupation that we entered and shut the door without being observed. At length the shuttle missed the string and flew into a large waste-paper basket. The boy turned and confronted us, and was instantly covered with confusion.

"Allow me," said Thorndyke, rooting rather unnecessarily in the waste-paper basket, and handing the toy to its owner. "I need not ask if Mr. Barlow is in," he added, "nor if he is likely to return shortly."

"He won't be back to-day," said the boy, perspiring with embarrassment. "He left before I came. I was rather late."

"I see," said Thorndyke. "The early bird catches the worm, but the late bird catches the *diabolo*. How did you know he would not be back?"

"He left a note. Here it is."

He exhibited the document, which was neatly written in red ink. Thorndyke examined it attentively, and then asked, "Did you break the inkstand yesterday?"

The boy stared at him in amazement. "Yes, I did," he answered. "How did you know?"

"I didn't, or I should not have asked. But I see that he has used his stylo to write this note."

The boy regarded Thorndyke distrustfully, as he continued, "I really called to see if your Mr. Barlow was a gentleman whom I used to know, but I expect you can tell me. My friend was tall and thin, dark, and clean-shaved."

195

"This ain't him, then," said the boy. "He's thin, but he ain't tall or dark. He's got a sandy beard, and he wears spectacles and a wig. I know a wig when I see one," he added cunningly, "'cause my father wears one. He puts it on a peg to comb it, and he swears at me when I larf."

"My friend had injured his left hand," pursued Thorndyke.

"I dunno about that," said the youth. "Mr. Barlow nearly always wears gloves. He always wears one on his left hand, anyhow."

"Ah well! I'll just write him a note on the chance, if you will give me a piece of notepaper. Have you any ink?"

"There's some in the bottle. I'll dip the pen in for you."

He produced, from the cupboard, an opened packet of cheap notepaper and a packet of similar envelopes, and, having dipped the pen to the bottom of the ink-bottle, handed it to Thorndyke, who sat down and hastily scribbled a short note. He had folded the paper, and was about to address the envelope, when he appeared suddenly to alter his mind.

"I don't think I will leave it, after all," he said, slipping the folded paper into his pocket. "No. Tell him I called – Mr. Horace Budge – and say I will look in again in a day or two."

The youth watched our exit with an air of perplexity, and he even came out on to the landing, the better to observe us over the balusters, until, unexpectedly catching Thorndyke's eye, he withdrew his head with remarkable suddenness, and retired in disorder.

To tell the truth, I was now little less perplexed than the office-boy by Thorndyke's proceedings, in which I could discover no relevancy to the investigation that I presumed he was engaged upon, and the last straw was laid upon the burden of my curiosity when he stopped at a staircase window, drew the note out of his pocket, examined it with his lens, held it up to the light, and chuckled aloud.

"Luck," he observed, "though no substitute for care and intelligence, is a very pleasant addition. Really, my learned brother, we are doing uncommonly well."

When we reached the hall, Thorndyke stopped at the housekeeper's box, and looked in with a genial nod.

"I have just been up to see Mr. Barlow," said he. "He seems to have left quite early."

"Yes, sir," the man replied. "He went away about half-past-eight."

"That was very early, and presumably he came earlier still?"

"I suppose so," the man assented, with a grin, "but I had only just come on when he left."

"Had he any luggage with him?"

"Yes, sir. There was two cases, a square one and a long, narrow one, about five foot long. I helped him to carry them down to the cab."

"Which was a four-wheeler, I suppose?"

"Yes, sir."

"Mr. Barlow hasn't been here very long, has he?" Thorndyke inquired.

"No. He only came in last quarter-day – about six weeks ago."

"Ah well! I must call another day. Good-morning." And Thorndyke strode out of the building, and made directly for the cab-rank in the adjoining street. Here he stopped for a minute or two to parley with the driver of a four-wheeled cab, whom he finally commissioned to convey us to a shop in New Oxford Street. Having dismissed the cabman with his blessing and a half-sovereign, he vanished into the shop, leaving me to gaze at the lathes, drills, and bars of metal displayed in the window. Presently he emerged with a small parcel, and explained, in answer to my inquiring look: "A strip of tool steel and a block of metal for Polton."

His next purchase was rather more eccentric. We were proceeding along Holborn when his attention was suddenly arrested by the window of a furniture shop, in which was displayed a collection of obsolete French small-arms – relics of the tragedy of 1870 – which were being sold for decorative purposes. After a brief inspection, he entered the shop, and shortly reappeared carrying a long sword-bayonet and an old Chassepôt rifle.

"What may be the meaning of this martial display?" I asked, as we turned down Fetter Lane.

"House protection," he replied promptly. "You will agree that a discharge of musketry, followed by a bayonet charge, would disconcert the boldest of burglars."

I laughed at the absurd picture thus drawn of the strenuous house-protector, but nevertheless continued to speculate on the meaning of my friend's eccentric proceedings, which I felt sure were in some way related to the murder in Brackenhurst Chambers, though I could not trace the connection.

After a late lunch, I hurried out to transact such of my business as had been interrupted by the stirring events of the morning, leaving Thorndyke busy with a drawing-board, squares, scale, and compasses, making accurate, scaled drawings from his rough sketches, while Polton, with the brown-paper parcel in his hand, looked on at him with an air of anxious expectation.

As I was returning homeward in the evening by way of Mitre Court, I overtook Mr. Marchmont, who was also bound for our chambers, and we walked on together.

"I had a note from Thorndyke," he explained, "asking for a specimen of handwriting, so I thought I would bring it along myself, and hear if he has any news."

When we entered the chambers, we found Thorndyke in earnest consultation with Polton, and on the table before them I observed, to my great surprise, the dagger with which the murder had been committed.

The Aluminium Dagger

"I have got you the specimen that you asked for," said Marchmont. "I didn't think I should be able to, but, by a lucky chance, Curtis kept the only letter he ever received from the party in question."

He drew the letter from his wallet, and handed it to Thorndyke, who looked at it attentively and with evident satisfaction.

"By the way," said Marchmont, taking up the dagger, "I thought the inspector took this away with him."

"He took the original," replied Thorndyke. "This is a duplicate, which Polton has made, for experimental purposes, from my drawings."

"Really!" exclaimed Marchmont, with a glance of respectful admiration at Polton. "It is a perfect replica – and you have made it so quickly, too."

"It was quite easy to make," said Polton, "to a man accustomed to work in metal."

"Which," added Thorndyke, "is a fact of some evidential value."

At this moment a hansom drew up outside. A moment later flying footsteps were heard on the stairs. There was a furious battering at the door, and, as Polton threw it open, Mr. Curtis burst wildly into the room.

"Here is a frightful thing, Marchmont!" he gasped. "Edith – my daughter – arrested for the murder. Inspector Badger came to our house and took her. My God! I shall go mad!"

Thorndyke laid his hand on the excited man's shoulder. "Don't distress yourself, Mr. Curtis," said he. "There is no occasion, I assure you. I suppose," he added, "your daughter is left-handed?"

"Yes, she is, by a most disastrous coincidence. But what are we to do? Good God! Dr. Thorndyke, they have taken her to prison – to prison – think of it! My poor Edith!"

"We'll soon have her out," said Thorndyke. "But listen, there is someone at the door."

A brisk rat-tat confirmed his statement, and when I rose to open the door, I found myself confronted by Inspector Badger. There was a moment of extreme awkwardness, and then both the detective and Mr. Curtis proposed to retire in favour of the other.

"Don't go, Inspector," said Thorndyke. "I want to have a word with you. Perhaps Mr. Curtis would look in again, say, in an hour. Will you? We shall have news for you by then, I hope."

Mr. Curtis agreed hastily, and dashed out of the room with his characteristic impetuosity. When he had gone, Thorndyke turned to the detective, and remarked dryly, "You seem to have been busy, inspector?"

"Yes," replied Badger. "I haven't let the grass grow under my feet, and I've got a pretty strong case against Miss Curtis already. You see, she was the last person seen in the company of the deceased. She had a grievance against him. She is left-handed, and you remember that the murder was committed by a left-handed person."

"Anything else?"

"Yes. I have seen those Italians, and the whole thing was a put-up job. A woman, in a widow's dress and veil, paid them to go and play the fool outside the building, and she gave them the letter that was left with the porter. They haven't identified her yet, but she seems to agree in size with Miss Curtis."

"And how did she get out of the chambers, with the door bolted on the inside?"

"Ah, there you are! That's a mystery at present – unless you can give us an explanation." The inspector made this qualification with a faint grin, and added, "As there was no one in the place when we broke into it, the murderer must have got out somehow. You can't deny that."

"I do deny it, nevertheless," said Thorndyke. "You look surprised," he continued (which was undoubtedly true), "but yet the whole thing is exceedingly obvious. The explanation struck me directly I looked at the body. There was evidently no practicable exit from the flat, and there was certainly no one in it when you entered. Clearly, then, the murderer had never been in the place at all."

"I don't follow you in the least," said the inspector.

"Well," said Thorndyke, "as I have finished with the case, and am handing it over to you, I will put the evidence before you *seriatim*. Now, I think we are agreed that, at the moment when the blow was struck, the deceased was standing before the fireplace, winding the clock. The dagger entered obliquely from the left, and, if you recall its position, you will remember that its hilt pointed directly towards an open window."

"Which was forty feet from the ground."

"Yes. And now we will consider the very peculiar character of the weapon with which the crime was committed."

He had placed his hand upon the knob of a drawer, when we were interrupted by a knock at the door. I sprang up, and, opening it, admitted no less a person than the porter of Brackenhurst Chambers. The man looked somewhat surprised on recognizing our visitors, but advanced to Thorndyke, drawing a folded paper from his pocket.

"I've found the article you were looking for, sir," said he, "and a rare hunt I had for it. It had stuck in the leaves of one of them shrubs."

Thorndyke opened the packet, and, having glanced inside, laid it on the table.

"Thank you," said he, pushing a sovereign across to the gratified official. "The inspector has your name, I think?"

"He have, sir," replied the porter, and, pocketing his fee, he departed, beaming.

"To return to the dagger," said Thorndyke, opening the drawer. "It was a very peculiar one, as I have said, and as you will see from this model, which is an exact duplicate." Here he exhibited Polton's production to the astonished detective. "You see that it is extraordinarily slender, and free from projections, and of unusual materials. You also see that it was obviously not made by an ordinary dagger-maker. That, in spite of the Italian word scrawled on it, there is plainly written all over it 'British mechanic.' The blade is made from a strip of common three-quarter-inch tool steel. The hilt is turned from an aluminium rod, and there is not a line of engraving on it that could not be produced in a lathe by any engineer's apprentice. Even the boss at the top is mechanical, for it is just like an ordinary hexagon nut. Then, notice the dimensions, as shown on my drawing. The parts *A* and *B*, which just project beyond the blade, are exactly similar in diameter – and such exactness could hardly be accidental. They are each parts of a circle having a diameter of 10.9 millimetres – a dimension which happens, by a singular coincidence, to be exactly the calibre of the old Chassepôt rifle, specimens of which are now on sale at several shops in London. Here is one, for instance."

He fetched the rifle that he had bought, from the corner in which it was standing, and, lifting the dagger by its point, slipped the hilt into the muzzle. When he let go, the dagger slid quietly down the barrel, until its hilt appeared in the open breech.

"Good God!" exclaimed Marchmont. "You don't suggest that the dagger was shot from a gun?"

"I do, indeed, and you now see the reason for the aluminium hilt – to diminish the weight of the already heavy projectile – and also for this hexagonal boss on the end?"

"No, I do not," said the inspector, "but I say that you are suggesting an impossibility."

"Then," replied Thorndyke, "I must explain and demonstrate. To begin with, this projectile had to travel point foremost. Therefore it had to be made to spin – and it certainly was spinning when it entered the body, as the clothing and the wound showed us. Now, to make it spin, it had to be fired from a rifled barrel, but as the hilt would not engage in the rifling, it had to be fitted with something that would. That something was evidently a soft metal washer, which fitted on to this hexagon, and which would be pressed into the grooves of the rifling, and so spin the dagger, but would drop off as soon as the weapon left the barrel. Here is such a washer, which Polton has made for us."

He laid on the table a metal disc, with a hexagonal hole through it.

"This is all very ingenious," said the inspector, "but I say it is impossible and fantastic."

"It certainly sounds rather improbable," Marchmont agreed.

"We will see," said Thorndyke. "Here is a makeshift cartridge of Polton's manufacture, containing an eighth charge of smokeless powder for a 20-bore gun."

He fitted the washer on to the boss of the dagger in the open breech of the rifle, pushed it into the barrel, inserted the cartridge, and closed the breech. Then, opening the office-door, he displayed a target of padded strawboard against the wall.

"The length of the two rooms," said he, "gives us a distance of thirty-two feet. Will you shut the windows, Jervis?"

I complied, and he then pointed the rifle at the target. There was a dull report – much less loud than I had expected – and when we looked at the target, we saw the dagger driven in up to its hilt at the margin of the bull's-eye.

"You see," said Thorndyke, laying down the rifle, "that the thing is practicable. Now for the evidence as to the actual occurrence. First, on the original dagger there are linear scratches which exactly correspond with the grooves of the rifling. Then there is the fact that the dagger was certainly spinning from left to right – in the direction of the rifling, that is – when it entered the body. And then there is this, which, as you heard, the porter found in the garden."

He opened the paper packet. In it lay a metal disc, perforated by a hexagonal hole. Stepping into the office, he picked up from the floor the washer that he had put on the dagger, and laid it on the paper beside the other. The two discs were identical in size, and the margin of each was indented with identical markings, corresponding to the rifling of the barrel.

The inspector gazed at the two discs in silence for a while. Then, looking up at Thorndyke, he said, "I give in, Doctor. You're right, beyond all doubt, but how you came to think of it beats me into fits. The only question now is, *who fired the gun*, and *why wasn't the report heard*?"

"As to the latter," said Thorndyke, "it is probable that he used a compressed-air attachment, not only to diminish the noise, but also to prevent any traces of the explosive from being left on the dagger. As to the former, I think I can give you the murderer's name, but we had better take the evidence in order. You may remember," he continued, "that when Dr. Jervis stood as if winding the clock, I chalked a mark on the floor where he stood. Now, standing on that marked spot, and looking out of the open window, I could see two of the windows of a house nearly opposite. They were the second- and third-floor windows of No. 6, Cotman Street. The second-floor is occupied by a firm of architects. The third-floor by a commission agent named Thomas Barlow. I called on Mr. Barlow, but before describing my visit, I will refer to another matter. You haven't those threatening letters about you, I suppose?"

"Yes, I have," said the inspector, and he drew forth a wallet from his breast-pocket.

"Lot us take the first one, then," said Thorndyke. "You see that the paper and envelope are of the very commonest, and the writing illiterate. But the ink does not agree with this. Illiterate people usually buy their ink in penny bottles. Now, this envelope is addressed with Draper's dichroic ink – a superior office ink, sold only in large bottles – and the red ink in which the note is written is an unfixed, scarlet ink, such as is used by draughtsmen, and has been used, as you can see, in a stylographic pen. But the most interesting thing about this letter is the design drawn at the top. In an artistic sense, the man could not draw, and the anatomical details of the skull are ridiculous. Yet the drawing is very neat. It has the clean, wiry line of a machine drawing, and is done with a steady, practised hand. It is also perfectly symmetrical. The skull, for instance, is exactly in the centre, and, when we examine it through a lens, we see why it is so, for we discover traces of a pencilled centre-line and ruled cross-lines. Moreover, the lens reveals a tiny particle of draughtsman's soft, red, rubber, with which the pencil lines were taken out, and all these facts, taken together, suggest that the drawing was made by someone accustomed to making accurate mechanical drawings. And now we will return to Mr. Barlow. He was out when I called, but I took the liberty of glancing round the office, and this is what I saw. On the mantelshelf was a twelve-inch flat boxwood rule, such as engineers use, a piece of soft, red rubber, and a stone bottle of Draper's dichroic ink. I obtained, by a simple ruse, a specimen of the office notepaper and the ink. We will examine it presently. I found that Mr. Barlow is a new tenant, that he is rather short, wears a wig and spectacles, and always wears a glove on his left hand. He left the office at 8:30 this morning, and no one saw him arrive. He had with him a square case, and a narrow, oblong one about five feet in length, and he took a cab to Victoria, and apparently caught the 8:51 train to Chatham."

"Ah!" exclaimed the inspector.

"But," continued Thorndyke, "now examine those three letters, and compare them with this note that I wrote in Mr. Barlow's office. You see that the paper is of the same make, with the same water-mark, but that is of no great significance. What is of crucial importance is this: You see, in each of these letters, two tiny indentations near the bottom corner. Somebody has used compasses or drawing-pins over the packet of notepaper, and the points have made little indentations, which have marked several of the sheets. Now, notepaper is cut to its size after it is folded, and if you stick a pin into the top sheet of a section, the indentations on all the underlying sheets will be at exactly similar distances from the edges and corners of the sheet. But you see that these little dents are all at the same distance from the edges and the corner." He demonstrated the fact with a pair of compasses. "And now look at this sheet, which I obtained at Mr. Barlow's office. There are two little indentations – rather faint, but quite visible – near the bottom corner, and when we measure them with the compasses, we find that they are exactly the same distance apart as the others, and the same distance from the edges and the bottom corner. The irresistible conclusion is that these four sheets came from the same packet."

The inspector started up from his chair, and faced Thorndyke. "Who is this Mr. Barlow?" he asked.

"That," replied Thorndyke, "is for you to determine, but I can give you a useful hint. There is only one person who benefits by the death of Alfred Hartridge, but he benefits to the extent of twenty thousand pounds. His name is Leonard Wolfe, and I learn from Mr. Marchmont that he is a man of indifferent character – a gambler and a spendthrift. By profession he is an engineer, and he is a capable mechanician. In appearance he is thin, short, fair, and clean-shaven, and he has lost the middle finger of his left hand. Mr. Barlow is also short, thin, and fair, but wears a wig, a beard, and spectacles, and always wears a glove on his left hand. I have seen the handwriting of both these gentlemen, and should say that it would be difficult to distinguish one from the other."

"That's good enough for me," said the inspector. "Give me his address, and I'll have Miss Curtis released at once."

The same night Leonard Wolfe was arrested at Eltham, in the very act of burying in his garden a large and powerful compressed-air rifle. He was never brought to trial, however, for he had in his pocket a more portable weapon – a large-bore Derringer pistol – with which he managed to terminate an exceedingly ill-spent life.

"And, after all," was Thorndyke's comment, when he heard of the event, "he had his uses. He has relieved society of two very bad men, and he has given us a most instructive case. He has shown us how a clever and ingenious criminal may take endless pains to mislead and delude the police, and yet, by inattention to trivial details, may scatter clues broadcast. We can only say to the criminal class generally, in both respects, 'Go thou and do likewise.'"

204

A Message From the Deep Sea

The Whitechapel Road, though redeemed by scattered relics of a more picturesque past from the utter desolation of its neighbour the Commercial Road, is hardly a gay thoroughfare. Especially at its eastern end, where its sordid modernity seems to reflect the colourless lives of its inhabitants, does its grey and dreary length depress the spirits of the wayfarer. But the longest and dullest road can be made delightful by sprightly discourse seasoned with wit and wisdom, and so it was that, as I walked westward by the side of my friend John Thorndyke, the long, monotonous road seemed all too short.

We had been to the London Hospital to see a remarkable case of acromegaly, and, as we returned, we discussed this curious affection, and the allied condition of gigantism, in all their bearings, from the origin of the "Gibson chin" to the physique of Og, King of Bashan.

"It would have been interesting," Thorndyke remarked as we passed up Aldgate High Street, "to have put one's finger into His Majesty's *pituitary fossa* – after his decease, of course. By the way, here is Harrow Alley – you remember Defoe's description of the dead-cart waiting out here, and the ghastly procession coming down the alley." He took my arm and led me up the narrow thoroughfare as far as the sharp turn by the "Star and Still" public-house, where we turned to look back.

"I never pass this place," he said musingly, "but I seem to hear the clang of the bell and the dismal cry of the carter – "

He broke off abruptly. Two figures had suddenly appeared framed in the archway, and now advanced at headlong speed. One, who led, was a stout, middle-aged Jewess, very breathless and disheveled. The other was a well-dressed young man, hardly less agitated than his companion. As they approached, the young man suddenly recognized my colleague, and accosted him in agitated tones.

"I've just been sent for to a case of murder or suicide. Would you mind looking at it for me, sir? It's my first case, and I feel rather nervous."

Here the woman darted back, and plucked the young doctor by the arm.

"Hurry! hurry!" she exclaimed, "don't stop to talk." Her face was as white as lard, and shiny with sweat, her lips twitched, her hands shook, and she stared with the eyes of a frightened child.

"Of course I will come, Hart," said Thorndyke, and, turning back, we followed the woman as she elbowed her way frantically among the foot-passengers.

"Have you started in practice here?" Thorndyke asked as we hurried along.

"No, sir," replied Dr. Hart. "I am an assistant. My principal is the police-surgeon, but he is out just now. It's very good of you to come with me, sir."

"Tut, tut," rejoined Thorndyke. "I am just coming to see that you do credit to my teaching. That looks like the house."

We had followed our guide into a side street, halfway down which we could see a knot of people clustered round a doorway. They watched us as we approached, and drew aside to let us enter. The woman whom we were following rushed into the passage with the same headlong haste with which she had traversed the streets, and so up the stairs. But as she neared the top of the flight she slowed down suddenly, and began to creep up on tiptoe with noiseless and hesitating steps. On the landing she turned to face us, and, pointing a shaking forefinger at the door of the back room, whispered almost inaudibly, "She's in there," and then sank half-fainting on the bottom stair of the next flight.

I laid my hand on the knob of the door, and looked back at Thorndyke. He was coming slowly up the stairs, closely scrutinizing floor, walls, and handrail as he came. When he reached the landing, I turned the handle, and we entered the room together, closing the door after us. The blind was still down, and in the dim, uncertain light nothing out of the common was, at first, to be seen. The shabby little room looked trim and orderly enough, save for a heap of cast-off feminine clothing piled upon a chair. The bed appeared undisturbed except by the half-seen shape of its occupant, and the quiet face, dimly visible in its shadowy corner, might have been that of a sleeper but for its utter stillness and for a dark stain on the pillow by its side.

Dr. Hart stole on tiptoe to the bedside, while Thorndyke drew up the blind, and as the garish daylight poured into the room, the young surgeon fell back with a gasp of horror.

"Good God!" he exclaimed. "Poor creature! But this is a frightful thing, sir!"

The light streamed down upon the white face of a handsome girl of twenty-five, a face peaceful, placid, and beautiful with the austere and almost unearthly beauty of the youthful dead. The lips were slightly parted, the eyes half closed and drowsy, shaded with sweeping lashes, and a wealth of dark hair in massive plaits served as a foil to the translucent skin.

206

Our friend had drawn back the bedclothes a few inches, and now there was revealed, beneath the comely face, so serene and inscrutable, and yet so dreadful in its fixity and waxen pallor, a horrible, yawning wound that almost divided the shapely neck.

Thorndyke looked down with stern pity at the plump white face.

"It was savagely done," said he, "and yet mercifully, by reason of its very savagery. She must have died without waking."

"The brute!" exclaimed Hart, clenching his fists and turning crimson with wrath. "The infernal cowardly beast! He shall hang! By God, he shall hang!" In his fury the young fellow shook his fists in the air, even as the moisture welled up into his eyes.

Thorndyke touched him on the shoulder. "That is what we are here for, Hart," said he. "Get out your notebook." And with this he bent down over the dead girl.

At the friendly reproof the young surgeon pulled himself together, and, with open notebook, commenced his investigation, while I, at Thorndyke's request, occupied myself in making a plan of the room, with a description of its contents and their arrangements. But this occupation did not prevent me from keeping an eye on Thorndyke's movements, and presently I suspended my labours to watch him as, with his pocket-knife, he scraped together some objects that he had found on the pillow.

"What do you make of this?" he asked, as I stepped over to his side. He pointed with the blade to a tiny heap of what looked like silver sand, and, as I looked more closely, I saw that similar particles were sprinkled on other parts of the pillow.

"Silver sand!" I exclaimed. "I don't understand at all how it can have got there. Do you?"

Thorndyke shook his head. "We will consider the explanation later," was his reply. He had produced from his pocket a small metal box which he always carried, and which contained such requisites as cover-slips, capillary tubes, moulding wax, and other "diagnostic materials". He now took from it a seed-envelope, into which he neatly shovelled the little pinch of sand with his knife. He had closed the envelope, and was writing a pencilled description on the outside, when we were startled by a cry from Hart.

"Good God, sir! Look at this! It was done by a woman!"

He had drawn back the bedclothes, and was staring aghast at the dead girl's left hand. It held a thin tress of long, red hair.

Thorndyke hastily pocketed his specimen, and, stepping round the little bedside table, bent over the hand with knitted brows. It was closed, though not tightly clenched, and when an attempt was made gently to separate the fingers, they were found to be as rigid as the fingers of a wooden hand. Thorndyke stooped yet more closely, and, taking out his lens, scrutinized the wisp of hair throughout its entire length.

"There is more here than meets the eye at the first glance," he remarked. "What say you, Hart?" He held out his lens to his quondam pupil, who was about to take it from him when the door opened, and three men entered. One was a police-inspector, the second appeared to be a plain-clothes officer, while the third was evidently the divisional surgeon.

"Friends of yours, Hart?" inquired the latter, regarding us with some disfavour.

Thorndyke gave a brief explanation of our presence to which the newcomer rejoined, "Well, sir, your *locus standi* here is a matter for the inspector. My assistant was not authorized to call in outsiders. You needn't wait, Hart."

With this he proceeded to his inspection, while Thorndyke withdrew the pocket-thermometer that he had slipped under the body, and took the reading.

The inspector, however, was not disposed to exercise the prerogative at which the surgeon had hinted, for an expert has his uses.

"How long should you say she'd been dead, sir?" he asked affably.

"About ten hours," replied Thorndyke.

The inspector and the detective simultaneously looked at their watches. "That fixes it at two o'clock this morning," said the former. "What's that, sir?"

The surgeon was pointing to the wisp of hair in the dead girl's hand.

"My word!" exclaimed the inspector. "A woman, eh? She must be a tough customer. This looks like a soft job for you, sergeant."

"Yes," said the detective. "That accounts for that box with the hassock on it at the head of the bed. She had to stand on them to reach over. But she couldn't have been very tall."

"She must have been mighty strong, though," said the inspector. "Why, she has nearly cut the poor wench's head off." He moved round to the head of the bed, and, stooping over, peered down at the gaping wound. Suddenly he began to draw his hand over the pillow, and then rub his fingers together. "Why," he exclaimed, "there's sand on the pillow – silver sand! Now, how can that have come there?"

The surgeon and the detective both came round to verify this discovery, and an earnest consultation took place as to its meaning.

"Did you notice it, sir?" the inspector asked Thorndyke.

"Yes," replied the latter. "It's an unaccountable thing, isn't it?"

"I don't know that it is, either," said the detective, he ran over to the washstand, and then uttered a grunt of satisfaction. "It's quite a simple matter, after all, you see," he said, glancing complacently at my colleague.

208

"There's a ball of sand-soap on the washstand, and the basin is full of blood-stained water. You see, she must have washed the blood off her hands, and off the knife, too – a pretty cool customer she must be – and she used the sand-soap. Then, while she was drying her hands, she must have stood over the head of the bed, and let the sand fall on to the pillow. I think that's clear enough."

"Admirably clear," said Thorndyke, "and what do you suppose was the sequence of events?"

The gratified detective glanced round the room. "I take it," said he, "that the deceased read herself to sleep. There is a book on the table by the bed, and a candlestick with nothing in it but a bit of burnt wick at the bottom of the socket. I imagine that the woman came in quietly, lit the gas, put the box and the hassock at the bedhead, stood on them, and cut her victim's throat. Deceased must have waked up and clutched the murderess's hair – though there doesn't seem to have been much of a struggle, but no doubt she died almost at once. Then the murderess washed her hands, cleaned the knife, tidied up the bed a bit, and went away. That's about how things happened, I think, but how she got in without anyone hearing, and how she got out, and where she went to, are the things that we've got to find out."

"Perhaps," said the surgeon, drawing the bedclothes over the corpse, "we had better have the landlady in and make a few inquiries." He glanced significantly at Thorndyke, and the inspector coughed behind his hand. My colleague, however, chose to be obtuse to these hints: Opening the door, he turned the key backwards and forwards several times, drew it out, examined it narrowly, and replaced it.

"The landlady is outside on the landing," he remarked, holding the door open.

Thereupon the inspector went out, and we all followed to hear the result of his inquiries.

"Now, Mrs. Goldstein," said the officer, opening his notebook, "I want you to tell us all that you know about this affair, and about the girl herself. What was her name?"

The landlady, who had been joined by a white-faced, tremulous man, wiped her eyes, and replied in a shaky voice, "Her name, poor child, was Minna Adler. She was a German. She came from Bremen about two years ago. She had no friends in England – no relatives, I mean. She was a waitress at a restaurant in Fenchurch Street, and a good, quiet, hard-working girl."

"When did you discover what had happened?"

"About eleven o'clock. I thought she had gone to work as usual, but my husband noticed from the back yard that her blind was still down. So I went up and knocked, and when I got no answer, I opened the door and went in, and then I saw – " Here the poor soul, overcome by the dreadful recollection, burst into hysterical sobs.

"Her door was unlocked, then. Did she usually lock it?"

"I think so," sobbed Mrs. Goldstein. "The key was always inside."

"And the street door – was that secure when you came down this morning?"

"It was shut. We don't bolt it because some of the lodgers come home rather late."

"And now tell us, had she any enemies? Was there anyone who had a grudge against her?"

"No, no, poor child! Why should anyone have a grudge against her? No, she had no quarrel – no real quarrel – with anyone, not even with Miriam."

"Miriam!" inquired the inspector. "Who is she?"

"That was nothing," interposed the man hastily. "That was not a quarrel."

"Just a little unpleasantness, I suppose, Mr. Goldstein?" suggested the inspector.

"Just a little foolishness about a young man," said Mr. Goldstein. "That was all. Miriam was a little jealous. But it was nothing."

"No, no. Of course. We all know that young women are apt to – "

A soft footstep had been for some time audible, slowly descending the stair above, and at this moment a turn of the staircase brought the newcomer into view. And at that vision the inspector stopped short as if petrified, and a tense, startled silence fell upon us all. Down the remaining stairs there advanced towards us a young woman, powerful though short, wild-eyed, dishevelled, horror-stricken, and of a ghastly pallor, and her hair was a fiery red.

Stock still and speechless we all stood as this apparition came slowly towards us, but suddenly the detective slipped back into the room, closing the door after him, to reappear a few moments later holding a small paper packet, which, after a quick glance at the inspector, he placed in his breast pocket.

"This is my daughter Miriam that we spoke about, gentlemen," said Mr. Goldstein. "Miriam, those are the doctors and the police."

The girl looked at us from one to the other. "You have seen her, then," she said in a strange, muffled voice, and added, "She isn't dead, is she? Not really dead?" The question was asked in a tone at once coaxing and despairing, such as a distracted mother might use over the corpse of her child. It filled me with vague discomfort, and, unconsciously, I looked round towards Thorndyke.

To my surprise he had vanished.

Noiselessly backing towards the head of the stairs, where I could command a view of the hall, or passage, I looked down, and saw him in the act of reaching up to a shelf behind the street door. He caught my eye, and beckoned, whereupon I crept away unnoticed by the party on the landing. When I reached the hall, he was wrapping up three small objects, each in a separate cigarette-paper, and I noticed that he handled them with more than ordinary tenderness.

"We didn't want to see that poor devil of a girl arrested," said he, as he deposited the three little packets gingerly in his pocket-box. "Let us be off." He opened the door noiselessly, and stood for a moment, turning the latch backwards and forwards, and closely examining its bolt.

I glanced up at the shelf behind the door. On it were two flat china candlesticks, in one of which I had happened to notice, as we came in, a short end of candle lying in the tray, and I now looked to see if that was what Thorndyke had annexed, but it was still there.

I followed my colleague out into the street, and for some time we walked on without speaking. "You guessed what the sergeant had in that paper, of course," said Thorndyke at length.

"Yes. It was the hair from the dead woman's hand, and I thought that he had much better have left it there."

"Undoubtedly. But that is the way in which well-meaning policemen destroy valuable evidence. Not that it matters much in this particular instance, but it might have been a fatal mistake."

"Do you intend to take any active part in this case?" I asked.

"That depends on circumstances. I have collected some evidence, but what it is worth I don't yet know. Neither do I know whether the police have observed the same set of facts, but I need not say that I shall do anything that seems necessary to assist the authorities. That is a matter of common citizenship."

The inroads made upon our time by the morning's adventures made it necessary that we should go each about his respective business without delay, so, after a perfunctory lunch at a tea-shop, we separated, and I did not see my colleague again until the day's work was finished, and I turned into our chambers just before dinner-time.

Here I found Thorndyke seated at the table, and evidently full of business. A microscope stood close by, with a condenser throwing a spot of light on to a pinch of powder that had been sprinkled on to the slide. His collecting-box lay open before him, and he was engaged, rather mysteriously, in squeezing a thick white cement from a tube on to three little pieces of moulding-wax.

"Useful stuff, this Fortafix," he remarked, "it makes excellent casts, and saves the trouble and mess of mixing plaster, which is a consideration for small work like this. By the way, if you want to know what was on that poor girl's pillow, just take a peep through the microscope. It is rather a pretty specimen."

I stepped across, and applied my eye to the instrument. The specimen was, indeed, pretty in more than a technical sense. Mingled with crystalline grains of quartz, glassy spicules, and water-worn fragments of coral, were a number of lovely little shells, some of the texture of fine porcelain, others like blown Venetian glass.

The Sand From the Murdered Woman's Pillow
Magnified 25 Diameters

"These are *Foraminifera*!" I exclaimed.
"Yes."

212

"Then it is not silver sand, after all?"

"Certainly not."

"But what is it, then?"

Thorndyke smiled. "It is a message to us from the deep sea, Jervis, from the floor of the Eastern Mediterranean."

"And can you read the message?"

"I think I can," he replied, "but I shall know soon, I hope."

I looked down the microscope again, and wondered what message these tiny shells had conveyed to my friend. Deep-sea sand on a dead woman's pillow! What could be more incongruous? What possible connection could there be between this sordid crime in the east of London and the deep bed of the "tideless sea"?

Meanwhile Thorndyke squeezed out more cement on to the three little pieces of moulding-wax (which I suspected to be the objects that I had seen him wrapping up with such care in the hall of the Goldsteins' house). Then, laying one of them down on a glass slide, with its cemented side uppermost, he stood the other two upright on either side of it. Finally he squeezed out a fresh load of the thick cement, apparently to bind the three objects together, and carried the slide very carefully to a cupboard, where he deposited it, together with the envelope containing the sand and the slide from the stage of the microscope.

He was just locking the cupboard when a sharp rat-tat on our knocker sent him hurriedly to the door. A messenger-boy, standing on the threshold, held out a dirty envelope.

"Mr. Goldstein kept me a awful long time, sir," said he. "I haven't been a-loitering."

Thorndyke took the envelope over to the gas-light, and, opening it, drew forth a sheet of paper, which he scanned quickly and almost eagerly, and, though his face remained as inscrutable as a mask of stone, I felt a conviction that the paper had told him something that he wished to know.

The boy having been sent on his way rejoicing, Thorndyke turned to the bookshelves, along which he ran his eye thoughtfully until it alighted on a shabbily-bound volume near one end. This he reached down, and as he laid it open on the table, I glanced at it, and was surprised to observe that it was a bi-lingual work, the opposite pages being apparently in Russian and Hebrew.

"The *Old Testament* in Russian and Yiddish," he remarked, noting my surprise. "I am going to get Polton to photograph a couple of specimen pages – is that the postman or a visitor?"

It turned out to be the postman, and as Thorndyke extracted from the letter-box a blue official envelope, he glanced significantly at me.

"This answers your question, I think, Jervis," said he. "Yes, coroner's subpoena and a very civil letter: '*Sorry to trouble you, but I had no choice under the circumstances*' – of course he hadn't – '*Dr. Davidson has arranged to make the autopsy to-morrow at four p.m., and I should be glad if you could be present. The mortuary is in Barker Street, next to the school.*' Well, we must go, I suppose, though Davidson will probably resent it." He took up the *Testament,* and went off with it to the laboratory.

We lunched at our chambers on the following day, and, after the meal, drew up our chairs to the fire and lit our pipes. Thorndyke was evidently preoccupied, for he laid his open notebook on his knee, and, gazing meditatively into the fire, made occasional entries with his pencil as though he were arranging the points of an argument. Assuming that the Aldgate murder was the subject of his cogitations, I ventured to ask, "Have you any material evidence to offer the coroner?"

He closed his notebook and put it away. "The evidence that I have," he said, "is material and important, but it is disjointed and rather inconclusive. If I can join it up into a coherent whole, as I hope to do before I reach the court, it will be very important indeed – but here is my invaluable familiar, with the instruments of research." He turned with a smile towards Polton, who had just entered the room, and master and man exchanged a friendly glance of mutual appreciation. The relations of Thorndyke and his assistant were a constant delight to me: On the one side, service, loyal and whole-hearted. On the other, frank and full recognition.

"I should think those will do, sir," said Polton, handing his principal a small cardboard box such as playing-cards are carried in. Thorndyke pulled off the lid, and I then saw that the box was fitted internally with grooves for plates, and contained two mounted photographs. The latter were very singular productions indeed. They were copies each of a page of the Testament, one Russian and the other Yiddish, but the lettering appeared white on a black ground, of which it occupied only quite a small space in the middle, leaving a broad black margin. Each photograph was mounted on a stiff card, and each card had a duplicate photograph pasted on the back.

Thorndyke exhibited them to me with a provoking smile, holding them daintily by their edges, before he slid them back into the grooves of their box.

"We are making a little digression into philology, you see," he remarked, as he pocketed the box. "But we must be off now, or we shall keep Davidson waiting. Thank you, Polton."

The District Railway carried us swiftly eastward, and we emerged from Aldgate Station a full half-hour before we were due. Nevertheless, Thorndyke stepped out briskly, but instead of making directly for the

214

mortuary, he strayed off unaccountably into Mansell Street, scanning the numbers of the houses as he went. A row of old houses, picturesque but grimy, on our right seemed specially to attract him, and he slowed down as we approached them.

"There is a quaint survival, Jervis," he remarked, pointing to a crudely painted, wooden effigy of an Indian standing on a bracket at the door of a small old-fashioned tobacconist's shop. We halted to look at the little image, and at that moment the side door opened, and a woman came out on to the doorstep, where she stood gazing up and down the street.

Thorndyke immediately crossed the pavement, and addressed her, apparently with some question, for I heard her answer presently: "A quarter-past six is his time, sir, and he is generally punctual to the minute."

"Thank you," said Thorndyke. "I'll bear that in mind." And, lifting his hat, he walked on briskly, turning presently up a side-street which brought us out into Aldgate. It was now but five minutes to four, so we strode off quickly to keep our tryst at the mortuary, but although we arrived at the gate as the hour was striking, when we entered the building we found Dr. Davidson hanging up his apron and preparing to depart.

"Sorry I couldn't wait for you," he said, with no great show of sincerity, "but a post-mortem is a mere farce in a case like this. You have seen all that there was to see. However, there is the body. Hart hasn't closed it up yet."

With this and a curt "Good-afternoon," he departed.

"I must apologize for Dr. Davidson, sir," said Hart, looking up with a vexed face from the desk at which he was writing out his notes.

"You needn't," said Thorndyke. "You didn't supply him with manners, and don't let me disturb you. I only want to verify one or two points."

Accepting the hint, Hart and I remained at the desk, while Thorndyke, removing his hat, advanced to the long slate table, and bent over its burden of pitiful tragedy. For some time he remained motionless, running his eye gravely over the corpse, in search, no doubt, of bruises and indications of a struggle. Then he stooped and narrowly examined the wound, especially at its commencement and end. Suddenly he drew nearer, peering intently as if something had attracted his attention, and having taken out his lens, fetched a small sponge, with which he dried an exposed process of the spine. Holding his lens before the dried spot, he again scrutinized it closely, and then, with a scalpel and forceps, detached some object, which he carefully washed, and then once more examined through his lens as it lay in the palm of his hand. Finally, as I expected, he brought forth his "collecting-box," took from it a seed-envelope, into which he dropped the object – evidently something quite small – closed up the envelope, wrote on the outside of it, and replaced it in the box.

"I think I have seen all that I wanted to see," he said, as he pocketed the box and took up his hat. "We shall meet to-morrow morning at the inquest." He shook hands with Hart, and we went out into the relatively pure air.

On one pretext or another, Thorndyke lingered about the neighbourhood of Aldgate until a church bell struck six, when he bent his steps towards Harrow Alley. Through the narrow, winding passage he walked, slowly and with a thoughtful mien, along Little Somerset Street and out into Mansell Street, until just on the stroke of a quarter-past we found ourselves opposite the little tobacconist's shop.

Thorndyke glanced at his watch and halted, looking keenly up the street. A moment later he hastily took from his pocket the cardboard box, from which he extracted the two mounted photographs which had puzzled me so much. They now seemed to puzzle Thorndyke equally, to judge by his expression, for he held them close to his eyes, scrutinizing them with an anxious frown, and backing by degrees into the doorway at the side of the tobacconist's. At this moment I became aware of a man who, as he approached, seemed to eye my friend with some curiosity and more disfavor – a very short, burly young man, apparently a foreign Jew, whose face, naturally sinister and unprepossessing, was further disfigured by the marks of smallpox.

"Excuse me," he said brusquely, pushing past Thorndyke. "I live here."

"I am sorry," responded Thorndyke. He moved aside, and then suddenly asked, "By the way, I suppose you do not by any chance understand Yiddish?"

"Why do you ask?" the newcomer demanded gruffly.

"Because I have just had these two photographs of lettering given to me. One is in Greek, I think, and one in Yiddish, but I have forgotten which is which." He held out the two cards to the stranger, who took them from him, and looked at them with scowling curiosity.

"This one is Yiddish," said he, raising his right hand, "and this other is Russian, not Greek." He held out the two cards to Thorndyke, who took them from him, holding them carefully by the edges as before.

"I am greatly obliged to you for your kind assistance," said Thorndyke, but before he had time to finish his thanks, the man had entered, by means of his latchkey, and slammed the door.

Thorndyke carefully slid the photographs back into their grooves, replaced the box in his pocket, and made an entry in his notebook.

216

"That," said he, "finishes my labours, with the exception of a small experiment which I can perform at home. By the way, I picked up a morsel of evidence that Davidson had overlooked. He will be annoyed, and I am not very fond of scoring off a colleague, but he is too uncivil for me to communicate with."

The coroner's subpoena had named ten o'clock as the hour at which Thorndyke was to attend to give evidence, but a consultation with a well-known solicitor so far interfered with his plans that we were a quarter-of an-hour late in starting from the Temple. My friend was evidently in excellent spirits, though silent and preoccupied, from which I inferred that he was satisfied with the results of his labours, but, as I sat by his side in the hansom, I forbore to question him, not from mere unselfishness, but rather from the desire to hear his evidence for the first time in conjunction with that of the other witnesses.

The room in which the inquest was held formed part of a school adjoining the mortuary. Its vacant bareness was on this occasion enlivened by a long, baize-covered table, at the head of which sat the coroner, while one side was occupied by the jury, and I was glad to observe that the latter consisted, for the most part, of genuine working men, instead of the stolid-faced, truculent "professional jurymen" who so often grace these tribunals.

A row of chairs accommodated the witnesses, a corner of the table was allotted to the accused woman's solicitor – a smart dapper gentleman in gold pince-nez, a portion of one side to the reporters, and several ranks of benches were occupied by a miscellaneous assembly representing the public.

There were one or two persons present whom I was somewhat surprised to see. There was, for instance, our pock-marked acquaintance of Mansell Street, who greeted us with a stare of hostile surprise, and there was Superintendent Miller of Scotland Yard, in whose manner I seemed to detect some kind of private understanding with Thorndyke. But I had little time to look about me, for when we arrived, the proceedings had already commenced. Mrs. Goldstein, the first witness, was finishing her recital of the circumstances under which the crime was discovered, and, as she retired, weeping hysterically, she was followed by looks of commiseration from the sympathetic jurymen.

The next witness was a young woman named Kate Silver. As she stepped forward to be sworn she flung a glance of hatred and defiance at Miriam Goldstein, who, white-faced and wild of aspect, with her red hair streaming in dishevelled masses on to her shoulders, stood apart in custody of two policemen, staring about her as if in a dream.

217

"You were intimately acquainted with the deceased, I believe?" said the coroner.

"I was. We worked at the same place for a long time – the Empire Restaurant in Fenchurch Street – and we lived in the same house. She was my most intimate friend."

"Had she, as far as you know, any friends or relations in England?"

"No. She came to England from Bremen about three years ago. It was then that I made her acquaintance. All her relations were in Germany, but she had many friends here, because she was a very lively, amiable girl."

"Had she, as far as you know, any enemies – any persons, I mean, who bore any grudge against her and were likely to do her an injury?"

"Yes. Miriam Goldstein was her enemy. She hated her."

"You say Miriam Goldstein hated the deceased. How do you know that?"

"She made no secret of it. They had had a violent quarrel about a young man named Moses Cohen. He was formerly Miriam's sweetheart, and I think they were very fond of one another until Minna Adler came to lodge at the Goldsteins' house about three months ago. Then Moses took a fancy to Minna, and she encouraged him, although she had a sweetheart of her own, a young man named Paul Petrofsky, who also lodged in the Goldsteins' house. At last Moses broke off with Miriam, and engaged himself to Minna. Then Miriam was furious, and complained to Minna about what she called her perfidious conduct, but Minna only laughed, and told her she could have Petrofsky instead."

"And what did Minna say to that?" asked the coroner.

"She was still more angry, because Moses Cohen is a smart, good-looking young man, while Petrofsky is not much to look at. Besides, Miriam did not like Petrofsky. He had been rude to her, and she had made her father send him away from the house. So they were not friends, and it was just after that that the trouble came."

"The trouble?"

"I mean about Moses Cohen. Miriam is a very passionate girl, and she was furiously jealous of Minna, so when Petrofsky annoyed her by taunting her about Moses Cohen and Minna, she lost her temper, and said dreadful things about both of them."

"As, for instance – ?"

"She said that she would kill them both, and that she would like to cut Minna's throat."

"When was this?"

"It was the day before the murder."

"Who heard her say these things besides you?"

218

"Another lodger named Edith Bryant and Petrofsky. We were all standing in the hall at the time."

"But I thought you said Petrofsky had been turned away from the house."

"So he had, a week before, but he had left a box in his room, and on this day he had come to fetch it. That was what started the trouble. Miriam had taken his room for her bedroom, and turned her old one into a workroom. She said he should not go to her room to fetch his box."

"And did he?"

"I think so. Miriam and Edith and I went out, leaving him in the hall. When we came back the box was gone, and, as Mrs. Goldstein was in the kitchen and there was nobody else in the house, he must have taken it."

"You spoke of Miriam's workroom. What work did she do?"

"She cut stencils for a firm of decorators."

Here the coroner took a peculiarly shaped knife from the table before him, and handed it to the witness.

"Have you ever seen that knife before?" he asked.

"Yes. It belongs to Miriam Goldstein. It is a stencil-knife that she used in her work."

This concluded the evidence of Kate Silver, and when the name of the next witness, Paul Petrofsky, was called, our Mansell Street friend came forward to be sworn. His evidence was quite brief, and merely corroborative of that of Kate Silver, as was that of the next witness, Edith Bryant. When these had been disposed of, the coroner announced, "Before taking the medical evidence, gentlemen, I propose to hear that of the police-officers, and first we will call Detective-sergeant Alfred Bates."

The sergeant stepped forward briskly, and proceeded to give his evidence with official readiness and precision.

"I was called by Constable Simmonds at eleven-forty-nine, and reached the house at two minutes to twelve in company with Inspector Harris and Divisional Surgeon Davidson. When I arrived Dr. Hart, Dr. Thorndyke, and Dr. Jervis were already in the room. I found the deceased woman, Minna Adler, lying in bed with her throat cut. She was dead and cold. There were no signs of a struggle, and the bed did not appear to have been disturbed. There was a table by the bedside on which was a book and an empty candlestick. The candle had apparently burnt out, for there was only a piece of charred wick at the bottom of the socket. A box had been placed on the floor at the head of the bed and a hassock stood on it. Apparently the murderer had stood on the hassock and leaned over the head of the bed to commit the murder. This was rendered necessary by the position of the table, which could not have been moved without making some noise and perhaps disturbing the deceased. I infer from the presence of the box and hassock that the murderer is a short person."

"Was there anything else that seemed to fix the identity of the murderer?"

"Yes. A tress of a woman's red hair was grasped in the left hand of the deceased."

As the detective uttered this statement, a simultaneous shriek of horror burst from the accused woman and her mother. Mrs. Goldstein sank half-fainting on to a bench, while Miriam, pale as death, stood as one petrified, fixing the detective with a stare of terror, as he drew from his pocket two small paper packets, which he opened and handed to the coroner.

"The hair in the packet marked *A*," said he, "is that which was found in the hand of the deceased – that in the packet marked *B* is the hair of Miriam Goldstein."

Here the accused woman's solicitor rose. "Where did you obtain the hair in the packet marked *B*?" he demanded.

"I took it from a bag of combings that hung on the wall of Miriam Goldstein's bedroom," answered the detective.

"I object to this," said the solicitor. "There is no evidence that the hair from that bag was the hair of Miriam Goldstein at all."

Thorndyke chuckled softly. "The lawyer is as dense as the policeman," he remarked to me in an undertone. "Neither of them seems to see the significance of that bag in the least."

"Did you know about the bag, then?" I asked in surprise.

"No. I thought it was the hair-brush."

I gazed at my colleague in amazement, and was about to ask for some elucidation of this cryptic reply, when he held up his finger and turned again to listen.

"Very well, Mr. Horwitz," the coroner was saying, "I will make a note of your objection, but I shall allow the sergeant to continue his evidence."

The solicitor sat down, and the detective resumed his statement.

"I have examined and compared the two samples of hair, and it is my opinion that they are from the head of the same person. The only other observation that I made in the room was that there was a small quantity of silver sand sprinkled on the pillow around the deceased woman's head."

"Silver sand!" exclaimed the coroner. "Surely that is a very singular material to find on a woman's pillow?"

"I think it is easily explained," replied the sergeant. "The wash-hand basin was full of bloodstained water, showing that the murderer had washed his – or her – hands, and probably the knife, too, after the crime.

220

On the washstand was a ball of sand-soap, and I imagine that the murderer used this to cleanse his – or her – hands, and, while drying them, must have stood over the head of the bed and let the sand sprinkle down on to the pillow."

"A simple but highly ingenious explanation," commented the coroner approvingly, and the jurymen exchanged admiring nods and nudges.

"I searched the rooms occupied by the accused woman, Miriam Goldstein, and found there a knife of the kind used by stencil cutters, but larger than usual. There were stains of blood on it which the accused explained by saying that she cut her finger some days ago. She admitted that the knife was hers."

This concluded the sergeant's evidence, and he was about to sit down when the solicitor rose.

"I should like to ask this witness one or two questions," said he, and the coroner having nodded assent, he proceeded, "Has the finger of the accused been examined since her arrest?"

"I believe not," replied the sergeant. "Not to my knowledge, at any rate."

The solicitor noted the reply, and then asked, "With reference to the silver sand, did you find any at the bottom of the wash-hand basin?"

The sergeant's face reddened. "I did not examine the wash-hand basin," he answered.

"Did anybody examine it?"

"I think not."

"Thank you." Mr. Horwitz sat down, and the triumphant squeak of his quill pen was heard above the muttered disapproval of the jury.

"We shall now take the evidence of the doctors, gentlemen," said the coroner, "and we will begin with that of the divisional surgeon. You saw the deceased, I believe, Doctor," he continued, when Dr. Davidson had been sworn, "soon after the discovery of the murder, and you have since then made an examination of the body?"

"Yes. I found the body of the deceased lying in her bed, which had apparently not been disturbed. She had been dead about ten hours, and rigidity was complete in the limbs but not in the trunk. The cause of death was a deep wound extending right across the throat and dividing all the structures down to the spine. It had been inflicted with a single sweep of a knife while deceased was lying down, and was evidently homicidal. It was not possible for the deceased to have inflicted the wound herself. It was made with a single-edged knife, drawn from left to right. The assailant stood on a hassock placed on a box at the head of the bed and leaned over to strike the blow. The murderer is probably quite a short person, very muscular, and right-handed. There was no sign of a struggle, and, judging

221

by the nature of the injuries, I should say that death was almost instantaneous. In the left hand of the deceased was a small tress of a woman's red hair. I have compared that hair with that of the accused, and am of opinion that it is her hair."

"You were shown a knife belonging to the accused?"

"Yes, a stencil-knife. There were stains of dried blood on it which I have examined and find to be mammalian blood. It is probably human blood, but I cannot say with certainty that it is."

"Could the wound have been inflicted with this knife?"

"Yes, though it is a small knife to produce so deep a wound. Still, it is quite possible."

The coroner glanced at Mr. Horwitz. "Do you wish to ask this witness any questions?" he inquired.

"If you please, sir," was the reply. The solicitor rose, and, having glanced through his notes, commenced, "You have described certain blood-stains on this knife. But we have heard that there was blood-stained water in the wash-hand basin, and it is suggested, most reasonably, that the murderer washed his hands and the knife. But if the knife was washed, how do you account for the bloodstains on it?"

"Apparently the knife was not washed, only the hands."

"But is not that highly improbable?"

"No, I think not."

"You say that there was no struggle, and that death was practically instantaneous, but yet the deceased had torn out a lock of the murderess's hair. Are not those two statements inconsistent with one another?"

"No. The hair was probably grasped convulsively at the moment of death. At any rate, the hair was undoubtedly in the dead woman's hand."

"Is it possible to identify positively the hair of any individual?"

"No. Not with certainty. But this is very peculiar hair."

The solicitor sat down, and, Dr. Hart having been called, and having briefly confirmed the evidence of his principal, the coroner announced, "The next witness, gentleman, is Dr. Thorndyke, who was present almost accidentally, but was actually the first on the scene of the murder. He has since made an examination of the body, and will, no doubt, be able to throw some further light on this horrible crime."

Thorndyke stood up, and, having been sworn, laid on the table a small box with a leather handle. Then, in answer to the coroner's questions, he described himself as the lecturer on Medical Jurisprudence at St. Margaret's Hospital, and briefly explained his connection with the case. At this point the foreman of the jury interrupted to ask that his opinion might be taken on the hair and the knife, as these were matters of contention, and the objects in question were accordingly handed to him.

"Is the hair in the packet marked *A* in your opinion from the same person as that in the packet marked *B*?" the coroner asked.

"I have no doubt that they are from the same person," was the reply.

"Will you examine this knife and tell us if the wound on the deceased might have been inflicted with it?"

Thorndyke examined the blade attentively, and then handed the knife back to the coroner.

"The wound might have been inflicted with this knife," said he, "but I am quite sure it was not."

"Can you give us your reasons for that very definite opinion?"

"I think," said Thorndyke, "that it will save time if I give you the facts in a connected order." The coroner bowed assent, and he proceeded. "I will not waste your time by reiterating facts already stated. Sergeant Bates has fully described the state of the room, and I have nothing to add on that subject. Dr. Davidson's description of the body covers all the facts: the woman had been dead about ten hours, the wound was unquestionably homicidal, and was inflicted in the manner that he has described. Death was apparently instantaneous, and I should say that the deceased never awakened from her sleep."

"But," objected the coroner, "the deceased held a lock of hair in her hand."

"That hair," replied Thorndyke, "was not the hair of the murderer. It was placed in the hand of the corpse for an obvious purpose, and the fact that the murderer had brought it with him shows that the crime was premeditated, and that it was committed by someone who had had access to the house and was acquainted with its inmates."

As Thorndyke made this statement, coroner, jurymen, and spectators alike gazed at him in open-mouthed amazement. There was an interval of intense silence, broken by a wild, hysteric laugh from Mrs. Goldstein, and then the coroner asked, "How did you know that the hair in the hand of the corpse was not that of the murderer?"

"The inference was very obvious. At the first glance the peculiar and conspicuous colour of the hair struck me as suspicious. But there were three facts, each of which was in itself sufficient to prove that the hair was probably not that of the murderer.

"In the first place there was the condition of the hand. When a person, at the moment of death, grasps any object firmly, there is set up a condition known as cadaveric spasm. The muscular contraction passes immediately into rigor mortis, or death-stiffening, and the object remains grasped by the dead hand until the rigidity passes off. In this case the hand was perfectly rigid, but it did not grasp the hair at all. The little tress lay in the palm quite loosely and the hand was only partially closed. Obviously the hair had been placed in it after death. The other two facts had reference to the condition of the hair itself. Now, when a lock of hair is torn from the head, it is evident that all the roots will be found at the same end of the lock. But in the present instance this was not the case. The lock of hair which lay in the dead woman's hand had roots at both ends, and so could not have been torn from the head of the murderer. But the third fact that I observed was still more conclusive. The hairs of which that little tress was composed had not been pulled out at all. They had fallen out spontaneously. They were, in fact, shed hairs – probably combings. Let me explain the difference. When a hair is shed naturally, it drops out of the little tube in the skin called the root sheath, having been pushed out by the young hair growing up underneath. The root end of such a shed hair shows nothing but a small bulbous enlargement – the root bulb. But when a hair is forcibly pulled out, its root drags out the root sheath with it, and this can be plainly seen as a glistening mass on the end of the hair. If Miriam Goldstein will pull out a hair and pass it to me, I will show you the great difference between hair which is pulled out and hair which is shed."

The unfortunate Miriam needed no pressing. In a twinkling she had tweaked out a dozen hairs, which a constable handed across to Thorndyke, by whom they were at once fixed in a paper-clip. A second clip being produced from the box, half-a-dozen hairs taken from the tress which had been found in the dead woman's hand were fixed in it. Then Thorndyke handed the two clips, together with a lens, to the coroner.

"Remarkable!" exclaimed the latter, "and most conclusive." He passed the objects on to the foreman, and there was an interval of silence while the jury examined them with breathless interest and much facial contortion.

"The next question," resumed Thorndyke, "was, *Whence did the murderer obtain these hairs*? I assumed that they had been taken from Miriam Goldstein's hair-brush, but the sergeant's evidence makes it pretty clear that they were obtained from the very bag of combings from which he took a sample for comparison."

"I think, Doctor," remarked the coroner, "you have disposed of the hair clue pretty completely. May I ask if you found anything that might throw any light on the identity of the murderer?"

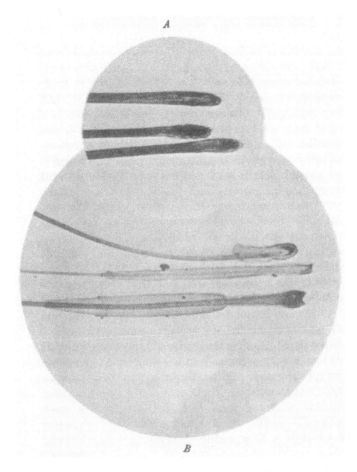

A – Shed Hairs Showing the Naked Bulb
Magnified 32 Diameters

B – Hairs Plucked From Scalp, Showing the Adherent Root-Sheathes
Magnified 20 Diameters

"Yes," replied Thorndyke, "I observed certain things which determine the identity of the murderer quite conclusively." He turned a significant glance on Superintendent Miller, who immediately rose, stepped quietly to the door, and then returned, putting something into his pocket. "When I entered the hall," Thorndyke continued, "I noted the following facts: Behind the door was a shelf on which were two china candlesticks. Each was fitted with a candle, and in one was a short candle-end, about an inch long, lying in the tray. On the floor, close to the mat, was a spot of candle-wax and some faint marks of muddy feet. The oil-cloth on the stairs also bore faint footmarks, made by wet goloshes. They

225

were ascending the stairs, and grew fainter towards the top. There were two more spots of candle-wax on the stairs, and one on the handrail, a burnt end of a wax match halfway up the stairs, and another on the landing. There were no descending footmarks, but one of the spots of wax close to the balusters had been trodden on while warm and soft, and bore the mark of the front of the heel of a golosh descending the stairs. The lock of the street door had been recently oiled, as had also that of the bedroom door, and the latter had been unlocked from outside with a bent wire, which had made a mark on the key. Inside the room I made two further observations. One was that the dead woman's pillow was lightly sprinkled with sand, somewhat like silver sand, but greyer and less gritty. I shall return to this presently.

"The other was that the candlestick on the bedside table was empty. It was a peculiar candlestick, having a skeleton socket formed of eight flat strips of metal. The charred wick of a burnt-out candle was at the bottom of the socket, but a little fragment of wax on the top edge showed that another candle had been stuck in it and had been taken out, for otherwise that fragment would have been melted. I at once thought of the candle-end in the hall, and when I went down again I took that end from the tray and examined it. On it I found eight distinct marks corresponding to the eight bars of the candlestick in the bedroom. It had been carried in the right hand of some person, for the warm, soft wax had taken beautifully clear impressions of a right thumb and forefinger. I took three moulds of the candle-end in moulding wax, and from these moulds have made this cement cast, which shows both the fingerprints and the marks of the candlestick." He took from his box a small white object, which he handed to the coroner.

"And what do you gather from these facts?" asked the coroner.

"I gather that at about a quarter-to-two on the morning of the crime, a man (who had, on the previous day visited the house to obtain the tress of hair and oil the locks) entered the house by means of a latchkey. We can fix the time by the fact that it rained on that morning from half-past-one to a quarter-to-two, this being the only rain that has fallen for a fortnight, and the murder was committed at about two o'clock. The man lit a wax match in the hall and another halfway up the stairs. He found the bedroom door locked, and turned the key from outside with a bent wire. He entered, lit the candle, placed the box and hassock, murdered his victim, washed his hands and knife, took the candle-end from the socket and went downstairs, where he blew out the candle and dropped it into the tray.

"The next clue is furnished by the sand on the pillow. I took a little of it, and examined it under the microscope, when it turned out to be deep-sea sand from the Eastern Mediterranean. It was full of the minute shells called '*Foraminifera*,' and as one of these happened to belong to a species which is found only in the Levant, I was able to fix the locality."

"But this is very remarkable," said the coroner. "How on earth could deep-sea sand have got on to this woman's pillow?"

"The explanation," replied Thorndyke, "is really quite simple. Sand of this kind is contained in considerable quantities in Turkey sponges. The warehouses in which the sponges are unpacked are often strewn with it ankle deep. The men who unpack the cases become dusted over with it, their clothes saturated and their pockets filled with it. If such a person, with his clothes and pockets full of sand, had committed this murder, it is pretty certain that in leaning over the head of the bed in a partly inverted position he would have let fall a certain quantity of the sand from his pockets and the interstices of his clothing. Now, as soon as I had examined this sand and ascertained its nature, I sent a message to Mr. Goldstein asking him for a list of the persons who were acquainted with the deceased, with their addresses and occupations. He sent me the list by return, and among the persons mentioned was a man who was engaged as a packer in a wholesale sponge warehouse in the Minories. I further ascertained that the new season's crop of Turkey sponges had arrived a few days before the murder.

"The question that now arose was, whether this sponge-packer was the person whose fingerprints I had found on the candle-end. To settle this point, I prepared two mounted photographs, and having contrived to meet the man at his door on his return from work, I induced him to look at them and compare them. He took them from me, holding each one between a forefinger and thumb. When he returned them to me, I took them home and carefully dusted each on both sides with a certain surgical dusting-powder. The powder adhered to the places where his fingers and thumbs had pressed against the photographs, showing the fingerprints very distinctly. Those of the right hand were identical with the prints on the candle, as you will see if you compare them with the cast." He produced from the box the photograph of the Yiddish lettering, on the black margin of which there now stood out with startling distinctness a yellowish-white print of a thumb.

Thorndyke had just handed the card to the coroner when a very singular disturbance arose. While my friend had been giving the latter part of his evidence, I had observed the man Petrofsky rise from his seat and walk stealthily across to the door. He turned the handle softly and pulled, at first gently, and then with more force. But the door was locked. As he realized this, Petrofsky seized the handle with both hands and tore at it furiously, shaking it to and fro with the violence of a madman, and his shaking limbs, his starting eyes, glaring insanely at the astonished spectators, his ugly face, dead white, running with sweat and hideous with terror, made a picture that was truly shocking.

Suddenly he let go the handle, and with a horrible cry thrust his hand under the skirt of his coat and rushed at Thorndyke. But the superintendent was ready for this. There was a shout and a scuffle, and then Petrofsky was born down, kicking and biting like a maniac, while Miller hung on to his right hand and the formidable knife that it grasped.

"I will ask you to hand that knife to the coroner," said Thorndyke, when Petrofsky had been secured and handcuffed, and the superintendent had readjusted his collar. "Will you kindly examine it, sir," he continued, "and tell me if there is a notch in the edge, near to the point – a triangular notch about an eighth of an inch long?"

The coroner looked at the knife, and then said in a tone of surprise, "Yes, there is. You have seen this knife before, then?"

"No, I have not," replied Thorndyke. "But perhaps I had better continue my statement. There is no need for me to tell you that the fingerprints on the card and on the candle are those of Paul Petrofsky. I will proceed to the evidence furnished by the body.

"In accordance with your order, I went to the mortuary and examined the corpse of the deceased. The wound has been fully and accurately described by Dr. Davidson, but I observed one fact which I presume he had overlooked. Embedded in the bone of the spine – in the left transverse process of the fourth vertebra – I discovered a small particle of steel, which I carefully extracted."

He drew his collecting-box from his pocket, and taking from it a seed-envelope, handed the latter to the coroner. "That fragment of steel is in this envelope," he said, "and it is possible that it may correspond to the notch in the knife-blade."

Amidst an intense silence the coroner opened the little envelope, and let the fragment of steel drop on to a sheet of paper. Laying the knife on the paper, he gently pushed the fragment towards the notch. Then he looked up at Thorndyke.

"It fits exactly," said he.

There was a heavy thud at the other end of the room and we all looked round.

Petrofsky had fallen on to the floor insensible.

Superintendent Miller Rises
To the Occasion

229

"An instructive case, Jervis," remarked Thorndyke, as we walked homewards – "a case that reiterates the lesson that the authorities still refuse to learn."

"What is that?" I asked.

"It is this. When it is discovered that a murder has been committed, the scene of that murder should instantly become as the Palace of the Sleeping Beauty. Not a grain of dust should be moved, not a soul should be allowed to approach it, until the scientific observer has seen everything *in situ* and absolutely undisturbed. No tramplings of excited constables, no rummaging by detectives, no scrambling to and fro of bloodhounds. Consider what would have happened in this case if we had arrived a few hours later. The corpse would have been in the mortuary, the hair in the sergeant's pocket, the bed rummaged and the sand scattered abroad, the candle probably removed, and the stairs covered with fresh tracks.

"There would not have been the vestige of a clue."

"And," I added, "the deep sea would have uttered its message in vain."

THE SINGING BONE

R. AUSTIN FREEMAN

1923 Dodd, Mead Cover

Preface

The peculiar construction of the first four stories in the present collection will probably strike both reader and critic and seem to call for some explanation, which I accordingly proceed to supply.

In the conventional "detective story" the interest is made to focus on the question, "Who did it?" The identity of the criminal is a secret that is jealously guarded up to the very end of the book, and its disclosure forms the final climax.

This I have always regarded as somewhat of a mistake. In real life, the identity of the criminal is a question of supreme importance for practical reasons, but in fiction, where no such reasons exist, I conceive the interest of the reader to be engaged chiefly by the demonstration of unexpected consequences of simple actions, of unsuspected causal connections, and by the evolution of an ordered train of evidence from a mass of facts apparently incoherent and unrelated. The reader's curiosity is concerned not so much with the question "Who did it?" as with the question "How was the discovery achieved?" That is to say, the ingenious reader is interested more in the intermediate action than in the ultimate result.

The offer by a popular author of a prize to the reader who should identify the criminal in a certain "detective story", exhibiting as it did the opposite view, suggested to me an interesting question.

Would it be possible to write a detective story in which from the outset the reader was taken entirely into the author's confidence, was made an actual witness of the crime and furnished with every fact that could possibly be used in its detection? Would there be any story left when the reader had all the facts? I believed that there would, and as an experiment to test the justice of my belief, I wrote "The Case of Oscar Brodski." Here the usual conditions are reversed, the reader knows everything, the detective knows nothing, and the interest focuses on the unexpected significance of trivial circumstances.

By excellent judges on both sides of the Atlantic – including the editor of Pearson's Magazine – this story was so far approved of that I was invited to produce others of the same type.

Three more were written and are here included together with one of the more orthodox characters, so that the reader can judge of the respective merits of the two methods of narration.

Nautical readers will observe that I have taken the liberty (for obvious reasons connected with the law of libel) of planting a screw-pile *lighthouse on the Girdler Sand in place of the light-vessel. I mention the matter to forestall criticism and save readers the trouble of writing to point out the error.*

R.A.F.
Gravesend

The Case of Oscar Brodski
Part I – The Mechanism of the Crime

A surprising amount of nonsense has been talked about conscience. On the one hand remorse (or the "again-bite", as certain scholars of ultra-Teutonic leanings would prefer to call it), on the other hand "an easy conscience" – these have been accepted as the determining factors of happiness or the reverse.

Of course there is an element of truth in the "easy conscience" view, but it begs the whole question. A particularly hardy conscience may be quite easy under the most unfavourable conditions – conditions in which the more feeble conscience might be severely afflicted with the "again-bite". And, then, it seems to be the fact that some fortunate persons have no conscience at all, a negative gift that raises them above the mental vicissitudes of the common herd of humanity.

Now, Silas Hickler was a case in point. No one, looking into his cheerful, round face, beaming with benevolence and wreathed in perpetual smiles, would have imagined him to be a criminal. Least of all, his worthy, high-church housekeeper, who was a witness to his unvarying amiability, who constantly heard him carolling light-heartedly about the house and noted his appreciative zest at meal-times.

Yet it is a fact that Silas earned his modest, though comfortable, income by the gentle art of burglary. A precarious trade and risky withal, yet not so very hazardous if pursued with judgment and moderation. And Silas was eminently a man of judgment. He worked invariably alone. He kept his own counsel. No confederate had he to turn King's Evidence at a pinch, no one he knew would bounce off in a fit of temper to Scotland Yard. Nor was he greedy and thriftless, as most criminals are. His "scoops" were few and far between, carefully planned, secretly executed, and the proceeds judiciously invested in "weekly property".

In early life Silas had been connected with the diamond industry, and he still did a little rather irregular dealing. In the trade he was suspected of transactions with I.D.B.'s, and one or two indiscreet dealers had gone so far as to whisper the ominous word "fence". But Silas smiled a benevolent smile and went his way. He knew what he knew, and his clients in Amsterdam were not inquisitive.

Such was Silas Hickler. As he strolled round his garden in the dusk of an October evening, he seemed the very type of modest, middle-class prosperity. He was dressed in the travelling suit that he wore on his little

Continental trips, his bag was packed and stood in readiness on the sitting-room sofa. A parcel of diamonds (purchased honestly, though without impertinent questions, at Southampton) was in the inside pocket of his waistcoat, and another more valuable parcel was stowed in a cavity in the heel of his right boot. In an hour-and-a-half it would be time for him to set out to catch the boat train at the junction. Meanwhile, there was nothing to do but to stroll round the fading garden and consider how he should invest the proceeds of the impending deal. His housekeeper had gone over to Welham for the week's shopping, and would probably not be back until eleven o'clock. He was alone in the premises and just a trifle dull.

He was about to turn into the house when his ear caught the sound of footsteps on the unmade road that passed the end of the garden. He paused and listened. There was no other dwelling near, and the road led nowhere, fading away into the waste land beyond the house. Could this be a visitor? It seemed unlikely, for visitors were few at Silas Hickler's house. Meanwhile the footsteps continued to approach, ringing out with increasing loudness on the hard, stony path.

Silas strolled down to the gate, and, leaning on it, looked out with some curiosity. Presently a glow of light showed him the face of a man, apparently lighting his pipe, then a dim figure detached itself from the enveloping gloom, advanced towards him and halted opposite the garden. The stranger removed a cigarette from his mouth and, blowing out a cloud of smoke, asked –

"Can you tell me if this road will take me to Badsham Junction?"

"No," replied Hickler, "but there is a footpath farther on that leads to the station."

"Footpath!" growled the stranger. "I've had enough of footpaths. I came down from town to Catley intending to walk across to the junction. I started along the road, and then some fool directed me to a short cut, with the result that I have been blundering about in the dark for the last half-hour. My sight isn't very good, you know," he added.

"What train do you want to catch?" asked Hickler.

"Seven-fifty-eight," was the reply.

"I am going to catch that train myself," said Silas, "but I shan't be starting for another hour. The station is only three-quarters of a mile from here. If you like to come in and take a rest, we can walk down together and then you'll be sure of not missing your way."

"It's very good of you," said the stranger, peering, with spectacled eyes, at the dark house, "but – I think – ?"

"Might as well wait here as at the station," said Silas in his genial way, holding the gate open, and the stranger, after a momentary hesitation, entered and, flinging away his cigarette, followed him to the door of the cottage.

The sitting-room was in darkness, save for the dull glow of the expiring fire, but, entering before his guest, Silas applied a match to the lamp that hung from the ceiling. As the flame leaped up, flooding the little interior with light, the two men regarded one another with mutual curiosity.

"Brodski, by Jingo!" was Hickler's silent commentary, as he looked at his guest. "Doesn't know me, evidently – wouldn't, of course, after all these years and with his bad eyesight. Take a seat, sir," he added aloud. "Will you join me in a little refreshment to while away the time?"

Brodski murmured an indistinct acceptance, and, as his host turned to open a cupboard, he deposited his hat (a hard, grey felt) on a chair in a corner, placed his bag on the edge of the table, resting his umbrella against it, and sat down in a small arm-chair.

"Have a biscuit?" said Hickler, as he placed a whisky bottle on the table together with a couple of his best star-pattern tumblers and a siphon.

"Thanks, I think I will," said Brodski. "The railway journey and all this confounded tramping about, you know – ?"

"Yes," agreed Silas. "Doesn't do to start with an empty stomach. Hope you don't mind oat-cakes. I see they're the only biscuits I have."

Brodski hastened to assure him that oat-cakes were his special and peculiar fancy, and in confirmation, having mixed himself a stiff jorum, he fell to upon the biscuits with evident gusto.

Brodski was a deliberate feeder, and at present appeared to be somewhat sharp set. His measured munching being unfavourable to conversation, most of the talking fell to Silas, and, for once, that genial transgressor found the task embarrassing. The natural thing would have been to discuss his guest's destination and perhaps the object of his journey, but this was precisely what Hickler avoided doing. For he knew both, and instinct told him to keep his knowledge to himself.

Brodski was a diamond merchant of considerable reputation, and in a large way of business. He bought stones principally in the rough, and of these he was a most excellent judge. His fancy was for stones of somewhat unusual size and value, and it was well known to be his custom, when he had accumulated a sufficient stock, to carry them himself to Amsterdam and supervise the cutting of the rough stones. Of this Hickler was aware, and he had no doubt that Brodski was now starting on one of his periodical excursions, that somewhere in the recesses of his rather shabby clothing was concealed a paper packet possibly worth several thousand pounds.

Brodski sat by the table munching monotonously and talking little. Hickler sat opposite him, talking nervously and rather wildly at times, and watching his guest with a growing fascination. Precious stones, and especially diamonds, were Hickler's specialty. "Hard stuff" – silver plate – he avoided entirely. Gold, excepting in the form of specie, he seldom touched. But stones, of which he could carry off a whole consignment in the heel of his boot and dispose of with absolute safety, formed the staple of his industry. And here was a man sitting opposite him with a parcel in his pocket containing the equivalent of a dozen of his most successful "scoops", stones worth perhaps – ? Here he pulled himself up short and began to talk rapidly, though without much coherence. For, even as he talked, other words, formed subconsciously, seemed to insinuate themselves into the interstices of the sentences, and to carry on a parallel train of thought.

"Gets chilly in the evenings now, doesn't it?" said Hickler.

"It does indeed," Brodski agreed, and then resumed his slow munching, breathing audibly through his nose.

"Five-thousand at least," the subconscious train of thought resumed, "probably six or seven, perhaps ten." Silas fidgeted in his chair and endeavoured to concentrate his ideas on some topic of interest. He was growing disagreeably conscious of a new and unfamiliar state of mind.

"Do you take any interest in gardening?" he asked. Next to diamonds and weekly "property", his besetting weakness was fuchsias.

Brodski chuckled sourly. "Hatton Garden is the nearest approach – ?" He broke off suddenly, and then added, "I am a Londoner, you know."

The abrupt break in the sentence was not unnoticed by Silas, nor had he any difficulty in interpreting it. A man who carries untold wealth upon his person must needs be wary in his speech.

"Yes," he answered absently, "it's hardly a Londoner's hobby." And then, half consciously, he began a rapid calculation. Put it at five thousand pounds. What would that represent in weekly property? His last set of houses had cost two hundred and fifty pounds apiece, and he had let them at ten shillings and sixpence a week. At that rate, five thousand pounds represented twenty houses at ten and sixpence a week – say ten pounds a week – one pound eight shillings a day – five hundred and twenty pounds a year – for life. It was a competency. Added to what he already had, it was wealth. With that income he could fling the tools of his trade into the river and live out the remainder of his life in comfort and security.

He glanced furtively at his guest across the table, and then looked away quickly as he felt stirring within him an impulse the nature of which he could not mistake. This must be put an end to. Crimes against the person he had always looked upon as sheer insanity. There was, it is true, that little affair of the Weybridge policeman, but that was unforeseen and unavoidable, and it was the constable's doing after all. And there was the

240

old housekeeper at Epsom, too, but, of course, if the old idiot would shriek in that insane fashion – well, it was an accident, very regrettable, to be sure, and no one could be more sorry for the mishap than himself. But deliberate homicide! Robbery from the person! It was the act of a stark lunatic.

Of course, if he had happened to be that sort of person, here was the opportunity of a lifetime. The immense booty, the empty house, the solitary neighbourhood, away from the main road and from other habitations, the time, the darkness – but, of course, there was the body to be thought of – that was always the difficulty. What to do with the body? Here he caught the shriek of the up express, rounding the curve in the line that ran past the waste land at the back of the house. The sound started a new train of thought, and, as he followed it out, his eyes fixed themselves on the unconscious and taciturn Brodski, as he sat thoughtfully sipping his whisky. At length, averting his gaze with an effort, he rose suddenly from his chair and turned to look at the clock on the mantelpiece, spreading out his hands before the dying fire. A tumult of strange sensations warned him to leave the house. He shivered slightly, though he was rather hot than chilly, and, turning his head, looked at the door.

"Seems to be a confounded draught," he said, with another slight shiver. "Did I shut the door properly, I wonder?" He strode across the room and, opening the door wide, looked out into the dark garden. A desire, sudden and urgent, had come over him to get out into the open air, to be on the road and have done with this madness that was knocking at the door of his brain.

"I wonder if it is worthwhile to start yet," he said, with a yearning glance at the murky, starless sky.

Brodski roused himself and looked round. "Is your clock right?" he asked.

Silas reluctantly admitted that it was.

"How long will it take us to walk to the station?" inquired Brodski.

"Oh, about twenty-five minutes to half-an-hour," replied Silas, unconsciously exaggerating the distance.

"Well," said Brodski, "we've got more than an hour yet, and it's more comfortable here than hanging about the station. I don't see the use of starting before we need."

"No, of course not," Silas agreed. A wave of strange emotion, half-regretful, half-triumphant, surged through his brain. For some moments he remained standing on the threshold, looking out dreamily into the night. Then he softly closed the door, and, seemingly without the exercise of his volition, the key turned noiselessly in the lock.

241

He returned to his chair and tried to open a conversation with the taciturn Brodski, but the words came faltering and disjointed. He felt his face growing hot, his brain full and intense, and there was a faint, high-pitched singing in his ears. He was conscious of watching his guest with a new and fearful interest, and, by sheer force of will, turned away his eyes, only to find them a moment later involuntarily returning to fix the unconscious man with yet more horrible intensity. And ever through his mind walked, like a dreadful procession, the thoughts of what that other man – the man of blood and violence – would do in these circumstances. Detail by detail the hideous synthesis fitted together the parts of the imagined crime, and arranged them in due sequence until they formed a succession of events, rational, connected and coherent.

He rose uneasily from his chair, with his eyes still riveted upon his guest. He could not sit any longer opposite that man with his hidden store of precious gems. The impulse that he recognized with fear and wonder was growing more ungovernable from moment to moment. If he stayed it would presently overpower him, and then? He shrank with horror from the dreadful thought, but his fingers itched to handle the diamonds. For Silas was, after all, a criminal by nature and habit. He was a beast of prey. His livelihood had never been earned, it had been taken by stealth or, if necessary, by force. His instincts were predacious, and the proximity of unguarded valuables suggested to him, as a logical consequence, their abstraction or seizure. His unwillingness to let these diamonds go away beyond his reach was fast becoming overwhelming.

But he would make one more effort to escape. He would keep out of Brodski's actual presence until the moment for starting came.

"If you'll excuse me," he said, "I will go and put on a thicker pair of boots. After all this dry weather we may get a change, and damp feet are very uncomfortable when you are travelling."

"Yes, dangerous too," agreed Brodski.

Silas walked through into the adjoining kitchen, where, by the light of the little lamp that was burning there, he had seen his stout, country boots placed, cleaned and in readiness, and sat down upon a chair to make the change. He did not, of course, intend to wear the country boots, for the diamonds were concealed in those he had on. But he would make the change and then alter his mind, it would all help to pass the time. He took a deep breath. It was a relief, at any rate, to be out of that room. Perhaps if he stayed away, the temptation would pass. Brodski would go on his way – he wished that he was going alone – and the danger would be over – at least – and the opportunity would have gone – the diamonds – ?

He looked up as he slowly unlaced his boot. From where he sat he could see Brodski sitting by the table with his back towards the kitchen

242

door. He had finished eating, now, and was composedly rolling a cigarette. Silas breathed heavily, and, slipping off his boot, sat for a while motionless, gazing steadily at the other man's back. Then he unlaced the other boot, still staring abstractedly at his unconscious guest, drew it off, and laid it very quietly on the floor.

Brodski calmly finished rolling his cigarette, licked the paper, put away his pouch, and, having dusted the crumbs of tobacco from his knees, began to search his pockets for a match. Suddenly, yielding to an uncontrollable impulse, Silas stood up and began stealthily to creep along the passage to the sitting-room. Not a sound came from his stockinged feet. Silently as a cat he stole forward, breathing softly with parted lips, until he stood at the threshold of the room. His face flushed duskily, his eyes, wide and staring, glittered in the lamplight, and the racing blood hummed in his ears.

Brodski struck a match – Silas noted that it was a wooden vesta – lighted his cigarette, blew out the match, and flung it into the fender. Then he replaced the box in his pocket and commenced to smoke.

Slowly and without a sound Silas crept forward into the room, step by step, with catlike stealthiness, until he stood close behind Brodski's chair – so close that he had to turn his head that his breath might not stir the hair upon the other man's head. So, for half-a-minute, he stood

243

motionless, like a symbolical statue of Murder, glaring down with horrible, glittering eyes upon the unconscious diamond merchant, while his quick breath passed without a sound through his open mouth and his fingers writhed slowly like the tentacles of a giant hydra. And then, as noiselessly as ever, he backed away to the door, turned quickly and walked back into the kitchen.

He drew a deep breath. It had been a near thing. Brodski's life had hung upon a thread. For it had been so easy. Indeed, if he had happened, as he stood behind the man's chair, to have a weapon – a hammer, for instance, or even a stone?

He glanced round the kitchen and his eyes lighted on a bar that had been left by the workmen who had put up the new greenhouse. It was an odd piece cut off from a square, wrought-iron stanchion, and was about a foot long and perhaps three-quarters of an inch thick. Now, if he had had that in his hand a minute ago –

He picked the bar up, balanced it in his hand and swung it round his head. A formidable weapon this. Silent, too. And it fitted the plan that had passed through his brain. Bah! He had better put the thing down.

But he did not. He stepped over to the door and looked again at Brodski, sitting, as before, meditatively smoking, with his back towards the kitchen.

Suddenly a change came over Silas. His face flushed, the veins of his neck stood out and a sullen scowl settled on his face. He drew out his watch, glanced at it earnestly and replaced it. Then he strode swiftly but silently along the passage into the sitting-room.

A pace away from his victim's chair he halted and took deliberate aim. The bar swung aloft, but not without some faint rustle of movement, for Brodski looked round quickly even as the iron whistled through the air. The movement disturbed the murderer's aim, and the bar glanced off his victim's head, making only a trifling wound. Brodski sprang up with a tremulous, bleating cry, and clutched his assailant's arms with the tenacity of mortal terror.

Then began a terrible struggle, as the two men, locked in a deadly embrace, swayed to and fro and trampled backwards and forwards. The chair was overturned, an empty glass swept from the table and, with Brodski's spectacles, crushed beneath stamping feet. And thrice that dreadful, pitiful, bleating cry rang out into the night, filling Silas, despite his murderous frenzy, with terror lest some chance wayfarer should hear it. Gathering his great strength for a final effort, he forced his victim backwards onto the table and, snatching up a corner of the tablecloth, thrust it into his face and crammed it into his mouth as it opened to utter another shriek. And thus they remained for a full two minutes, almost

244

motionless, like some dreadful group of tragic allegory. Then, when the last faint twitchings had died away, Silas relaxed his grasp and let the limp body slip softly onto the floor.

It was over. For good or for evil, the thing was done. Silas stood up, breathing heavily, and, as he wiped the sweat from his face, he looked at the clock. The hands stood at one minute to seven. The whole thing had taken a little over three minutes. He had nearly an hour in which to finish his task. The goods train that entered into his scheme came by at twenty minutes past, and it was only three-hundred yards to the line. Still, he must not waste time. He was now quite composed, and only disturbed by the thought that Brodski's cries might have been heard. If no one had heard them it was all plain sailing.

He stooped, and, gently disengaging the table-cloth from the dead man's teeth, began a careful search of his pockets. He was not long finding what he sought, and, as he pinched the paper packet and felt the little hard bodies grating on one another inside, his faint regrets for what had happened were swallowed up in self-congratulations.

He now set about his task with business-like briskness and an attentive eye on the clock. A few large drops of blood had fallen on the table-cloth, and there was a small bloody smear on the carpet by the dead man's head. Silas fetched from the kitchen some water, a nail-brush and a dry cloth, and, having washed out the stains from the table-cover – not forgetting the deal table-top underneath – and cleaned away the smear from the carpet and rubbed the damp places dry, he slipped a sheet of paper under the head of the corpse to prevent further contamination. Then he set the tablecloth straight, stood the chair upright, laid the broken spectacles on the table and picked up the cigarette, which had been trodden flat in the struggle, and flung it under the grate. Then there was the broken glass, which he swept up into a dust-pan. Part of it was the remains of the shattered tumbler, and the rest the fragments of the broken spectacles. He turned it out onto a sheet of paper and looked it over carefully, picking out the larger recognizable pieces of the spectacle-glasses and putting them aside on a separate slip of paper, together with a sprinkling of the minute fragments. The remainder he shot back into the dust-pan and, having hurriedly put on his boots, carried it out to the rubbish-heap at the back of the house.

It was now time to start. Hastily cutting off a length of string from his string-box – for Silas was an orderly man and despised the oddments of string with which many people make shift – he tied it to the dead man's bag and umbrella and slung them from his shoulder. Then he folded up the paper of broken glass, and, slipping it and the spectacles into his pocket, picked up the body and threw it over his shoulder. Brodski was a small, spare man, weighing not more than nine stone, not a very formidable burden for a big, athletic man like Silas.

The night was intensely dark, and, when Silas looked out of the back gate over the waste land that stretched from his house to the railway, he could hardly see twenty yards ahead. After listening cautiously and hearing no sound, he went out, shut the gate softly behind him and set forth at a good pace, though carefully, over the broken ground. His progress was not as silent as he could have wished for, though.

The scanty turf that covered the gravelly land was thick enough to deaden his footfalls, the swinging bag and umbrella made an irritating noise, indeed, his movements were more hampered by them than by the weightier burden.

The distance to the line was about three-hundred yards. Ordinarily he would have walked it in from three to four minutes, but now, going cautiously with his burden and stopping now and again to listen, it took him just six minutes to reach the three-bar fence that separated the waste land from the railway. Arrived here he halted for a moment and once more listened attentively, peering into the darkness on all sides. Not a living creature was to be seen or heard in this desolate spot, but far away, the shriek of an engine's whistle warned him to hasten.

Lifting the corpse easily over the fence, he carried it a few yards farther to a point where the line curved sharply.

Here he laid it face downwards, with the neck over the near rail. Drawing out his pocket-knife, he cut through the knot that fastened the umbrella to the string and also secured the bag, and when he had flung the bag and umbrella on the track beside the body, he carefully pocketed the string, excepting the little loop that had fallen to the ground when the knot was cut.

The quick snort and clanking rumble of an approaching goods train began now to be clearly audible. Rapidly, Silas, drew from his pockets the battered spectacles and the packet of broken glass. The former he threw down by the dead man's head, and then, emptying the packet into his hand, sprinkled the fragments of glass around the spectacles.

He was none too soon. Already the quick, laboured puffing of the engine sounded close at hand. His impulse was to stay and watch, to witness the final catastrophe that should convert the murder into an accident or suicide. But it was hardly safe. It would be better that he should not be near lest he should not be able to get away without being seen. Hastily he climbed back over the fence and strode away across the rough fields, while the train came snorting and clattering towards the curve.

He had nearly reached his back gate when a sound from the line brought him to a sudden halt, it was a prolonged whistle accompanied by the groan of brakes and the loud clank of colliding trucks. The snorting of the engine had ceased and was replaced by the penetrating hiss of escaping steam.

The train had stopped!

For one brief moment Silas stood with bated breath and mouth agape like one petrified, then he strode forward quickly to the gate, and, letting himself in, silently slid the bolt. He was undeniably alarmed. What could have happened on the line? It was practically certain that the body had been seen, but what was happening now? And would they come to the house? He entered the kitchen, and having paused again to listen – for somebody might come and knock at the door at any moment – he walked through the sitting-room and looked round. All seemed in order there. There was the bar, though, lying where he had dropped it in the scuffle. He picked it up and held it under the lamp. There was no blood on it, only one or two hairs. Somewhat absently he wiped it with the table-cover, and then, running out through the kitchen into the back garden, dropped it over the wall into a bed of nettles. Not that there was anything incriminating in the bar, but, since he had used it as a weapon, it had somehow acquired a sinister aspect to his eye.

He now felt that it would be well to start for the station at once. It was not time yet, for it was barely twenty-five minutes past seven, but he did not wish to be found in the house if anyone should come. His soft hat was on the sofa with his bag, to which his umbrella was strapped. He put on the hat, caught up the bag, and stepped over to the door, then he came back to turn down the lamp. And it was at this moment, when he stood with his hand raised to the burner, that his eyes, travelling by chance into the dim

247

corner of the room, lighted on Brodski's grey felt hat, reposing on the chair where the dead man had placed it when he entered the house.

Silas stood for a few moments as if petrified, with the chilly sweat of mortal fear standing in beads upon his forehead. Another instant and he would have turned the lamp down and gone on his way, and then – ? He strode over to the chair, snatched up the hat and looked inside it. Yes, there was the name, "*Oscar Brodski*", written plainly on the lining. If he had gone away, leaving it to be discovered, he would have been lost. Indeed, even now, if a search-party should come to the house, it was enough to send him to the gallows.

His limbs shook with horror at the thought, but in spite of his panic he did not lose his self-possession. Darting through into the kitchen, he grabbed up a handful of the dry brush-wood that was kept for lighting fires and carried it to the sitting-room grate where he thrust it on the extinct, but still hot, embers, and crumpling up the paper that he had placed under Brodski's head – on which paper he now noticed, for the first time, a minute bloody smear – he poked it in under the wood, and striking a wax match, set light to it. As the wood flared up, he hacked at the hat with his pocket knife and threw the ragged strips into the blaze.

And all the while his heart was thumping and his hands a-tremble with the dread of discovery. The fragments of felt were far from inflammable, tending rather to fuse into cindery masses that smoked and smouldered than to burn away into actual ash. Moreover, to his dismay, they emitted a powerful resinous stench mixed with the odour of burning hair, so that he had to open the kitchen window (since he dared not unlock the front door) to disperse the reek. And still, as he fed the fire with small cut fragments, he strained his ears to catch, above the crackling of the wood, the sound of the dreaded footsteps, the knock on the door that should be as the summons of Fate.

The time, too, was speeding on. Twenty-one minutes to eight! In a few minutes more he must set out or he would miss the train. He dropped the dismembered hat-brim on the blazing wood and ran upstairs to open a window, since he must close that in the kitchen before he left. When he came back, the brim had already curled up into a black, clinkery mass that bubbled and hissed as the fat, pungent smoke rose from it sluggishly to the chimney.

Nineteen minutes to eight! It was time to start. He took up the poker and carefully beat the cinders into small particles, stirring them into the glowing embers of the wood and coal. There was nothing unusual in the appearance of the grate. It was his constant custom to burn letters and other discarded articles in the sitting-room fire. His housekeeper would notice nothing out of the common. Indeed, the cinders would probably be reduced to ashes before she returned. He had been careful to notice that there were no metallic fittings of any kind in the hat, which might have escaped burning.

Once more he picked up his bag, took a last look round, turned down the lamp and, unlocking the door, held it open for a few moments. Then he went out, locked the door, pocketed the key (of which his housekeeper had a duplicate) and set off at a brisk pace for the station.

He arrived in good time after all, and, having taken his ticket, strolled through onto the platform. The train was not yet signalled, but there seemed to be an unusual stir in the place. The passengers were collected in a group at one end of the platform, and were all looking in one direction down the line, and, even as he walked towards them, with a certain tremulous, nauseating curiosity, two men emerged from the darkness and ascended the slope to the platform, carrying a stretcher covered with a tarpaulin. The passengers parted to let the bearers pass, turning fascinated eyes upon the shape that showed faintly through the rough pall, and, when the stretcher had been borne into the lamp-room, they fixed their attention upon a porter who followed carrying a hand-bag and an umbrella.

Suddenly one of the passengers started forward with an exclamation. "Is that his umbrella?" he demanded.

"Yes, sir," answered the porter, stopping and holding it out for the speaker's inspection.

"My God!" ejaculated the passenger, then, turning sharply to a tall man who stood close by, he said excitedly, "That's Brodski's umbrella. I could swear to it. You remember Brodski?" The tall man nodded, and the passenger, turning once more to the porter, said, "I identify that umbrella. It belongs to a gentleman named Brodski. If you look in his hat you will see his name written in it. He always writes his name in his hat."

"We haven't found his hat yet," said the porter, "but here is the station-master coming up the line." He awaited the arrival of his superior and then announced, "This gentleman, sir, has identified the umbrella."

"Oh," said the station-master, "you recognize the umbrella, sir, do you? Then perhaps you would step into the lamp-room and see if you can identify the body."

"Is it – is he – very much injured?" the passenger asked tremulously.

"Well, yes," was the reply. "You see, the engine and six of the trucks went over him before they could stop the train. Took his head clean off, in fact."

"Shocking! Shocking!" gasped the passenger. "I think, if you don't mind – I'd – I'd rather not. You don't think it's necessary, Doctor, do you?"

249

"Yes, I do," replied the tall man. "Early identification may be of the first importance."

"Then I suppose I must," said the passenger.

Very reluctantly he allowed himself to be conducted by the station-master to the lamp-room, as the clang of the bell announced the approaching train. Silas Hickler followed and took his stand with the expectant crowd outside the closed door. In a few moments the passenger burst out, pale and awe-stricken, and rushed up to his tall friend. "It is!" he exclaimed breathlessly. "It's Brodski! Poor old Brodski! Horrible! Horrible! He was to have met me here and come on with me to Amsterdam."

"Had he any – merchandize about him?" the tall man asked, and Silas strained his ears to catch the reply.

"He had some stones, no doubt, but I don't know what. His clerk will know, of course. By the way, Doctor, could you watch the case for me? Just to be sure it was really an accident or – you know what. We were old friends, you know, fellow townsmen, too. We were both born in Warsaw. I'd like you to give an eye to the case."

"Very well," said the other. "I will satisfy myself that – there is nothing more than appears, and let you have a report. Will that do?"

"Thank you. It's excessively good of you, Doctor. Ah! Here comes the train. I hope it won't inconvenience you to stay and see to this matter."

"Not in the least," replied the Doctor. "We are not due at Warmington until to-morrow afternoon, and I expect we can find out all that is necessary to know before that."

Silas looked long and curiously at the tall, imposing man who was, as it were, taking his seat at the chessboard, to play against him for his life. A formidable antagonist he looked, with his keen, thoughtful face, so resolute and calm. As Silas stepped into his carriage he thought with deep discomfort of Brodski's hat, and hoped that he had made no other oversight.

250

Part II – The Mechanism of Detection
(Related by Christopher Jervis, M.D.)

The singular circumstances that attended the death of Mr. Oscar Brodski, the well-known diamond merchant of Hatton Garden, illustrated very forcibly the importance of one or two points in medico-legal practice which Thorndyke was accustomed to insist were not sufficiently appreciated. What those points were, I shall leave my friend and teacher to state at the proper place, and meanwhile, as the case is in the highest degree instructive, I shall record the incidents in the order of their occurrence.

The dusk of an October evening was closing in as Thorndyke and I, the sole occupants of a smoking compartment, found ourselves approaching the little station of Ludham, and, as the train slowed down, we peered out at the knot of country, people who were waiting on the platform. Suddenly Thorndyke exclaimed in a tone of surprise, "Why, that is surely Boscovitch!" And almost at the same moment a brisk, excitable little man darted at the door of our compartment and literally tumbled in.

"I hope I don't intrude on this learned conclave," he said, shaking hands genially and banging his Gladstone with impulsive violence into the rack, "but I saw your faces at the window, and naturally jumped at the chance of such pleasant companionship."

"You are very flattering," said Thorndyke, "so flattering that you leave us nothing to say. But what in the name of fortune are you doing at – what's the name of the place – Ludham?"

"My brother has a little place a mile or so from here, and I have been spending a couple of days with him," Mr. Boscovitch explained. "I shall change at Badsham Junction and catch the boat train for Amsterdam. But whither are you two bound? I see you have your mysterious little green box up on the hat-rack, so I infer that you are on some romantic quest, eh? Going to unravel some dark and intricate crime?"

"No," replied Thorndyke. "We are bound for Warmington on a quite prosaic errand. I am instructed to watch the proceedings at an inquest there to-morrow on behalf of the Griffin Life Insurance Office, and we are travelling down to-night as it is rather a cross-country journey."

"But why the box of magic?" asked Boscovitch, glancing up at the hat-rack.

"I never go away from home without it," answered Thorndyke. "One never knows what may turn up, the trouble of carrying it is small when set off against the comfort of having appliances at hand in an emergency."

251

Boscovitch continued to stare up at the little square case covered with Willesden canvas. Presently he remarked, "I often used to wonder what you had in it when you were down at Chelmsford in connection with that bank murder – what an amazing case that was, by the way, and didn't your methods of research astonish the police!" As he still looked up wistfully at the case, Thorndyke good-naturedly lifted it down and unlocked it. As a matter of fact he was rather proud of his "portable laboratory", and certainly it was a triumph of condensation, for, small as it was – only a foot square by four inches deep – it contained a fairly complete outfit for a preliminary investigation.

"Wonderful!" exclaimed Boscovitch, when the case lay open before him, displaying its rows of little re-agent bottles, tiny test-tubes, diminutive spirit-lamp, dwarf microscope, and assorted instruments on the same Lilliputian scale, "It's like a doll's house – everything looks as if it was seen through the wrong end of a telescope. But are these tiny things really efficient? That microscope now – ?"

"Perfectly efficient at low and moderate magnifications," said Thorndyke. "It looks like a toy, but it isn't one, the lenses are the best that can be had. Of course a full-sized instrument would be infinitely more convenient – but I shouldn't have it with me, and should have to make shift with a pocket-lens. And so with the rest of the under-sized appliances, they are the alternative to no appliances."

Boscovitch pored over the case and its contents, fingering the instruments delicately and asking questions innumerable about their uses – indeed, his curiosity was but half-appeased when, half-an-hour later, the train began to slow down.

"By Jove!" he exclaimed, starting up and seizing his bag, "here we are at the junction already. You change here too, don't you?"

"Yes," replied Thorndyke. "We take the branch train on to Warmington."

As we stepped out onto the platform, we became aware that something unusual was happening or had happened. All the passengers and most of the porters and supernumeraries were gathered at one end of the station, and all were looking intently into the darkness down the line.

"Anything wrong?" asked Mr. Boscovitch, addressing the station-inspector.

"Yes, sir," the official replied, "a man has been run over by the goods train about a mile down the line. The station-master has gone down with a stretcher to bring him in, and I expect that is his lantern that you see coming this way."

As we stood watching the dancing light grow momentarily brighter, flashing fitful reflections from the burnished rails, a man came out of the booking-office and joined the group of onlookers. He attracted my attention, as I afterwards remembered, for two reasons: In the first place his round, jolly face was excessively pale and bore a strained and wild expression, and, in the second, though he stared into the darkness with eager curiosity he asked no questions.

The swinging lantern continued to approach, and then suddenly two men came into sight bearing a stretcher covered with a tarpaulin, through which the shape of a human figure was dimly discernible. They ascended the slope to the platform, and proceeded with their burden to the lamp-room, when the inquisitive gaze of the passengers was transferred to a porter who followed carrying a handbag and umbrella and to the station-master who brought up the rear with his lantern.

As the porter passed, Mr. Boscovitch started forward with sudden excitement.

"Is that his umbrella?" he asked.

"Yes, sir," answered the porter, stopping and holding it out for the speaker's inspection.

"My God!" ejaculated Boscovitch, then, turning sharply to Thorndyke, he exclaimed, "That's Brodski's umbrella. I could swear to it. You remember Brodski?"

Thorndyke nodded, and Boscovitch, turning once more to the porter, said, "I identify that umbrella. It belongs to a gentleman named Brodski. If you look in his hat, you will see his name written in it. He always writes his name in his hat."

"We haven't found his hat yet," said the porter, "but here is the station-master." He turned to his superior and announced, "This gentleman, sir, has identified the umbrella."

"Oh," said the station-master, "you recognize the umbrella, sir, do you? Then perhaps you would step into the lamp-room and see if you can identify the body."

Mr. Boscovitch recoiled with a look of alarm. "Is it? Is he – very much injured?" he asked nervously.

"Well, yes," was the reply. "You see, the engine and six of the trucks went over him before they could stop the train. Took his head clean off, in fact."

"Shocking! Shocking!" gasped Boscovitch. "I think? If you don't mind – I'd – I'd rather not. You don't think it necessary, Doctor, do you?"

"Yes, I do," replied Thorndyke. "Early identification may be of the first importance."

"Then I suppose I must," said Boscovitch, and, with extreme reluctance, he followed the station-master to the lamp-room, as the loud ringing of the bell announced the approach of the boat train. His inspection must have been of the briefest, for, in a few moments, he burst out, pale and awe-stricken, and rushed up to Thorndyke.

"It is!" he exclaimed breathlessly. "It's Brodski! Poor old Brodski! Horrible! Horrible! He was to have met me here and come on with me to Amsterdam."

"Had he any – merchandize about him?" Thorndyke asked, and, as he spoke, the stranger whom I had previously noticed edged up closer as if to catch the reply.

"He had some stones, no doubt," answered Boscovitch, "but I don't know what they were. His clerk will know, of course. By the way, Doctor, could you watch the case for me? Just to be sure it was really an accident or – you know what. We were old friends, you know, fellow townsmen, too. We were both born in Warsaw. I'd like you to give an eye to the case."

"Very well," said Thorndyke. "I will satisfy myself that there is nothing more than appears, and let you have a report. Will that do?"

"Thank you," said Boscovitch. "It's excessively good of you, Doctor. Ah, here comes the train. I hope it won't inconvenience you to stay and see to the matter."

"Not in the least," replied Thorndyke. "We are not due at Warmington until to-morrow afternoon, and I expect we can find out all that is necessary to know and still keep our appointment."

As Thorndyke spoke, the stranger, who had kept close to us with the evident purpose of hearing what was said, bestowed on him a very curious and attentive look, and it was only when the train had actually come to rest by the platform that he hurried away to find a compartment.

No sooner had the train left the station than Thorndyke sought out the station-master and informed him of the instructions that he had received from Boscovitch. "Of course," he added, in conclusion, "we must not move in the matter until the police arrive. I suppose they have been informed?"

"Yes," replied the station-master, "I sent a message at once to the Chief Constable, and I expect him or an inspector at any moment. In fact, I think I will slip out to the approach and see if he is coming." He evidently wished to have a word in private with the police officer before committing himself to any statement.

As the official departed, Thorndyke and I began to pace the now empty platform, and my friend, as was his wont, when entering on a new inquiry, meditatively reviewed the features of the problem.

"In a case of this kind," he remarked, "we have to decide on one of three possible explanations: Accident, suicide or homicide, and our decision will be determined by inferences from three sets of facts. First, the general facts of the case; second, the special data obtained by examination of the body; and, third, the special data obtained by examining the spot on which the body was found. Now the only general facts at present in our possession are that the deceased was a diamond merchant making a journey for a specific purpose and probably having on his person property of small bulk and great value. These facts are somewhat against the hypothesis of suicide and somewhat favourable to that of homicide. Facts relevant to the question of accident would be the existence or otherwise of a level crossing, a road or path leading to the line, an enclosing fence with or without a gate, and any other facts rendering probable or otherwise the accidental presence of the deceased at the spot where the body was found. As we do not possess these facts, it is desirable that we extend our knowledge."

"Why not put a few discreet questions to the porter who brought in the bag and umbrella?" I suggested. "He is at this moment in earnest conversation with the ticket collector and would, no doubt, be glad of a new listener."

"An excellent suggestion, Jervis," answered Thorndyke. "Let us see what he has to tell us." We approached the porter and found him, as I had anticipated, bursting to unburden himself of the tragic story.

"The way the thing happened, sir, was this," he said, in answer to Thorndyke's question: "There's a sharpish bend in the road just at that place, and the goods train was just rounding the curve when the driver suddenly caught sight of something lying across the rails. As the engine turned, the head-lights shone on it and then he saw it was a man. He shut off steam at once, blew his whistle, and put the brakes down hard, but, as you know, sir, a goods train takes some stopping, before they could bring her up, the engine and half-a-dozen trucks had gone over the poor beggar."

"Could the driver see how the man was lying?" Thorndyke asked.

"Yes, he could see him quite plain, because the headlights were full on him. He was lying on his face with his neck over the near rail on the downside. His head was in the four-foot and his body by the side of the track. It looked as if he had laid himself out a-purpose."

"Is there a level crossing thereabouts?" asked Thorndyke.

"No, sir. No crossing, no road, no path, no nothing," said the porter, ruthlessly sacrificing grammar to emphasis. "He must have come across the fields and climbed over the fence to get onto the permanent way. Deliberate suicide is what it looks like."

"How did you learn all this?" Thorndyke inquired.

"Why, the driver, you see, sir, when him and his mate had lifted the body off the track, went on to the next signal-box and sent in his report by telegram. The station-master told me all about it as we walked down the line."

Thorndyke thanked the man for his information, and, as we strolled back towards the lamp-room, discussed the bearing of these new facts.

"Our friend is unquestionably right in one respect," he said, "this was not an accident. The man might, if he were near-sighted, deaf, or stupid, have climbed over the fence and got knocked down by the train. But his position, lying across the rails, can only be explained by one of two hypotheses: Either it was, as the porter says, deliberate suicide, or else the man was already dead or insensible. We must leave it at that until we have seen the body, that is, if the police will allow us to see it. But here comes the station-master and an officer with him. Let us hear what they have to say."

The two officials had evidently made up their minds to decline any outside assistance. The divisional surgeon would make the necessary examination, and information could be obtained through the usual channels. The production of Thorndyke's card, however, somewhat altered the situation. The police inspector hummed and hawed irresolutely, with the card in his hand, but finally agreed to allow us to view the body, and we entered the lamp-room together, the station-master leading the way to turn up the gas.

The stretcher stood on the floor by one wall, its grim burden still hidden by the tarpaulin, and the hand-bag and umbrella lay on a large box, together with the battered frame of a pair of spectacles from which the glasses had fallen out.

"Were these spectacles found by the body?" Thorndyke inquired.

"Yes," replied the station-master. "They were close to the head and the glass was scattered about on the ballast."

Thorndyke made a note in his pocket-book, and then, as the inspector removed the tarpaulin, he glanced down on the corpse, lying limply on the stretcher and looking grotesquely horrible with its displaced head and distorted limbs. For fully a minute he remained silently stooping over the uncanny object, on which the inspector was now throwing the light of a large lantern. Then he stood up and said quietly to me, "I think we can eliminate two out of the three hypotheses."

The inspector looked at him quickly, and was about to ask a question, when his attention was diverted by the travelling-case which Thorndyke had laid on a shelf and now opened to abstract a couple of pairs of dissecting forceps.

"We've no authority to make a *post-mortem*, you know," said the inspector.

"No, of course not," said Thorndyke. "I am merely going to look into the mouth." With one pair of forceps he turned back the lip and, having scrutinized its inner surface, closely examined the teeth.

"May I trouble you for your lens, Jervis?" he said, and, as I handed him my doublet ready opened, the inspector brought the lantern close to the dead face and leaned forward eagerly. In his usual systematic fashion, Thorndyke slowly passed the lens along the whole range of sharp, uneven teeth, and then, bringing it back to the centre, examined with more minuteness the upper incisors. At length, very delicately, he picked out with his forceps some minute object from between two of the upper front teeth and held it in the focus of the lens. Anticipating his next move, I took a labelled microscope-slide from the case and handed it to him, together with a dissecting needle, and, as he transferred the object to the slide and spread it out with the needle, I set up the little microscope on the shelf.

"A drop of Farrant and a cover-glass, please, Jervis," said Thorndyke.

I handed him the bottle, and, when he had let a drop of the mounting fluid fall gently on the object and put on the cover-slip, he placed the slide on the stage of the microscope and examined it attentively.

Happening to glance at the inspector, I observed on his countenance a faint grin, which he politely strove to suppress when he caught my eye.

"I was thinking, sir," he said apologetically, "that it's a bit off the track to be finding out what he had for dinner. He didn't die of unwholesome feeding."

Thorndyke looked up with a smile. "It doesn't do, Inspector, to assume that anything is off the track in an inquiry of this kind. Every fact must have some significance, you know."

"I don't see any significance in the diet of a man who has had his head cut off," the inspector rejoined defiantly.

"Don't you?" said Thorndyke. "Is there no interest attaching to the last meal of a man who has met a violent death? These crumbs, for instance, that are scattered over the dead man's waistcoat. Can we learn nothing from them?"

"I don't see what you can learn," was the dogged rejoinder.

Thorndyke picked off the crumbs, one by one, with his forceps, and having deposited them on a slide, inspected them, first with the lens and then through the microscope.

"I learn," said he, "that shortly before his death, the deceased partook of some kind of whole-meal biscuits, apparently composed partly of oatmeal."

"I call that nothing," said the inspector. "The question that we have got to settle is not what refreshments had the deceased been taking, but what was the cause of his death: Did he commit suicide? Was he killed by accident? Or was there any foul play?"

"I beg your pardon," said Thorndyke. "The questions that remain to be settled are, who killed the deceased, and with what motive? The others are already answered as far as I am, concerned."

The inspector stared in sheer amazement not unmixed with incredulity.

"You haven't been long coming to a conclusion, sir," he said.

"No, it was a pretty obvious case of murder," said Thorndyke. "As to the motive, the deceased was a diamond merchant and is believed to have had a quantity of stones about his person. I should suggest that you search the body."

The inspector gave vent to an exclamation of disgust. "I see," he said. "It was just a guess on your part. The dead man was a diamond merchant and had valuable property about him. Therefore he was murdered." He drew himself up, and, regarding Thorndyke with stern reproach, added, "But you must understand, sir, that this is a judicial inquiry, not a prize competition in a penny paper. And, as to searching the body – why, that is what I principally came for." He ostentatiously turned his back on us and proceeded systematically to turn out the dead man's pockets, laying the articles, as he removed them, on the box by the side of the hand-bag and umbrella.

While he was thus occupied, Thorndyke looked over the body generally, paying special attention to the soles of the boots, which, to the inspector's undissembled amusement, he very thoroughly examined with the lens.

"I should have thought, sir, that his feet were large enough to be seen with the naked eye," was his comment, "but perhaps," he added, with a sly glance at the station-master, "you're a little near-sighted."

Thorndyke chuckled good-humouredly, and, while the officer continued his search, he looked over the articles that had already been laid on the box. The purse and pocket-book he naturally left for the inspector to open, but the reading-glasses, pocket-knife and card-case, and other small pocket articles were subjected to a searching scrutiny. The inspector watched him out of the corner of his eye with furtive amusement, saw him hold up the glasses to the light to estimate their refractive power, peer into the tobacco pouch, open the cigarette book and examine the watermark of the paper, and even inspect the contents of the silver match-box.

"What might you have expected to find in his tobacco pouch?" the officer asked, laying down a bunch of keys from the dead man's pocket.

"Tobacco," Thorndyke replied stolidly, "but I did not expect to find fine-cut Latakia. I don't remember ever having seen pure Latakia smoked in cigarettes."

258

"You do take an interest in things, sir," said the inspector, with a side glance at the stolid station-master.

"I do," Thorndyke agreed, "and I note that there are no diamonds among this collection."

"No, and we don't know that he had any about him, but there's a gold watch and chain, a diamond scarf-pin, and a purse containing" – he opened it and tipped out its contents into his hand – "twelve pounds in gold. That doesn't look much like robbery, does it? What do you say to the murder theory now?"

"My opinion is unchanged," said Thorndyke, "and I should like to examine the spot where the body was found. Has the engine been inspected?" he added, addressing the station-master.

"I telegraphed to Bradfield to have it examined," the official answered. "The report has probably come in by now. I'd better see before we start down the line."

We emerged from the lamp-room and, at the door, found the station-inspector waiting with a telegram. He handed it to the station-master, who read it aloud.

"The engine has been carefully examined by me. I find small smears of blood on near leading wheel and smaller one on next wheel following. No other marks." He glanced questioningly at Thorndyke, who nodded and remarked, "It will be interesting to see if the line tells the same tale."

The station-master looked puzzled and was apparently about to ask for an explanation, but the inspector, who had carefully pocketed the dead man's property, was impatient to start and, accordingly, when Thorndyke had repacked his case and had, at his own request, been furnished with a lantern, we set off down the permanent way, Thorndyke carrying the light and I the indispensable green case.

"I am a little in the dark about this affair," I said, when we had allowed the two officials to draw ahead out of earshot. "You came to a conclusion remarkably quickly. What was it that so immediately determined the opinion of murder as against suicide?"

"It was a small matter but very conclusive," replied Thorndyke. "You noticed a small scalp-wound above the left temple? It was a glancing wound, and might easily have been made by the engine. But the wound had bled, and it had bled for an appreciable time. There were two streams of blood from it, and in both the blood was firmly clotted and partially dried. But the man had been decapitated, and this wound, if inflicted by the engine, must have been made after the decapitation, since it was on the side most distant from the engine as it approached. Now, a decapitated head does not bleed. Therefore, this wound was inflicted *before* the decapitation.

259

"But not only had the wound bled. The blood had trickled down in two streams at right angles to one another. First, in the order of time as shown by the appearance of the stream, it had trickled down the side of the face and dropped on the collar. The second stream ran from the wound to the back of the head. Now, you know, Jervis, there are no exceptions to the law of gravity. If the blood ran down the face towards the chin, the face must have been upright at the time, and if the blood trickled from the front to the back of the head, the head must have been horizontal and face upwards. But the man when he was seen by the engine-driver, was lying face downwards. The only possible inference is that when the wound was inflicted, the man was in the upright position – standing or sitting, and that subsequently, and while he was still alive, he lay on his back for a sufficiently long time for the blood to have trickled to the back of his head."

"I see. I was a duffer not to have reasoned this out for myself," I remarked contritely.

"Quick observation and rapid inference come by practice," replied Thorndyke. "What did you notice about the face?"

"I thought there was a strong suggestion of asphyxia."

"Undoubtedly," said Thorndyke. "It was the face of a suffocated man. You must have noticed, too, that the tongue was very distinctly swollen and that on the inside of the upper lip were deep indentations made by the teeth, as well as one or two slight wounds, obviously caused by heavy pressure on the mouth. And now observe how completely these facts and inferences agree with those from the scalp wound. If we knew that the deceased had received a blow on the head, had struggled with his assailant, and been finally borne down and suffocated, we should look for precisely those signs which we have found."

"By the way, what was it that you found wedged between the teeth? I did not get a chance to look through the microscope."

"Ah!" said Thorndyke, "there we not only get confirmation, but we carry our inferences a stage further. The object was a little tuft of some textile fabric. Under the microscope, I found it to consist of several different fibres, differently dyed. The bulk of it consisted of wool fibres dyed crimson, but there were also cotton fibres dyed blue and a few which looked like jute, dyed yellow. It was obviously a parti-coloured fabric and might have been part of a woman's dress, though the presence of the jute is much more suggestive of a curtain or rug of inferior quality."

"And its importance?"

"Is that, if it is not part of an article of clothing, then it must have come from an article of furniture, and furniture suggests a habitation."

"That doesn't seem very conclusive," I objected.

260

"It is not, but it is valuable corroboration."

"Of what?"

"Of the suggestion offered by the soles of the dead man's boots. I examined them most minutely and could find no trace of sand, gravel, or earth, in spite of the fact that he must have crossed fields and rough land to reach the place where he was found. What I did find was fine tobacco ash, a charred mark as if a cigar or cigarette had been trodden on, several crumbs of biscuit, and, on a projecting brad, some coloured fibres, apparently from a carpet. The manifest suggestion is that the man was killed in a house with a carpeted floor, and carried from thence to the railway."

I was silent for some moments. Well as I knew Thorndyke, I was completely taken by surprise, a sensation, indeed, that I experienced anew every time that I accompanied him on one of his investigations. His marvellous power of co-ordinating apparently insignificant facts, of arranging them into an ordered sequence, and making them tell a coherent story, was a phenomenon that I never got used to. Every exhibition of it astonished me afresh.

"If your inferences are correct," I said, "the problem is practically solved. There must be abundant traces inside the house. The only question is, which house is it?"

"Quite so," replied Thorndyke, "that is the question, and a very difficult question it is. A glance at that interior would doubtless clear up the whole mystery. But how are we to get that glance? We cannot enter houses speculatively to see if they present traces of a murder. At present, our clue breaks off abruptly. The other end of it is in some unknown house, and, if we cannot join up the two ends, our problem remains unsolved. For the question is, you remember, Who killed Oscar Brodski?"

"Then what do you propose to do?" I asked.

"The next stage of the inquiry is to connect some particular house with this crime. To that end, I can only gather up all available facts and consider each in all its possible bearings. If I cannot establish any such connection, then the inquiry will have failed and we shall have to make a fresh start – say, at Amsterdam, if it turns out that Brodski really had diamonds on his person, as I have no doubt he had."

Here our conversation was interrupted by our arrival at the spot where the body had been found. The station-master had halted, and he and the inspector were now examining the near rail by the light of their lanterns.

"There's remarkably little blood about," said the former. "I've seen a good many accidents of this kind and there has always been a lot of blood, both on the engine and on the road. It's very curious."

Thorndyke glanced at the rail with but slight attention. That question had ceased to interest him. But the light of his lantern flashed onto the ground at the side of the track – a loose, gravelly soil mixed with fragments of chalk – and from thence to the soles of the inspector's boots, which were displayed as he knelt by the rail.

"You observe, Jervis?" he said in a low voice, and I nodded. The inspector's boot-soles were covered with adherent particles of gravel and conspicuously marked by the chalk on which he had trodden.

"You haven't found the hat, I suppose?" Thorndyke asked, stooping to pick up a short piece of string that lay on the ground at the side of the track.

"No," replied the inspector, "but it can't be far off. You seem to have found another clue, sir," he added, with a grin, glancing at the piece of string.

"Who knows," said Thorndyke. "A short end of white twine with a green strand in it. It may tell us something later. At any rate we'll keep it," and, taking from his pocket a small tin box containing, among other things, a number of seed envelopes, he slipped the string into one of the latter and scribbled a note in pencil on the outside. The inspector watched his proceedings with an indulgent smile, and then returned to his examination of the track, in which Thorndyke now joined.

"I suppose the poor chap was near-sighted," the officer remarked, indicating the remains of the shattered spectacles. "That might account for his having strayed onto the line."

"Possibly," said Thorndyke. He had already noticed the fragments scattered over a sleeper and the adjacent ballast, and now once more produced his "collecting-box," from which he took another seed envelope. "Would you hand me a pair of forceps, Jervis?" he said. "And perhaps you wouldn't mind taking a pair yourself and helping me to gather up these fragments."

As I complied, the inspector looked up curiously.

"There isn't any doubt that these spectacles belonged to the deceased, is there?" he asked. "He certainly wore spectacles, for I saw the mark on his nose."

"Still, there is no harm in verifying the fact," said Thorndyke, and he added to me in a lower tone, "Pick up every particle you can find, Jervis. It may be most important."

"I don't quite see how," I said, groping amongst the shingle by the light of the lantern in search of the tiny splinters of glass.

"Don't you?" returned Thorndyke. "Well, look at these fragments. Some of them are a fair size, but many of these on the sleeper are mere grains. And consider their number. Obviously, the condition of the glass does not agree with the circumstances in which we find it. These are thick concave spectacle-lenses broken into a great number of minute fragments. Now how were they broken? Not merely by falling, evidently. Such a lens, when it is dropped, breaks into a small number of large pieces. Nor were they broken by the wheel passing over them, for they would then have been reduced to fine powder, and that powder would have been visible on the rail, which it is not. The spectacle-frames, you may remember, presented the same incongruity – they were battered and damaged more than they would have been by falling, but not nearly so much as they would have been if the wheel had passed over them."

"What do you suggest, then?" I asked.

"The appearances suggest that the spectacles had been trodden on. But, if the body was carried here, the probability is that the spectacles were carried here too, and that they were then already broken, for it is more likely that they were trodden on during the struggle than that the murderer trod on them after bringing them here. Hence the importance of picking up every fragment."

"But why?" I inquired, rather foolishly, I must admit.

263

"Because, if, when we have picked up every fragment that we can find, there still remains missing a larger portion of the lenses than we could reasonably expect, that would tend to support our hypothesis and we might find the missing remainder elsewhere. If, on the other hand, we find as much of the lenses as we could expect to find, we must conclude that they were broken on this spot."

While we were conducting our search, the two officials were circling around with their lanterns in quest of the missing hat, and, when we had at length picked up the last fragment, and a careful search, even aided by a lens, failed to reveal any other, we could see their lanterns moving, like will-o'-the-wisps, some distance down the line.

"We may as well see what we have got before our friends come back," said Thorndyke, glancing at the twinkling lights. "Lay the case down on the grass by the fence. It will serve for a table."

I did so, and Thorndyke, taking a letter from his pocket, opened it, spread it out flat on the case, securing it with a couple of heavy stones, although the night was quite calm. Then he tipped the contents of the seed envelope out on the paper, and carefully spreading out the pieces of glass, looked at them for some moments in silence. And, as he looked, there stole over his face a very curious expression, with sudden eagerness he began picking out the large fragments and laying them on two visiting-cards which he had taken from his card-case. Rapidly and with wonderful deftness he fitted the pieces together, and, as the reconstituted lenses began gradually to take shape on their cards I looked on with growing excitement, for something in my colleague's manner told me that we were on the verge of a discovery.

At length the two ovals of glass lay on their respective cards, complete save for one or two small gaps, and the little heap that remained consisted of fragments so minute as to render further reconstruction impossible. Then Thorndyke leaned back and laughed softly.

"This is certainly an unlooked-for result," said he.

"What is?" I asked.

"Don't you see, my dear fellow? There's too much glass. We have almost completely built up the broken lenses, and the fragments that are left over are considerably more than are required to fill up the gaps."

I looked at the little heap of small fragments and saw at once that it was as he had said. There was a surplus of small pieces.

"This is very extraordinary," I said. "What do you think can be the explanation?"

"The fragments will probably tell us," he replied, "if we ask them intelligently."

264

He lifted the paper and the two cards carefully onto the ground, and, opening the case, took out the little microscope, to which he fitted the lowest-power objective and eye-piece – having a combined magnification of only ten diameters. Then he transferred the minute fragments of glass to a slide, and, having arranged the lantern as a microscope-lamp, commenced his examination.

"Ha!" he exclaimed presently. "The plot thickens. There is too much glass and yet too little – that is to say, there are only one or two fragments here that belong to the spectacles, not nearly enough to complete the building up of the lenses. The remainder consists of a soft, uneven, moulded glass, easily distinguished from the clear, hard optical glass. These foreign fragments are all curved, as if they had formed part of a cylinder, and are, I should say, portions of a wine-glass or tumbler." He moved the slide once or twice, and then continued, "We are in luck, Jervis. Here is a fragment with two little diverging lines etched on it, evidently the points of an eight-rayed star – and here is another with three points – the ends of three rays. This enables us to reconstruct the vessel perfectly. It was a clear, thin glass – probably a tumbler – decorated with scattered stars, I dare say you know the pattern. Sometimes there is an ornamented band in addition, but generally the stars form the only decoration. Have a look at the specimen."

I had just applied my eye to the microscope when the station-master and the inspector came up. Our appearance, seated on the ground with the microscope between us, was too much for the police officer's gravity, and he laughed long and joyously.

"You must excuse me, gentlemen," he said apologetically, "but really, you know, to an old hand, like myself, it does look a little – well – you understand – I dare say a microscope is a very interesting and amusing thing, but it doesn't get you much forwarder in a case like this, does it?"

"Perhaps not," replied Thorndyke. "By the way, where did you find the hat, after all?"

"We haven't found it," the inspector replied.

"Then we must help you to continue the search," said Thorndyke. "If you will wait a few moments, we will come with you." He poured a few drops of xylol balsam on the cards to fix the reconstituted lenses to their supports and then, packing them and the microscope in the case, announced that he was ready to start.

"Is there any village or hamlet near?" he asked the station-master.

"None nearer than Corfield. That is about half-a-mile from here."

"And where is the nearest road?"

"There is a half-made road that runs past a house about three hundred yards from here. It belonged to a building estate that was never built. There is a footpath from it to the station."

"Are there any other houses near?"

"No. That is the only house for half-a-mile round, and there is no other road near here."

"Then the probability is that Brodski approached the railway from that direction, as he was found on that side of the permanent way."

The inspector agreeing with this view, we all set off slowly towards the house, piloted by the station-master and searching the ground as we went. The waste land over which we passed was covered with patches of docks and nettles, through each of which the inspector kicked his way, searching with feet and lantern for the missing hat. A walk of three hundred yards brought us to a low wall enclosing a garden, beyond which we could see a small house, and here we halted while the inspector waded into a large bed of nettles beside the wall and kicked vigorously. Suddenly there came a clinking sound mingled with objurgations, and the inspector hopped out holding one foot and soliloquizing profanely.

"I wonder what sort of a fool put a thing like that into a bed of nettles!" he exclaimed, stroking the injured foot. Thorndyke picked the object up and held it in the light of the lantern, displaying a piece of three-quarter inch rolled iron bar about a foot long. "It doesn't seem to have been there very long," he observed, examining it closely. "There is hardly any rust on it."

"It has been there long enough for me," growled the inspector, "and I'd like to bang it on the head of the blighter that put it there."

Callously indifferent to the inspector's sufferings, Thorndyke continued calmly to examine the bar. At length, resting his lantern on the wall, he produced his pocket-lens, with which he resumed his investigation, a proceeding that so exasperated the inspector that that afflicted official limped off in dudgeon, followed by the station-master, and we heard him, presently, rapping at the front door of the house.

"Give me a slide, Jervis, with a drop of Farrant on it," said Thorndyke. "There are some fibres sticking to this bar."

I prepared the slide, and, having handed it to him together with a cover-glass, a pair of forceps and a needle, set up the microscope on the wall.

"I'm sorry for the inspector," Thorndyke remarked, with his eye applied to the little instrument, "but that was a lucky kick for us. Just take a look at the specimen."

I did so, and, having moved the slide about until I had seen the whole of the object, I gave my opinion. "Red wool fibres, blue cotton fibres, and some yellow vegetable fibres that look like jute."

"Yes," said Thorndyke, "the same combination of fibres as that which we found on the dead man's teeth, and probably from the same source. This bar has probably been wiped on that very curtain or rug with which poor Brodski was stifled. We will place it on the wall for future reference, and meanwhile, by hook or by crook, we must get into that house. This is much too plain a hint to be disregarded."

Hastily repacking the case, we hurried to the front of the house, where we found the two officials looking rather vaguely up the unmade road.

"There's a light in the house," said the inspector, "but there's no one at home. I have knocked a dozen times and got no answer. And I don't see what we are hanging about here for at all. The hat is probably close to where the body was found, and we shall find it in the morning."

Thorndyke made no reply, but, entering the garden, stepped up the path, and having knocked gently at the door, stooped and listened attentively at the key-hole.

"I tell you there's no one in the house, sir," said the inspector irritably, and, as Thorndyke continued to listen, he walked away, muttering angrily. As soon as he was gone, Thorndyke flashed his lantern over the door, the threshold, the path and the small flower-beds, and, from one of the latter, I presently saw him stoop and pick something up.

"Here is a highly instructive object, Jervis," he said, coming out to the gate, and displaying a cigarette of which only half-an-inch had been smoked.

"How instructive?" I asked. "What do you learn from it?"

"Many things," he replied. "It has been lit and thrown away unsmoked, that indicates a sudden change of purpose. It was thrown away at the entrance to the house, almost certainly by someone entering it. That person was probably a stranger, or he would have taken it in with him. But he had not expected to enter the house, or he would not have lit it. These are the general suggestions, now as to the particular ones. The paper of the cigarette is of the kind known as the 'Zig-Zag' brand, the very conspicuous water-mark is quite easy to see. Now Brodski's cigarette book was a 'Zig-Zag' book – so called from the way in which the papers pull out. But let us see what the tobacco is like." With a pin from his coat, he hooked out from the unburned end a wisp of dark, dirty brown tobacco, which he held out for my inspection.

"Fine-cut Latakia," I pronounced, without hesitation.

"Very well," said Thorndyke. "Here is a cigarette made of an unusual tobacco similar to that in Brodski's pouch and wrapped in an unusual paper similar to those in Brodski's cigarette book. With due regard to the fourth rule of the syllogism, I suggest that this cigarette was made by Oscar Brodski. But, nevertheless, we will look for corroborative detail."

"What is that?" I asked.

"You may have noticed that Brodski's match-box contained round wooden vestas – which are also rather unusual. As he must have lighted the cigarette within a few steps of the gate, we ought to be able to find the match with which he lighted it. Let us try up the road in the direction from which he would probably have approached."

We walked very slowly up the road, searching the ground with the lantern, and we had hardly gone a dozen paces when I espied a match lying on the rough path and eagerly picked it up. It was a round wooden vesta.

Thorndyke examined it with interest and having deposited it, with the cigarette, in his "collecting-box", turned to retrace his steps. "There is now, Jervis, no reasonable doubt that Brodski was murdered in that house. We have succeeded in connecting that house with the crime, and now we have got to force an entrance and join up the other clues." We walked quickly back to the rear of the premises, where we found the inspector conversing disconsolately with the station-master.

"I think, sir," said the former, "we had better go back now. In fact, I don't see what we came here for, but – here! I say, sir, you mustn't do that!" For Thorndyke, without a word of warning, had sprung up lightly and thrown one of his long legs over the wall.

"I can't allow you to enter private premises, sir," continued the inspector, but Thorndyke quietly dropped down on the inside and turned to face the officer over the wall.

"Now, listen to me, Inspector," said he. "I have good reasons for believing that the dead man, Brodski, has been in this house. In fact, I am prepared to swear an information to that effect. But time is precious, we must follow the scent while it is hot. And I am not proposing to break into the house off-hand. I merely wish to examine the dust-bin."

"The dust-bin!" gasped the inspector. "Well, you really are a most extraordinary gentleman! What do you expect to find in the dust-bin?"

"I am looking for a broken tumbler or wine-glass. It is a thin glass vessel decorated with a pattern of small, eight-pointed stars. It may be in the dust-bin or it may be inside the house."

The inspector hesitated, but Thorndyke's confident manner had evidently impressed him.

"We can soon see what is in the dust-bin," he said, "though what in creation a broken tumbler has to do with the case is more than I can understand. However, here goes." He sprang up onto the wall, and, as he dropped down into the garden, the station-master and I followed.

Thorndyke lingered a few moments by the gate examining the ground, while the two officials hurried up the path. Finding nothing of interest, however, he walked towards the house, looking keenly about him as he went, but we were hardly half-way up the path when we heard the voice of the inspector calling excitedly.

"Here you are, sir, this way," he sang out, and, as we hurried forward, we suddenly came on the two officials standing over a small rubbish-heap and looking the picture of astonishment. The glare of their lanterns illuminated the heap, and showed us the scattered fragments of a thin glass, star-pattern tumbler.

"I can't imagine how you guessed it was here, sir," said the inspector, with a new-born respect in his tone, "nor what you're going to do with it now you have found it."

"It is merely another link in the chain of evidence," said Thorndyke, taking a pair of forceps from the case and stooping over the heap. "Perhaps we shall find something else." He picked up several small fragments of glass, looked at them closely and dropped them again. Suddenly his eye caught a small splinter at the base of the heap. Seizing it with the forceps, he held it close to his eye in the strong lamplight, and, taking out his lens, examined it with minute attention. "Yes," he said at length, "this is what I was looking for. Let me have those two cards, Jervis."

I produced the two visiting-cards with the reconstructed lenses stuck to them, and, laying them on the lid of the case, threw the light of the lantern on them. Thorndyke looked at them intently for some time, and from them to the fragment that he held. Then, turning to the inspector, he said, "You saw me pick up this splinter of glass?"

"Yes, sir," replied the officer.

"And you saw where we found these spectacle-glasses and know whose they were?"

"Yes, sir. They are the dead man's spectacles, and you found them where the body had been."

"Very well," said Thorndyke, "now observe." And, as the two officials craned forward with parted lips, he laid the little splinter in a gap in one of the lenses and then gave it a gentle push forward, when it occupied the gap perfectly, joining edge to edge with the adjacent fragments and rendering that portion of the lens complete.

"My God!" exclaimed the inspector. "How on earth did you know?"

"I must explain that later," said Thorndyke. "Meanwhile, we had better have a look inside the house. I expect to find there a cigarette – or possibly a cigar – which has been trodden on, some whole-meal biscuits, possibly a wooden vesta, and perhaps even the missing hat."

At the mention of the hat, the inspector stepped eagerly to the back door, but, finding it bolted, he tried the window. This also was securely fastened and, on Thorndyke's advice, we went round to the front door.

"This door is locked too," said the inspector. "I'm afraid we shall have to break in. It's a nuisance, though."

"Have a look at the window," suggested Thorndyke.

The officer did so, struggling vainly to undo the patent catch with his pocket-knife.

"It's no go," he said, coming back to the door. "We shall have to – ?" He broke off with an astonished stare, for the door stood open and Thorndyke was putting something in his pocket.

"Your friend doesn't waste much time – even in picking a lock," he remarked to me, as we followed Thorndyke into the house, but his reflections were soon merged in a new surprise. Thorndyke had preceded us into a small sitting-room dimly lighted by a hanging lamp turned down low.

As we entered he turned up the light and glanced about the room. A whisky bottle was on the table, with a siphon, a tumbler, and a biscuit-box. Pointing to the latter, Thorndyke said to the inspector, "See what is in that box."

The inspector raised the lid and peeped in. The station-master peered over his shoulder, and then both stared at Thorndyke.

"How in the name of goodness did you know that there were whole-meal biscuits in the house, sir?" exclaimed the station-master.

"You'd be disappointed if I told you," replied Thorndyke. "But look at this." He pointed to the hearth, where lay a flattened, half-smoked cigarette and a round wooden vesta. The inspector gazed at these objects in silent wonder, while, as to the station-master, he continued to stare at Thorndyke with what I can only describe as superstitious awe.

"You have the dead man's property with you, I believe?" said my colleague.

"Yes," replied the inspector. "I put the things in my pocket for safety."

"Then," said Thorndyke, picking up the flattened cigarette, "let us have a look at his tobacco-pouch."

As the officer produced and opened the pouch, Thorndyke neatly cut open the cigarette with his sharp pocket-knife. "Now," said he, "what kind of tobacco is in the pouch?"

The inspector took out a pinch, looked at it and smelt it distastefully. "It's one of those stinking tobaccos," he said, "that they put in mixtures – Latakia, I think."

"And what is this?" asked Thorndyke, pointing to the open cigarette.

270

"Same stuff, undoubtedly," replied the inspector.

"And now let us see his cigarette papers," said Thorndyke.

The little book, or rather packet – for it consisted of separated papers – was produced from the officer's pocket and a sample paper abstracted. Thorndyke laid the half-burnt paper beside it, and the inspector, having examined the two, held them up to the light.

"There isn't much chance of mistaking that 'Zig-Zag' watermark," he said. "This cigarette was made by the deceased. There can't be the shadow of a doubt."

"One more point," said Thorndyke, laying the burnt wooden vesta on the table. "You have his match-box?"

The inspector brought forth the little silver casket, opened it, and compared the wooden vestas that it contained with the burnt end. Then he shut the box with a snap.

"You've proved it up to the hilt," said he. "If we could only find the hat, we should have a complete case."

"I'm not sure that we haven't found the hat," said Thorndyke. "You notice that something besides coal has been burned in the grate."

The inspector ran eagerly to the fire-place and began with feverish hands, to pick out the remains of the extinct fire. "The cinders are still warm," he said, "and they are certainly not all coal cinders. There has been wood burned here on top of the coal, and these little black lumps are neither coal nor wood. They may quite possibly be the remains of a burnt hat, but, Lord! Who can tell? You can put together the pieces of broken spectacle-glasses, but you can't build up a hat out of a few cinders." He held out a handful of little, black, spongy cinders and looked ruefully at Thorndyke, who took them from him and laid them out on a sheet of paper.

"We can't reconstitute the hat, certainly," my friend agreed, "but we may be able to ascertain the origin of these remains. They may not be cinders of a hat, after all." He lit a wax match and, taking up one of the charred fragments, applied the flame to it. The cindery mass fused at once with a crackling, seething sound, emitting a dense smoke, and instantly the air became charged with a pungent, resinous odour mingled with the smell of burning animal matter.

"Smells like varnish," the station-master remarked.

"Yes. Shellac," said Thorndyke, "so the first test gives a positive result. The next test will take more time."

He opened the green case and took from it a little flask, fitted for Marsh's arsenic test, with a safety funnel and escape tube, a small folding tripod, a spirit lamp, and a disc of asbestos to serve as a sand-bath. Dropping into the flask several of the cindery masses, selected after careful inspection, he filled it up with alcohol and placed it on the disc, which he rested on the tripod. Then he lighted the spirit lamp underneath and sat down to wait for the alcohol to boil.

"There is one little point that we may as well settle," he said presently, as the bubbles began to rise in the flask. "Give me a slide with a drop of Farrant on it, Jervis."

I prepared the slide while Thorndyke, with a pair of forceps, picked out a tiny wisp from the table-cloth. "I fancy we have seen this fabric before," he remarked, as he laid the little pinch of fluff in the mounting fluid and slipped the slide onto the stage of the microscope. "Yes," he continued, looking into the eye-piece, "here are our old acquaintances, the red wool fibres, the blue cotton, and the yellow jute. We must label this at once or we may confuse it with the other specimens."

"Have you any idea how the deceased met his death?" the inspector asked.

"Yes," replied Thorndyke. "I take it that the murderer enticed him into this room and gave him some refreshments. The murderer sat in the chair in which you are sitting, Brodski sat in that small arm-chair. Then I imagine the murderer attacked him with that iron bar that you found among the nettles, failed to kill him at the first stroke, struggled with him, and finally suffocated him with the table-cloth. By the way, there is just one more point. You recognize this piece of string?" He took from his "collecting-box" the little end of twine that had been picked up by the line. The inspector nodded. "Look behind you. You will see where it came from."

The officer turned sharply and his eye lighted on a string-box on the mantelpiece. He lifted it down, and Thorndyke drew out from it a length of white twine with one green strand, which he compared with the piece in his hand. "The green strand in it makes the identification fairly certain," he said. "Of course the string was used to secure the umbrella and hand-bag. He could not have carried them in his hand, encumbered as he was with the corpse. But I expect our other specimen is ready now." He lifted the flask off the tripod, and, giving it a vigorous shake, examined the contents through his lens. The alcohol had now become dark-brown in colour, and was noticeably thicker and more syrupy in consistence.

"I think we have enough here for a rough test," said he, selecting a pipette and a slide from the case. He dipped the former into the flask and, having sucked up a few drops of the alcohol from the bottom, held the pipette over the slide on which he allowed the contained fluid to drop.

Laying a cover-glass on the little pool of alcohol, he put the slide on the microscope stage and examined it attentively, while we watched him in expectant silence.

At length he looked up, and, addressing the inspector, asked, "Do you know what felt hats are made of?"

"I can't say that I do, sir," replied the officer.

"Well, the better quality hats are made of rabbits' and hares' wool – the soft under-fur, you know – cemented together with shellac. Now there is very little doubt that these cinders contain shellac, and with the microscope I find a number of small hairs of a rabbit. I have, therefore, little hesitation in saying that these cinders are the remains of a hard felt hat, and, as the hairs do not appear to be dyed, I should say it was a grey hat."

At this moment our conclave was interrupted by hurried footsteps on the garden path and, as we turned with one accord, an elderly woman burst into the room.

She stood for a moment in mute astonishment, and then, looking from one to the other, demanded, "Who are you? And what are you doing here?"

The inspector rose. "I am a police officer, madam," said he. "I can't give you any further information just now, but, if you will excuse me asking, who are you?"

"I am Mr. Hickler's housekeeper," she replied.

"And Mr. Hickler? Are you expecting him home shortly?"

"No, I am not," was the curt reply. "Mr. Hickler is away from home just now. He left this evening by the boat train."

"For Amsterdam?" asked Thorndyke.

"I believe so, though I don't see what business it is of yours," the housekeeper answered.

"I thought he might, perhaps, be a diamond broker or merchant," said Thorndyke. "A good many of them travel by that train."

"So he is," said the woman. "At least, he has something to do with diamonds."

"Ah. Well, we must be going, Jervis," said Thorndyke. "We have finished here, and we have to find an hotel or inn. Can I have a word with you, Inspector?"

The officer, now entirely humble and reverent, followed us out into the garden to receive Thorndyke's parting advice.

"You had better take possession of the house at once, and get rid of the housekeeper. Nothing must be removed. Preserve those cinders and see that the rubbish-heap is not disturbed. And, above all, don't have the room swept. An officer will be sent to relieve you."

With a friendly "Good-night" we went on our way, guided by the station-master, and here our connection with the case came to an end. Hickler (whose Christian name turned out to be Silas) was, it is true, arrested as he stepped ashore from the steamer, and a packet of diamonds, subsequently identified as the property of Oscar Brodski, found upon his person. But he was never brought to trial, for on the return voyage he contrived to elude his guards for an instant as the ship was approaching the English coast, and it was not until three days later, when a hand-cuffed body was cast up on the lonely shore by Orfordness, that the authorities knew the fate of Silas Hickler.

"An appropriate and dramatic end to a singular and yet typical case," said Thorndyke, as he put down the newspaper. "I hope it has enlarged your knowledge, Jervis, and enabled you to form one or two useful corollaries."

"I prefer to hear you sing the medico-legal doxology," I answered, turning upon him like the proverbial worm and grinning derisively (which the worm does not).

"I know you do," he retorted, with mock gravity, "and I lament your lack of mental initiative. However, the points that this case illustrates are these: First, the danger of delay, the vital importance of instant action before that frail and fleeting thing that we call a clue has time to evaporate. A delay of a few hours would have left us with hardly a single datum. Second, the necessity of pursuing the most trivial clue to an absolute finish, as illustrated by the spectacles. Third, the urgent need of a trained scientist to aid the police, and, last," he concluded, with a smile, "we learn never to go abroad without the invaluable green case."

A Case of Premeditation
Part I – The Elimination of Mr. Pratt

The wine merchant who should supply a consignment of *petit vin* to a customer who had ordered, and paid for, a vintage wine, would render himself subject to unambiguous comment. Nay! More, he would be liable to certain legal penalties. And yet his conduct would be morally indistinguishable from that of the railway company which, having accepted a first-class fare, inflicts upon the passenger that kind of company which he has paid to avoid. But the corporate conscience, as Herbert Spencer was wont to explain, is an altogether inferior product to that of the individual.

Such were the reflections of Mr. Rufus Pembury when, as the train was about to move out of Maidstone (West) Station, a coarse and burly man (clearly a denizen of the third-class) was ushered into his compartment by the guard. He had paid the higher fare, not for cushioned seats, but for seclusion or, at least, select companionship. The man's entry had deprived him of both, and he resented it.

But if the presence of this stranger involved a breach of contract, his conduct was a positive affront – an indignity, for, no sooner had the train started than he fixed upon Mr. Pembury a gaze of impertinent intensity, and continued thereafter to regard him with a stare as steady and unwinking as that of a Polynesian idol.

It was offensive to a degree, and highly disconcerting withal. Mr. Pembury fidgeted in his seat with increasing discomfort and rising temper. He looked into his pocket-book, read one or two letters, and sorted a collection of visiting-cards. He even thought of opening his umbrella. Finally, his patience exhausted and his wrath mounting to boiling-point, he turned to the stranger with frosty remonstrance.

"I imagine, sir, that you will have no difficulty in recognizing me, should we ever meet again – which God forbid."

"I should recognize you among ten-thousand," was the reply, so unexpected as to leave Mr. Pembury speechless.

"You see," the stranger continued impressively, "I've got the gift of faces. I never forget."

"That must be a great consolation," said Pembury.

"It's very useful to me," said the stranger. "At least, it used to be, when I was a warder at Portland – you remember me, I dare say. My name is Pratt. I was Assistant-Warder in your time. God-forsaken hole, Portland, and mighty glad I was when they used to send me up to town on reckernizing duty. Holloway was the house of detention then. You remember, that was before they moved to Brixton."

Pratt paused in his reminiscences, and Pembury, pale and gasping with astonishment, pulled himself together.

"I think," said he, "you must be mistaking me for someone else."

"I don't," replied Pratt. "You're Francis Dobbs, that's who you are. Slipped away from Portland one evening about twelve years ago. Clothes washed up on the Bill next day. No trace of fugitive. As neat a mizzle as ever I heard of. But there are a couple of photographs and a set of fingerprints at the Habitual Criminals Register. P'r'aps you'd like to come and see 'em?"

"Why should I go to the Habitual Criminals Register?" Pembury demanded faintly.

"Ah! Exactly. Why should you? When you are a man of means, and a little judiciously invested capital would render it unnecessary?"

Pembury looked out of the window, and for a minute or more preserved a stony silence. At length he turned suddenly to Pratt. "How much?" he asked.

"I shouldn't think a couple of hundred a year would hurt you," was the calm reply.

Pembury reflected awhile. "What makes you think I am a man of means?" he asked presently.

Pratt smiled grimly. "Bless you, Mr. Pembury," said he, "I know all about you. Why, for the last six months I have been living within half-a-mile of your house."

"The devil you have!"

"Yes. When I retired from the service, General O'Gorman engaged me as a sort of steward or caretaker of his little place at Baysford – he's very seldom there himself – and the very day after I came down, I met you and spotted you, but, naturally, I kept out of sight myself. Thought I'd find out whether you were good for anything before I spoke, so I've been keeping my ears open and I find you are good for a couple of hundred."

There was an interval of silence, and then the ex-warder resumed – "That's what comes of having a memory for faces. Now there's Jack Ellis, on the other hand. He must have had you under his nose for a couple of years, and yet he's never twigged – he never will either," added Pratt, already regretting the confidence into which his vanity had led him.

"Who is Jack Ellis?" Pembury demanded sharply.

"Why, he's a sort of supernumerary at the Baysford Police Station – does odd jobs, rural detective, helps in the office, and that sort of thing. He was in the Civil Guard at Portland, in your time, but he got his left forefinger chopped off, so they pensioned him, and, as he was a Baysford man, he got this billet. But he'll never reckernize you, don't you fear."

"Unless you direct his attention to me," suggested Pembury.

"There's no fear of that," laughed Pratt. "You can trust me to sit quiet on my own nest-egg. Besides, we're not very friendly. He came nosing round our place after the parlourmaid – him a married man, mark you! But I soon boosted him out, I can tell you, and Jack Ellis don't like me now."

"I see," said Pembury reflectively, then, after a pause, he asked, "Who is this General O'Gorman? I seem to know the name."

"I expect you do," said Pratt. "He was Governor of Dartmoor when I was there – that was my last billet – and, let me tell you, if he'd been at Portland in your time, you'd never have got away."

"How is that?"

"Why, you see, the general is a great man on bloodhounds. He kept a pack at Dartmoor and, you bet, those lags knew it. There were no attempted escapes in those days. They wouldn't have had a chance."

"He has the pack still, hasn't he?" asked Pembury.

"Rather. Spends any amount of time on training 'em, too. He's always hoping there'll be a burglary or a murder in the neighbourhood so as he can try 'em, but he's never got a chance yet. P'r'aps the crooks have heard about 'em. But, to come back to our little arrangement. What do you say to a couple of hundred, paid quarterly, if you like?"

"I can't settle the matter off-hand," said Pembury. "You must give me time to think it over."

"Very well," said Pratt. "I shall be back at Baysford to-morrow evening. That will give you a clear day to think it over. Shall I look in at your place to-morrow night?"

"No," replied Pembury, "You'd better not be seen at my house, nor I at yours. If I meet you at some quiet spot, where we shan't be seen, we can settle our business without anyone knowing that we have met. It won't take long, and we can't be too careful."

"That's true," agreed Pratt. "Well, I'll tell you what. There's an avenue leading up to our house, you know it, I expect. There's no lodge, and the gates are always ajar, excepting at night. Now I shall be down by the six-thirty at Baysford. Our place is a quarter-of-an-hour from the station. Say you meet me in the avenue at a quarter-to-seven."

"That will suit me," said Pembury. "That is, if you are sure the bloodhounds won't be straying about the grounds."

"Lord bless you, no!" laughed Pratt. "D'you suppose the general lets his precious hounds stray about for any casual crook to feed with poisoned sausage? No, they're locked up safe in the kennels at the back of the house. Hallo! This'll be Swanley, I expect. I'll change into a smoker here and leave you time to turn the matter over in your mind. So long. To-morrow evening in the avenue at a quarter-to-seven. And, I say, Mr. Pembury, you might as well bring the first installment with you – fifty, in small notes or gold."

"Very well," said Mr. Pembury. He spoke coldly enough, but there was a flush on his cheeks and an angry light in his eyes, which, perhaps, the ex-warder noticed, for when he had stepped out and shut the door, he thrust his head in at the window and said threateningly. "One more word, Mr. Pembury-Dobbs. No hanky-panky, you know. I'm an old hand and pretty fly, I am. So don't you try any chickery-pokery on me. That's all." He withdrew his head and disappeared, leaving Pembury to his reflections.

The nature of those reflections – if some telepathist transferring his attention for the moment from hidden courtyards or missing thimbles to more practical matters – could have conveyed them into the mind of Mr. Pratt, would have caused that quondam official some surprise and, perhaps, a little disquiet. For long experience of the criminal, as he appears

279

when in durance, had produced some rather misleading ideas as to his behaviour when at large. In fact, the ex-warder had considerably under-estimated the ex-convict.

Rufus Pembury, to give his real name – for Dobbs was literally a *nom de guerre* – was a man of strong character and intelligence. So much so that, having tried the criminal career and found it not worth pursuing, he had definitely abandoned it. When the cattle-boat that picked him up off Portland Bill had landed him at an American port, he brought his entire ability and energy to bear on legitimate commercial pursuits, and with such success that, at the end of ten years, he was able to return to England with a moderate competence. Then he had taken a modest house near the little town of Baysford, where he had lived quietly on his savings for the last two years, holding aloof without much difficulty from the rather exclusive local society, and here he might have lived out the rest of his life in peace but for the unlucky chance that brought the man Pratt into the neighbourhood. With the arrival of Pratt his security was utterly destroyed.

There is something eminently unsatisfactory about a blackmailer. No arrangement with him has any permanent validity. No undertaking that he gives is binding. The thing which he has sold remains in his possession to sell over again. He pockets the price of emancipation, but retains the key of the fetters. In short, the blackmailer is a totally impossible person.

Such were the considerations that had passed through the mind of Rufus Pembury, even while Pratt was making his proposals, and those proposals he had never for an instant entertained. The ex-warder's advice to him to "turn the matter over in his mind" was unnecessary. For his mind was already made up. His decision was arrived at in the very moment when Pratt had disclosed his identity. The conclusion was self-evident. Before Pratt appeared he was living in peace and security. While Pratt remained, his liberty was precarious from moment to moment. If Pratt should disappear, his peace and security would return. Therefore Pratt must be eliminated.

It was a logical consequence.

The profound meditations, therefore, in which Pembury remained immersed for the remainder of the journey had nothing whatever to do with the quarterly allowance. They were concerned exclusively with the elimination of ex-warder Pratt.

Now Rufus Pembury was not a ferocious man. He was not even cruel. But he was gifted with a certain magnanimous cynicism which ignored the trivialities of sentiment and regarded only the main issues. If a wasp hummed over his tea-cup, he would crush that wasp, but not with his bare hand. The wasp carried the means of aggression. That was the wasp's look-out. His concern was to avoid being stung.

So it was with Pratt. The man had elected, for his own profit, to threaten Pembury's liberty. Very well. He had done it at his own risk. That risk was no concern of Pembury's. His concern was his own safety.

When Pembury alighted at Charing Cross, he directed his steps (after having watched Pratt's departure from the station) to Buckingham Street, Strand, where he entered a quiet private hotel. He was apparently expected, for the manageress greeted him by his name as she handed him his key.

"Are you staying in town, Mr. Pembury?" she asked.

"No," was the reply. "I go back to-morrow morning, but I may be coming up again shortly. By the way, you used to have an encyclopaedia in one of the rooms. Could I see it for a moment?"

"It is in the drawing-room," said the manageress. "Shall I show you – but you know the way, don't you?"

Certainly Mr. Pembury knew the way. It was on the first floor, a pleasant old-world room looking on the quiet old street, and on a shelf, amidst a collection of novels, stood the sedate volumes of *Chambers's Encyclopaedia*.

That a gentleman from the country should desire to look up the subject of "hounds" would not, to a casual observer, have seemed unnatural. But when from hounds the student proceeded to the article on blood, and thence to one devoted to perfumes, the observer might reasonably have felt some surprise, and this surprise might have been augmented if he had followed Mr. Pembury's subsequent proceedings, and specially if he had considered them as the actions of a man whose immediate aim was the removal of a superfluous unit of the population.

Having deposited his bag and umbrella in his room, Pembury set forth from the hotel as one with a definite purpose, and his footsteps led, in the first place, to an umbrella shop on the Strand, where he selected a thick rattan cane. There was nothing remarkable in this, perhaps, but the cane was of an uncomely thickness and the salesman protested. "I like a thick cane," said Pembury.

"Yes, sir, but for a gentleman of your height" (Pembury was a small, slightly-built man) "I would venture to suggest – ?"

"I like a thick cane," repeated Pembury. "Cut it down to the proper length and don't rivet the ferrule on. I'll cement it on when I get home."

His next investment would have seemed more to the purpose, though suggestive of unexpected crudity of method. It was a large Norwegian knife. But not content with this, he went on forthwith to a second cutler's and purchased a second knife, the exact duplicate of the first. Now, for what purpose could he want two identically similar knives? And why not have bought them both at the same shop? It was highly mysterious.

Shopping appeared to be a positive mania with Rufus Pembury. In the course of the next half-hour he acquired a cheap hand-bag, an artist's black-japanned brush-case, a three-cornered file, a stick of elastic glue, and a pair of iron crucible-tongs. Still insatiable, he repaired to an old-fashioned chemist's shop in a by-street, where he further enriched himself with a packet of absorbent cotton-wool and an ounce of permanganate of potash, and, as the chemist wrapped up these articles, with the occult and necromantic air peculiar to chemists, Pembury watched him impassively.

"I suppose you don't keep musk?" he asked carelessly.

The chemist paused in the act of heating a stick of sealing-wax, and appeared as if about to mutter an incantation. But he merely replied, "No, sir. Not the solid musk, it's so very costly. But I have the essence."

"That isn't as strong as the pure stuff, I suppose?"

"No," replied the chemist, with a cryptic smile, "not so strong, but strong enough. These animal perfumes are so very penetrating, you know, and so lasting. Why, I venture to say that if you were to sprinkle a table-spoonful of the essence in the middle of St. Paul's, the place would smell of it six months hence."

"You don't say so!" said Pembury. "Well, that ought to be enough for anybody. I'll take a small quantity, please, and, for goodness' sake, see that there isn't any on the outside of the bottle. The stuff isn't for myself, and I don't want to go about smelling like a civet cat."

"Naturally you don't, sir," agreed the chemist. He then produced an ounce bottle, a small glass funnel and a stoppered bottle labelled "*Ess. Moschi*", with which he proceeded to perform a few trifling feats of legerdemain.

"There, sir," said he, when he had finished the performance. "There is not a drop on the outside of the bottle, and, if I fit it with a rubber cork, you will be quite secure."

Pembury's dislike of musk appeared to be excessive, for, when the chemist had retired into a secret cubicle as if to hold converse with some familiar spirit (but actually to change half-a-crown), he took the brush-case from his bag, pulled off its lid, and then, with the crucible-tongs, daintily lifted the bottle off the counter, slid it softly into the brush-case, and, replacing the lid, returned the case and tongs to the bag. The other two packets he took from the counter and dropped into his pocket, and, when the presiding wizard, having miraculously transformed a single half-crown into four pennies, handed him the product, he left the shop and walked thoughtfully back towards the Strand. Suddenly a new idea seemed to strike him. He halted, considered for a few moments, and then strode away northward to make the oddest of all his purchases.

The transaction took place in a shop in the Seven Dials, whose strange stock-in-trade ranged the whole zoological gamut, from water-snails to Angora cats. Pembury looked at a cage of guinea-pigs in the window and entered the shop.

"Do you happen to have a dead guinea-pig?" he asked.

"No, mine are all alive," replied the man, adding, with a sinister grin, "But they're not immortal, you know."

Pembury looked at the man distastefully. There is an appreciable difference between a guinea-pig and a blackmailer. "Any small mammal would do," he said.

"There's a dead rat in that cage, if he's any good," said the man. "Died this morning, so he's quite fresh."

"I'll take the rat," said Pembury. "He'll do quite well."

The little corpse was accordingly made into a parcel and deposited in the bag, and Pembury, having tendered a complimentary fee, made his way back to the hotel.

After a modest lunch, he went forth and spent the remainder of the day transacting the business which had originally brought him to town. He dined at a restaurant and did not return to his hotel until ten o'clock, when he took his key and, tucking under his arm a parcel that he had brought in with him, retired for the night. But before undressing – and after locking his door – he did a very strange and unaccountable thing. Having pulled off the loose ferrule from his newly-purchased cane, he bored a hole in the bottom of it with the spike end of the file. Then, using the latter as a broach, he enlarged the hole until only a narrow rim of the bottom was left. He next rolled up a small ball of cottonwool and pushed it into the ferrule, and having smeared the end of the cane with elastic glue, he replaced the ferrule, warming it over the gas to make the glue stick.

When he had finished with the cane, he turned his attention to one of the Norwegian knives. First, he carefully removed with the file most of the bright, yellow varnish from the wooden case or handle.

Then he opened the knife, and, cutting the string of the parcel that he had brought in, took from it the dead rat which he had bought at the zoologist's. Laying the animal on a sheet of paper, he cut off its head, and, holding it up by the tail, allowed the blood that oozed from the neck to drop on the knife, spreading it over both sides of the blade and handle with his finger.

Then he laid the knife on the paper and softly opened the window. From the darkness below came the voice of a cat, apparently perfecting itself in the execution of chromatic scales, and in that direction Pembury flung the body and head of the rat, and closed the window. Finally, having washed his hands and stuffed the paper from the parcel into the fire-place, he went to bed.

But his proceedings in the morning were equally mysterious. Having breakfasted betimes, he returned to his bedroom and locked himself in. Then he tied his new cane, handle downwards, to the leg of the dressing-table. Next, with the crucible-tongs, he drew the little bottle of musk from the brush-case, and, having assured himself, by sniffing at it, that the exterior was really free from odour, he withdrew the rubber cork. Then, slowly and with infinite care, he poured a few drops – perhaps half-a-teaspoonful – of the essence on the cotton-wool that bulged through the hole in the ferrule, watching the absorbent material narrowly as it soaked up the liquid. When it was saturated he proceeded to treat the knife in the same fashion, letting fall a drop of the essence on the wooden handle – which soaked it up readily. This done, he slid up the window and looked out. Immediately below was a tiny yard in which grew, or rather survived, a couple of faded laurel bushes. The body of the rat was nowhere to be seen, it had apparently been spirited away in the night. Holding out the bottle, which he still held, he dropped it into the bushes, flinging the rubber cork after it.

His next proceeding was to take a tube of vaseline from his dressing-bag and squeeze a small quantity onto his fingers. With this he thoroughly smeared the shoulder of the brush-case and the inside of the lid, so as to ensure an air-tight joint. Having wiped his fingers, he picked the knife up with the crucible-tongs, and, dropping it into the brush-case, immediately pushed on the lid. Then he heated the tips of the tongs in the gas flame to destroy the scent, packed the tongs and brush-case in the bag, untied the cane – carefully avoiding contact with the ferrule – and, taking up the two bags, went out, holding the cane by its middle.

There was no difficulty in finding an empty compartment, for first-class passengers were few at that time in the morning. Pembury waited on the platform until the guard's whistle sounded, when he stepped into the compartment, shut the door and laid the cane on the seat with its ferrule projecting out of the off-side window, in which position it remained until the train drew up in Baysford Station.

Pembury left his dressing-bag at the cloak-room, and, still grasping the cane by its middle, he sallied forth. The town of Baysford lay some half-a-mile to the east of the station, his own house was a mile along the road to the west, and half-way between his house and the station was the residence of General O'Gorman. He knew the place well. Originally a farmhouse, it stood on the edge of a great expanse of flat meadows and communicated with the road by an avenue, nearly three hundred yards long, of ancient trees. The avenue was shut off from the road by a pair of iron gates, but these were merely ornamental, for the place was unenclosed and accessible from the surrounding meadows – indeed, an indistinct footpath crossed the meadows and intersected the avenue about half-way up.

On this occasion Pembury, whose objective was the avenue, elected to approach it by the latter route, and at each stile or fence that he surmounted, he paused to survey the country. Presently the avenue arose before him, lying athwart the narrow track, and, as he entered it between two of the trees, he halted and looked about him.

He stood listening for a while. Beyond the faint rustle of leaves no sound was to be heard. Evidently there was no one about, and, as Pratt was at large, it was probable that the general was absent.

And now Pembury began to examine the adjacent trees with more than a casual interest. The two between which he had entered were respectively an elm and a great pollard oak, the latter being an immense tree whose huge, warty bole divided about seven feet from the ground into three limbs, each as large as a fair-sized tree, of which the largest swept outward in a great curve half-way across the avenue. On this patriarch Pembury bestowed especial attention, walking completely round it and finally laying down his bag and cane (the latter resting on the bag with the ferrule off the ground) that he might climb up, by the aid of the warty outgrowths, to examine the crown, and he had just stepped up into the space between the three limbs, when the creaking of the iron gates was followed by a quick step in the avenue. Hastily he let himself down from the tree, and, gathering up his possessions, stood close behind the great bole.

"Just as well not to be seen," was his reflection, as he hugged the tree closely and waited, peering cautiously round the trunk. Soon a streak of moving shadow heralded the stranger's approach, and he moved round to keep the trunk between himself and the intruder. On the footsteps came, until the stranger was abreast of the tree, and when he had passed Pembury peeped round at the retreating figure. It was only the postman, but then the man knew him, and he was glad he had kept out of sight.

Apparently the oak did not meet his requirements, for he stepped out and looked up and down the avenue. Then, beyond the elm, he caught sight of an ancient pollard hornbeam – a strange, fantastic tree whose trunk widened out trumpet-like above into a broad crown, from the edge of which multitudinous branches uprose like the limbs of some weird hamadryad.

That tree he approved at a glance, but he lingered behind the oak until the postman, returning with brisk step and cheerful whistle, passed down the avenue and left him once more in solitude. Then he moved on with a resolute air to the hornbeam.

The crown of the trunk was barely six feet from the ground. He could reach it easily, as he found on trying. Standing the cane against the tree – ferrule downwards, this time – he took the brush-case from the bag, pulled off the lid, and, with the crucible-tongs, lifted out the knife and laid it on the crown of the tree, just out of sight, leaving the tongs also invisible – still grasping the knife. He was about to replace the brush-case in the bag,

286

when he appeared to alter his mind. Sniffing at it, and finding it reeking with the sickly perfume, he pushed the lid on again and threw the case up into the tree, where he heard it roll down into the central hollow of the crown. Then he closed the bag, and, taking the cane by its handle, moved slowly away in the direction whence he had come, passing out of the avenue between the elm and the oak.

His mode of progress was certainly peculiar. He walked with excessive slowness, trailing the cane along the ground, and every few paces he would stop and press the ferrule firmly against the earth, so that, to anyone who should have observed him, he would have appeared to be wrapped in an absorbing reverie.

Thus he moved on across the fields – not, however, returning to the high road, but crossing another stretch of fields until he emerged into a narrow lane that led out into the High Street. Immediately opposite to the lane was the police station, distinguished from the adjacent cottages only by its lamp, its open door, and the notices pasted up outside. Straight across the road Pembury walked, still trailing the cane, and halted at the station door to read the notices, resting his cane on the doorstep as he did so. Through the open doorway he could see a man writing at a desk. The man's back was towards him, but, presently, a movement brought his left hand into view, and Pembury noted that the forefinger was missing. This, then, was Jack Ellis, late of the Civil Guard at Portland.

Even while he was looking the man turned his head, and Pembury recognized him at once. He had frequently met him on the road between Baysford and the adjoining village of Thorpe, and always at the same time. Apparently Ellis paid a daily visit to Thorpe – perhaps to receive a report from the rural constable – and he started between three and four and returned between seven and a quarter past.

Pembury looked at his watch. It was a quarter-past-three. He moved away thoughtfully (holding his cane, now, by the middle), and began to walk slowly in the direction of Thorpe – westward.

For a while he was deeply meditative, and his face wore a puzzled frown. Then, suddenly, his face cleared and he strode forward at a brisker pace. Presently he passed through a gap in the hedge, and, walking in a field parallel with the road, took out his purse – a small pigskin pouch.

Having frugally emptied it of its contents, excepting a few shillings, he thrust the ferrule of his cane into the small compartment ordinarily reserved for gold or notes.

And thus he continued to walk on slowly, carrying the cane by the middle and the purse jammed on the end.

At length he reached a sharp double curve in the road whence he could see back for a considerable distance, and here opposite a small opening, he sat down to wait. The hedge screened him effectually from the gaze of passers-by – though these were few enough – without interfering with his view.

A quarter-of-an-hour passed. He began to be uneasy. Had he been mistaken? Were Ellis's visits only occasional instead of daily, as he had thought? That would be tiresome though not actually disastrous. But at this point in his reflections a figure came into view, advancing along the road with a steady swing. He recognized the figure. It was Ellis.

But there was another figure advancing from the opposite direction – A labourer, apparently. He prepared to shift his ground, but another glance showed him that the labourer would pass first. He waited. The labourer came on and, at length, passed the opening, and, as he did so, Ellis disappeared for a moment in a bend of the road. Instantly Pembury passed his cane through the opening in the hedge, shook off the purse and pushed it into the middle of the foot-way. Then he crept forward, behind the hedge, towards the approaching official, and again sat down to wait. On came the steady tramp of the unconscious Ellis, and, as it passed, Pembury drew aside an obstructing branch and peered out at the retreating figure. The question now was, would Ellis see the purse? It was not a very conspicuous object.

The footsteps stopped abruptly. Looking out, Pembury saw the police official stoop, pick up the purse, examine its contents and finally stow it in his trousers pocket. Pembury heaved a sigh of relief, and, as the dwindling figure passed out of sight round a curve in the road, he rose, stretched himself and strode away briskly.

Near the gap was a group of ricks, and, as he passed them, a fresh idea suggested itself. Looking round quickly he passed to the farther side of one and, thrusting his cane deeply into it, pushed it home with a piece of stick that he picked up near the rick, until the handle was lost among the straw. The bag was now all that was left, and it was empty – for his other purchases were in the dressing-bag, which, by the way, he must fetch from the station. He opened it and smelt the interior, but, though he could detect no odour, he resolved to be rid of it if possible.

As he emerged from the gap a wagon jogged slowly past. It was piled high with sacks, and the tail-board was down. Stepping into the road, he quickly overtook the wagon, and, having glanced round, laid the bag lightly on the tail-board. Then he set off for the station.

On arriving home, he went straight up to his bedroom and, ringing for his housekeeper, ordered a substantial meal. Then he took off his clothes and deposited them, even to his shirt, socks and necktie, in a trunk, wherein his summer clothing was stored with a plentiful sprinkling of naphthol to preserve it from the moth. Taking the packet of permanganate of potash from his dressing-bag, he passed into the adjoining bathroom, and, tipping the crystals into the bath, turned on the water. Soon the bath was filled with a pink solution of the salt, and into this he plunged, immersing his entire body and thoroughly soaking his hair. Then he emptied the bath and rinsed himself in clear water, and, having dried himself, returned to the bedroom and dressed himself in fresh clothing. Finally he took a hearty meal, and then lay down on the sofa to rest until it should be time to start for the rendezvous.

Half-past-six found him lurking in the shadow by the station-approach, within sight of the solitary lamp. He heard the train come in, saw the stream of passengers emerge, and noted one figure detach itself from the throng and turn on to the Thorpe road. It was Pratt, as the lamplight showed him, Pratt, striding forward to the meeting-place with an air of jaunty satisfaction and an uncommonly creaky pair of boots.

Pembury followed him at a safe distance, and rather by sound than sight, until he was well past the stile at the entrance to the footpath. Evidently he was going on to the gates. Then Pembury vaulted over the stile and strode away swiftly across the dark meadows.

When he plunged into the deep gloom of the avenue, his first act was to grope his way to the hornbeam and slip his hand up onto the crown and satisfy himself that the tongs were as he had left them. Reassured by the touch of his fingers on the iron loops, he turned and walked slowly down the avenue. The duplicate knife – ready opened – was in his left inside breast-pocket, and he fingered its handle as he walked.

Presently the iron gate squeaked mournfully, and then the rhythmical creak of a pair of boots was audible, coming up the avenue. Pembury walked forward slowly until a darker smear emerged from the surrounding gloom, when he called out, "Is that you, Pratt?"

"That's me," was the cheerful, if ungrammatical response, and, as he drew nearer, the ex-warder asked, "Have you brought the rhino, old man?"

The insolent familiarity of the man's tone was agreeable to Pembury – it strengthened his nerve and hardened his heart. "Of course," he replied, "but we must have a definite understanding, you know."

"Look here," said Pratt, "I've got no time for jaw. The General will be here presently. He's riding over from Bingfield with a friend. You hand over the dibs and we'll talk some other time."

"That is all very well," said Pembury, "but you must understand – ?" He paused abruptly and stood still. They were now close to the hornbeam, and, as he stood, he stared up into the dark mass of foliage.

"What's the matter?" demanded Pratt. "What are you staring at?" He, too, had halted and stood gazing intently into the darkness.

Then, in an instant, Pembury whipped out the knife and drove it, with all his strength, into the broad back of the ex-warder, below the left shoulder-blade.

With a hideous yell Pratt turned and grappled with his assailant. A powerful man and a competent wrestler, too, he was far more than a match for Pembury unarmed, and, in a moment, he had him by the throat. But Pembury clung to him tightly, and, as they trampled to-and-fro and round-and-round, he stabbed again and again with the viciousness of a scorpion, while Pratt's cries grew more gurgling and husky. Then they fell heavily to the ground, Pembury underneath. But the struggle was over. With a last bubbling groan, Pratt relaxed his hold and in a moment grew limp and inert. Pembury pushed him off and rose, trembling and breathing heavily.

But he wasted no time. There had been more noise than he had bargained for. Quickly stepping up to the hornbeam, he reached up for the tongs. His fingers slid into the looped handles, the tongs grasped the knife, and he lifted it out from its hiding-place and carried it to where the corpse lay, depositing it on the ground a few feet from the body. Then he went back to the tree and carefully pushed the tongs over into the hollow of the crown.

At this moment a woman's voice sounded shrilly from the top of the avenue.

"Is that you, Mr. Pratt?" it called.

290

Pembury started and then stepped back quickly, on tiptoe, to the body. For there was the duplicate knife. He must take that away at all costs.

The corpse was lying on its back. The knife was underneath it, driven in to the very haft. He had to use both hands to lift the body, and even then he had some difficulty in disengaging the weapon. And, meanwhile, the voice, repeating its question, drew nearer.

At length he succeeded in drawing out the knife and thrust it into his breast-pocket. The corpse fell back, and he stood up gasping.

"Mr. Pratt! Are you there?" The nearness of the voice startled Pembury, and, turning sharply, he saw a light twinkling between the trees. And then the gates creaked loudly and he heard the crunch of a horse's hoofs on the gravel.

He stood for an instant bewildered – utterly taken by surprise. He had not reckoned on a horse. His intended flight across the meadows towards Thorpe was now impracticable. If he were overtaken he was lost, for he knew there was blood on his clothes and his hands were wet and slippery – to say nothing of the knife in his pocket.

But his confusion lasted only for an instant. He remembered the oak tree, and, turning out of the avenue, he ran to it, and, touching it as little as he could with his bloody hands, climbed quickly up into the crown. The great horizontal limb was nearly three feet in diameter, and, as he lay out on it, gathering his coat closely round him, he was quite invisible from below.

He had hardly settled himself when the light which he had seen came into full view, revealing a woman advancing with a stable lantern in her hand. And, almost at the same moment, a streak of brighter light burst from the opposite direction. The horseman was accompanied by a man on a bicycle.

The two men came on apace, and the horseman, sighting the woman, called out, "Anything the matter, Mrs. Parton?" But, at that moment, the light of the bicycle lamp fell full on the prostrate corpse. The two men uttered a simultaneous cry of horror, the woman shrieked aloud, and then the horseman sprang from the saddle and ran forward to the body.

"Why," he exclaimed, stooping over it, "it's Pratt!" And, as the cyclist came up and the glare of his lamp shone on a great pool of blood, he added, "There's been foul play here, Hanford."

Hanford flashed his lamp around the body, lighting up the ground for several yards.

"What is that behind you, O'Gorman?" he said suddenly. "Isn't it a knife?" He was moving quickly towards it when O'Gorman held up his hand.

291

"Don't touch it!" he exclaimed. "We'll put the hounds onto it. They'll soon track the scoundrel, whoever he is. By God! Hanford, this fellow has fairly delivered himself into our hands." He stood for a few moments looking down at the knife with something uncommonly like exultation, and then, turning quickly to his friend, said, "Look here, Hanford, you ride off to the police station as hard as you can pelt. It is only three-quarters of a mile, you'll do it in five minutes. Send or bring an officer and I'll scour the meadows meanwhile. If I haven't got the scoundrel when you come back, we'll put the hounds onto this knife and run the beggar down."

"Right," replied Hanford, and without another word he wheeled his machine about, mounted, and rode away into the darkness.

"Mrs. Parton," said O'Gorman, "watch that knife. See that nobody touches it while I go and examine the meadows."

"Is Mr. Pratt dead, sir?" whimpered Mrs. Parton.

"Gad! I hadn't thought of that," said the general. "You'd better have a look at him, but mind! Nobody is to touch that knife or they will confuse the scent."

He scrambled into the saddle and galloped away across the meadows in the direction of Thorpe, and, as Pembury listened to the diminuendo of the horse's hoofs, he was glad that he had not attempted to escape, for that was the direction in which he had meant to go, and he would surely have been overtaken.

As soon as the general was gone, Mrs. Parton, with many a terror-stricken glance over her shoulder, approached the corpse and held the lantern close to the dead face. Suddenly she stood up, trembling violently, for footsteps were audible coming down the avenue. A familiar voice reassured her.

"Is anything wrong, Mrs. Parton?" The question proceeded from one of the maids who had come in search of the elder woman, escorted by a young man, and the pair now came out into the circle of light.

"Good God!" ejaculated the man. "Who's that?"

"It's Mr. Pratt," replied Mrs. Parton. "He's been murdered."

The girl screamed, and then the two domestics approached on tiptoe, staring at the corpse with the fascination of horror.

"Don't touch that knife," said Mrs. Parton, for the man was about to pick it up. "The general's going to put the bloodhounds onto it."

"Is the general here, then?" asked the man, and, as he spoke, the drumming of hoofs, growing momentarily louder, answered him from the meadow.

O'Gorman reined in his horse as he perceived the group of servants gathered about the corpse. "Is he dead, Mrs. Parton?" he asked.

"I am afraid so, sir," was the reply.

"Ha! Somebody ought to go for the doctor, but not you, Bailey. I want you to get the hounds ready and wait with them at the top of the avenue until I call you."

He was off again into the Baysford meadows, and Bailey hurried away, leaving the two women staring at the body and talking in whispers.

Pembury's position was cramped and uncomfortable. He dared not move, hardly dared to breathe, for the women below him were not a dozen yards away, and it was with mingled feelings of relief and apprehension that he presently saw from his elevated station a group of lights approaching rapidly along the road from Baysford. Presently they were hidden by the trees, and then, after a brief interval, the whirr of wheels sounded on the drive and streaks of light on the tree-trunks announced the new arrivals. There were three bicycles, ridden respectively by Mr. Hanford, a police inspector, and a sergeant, and, as they drew up, the general came thundering back into the avenue.

"Is Ellis with you?" he asked, as he pulled up.

"No, sir," was the reply. "He hadn't come in from Thorpe when we left. He's rather late to-night."

"Have you sent for a doctor?"

"Yes, sir, I've sent for Dr. Hills," said the inspector, resting his bicycle against the oak. Pembury could smell the reek of the lamp as he crouched. "Is Pratt dead?"

"Seems to be," replied O'Gorman, "but we'd better leave that to the doctor. There's the murderer's knife. Nobody has touched it. I'm going to fetch the bloodhounds now."

"Ah! That's the thing," said the inspector. "The man can't be far away." He rubbed his hands with a satisfied air as O'Gorman cantered away up the avenue.

In less than a minute, there came out from the darkness the deep baying of a hound followed by quick footsteps on the gravel. Then into the circle of light emerged three sinister shapes, loose-limbed and gaunt, and two men advancing at a shambling trot.

"Here, Inspector," shouted the general, "you take one, I can't hold 'em both."

The inspector ran forward and seized one of the leashes, and the general led his hound up to the knife, as it lay on the ground. Pembury, peering cautiously round the bough, watched the great brute with almost impersonal curiosity, noted its high poll, its wrinkled forehead, and melancholy face as it stooped to snuff suspiciously at the prostrate knife.

For some moments the hound stood motionless, sniffing at the knife. Then it turned away and walked to and fro with its muzzle to the ground. Suddenly it lifted its head, bayed loudly, lowered its muzzle, and started forward between the oak and the elm, dragging the general after it at a run.

The inspector next brought his hound to the knife, and was soon bounding away to the tug of the leash in the general's wake.

"They don't make no mistakes, they don't," said Bailey, addressing the gratified sergeant, as he brought forward the third hound. "You'll see – ?" But his remark was cut short by a violent jerk of the leash, and the next moment he was flying after the others, followed by Mr. Hanford.

The sergeant daintily picked the knife up by its ring, wrapped it in his handkerchief and bestowed it in his pocket. Then he ran off after the hounds.

294

Pembury smiled grimly. His scheme was working out admirably in spite of the unforeseen difficulties. If those confounded women would only go away, he could come down and take himself off while the course was clear. He listened to the baying of the hounds, gradually growing fainter in the increasing distance, and cursed the dilatoriness of the doctor. Confound the fellow! Didn't he realize that this was a case of life or death?

Suddenly his ear caught the tinkle of a bicycle bell. A fresh light appeared coming up the avenue and then a bicycle swept up swiftly to the scene of the tragedy, and a small elderly man jumped down by the side of the body. Giving his machine to Mrs. Parton, he stooped over the dead man, felt the wrist, pushed back an eyelid, held a match to the eye and then rose. "This is a shocking affair, Mrs. Parton," said he. "The poor fellow is quite dead. You had better help me to carry him to the house. If you two take the feet I will take the shoulders."

Pembury watched them raise the body and stagger away with it up the avenue. He heard their shuffling steps die away and the door of the house shut. And still he listened. From far away in the meadows came, at intervals, the baying of the hounds. Other sounds there was none. Presently the doctor would come back for his bicycle, but, for the moment, the coast was clear. Pembury rose stiffly. His hands had stuck to the tree where they had pressed against it, and they were still sticky and damp. Quickly he let himself down to the ground, listened again for a moment, and then, making a small circuit to avoid the lamplight, softly crossed the avenue and stole away across the Thorpe meadows.

The night was intensely dark, and not a soul was stirring in the meadows. He strode forward quickly, peering into the darkness and stopping now and again to listen, but no sound came to his ears, save the now faint baying of the distant hounds. Not far from his house, he remembered, was a deep ditch spanned by a wooden bridge, and towards this he now made his way, for he knew that his appearance was such as to convict him at a glance. Arrived at the ditch, he stooped to wash his hands and wrists, and, as he bent forward, the knife fell from his breast-pocket into the shallow water at the margin. He groped for it, and, having found it, drove it deep into the mud as far out as he could reach. Then he wiped his hands on some water-weed, crossed the bridge, and started homewards.

He approached his house from the rear, satisfied himself that his housekeeper was in the kitchen and, letting himself in very quietly with his key, went quickly up to his bedroom. Here he washed thoroughly – in the bath, so that he could get rid of the discoloured water – changed his clothes, and packed those that he took off in a portmanteau.

By the time he had done this the gong sounded for supper. As he took his seat at the table, spruce and fresh in appearance, quietly cheerful in manner, he addressed his housekeeper. "I wasn't able to finish my business in London," he said. "I shall have to go up again to-morrow."

"Shall you come home the same day?" asked the housekeeper.

"Perhaps," was the reply, "and perhaps not. It will depend on circumstances."

He did not say what the circumstances might be, nor did the housekeeper ask. Mr. Pembury was not addicted to confidences. He was an eminently discreet man, and discreet men say little.

Part II – Rival Sleuth-Hounds
(Related by Christopher Jervis, M.D.)

The half-hour that follows breakfast, when the fire has, so to speak, got into its stride, and the morning pipe throws up its clouds of incense, is, perhaps, the most agreeable in the whole day. Especially so when a sombre sky, brooding over the town, hints at streets pervaded by the chilly morning air, and hoots from protesting tugs upon the river tell of lingering mists, the legacy of the lately-vanished night.

The autumn morning was raw. The fire burned jovially. I thrust my slippered feet towards the blaze and meditated, on nothing in particular, with cat-like enjoyment. Presently a disapproving grunt from Thorndyke attracted my attention, and I looked round lazily. He was extracting, with a pair of office shears, the readable portions of the morning paper, and had paused with a small cutting between his finger and thumb. "Bloodhounds again," said he. "We shall be hearing presently of the revival of the ordeal by fire."

"And a deuced comfortable ordeal, too, on a morning like this," I said, stroking my legs ecstatically. "What is the case?"

He was about to reply when a sharp rat-tat from the little brass knocker announced a disturber of our peace. Thorndyke stepped over to the door and admitted a police inspector in uniform, and I stood up, and, presenting my dorsal aspect to the fire, prepared to combine bodily comfort with attention to business.

"I believe I am speaking to Dr. Thorndyke," said the officer, and, as Thorndyke nodded, he went on, "My name, sir, is Fox, Inspector Fox of the Baysford Police. Perhaps you've seen the morning paper?"

Thorndyke held up the cutting, and, placing a chair by the fire, asked the inspector if he had breakfasted.

"Thank you, sir, I have," replied Inspector Fox. "I came up to town by the late train last night so as to be here early, and stayed at an hotel. You see, from the paper, that we have had to arrest one of our own men. That's rather awkward, you know, sir."

"Very," agreed Thorndyke.

"Yes, it's bad for the force and bad for the public too. But we had to do it. There was no way out that we could see. Still, we should like the accused to have every chance, both for our sake and his own, so the chief constable thought he'd like to have your opinion on the case, and he thought that, perhaps, you might be willing to act for the defence."

"Let us have the particulars," said Thorndyke, taking a writing-pad from a drawer and dropping into his armchair. "Begin at the beginning," he added, "and tell us all you know."

"Well," said the inspector, after a preliminary cough, "to begin with the murdered man. His name is Pratt. He was a retired prison warder, and was employed as steward by General O'Gorman, who is a retired prison governor – you may have heard of him in connection with his pack of bloodhounds. Well, Pratt came down from London yesterday evening by a train arriving at Baysford at six-thirty. He was seen by the guard, the ticket collector, and the outside porter. The porter saw him leave the station at six-thirty-seven. General O'Gorman's house is about half-a-mile from the station. At five-minutes-to-seven, the general and a gentleman named Hanford and the general's housekeeper, a Mrs. Parton, found Pratt lying dead in the avenue that leads up to the house. He had apparently been stabbed, for there was a lot of blood about, and a knife – a Norwegian knife – was lying on the ground near the body. Mrs. Parton had thought she heard someone in the avenue calling out for help, and, as Pratt was just due, she came out with a lantern. She met the general and Mr. Hanford, and all three seem to have caught sight of the body at the same moment. Mr. Hanford cycled down to us, at once, with the news, we sent for a doctor, and I went back with Mr. Hanford and took a sergeant with me. We arrived at twelve-minutes-past-seven, and then the general, who had galloped his horse over the meadows each side of the avenue without having seen anybody, fetched out his bloodhounds and led them up to the knife. All three hounds took up the scent at once – I held the leash of one of them – and they took us across the meadows without a pause or a falter, over stiles and fences, along a lane, out into the town, and then, one after the other, they crossed the road in a bee-line to the police station, bolted in at the door, which stood open, and made straight for the desk, where a supernumerary officer named Ellis was writing. They made a rare to-do, struggling to get at him, and it was as much as we could manage to hold them back. As for Ellis, he turned as pale as a ghost."

"Was anyone else in the room?" asked Thorndyke.

"Oh, yes. There were two constables and a messenger. We led the hounds up to them, but the brutes wouldn't take any notice of them. They wanted Ellis."

"And what did you do?"

"Why, we arrested Ellis, of course. Couldn't do anything else – especially with the general there."

"What had the general to do with it?" asked Thorndyke.

"He's a J.P. and a late governor of Dartmoor, and it was his hounds that had run the man down. But we must have arrested Ellis in any case."

"Is there anything against the accused man?"

"Yes, there is. He and Pratt were on distinctly unfriendly terms. They were old comrades, for Ellis was in the Civil Guard at Portland when Pratt was warder there – he was pensioned off from the service because he got his left forefinger chopped off – but lately they had had some unpleasantness about a woman, a parlourmaid of the general's. It seems that Ellis, who is a married man, paid the girl too much attention – or Pratt thought he did – and Pratt warned Ellis off the premises. Since then they had not been on speaking terms."

"And what sort of a man is Ellis?"

"A remarkably decent fellow he always seemed – quiet, steady, good-natured, I should have said he wouldn't have hurt a fly. We all liked him – better than we liked Pratt, in fact. Poor Pratt was what you'd call an old soldier – sly, you know, sir – and a bit of a sneak."

"You searched and examined Ellis, of course?"

"Yes. There was nothing suspicious about him except that he had two purses. But he says he picked up one of them? a small, pigskin pouch – on the footpath of the Thorpe road yesterday afternoon, and there's no reason to disbelieve him. At any rate, the purse was not Pratt's."

Thorndyke made a note on his pad, and then asked, "There were no blood-stains or marks on his clothing?"

"No. His clothing was not marked or disarranged in any way."

"Any cuts, scratches, or bruises on his person?"

"None whatever," replied the inspector.

"At what time did you arrest Ellis?"

"Half-past seven exactly."

"Have you ascertained what his movements were? Had he been near the scene of the murder?"

"Yes, he had been to Thorpe and would pass the gates of the avenue on his way back. And he was later than usual in returning, though not later than he has often been before."

"And now, as to the murdered man: Has the body been examined?"

"Yes, I had Dr. Hills's report before I left. There were no less than seven deep knife-wounds, all on the left side of the back. There was a great deal of blood on the ground, and Dr. Hills thinks Pratt must have bled to death in a minute or two."

"Do the wounds correspond with the knife that was found?"

"I asked the doctor that, and he said 'Yes,' though he wasn't going to swear to any particular knife. However, that point isn't of much importance. The knife was covered with blood, and it was found close to the body."

"What has been done with it, by the way?" asked Thorndyke.

"The sergeant who was with me picked it up and rolled it in his handkerchief to carry in his pocket. I took it from him, just as it was, and locked it in a dispatch-box."

"Has the knife been recognized as Ellis's property?"

"No, sir, it has not."

"Were there any recognizable footprints or marks of a struggle?" Thorndyke asked.

The inspector grinned sheepishly. "I haven't examined the spot, of course, sir," said he, "but, after the general's horse and the bloodhounds and the general on foot and me and the gardener and the sergeant and Mr. Hanford had been over it twice, going and returning, why, you see, sir – ?"

"Exactly, exactly," said Thorndyke. "Well, Inspector, I shall be pleased to act for the defence. Tt seems to me that the case against Ellis is in some respects rather inconclusive."

The inspector was frankly amazed. "It certainly hadn't struck me in that light, sir," he said.

"No? Well, that is my view, and I think the best plan will be for me to come down with you and investigate matters on the spot."

The inspector assented cheerfully, and, when we had provided him with a newspaper, we withdrew to the laboratory to consult time-tables and prepare for the expedition.

"You are coming, I suppose, Jervis?" said Thorndyke.

"If I shall be of any use," I replied.

"Of course you will," said he. "Two heads are better than one, and, by the look of things, I should say that ours will be the only ones with any sense in them. We will take the research case, of course, and we may as well have a camera with us. I see there is a train from Charing Cross in twenty minutes."

For the first half-hour of the journey Thorndyke sat in his corner, alternately conning over his notes and gazing with thoughtful eyes out of the window. I could see that the case pleased him, and was careful not to break in upon his train of thought. Presently, however, he put away his notes and began to fill his pipe with a more companionable air, and then the inspector, who had been wriggling with impatience, opened fire.

"So you think, sir, that you see a way out for Ellis?"

"I think there is a case for the defence," replied Thorndyke. "In fact, I call the evidence against him rather flimsy."

The inspector gasped. "But the knife, sir? What about the knife?"

"Well," said Thorndyke, "what about the knife? Whose knife was it? You don't know. It was covered with blood. Whose blood? You don't know. Let us assume, for the sake of argument, that it was the murderer's knife. Then the blood on it was Pratt's blood. But if it was Pratt's blood, when the hounds had smelt it they should have led you to Pratt's body, for blood gives a very strong scent. But they did not. They ignored the body. The inference seems to be that the blood on the knife was not Pratt's blood."

The inspector took off his cap and gently scratched the back of his head. "You're perfectly right, sir," he said. "I'd never thought of that. None of us had."

"Then," pursued Thorndyke, "let us assume that the knife was Pratt's. If so, it would seem to have been used in self-defence. But this was a Norwegian knife, a clumsy tool – not a weapon at all – which takes an appreciable time to open and requires the use of two free hands. Now, had Pratt both hands free? Certainly not after the attack had commenced. There were seven wounds, all on the left side of the back, which indicates that he held the murderer locked in his arms and that the murderer's arms were around him. Also, incidentally, that the murderer is right-handed. But, still, let us assume that the knife was Pratt's. Then the blood on it was that of the murderer. Then the murderer must have been wounded. But Ellis was not wounded. Then Ellis is not the murderer. The knife doesn't help us at all."

The inspector puffed out his cheeks and blew softly. "This is getting out of my depth," he said. "Still, sir, you can't get over the bloodhounds. They tell us distinctly that the knife is Ellis's knife and I don't see any answer to that."

"There is no answer because there has been no statement. The bloodhounds have told you nothing. You have drawn certain inferences from their actions, but those inferences may be totally wrong and they are certainly not evidence."

"You don't seem to have much opinion of bloodhounds," the inspector remarked.

"As agents for the detection of crime," replied Thorndyke, "I regard them as useless. You cannot put a bloodhound in the witness-box. You can get no intelligible statement from it. If it possesses any knowledge, it has no means of communicating it. The fact is," he continued, "that the entire system of using bloodhounds for criminal detection is based on a fallacy. In the American plantations these animals were used with great success for tracking runaway slaves. But the slave was a known individual. All that was required was to ascertain his whereabouts. That is not the problem that is presented in the detection of a crime. The detective is not concerned in establishing the whereabouts of a known individual, but in discovering the identity of an unknown individual. And for this purpose bloodhounds are useless. They may discover such identity, but they cannot communicate their knowledge. If the criminal is unknown, they cannot identify him. If he is known, the police have no need of the bloodhound.

"To return to our present case," Thorndyke resumed, after a pause, "we have employed certain agents – the hounds – with whom we are not *en rapport*, as the spiritualists would say, and we have no 'medium'. The hound possesses a special sense – the olfactory – which in man is quite rudimentary. He thinks, so to speak, in terms of smell, and his thoughts are untranslatable to beings in whom the sense of smell is undeveloped. We have presented to the hound a knife, and he discovers in it certain odorous properties. He discovers similar or related odorous properties in a tract of land and a human individual – Ellis. We cannot verify his discoveries or ascertain their nature. What remains? All that we can say is that there appears to exist some odorous relation between the knife and the man Ellis. But until we can ascertain the nature of that relation, we cannot estimate its evidential value or bearing. All the other 'evidence' is the product of your imagination and that of the general. There is, at present, no case against Ellis."

"He must have been pretty close to the place when the murder happened," said the inspector.

"So, probably, were many other people," answered Thorndyke, "but had he time to wash and change? Because he would have needed it."

"I suppose he would," the inspector agreed dubiously.

"Undoubtedly. There were seven wounds which would have taken some time to inflict. Now we can't suppose that Pratt stood passively while

302

the other man stabbed him. Indeed, as I have said, the position of the wounds shows that he did not. There was a struggle. The two men were locked together. One of the murderer's hands was against Pratt's back, probably both hands were, one clasping and the other stabbing. There must have been blood on one hand and probably on both. But you say there was no blood on Ellis, and there doesn't seem to have been time or opportunity for him to wash."

"Well, it's a mysterious affair," said the inspector, "but I don't see how you are going to get over the bloodhounds."

Thorndyke shrugged his shoulders impatiently. "The bloodhounds are an obsession," he said. "The whole problem really centres around the knife. The questions are, Whose knife was it? And what was the connection between it and Ellis? There is a problem, Jervis," he continued, turning to me, "that I submit for your consideration. Some of the possible solutions are exceedingly curious."

As we set out from Baysford Station, Thorndyke looked at his watch and noted the time. "You will take us the way that Pratt went," he said.

"As to that," said the inspector, "he may have gone by the road or by the footpath, but there's very little difference in the distance."

Turning away from Baysford, we walked along the road westward, towards the village of Thorpe, and presently passed on our right a stile at the entrance to a footpath.

"That path," said the inspector, "crosses the avenue about half-way up. But we'd better keep to the road." A quarter-of-a-mile further on we came to a pair of rusty iron gates one of which stood open, and, entering, we found ourselves in a broad drive bordered by two rows of trees, between the trunks of which a long stretch of pasture meadows could be seen on either hand. It was a fine avenue, and, late in the year as it was, the yellowing foliage clustered thickly overhead.

When we had walked about a hundred-and-fifty yards from the gates, the inspector halted.

"This is the place," he said, and Thorndyke again noted the time.

"Nine minutes exactly," said he. "Then Pratt arrived here about fourteen-minutes-to-seven, and his body was found at five-minutes-to-seven – nine minutes after his arrival. The murderer couldn't have been far away then."

"No, it was a pretty fresh scent," replied the inspector. "You'd like to see the body first, I think you said, sir?"

"Yes, and the knife, if you please."

"I shall have to send down to the station for that. It's locked up in the office."

He entered the house, and, having dispatched a messenger to the police station, came out and conducted us to the outbuilding where the corpse had been deposited. Thorndyke made a rapid examination of the wounds and the holes in the clothing, neither of which presented anything particularly suggestive. The weapon used had evidently been a thick-backed, single-edged knife similar to the one described, and the discolouration around the wounds indicated that the weapon had a definite shoulder like that of a Norwegian knife, and that it had been driven in with savage violence.

"Do you find anything that throws any light on the case?" the inspector asked, when the examination was concluded.

"That is impossible to say until we have seen the knife," replied Thorndyke, "but while we are waiting for it, we may as well go and look at the scene of the tragedy. These are Pratt's boots, I think?" He lifted a pair of stout laced boots from the table and turned them up to inspect the soles.

"Yes, those are his boots," replied Fox, "and pretty easy they'd have been to track, if the case had been the other way about. Those Blakey's protectors are as good as a trademark."

"We'll take them, at any rate," said Thorndyke, and, the inspector having taken the boots from him, we went out and retraced our steps down the avenue.

The place where the murder had occurred was easily identified by a large dark stain on the gravel at one side of the drive, half-way between two trees – an ancient pollard hornbeam and an elm. Next to the elm was a pollard oak with a squat, warty bole about seven feet high, and three enormous limbs, of which one slanted half-way across the avenue, and between these two trees the ground was covered with the tracks of men and hounds superimposed upon the hoof-prints of a horse.

"Where was the knife found?" Thorndyke asked.

The inspector indicated a spot near the middle of the drive, almost opposite the hornbeam and Thorndyke, picking up a large stone, laid it on the spot. Then he surveyed the scene thoughtfully, looking up and down the drive and at the trees that bordered it, and, finally, walked slowly to the space between the elm and the oak, scanning the ground as he went. "There is no dearth of footprints," he remarked grimly, as he looked down at the trampled earth.

"No, but the question is, whose are they?" said the inspector.

"Yes, that is the question," agreed Thorndyke, "and we will begin the solution by identifying those of Pratt."

"I don't see how that will help us," said the inspector. "We know he was here."

Thorndyke looked at him in surprise, and I must confess that the foolish remark astonished me too, accustomed as I was to the quick-witted officers from Scotland Yard.

"The hue-and-cry procession," remarked Thorndyke, "seems to have passed out between the elm and the oak. Elsewhere the ground seems pretty clear." He walked round the elm, still looking earnestly at the ground, and presently continued, "Now here, in the soft earth bordering the turf, are the prints of a pair of smallish feet wearing pointed boots – a rather short man, evidently, by the size of foot and length of stride, and he doesn't seem to have belonged to the procession. But I don't see any of Pratt's. He doesn't seem to have come off the hard gravel." He continued to walk slowly towards the hornbeam with his eyes fixed on the ground. Suddenly he halted and stooped with an eager look at the earth, and, as Fox and I approached, he stood up and pointed. "Pratt's footprints – faint and fragmentary, but unmistakable. And now, Inspector, you see their importance. They furnish the time factor in respect of the other footprints. Look at this one and then look at that." He pointed from one to another of the faint impressions of the dead man's foot.

"You mean that there are signs of a struggle?" said Fox.

"I mean more than that," replied Thorndyke. "Here is one of Pratt's footprints treading into the print of a small, pointed foot, and there at the edge of the gravel is another of Pratt's nearly obliterated by the tread of a pointed foot. Obviously the first pointed footprint was made before Pratt's, and the second one after his, and the necessary inference is that the owner of the pointed foot was here at the same time as Pratt."

"Then he must have been the murderer!" exclaimed Fox.

"Presumably," answered Thorndyke, "but let us see whither he went. You notice, in the first place, that the man stood close to this tree" – he indicated the hornbeam – "and that he went towards the elm. Let us follow him. He passes the elm, you see, and you will observe that these tracks form a regular series leading from the hornbeam and not mixed up with the marks of the struggle. They were, therefore, probably made after the murder had been perpetrated. You will also notice that they pass along the backs of the trees – outside the avenue, that is. What does that suggest to you?"

"It suggests to me," I said, when the inspector had shaken his head hopelessly, "that there was possibly someone in the avenue when the man was stealing off."

"Precisely," said Thorndyke. "The body was found not more than nine minutes after Pratt arrived here. But the murder must have taken some time. Then the housekeeper thought she heard someone calling and came out with a lantern, and, at the same time, the general and Mr. Hanford came up the drive. The suggestion is that the man sneaked along outside the trees to avoid being seen. However, let us follow the tracks. They pass the elm and they pass on behind the next tree – but wait! There is something odd here." He passed behind the great pollard oak and looked down at the soft earth by its roots. "Here is a pair of impressions much deeper than the rest, and they are not a part of the track since their toes point towards the tree. What do you make of that?" Without waiting for an answer he began closely to scan the bole of the tree and especially a large, warty protuberance about three feet from the ground. On the bark above this was a vertical mark, as if something had scraped down the tree, and from the wart itself a dead twig had been newly broken off and lay upon the ground. Pointing to these marks Thorndyke set his foot on the protuberance, and, springing up, brought his eye above the level of the crown, whence the great boughs branched off.

"Ah!" he exclaimed. "Here is something much more definite." With the aid of another projection, he scrambled up into the crown of the tree, and, having glanced quickly round, beckoned to us. I stepped up on the projecting lump and, as my eyes rose above the crown, I perceived the brown, shiny impression of a hand on the edge. Climbing into the crown, I was quickly followed by the inspector, and we both stood up by Thorndyke between the three boughs. From where we stood we looked on the upper side of the great limb that swept out across the avenue, and there on its lichen-covered surface, we saw the imprints in reddish-brown of a pair of open hands.

"You notice," said Thorndyke, leaning out upon the bough, "that he is a short man. I cannot conveniently place my hands so low. You also note that he has both forefingers intact, and so is certainly not Ellis."

"If you mean to say, sir, that these marks were made by the murderer," said Fox, "I say it's impossible. Why, that would mean that he was here looking down at us when we were searching for him with the hounds. The presence of the hounds proves that this man could not have been the murderer."

"On the contrary," said Thorndyke, "the presence of this man with bloody hands confirms the other evidence, which all indicates that the hounds were never on the murderer's trail at all. Come now, Inspector. I put it to you: Here is a murdered man, the murderer has almost certainly blood upon his hands, and here is a man with bloody hands, lurking in a tree within a few feet of the corpse and within a few minutes of its discovery (as is shown by the footprints), what are the reasonable probabilities?"

"But you are forgetting the bloodhounds, sir, and the murderer's knife!" urged the inspector.

306

"Tut, tut, man!" exclaimed Thorndyke, "those bloodhounds are a positive obsession. But I see a sergeant coming up the drive, with the knife, I hope. Perhaps that will solve the riddle for us."

The sergeant, who carried a small dispatch-box, halted opposite the tree in some surprise while we descended, when he came forward with a military salute and handed the box to the inspector, who forthwith unlocked it and, opening the lid, displayed an object wrapped in a pocket-handkerchief.

"There is the knife, sir," said he, "just as I received it. The handkerchief is the sergeant's."

Thorndyke unrolled the handkerchief and took from it a large-sized Norwegian knife, which he looked at critically and then handed to me. While I was inspecting the blade, he shook out the handkerchief and, having looked it over on both sides, turned to the sergeant.

"At what time did you pick up this knife?" he asked.

"About seven-fifteen, sir, directly after the hounds had started. I was careful to pick it up by the ring, and I wrapped it in the handkerchief at once."

"Seven-fifteen," said Thorndyke. "Less than half-an-hour after the murder. That is very singular. Do you observe the state of this handkerchief? There is not a mark on it. Not a trace of any bloodstain, which proves that when the knife was picked up, the blood on it was already dry. But things dry slowly, if they dry at all, in the saturated air of an autumn evening. The appearances seem to suggest that the blood on the knife was dry when it was thrown down. By the way, sergeant, what do you scent your handkerchief with?"

"Scent, sir!" exclaimed the astonished officer in indignant accents, "me scent my handkerchief! No, sir, certainly not. Never used scent in my life, sir."

Thorndyke held out the handkerchief, and the sergeant sniffed at it incredulously. "It certainly does seem to smell of scent," he admitted, "but it must be the knife." The same idea having occurred to me, I applied the handle of the knife to my nose and instantly detected the sickly-sweet odour of musk.

"The question is," said the inspector, when the two articles had been tested by us all, "was it the knife that scented the handkerchief, or the handkerchief that scented the knife?"

"You heard what the sergeant said," replied Thorndyke. "There was no scent on the handkerchief when the knife was wrapped in it. Do you know, inspector, this scent seems to me to offer a very curious suggestion. Consider the facts of the case: The distinct trail leading straight to Ellis, who is, nevertheless, found to be without a scratch or a spot of blood, the

307

inconsistencies in the case that I pointed out in the train, and now this knife, apparently dropped with dried blood on it and scented with musk. To me it suggests a carefully-planned, coolly-premeditated crime. The murderer knew about the general's bloodhounds and made use of them as a blind. He planted this knife, smeared with blood and tainted with musk, to furnish a scent. No doubt some object, also scented with musk, would be drawn over the ground to give the trail. It is only a suggestion, of course, but it is worth considering."

"But, sir," the inspector objected eagerly, "if the murderer had handled the knife, it would have scented him too."

"Exactly, so, as we are assuming that the man is not a fool, we may assume that he did not handle it. He will have left it here in readiness, hidden in some place whence he could knock it down, say, with a stick, without touching it."

"Perhaps in this very tree, sir," suggested the sergeant, pointing to the oak.

"No," said Thorndyke, "he would hardly have hidden in the tree where the knife had been. The hounds might have scented the place instead of following the trail at once. The most likely hiding-place for the knife is the one nearest the spot where it was found." He walked over to the stone that marked the spot, and looking round, continued, "You see, that hornbeam is much the nearest, and its flat crown would be very convenient for the purpose – easily reached even by a short man, as he appears to be. Let us see if there are any traces of it. Perhaps you will give me a 'back up', sergeant, as we haven't a ladder."

The sergeant assented with a faint grin, and stooping beside the tree in an attitude suggesting the game of leapfrog, placed his hands firmly on his knees. Grasping a stout branch, Thorndyke swung himself up on the sergeant's broad back, whence he looked down into the crown of the tree. Then, parting the branches, he stepped onto the ledge and disappeared into the central hollow.

When he re-appeared he held in his hands two very singular objects: A pair of iron crucible-tongs and an artist's brush-case of black-japanned tin. The former article he handed down to me, but the brush-case he held carefully by its wire handle as he dropped to the ground.

"The significance of these things is, I think, obvious," he said. "The tongs were used to handle the knife with and the case to carry it in, so that it should not scent his clothes or bag. It was very carefully planned."

"If that is so," said the inspector, "the inside of the case ought to smell of musk."

308

"No doubt," said Thorndyke, "but before we open it, there is a rather important matter to be attended to. Will you give me the Vitogen powder, Jervis?"

I opened the canvas-covered "research case" and took from it an object like a diminutive pepper-caster – an iodo-form dredger in fact – and handed it to him. Grasping the brush-case by its wire handle, he sprinkled the pale yellow powder from the dredger freely all round the pull-off lid, tapping the top with his knuckles to make the fine particles spread. Then he blew off the superfluous powder, and the two police officers gave a simultaneous gasp of joy, for now, on the black background, there stood out plainly a number of finger-prints, so clear and distinct that the ridge-pattern could be made out with perfect ease.

"These will probably be his right hand," said Thorndyke. "Now for the left." He treated the body of the case in the same way, and, when he had blown off the powder, the entire surface was spotted with yellow, oval impressions. "Now, Jervis," said he, "if you will put on a glove and pull off the lid, we can test the inside."

There was no difficulty in getting the lid off, for the shoulder of the case had been smeared with vaseline – apparently to produce an airtight joint – and, as it separated with a hollow sound, a faint, musky odour exhaled from its interior.

"The remainder of the inquiry," said Thorndyke, when I pushed the lid on again, "will be best conducted at the police station, where, also, we can photograph these fingerprints."

"The shortest way will be across the meadows," said Fox, "the way the hounds went."

By this route we accordingly travelled, Thorndyke carrying the brush-case tenderly by its handle.

"I don't quite see where Ellis comes in in this job," said the inspector, as we walked along, "if the fellow had a grudge against Pratt. They weren't chums."

"I think I do," said Thorndyke. "You say that both men were prison officers at Portland at the same time. Now doesn't it seem likely that this is the work of some old convict who had been identified – and perhaps blackmailed – by Pratt, and possibly by Ellis too? That is where the value of the finger-prints comes in. If he is an old 'lag', his prints will be at Scotland Yard. Otherwise they are not of much value as a clue."

"That's true, sir," said the inspector. "I suppose you want to see Ellis."

"I want to see that purse that you spoke of, first," replied Thorndyke. "That is probably the other end of the clue."

As soon as we arrived at the station, the inspector unlocked a safe and brought out a parcel. "These are Ellis's things," said he, as he unfastened it, "and that is the purse."

He handed Thorndyke a small pigskin pouch, which my colleague opened, and having smelt the inside, passed to me. The odour of musk was plainly perceptible, especially in the small compartment at the back.

"It has probably tainted the other contents of the parcel," said Thorndyke, sniffing at each article in turn, "but my sense of smell is not keen enough to detect any scent. They all seem odourless to me, whereas the purse smells quite distinctly. Shall we have Ellis in now?"

The sergeant took a key from a locked drawer and departed for the cells, whence he presently re-appeared accompanied by the prisoner – a stout, burly man, in the last stage of dejection.

"Come, cheer up, Ellis," said the inspector. "Here's Dr. Thorndyke come down to help us and he wants to ask you one or two questions."

Ellis looked piteously at Thorndyke, and exclaimed, "I know nothing whatever about this affair, sir, I swear to God I don't."

"I never supposed you did," said Thorndyke. "But there are one or two things that I want you to tell me. To begin with, that purse: Where did you find it?"

"On the Thorpe Road, sir. It was lying in the middle of the footway."

"Had anyone else passed the spot lately? Did you meet or pass anyone?"

"Yes, sir, I met a labourer about a minute before I saw the purse. I can't imagine why he didn't see it."

"Probably because it wasn't there," said Thorndyke. "Is there a hedge there?"

"Yes, sir, a hedge on a low bank."

"Ha! Well, now, tell me. Is there anyone about here whom you knew when you and Pratt were together at Portland? Any old lag – to put it bluntly – whom you and Pratt have been putting the screw on."

"No, sir, I swear there isn't. But I wouldn't answer for Pratt. He had a rare memory for faces."

Thorndyke reflected. "Were there any escapes from Portland in your time?" he asked.

"Only one – a man named Dobbs. He made off to the sea in a sudden fog and he was supposed to be drowned. His clothes washed up on the Bill, but not his body. At any rate, he was never heard of again."

"Thank you, Ellis. Do you mind my taking your fingerprints?"

"Certainly not, sir," was the almost eager reply, and the office inking-pad being requisitioned, a rough set of finger-prints was produced, and when Thorndyke had compared them with those on the brush-case and found no resemblance, Ellis returned to his cell in quite buoyant spirits.

Having made several photographs of the strange fingerprints, we returned to town that evening, taking the negatives with us, and while we waited for our train, Thorndyke gave a few parting injunctions to the inspector. "Remember," he said, "that the man must have washed his hands before he could appear in public. Search the banks of every pond, ditch, and stream in the neighbourhood for footprints like those in the avenue, and, if you find any, search the bottom of the water thoroughly, for he is quite likely to have dropped the knife into the mud."

The photographs, which we handed in at Scotland Yard that same night, enabled the experts to identify the fingerprints as those of Francis Dobbs, an escaped convict. The two photographs – profile and full-face – which were attached to his record, were sent down to Baysford with a description of the man, and were, in due course, identified with a somewhat mysterious individual who passed by the name of Rufus Pembury and who had lived in the neighbourhood as a private gentleman for some two years. But Rufus Pembury was not to be found either at his genteel house or elsewhere. All that was known was, that on the day after the murder, he had converted his entire "personalty" into "bearer securities", and then vanished from mortal ken. Nor has he ever been heard of to this day.

"And, between ourselves," said Thorndyke, when we were discussing the case some time after, "he deserved to escape. It was clearly a case of blackmail, and to kill a blackmailer – when you have no other defence against him – is hardly murder. As to Ellis, he could never have been convicted, and Dobbs, or Pembury, must have known it. But he would have been committed to the Assizes, and that would have given time for all traces to disappear. No, Dobbs was a man of courage, ingenuity and resource, and, above all, he knocked the bottom out of the great bloodhound superstition."

The Echo of a Mutiny
Part I – Death on the Girdler

Popular belief ascribes to infants and the lower animals certain occult powers of divining character denied to the reasoning faculties of the human adult, and is apt to accept their judgment as finally overriding the pronouncements of mere experience.

Whether this belief rests upon any foundation other than the universal love of paradox it is unnecessary to inquire. It is very generally entertained, especially by ladies of a certain social status, and by Mrs. Thomas Solly it was loyally maintained as an article of faith.

"Yes," she moralized, "it's surprisin' how they know, the little children and the dumb animals. But they do. There's no deceivin' them. They can tell the gold from the dross in a moment, they can, and they reads the human heart like a book. Wonderful, I call it. I suppose it's instinct."

Having delivered herself of this priceless gem of philosophic thought, she thrust her arms elbow-deep into the foaming wash-tub and glanced admiringly at her lodger as he sat in the doorway, supporting on one knee an obese infant of eighteen months and on the other a fine tabby cat.

James Brown was an elderly seafaring man, small and slight in build and in manner suave, insinuating and perhaps a trifle sly. But he had all the sailor's love of children and animals, and the sailor's knack of making himself acceptable to them, for, as he sat with an empty pipe wobbling in the grasp of his toothless gums, the baby beamed with humid smiles, and the cat, rolled into a fluffy ball and purring like a stocking-loom, worked its fingers ecstatically as if it were trying on a new pair of gloves.

"It must be mortal lonely out at the lighthouse," Mrs. Solly resumed. "Only three men and never a neighbour to speak to, and, Lord! What a muddle they must be in with no woman to look after them and keep 'em tidy. But you won't be overworked, Mr. Brown, in these long days, daylight till past nine o'clock. I don't know what you'll do to pass the time."

"Oh, I shall find plenty to do, I expect," said Brown, "what with cleanin' the lamps and glasses and paintin' up the ironwork. And that reminds me," he added, looking round at the clock, "that time's getting on. High water at half-past ten, and here it's gone eight o'clock."

Mrs. Solly, acting on the hint, began rapidly to fish out the washed garments and wring them out into the form of short ropes. Then, having dried her hands on her apron, she relieved Brown of the protesting baby.

312

"Your room will be ready for you, Mr. Brown," said she, "when your turn comes for a spell ashore, and main glad me and Tom will be to see you back."

"Thank you, Mrs. Solly, ma'am," answered Brown, tenderly placing the cat on the floor. "You won't be more glad than what I will." He shook hands warmly with his landlady, kissed the baby, chucked the cat under the chin, and, picking up his little chest by its becket, swung it onto his shoulder and strode out of the cottage.

His way lay across the marshes, and, like the ships in the offing, he shaped his course by the twin towers of Reculver that stood up grotesquely on the rim of the land, and as he trod the springy turf, Tom Solly's fleecy charges looked up at him with vacant stares and valedictory bleatings. Once, at a dyke-gate, he paused to look back at the fair Kentish landscape. At the grey tower of St. Nicholas-at-Wade peeping above the trees and the faraway mill at Sarre, whirling slowly in the summer breeze, and, above all, at the solitary cottage where, for a brief spell in his stormy life, he had known the homely joys of domesticity and peace. Well, that was over for the present, and the lighthouse loomed ahead. With a half-sigh he passed through the gate and walked on towards Reculver.

Outside the whitewashed cottages with their official black chimneys, a petty-officer of the coast-guard was adjusting the halyards of the flagstaff. He looked round as Brown approached, and hailed him cheerily.

"Here you are, then," said he, "all figged out in your new togs, too. But we're in a bit of a difficulty, d'ye see. We've got to pull up to Whitstable this morning, so I can't send a man out with you and I can't spare a boat."

"Have I got to swim out, then?" asked Brown.

The coast-guard grinned. "Not in them new clothes, mate," he answered. "No, but there's old Willett's boat. He isn't using her to-day. He's going over to Minster to see his daughter, and he'll let us have the loan of the boat. But there's no one to go with you, and I'm responsible to Willett."

"Well, what about it?" asked Brown, with the deep-sea sailor's (usually misplaced) confidence in his power to handle a sailing-boat. "D'ye think I can't manage a tub of a boat? Me what's used the sea since I was a kid of ten?"

"Yes," said the coast-guard, "but who's to bring her back?"

"Why, the man that I'm going to relieve," answered Brown. "He don't want to swim no more than what I do."

The coast-guard reflected with his telescope pointed at a passing barge. "Well, I suppose it'll be all right," he concluded, "but it's a pity they couldn't send the tender round. However, if you undertake to send the boat back, we'll get her afloat. It's time you were off."

He strolled away to the back of the cottages, whence he presently returned with two of his mates, and the four men proceeded along the shore to where Willett's boat lay just above high-water mark.

The *Emily* was a beamy craft of the type locally known as a "half-share skiff", solidly built of oak, with varnished planking and fitted with main and mizzen lugs. She was a good handful for four men, and, as she slid over the soft chalk rocks with a hollow rumble, the coast-guards debated the advisability of lifting out the bags of shingle with which she was ballasted. However, she was at length dragged down, ballast and all, to the water's edge, and then, while Brown stepped the mainmast, the petty-officer gave him his directions. "What you've got to do," said he, "is to make use of the flood-tide. Keep her nose nor'-east, and with this trickle of nor'-westerly breeze you ought to make the light-house in one board. Anyhow don't let her get east of the lighthouse, or, when the ebb sets in, you'll be in a fix."

To these admonitions Brown listened with jaunty indifference as he hoisted the sails and watched the incoming tide creep over the level shore. Then the boat lifted on the gentle swell. Putting out an oar, he gave a vigorous shove off that sent the boat, with a final scrape, clear of the beach, and then, having dropped the rudder onto its pintles, he seated himself and calmly belayed the main-sheet.

"There he goes," growled the coast-guard, "makin' fast his sheet. They will do it" (he invariably did it himself), "and that's how accidents happen. I hope old Willett'll see his boat back all right."

He stood for some time watching the dwindling boat as it sidled across the smooth water, then he turned and followed his mates towards the station.

Out on the south-western edge of the Girdler Sand, just inside the two-fathom line, the spindle-shanked lighthouse stood a-straddle on its long screw-piles like some uncouth red-bodied wading bird. It was now nearly half-flood tide. The highest shoals were long since covered, and the lighthouse rose above the smooth sea as solitary as a slaver becalmed in the "middle passage".

On the gallery outside the lantern were two men, the entire staff of the building, of whom one sat huddled in a chair with his left leg propped up with pillows on another, while his companion rested a telescope on the rail and peered at the faint grey line of the distant land and the two tiny points that marked the twin spires of Reculver.

"I don't see any signs of the boat, Harry," said he.

314

The other man groaned. "I shall lose the tide," he complained, "and then there's another day gone."

"They can pull you down to Birchington and put you in the train," said the first man.

"I don't want no trains," growled the invalid. "The boat'll be bad enough. I suppose there's nothing coming our way, Tom?"

Tom turned his face eastward and shaded his eyes. "There's a brig coming across the tide from the north," he said. "Looks like a collier." He pointed his telescope at the approaching vessel, and added, "She's got two new cloths in her upper fore top-sail, one on each leech."

The other man sat up eagerly. "What's her trysail like, Tom?" he asked.

"Can't see it," replied Tom. "Yes, I can, now. It's tanned. Why, that'll be the old *Utopia*, Harry. She's the only brig I know that's got a tanned trysail."

"Look here, Tom," exclaimed the other, "If that's the *Utopia*, she's going to my home and I'm going aboard of her. Captain Mockett'll give me a passage, I know."

"You oughtn't to go until you're relieved, you know, Barnett," said Tom doubtfully, "it's against regulations to leave your station."

"Regulations be blowed!" exclaimed Barnett. "My leg's more to me than the regulations. I don't want to be a cripple all my life. Besides, I'm no good here, and this new chap, Brown, will be coming out presently. You run up the signal, Tom, like a good comrade, and hail the brig."

"Well, it's your look-out," said Tom, "and I don't mind saying that if I was in your place I should cut off home and see a doctor, if I got the chance." He sauntered off to the flag-locker, and, selecting the two code-flags, deliberately toggled them onto the halyards. Then, as the brig swept up within range, he hoisted the little balls of bunting to the flagstaff-head and jerked the halyards, when the two flags blew out making the signal "Need assistance."

Promptly a coal-soiled answering pennant soared to the brig's main-truck, less promptly the collier went about, and, turning her nose down stream, slowly drifted stern-forwards towards the lighthouse. Then a boat slid out through her gangway, and a couple of men plied the oars vigorously.

"Lighthouse ahoy!" roared one of them, as the boat came within hail. "What's amiss?"

"Harry Barnett has broke his leg," shouted the lighthouse keeper, "and he wants to know if Captain Mockett will give him a passage to Whitstable."

The boat turned back to the brig, and after a brief and bellowed consultation, once more pulled towards the lighthouse.

"Skipper says yus," roared the sailor, when he was within ear-shot, "and he says look alive, 'cause he don't want to miss his tide."

The injured man heaved a sigh of relief. "That's good news," said he, "though, how the blazes I'm going to get down the ladder is more than I can tell. What do you say, Jeffreys?"

"I say you'd better let me lower you with the tackle," replied Jeffreys. "You can sit in the bight of a rope and I'll give you a line to steady yourself with."

"Ah, that'll do, Tom," said Barnett, "but, for the Lord's sake, pay out the fall-rope gently."

The arrangements were made so quickly that by the time the boat was fast alongside everything was in readiness, and a minute later the injured man, dangling like a gigantic spider from the end of the tackle, slowly descended, cursing volubly to the accompaniment of the creaking of the blocks. His chest and kit-bag followed, and, as soon as these were unhooked from the tackle, the boat pulled off to the brig, which was now slowly creeping stern-foremost past the lighthouse. The sick man was hoisted up the side, his chest handed up after him, and then the brig was put on her course due south across the Kentish Flats.

Jeffreys stood on the gallery watching the receding vessel and listening to the voices of her crew as they grew small and weak in the increasing distance. Now that his gruff companion was gone, a strange loneliness had fallen on the lighthouse. The last of the homeward-bound ships had long since passed up the Princes Channel and left the calm sea desolate and blank. The distant buoys, showing as tiny black dots on the glassy surface, and the spindly shapes of the beacons which stood up from invisible shoals, but emphasized the solitude of the empty sea, and the tolling of the bell buoy on the Shivering Sand, stealing faintly down the wind, sounded weird and mournful. The day's work was already done. The lenses were polished, the lamps had been trimmed, and the little motor that worked the foghorn had been cleaned and oiled. There were several odd jobs, it is true, waiting to be done, as there always are in a lighthouse, but, just now, Jeffreys was not in a working humour. A new comrade was coming into his life to-day, a stranger with whom he was to be shut up alone, night and day, for a month on end, and whose temper and tastes and habits might mean for him pleasant companionship or jangling and discord without end. Who was this man Brown? What had he been? And what was he like? These were the questions that passed, naturally enough, through the lighthouse keeper's mind and distracted him from his usual thoughts and occupations.

Presently a speck on the landward horizon caught his eye. He snatched up the telescope eagerly to inspect it. Yes, it was a boat, but not the coast-guard's cutter, for which he was looking. Evidently a fisherman's boat and with only one man in it. He laid down the telescope with a sigh of disappointment and, filling his pipe, leaned on the rail with a dreamy eye bent on the faint grey line of the land.

Three long years had he spent in this dreary solitude, so repugnant to his active, restless nature – three blank, interminable years, with nothing to look back on but the endless succession of summer calms, stormy nights, and the chilly fogs of winter, when the unseen steamers hooted from the void and the fog-horn bellowed its hoarse warning.

Why had he come to this God-forsaken spot? And why did he stay, when the wide world called to him? And then memory painted him a picture on which his mind's eye had often looked before and which once again arose before him, shutting out the vision of the calm sea and the distant land. It was a brightly-coloured picture. It showed a cloudless sky brooding over the deep blue tropic sea, and in the middle of the picture, see-sawing gently on the quiet swell, a white-painted barque.

Her sails were clewed up untidily, her swinging yards jerked at the slack braces, and her untended wheel revolved to and fro to the oscillations of the rudder.

She was not a derelict, for more than a dozen men were on her deck, but the men were all drunk and mostly asleep, and there was never an officer among them.

Then he saw the interior of one of her cabins. The chart-rack, the tell-tale compass, and the chronometers marked it as the captain's cabin. In it were four men, and two of them lay dead on the deck. Of the other two, one was a small, cunning-faced man, who was, at the moment, kneeling beside one of the corpses to wipe a knife upon its coat. The fourth man was himself.

Again, he saw the two murderers stealing off in a quarter-boat, as the barque with her drunken crew drifted towards the spouting surf of a river-bar. He saw the ship melt away in the surf like an icicle in the sunshine, and, later, two shipwrecked mariners, picked up in an open boat and set ashore at an American port.

That was why he was here. Because he was a murderer. The other scoundrel, Amos Todd, had turned Queen's Evidence and denounced him, and he had barely managed to escape. Since then he had hidden himself from the great world, and here he must continue to hide, not from the law – for his person was unknown now that his shipmates were dead – but from the partner of his crime. It was the fear of Todd that had changed him from Jeffrey Rorke to Tom Jeffreys and had sent him to the Girdler, a prisoner

317

for life. Todd might die – might even now be dead – but he would never hear of it, would never hear the news of his release.

He roused himself and once more pointed his telescope at the distant boat. She was considerably nearer now and seemed to be heading out towards the lighthouse. Perhaps the man in her was bringing a message. At any rate, there was no sign of the coast-guard's cutter.

He went in, and, betaking himself to the kitchen, busied himself with a few simple preparations for dinner. But there was nothing to cook, for there remained the cold meat from yesterday's cooking, which he would make sufficient, with some biscuit in place of potatoes. He felt restless and unstrung. The solitude irked him, and the everlasting wash of the water among the piles jarred on his nerves.

When he went out again into the gallery the ebb-tide had set in strongly and the boat was little more than a mile distant, and now, through the glass, he could see that the man in her wore the uniform cap of the Trinity House. Then the man must be his future comrade, Brown, but this was very extraordinary. What were they to do with the boat? There was no one to take her back.

The breeze was dying away. As he watched the boat, he saw the man lower the sail and take to his oars, and something of hurry in the way the man pulled over the gathering tide, caused Jeffreys to look round the horizon. And then, for the first time, he noticed a bank of fog creeping up from the east and already so near that the beacon on the East Girdler had faded out of sight. He hastened in to start the little motor that compressed the air for the fog-horn and waited awhile to see that the mechanism was running properly. Then, as the deck vibrated to the roar of the horn, he went out once more into the gallery.

The fog was now all round the lighthouse and the boat was hidden from view. He listened intently. The enclosing wall of vapour seemed to have shut out sound as well as vision. At intervals the horn bellowed its note of warning, and then all was still save the murmur of the water among the piles below, and, infinitely faint and far away, the mournful tolling of the bell on the Shivering Sand.

At length there came to his ear the muffled sound of oars working in the holes, then, at the very edge of the circle of grey water that was visible, the boat appeared through the fog, pale and spectral, with a shadowy figure pulling furiously. The horn emitted a hoarse growl, the man looked round, perceived the lighthouse and altered his course towards it.

Jeffreys descended the iron stairway, and, walking along the lower gallery, stood at the head of the ladder earnestly watching the approaching stranger. Already he was tired of being alone. The yearning for human companionship had been growing ever since Barnett left. But what sort of

318

comrade was this stranger who was coming into his life? And coming to occupy so dominant a place in it.

The boat swept down swiftly athwart the hurrying tide. Nearer it came and yet nearer, and still Jeffreys could catch no glimpse of his new comrade's face. At length it came fairly alongside and bumped against the fender-posts, the stranger whisked in an oar and grabbed a rung of the ladder, and Jeffreys dropped a coil of rope into the boat. And still the man's face was hidden.

Jeffreys leaned out over the ladder and watched him anxiously, as he made fast the rope, unhooked the sail from the traveller and unstepped the mast. When he had set all in order, the stranger picked up a small chest, and, swinging it over his shoulder, stepped onto the ladder. Slowly, by reason of his encumbrance, he mounted, rung by rung, with never an upward glance, and Jeffreys gazed down at the top of his head with growing curiosity. At last he reached the top of the ladder and Jeffreys stooped to lend him a hand. Then, for the first time, he looked up, and Jeffreys started back with a blanched face.

"God Almighty!" he gasped. "It's Amos Todd!"

As the newcomer stepped on the gallery, the fog-horn emitted a roar like that of some hungry monster. Jeffreys turned abruptly without a word, and walked to the stairs, followed by Todd, and the two men ascended with never a sound but the hollow clank of their footsteps on the iron plates. Silently Jeffreys stalked into the living-room and, as his companion followed, he turned and motioned to the latter to set down his chest.

"You ain't much of a talker, mate," said Todd, looking round the room in some surprise. "Ain't you going to say 'Good-morning'? We're going to be good comrades, I hope. I'm Jim Brown, the new hand, I am. What might your name be?"

Jeffreys turned on him suddenly and led him to the window. "Look at me carefully, Amos Todd," he said sternly, "and then ask yourself what my name is."

At the sound of his voice Todd looked up with a start and turned pale as death. "It can't be," he whispered. "It can't be Jeff Rorke!"

The other man laughed harshly, and leaning forward, said in a low voice, "Hast thou found me, O mine enemy!"

"Don't say that!" exclaimed Todd. "Don't call me your enemy, Jeff. Lord knows but I'm glad to see you, though I'd never have known you without your beard and with that grey hair. I've been to blame, Jeff, and I know it, but it ain't no use raking up old grudges. Let bygones be bygones, Jeff, and let us be pals as we used to be." He wiped his face with his handkerchief and watched his companion apprehensively.

319

"Sit down," said Rorke, pointing to a shabby rep-covered arm-chair, "sit down and tell me what you've done with all that money. You've blued it all, I suppose, or you wouldn't be here."

"Robbed, Jeff," answered Todd, "robbed of every penny. Ah! That was an unfortunate affair, that job on board the old *Seaflower*. But it's over and done with and we'd best forget it. They're all dead but us, Jeff, so we're safe enough so long as we keep our mouths shut, all at the bottom of the sea – and the best place for 'em too."

"Yes," Rorke replied fiercely, "that's the best place for your shipmates when they know too much, at the bottom of the sea or swinging at the end of a rope." He paced up and down the little room with rapid strides, and each time that he approached Todd's chair the latter shrank back with an expression of alarm.

"Don't sit there staring at me," said Rorke. "Why don't you smoke or do something?"

Todd hastily produced a pipe from his pocket, and having filled it from a moleskin pouch, stuck it in his mouth while he searched for a match. Apparently he carried his matches loose in his pocket, for he presently brought one forth – a red-headed match, which, when he struck it on the wall, lighted with a pale-blue flame. He applied it to his pipe, sucking in his cheeks while he kept his eyes fixed on his companion. Rorke, meanwhile, halted in his walk to cut some shavings from a cake of hard tobacco with a large clasp-knife, and, as he stood, he gazed with frowning abstraction at Todd.

"This pipe's stopped," said the latter, sucking ineffectually at the mouthpiece. "Have you got such a thing as a piece of wire, Jeff?"

"No, I haven't," replied Rorke, "not up here. I'll get a bit from the store presently. Here, take this pipe till you can clean your own. I've got another in the rack there." The sailor's natural hospitality overcoming for the moment his animosity, he thrust the pipe that he had just filled towards Todd, who took it with a mumbled "Thank you" and an anxious eye on the open knife. On the wall beside the chair was a roughly-carved pipe-rack containing several pipes, one of which Rorke lifted out, and as he leaned over the chair to reach it, Todd's face went several shades paler.

"Well, Jeff," he said, after a pause, while Rorke cut a fresh "fill" of tobacco, "are we going to be pals same as what we used to be?"

Rorke's animosity lighted up afresh. "Am I going to be pals with the man that tried to swear away my life?" he said sternly, and after a pause he added, "That wants thinking about, that does, and meantime I must go and look at the engine."

When Rorke had gone the new hand sat, with the two pipes in his hands, reflecting deeply. Abstractedly he stuck the fresh pipe into his mouth, and, dropping the stopped one into the rack, felt for a match. Still with an air of abstraction he lit the pipe, and having smoked for a minute or two, rose from the chair and began softly to creep across the room, looking about him and listening intently. At the door he paused to look out into the fog, and then, having again listened attentively, he stepped on tip-toe out onto the gallery and along towards the stairway. Of a sudden the voice of Rorke brought him up with a start.

"Hallo, Todd! Where are you off to?"

"I'm just going down to make the boat secure," was the reply.

"Never you mind about the boat," said Rorke. "I'll see to her."

"Right-o, Jeff," said Todd, still edging towards the stairway. "But, I say, mate, where's the other man – the man that I'm to relieve?"

"There ain't any other man," replied Rorke. "He went off aboard a collier."

Todd's face suddenly became grey and haggard. "Then there's no one here but us two!" he gasped, and then, with an effort to conceal his fear, he asked, "But who's going to take the boat back?"

"We'll see about that presently," replied Rorke, "you get along in and unpack your chest."

He came out on the gallery as he spoke, with a lowering frown on his face. Todd cast a terrified glance at him, and then turned and ran for his life towards the stairway.

"Come back!" roared Rorke, springing forward along the gallery, but Todd's feet were already clattering down the iron steps. By the time Rorke reached the head of the stairs, the fugitive was near the bottom, but here, in his haste, he stumbled, barely saving himself by the handrail, and when he recovered his balance Rorke was upon him. Todd darted to the head of the ladder, but, as he grasped the stanchion, his pursuer seized him by the collar. In a moment he had turned with his hand under his coat. There was a quick blow, a loud curse from Rorke, an answering yell from Todd, and a knife fell spinning through the air and dropped into the fore-peak of the boat below.

"You murderous little devil!" said Rorke in an ominously quiet voice, with his bleeding hand gripping his captive by the throat. "Handy with your knife as ever, eh? So you were off to give information, were you?"

"No, I wasn't Jeff," replied Todd in a choking voice. "I wasn't, s'elp me, God. Let go, Jeff. I didn't mean no harm. I was only – " With a sudden wrench he freed one hand and struck out frantically at his captor's face. But Rorke warded off the blow, and, grasping the other wrist, gave a violent push and let go. Todd staggered backward a few paces along the staging, bringing up at the extreme edge, and here, for a sensible time, he stood with wide-open mouth and starting eye-balls, swaying and clutching

321

wildly at the air. Then, with a shrill scream, he toppled backwards and fell, striking a pile in his descent and rebounding into the water.

In spite of the audible thump of his head on the pile, he was not stunned, for when he rose to the surface, he struck out vigorously, uttering short, stifled cries for help. Rorke watched him with set teeth and quickened breath, but made no move. Smaller and still smaller grew the head with its little circle of ripples, swept away on the swift ebb-tide, and fainter the bubbling cries that came across the smooth water. At length as the small black spot began to fade in the fog, the drowning man, with a final effort, raised his head clear of the surface and sent a last, despairing shriek towards the lighthouse. The fog-horn sent back an answering bellow, the head sank below the surface and was seen no more, and in the dreadful stillness that settled down upon the sea there sounded faint and far away the muffled tolling of a bell.

Rorke stood for some minutes immovable, wrapped in thought. Presently the distant hoot of a steamer's whistle aroused him. The ebb-tide shipping was beginning to come down and the fog might lift at any moment, and there was the boat still alongside. She must be disposed of at once. No one had seen her arrive and no one must see her made fast to the lighthouse. Once get rid of the boat and all traces of Todd's visit would be destroyed. He ran down the ladder and stepped into the boat. It was simple. She was heavily ballasted, and would go down if she filled.

He shifted some of the bags of shingle, and, lifting the bottom boards, pulled out the plug. Instantly a large jet of water spouted up into the bottom. Rorke looked at it critically, and, deciding that it would fill her in a few minutes, replaced the bottom boards, and having secured the mast and sail with a few turns of the sheet round a thwart, to prevent them from floating away, he cast off the mooring-rope and stepped on the ladder.

As the released boat began to move away on the tide, he ran up and mounted to the upper gallery to watch her disappearance. Suddenly he remembered Todd's chest. It was still in the room below. With a hurried glance around into the fog, he ran down to the room, and snatching up the chest, carried it out on the lower gallery. After another nervous glance around to assure himself that no craft was in sight, he heaved the chest over the handrail, and, when it fell with a loud splash into the sea, he waited to watch it float away after its owner and the sunken boat. But it never rose, and presently he returned to the upper gallery.

The fog was thinning perceptibly now, and the boat remained plainly visible as she drifted away. But she sank more slowly than he had expected, and presently as she drifted farther away, he fetched the telescope and peered at her with growing anxiety. It would be unfortunate

322

if anyone saw her, if she should be picked up here, with her plug out, it would be disastrous.

He was beginning to be really alarmed. Through the glass he could see that the boat was now rolling in a sluggish, water-logged fashion, but she still showed some inches of free-board, and the fog was thinning every moment.

Presently the blast of a steamer's whistle sounded close at hand. He looked round hurriedly and, seeing nothing, again pointed the telescope eagerly at the dwindling boat. Suddenly he gave a gasp of relief. The boat had rolled gunwale under, had staggered back for a moment and then rolled again, slowly, finally, with the water pouring in over the submerged gunwale.

In a few more seconds she had vanished. Rorke lowered the telescope and took a deep breath. Now he was safe. The boat had sunk unseen. But he was better than safe. He was free. His evil spirit, the standing menace of his life, was gone, and the wide world, the world of life, of action, of pleasure, called to him.

In a few minutes the fog lifted. The sun shone brightly on the red-funnelled cattle-boat whose whistle had startled him just now, the summer blue came back to sky and sea, and the land peeped once more over the edge of the horizon.

He went in, whistling cheerfully, and stopped the motor, returned to coil away the rope that he had thrown to Todd, and, when he had hoisted a signal for assistance, he went in once more to eat his solitary meal in peace and gladness.

Part II – The Singing Bone
(Related by Christopher Jervis, M.D.)

In every kind of scientific work a certain amount of manual labour naturally appertains, labour that cannot be performed by the scientist himself, since art is long but life is short. A chemical analysis involves a laborious "clean up" of apparatus and laboratory, for which the chemist has no time, the preparation of a skeleton – the maceration, bleaching, "assembling," and riveting together of bones – must be carried out by someone whose time is not too precious. And so with other scientific activities. Behind the man of science with his outfit of knowledge is the indispensable mechanic with his outfit of manual skill.

Thorndyke's laboratory assistant, Polton, was a fine example of the latter type: Deft, resourceful, ingenious, and untiring. He was somewhat of an inventive genius, too, and it was one of his inventions that connected us with the singular case that I am about to record.

Though by trade a watchmaker, Polton was, by choice, an optician. Optical apparatus was the passion of his life, and when, one day, he produced for our inspection an improved prism for increasing the efficiency of gas-buoys, Thorndyke at once brought the invention to the notice of a friend at the Trinity House.

As a consequence, we three – Thorndyke, Polton, and I – found ourselves early on a fine July morning making our way down Middle Temple Lane bound for the Temple Pier. A small oil-launch lay alongside the pontoon, and, as we made our appearance, a red-faced, white-whiskered gentleman stood up in the cockpit.

"Here's a delightful morning, Doctor," he sang out in a fine, brassy, resonant, sea-faring voice, "sort of day for a trip to the lower river, hey? Hallo, Polton! Coming down to take the bread out of our mouths, are you? Ha, ha!" The cheery laugh rang out over the river and mingled with the throb of the engine as the launch moved off from the pier.

Captain Grumpass was one of the Elder Brethren of the Trinity House. Formerly a client of Thorndyke's he had subsided, as Thorndyke's clients were apt to do, into the position of a personal friend, and his hearty regard included our invaluable assistant.

"Nice state of things," continued the captain, with a chuckle, "when a body of nautical experts have got to be taught their business by a parcel of lawyers or doctors, what? I suppose trade's slack and '*Satan findeth mischief still*,' hey, Polton?"

"There isn't much doing on the civil side, sir," replied Polton, with a quaint, crinkly smile, "but the criminals are still going strong."

"Ha! Mystery department still flourishing, what? And, by Jove! Talking of mysteries, Doctor, our people have got a queer problem to work out, something quite in your line – quite. Yes, and, by the Lord Moses, since I've got you here, why shouldn't I suck your brains?"

"Exactly," said Thorndyke. "Why shouldn't you?"

"Well, then, I will," said the captain, "so here goes. All hands to the pump!" He lit a cigar, and, after a few preliminary puffs, began. "The mystery, shortly stated, is this: One of our lighthousemen has disappeared – vanished off the face of the earth and left no trace. He may have bolted, he may have been drowned accidentally or he may have been murdered. But I'd rather give you the particulars in order. At the end of last week a barge brought into Ramsgate a letter from the screw-pile lighthouse on the Girdler. There are only two men there, and it seems that one of them, a man named Barnett, had broken his leg, and he asked that the tender should be sent to bring him ashore. Well, it happened that the local tender, the Warden, was up on the slip in Ramsgate Harbour, having a scrape down, and wouldn't be available for a day or two, so, as the case was urgent, the officer at Ramsgate sent a letter to the lighthouse by one of the pleasure steamers saying that the man should be relieved by boat on the following morning, which was Saturday. He also wrote to a new hand who had just been taken on, a man named James Brown, who was lodging near Reculver, waiting his turn, telling him to go out on Saturday morning in the coast-guard's boat, and he sent a third letter to the coast-guard at Reculver asking him to take Brown out to the lighthouse and bring Barnett ashore. Well, between them, they made a fine muddle of it. The coast-guard couldn't spare either a boat or a man, so they borrowed a fisherman's boat, and in this the man Brown started off alone, like an idiot, on the chance that Barnett would be able to sail the boat back in spite of his broken leg.

"Meanwhile Barnett, who is a Whitstable man, had signalled a collier bound for his native town, and got taken off, so that the other keeper, Thomas Jeffreys, was left alone until Brown should turn up.

"But Brown never did turn up. The coast-guard helped him to put off and saw him well out to sea, and the keeper, Jeffreys, saw a sailing-boat with one man in her making for the lighthouse. Then a bank of fog came up and hid the boat, and when the fog cleared she was nowhere to be seen. Man and boat had vanished and left no sign."

"He may have been run down," Thorndyke suggested.

"He may," agreed the captain, "but no accident has been reported. The coast-guards think he may have capsized in a squall – they saw him make the sheet fast. But there weren't any squalls, the weather was quite calm."

"Was he all right and well when he put off?" inquired Thorndyke.

"Yes," replied the captain. "The coast-guards' report is highly circumstantial – in fact, it's full of silly details that have no bearing on anything. This is what they say." He pulled out an official letter and read: "'*When last seen, the missing man was seated in the boat's stern to windward of the helm. He had belayed the sheet. He was holding a pipe and tobacco-pouch in his hands and steering with his elbow. He was filling the pipe from the tobacco-pouch.*' There! '*He was holding the pipe in his hand,*' mark you! Not with his toes, and he was filling it from a tobacco-pouch, whereas you'd have expected him to fill it from a coalscuttle or a feeding-bottle. Bah!" The captain rammed the letter back in his pocket and puffed scornfully at his cigar.

"You are hardly fair to the coast-guard," said Thorndyke, laughing at the captain's vehemence. "The duty of a witness is to give all the facts, not a judicious selection."

"But, my dear sir," said Captain Grumpass, "what the deuce can it matter what the poor devil filled his pipe from?"

"Who can say?" answered Thorndyke. "It may turn out to be a highly material fact. One never knows beforehand. The value of a particular fact depends on its relation to the rest of the evidence."

"I suppose it does," grunted the captain, and he continued to smoke in reflective silence until we opened Blackwall Point, when he suddenly stood up.

"There's a steam trawler alongside our wharf," he announced. "Now what the deuce can she be doing there?" He scanned the little steamer attentively, and continued, "They seem to be landing something, too. Just pass me those glasses, Polton. Why, hang me! It's a dead body! But why on earth are they landing it on our wharf? They must have known you were coming, Doctor."

As the launch swept alongside the wharf, the captain sprang up lightly and approached the group gathered round the body. "What's this?" he asked. "Why have they brought this thing here?"

The master of the trawler, who had superintended the landing, proceeded to explain.

"It's one of your men, sir," said he. "We saw the body lying on the edge of the South Shingles Sand, close to the beacon, as we passed at low water, so we put off the boat and fetched it aboard. As there was nothing to identify the man by, I had a look in his pockets and found this letter."

He handed the captain an official envelope addressed to "*Mr. J. Brown, c/o Mr. Solly, Shepherd, Reculver, Kent*".

"Why, this is the man we were speaking about, Doctor," exclaimed Captain Grumpass. "What a very singular coincidence. But what are we to do with the body?"

"You will have to write to the coroner," replied Thorndyke. "By the way, did you turn out all the pockets?" he asked, turning to the skipper of the trawler.

"No, sir," was the reply. "I found the letter in the first pocket that I felt in, so I didn't examine any of the others. Is there anything more that you want to know, sir?"

"Nothing but your name and address, for the coroner," replied Thorndyke, and the skipper, having given this information and expressed the hope that the coroner would not keep him "hanging about", returned to his vessel, and pursued his way to Billingsgate.

"I wonder if you would mind having a look at the body of this poor devil, while Polton is showing us his contraptions," said Captain Grumpass.

"I can't do much without a coroner's order," replied Thorndyke, "but if it will give you any satisfaction, Jervis and I will make a preliminary inspection with pleasure."

"I should be glad if you would," said the captain. "We should like to know that the poor beggar met his end fairly."

The body was accordingly moved to a shed, and, as Polton was led away, carrying the black bag that contained his precious model, we entered the shed and commenced our investigation.

The deceased was a small, elderly man, decently dressed in a somewhat nautical fashion. He appeared to have been dead only two or three days, and the body, unlike the majority of sea-borne corpses, was uninjured by fish or crabs. There were no fractured bones or other gross injuries, and no wounds, excepting a rugged tear in the scalp at the back of the head.

"The general appearance of the body," said Thorndyke, when he had noted these particulars, "suggests death by drowning, though, of course, we can't give a definite opinion until a *post-mortem* has been made."

"You don't attach any significance to that scalp-wound, then?" I asked.

"As a cause of death? No. It was obviously inflicted during life, but it seems to have been an oblique blow that spent its force on the scalp, leaving the skull uninjured. But it is very significant in another way."

"In what way?" I asked.

Thorndyke took out his pocket-case and extracted a pair of forceps. "Consider the circumstances," said he. "This man put off from the shore to go to the lighthouse, but never arrived there. The question is, where did

327

he arrive?" As he spoke he stooped over the corpse and turned back the hair round the wound with the beak of the forceps. "Look at those white objects among the hair, Jervis, and inside the wound. They tell us something, I think."

I examined, through my lens, the chalky fragments to which he pointed. "These seem to be bits of shells and the tubes of some marine worm," I said.

"Yes," he answered. "The broken shells are evidently those of the acorn barnacle, and the other fragments are mostly pieces of the tubes of the common *serpula*. The inference that these objects suggest is an important one. It is that this wound was produced by some body encrusted by acorn barnacles and serpula, that is to say, by a body that is periodically submerged. Now, what can that body be, and how can the deceased have knocked his head against it?"

"It might be the stem of a ship that ran him down," I suggested.

"I don't think you would find many *serpulae* on the stem of a ship," said Thorndyke. "The combination rather suggests some stationary object between tidemarks, such as a beacon. But one doesn't see how a man could knock his head against a beacon, while, on the other hand, there are no other stationary objects out in the estuary to knock against except buoys, and a buoy presents a flat surface that could hardly have produced this wound. By the way, we may as well see what there is in his pockets, though it is not likely that robbery had anything to do with his death."

"No," I agreed, "and I see his watch is in his pocket, quite a good silver one," I added, taking it out. "It has stopped at 12:13."

"That may be important," said Thorndyke, making a note of the fact, "but we had better examine the pockets one at a time, and put the things back when we have looked at them."

The first pocket that we turned out was the left hip-pocket of the monkey jacket. This was apparently the one that the skipper had rifled, for we found in it two letters, both bearing the crest of the Trinity House. These, of course, we returned without reading, and then passed on to the right pocket. The contents of this were common-place enough, consisting of a briar pipe, a moleskin pouch, and a number of loose matches.

"Rather a casual proceeding, this," I remarked, "to carry matches loose in the pocket, and a pipe with them, too."

"Yes," agreed Thorndyke, "especially with these very inflammable matches. You notice that the sticks had been coated at the upper end with sulphur before the red phosphorous heads were put on. They would light with a touch, and would be very difficult to extinguish, which, no doubt, is the reason that this type of match is so popular among seamen, who have to light their pipes in all sorts of weather." As he spoke he picked up the

328

pipe and looked at it reflectively, turning it over in his hand and peering into the bowl. Suddenly he glanced from the pipe to the dead man's face and then, with the forceps, turned back the lips to look into the mouth.

"Let us see what tobacco he smokes," said he.

I opened the sodden pouch and displayed a mass of dark, fine-cut tobacco. "It looks like shag," I said.

"Yes, it is shag," he replied, "and now we will see what is in the pipe. It has been only half-smoked out." He dug out the "dottle" with his pocket-knife onto a sheet of paper, and we both inspected it. Clearly it was not shag, for it consisted of coarsely-cut shreds and was nearly black.

"Shavings from a cake of 'hard'," was my verdict, and Thorndyke agreed as he shot the fragments back into the pipe.

The other pockets yielded nothing of interest, except a pocket-knife, which Thorndyke opened and examined closely. There was not much money, though as much as one would expect, and enough to exclude the idea of robbery.

"Is there a sheath-knife on that strap?" Thorndyke asked, pointing to a narrow leather belt. I turned back the jacket and looked.

"There is a sheath," I said, "but no knife. It must have dropped out."

"That is rather odd," said Thorndyke. "A sailor's sheath-knife takes a deal of shaking out as a rule. It is intended to be used in working on the rigging when the man is aloft, so that he can get it out with one hand while he is holding on with the other. It has to be and usually is very secure, for the sheath holds half the handle as well as the blade. What makes one notice the matter in this case is that the man, as you see, carried a pocket-knife, and, as this would serve all the ordinary purposes of a knife, it seems to suggest that the sheath-knife was carried for defensive purposes – as a weapon, in fact. However, we can't get much further in the case without a *post-mortem*, and here comes the captain."

Captain Grumpass entered the shed and looked down commiseratingly at the dead seaman.

"Is there anything, Doctor, that throws any light on the man's disappearance?" he asked.

"There are one or two curious features in the case," Thorndyke replied, "but, oddly enough, the only really important point arises out of that statement of the coast guard's, concerning which you were so scornful."

"You don't say so!" exclaimed the captain.

"Yes," said Thorndyke, "the coast-guard states that when last seen deceased was filling his pipe from his tobacco-pouch. Now his pouch contains shag, but the pipe in his pocket contains hard cut."

"Is there no cake tobacco in any of the pockets?"

"Not a fragment. Of course, it is possible that he might have had a piece and used it up to fill the pipe, but there is no trace of any on the blade of his pocket-knife, and you know how this juicy black cake stains a knife-blade. His sheath-knife is missing, but he would hardly have used that to shred tobacco when he had a pocket-knife."

"No," assented the captain. "But are you sure he hadn't a second pipe?"

"There was only one pipe," replied Thorndyke, "and that was not his own."

"Not his own!" exclaimed the captain, halting by a huge, chequered buoy, to stare at my colleague. "How do you know it was not his own?"

"By the appearance of the vulcanite mouthpiece," said Thorndyke. "It showed deep tooth-marks, in fact, it was nearly bitten through. Now a man who bites through his pipe usually presents certain definite physical peculiarities, among which is, necessarily, a fairly good set of teeth. But the dead man had not a tooth in his head."

The captain cogitated a while, and then remarked, "I don't quite see the bearing of this."

"Don't you?" said Thorndyke. "It seems to me highly suggestive. Here is a man who, when last seen, was filling his pipe with a particular kind of tobacco. He is picked up dead, and his pipe contains a totally different kind of tobacco. Where did that tobacco come from? The obvious suggestion is that he had met someone."

"Yes, it does look like it," agreed the captain.

"Then," continued Thorndyke, "there is the fact that his sheath-knife is missing. That may mean nothing, but we have to bear it in mind. And there is another curious circumstance. There is a wound on the back of the head caused by a heavy bump against some body that was covered with acorn barnacles and marine worms. Now there are no piers or stages out in the open estuary. The question is, what could he have struck?"

"Oh, there is nothing in that," said the captain. "When a body has been washing about in a tide-way for close on three days – "

"But this is not a question of a body," Thorndyke interrupted. "The wound was made during life."

"The deuce it was!" exclaimed the captain. "Well, all I can suggest is that he must have fouled one of the beacons in the fog, stove in his boat and bumped his head, though, I must admit, that's rather a lame explanation." He stood for a minute gazing at his toes with a cogitative frown and then looked up at Thorndyke.

"I have an idea," he said. "From what you say, this matter wants looking into pretty carefully. Now, I am going down on the tender to-day to make inquiries on the spot. What do you say to coming with me as

330

adviser – as a matter of business, of course – you and Dr. Jervis? I shall start about eleven, we shall be at the lighthouse by three o'clock, and you can get back to town to-night, if you want to. What do you say?"

"There's nothing to hinder us," I put in eagerly, for even at Bugsby's Hole the river looked very alluring on this summer morning.

"Very well," said Thorndyke, "we will come. Jervis is evidently hankering for a sea-trip, and so am I, for that matter."

"It's a business engagement, you know," the captain stipulated.

"Nothing of the kind," said Thorndyke. "It's unmitigated pleasure – the pleasure of the voyage and your high well-born society."

"I didn't mean that," grumbled the captain, "but, if you are coming as guests, send your man for your nightgear and let us bring you back to-morrow evening."

"We won't disturb Polton," said my colleague. "We can take the train from Blackwall and fetch our things ourselves. Eleven o'clock, you said?"

"Thereabouts," said Captain Grumpass, "but don't put yourselves out."

The means of communication in London have reached an almost undesirable state of perfection. With the aid of the snorting train and the tinkling, two-wheeled "gondola", we crossed and re-crossed the town with such celerity that it was barely eleven when we re-appeared on Trinity Wharf with a joint Gladstone and Thorndyke's little green case.

The tender had hauled out of Bow Creek, and now lay alongside the wharf with a great striped can buoy dangling from her derrick, and Captain Grumpass stood at the gangway, his jolly, red face beaming with pleasure. The buoy was safely stowed forward, the derrick hauled up to the mast, the loose shrouds rehooked to the screw-lanyards, and the steamer, with four jubilant hoots, swung round and shoved her sharp nose against the incoming tide.

For near upon four hours the ever-widening stream of the "London River" unfolded its moving panorama. The smoke and smell of Woolwich Reach gave place to lucid air made soft by the summer haze, the grey huddle of factories fell away and green levels of cattle-spotted marsh stretched away to the high land bordering the river valley. Venerable training ships displayed their chequered hulls by the wooded shore, and whispered of the days of oak and hemp, when the tall three-decker, comely and majestic, with her soaring heights of canvas, like towers of ivory, had not yet given place to the mud-coloured saucepans that fly the white ensign now-a-days and devour the substance of the British taxpayer – when a sailor was a sailor and not a mere seafaring mechanic. Sturdily breasting the flood tide, the tender threaded her way through the endless procession of shipping, barges, billy-boys, schooners, brigs, lumpish Black-seamen,

331

blue-funnelled China tramps, rickety Baltic barques with twirling windmills, gigantic liners, staggering under a mountain of top-hamper. Erith, Purfleet, Greenhithe, Grays greeted us and passed astern. The chimneys of Northfleet, the clustering roofs of Gravesend, the populous anchorage and the lurking batteries, were left behind, and, as we swung out of the Lower Hope, the wide expanse of sea reach spread out before us like a great sheet of blue-shot satin.

About half-past-twelve, the ebb overtook us and helped us on our way, as we could see by the speed with which the distant land slid past, and the freshening of the air as we passed through it.

But sky and sea were hushed in a summer calm. Balls of fleecy cloud hung aloft, motionless in the soft blue, the barges drifted on the tide with drooping sails, and a big, striped bell buoy – surmounted by a staff and cage and labelled "Shivering Sand" – sat dreaming in the sun above its motionless reflection, to rouse for a moment as it met our wash, nod its cage drowsily, utter a solemn ding-dong, and fall asleep again.

It was shortly after passing the buoy that the gaunt shape of a screw-pile lighthouse began to loom up ahead, its dull-red paint turned to vermilion by the early afternoon sun. As we drew nearer, the name *Girdler*, painted in huge, white letters, became visible, and two men could be seen in the gallery around the lantern, inspecting us through a telescope.

"Shall you be long at the lighthouse, sir?" the master of the tender inquired of Captain Grumpass, "because we're going down to the North-East Pan Sand to fix this new buoy and take up the old one."

"Then you'd better put us off at the lighthouse and come back for us when you've finished the job," was the reply. "I don't know how long we shall be."

The tender was brought to, a boat lowered, and a couple of hands pulled us across the intervening space of water.

"It will be a dirty climb for you in your shore-going clothes," the captain remarked – he was as spruce as a new pin himself, "but the stuff will all wipe off." We looked up at the skeleton shape. The falling tide had exposed some fifteen feet of the piles, and piles and ladder alike were swathed in sea-grass and encrusted with barnacles and worm-tubes. But we were not such town-sparrows as the captain seemed to think, for we both followed his lead without difficulty up the slippery ladder, Thorndyke clinging tenaciously to his little green case, from which he refused to be separated even for an instant.

"These gentlemen and I," said the captain, as we stepped on the stage at the head of the ladder, "have come to make inquiries about the missing man, James Brown. Which of you is Jeffreys?"

332

"I am, sir," replied a tall, powerful, square-jawed, beetle-browed man, whose left hand was tied up in a rough bandage.

"What have you been doing to your hand?" asked the captain.

"I cut it while I was peeling some potatoes," was the reply. "It isn't much of a cut, sir."

"Well, Jeffreys," said the captain, "Brown's body has been picked up and I want particulars for the inquest. You'll be summoned as a witness, I suppose, so come in and tell us all you know."

We entered the living-room and seated ourselves at the table. The captain opened a massive pocket-book, while Thorndyke, in his attentive, inquisitive fashion, looked about the odd, cabin-like room as if making a mental inventory of its contents.

Jeffreys' statement added nothing to what we already knew. He had seen a boat with one man in it making for the lighthouse. Then the fog had drifted up and he had lost sight of the boat. He started the fog-horn and kept a bright look-out, but the boat never arrived. And that was all he knew. He supposed that the man must have missed the lighthouse and been carried away on the ebb-tide, which was running strongly at the time.

"What time was it when you last saw the boat?" Thorndyke asked.

"About half-past eleven," replied Jeffreys.

"What was the man like?" asked the captain.

"I don't know, sir. He was rowing, and his back was towards me."

"Had he any kit-bag or chest with him?" asked Thorndyke.

"He'd got his chest with him," said Jeffreys.

"What sort of chest was it?" inquired Thorndyke.

"A small chest, painted green, with rope beckets."

"Was it corded?"

"It had a single cord round, to hold the lid down."

"Where was it stowed?"

"In the stern-sheets, sir."

"How far off was the boat when you last saw it?"

"About half-a-mile."

"Half-a-mile!" exclaimed the captain. "Why, how the deuce could you see that chest half-a-mile away?"

The man reddened and cast a look of angry suspicion at Thorndyke. "I was watching the boat through the glass, sir," he replied sulkily.

"I see," said Captain Grumpass. "Well, that will do, Jeffreys. We shall have to arrange for you to attend the inquest. Tell Smith I want to see him."

The examination concluded, Thorndyke and I moved our chairs to the window, which looked out over the sea to the east. But it was not the sea or the passing ships that engaged my colleague's attention. On the wall, beside the window, hung a rudely-carved pipe-rack containing five pipes.

Thorndyke had noted it when we entered the room, and now, as we talked, I observed him regarding it from time to time with speculative interest.

"You men seem to be inveterate smokers," he remarked to the keeper, Smith, when the captain had concluded the arrangements for the "shift."

"Well, we do like our bit of 'baccy, sir, and that's a fact," answered Smith. "You see, sir," he continued, "it's a lonely life, and tobacco's cheap out here."

"How is that?" asked Thorndyke.

"Why, we get it given to us. The small craft from foreign, especially the Dutchmen, generally heave us a cake or two when they pass close. We're not ashore, you see, so there's no duty to pay."

"So you don't trouble the tobacconists much? Don't go in for cut tobacco?"

"No, sir, we'd have to buy it, and then the cut stuff wouldn't keep. No, it's hard-tack to eat out here and hard tobacco to smoke."

"I see you've got a pipe-rack, too, quite a stylish affair."

"Yes," said Smith, "I made it in my off-time. Keeps the place tidy and looks more ship-shape than letting the pipes lay about anywhere."

"Someone seems to have neglected his pipe," said Thorndyke, pointing to one at the end of the rack which was coated with green mildew.

"Yes, that's Parsons, my mate. He must have left it when he went off near a month ago. Pipes do go mouldy in the damp air out here."

"How soon does a pipe go mouldy if it is left untouched?" Thorndyke asked.

"It's according to the weather," said Smith. "When it's warm and damp they'll begin to go in about a week. Now here's Barnett's pipe that he's left behind – the man that broke his leg, you know, sir – it's just beginning to spot a little. He couldn't have used it for a day or two before he went."

"And are all these other pipes yours?"

"No, sir. This here one is mine. The end one is Jeffreys', and I suppose the middle one is his too, but I don't know it."

"You're a demon for pipes, Doctor," said the captain, strolling up at this moment. "You seem to make a special study of them."

"'*The proper study of mankind is man*,'" replied Thorndyke, as the keeper retired, "and '*man*' includes those objects on which his personality is impressed. Now a pipe is a very personal thing. Look at that row in the rack. Each has its own physiognomy which, in a measure, reflects the peculiarities of the owner. There is Jeffreys' pipe at the end, for instance. The mouth-piece is nearly bitten through, the bowl scraped to a shell and scored inside and the brim battered and chipped. The whole thing speaks of rude strength and rough handling. He chews the stem as he smokes, he

334

scrapes the bowl violently, and he bangs the ashes out with unnecessary force. And the man fits the pipe exactly. Powerful, square-jawed and, I should say, violent on occasion."

"Yes, he looks a tough customer, does Jeffreys," agreed the captain.

"Then," continued Thorndyke, "there is Smith's pipe, next to it, 'coked' up until the cavity is nearly filled and burnt all round the edge – a talker's pipe, constantly going out and being relit. But the one that interests me most is the middle one."

"Didn't Smith say that was Jeffreys' too?" I said.

"Yes," replied Thorndyke, "but he must be mistaken. It is the very opposite of Jeffreys' pipe in every respect. To begin with, although it is an old pipe, there is not a sign of any tooth-mark on the mouth-piece. It is the only one in the rack that is quite unmarked. Then the brim is quite uninjured – it has been handled gently, and the silver band is jet-black, whereas the band on Jeffreys' pipe is quite bright."

"I hadn't noticed that it had a band," said the captain. "What has made it so black?"

Thorndyke lifted the pipe out of the rack and looked at it closely. "Silver sulphide," said he, "the sulphur no doubt derived from something carried in the pocket."

"I see," said Captain Grumpass, smothering a yawn and gazing out of the window at the distant tender. "Incidentally it's full of tobacco. What moral do you draw from that?"

Thorndyke turned the pipe over and looked closely at the mouth-piece. "The moral is," he replied, "that you should see that your pipe is clear before you fill it." He pointed to the mouth-piece, the bore of which was completely stopped up with fine fluff.

"An excellent moral too," said the captain, rising with another yawn. "If you'll excuse me a minute I'll just go and see what the tender is up to. She seems to be crossing to the East Girdler." He reached the telescope down from its brackets and went out onto the gallery.

As the captain retreated, Thorndyke opened his pocket-knife, and, sticking the blade into the bowl of the pipe, turned the tobacco out into his hand.

"Shag, by Jove!" I exclaimed.

"Yes," he answered, poking it back into the bowl. "Didn't you expect it to be shag?"

"I don't know that I expected anything," I admitted. "The silver band was occupying my attention."

"Yes, that is an interesting point," said Thorndyke, "but let us see what the obstruction consists of." He opened the green case, and, taking out a dissecting needle, neatly extracted a little ball of fluff from the bore of the pipe. Laying this on a glass slide, he teased it out in a drop of glycerine and put on a cover-glass while I set up the microscope.

"Better put the pipe back in the rack," he said, as he laid the slide on the stage of the instrument. I did so and then turned, with no little excitement, to watch him as he examined the specimen. After a brief inspection he rose and waved his hand towards the microscope.

"Take a look at it, Jervis," he said.

I applied my eye to the instrument, and, moving the slide about, identified the constituents of the little mass of fluff. The ubiquitous cotton fibre was, of course, in evidence, and a few fibres of wool, but the most remarkable objects were two or three hairs – very minute hairs of a definite zigzag shape and having a flat expansion near the free end like the blade of a paddle.

"These are the hairs of some small animal," I said. "Not a mouse or rat or any rodent, I should say. Some small insectivorous animal, I fancy. Yes! Of course! They are the hairs of a mole." I stood up, and, as the importance of the discovery flashed on me, I looked at my colleague in silence.

"Yes," he said, "they are unmistakable, and they furnish the keystone of the argument."

"You think that this is really the dead man's pipe, then?" I said.

"According to the law of multiple evidence," he replied, "it is practically a certainty. Consider the facts in sequence. Since there is no sign of mildew on it, this pipe can have been here only a short time, and must belong either to Barnett, Smith, Jeffreys, or Brown. It is an old pipe, but it has no tooth-marks on it. Therefore it has been used by a man who has no teeth. But Barnett, Smith, and Jeffreys all have teeth and mark their pipes, whereas Brown has no teeth. The tobacco in it is shag. But these three men do not smoke shag, whereas Brown had shag in his pouch. The silver band is encrusted with sulphide, and Brown carried sulphur-tipped matches loose in his pocket with his pipe. We find hairs of a mole in the bore of the pipe, and Brown carried a moleskin pouch in the pocket in which he appears to have carried his pipe. Finally, Brown's pocket contained a pipe which was obviously not his and which closely resembled that of Jeffreys, it contained tobacco similar to that which Jeffreys smokes and different from that in Brown's pouch. It appears to me quite conclusive, especially when we add to this evidence the other items that are in our possession."

"What items are they?" I asked.

"First there is the fact that the dead man had knocked his head heavily against some periodically submerged body covered with acorn barnacles and serpulae. Now the piles of this lighthouse answer to the description exactly, and there are no other bodies in the neighbourhood that do, for even the beacons are too large to have produced that kind of wound. Then the dead man's sheath-knife is missing, and Jeffreys has a knife-wound on his hand. You must admit that the circumstantial evidence is overwhelming."

At this moment the captain bustled into the room with the telescope in his hand. "The tender is coming up towing a strange boat," he said. "I expect it's the missing one, and, if it is, we may learn something. You'd better pack up your traps and get ready to go on board."

We packed the green case and went out into the gallery, where the two keepers were watching the approaching tender, Smith frankly curious and interested, Jeffreys restless, fidgety and noticeably pale. As the steamer came opposite the lighthouse, three men dropped into the boat and pulled across, and one of them – the mate of the tender – came climbing up the ladder.

"Is that the missing boat?" the captain sang out.

"Yes, sir," answered the officer, stepping onto the staging and wiping his hands on the reverse aspect of his trousers. "We saw her lying on the dry patch of the East Girdler. There's been some hanky-panky in this job, sir."

"Foul play, you think, hey?"

"Not a doubt of it, sir. The plug was out and lying loose in the bottom, and we found a sheath-knife sticking into the kelson forward among the coils of the painter. It was stuck in hard as if it had dropped from a height."

"That's odd," said the captain. "As to the plug, it might have got out by accident."

"But it hadn't sir," said the mate. "The ballast-bags had been shifted along to get the bottom boards up. Besides, sir, a seaman wouldn't let the boat fill – he'd have put the plug back and baled out."

"That's true," replied Captain Grumpass, "and certainly the presence of the knife looks fishy. But where the deuce could it have dropped from, out in the open sea? Knives don't drop from the clouds – fortunately. What do you say, Doctor?"

"I should say that it is Brown's own knife, and that it probably fell from this staging."

Jeffreys turned swiftly, crimson with wrath. "What d'ye mean?" he demanded. "Haven't I said that the boat never came here?"

"You have," replied Thorndyke, "but if that is so, how do you explain the fact that your pipe was found in the dead man's pocket and that the dead man's pipe is at this moment in your pipe-rack?"

The crimson flush on Jeffreys' face faded as quickly as it had come. "I don't know what you're talking about," he faltered.

337

"I'll tell you," said Thorndyke. "I will relate what happened and you shall check my statements. Brown brought his boat alongside and came up into the living-room, bringing his chest with him. He filled his pipe and tried to light it, but it was stopped and wouldn't draw. Then you lent him a pipe of yours and filled it for him. Soon afterwards you came out on this staging and quarrelled. Brown defended himself with his knife, which dropped from his hand into the boat. You pushed him off the staging and he fell, knocking his head on one of the piles. Then you took the plug out of the boat and sent her adrift to sink, and you flung the chest into the sea. This happened about ten minutes past twelve. Am I right?"

Jeffreys stood staring at Thorndyke, the picture of amazement and consternation, but he uttered no word in reply. "Am I right?" Thorndyke repeated.

"Strike me blind!" muttered Jeffreys. "Was you here, then? You talk as if you had been. Anyhow," he continued, recovering somewhat, "you seem to know all about it. But you're wrong about one thing. There was no quarrel. This chap, Brown, didn't take to me and he didn't mean to stay out here. He was going to put off and go ashore again and I wouldn't let him. Then he hit out at me with his knife and I knocked it out of his hand and he staggered backwards and went overboard."

"And did you try to pick him up?" asked the captain.

"How could I," demanded Jeffreys, "with the tide racing down and me alone on the station? I'd never have got back."

"But what about the boat, Jeffreys? Why did you scuttle her?"

"The fact is," replied Jeffreys, "I got in a funk, and I thought the simplest plan was to send her to the cellar and know nothing about it. But I never shoved him over. It was an accident, sir, I swear it!"

"Well, that sounds a reasonable explanation," said the captain. "What do you say, Doctor?"

"Perfectly reasonable," replied Thorndyke, "and, as to its truth, that is no affair of ours."

"No. But I shall have to take you off, Jeffreys, and hand you over to the police. You understand that?"

"Yes, sir, I understand," answered Jeffreys.

"That was a queer case, that affair on the Girdler," remarked Captain Grumpass, when he was spending an evening with us some six months later. "A pretty easy let off for Jeffreys, too – eighteen months, wasn't it?"

"Yes, it was a very queer case indeed," said Thorndyke. "There was something behind that 'accident,' I should say. Those men had probably met before."

"So I thought," agreed the captain. "But the queerest part of it to me was the way you nosed it all out. I've had a deep respect for briar pipes

338

since then. It was a remarkable case," he continued. "The way in which you made that pipe tell the story of the murder seems to me like sheer enchantment."

"Yes," said I, "it spoke like the magic pipe – only that wasn't a tobacco-pipe – in the German folk-story of 'The Singing Bone'. Do you remember it? A peasant found the bone of a murdered man and fashioned it into a pipe. But when he tried to play on it, it burst into a song of its own –

>"*My brother slew me and buried my bones*
>*Beneath the sand and under the stones.*'"

"A pretty story," said Thorndyke, "and one with an excellent moral. The inanimate things around us have each of them a song to sing to us if we are but ready with attentive ears."

A Wastrel's Romance
Part I – The Spinster's Guest

The lingering summer twilight was fast merging into night as a solitary cyclist, whose evening-dress suit was thinly disguised by an overcoat, rode slowly along a pleasant country road. From time to time he had been overtaken and passed by a carriage, a car, or a closed cab from the adjacent town, and from the festive garb of the occupants he had made shrewd guesses at their destination. His own objective was a large house, standing in somewhat extensive grounds just off the road, and the peculiar circumstances that surrounded his visit to it caused him to ride more and more slowly as he approached his goal.

Willowdale – such was the name of the house – was, tonight, witnessing a temporary revival of its past glories. For many months it had been empty and a notice-board by the gate-keeper's lodge had silently announced its forlorn state, but to-night, its rooms, their bare walls clothed in flags and draperies, their floors waxed or carpeted, would once more echo the sound of music and cheerful voices and vibrate to the tread of many feet. For on this night the spinsters of Raynesford were giving a dance, and chief amongst the spinsters was Miss Halliwell, the owner of Willowdale.

It was a great occasion. The house was large and imposing, the spinsters were many, and their purses were long. The guests were numerous and distinguished, and included no less a person than Mrs. Jehu B. Chater. This was the crowning triumph of the function, for the beautiful American widow was the lion (or should we say lioness?) of the season. Her wealth was, if not beyond the dreams of avarice, at least beyond the powers of common British arithmetic, and her diamonds were, at once, the glory and the terror of her hostesses.

All these attractions notwithstanding, the cyclist approached the vicinity of Willowdale with a slowness almost hinting at reluctance, and when, at length, a curve of the road brought the gates into view, he dismounted and halted irresolutely. He was about to do a rather risky thing, and, though by no means a man of weak nerve, he hesitated to make the plunge.

The fact is, he had not been invited.

Why, then, was he going? And how was he to gain admittance? To which questions the answer involves a painful explanation.

Augustus Bailey lived by his wits. That is the common phrase, and a stupid phrase it is. For do we not all live by our wits, if we have any? And does it need any specially brilliant wits to be a common rogue? However, such as his wits were, Augustus Bailey lived by them, and he had not hitherto made a fortune.

The present venture arose out of a conversation overheard at a restaurant table and an invitation-card carelessly laid down and adroitly covered with the menu. Augustus had accepted the invitation that he had not received (on a sheet of Hotel Cecil notepaper that he had among his collection of stationery) in the name of Geoffrey Harrington-Baillie, and the question that exercised his mind at the moment was, would he or would he not be spotted? He had trusted to the number of guests and the probable inexperience of the hostesses. He knew that the cards need not be shown, though there was the awkward ceremony of announcement.

But perhaps it wouldn't get as far as that. Probably not, if his acceptance had been detected as emanating from an uninvited stranger.

He walked slowly towards the gates with growing discomfort. Added to his nervousness as to the present were certain twinges of reminiscence. He had once held a commission in a line regiment – not for long, indeed, his "wits" had been too much for his brother officers – but there had been a time when he would have come to such a gathering as this an invited guest. Now, a common thief, he was sneaking in under a false name, with a fair prospect of being ignominiously thrown out by the servants.

As he stood hesitating, the sound of hoofs on the road was followed by the aggressive bellow of a motor-horn. The modest twinkle of carriage lamps appeared round the curve and then the glare of acetylene headlights. A man came out of the lodge and drew open the gates, and Mr. Bailey, taking his courage in both hands, boldly trundled his machine up the drive.

Half-way up – it was quite a steep incline – the car whizzed by, a large Napier filled with a bevy of young men who economized space by sitting on the backs of the seats and on one another's knees. Bailey looked at them and decided that this was his chance, and, pushing forward, he saw his bicycle safely bestowed in the empty coach-house and then hurried on to the cloak-room. The young men had arrived there before him and, as he entered, were gaily peeling off their overcoats and flinging them down on a table. Bailey followed their example, and, in his eagerness to enter the reception-room with the crowd, let his attention wander from the business of the moment, and, as he pocketed the ticket and hurried away, he failed to notice that the bewildered attendant had put his hat with another man's coat and affixed his duplicate to them both.

"Major Podbury, Captain Barker-Jones, Captain Sparker, Mr. Watson, Mr. Goldsmith, Mr. Smart, Mr. Harrington-Baillie!"

As Augustus swaggered up the room, hugging the party of officers and quaking inwardly, he was conscious that his hostesses glanced from one man to another with more than common interest.

But at that moment the footman's voice rang out, sonorous and clear —

"Mrs. Chater, Colonel Grumpier!" and, as all eyes were turned towards the new arrivals, Augustus made his bow and passed into the throng. His little game of bluff had "come off", after all.

He withdrew modestly into the more crowded portion of the room, and there took up a position where he would be shielded from the gaze of his hostesses. Presently, he reflected, they would forget him, if they had really thought about him at all, and then he would see what could be done in the way of business. He was still rather shaky, and wondered how soon it would be decent to steady his nerves with a "refresher". Meanwhile he kept a sharp look-out over the shoulders of neighbouring guests, until a movement in the crowd of guests disclosed Mrs. Chater shaking hands with the presiding spinster. Then Augustus got a most uncommon surprise.

He knew her at the first glance. He had a good memory for faces, and Mrs. Chater's face was one to remember. Well did he recall the frank and lovely American girl with whom he had danced at the regimental ball years ago. That was in the old days when he was a subaltern, and before that little affair of the pricked court-cards that brought his military career to an end. They had taken a mutual liking, he remembered, that sweet-faced Yankee maid and he had danced many dances and had sat out others, to talk mystical nonsense which, in their innocence, they had believed to be philosophy. He had never seen her since. She had come into his life and gone out of it again, and he had forgotten her name, if he had ever known it. But here she was, middle-aged now, it was true, but still beautiful and a great personage withal. And, ye gods! What diamonds! And here was he, too, a common rogue, lurking in the crowd that he might, perchance, snatch a pendant or "pinch" a loose brooch.

Perhaps she might recognize him. Why not? He had recognized her. But that would never do. And thus reflecting, Mr. Bailey slipped out to stroll on the lawn and smoke a cigarette. Another man, somewhat older than himself, was pacing to and fro thoughtfully, glancing from time to time through the open windows into the brilliantly-lighted rooms. When they had passed once or twice, the stranger halted and addressed him.

"This is the best place on a night like this," he remarked. "It's getting hot inside already. But perhaps you're keen on dancing."

"Not so keen as I used to be," replied Bailey, and then, observing the hungry look that the other man was bestowing on his cigarette, he produced his case and offered it.

342

"Thanks awfully!" exclaimed the stranger, pouncing with avidity on the open case. "Good Samaritan, by Jove. Left my case in my overcoat. Hadn't the cheek to ask, though I was starving for a smoke." He inhaled luxuriously, and, blowing out a cloud of smoke, resumed, "These chits seem to be running the show pretty well, h'm? Wouldn't take it for an empty house to look at it, would you?"

"I have hardly seen it," said Bailey. "Only just come, you know."

"We'll have a look round, if you like," said the genial stranger, "when we've finished our smoke, that is. Have a drink too, may cool us a bit. Know many people here?"

"Not a soul," replied Bailey. "My hostess doesn't seem to have turned up."

"Well, that's easily remedied," said the stranger. "My daughter's one of the spinsters – Granby, my name. When we've had a drink, I'll make her find you a partner – that is, if you care for the light fantastic."

"I should like a dance or two," said Bailey, "though I'm getting a bit past it now, I suppose. Still, it doesn't do to chuck up the sponge prematurely."

"Certainly not," Granby agreed jovially, "a man's as young as he feels. Well, come and have a drink and then we'll hunt up my little girl." The two men flung away the stumps of their cigarettes and headed for the refreshments.

The spinsters' champagne was light, but it was well enough if taken in sufficient quantity, a point to which Augustus – and Granby too – paid judicious attention, and when he had supplemented the wine with a few sandwiches, Mr. Bailey felt in notably better spirits. For to tell the truth, his diet, of late, had been somewhat meagre. Miss Granby, when found, proved to be a blonde and guileless "flapper" of some seventeen summers, childishly eager to play her part of hostess with due dignity, and presently Bailey found himself gyrating through the eddying crowd in company with a comely matron of thirty or thereabouts.

The sensations that this novel experience aroused rather took him by surprise. For years past he had been living a precarious life of mean and sordid shifts that oscillated between mere shabby trickery and downright crime, now conducting a paltry swindle just inside the pale of the law, and now, when hard pressed, descending to actual theft, consorting with shady characters, swindlers and knaves and scurvy rogues like himself, gambling, borrowing, cadging and, if need be, stealing, and always slinking abroad with an apprehensive eye upon "the man in blue".

And now, amidst the half-forgotten surroundings, once so familiar – the gaily-decorated rooms, the rhythmic music, the twinkle of jewels, the murmur of gliding feet and the rustle of costly gowns, the moving vision of honest gentlemen and fair ladies – the shameful years seemed to drop away and leave him to take up the thread of his life where it had snapped so disastrously. After all, these were his own people. The seedy knaves in whose steps he had walked of late were but aliens met by the way.

He surrendered his partner, in due course, with regret – which was mutual – to an inarticulate subaltern, and was meditating another pilgrimage to the refreshment-room, when he felt a light touch upon his arm. He turned swiftly. A touch on the arm meant more to him than to some men. But it was no wooden-faced plain-clothes man that he confronted – it was only a lady. In short, it was Mrs. Chater, smiling nervously and a little abashed by her own boldness.

"I expect you've forgotten me," she began apologetically, but Augustus interrupted her with an eager disclaimer.

"Of course I haven't," he said, "though I have forgotten your name, but I remember that Portsmouth dance as well as if it were yesterday – at least one incident in it – the only one that was worth remembering. I've often hoped that I might meet you again, and now, at last, it has happened."

"It's nice of you to remember," she rejoined. "I've often and often thought of that evening and all the wonderful things that we talked about. You were a nice boy then, I wonder what you are like now. What a long time ago it is!"

"Yes," Augustus agreed gravely, "it is a long time. I know it myself, but when I look at you, it seems as if it could only have been last season."

"Oh, fie!" she exclaimed. "You are not simple as you used to be. You didn't flatter then, but perhaps there wasn't the need." She spoke with gentle reproach, but her pretty face flushed with pleasure nevertheless, and there was a certain wistfulness in the tone of her concluding sentence.

"I wasn't flattering," Augustus replied, quite sincerely, "I knew you directly you entered the room and marvelled that Time had been so gentle with you. He hasn't been as kind to me."

"No. You have gotten a few grey hairs, I see, but after all, what are grey hairs to a man? Just the badges of rank, like the crown on your collar or the lace on your cuffs, to mark the steps of your promotion – for I guess you'll be a colonel by now."

"No," Augustus answered quickly, with a faint flush, "I left the army some years ago."

"My! What a pity!" exclaimed Mrs. Chater. "You must tell me all about it – but not now. My partner will be looking for me. We will sit out a dance and have a real gossip. But I've forgotten your name – never could recall it, in fact, though that didn't prevent me from remembering you. But, as our dear W. S. remarks, '*What's in a name –* '"

"Ah, indeed," said Mr. Harrington-Baillie, and apropos of that sentiment, he added, "Mine is Rowland – Captain Rowland. You may remember it now."

Mrs. Chater did not, however, and said so. "Will Number Six do?" she asked, opening her programme, and, when Augustus had assented, she entered his provisional name, remarking complacently, "We'll sit out and have a right-down good talk, and you shall tell me all about yourself and if you still think the same about free-will and personal responsibility. You had very lofty ideals, I remember, in those days, and I hope you have still. But one's ideals get rubbed down rather faint in the friction of life. Don't you think so?"

"Yes, I am afraid you're right," Augustus assented gloomily. "The wear-and-tear of life soon fetches the gilt off the gingerbread. Middle-age is apt to find us a bit patchy, not to say naked."

"Oh, don't be pessimistic," said Mrs. Chater. "That is the attitude of the disappointed idealist, and I am sure you have no reason, really, to be disappointed in yourself. But I must run away now. Think over all the things you have to tell me, and don't forget that it is Number Six." With a bright smile and a friendly nod she sailed away, a vision of glittering splendour, compared with which Solomon in all his glory was a mere matter of commonplace bullion.

The interview, evidently friendly and familiar, between the unknown guest and the famous American widow had by no means passed unnoticed, and in other circumstances, Bailey might have endeavoured to profit by the reflected glory that enveloped him. But he was not in search of notoriety, and the same evasive instinct that had led him to sink Mr. Harrington-Baillie in Captain Rowland now advised him to withdraw his dual personality from the vulgar gaze. He had come here on very definite business. For the hundredth time he was "stony-broke", and it was the hope of picking up some "unconsidered trifles" that had brought him. But, somehow, the atmosphere of the place had proved unfavourable. Either opportunities were lacking or he failed to seize them. In any case, the game pocket that formed an unconventional feature of his dress-coat was still empty, and it looked as if a pleasant evening and a good supper were all that he was likely to get. Nevertheless, be his conduct never so blameless, the fact remained that he was an uninvited guest, liable at any moment to be ejected as an impostor, and his recognition by the widow had not rendered this possibility any the more remote.

He strayed out onto the lawn, whence the grounds fell away on all sides. But there were other guests there, cooling themselves after the last dance, and the light from the rooms streamed through the windows, illuminating their figures, and among them, that of the too-companionable

Granby. Augustus quickly drew away from the lighted area, and, chancing upon a narrow path, strolled away along it in the direction of a copse or shrubbery that he saw ahead. Presently he came to an ivy-covered arch, lighted by one or two fairy lamps, and, passing through this, he entered a winding path, bordered by trees and shrubs and but faintly lighted by an occasional coloured lamp suspended from a branch.

Already he was quite clear of the crowd – indeed, the deserted condition of the pleasant retreat rather surprised him, until he reflected that to couples desiring seclusion there were whole ranges of untenanted rooms and galleries available in the empty house.

The path sloped gently downwards for some distance, then came a long flight of rustic steps and, at the bottom, a seat between two trees. In front of the seat the path extended in a straight line, forming a narrow terrace. On the right the ground sloped up steeply towards the lawn, on the left it fell away still more steeply towards the encompassing wall of the grounds, and on both sides it was covered with trees and shrubs.

Bailey sat down on the seat to think over the account of himself that he should present to Mrs. Chater. It was a comfortable seat, built into the trunk of an elm, which formed one end and part of the back. He leaned against the tree, and, taking out his silver case, selected a cigarette. But it remained unlighted between his fingers as he sat and meditated upon his unsatisfactory past and the melancholy tale of what might have been. Fresh from the atmosphere of refined opulence that pervaded the dancing-rooms, the throng of well-groomed men and dainty women, his mind travelled back to his sordid little flat in Bermondsey, encompassed by poverty and squalor, jostled by lofty factories, grimy with the smoke of the river and the reek from the great chimneys. It was a hideous contrast. Verily the way of the transgressor was not strewn with flowers.

At that point in his meditations he caught the sound of voices and footsteps on the path above and rose to walk on along the path. He did not wish to be seen wandering alone in the shrubbery. But now a woman's laugh sounded from somewhere down the path. There were people approaching that way too. He put the cigarette back in the case and stepped round behind the seat, intending to retreat in that direction, but here the path ended, and beyond was nothing but a rugged slope down to the wall thickly covered with bushes. And while he was hesitating, the sound of feet descending the steps and the rustle of a woman's dress left him to choose between staying where he was or coming out to confront the new-comers. He chose the former, drawing up close behind the tree to wait until they should have passed on.

But they were not going to pass on. One of them – a woman – sat down on the seat, and then a familiar voice smote on his ear.

"I guess I'll rest here quietly for a while. This tooth of mine is aching terribly, and, see here, I want you to go and fetch me something. Take this ticket to the cloak-room and tell the woman to give you my little velvet bag. You'll find in it a bottle of chloroform and a packet of cotton-wool."

"But I can't leave you here all alone, Mrs. Chater," her partner expostulated.

"I'm not hankering for society just now," said Mrs. Chater. "I want that chloroform. Just you hustle off and fetch it, like a good boy. Here's the ticket."

The young officer's footsteps retreated rapidly, and the voices of the couple advancing along the path grew louder. Bailey, cursing the chance that had placed him in his ridiculous and uncomfortable position, heard them approach and pass on up the steps, and then all was silent, save for an occasional moan from Mrs. Chater and the measured creaking of the seat as she rocked uneasily to and fro. But the young man was uncommonly prompt in the discharge of his mission, and in a very few minutes Bailey heard him approaching at a run along the path above and then bounding down the steps.

"Now I call that real good of you," said the widow gratefully. "You must have run like the wind. Cut the string of the packet and then leave me to wrestle with this tooth."

"But I can't leave you here all – "

"Yes, you can," interrupted Mrs. Chater. "There won't be anyone about – the next dance is a waltz. Besides, you must go and find your partners."

"Well, if you'd really rather be alone," the subaltern began, but Mrs. Chater interrupted him.

"Of course I would, when I'm fixing up my teeth. Now go along, and a thousand thanks for your kindness."

With mumbled protestations the young officer slowly retired, and Bailey heard his reluctant feet ascending the steps. Then a deep silence fell on the place in which the rustle of paper and the squeak of a withdrawn cork seemed loud and palpable. Bailey had turned with his face towards the tree, against which he leaned with his lips parted scarcely daring to breathe. He cursed himself again and again for having thus entrapped himself for no tangible reason, and longed to get away. But there was no escape now without betraying himself. He must wait for the woman to go.

Suddenly, beyond the edge of the tree, a hand appeared holding an open packet of cotton-wool. It laid the wool down on the seat, and, pinching off a fragment, rolled it into a tiny ball. The fingers of the hand were encircled by rings, its wrist enclosed by a broad bracelet, and from rings and bracelet the light of the solitary fairy-lamp, that hung from a

347

branch of the tree, was reflected in prismatic sparks. The hand was withdrawn and Bailey stared dreamily at the square pad of cotton-wool. Then the hand came again into view. This time it held a small phial which it laid softly on the seat, setting the cork beside it. And again the light flashed in many-coloured scintillations from the encrusting gems.

Bailey's knees began to tremble, and a chilly moisture broke out upon his forehead.

The hand drew back, but, as it vanished, Bailey moved his head silently until his face emerged from behind the tree. The woman was leaning back, her head resting against the trunk only a few inches away from his face. The great stones of the tiara flashed in his very eyes. Over her shoulder, he could even see the gorgeous pendant, rising and falling on her bosom with ever-changing fires, and both her raised hands were a mass of glitter and sparkle, only the deeper and richer for the subdued light.

His heart throbbed with palpable blows that drummed aloud in his ears. The sweat trickled clammily down his face, and he clenched his teeth to keep them from chattering. An agony of horror – of deadly fear – was creeping over him. A terror of the dreadful impulse that was stealing away his reason and his will.

The silence was profound. The woman's soft breathing, the creak of her bodice, were plainly – grossly – audible, and he checked his own breath until he seemed on the verge of suffocation.

Of a sudden through the night air was borne faintly the dreamy music of a waltz. The dance had begun. The distant sound but deepened the sense of solitude in this deserted spot.

Bailey listened intently. He yearned to escape from the invisible force that seemed to be clutching at his wrists, and dragging him forward inexorably to his doom.

He gazed down at the woman with a horrid fascination. He struggled to draw back out of sight – and struggled in vain.

Then, at last, with a horrible, stealthy deliberation, a clammy, shaking hand crept forward towards the seat. Without a sound it grasped the wool, and noiselessly, slowly drew back. Again it stole forth. The fingers twined snakily around the phial, lifted it from the seat and carried it back into the shadow.

After a few seconds it reappeared and softly replaced the bottle – now half empty. There was a brief pause. The measured cadences of the waltz stole softly through the quiet night and seemed to keep time with the woman's breathing. Other sound there was none. The place was wrapped in the silence of the grave.

Suddenly, from the hiding-place, Bailey leaned forward over the back of the seat. The pad of cotton-wool was in his hand.

The woman was now leaning back as if dozing, and her hands rested in her lap. There was a swift movement. The pad was pressed against her face and her head dragged back against the chest of the invisible assailant. A smothered gasp burst from her hidden lips as her hands flew up to clutch at the murderous arm, and then came a frightful struggle, made even more frightful by the gay and costly trappings of the writhing victim. And still there was hardly a sound, only muffled gasps – the rustle of silk, the creaking of the seat, the clink of the falling bottle and, afar off, with dreadful irony, the dreamy murmur of the waltz.

The struggle was but brief. Quite suddenly the jewelled hands dropped, the head lay resistless on the crumpled shirt-front, and the body, now limp and inert, began to slip forward off the seat. Bailey, still grasping the passive head, climbed over the back of the seat and, as the woman slid gently to the ground, he drew away the pad and stooped over her. The struggle was over now. The mad fury of the moment was passing swiftly into the chill of mortal fear.

He stared with incredulous horror into the swollen face, but now so comely, the sightless eyes that but a little while since had smiled into his with such kindly recognition.

He had done this! He, the sneaking wastrel, discarded of all the world, to whom this sweet woman had held out the hand of friendship. She had cherished his memory, when to all others he was sunk deep under the waters of oblivion. And he had killed her – for to his ear no breath of life seemed to issue from those purple lips.

A sudden hideous compunction for this irrevocable thing that he had done surged through him, and he stood up clutching at his damp hair with a hoarse cry that was like the cry of the damned.

The jewels passed straightaway out of his consciousness. Everything was forgotten now but the horror of this unspeakable thing that he had done. Remorse incurable and haunting fear were all that were left to him.

The sound of voices far away along the path aroused him, and the vague horror that possessed him materialized into abject bodily fear. He lifted the limp body to the edge of the path and let it slip down the steep declivity among the bushes. A soft, shuddering sigh came from the parted lips as the body turned over, and he paused a moment to listen. But there was no other sound of life. Doubtless that sigh was only the result of the passive movement.

Again he stood for an instant as one in a dream, gazing at the huddled shape half-hidden by the bushes, before he climbed back to the path, and

349

even then he looked back once more, but now she was hidden from sight. And, as the voices drew nearer, he turned, and ran up the rustic steps.

As he came out on the edge of the lawn the music ceased, and, almost immediately, a stream of people issued from the house. Shaken as he was, Bailey yet had wits enough left to know that his clothes and hair were disordered and that his appearance must be wild. Accordingly he avoided the dancers, and, keeping to the margin of the lawn, made his way to the cloak-room by the least frequented route. If he had dared, he would have called in at the refreshment-room, for he was deadly faint and his limbs shook as he walked. But a haunting fear pursued him and, indeed, grew from moment to moment. He found himself already listening for the rumour of the inevitable discovery.

He staggered into the cloak-room, and, flinging his ticket down on the table, dragged out his watch. The attendant looked at him curiously and, pausing with the ticket in his hand, asked sympathetically, "Not feeling very well, sir?"

"No," said Bailey. "So beastly hot in there."

"You ought to have a glass of champagne, sir, before you start," said the man.

"No time," replied Bailey, holding out a shaky hand for his coat. "Shall lose my train if I'm not sharp."

At this hint the attendant reached down the coat and hat, holding up the former for its owner to slip his arms into the sleeves. But Bailey snatched it from him, and, flinging it over his arm, put on his hat and hurried away to the coachhouse. Here, again, the attendant stared at him in astonishment, which was not lessened when Bailey, declining his offer to help him on with his coat, bundled the latter under his arm, clicked the lever of the "variable" on to the ninety gear, sprang onto the machine and whirled away down the steep drive, a grotesque vision of flying coat-tails.

"You haven't lit your lamp, sir," roared the attendant, but Bailey's ears were deaf to all save the clamour of the expected pursuit.

Fortunately the drive entered the road obliquely, or Bailey must have been flung into the opposite hedge. As it was, the machine, rushing down the slope, flew out into the road with terrific velocity, nor did its speed diminish then, for its rider, impelled by mortal terror, trod the pedals with the fury of a madman. And still, as the machine whizzed along the dark and silent road, his ears were strained to catch the clatter of hoofs or the throb of a motor from behind.

He knew the country – well, in fact, as a precaution, he had cycled over the district only the day before, and he was ready, at any suspicious sound, to slip down any of the lanes or byways, secure of finding his way.

350

But still he sped on, and still no sound from the rear came to tell him of the dread discovery.

When he had ridden about three miles, he came to the foot of a steep hill. Here he had to dismount and push his machine up the incline, which he did at such speed that he arrived at the top quite breathless. Before mounting again he determined to put on his coat, for his appearance was calculated to attract attention, if nothing more. It was only half-past eleven, and presently he would pass through the streets of a small town. Also he would light his lamp. It would be fatal to be stopped by a patrol or rural constable.

Having lit his lamp and hastily put on his coat he once more listened intently, looking back over the country that was darkly visible from the summit of the hill. No moving lights were to be seen, no ringing hoofs or throbbing engines to be heard, and, turning to mount, he instinctively felt in his overcoat pocket for his gloves.

A pair of gloves came out in his hand, but he was instantly conscious that they were not his. A silk muffler was there also, a white one. But his muffler was black.

With a sudden shock of terror he thrust his hand into the ticket-pocket, where he had put his latch-key. There was no key there, only an amber cigar-holder, which he had never seen before. He stood for a few moments in utter consternation. He had taken the wrong coat. Then he had left his own coat behind. A cold sweat of fear broke out afresh on his face as he realized this. His Yale latch-key was in its pocket, not that that mattered very much. He had a duplicate at home, and, as to getting in, well, he knew his own outside door and his tool-bag contained one or two trifles not usually found in cyclists' tool-bags. The question was whether that coat contained anything that could disclose his identity. And then suddenly he remembered, with a gasp of relief, that he had carefully turned the pockets out before starting.

No, once let him attain the sanctuary of his grimy little flat, wedged in as it was between the great factories by the river-side, and he would be safe – safe from everything but the horror of himself, and the haunting vision of a jewelled figure huddled up in a silken heap beneath the bushes.

With a last look round he mounted his machine, and, driving it over the brow of the hill, swept away into the darkness.

Part II – *Munera Pulveris*
(Related by Christopher Jervis, M.D.)

It is one of the drawbacks of medicine as a profession that one is never rid of one's responsibilities. The merchant, the lawyer, the civil servant, each at the appointed time locks up his desk, puts on his hat and goes forth a free man with an interval of uninterrupted leisure before him. Not so the doctor. Whether at work or at play, awake or asleep, he is the servant of humanity, at the instant disposal of friend or stranger alike whose need may make the necessary claim.

When I agreed to accompany my wife to the spinsters' dance at Raynesford, I imagined that, for that evening, at least, I was definitely off-duty, and in that belief I continued until the conclusion of the eighth dance. To be quite truthful, I was not sorry when the delusion was shattered. My last partner was a young lady of a slanginess of speech that verged on the inarticulate. Now it is not easy to exchange ideas in "pidgin" English, and the conversation of a person to whom all things are either "ripping" or "rotten" is apt to lack subtlety. In fact, I was frankly bored, and, reflecting on the utility of the humble sandwich as an aid to conversation, I was about to entice my partner to the refreshment-room when I felt someone pluck at my sleeve. I turned quickly and looked into the anxious and rather frightened face of my wife.

"Miss Halliwell is looking for you," she said. "A lady has been taken ill. Will you come and see what is the matter?" She took my arm and, when I had made my apologies to my partner, she hurried me on to the lawn.

"It's a mysterious affair," my wife continued. "The sick lady is a Mrs. Chater, a very wealthy American widow. Edith Halliwell and Major Podbury found her lying in the shrubbery all alone and unable to give any account of herself. Poor Edith is dreadfully upset. She doesn't know what to think."

"What do you mean?" I began, but at this moment Miss Halliwell, who was waiting by an ivy-covered rustic arch, espied us and ran forward.

"Oh, do hurry, please, Dr. Jervis," she exclaimed. "Such a shocking thing has happened. Has Juliet told you?" Without waiting for an answer, she darted through the arch and preceded us along a narrow path at the curious, flat-footed, shambling trot common to most adult women. Presently we descended a flight of rustic steps which brought us to a seat, from whence extended a straight path cut like a miniature terrace on a steep slope, with a high bank rising to the right and declivity falling away to the left. Down in the hollow, his head and shoulders appearing above the bushes, was a man holding in his hand a fairy-lamp that he had apparently taken down from a tree. I climbed down to him, and, as I came round the bushes, I perceived a richly-dressed woman lying huddled on the ground. She was not completely insensible, for she moved slightly at my approach, muttering a few words in thick, indistinct accents. I took the lamp from the man, whom I assumed to be Major Podbury, and, as he delivered it to me with a significant glance and a faint lift of the eyebrows, I understood Miss Halliwell's agitation. Indeed – for one horrible moment I thought that she was right – that the prostrate woman was intoxicated. But when I approached nearer, the flickering light of the lamp made visible a square reddened patch on her face, like the impression of a mustard plaster, covering the nose and mouth, and then I scented mischief of a more serious kind.

"We had better carry her up to the seat," I said, handing the lamp to Miss Halliwell. "Then we can consider moving her to the house." The major and I lifted the helpless woman and, having climbed cautiously up to the path, laid her on the seat.

"What is it, Dr. Jervis?" Miss Halliwell whispered.

"I can't say at the moment," I replied, "but it's not what you feared."

"Thank God for that!" was her fervent rejoinder. "It would have been a shocking scandal."

I took the dim lamp and once more bent over the half-conscious woman.

Her appearance puzzled me not a little. She looked like a person recovering from an anaesthetic, but the square red patch on her face, recalling, as it did, the Burke murders, rather suggested suffocation. As I was thus reflecting, the light of the lamp fell on a white object lying on the ground behind the seat, and holding the lamp forward, I saw that it was a square pad of cotton-wool. The coincidence of its shape and size with that of the red patch on the woman's face instantly struck me, and I stooped down to pick it up, and then I saw, lying under the seat, a small bottle. This also I picked up and held in the lamplight. It was a one-ounce phial, quite empty, and was labelled "*Methylated Chloroform*". Here seemed to be a complete explanation of the thick utterance and drunken aspect, but it was an explanation that required, in its turn, to be explained. Obviously no robbery had been committed, for the woman literally glittered with diamonds. Equally obviously she had not administered the chloroform to herself.

There was nothing for it but to carry her indoors and await her further recovery, so, with the major's help, we conveyed her through the shrubbery and kitchen garden to a side door, and deposited her on a sofa in a half-furnished room.

353

Here, under the influence of water dabbed on her face and the plentiful use of smelling salts, she quickly revived, and was soon able to give an intelligible account of herself.

The chloroform and cotton-wool were her own. She had used them for an aching tooth, and she was sitting alone on the seat with the bottle and the wool beside her when the incomprehensible thing had happened. Without a moment's warning a hand had come from behind her and pressed the pad of wool over her nose and mouth. The wool was saturated with chloroform, and she had lost consciousness almost immediately.

"You didn't see the person, then?" I asked.

"No, but I know he was in evening dress, because I felt my head against his shirt-front."

"Then," said I, "he is either here still or he has been to the cloak-room. He couldn't have left the place without an overcoat."

"No, by Jove!" exclaimed the major, "that's true. I'll go and make inquiries." He strode away all agog, and I, having satisfied myself that Mrs. Chater could be left safely, followed him almost immediately.

I made my way straight to the cloak-room, and here I found the major and one or two of his brother officers putting on their coats in a flutter of gleeful excitement.

"He's gone," said Podbury, struggling frantically into his overcoat. "Went off nearly an hour ago on a bicycle. Seemed in a deuce of a stew, the attendant says, and no wonder. We're goin' after him in our car. Care to join the hunt?"

"No, thanks. I must stay with the patient. But how do you know you're after the right man?"

"Isn't any other. Only one Johnnie's left. Besides – here, confound it! You've given me the wrong coat!" He tore off the garment and handed it back to the attendant, who regarded it with an expression of dismay.

"Are you sure, sir?" he asked.

"Perfectly," said the major. "Come, hurry up, my man."

"I'm afraid, sir," said the attendant, "that the gentleman who has gone has taken your coat. They were on the same peg, I know. I am very sorry, sir."

The major was speechless with wrath. What the devil was the good of being sorry, and how the deuce was he to get his coat back –

"But," I interposed, "if the stranger has got your coat, then this coat must be his."

"I know," said Podbury, "but I don't want his beastly coat."

"No," I replied, "but it may be useful for identification."

This appeared to afford the bereaved officer little consolation, but as the car was now ready, he bustled away, and I, having directed the man to put the coat away in a safe place, went back to my patient.

Mrs. Chater was by now fairly recovered, and had developed a highly vindictive interest in her late assailant. She even went so far as to regret that he had not taken at least some of her diamonds, so that robbery might have been added to the charge of attempted murder, and expressed the earnest hope that the officers would not be foolishly gentle in their treatment of him when they caught him.

"By the way, Dr. Jervis," said Miss Halliwell, "I think I ought to mention a rather curious thing that happened in connection with this dance. We received an acceptance from a Mr. Harrington-Baillie, who wrote from the Hotel Cecil. Now I am certain that no such name was proposed by any of the spinsters."

"But didn't you ask them?" I inquired.

"Well, the fact is," she replied, "that one of them, Miss Waters, had to go abroad suddenly, and we had not got her address, and as it was possible that she might have invited him, I did not like to move in the matter. I am very sorry I didn't now. We may have let in a regular criminal? Though why he should have wanted to murder Mrs. Chater I cannot imagine."

It was certainly a mysterious affair, and the mystery was in no wise dispelled by the return of the search party an hour later. It seemed that the bicycle had been tracked for a couple of miles towards London, but then, at the cross-roads, the tracks had become hopelessly mixed with the impressions of other machines and the officers, after cruising about vaguely for a while, had given up the hunt and returned.

"You see, Mrs. Chater," Major Podbury explained apologetically, "the fellow must have had a good hour's start, and that would have brought him pretty close to London."

"Do you mean to tell me," exclaimed Mrs. Chater, regarding the major with hardly-concealed contempt, "that that villain has got off scot-free?"

"Looks rather like it," replied Podbury, "but if I were you I should get the man's description from the attendants who saw him and go up to Scotland Yard to-morrow. They may know the Johnny there, and they may even recognize the coat if you take it with you."

"That doesn't seem very likely," said Mrs. Chater, and it certainly did not, but since no better plan could be suggested the lady decided to adopt it, and I supposed that I had heard the last of the matter.

In this, however, I was mistaken. On the following day, just before noon, as I was drowsily considering the points in a brief dealing with a

355

question of survivorship, while Thorndyke drafted his weekly lecture, a smart rat-tat at the door of our chambers announced a visitor. I rose wearily – I had had only four hours' sleep – and opened the door, whereupon there sailed into the room no less a person than Mrs. Chater, followed by Superintendent Miller, with a grin on his face and a brown-paper parcel under his arm.

The lady was not in the best of tempers, though wonderfully lively and alert considering the severe shock that she had suffered so recently, and her disapproval of Miller was frankly obvious.

"Dr. Jervis has probably told you about the attempt to murder me last night," she said, when I had introduced her to my colleague. "Well, now, will you believe it? I have been to the police, I have given them a description of the murderous villain, and I have even shown them the very coat that he wore, and they tell me that nothing can be done. That, in short, this scoundrel must be allowed to go his way free and unmolested."

"You will observe, Doctor," said Miller, "that this lady has given us a description that would apply to fifty-percent, of the middle-class men of the United Kingdom, and has shown us a coat without a single identifying mark of any kind on it, and expects us to lay our hands on the owner without a solitary clue to guide us. Now we are not sorcerers at the Yard, we're only policemen. So I have taken the liberty of referring Mrs. Chater to you." He grinned maliciously and laid the parcel on the table.

"And what do you want me to do?" Thorndyke asked quietly.

"Why sir," said Miller, "there is a coat. In the pockets were a pair of gloves, a muffler, a box of matches, a tram-ticket, and a Yale key. Mrs. Chater would like to know whose coat it is." He untied the parcel with his eye cocked at our rather disconcerted client, and Thorndyke watched him with a faint smile.

"This is very kind of you, Miller," said he, "but I think a clairvoyant would be more to your purpose."

The superintendent instantly dropped his facetious manner.

"Seriously, sir," he said, "I should be glad if you would take a look at the coat. We have absolutely nothing to go on, and yet we don't want to give up the case. I have gone through it most thoroughly and can't find any clue to guide us. Now I know that nothing escapes you, and perhaps you might notice something that I have overlooked, something that would give us a hint where to start on, our inquiry. Couldn't you turn the microscope on it, for instance?" he added, with a deprecating smile.

Thorndyke reflected, with an inquisitive eye on the coat. I saw that the problem was not without its attractions to him, and when the lady seconded Miller's request with persuasive eagerness, the inevitable consequence followed.

356

"Very well," he said. "Leave the coat with me for an hour or so and I will look it over. I am afraid there is not the remotest chance of our learning anything from it, but even so, the examination will have done no harm. Come back at two o'clock. I shall be ready to report my failure by then."

He bowed our visitors out and, returning to the table, looked down with a quizzical smile on the coat and the large official envelope containing articles from the pockets.

"And what does my learned brother suggest?" he asked, looking up at me.

"I should look at the tram-ticket first," I replied, "and then – well, Miller's suggestion wasn't such a bad one, to explore the surface with the microscope."

"I think we will take the latter measure first," said he. "The tram-ticket might create a misleading bias. A man may take a tram anywhere, whereas the indoor dust on a man's coat appertains mostly to a definite locality."

"Yes," I replied, "but the information that it yields is excessively vague."

"That is true," he agreed, taking up the coat and envelope to carry them to the laboratory, "and yet, you know, Jervis, as I have often pointed out, the evidential value of dust is apt to be under-estimated. The naked-eye appearances – which are the normal appearances – are misleading. Gather the dust, say, from a table-top, and what have you? A fine powder of a characterless grey, just like any other dust from any other table-top. But, under the microscope, this grey powder is resolved into recognizable fragments of definite substances, which fragments may often be traced with certainty to the masses from which they have been detached. But you know all this as well as I do."

"I quite appreciate the value of dust as evidence in certain circumstances," I replied, "but surely the information that could be gathered from dust on the coat of an unknown man must be too general to be of any use in tracing the owner."

"I am afraid you are right," said Thorndyke, laying the coat on the laboratory bench, "but we shall soon see, if Polton will let us have his patent dust-extractor."

The little apparatus to which my colleague referred was the invention of our ingenious laboratory assistant, and resembled in principle the "vacuum cleaners" used for restoring carpets. It had, however, one special feature. The receiver was made to admit a microscope-slide, and on this the dust-laden air was delivered from a jet.

The "extractor" having been clamped to the bench by its proud inventor, and a wetted slide introduced into the receiver, Thorndyke applied the nozzle of the instrument to the collar of the coat while Polton worked the pump. The slide was then removed and, another having been substituted, the nozzle was applied to the right sleeve near the shoulder, and the exhauster again worked by Polton. By repeating this process, half-a-dozen slides were obtained charged with dust from different parts of the garment, and then, setting up our respective microscopes, we proceeded to examine the samples.

A very brief inspection showed me that this dust contained matter not usually met with – at any rate, in appreciable quantities. There were, of course, the usual fragments of wool, cotton, and other fibres derived from clothing and furniture, particles of straw, husk, hair, various mineral particles and, in fact, the ordinary constituents of dust from clothing. But, in addition to these, and in much greater quantity, were a number of other bodies, mostly of vegetable origin and presenting well-defined characters in considerable variety, and especially abundant were various starch granules.

I glanced at Thorndyke and observed he was already busy with a pencil and a slip of paper, apparently making a list of the objects visible in the field of the microscope. I hastened to follow his example, and for a time we worked on in silence. At length my colleague leaned back in his chair and read over his list.

"This is a highly interesting collection, Jervis," he remarked. "What do you find on your slides out of the ordinary?"

"I have quite a little museum here," I replied, referring to my list. "There is, of course, chalk from the road at Raynesford. In addition to this I find various starches, principally wheat and rice, especially rice, fragments of the cortices of several seeds, several different stone-cells, some yellow masses that look like turmeric, black pepper resin-cells, one 'port wine' pimento cell, and one or two particles of graphite."

"Graphite!" exclaimed Thorndyke. "I have found no graphite, but I have found traces of cocoa – spiral vessels and starch grains – and of hops – one fragment of leaf and several lupulin glands. May I see the graphite?"

I passed him the slide and he examined it with keen interest. "Yes," he said, "this is undoubtedly graphite, and no less than six particles of it. We had better go over the coat systematically. You see the importance of this?"

"I see that this is evidently factory dust and that it may fix a locality, but I don't see that it will carry us any farther."

"Don't forget that we have a touchstone," said he, and, as I raised my eyebrows inquiringly, he added, "The Yale latchkey. If we can narrow the locality down sufficiently, Miller can make a tour of the front doors."

"But can we?" I asked incredulously. "I doubt it."

"We can try," answered Thorndyke. "Evidently some of the substances are distributed over the entire coat, inside and out, while others, such as the graphite, are present only on certain parts. We must locate those parts exactly and then consider what this special distribution means." He rapidly sketched out on a sheet of paper a rough diagram of the coat, marking each part with a distinctive letter, and then, taking a number of labelled slides, he wrote a single letter on each. The samples of dust taken on the slides could thus be easily referred to the exact spots whence they had been obtained.

Once more we set to work with the microscope, making, now and again, an addition to our lists of discoveries, and, at the end of nearly an hour's strenuous search, every slide had been examined and the lists compared.

"The net result of the examination," said Thorndyke, "is this. The entire coat, inside and out, is evenly powdered with the following substances: Rice-starch in abundance, wheat-starch in less abundance, and smaller quantities of the starches of ginger, pimento, and cinnamon, bast fibre of cinnamon, various seed cortices, stone-cells of pimento, cinnamon, cassia, and black pepper, with other fragments of similar origin, such as resin-cells and ginger pigment – not turmeric. In addition there are, on the right shoulder and sleeve, traces of cocoa and hops, and on the back below the shoulders a few fragments of graphite. Those are the data, and now, what are the inferences? Remember this is not mere surface dust, but the accumulation of months, beaten into the cloth by repeated brushing – dust that nothing but a vacuum apparatus could extract."

"Evidently," I said, "the particles that are all over the coat represent dust that is floating in the air of the place where the coat habitually hangs. The graphite has obviously been picked up from a seat and the cocoa and hops from some factories that the man passes frequently, though I don't see why they are on the right side only."

"That is a question of time," said Thorndyke, "and incidentally throws some light on our friend's habits. Going from home, he passes the factories on his right, returning home, he passes them on his left, but they have then stopped work. However, the first group of substances is the more important as they indicate the locality of his dwelling – for he is clearly not a workman or factory employee. Now rice-starch, wheat-starch and a group of substances collectively designated 'spices' suggest a rice-mill, a flour-mill, and a spice factory. Polton, may I trouble you for the *Post Office Directory?*"

He turned over the leaves of the *"Trades"* section and resumed. "I see there are four rice-mills in London, of which the largest is Carbutt's at Dockhead. Let us look at the spice-factories." He again turned over the leaves and read down the list of names. "There are six spice-grinders in London," said he. "One of them, Thomas Williams and Co., is at Dockhead. None of the others is near any rice-mill. The next question is as to the flour-mill. Let us see. Here are the names of several flour millers, but none of them is near either a rice-mill or a spice-grinder, with one exception: Seth Taylor's, St. Saviour's Flour Mills, Dockhead."

"This is really becoming interesting," said I.

"It has become interesting," Thorndyke retorted. "You observe that at Dockhead we find the peculiar combination of factories necessary to produce the composite dust in which this coat has hung, and the directory shows us that this particular combination exists nowhere else in London. Then the graphite, the cocoa, and the hops tend to confirm the other suggestions. They all appertain to industries of the locality. The trams which pass Dockhead, also, to my knowledge, pass at no great distance from the black-lead works of Pearce Duff and Co. in Rouel Road, and will probably collect a few particles of black-lead on the seats in certain states of the wind. I see, too, that there is a cocoa factory – Payne's – in Goat Street, Horsleydown, which lies to the right of the tram line going west, and I have noticed several hop warehouses on the right side of Southwark Street, going west. But these are mere suggestions. The really important data are the rice and flour mills and the spice-grinders, which seem to point unmistakably to Dockhead."

"Are there any private houses at Dockhead?" I asked.

"We must look up the 'Street' list," he replied. "The Yale latch-key rather suggests a flat, and a flat with a single occupant, and the probable habits of our absent friend offer a similar suggestion." He ran his eye down the list and presently turned to me with his finger on the page.

"If the facts that we have elicited – the singular series of agreements with the required conditions – are only a string of coincidences, here is another. On the south side of Dockhead, actually next door to the spice-grinders and opposite to Carbutt's rice-mills, is a block of workmen's flats, Hanover Buildings. They fulfil the conditions exactly. A coat hung in a room in those flats, with the windows open (as they would probably be at this time of year), would be exposed to the air containing a composite dust of precisely the character of that which we have found. Of course, the same conditions obtain in other dwellings in this part of Dockhead, but the probability is in favour of the buildings. And that is all that we can say. It is no certainty. There may be some radical fallacy in our reasoning. But, on the face of it, the chances are a thousand-to-one that the door that that key will open is in some part of Dockhead, and most probably in Hanover Buildings. We must leave the verification to Miller."

"Wouldn't it be as well to look at the tram-ticket?" I asked.

"Dear me!" he exclaimed. "I had forgotten the ticket. Yes, by all means." He opened the envelope and, turning its contents out on the bench, picked up the dingy slip of paper. After a glance at it he handed it to me. It was punched for the journey from Tooley Street to Dockhead.

"Another coincidence," he remarked, "and by yet another, I think I hear Miller knocking at our door."

It was the superintendent, and, as we let him into the room, the hum of a motor-car entering from Tudor Street announced the arrival of Mrs. Chater. We waited for her at the open door, and, as she entered, she held out her hands impulsively.

"Say, now, Dr. Thorndyke," she exclaimed, "have you gotten something to tell us?"

"I have a suggestion to make," replied Thorndyke. "I think that if the superintendent will take this key to Hanover Buildings, Dockhead, Bermondsey, he may possibly find a door that it will fit."

"The deuce!" exclaimed Miller. "I beg your pardon, madam, but I thought I had gone through that coat pretty completely. What was it that I had overlooked, sir? Was there a letter hidden in it, after all?"

"You overlooked the dust on it, Miller, that is all," said Thorndyke.

"Dust!" exclaimed the detective, staring round-eyed at my colleague. Then he chuckled softly. "Well," said he, "as I said before, I'm not a sorcerer, I'm only a policeman." He picked up the key and asked, "Are you coming to see the end of it, sir?"

"Of course he is coming," said Mrs. Chater, "and Dr. Jervis too, to identify the man. Now that we have gotten the villain, we must leave him no loophole for escape."

Thorndyke smiled dryly. "We will come if you wish it, Mrs. Chater," he said, "but you mustn't look upon our quest as a certainty. We may have made an entire miscalculation, and I am, in fact, rather curious to see if the result works out correctly. But even if we run the man to earth, I don't see that you have much evidence against him. The most that you can prove is that he was at the house and that he left hurriedly."

Mrs. Chater regarded my colleague for a moment in scornful silence, and then, gathering up her skirts, stalked out of the room. If there is one thing that the average woman detests more than another, it is an entirely reasonable man.

The big car whirled us rapidly over Blackfriars Bridge into the region of the Borough, whence we presently turned down Tooley Street towards Bermondsey.

As soon as Dockhead came into view, the detective, Thorndyke, and I, alighted and proceeded on foot, leaving our client, who was now closely veiled, to follow at a little distance in the car. Opposite the head of St.

361

Saviour's Dock, Thorndyke halted and, looking over the wall, drew my attention to the snowy powder that had lodged on every projection on the backs of the tall buildings and on the decks of the barges that were loading with the flour and ground rice. Then, crossing the road, he pointed to the wooden lantern above the roof of the spice works, the louvres of which were covered with greyish-buff dust.

"Thus," he moralized, "does commerce subserve the ends of justice – at least, we hope it does," he added quickly, as Miller disappeared into the semi-basement of the buildings.

We met the detective returning from his quest as we entered the building.

"No go there," was his report. "We'll try the next floor."

This was the ground-floor, or it might be considered the first floor. At any rate, it yielded nothing of interest, and, after a glance at the doors that opened on the landing, he strode briskly up the stone stairs. The next floor was equally unrewarding, for our eager inspection disclosed nothing but the gaping keyhole associated with the common type of night-latch.

"What name was you wanting?" inquired a dusty knight of industry who emerged from one of the flats.

"Muggs," replied Miller, with admirable promptness.

"Don't know 'im," said the workman. "I expect it's farther up."

Farther up we accordingly went, but still from each door the artless grin of the invariable keyhole saluted us with depressing monotony. I began to grow uneasy, and when the fourth floor had been explored with no better result, my anxiety became acute. A mare's nest may be an interesting curiosity, but it brings no kudos to its discoverer.

"I suppose you haven't made any mistake, sir?" said Miller, stopping to wipe his brow.

"It's quite likely that I have." replied Thorndyke, with unmoved composure. "I only proposed this search as a tentative proceeding, you know."

The superintendent grunted. He was accustomed – as was I too, for that matter – to regard Thorndyke's "tentative suggestions" as equal to another man's certainties.

"It will be an awful suck-in for Mrs. Chater if we don't find him after all," he growled as we climbed up the last flight. "She's counted her chickens to a feather." He paused at the head of the stairs and stood for a few moments looking round the landing. Suddenly he turned eagerly, and, laying his hand on Thorndyke's arm, pointed to a door in the farthest corner.

"Yale lock!" he whispered impressively.

We followed him silently as he stole on tip-toe across the landing, and watched him as he stood for an instant with the key in his land looking gloatingly at the brass disc. We saw him softly apply the nose of the fluted key-blade to the crooked slit in the cylinder, and, as we watched, it slid noiselessly up to the shoulder. The detective looked round with a grin of triumph, and, silently withdrawing the key, stepped back to us.

"You've run him to earth, sir," he whispered, "but I don't think Mr. Fox is at home. He can't have got back yet."

"Why not?" asked Thorndyke.

Miller waved his hand towards the door. "Nothing has been disturbed," he replied. "There's not a mark on the paint. Now he hadn't got the key, and you can't pick a Yale lock. He'd have had to break in, and he hasn't broken in."

Thorndyke stepped up to the door and softly pushed in the flap of the letter-slit, through which he looked into the flat.

"There's no letter-box," said he. "My dear Miller, I would undertake to open that door in five minutes with a foot of wire and a bit of resined string."

Miller shook his head and grinned once more. "I am glad you're not on the lay, sir, you'd be one too many for us. Shall we signal to the lady?"

I went out onto the gallery and looked down at the waiting car. Mrs. Chater was staring intently up at the building, and the little crowd that the car had collected stared alternately at the lady and at the object of her regard. I wiped my face with my handkerchief – the signal agreed upon – and she instantly sprang out of the car, and in an incredibly short time she appeared on the landing, purple and gasping, but with the fire of battle flashing from her eyes.

"We've found his flat, madam," said Miller, "and we're going to enter. You're not intending to offer any violence, I hope," he added, noting with some uneasiness the lady's ferocious expression.

"Of course I'm not," replied Mrs. Chater. "In the States ladies don't have to avenge insults themselves. If you were American men, you'd hang the ruffian from his own bedpost."

"We're not American men, madam," said the superintendent stiffly. "We are law-abiding Englishmen, and, moreover, we are all officers of the law. These gentlemen are barristers and I am a police officer."

With this preliminary caution, he once more inserted the key, and as he turned it and pushed the door open, we all followed him into the sitting-room.

"I told you so, sir," said Miller, softly shutting the door. "He hasn't come back yet."

Apparently he was right. At any rate, there was no one in the flat, and we proceeded unopposed on our tour of inspection. It was a miserable spectacle, and, as we wandered from one squalid room to another, a feeling of pity for the starving wretch into whose lair we were intruding stole over me and began almost to mitigate the hideousness of his crime. On all sides poverty – utter, grinding poverty – stared us in the face. It looked at us hollow-eyed in the wretched sitting-room, with its bare floor, its solitary chair and tiny deal table, its unfurnished walls and windows destitute of blind or curtain. A piece of Dutch cheese-rind on the table, scraped to the thinness of paper, whispered of starvation, and famine lurked in the gaping cupboard, in the empty bread-tin, in the tea-caddy with its pinch of dust at the bottom, in the jam-jar, wiped clean, as a few crumbs testified, with a crust of bread. There was not enough food in the place to furnish a meal for a healthy mouse.

The bedroom told the same tale, but with a curious variation. A miserable truckle-bed with a straw mattress and a cheap jute rug for bed-clothes, an orange-case – stood on end – for a dressing-table, and another, bearing a tin washing-bowl, formed the wretched furniture. But the suit that hung from a couple of nails was well-cut and even fashionable, though shabby, and another suit lay on the floor, neatly folded and covered with a newspaper, and, most incongruous of all, a silver cigarette-case reposed on the dressing-table.

"Why on earth does this fellow starve," I exclaimed, "when he has a silver case to pawn?"

"Wouldn't do," said Miller. "A man doesn't pawn the implements of his trade."

Mrs. Chater, who had been staring about her with the mute amazement of a wealthy woman confronted, for the first time, with abject poverty, turned suddenly to the superintendent. "This can't be the man!" she exclaimed. "You have made some mistake. This poor creature could never have made his way into a house like Willowdale."

Thorndyke lifted the newspaper. Beneath it was a dress suit with the shirt, collar, and tie all carefully smoothed out and folded. Thorndyke unfolded the shirt and pointed to the curiously crumpled front. Suddenly he brought it close to his eye and then, from the sham diamond stud, he drew a single hair – a woman's hair.

"That is rather significant," said he, holding it up between his finger and thumb, and Mrs. Chater evidently thought so too, for the pity and compunction suddenly faded from her face, and once more her eyes flashed with vindictive fire.

364

"I wish he would come," she exclaimed viciously. "Prison won't be much hardship to him after this, but I want to see him in the dock all the same."

"No," the detective agreed, "it won't hurt him much to swap this for Portland. Listen!"

A key was being inserted into the outer door, and as we all stood like statues, a man entered and closed the door after him. He passed the door of the bedroom without seeing us, and with the dragging steps of a weary, dispirited man. Almost immediately we heard him go to the kitchen and draw water into some vessel. Then he went back to the sitting-room.

"Come along," said Miller, stepping silently towards the door. We followed closely, and as he threw the door open, we looked in over his shoulder.

The man had seated himself at the table, on which now lay a hunk of household bread resting on the paper in which he had brought it, and a tumbler of water. He half rose as the door opened, and as if petrified remained staring at Miller with a dreadful expression of terror upon his livid face.

At this moment I felt a hand on my arm, and Mrs. Chater brusquely pushed past me into the room. But at the threshold she stopped short, and a singular change crept over the man's ghastly face, a change so remarkable that I looked involuntarily from him to our client. She had turned, in a moment, deadly pale, and her face had frozen into an expression of incredulous horror.

The dramatic silence was broken by the matter-of-fact voice of the detective.

"I am a police officer," said he, "and I arrest you for – ?"

A peal of hysterical laughter from Mrs. Chater interrupted him, and he looked at her in astonishment. "Stop, stop!" she cried in a shaky voice. "I guess we've made a ridiculous mistake. This isn't the man. This gentleman is Captain Rowland, an old friend of mine."

"I'm sorry he's a friend of yours," said Miller, "because I shall have to ask you to appear against him."

"You can ask what you please," replied Mrs. Chater. "I tell you he's not the man."

The superintendent rubbed his nose and looked hungrily at his quarry. "Do I understand, madam," he asked stiffly, "that you refuse to prosecute?"

"Prosecute!" she exclaimed. "Prosecute my friends for offences that I know they have not committed? Certainly I refuse."

The superintendent looked at Thorndyke, but my colleague's countenance had congealed into a state of absolute immobility and was as devoid of expression as the face of a Dutch clock.

"Very well," said Miller, looking sourly at his watch. "Then we have had our trouble for nothing. I wish you good afternoon, madam."

"I am sorry I troubled you, now," said Mrs. Chater.

"I am sorry you did," was the curt reply, and the superintendent, flinging the key on the table, stalked out of the room.

As the outer door slammed, the man sat down with an air of bewilderment, and then, suddenly flinging his arms on the table, he dropped his head on them, and burst into a passion of sobbing.

It was very embarrassing. With one accord Thorndyke and I turned to go, but Mrs. Chater motioned us to stay. Stepping over to the man, she touched him lightly on the arm.

"Why did you do it?" she asked in a tone of gentle reproach.

The man sat up and flung out one arm in an eloquent gesture that comprehended the miserable room and the yawning cupboard.

"It was the temptation of a moment," he said. "I was penniless, and those accursed diamonds were thrust in my face. They were mine for the taking. I was mad, I suppose."

"But why didn't you take them?" she said. "Why didn't you?"

"I don't know. The madness passed, and then – when I saw you lying there – ? Oh, God! Why don't you give me up to the police?" He laid his head down and sobbed afresh.

Mrs. Chater bent over him with tears standing in her pretty grey eyes. "But tell me," she said, "why didn't you take the diamonds? You could if you'd liked, I suppose?"

"What good were they to me?" he demanded passionately. "What did anything matter to me? I thought you were dead."

"Well, I'm not, you see," she said, with a rather tearful smile, "I'm just as well as an old woman like me can expect to be. And I want your address, so that I can write and give you some good advice."

The man sat up and produced a shabby cardcase from his pocket, and, as he took out a number of cards and spread them out like the "hand" of a whist player, I caught a twinkle in Thorndyke's eye.

"My name is Augustus Bailey," said the man. He selected the appropriate card, and, having scribbled his address on it with a stump of lead pencil, relapsed into his former position.

"Thank you," said Mrs. Chater, lingering for a moment by the table. "Now we'll go. Good-bye, Mr. Bailey. I shall write to-morrow, and you must attend seriously to the advice of an old friend."

366

I held open the door for her to pass out and looked back before I turned to follow. Bailey still sat sobbing quietly, with his hand resting on his arms, and a little pile of gold stood on the corner of the table.

"I expect, Doctor," said Mrs. Chater, as Thorndyke handed her into the car, "you've written me down a sentimental fool."

Thorndyke looked at her with an unwonted softening of his rather severe face and answered quietly, "It is written: *Blessed are the Merciful.*"

The Old Lag
Part I – The Changed Immutable

Among the minor and purely physical pleasures of life, I am disposed to rank very highly that feeling of bodily comfort that one experiences on passing from the outer darkness of a wet winter's night to a cheerful interior made glad by mellow lamplight and blazing hearth. And so I thought when, on a dreary November night, I let myself into our chambers in the Temple and found my friend smoking his pipe in slippered ease, by a roaring fire, and facing an empty arm-chair evidently placed in readiness for me.

As I shed my damp overcoat, I glanced inquisitively at my colleague, for he held in his hand an open letter, and I seemed to perceive in his aspect something meditative and self-communing – something, in short, suggestive of a new case.

"I was just considering," he said, in answer to my inquiring look, "whether I am about to become an accessory after the fact. Read that and give me your opinion."

He handed me the letter, which I read aloud.

Dear Sir,

I am in great danger and distress. A warrant has been issued for my arrest on a charge of which I am entirely innocent. Can I come and see you, and will you let me leave in safety?

The bearer will wait for a reply.

"I said 'Yes,' of course, there was nothing else to do," said Thorndyke. "But if I let him go, as I have promised to do, I shall be virtually conniving at his escape."

"Yes, you are taking a risk," I answered. "When is he coming?"

"He was due five minutes ago – and I rather think – yes, here he is."

A stealthy tread on the landing was followed by a soft tapping on the outer door.

Thorndyke rose and, flinging open the inner door, unfastened the massive "oak".

"Dr. Thorndyke?" inquired a breathless, quavering voice.

"Yes, come in. You sent me a letter by hand?"

"I did, sir," was the reply, and the speaker entered, but at the sight of me he stopped short.

"This is my colleague, Dr. Jervis," Thorndyke explained. "You need have no – ?"

"Oh, I remember him," our visitor interrupted in a tone of relief. "I have seen you both before, you know, and you have seen me too – though I don't suppose you recognize me," he added, with a sickly smile.

"Frank Belfield?" asked Thorndyke, smiling also.

Our visitor's jaw fell and he gazed at my colleague in sudden dismay.

"And I may remark," pursued Thorndyke, "that for a man in your perilous position, you are running most unnecessary risks. That wig, that false beard and those spectacles – through which you obviously cannot see – are enough to bring the entire police force at your heels. It is not wise for a man who is wanted by the police to make up as though he had just escaped from a comic opera."

Mr. Belfield seated himself with a groan, and, taking off his spectacles, stared stupidly from one of us to the other.

"And now tell us about your little affair," said Thorndyke. "You say that you are innocent?"

"I swear it, Doctor," replied Belfield, adding, with great earnestness, "And you may take it from me, sir, that if I was not, I shouldn't be here. It was you that convicted me last time, when I thought myself quite safe, so I know your ways too well to try to gammon you."

"If you are innocent," rejoined Thorndyke, "I will do what I can for you, and if you are not – well, you would have been wiser to stay away."

"I know that well enough," said Belfield, "and I am only afraid that you won't believe what I am going to tell you."

"I shall keep an open mind, at any rate," replied Thorndyke.

"If you only will," groaned Belfield, "I shall have a look in, in spite of them all. You know, sir, that I have been on the crook, but I have paid in full. That job when you tripped me up was the last of it – it was, sir, so help me. It was a woman that changed me – the best and truest woman on God's earth. She said she would marry me when I came out if I promised her to go straight and live an honest life. And she kept her promise – and I have kept mine. She found me work as clerk in a warehouse and I have stuck to it ever since, earning fair wages and building up a good character as an honest, industrious man. I thought all was going well, and that I was settled for life, when only this very morning the whole thing comes tumbling about my ears like a house of cards."

"What happened this morning, then?" asked Thorndyke.

"Why, I was on my way to work when, as I passed the police station, I noticed a bill with the heading '*Wanted*' and a photograph. I stopped for a moment to look at it, and you may imagine my feelings when I recognized my own portrait – taken at Holloway – and read my own name and description. I did not stop to read the bill through, but ran back home and told my wife, and she ran down to the station and read the bill carefully. Good God, sir! What do you think I am wanted for?" He paused for a moment, and then replied in breathless tones to his own question: "The Camberwell murder!"

Thorndyke gave a low whistle.

"My wife knows I didn't do it," continued Belfield, "because I was at home all the evening and night, but what use is a man's wife to prove an alibi?"

"Not much, I fear," Thorndyke admitted. "And you have no other witness?"

"Not a soul. We were alone all the evening."

"However," said Thorndyke, "if you are innocent – as I am assuming – the evidence against you must be entirely circumstantial and your alibi may be quite sufficient. Have you any idea of the grounds of suspicion against you?"

"Not the faintest. The papers said that the police had an excellent clue, but they did not say what it was. Probably someone has given false information for the – ?"

A sharp rapping at the outer door cut short the explanation, and our visitor rose, trembling and aghast, with beads of sweat standing upon his livid face.

"You had better go into the office, Belfield, while we see who it is," said Thorndyke. "The key is on the inside."

The fugitive wanted no second bidding, but hurried into the empty apartment, and, as the door closed, we heard the key turn in the lock.

As Thorndyke threw open the outer door, he cast a meaning glance at me over his shoulder which I understood when the newcomer entered the room, for it was none other than Superintendent Miller of Scotland Yard.

"I have just dropped in," said the superintendent, in his brisk, cheerful way, "to ask you to do me a favour. Good evening, Dr. Jervis. I hear you are reading for the bar, learned counsel soon, sir, hey? Medico-legal expert. Dr. Thorndyke's mantle going to fall on you, sir?"

"I hope Dr. Thorndyke's mantle will continue to drape his own majestic form for many a long year yet," I answered, "though he is good enough to spare me a corner – but what on earth have you got there?" For during this dialogue the superintendent had been deftly unfastening a brown-paper parcel, from which he now drew a linen shirt, once white, but now of an unsavoury grey.

370

"I want to know what this is," said Miller, exhibiting a brownish-red stain on one sleeve. "Just look at that, sir, and tell me if it is blood, and, if so, is it human blood?"

"Really, Miller," said Thorndyke, with a smile, "you flatter me, but I am not like the wise woman of Bagdad who could tell you how many stairs the patient had tumbled down by merely looking at his tongue. I must examine this very thoroughly. When do you want to know?"

"I should like to know to-night," replied the detective.

"Can I cut a piece out to put under the microscope?"

"I would rather you did not," was the reply.

"Very well, you shall have the information in about an hour."

"It's very good of you, Doctor," said the detective, and he was taking up his hat preparatory to departing, when Thorndyke said suddenly, "By the way, there is a little matter that I was going to speak to you about. It refers to this Camberwell murder case. I understand you have a clue to the identity of the murderer?"

"Clue!" exclaimed the superintendent contemptuously. "We have spotted our man all right, if we could only lay hands on him, but he has given us the slip for the moment."

"Who is the man?" asked Thorndyke.

The detective looked doubtfully at Thorndyke for some seconds and then said, with evident reluctance, "I suppose there is no harm in telling you – especially as you probably know already," – this with a sly grin, "it's an old crook named Belfield."

"And what is the evidence against him?"

Again the superintendent looked doubtful and again relented.

"Why, the case is as clear as – as cold Scotch," he said. (Here Thorndyke, in illustration of this figure of speech, produced a decanter, a syphon, and a tumbler, which he pushed towards the officer.) "You see, sir, the silly fool went and stuck his sweaty hand on the window, and there we found the marks – four fingers and a thumb, as beautiful prints as you could wish to see. Of course we cut out the piece of glass and took it up to the Finger-print Department, they turned up their files, and out came Mr. Belfield's record, with his finger-prints and photograph all complete."

"And the finger-prints on the window-pane were identical with those on the prison form?"

"Identical."

"Hmm!" Thorndyke reflected for a while, and the superintendent watched him foxily over the edge of his tumbler.

"I guess you are retained to defend Belfield," the latter observed presently.

"To look into the case generally," replied Thorndyke.

"And I expect you know where the beggar is hiding," continued the detective.

"Belfield's address has not yet been communicated to me," said Thorndyke. "I am merely to investigate the case – and there is no reason, Miller, why you and I should be at cross purposes. We are both working at the case – you want to get a conviction *and* you want to convict the right man."

"That's so – and Belfield's the right man – but what do you want of us, Doctor?"

"I should like to see the piece of glass with the finger-prints on it, and the prison form, and take a photograph of each. And I should like to examine the room in which the murder took place – you have it locked up, I suppose?"

"Yes, we have the keys. Well, it's all rather irregular, letting you see the things. Still, you've always played the game fairly with us, so we might stretch a point. Yes, I will. I'll come back in an hour for your report and bring the glass and the form. I can't let them go out of my custody, you know. I'll be off now – no, thank you, not another drop."

The superintendent caught up his hat and strode away, the personification of mental alertness and bodily vigour.

No sooner had the door closed behind him than Thorndyke's stolid calm changed instantaneously into feverish energy. Darting to the electric bell that rang into the laboratories above, he pressed the button while he gave me my directions.

"Have a look at that blood-stain, Jervis, while I am finishing with Belfield. Don't wet it – scrape it into a drop of warm normal saline solution."

I hastened to reach down the microscope and set out on the table the necessary apparatus and reagents, and, as I was thus occupied, a latch-key turned in the outer door and our invaluable helpmate, Polton, entered the room in his habitual silent, unobtrusive fashion.

"Let me have the finger-print apparatus, please, Polton," said Thorndyke, "and have the copying camera ready by nine o'clock. I am expecting Mr. Miller with some documents."

As his laboratory assistant departed, Thorndyke rapped at the office door.

"It's all clear, Belfield," he called. "You can come out."

The key turned and the prisoner emerged, looking ludicrously woebegone in his ridiculous wig and beard.

"I am going to take your finger-prints, to compare with some that the police found on the window."

372

"Finger-prints!" exclaimed Belfield, in a tone of dismay. "They don't say they're my finger-prints, do they, sir?"

"They do indeed," replied Thorndyke, eyeing the man narrowly. "They have compared them with those taken when you were at Holloway, and they say that they are identical."

"Good God!" murmured Belfield, collapsing into a chair, faint and trembling. "They must have made some awful mistake. But are mistakes possible with finger-prints?"

"Now look here, Belfield," said Thorndyke. "Were you in that house that night, or were you not? It is of no use for you to tell me any lies."

"I was not there, sir, I swear to God I was not."

"Then they cannot be your finger-prints, that is obvious." Here he stepped to the door to intercept Polton, from whom he received a substantial box, which he brought in and placed on the table.

"Tell me all you know about this case," he continued, as he set out the contents of the box on the table.

"I know nothing about it whatever," replied Belfield, "nothing, at least, except – ?"

"Except what?" demanded Thorndyke, looking up sharply as he squeezed a drop from a tube of finger-print ink onto a smooth copper plate.

"Except that the murdered man, Caldwell, was a retired fence."

"A fence, was he?" said Thorndyke in a tone of interest.

"Yes, and I suspect he was a 'nark' too. He knew more than was wholesome for a good many."

"Did he know anything about you?"

"Yes, but nothing that the police don't know."

With a small roller, Thorndyke spread the ink upon the plate into a thin film. Then he laid on the edge of the table a smooth white card and, taking Belfield's right hand, pressed the forefinger firmly but quickly, first on the inked plate and then on the card, leaving on the latter a clear print of the finger-tip. This process he repeated with the other fingers and thumb, and then took several additional prints of each.

"That was a nasty injury to your forefinger, Belfield," said Thorndyke, holding the finger to the light and examining the tip carefully. "How did you do it?"

"Stuck a tin-opener into it – a dirty one, too. It was bad for weeks, in fact, Dr. Sampson thought at one time that he would have to amputate the finger."

"How long ago was that?"

"Oh, nearly a year ago, sir."

Thorndyke wrote the date of the injury by the side of the finger-print and then, having rolled up the inking plate afresh, laid on the table several larger cards. "I am now going to take the prints of the four fingers and the thumb all at once," he said.

"They only took the four fingers at once at the prison," said Belfield. "They took the thumb separately."

"I know," replied Thorndyke, "but I am going to take the impression just as it would appear on the window glass."

He took several impressions thus, and then, having looked at his watch, he began to repack the apparatus in its box. While doing this, he glanced, from time to time, in meditative fashion, at the suspected man who sat, the living picture of misery and terror, wiping the greasy ink from his trembling fingers with his handkerchief.

"Belfield," he said at length, "you have sworn to me that you are an innocent man and are trying to live an honest life. I believe you, but in a few minutes I shall know for certain."

"Thank God for that, sir," exclaimed Belfield, brightening up wonderfully.

"And now," said Thorndyke, "you had better go back into the office, for I am expecting Superintendent Miller, and he may be here at any moment."

Belfield hastily slunk back into the office, locking the door after him, and Thorndyke, having returned the box to the laboratory and deposited the cards bearing the finger-prints in a drawer, came round to inspect my work. I had managed to detach a tiny fragment of dried clot from the blood-stained garment, and this, in a drop of normal saline solution, I now had under the microscope.

"What do you make out, Jervis?" my colleague asked.

"Oval corpuscles with distinct nuclei," I answered.

"Ah," said Thorndyke, "that will be good hearing for some poor devil. Have you measured them?"

"Yes. Long diameter one-twenty-one-hundredth of an inch, short diameter about one-thirty-four-hundredth of an inch."

Thorndyke reached down an indexed note-book from a shelf of reference volumes and consulted a table of histological measurements.

"That would seem to be the blood of a pheasant, then, or it might, more probably, be that of a common fowl." He applied his eye to the microscope and, fitting in the eyepiece micrometer, verified my measurements. He was thus employed when a sharp tap was heard on the outer door, and rising to open it he admitted the superintendent.

"I see you are at work on my little problem, Doctor," said the latter, glancing at the microscope. "What do you make of that stain?"

"It is the blood of a bird – probably a pheasant, or perhaps a common fowl."

374

The superintendent slapped his thigh. "Well, I'm hanged!" he exclaimed. "You're a regular wizard, Doctor, that's what you are. The fellow said he got that stain through handling a wounded pheasant and here are you able to tell us yes or no without a hint from us to help you. Well, you've done my little job for me, sir, and I'm much obliged to you. Now I'll carry out my part of the bargain." He opened a hand-bag and drew forth a wooden frame and a blue foolscap envelope and laid them with extreme care on the table.

"There you are, sir," said he, pointing to the frame, "you will find Mr. Belfield's trade-mark very neatly executed, and in the envelope is the finger-print sheet for comparison."

Thorndyke took up the frame and examined it. It enclosed two sheets of glass, one being the portion of the window-pane and the other a cover-glass to protect the fingerprints. Laying a sheet of white paper on the table, where the light was strongest, Thorndyke held the frame over it and gazed at the glass in silence, but with that faint lighting up of his impassive face which I knew so well and which meant so much to me. I walked round, and looking over his shoulder saw upon the glass the beautifully distinct imprints of four fingers and a thumb – the finger-tips, in fact, of an open hand.

After regarding the frame attentively for some time, Thorndyke produced from his pocket a little wash-leather bag, from which he extracted a powerful doublet lens, and with the aid of this he again explored the finger-prints, dwelling especially upon the print of the forefinger.

"I don't think you will find much amiss with those finger-prints, Doctor," said the superintendent. "They are as clear as if he made them on purpose."

"They are indeed," replied Thorndyke, with an inscrutable smile. "Exactly as if he had made them on purpose. And how beautifully clean the glass is – as if he had polished it before making the impression."

The superintendent glanced at Thorndyke with quick suspicion, but the smile had faded and given place to a wooden immobility from which nothing could be gleaned.

When he had examined the glass exhaustively, Thorndyke drew the finger-print form from its envelope and scanned it quickly, glancing repeatedly from the paper to the glass and from the glass to the paper. At length he laid them both on the table, and turning to the detective looked him steadily in the face.

"I think, Miller," said he, "that I can give you a hint."

"Indeed, sir? And what might that be?"

"It is this: You are after the wrong man."

375

The superintendent snorted – not a loud snort, for that would have been rude, and no officer could be more polite than Superintendent Miller. But it conveyed a protest which he speedily followed up in words.

"You don't mean to say that the prints on that glass are not the finger-prints of Frank Belfield?"

"I say that those prints were not made by Frank Belfield," Thorndyke replied firmly.

"Do you admit, sir, that the finger-prints on the official form were made by him?"

"I have no doubt that they were."

"Well, sir, Mr. Singleton, of the Finger-print Department, has compared the prints on the glass with those on the form and he says they are identical, and I have examined them and I say they are identical."

"Exactly," said Thorndyke, "and I have examined them and I say they are identical – and that therefore those on the glass cannot have been made by Belfield."

The superintendent snorted again – somewhat louder this time – and gazed at Thorndyke with wrinkled brows.

"You are not pulling my leg, I suppose, sir?" he asked, a little sourly.

"I should as soon think of tickling a porcupine," Thorndyke answered, with a suave smile.

"Well," rejoined the bewildered detective, "if I didn't know you, sir, I should say you were talking confounded nonsense. Perhaps you wouldn't mind explaining what you mean."

"Supposing," said Thorndyke, "I make it clear to you that those prints on the window-pane were not made by Belfield. Would you still execute the warrant?"

"What do you think?" exclaimed Miller. "Do you suppose we should go into court to have you come and knock the bottom out of our case, like you did in that Hornby affair? By the way, that was a finger-print case too, now I come to think of it," and the superintendent suddenly became thoughtful.

"You have often complained," pursued Thorndyke, "that I have withheld information from you and sprung unexpected evidence on you at the trial. Now I am going to take you into my confidence, and when I have proved to you that this clue of yours is a false one, I shall expect you to let this poor devil Belfield go his way in peace."

The superintendent grunted – a form of utterance that committed him to nothing.

"These prints," continued Thorndyke, taking up the frame once more, "present several features of interest, one of which, at least, ought not to have escaped you and Mr. Singleton, as it seems to have done. Just look at that thumb."

The superintendent did so, and then pored over the official paper.

"Well," he said, "I don't see anything the matter with it. It's exactly like the print on the paper."

"Of course it is," rejoined Thorndyke, "and that is just the point. It ought not to be. The print of the thumb on the paper was taken separately from the fingers. And why? Because it was impossible to take it at the same time. The thumb is in a different plane from the fingers, when the hand is laid flat on any surface – as this window-pane, for instance – the palmar surfaces of the fingers touch it, whereas it is the side of the thumb which comes in contact and not the palmar surface. But in this" – he tapped the framed glass with his finger – "the prints show the palmar surfaces of all the five digits in contact at once, which is an impossibility. Just try to put your own thumb in that position and you will see that it is so."

The detective spread out his hand on the table and immediately perceived the truth of my colleague's statement.

"And what does that prove?" he asked.

"It proves that the thumb-print on the window-pane was not made at the same time as the finger-prints – that it was added separately, and that fact seems to prove that the prints were not made accidentally, but – as you ingeniously suggested just now – were put there for a purpose."

"I don't quite see the drift of all this," said the superintendent, rubbing the back of his head perplexedly, "and you said a while back that the prints on the glass can't be Belfield's because they are identical with the prints on the form. Now that seems to me sheer nonsense, if you will excuse my saying so."

"And yet," replied Thorndyke, "it is the actual fact. Listen: These prints" – here he took up the official sheet – "were taken at Holloway six years ago. These" – pointing to the framed glass – "were made within the present week. The one is, as regards the ridge-pattern, a perfect duplicate of the other. Is that not so?"

"That is so, Doctor," agreed the superintendent.

"Very well. Now suppose I were to tell you that within the last twelve months something had happened to Belfield that made an appreciable change in the ridge-pattern on one of his fingers?"

"But is such a thing possible?"

"It is not only possible but it has happened. I will show you."

He brought forth from the drawer the cards on which Belfield had made his finger-prints, and laid them before the detective.

"Observe the prints of the forefinger," he said, indicating them, "there are a dozen, in all, and you will notice in each a white line crossing the ridges and dividing them. That line is caused by a scar, which has destroyed a portion of the ridges, and is now an integral part of Belfield's finger-print. And since no such blank line is to be seen in this print on the glass – in which the ridges appear perfect, as they were before the injury – it follows that that print could not have been made by Belfield's finger."

"There is no doubt about the injury, I suppose?"

"None whatever. There is the scar to prove it, and I can produce the surgeon who attended Belfield at the time."

The officer rubbed his head harder than before, and regarded Thorndyke with puckered brows.

"This is a teaser," he growled, "it is indeed. What you say, sir, seems perfectly sound, and yet – there are those finger-prints on the window-glass. Now you can't get fingerprints without fingers, can you?"

"Undoubtedly you can," said Thorndyke.

"I should want to see that done before I could believe even you, sir," said Miller.

"You shall see it done now," was the calm rejoinder. "You have evidently forgotten the Hornby case – the case of the Red Thumb-mark, as the newspapers called it."

"I only heard part of it," replied Miller, "and I didn't really follow the evidence in that."

"Well, I will show you a relic of that case," said Thorndyke. He unlocked a cabinet and took from one of the shelves a small box labelled "*Hornby*", which, being opened, was seen to contain a folded paper, a little red-covered oblong book, and what looked like a large boxwood pawn.

"This little book," Thorndyke continued, "is a '*Thumb-o-graph*' – a sort of finger-print album. I dare say you know the kind of thing."

The superintendent nodded contemptuously at the little volume.

"Now while Dr. Jervis is finding us the print we want, I will run up to the laboratory for an inked slab."

He handed me the little book and, as he left the room, I began to turn over the leaves – not without emotion, for it was this very "*Thumb-o-graph*" that first introduced me to my wife, as is related elsewhere – glancing at the various prints above the familiar names and marvelling afresh at the endless variations of pattern that they displayed. At length I came upon two thumb-prints of which one – the left – was marked by a longitudinal white line – evidently the trace of a scar, and underneath them was written the signature "*Reuben Hornby*".

At this moment Thorndyke re-entered the room carrying the inked slab, which he laid on the table, and seating himself between the superintendent and me, addressed the former.

"Now, Miller, here are two thumb-prints made by a gentleman named Reuben Hornby. Just glance at the left one, it is a highly characteristic print."

"Yes," agreed Miller. "One could swear to that from memory, I should think."

"Then look at this." Thorndyke took the paper from the box and, unfolding it, handed it to the detective. It bore a pencilled inscription, and on it were two blood-smears and a very distinct thumb-print in blood. "What do you say to that thumb-print?"

"Why," answered Miller, "it's this one, of course, Reuben Hornby's left thumb."

"Wrong, my friend," said Thorndyke. "It was made by an ingenious gentleman named Walter Hornby (whom you followed from the Old Bailey and lost on Ludgate Hill), but not with his thumb."

"How, then?" demanded the superintendent incredulously.

"In this way." Thorndyke took the boxwood "pawn" from its receptacle and pressed its flat base onto the inked slab, then lifted it and pressed it onto the back of a visiting-card, and again raised it, and now the card was marked by a very distinct thumb-print.

"My God!" exclaimed the detective, picking up the card and viewing it with a stare of dismay, "this is the very devil, sir. This fairly knocks the bottom out of finger-print identification. May I ask, sir, how you made that stamp – for I suppose you did make it?"

"Yes, we made it here, and the process we used was practically that used by photo-engravers in making line blocks – that is to say, we photographed one of Mr. Hornby's thumb-prints, printed it on a plate of chrome-gelatine, developed the plate with hot water and this" – here he touched the embossed surface of the stamp – "is what remained. But we could have done it in various other ways – for instance, with common transfer paper and lithographic stone. Indeed, I assure you, Miller, that there is nothing easier to forge than a finger-print, and it can be done with such perfection that the forger himself cannot tell his own forgery from a genuine original, even when they are placed side by side."

"Well, I'm hanged," grunted the superintendent. "You've fairly knocked me, this time, Doctor." He rose gloomily and prepared to depart. "I suppose," he added, "your interest in this case has lapsed, now Belfield's out of it?"

"Professionally, yes, but I am disposed to finish the case for my own satisfaction. I am quite curious as to who our too-ingenious friend may be."

Miller's face brightened. "We shall give you every facility, you know – and that reminds me that Singleton gave me these two photographs for you, one of the official paper and one of the prints on the glass. Is there anything more that we can do for you?"

"I should like to have a look at the room in which the murder took place."

"You shall, Doctor. To-morrow, if you like. I'll meet you there in the morning at ten, if that will do."

It would do excellently, Thorndyke assured him, and with this the superintendent took his departure in renewed spirits.

We had only just closed the door when there came a hurried and urgent tapping upon it, whereupon I once more threw it open, and a quietly-dressed woman in a thick veil, who was standing on the threshold, stepped quickly past me into the room.

"Where is my husband?" she demanded, as I closed the door, and then, catching sight of Thorndyke, she strode up to him with a threatening air and a terrified but angry face.

"What have you done with my husband, sir?" she repeated. "Have you betrayed him, after giving your word? I met a man who looked like a police officer on the stairs."

"Your husband, Mrs. Belfield, is here and quite safe," replied Thorndyke. "He has locked himself in that room," indicating the office.

Mrs. Belfield darted across and rapped smartly at the door. "Are you there, Frank?" she called.

In immediate response the key turned, the door opened and Belfield emerged looking very pale and worn.

"You have kept me a long time in there, sir," he said.

"It took me a long time to prove to Superintendent Miller that he was after the wrong man. But I succeeded, and now, Belfield, you are free. The charge against you is withdrawn."

Belfield stood for a while as one stupefied, while his wife, after a moment of silent amazement, flung her arms round his neck and burst into tears. "But how did you know I was innocent, sir?" demanded the bewildered Belfield.

"Ah! How did I? Every man to his trade, you know. Well, I congratulate you, and now go home and have a square meal and get a good night's rest."

He shook hands with his clients – vainly endeavouring to prevent Mrs. Belfield from kissing his hand – and stood at the open door listening until the sound of their retreating footsteps died away.

"A noble little woman, Jervis," said he, as he closed the door. "In another moment she would have scratched my face – and I mean to find out the scoundrel who tried to wreck her happiness."

Part II – The Ship of the Desert

The case which I am now about to describe has always appeared to me a singularly instructive one, as illustrating the value and importance of that fundamental rule in the carrying out of investigations which Thorndyke had laid down so emphatically – the rule that all facts, in any way relating to a case, should be collected impartially and without reference to any theory, and each fact, no matter how trivial or apparently irrelevant, carefully studied. But I must not anticipate the remarks of my learned and talented friend on this subject which I have to chronicle anon. Rather let me proceed to the case itself.

I had slept at our chambers in King's Bench Walk – as I commonly did two or three nights a week – and on coming down to the sitting-room, found Thorndyke's man, Polton, putting the last touches to the breakfast-table, while Thorndyke himself was poring over two photographs of fingerprints, of which he seemed to be taking elaborate measurements with a pair of hair-dividers. He greeted me with his quiet, genial smile and, laying down the dividers, took his seat at the breakfast-table.

"You are coming with me this morning, I suppose," said he. "The Camberwell murder case, you know."

"Of course I am, if you will have me, but I know practically nothing of the case. Could you give me an outline of the facts that are known?"

Thorndyke looked at me solemnly, but with a mischievous twinkle. "This," he said, "is the old story of the fox and the crow, you 'bid me discourse,' and while I 'enchant thine ear,' you claw to windward with the broiled ham. A deep-laid plot, my learned brother."

"And such," I exclaimed, "is the result of contact with the criminal classes!"

"I am sorry that you regard yourself in that light," he retorted, with a malicious smile. "However, with regard to this case. The facts are briefly these: The murdered man, Caldwell, who seems to have been formerly a receiver of stolen goods and probably a police spy as well, lived a solitary life in a small house with only an elderly woman to attend him.

"A week ago, this woman went to visit a married daughter and stayed the night with her, leaving Caldwell alone in the house. When she returned on the following morning, she found her master lying dead on the floor of his office, or study, in a small pool of blood.

"The police surgeon found that he had been dead about twelve hours. He had been killed by a single blow, struck from behind, with some heavy implement, and a jemmy which lay on the floor beside him fitted the wound exactly. The deceased wore a dressing-gown and no collar, and a bedroom candlestick lay upside down on the floor, although gas was laid on in the room, and as the window of the office appears to have been forced with the jemmy that was found, and there were distinct footprints on the flower-bed outside the window, the police think that the deceased was undressing to go to bed when he was disturbed by the noise of the opening window, that he went down to the office and, as he entered, was struck down by the burglar who was lurking behind the door. On the window-glass the police found the greasy impression of an open right hand, and, as you know, the finger-prints were identified by the experts as those of an old convict named Belfield. As you also know, I proved that those finger-prints were, in reality, forgeries, executed with rubber or gelatine stamps. That is an outline of the case."

The close of this recital brought our meal to an end, and we prepared for our visit to the scene of the crime. Thorndyke slipped into his pocket his queer outfit – somewhat like that of a field geologist – locked up the photographs, and we set forth by way of the Embankment.

"The police have no clue, I suppose, to the identity of the murderer, now that the finger-prints have failed?" I asked, as we strode along together.

"I expect not," he replied, "though they might have if they examined their material. I made out a rather interesting point this morning, which is this: The man who made those sham finger-prints used two stamps, one for the thumb and the other for the four fingers, and the original from which those stamps were made was the official finger-print form."

"How did you discover that?" I inquired.

"It was very simple. You remember that Mr. Singleton of the Finger-print Department sent me, by Superintendent Miller, two photographs, one of the prints on the window and one of the official form with Belfield's finger-prints on it. Well, I have compared them and made the most minute measurements of each, and they are obviously duplicates. Not only are all the little imperfections on the form – due to defective inking – reproduced faithfully on the window-pane, but the relative positions of the four fingers on both cases agree to the hundredth of an inch. Of course, the thumb stamp was made by taking an oval out of the rolled impression on the form."

"Then do you suggest that this murder was committed by someone connected with the Finger-print Department at Scotland Yard?"

"Hardly. But someone has had access to the forms. There has been leakage somewhere."

When we arrived at the little detached house in which the murdered man had lived, the door was opened by an elderly woman, and our friend, Superintendent Miller, greeted us in the hall.

"We are all ready for you, Doctor," said he. "Of course, the things have all been gone over once, but we are turning them out more thoroughly now." He led the way into the small, barely-furnished office in which the tragedy had occurred. A dark stain on the carpet and a square hole in one of the window-panes furnished memorials of the crime, which were supplemented by an odd assortment of objects laid out on the newspaper-covered table. These included silver teaspoons, watches, various articles of jewellery from which the stones had been removed – none of them of any considerable value – and a roughly-made jemmy.

"I don't know why Caldwell should have kept all these odds and ends," said the detective superintendent. "There is stuff here, that I can identify, from six different burglaries – and not a conviction among the six."

Thorndyke looked over the collection with languid interest, he was evidently disappointed at finding the room so completely turned out.

"Have you any idea what has been taken?" he asked.

"Not the least. We don't even know if the safe was opened. The keys were on the writing-table, so I suppose he went through everything, though I don't see why he left these things if he did. We found them all in the safe."

"Have you powdered the jemmy?"

The superintendent turned very red. "Yes," he growled, "but some half-dozen blithering idiots had handled the thing before I saw it – been trying it on the window, the blighters – so, of course, it showed nothing but the marks of their beastly paws."

"The window had not really been forced, I suppose?" said Thorndyke.

"No," replied Miller, with a glance of surprise at my colleague. "That was a plant. So were the footprints. He must have put on a pair of Caldwell's boots and gone out and made them – unless Caldwell made them himself, which isn't likely."

"Have you found any letter or telegram?"

"A letter making an appointment for nine o'clock on the night of the murder. No signature or address, and the handwriting evidently disguised."

"Is there anything that furnishes any sort of clue?"

"Yes, sir, there is. There's this, which we found in the safe." He produced a small parcel which he proceeded to unfasten, looking somewhat queerly at Thorndyke the while. It contained various odds and ends of jewellery, and a smaller parcel formed of a pocket-handkerchief tied with tape. This the detective also unfastened, revealing half-a-dozen silver teaspoons, all engraved with the same crest, two salt-cellars, and a gold locket bearing a monogram. There was also a half-sheet of note-paper on which was written, in a manifestly disguised hand: *These are the goods I told you about. F. B.*" But what riveted Thorndyke's attention and mine was the handkerchief itself (which was not a very clean one and was sullied by one or two small blood-stains), for it was marked in one corner with the name "F. Belfield," legibly printed in marking-ink with a rubber stamp.

Thorndyke and the superintendent looked at one another and both smiled.

"I know what you are thinking, sir," said the latter.

"I am sure you do," was the reply, "and it is useless to pretend that you don't agree with me."

"Well, sir," said Miller doggedly, "if that handkerchief has been put there as a plant, it's Belfield's business to prove it. You see, Doctor," he added persuasively, "it isn't this job only that's affected. Those spoons, those salt-cellars, and that locket are part of the proceeds of the Winchmore Hill burglary, and we want the gentleman who did that crack – we want him very badly."

"No doubt you do," replied Thorndyke, "but this handkerchief won't help you. A sharp counsel – Mr. Anstey, for instance – would demolish it in five minutes. I assure you, Miller, that handkerchief has no evidential value whatever, whereas it might prove an invaluable instrument of research. The best thing you can do is to hand it over to me and let me see what I can learn from it."

The superintendent was obviously dissatisfied, but he eventually agreed, with manifest reluctance, to Thorndyke's suggestion.

"Very well, Doctor," he said, "you shall have it for a day or two. Do you want the spoons and things as well?"

"No. Only the handkerchief and the paper that was in it."

The two articles were accordingly handed to him and deposited in a tin box which he usually carried in his pocket, and, after a few more words with the disconsolate detective, we took our departure.

"A very disappointing morning," was Thorndyke's comment as we walked away. "Of course, the room ought to have been examined by an expert before anything was moved."

"Have you picked up anything in the way of information?" I asked.

"Very little, excepting confirmation of my original theory. You see, this man Caldwell was a receiver and evidently a police spy. He gave useful information to the police, and they, in return, refrained from inconvenient inquiries. But a spy, or 'nark', is nearly always a blackmailer

384

too, and the probabilities in this case are that some crook, on whom Caldwell was putting the screw rather too tightly, made an appointment for a meeting when the house was empty, and just knocked Caldwell on the head. The crime was evidently planned beforehand, and the murderer came prepared to kill several birds with one stone. Thus he brought with him the stamps to make the sham finger-prints on the window, and I have no doubt that he also brought this handkerchief and the various oddments of plate and jewellery from those burglaries that Miller is so keen about, and planted them in the safe. You noticed, I suppose, that none of the things were of any value, but all were capable of easy identification?"

"Yes, I noticed that. His object, evidently, was to put those burglaries as well as the murder onto poor Belfield."

"Exactly. And you see what Miller's attitude is: Belfield is the bird in the hand, whereas the other man – if there is another – is still in the bush, so Belfield is to be followed up and a conviction obtained if possible. If he is innocent, that is his affair, and it is for him to prove it."

"And what shall you do next?" I asked.

"I shall telegraph to Belfield to come and see us this evening. He may be able to tell us something about this handkerchief that, with the clue we already have, may put us on the right track. What time is your consultation?"

"Twelve-thirty – and here comes my 'bus. I shall be in to lunch." I sprang onto the footboard, and as I took my seat on the roof and looked back at my friend striding along with an easy swing, I knew that he was deep in thought, though automatically attentive to all that was happening. My consultation – it was a lunacy case of some importance – was over in time to allow of my return to our chambers punctually at the luncheon hour, and as I entered, I was at once struck by something new in Thorndyke's manner – a certain elation and gaiety which I had learned to associate with a point scored successfully in some intricate and puzzling case. He made no confidences, however, and seemed, in fact, inclined to put away, for a time, all his professional cares and business.

"Shall we have an afternoon off, Jervis?" he said gaily. "It is a fine day and work is slack just now. What say you to the Zoo? They have a splendid chimpanzee and several specimens of that remarkable fish *Periophthalmos Kolreuteri*. Shall we go?"

"By all means," I replied, "and we will mount the elephant, if you like, and throw buns to the grizzly bear, and generally renew our youth like the eagle."

But when, an hour later, we found ourselves in the gardens, I began to suspect my friend of some ulterior purpose in this holiday jaunt, for it was not the chimpanzee or even the wonderful fish that attracted his attention. On the contrary, he hung about the vicinity of the lamas and camels in a way that I could not fail to notice, and even there it appeared to be the sheds and houses rather than the animals themselves that interested him.

"Behold, Jervis," he said presently, as a saddled camel of seedy aspect was led towards its house, "behold the ship of the desert, with raised saloon-deck amidships, fitted internally with watertight compartments and displaying the effects of rheumatoid arthritis in his starboard hip-joint. Let us go and examine him before he hauls into dock." We took a cross-path to intercept the camel on its way to its residence, and Thorndyke moralized as we went.

"It is interesting," he remarked, "to note the way in which these specialized animals, such as the horse, the reindeer, and the camel, have been appropriated by man, and their special character made to subserve human needs. Think, for instance, of the part the camel has played in history, in ancient commerce – and modern too, for that matter – and in the diffusion of culture, and of the role he has enacted in war and conquest from the Egyptian campaign of Cambyses down to that of Kitchener. Yes, the camel is a very remarkable animal, though it must be admitted that this particular specimen is a scurvy-looking beast."

The camel seemed to be sensible of these disparaging remarks, for as it approached it saluted Thorndyke with a supercilious grin and then turned away its head.

"Your charge is not as young as he used to be," Thorndyke observed to the man who was leading the animal.

"No, sir, he isn't. He's getting old, and that's the fact. He shows it too."

"I suppose," said Thorndyke, strolling towards the house by the man's side, "these beasts require a deal of attention?"

"You're right, sir, and nasty-tempered brutes they are."

"So I have heard, but they are interesting creatures, the camels and lamas. Do you happen to know if complete sets of photographs of them are to be had here?"

"You can get a good many at the lodge, sir," the man replied, "but not all, I think. If you want a complete set, there's one of our men in the camel-house that could let you have them. He takes the photos himself, and very clever he is at it, too. But he isn't here just now."

"Perhaps you could give me his name so that I could write to him," said Thorndyke.

"Yes, sir. His name is Woodthorpe – Joseph Woodthorpe. He'll do anything for you to order. Thank you, sir, good-afternoon, sir," and pocketing an unexpected tip, the man led his charge towards its lair.

386

Thorndyke's absorbing interest in the camels seemed now suddenly to become extinct, and he suffered me to lead him to any part of the gardens that attracted me, showing an imperial interest in all the inmates from the insects to the elephants, and enjoying his holiday – if it was one – with the gaiety and high spirits of a schoolboy. Yet he never let slip a chance of picking up a stray hair or feather, but gathered up each with care, wrapped it in its separate paper, on which was written its description, and deposited it in his tin collecting-box.

"You never know," he remarked, as we turned away from the ostrich enclosure, "when a specimen for comparison may be of vital importance. Here, for instance, is a small feather of a cassowary, and here the hair of a wapiti deer. Now the recognition of either of those might, in certain circumstances, lead to the detection of a criminal or save the life of an innocent man. The thing has happened repeatedly, and may happen again to-morrow."

"You must have an enormous collection of hairs in your cabinet," I remarked, as we walked home.

"I have," he replied, "probably the largest in the world. And as to other microscopical objects of medico-legal interest, such as dust and mud from different localities and from special industries and manufactures, fibres, food-products and drugs, my collection is certainly unique."

"And you have found your collection useful in your work?" I asked.

"Constantly. Over and over again I have obtained, by reference to my specimens, the most unexpected evidence, and the longer I practise, the more I become convinced that the microscope is the sheet-anchor of the medical jurist."

"By the way," I said, "you spoke of sending a telegram to Belfield. Did you send it?"

"Yes. I asked him to come to see me to-night at half-past eight, and, if possible, bring his wife with him. I want to get to the bottom of that handkerchief mystery."

"But do you think he will tell you the truth about it?"

"That is impossible to judge. He will be a fool if he does not. But I think he will. He has a godly fear of me and my methods."

As soon as our dinner was finished and cleared away, Thorndyke produced the "collecting-box" from his pocket, and began to sort out the day's "catch". giving explicit directions to Polton for the disposal of each specimen. The hairs and small feathers were to be mounted as microscopic objects, while the larger feathers were to be placed, each in its separate labelled envelope, in its appropriate box. While these directions were being given, I stood by the window absently gazing out as I listened, gathering many a useful hint in the technique of preparation and preservation, and filled with admiration alike at my colleague's exhaustive knowledge of practical detail and the perfect manner in which he had trained his assistant. Suddenly I started, for a well-known figure was crossing from Crown Office Row and evidently bearing down on our chambers.

"My word, Thorndyke," I exclaimed, "here's a pretty mess!"

"What is the matter?" he asked, looking up anxiously.

"Superintendent Miller heading straight for our doorway. And it is now twenty-minutes-past-eight."

Thorndyke laughed. "It will be a quaint position," he remarked, "and somewhat of a shock for Belfield. But it really doesn't matter, in fact, I think, on the whole, I am rather pleased that he should have come."

The superintendent's brisk knock was heard a few moments later, and when he was admitted by Polton, he entered and looked round the room a little, sheepishly.

"I am ashamed to come worrying you like this, sir," he began apologetically.

"Not at all," replied Thorndyke, serenely slipping the cassowary's feather into an envelope, and writing the name, date, and locality on the outside. "I am your servant in this case, you know. Polton, whisky and soda for the superintendent."

"You see, sir," continued Miller, "our people are beginning to fuss about this case, and they don't approve of my having handed that handkerchief and the paper over to you, as they will have to be put in evidence."

"I thought they might object," remarked Thorndyke.

"So did I, sir, and they do. And, in short, they say that I have got to get them back at once. I hope it won't put you out, sir."

"Not in the least," said Thorndyke. "I have asked Belfield to come here to-night – I expect him in a few minutes – and when I have heard what he has to say, I shall have no further use for the handkerchief."

"You're not going to show it to him!" exclaimed the detective, aghast.

"Certainly I am."

"You mustn't do that, sir. I can't sanction it, I can't indeed."

"Now, look you here, Miller," said Thorndyke, shaking his forefinger at the officer, "I am working for you in this case, as I have told you. Leave the matter in my hands. Don't raise silly objections, and when you leave here tonight you will take with you not only the handkerchief and the paper, but probably also the name and address of the man who committed this murder and those various burglaries that you are so keen about."

"Is that really so, sir?" exclaimed the astonished detective. "Well, you haven't let the grass grow under your feet. Ah!" as a gentle rap at the door was heard. "Here's Belfield, I suppose."

It was Belfield – accompanied by his wife – and mightily disturbed they were when their eyes lighted on our visitor.

"You needn't be afraid of me, Belfield," said Miller, with ferocious geniality. "I am not here after you." Which was not literally true, though it served to reassure the affrighted ex-convict.

"The superintendent dropped in by chance," said Thorndyke, "but it is just as well that he should hear what passes. I want you to look at this handkerchief and tell me if it is yours. Don't be afraid, but just tell us the simple truth."

He took the handkerchief out of a drawer and spread it on the table, and I now observed that a small square had been cut out of one of the bloodstains.

Belfield took the handkerchief in his trembling hands, and as his eye fell on the stamped name in the corner he turned deadly pale.

"It looks like mine," he said huskily. "What do you say, Liz?" he added, passing it to his wife.

Mrs. Belfield examined first the name and then the hem. "It's yours, right enough, Frank," said she. "It's the one that got changed in the wash. You see, sir," she continued, addressing Thorndyke, "I bought him half-a-dozen new ones about six months ago, and I got a rubber stamp made and marked them all. Well, one day when I was looking over his things, I noticed that one of his handkerchiefs had got no mark on it. I spoke to the laundress about it, but she couldn't explain it, so as the right one never came back, I marked the one that we got in exchange."

"How long ago was that?" asked Thorndyke.

"About two months ago I noticed it."

"And you know nothing more about it."

"Nothing whatever, sir. Nor you, Frank, do you?"

Her husband shook his head gloomily, and Thorndyke replaced the handkerchief in the drawer.

"And now," said he, "I am going to ask you a question on another subject. When you were at Holloway, there was a warder – or assistant warder – there, named Woodthorpe. Do you remember him?"

"Yes, sir, very well indeed. In fact, it was him that – ?"

"I know," interrupted Thorndyke. "Have you seen him since you left Holloway?"

"Yes, sir, once. It was last Easter Monday. I met him at the Zoo. He is a keeper there now in the camel-house." (Here a sudden light dawned upon me and I chuckled aloud, to Belfield's great astonishment). "He gave my little boy a ride on one of the camels and made himself very pleasant."

"Do you remember anything else happening?" Thorndyke inquired.

"Yes, sir. The camel had a little accident. He kicked out – he was an ill-tempered beast – and his leg hit a post. There happened to be a nail sticking out from that post, and it tore up a little flap of skin. Then Woodthorpe got out his handkerchief to tie up the wound, but as it was none of the cleanest, I said to him, 'Don't use that, Woodthorpe, have mine,' which was quite a clean one. So he took it and bound up the camel's leg, and he said to me, 'I'll have it washed and send it to you if you give me your address.' But I told him there was no need for that, I should be passing the camel-house on my way out and I would look in for the handkerchief. And I did. I looked in about an hour later, and Woodthorpe gave me my handkerchief, folded up, but not washed."

"Did you examine it to see if it was yours?" asked Thorndyke.

"No, sir. I just slipped it in my pocket as it was."

"And what became of it afterwards?"

"When I got home I dropped it into the dirty-linen basket."

"Is that all you know about it?"

"Yes, sir, that is all I know."

"Very well, Belfield, that will do. Now you have no reason to be uneasy. You will soon know all about the Camberwell murder – that is, if you read the papers."

The ex-convict and his wife were obviously relieved by this assurance and departed in quite good spirits. When they were gone, Thorndyke produced the handkerchief and the half-sheet of paper and handed them to the superintendent, remarking, "This is highly satisfactory, Miller. The whole case seems to join up very neatly indeed. Two months ago, the wife first noticed the substituted handkerchief, and last Easter Monday – a little over two months ago – this very significant incident took place in the Zoological Gardens."

"That is all very well, sir," objected the superintendent, "but we've only their word for it, you know."

"Not so," replied Thorndyke. "We have excellent corroborative evidence. You noticed that I had cut a small piece out of the blood-stained portion of the handkerchief?"

"Yes, and I was sorry you had done it. Our people won't like that."

"Well, here it is, and we will ask Dr. Jervis to give us his opinion of it."

From the drawer in which the handkerchief had been hidden he brought forth a microscope slide, and setting the microscope on the table, laid the slide on the stage.

"Now, Jervis," he said, "tell us what you see there."

I examined the edge of the little square of fabric (which had been mounted in a fluid reagent) with a high-power objective, and was, for a time, a little puzzled by the appearance of the blood that adhered to it.

"It looks like bird's blood," I said presently, with some hesitation, "but yet I can make out no nuclei." I looked again, and then, suddenly, "By Jove!" I exclaimed, "I have it, of course! It's the blood of a camel!"

"Is that so, Doctor?" demanded the detective, leaning forward in his excitement.

"That is so," replied Thorndyke. "I discovered it after I came home this morning. You see," he explained, "it is quite unmistakable. The rule is that the blood corpuscles of mammals are circular. The one exception is the camel family, in which the corpuscles are elliptical."

"Why," exclaimed Miller, "that seems to connect Woodthorpe with this Camberwell job."

"It connects him with it very conclusively," said Thorndyke. "You are forgetting the finger-prints."

The detective looked puzzled. "What about them?" he asked.

"They were made with stamps – two stamps, as a matter of fact – and those stamps were made by photographic process from the official finger-print form. I can prove that beyond all doubt."

"Well, suppose they were. What then?"

Thorndyke opened a drawer and took out a photograph, which he handed to Miller. "Here," he said, "is the photograph of the official finger-print form which you were kind enough to bring me. What does it say at the bottom there?" and he pointed with his finger.

The superintendent read aloud: "*Impressions taken by Joseph Woodthorpe. Rank, Warder, Prison, Holloway*". He stared at the photograph for a moment, and then exclaimed, "Well, I'm hanged! You have worked this out neatly, Doctor! And so quick too. We'll have Mr. Woodthorpe under lock-and-key the first thing to-morrow morning. But how did he do it, do you think?"

"He might have taken duplicate finger-prints and kept one form. The prisoners would not know there was anything wrong, but he did not in this case. He must have contrived to take a photograph of the form before sending it in – it would take a skilful photographer only a minute or two with a suitable hand-camera placed on a table at the proper distance from the wall, and I have ascertained that he is a skilful photographer. You will probably find the apparatus, and the stamps too, when you search his rooms."

"Well, well. You do give us some surprises, Doctor. But I must be off now to see about this warrant. Good-night, sir, and many thanks for your help."

When the superintendent had gone, we sat for a while looking at one another in silence. At length Thorndyke spoke. "Here is a case, Jervis," he said, "which, simple as it is, teaches a most invaluable lesson – a lesson which you should take well to heart. It is this: The evidential value of any fact is an unknown quantity until the fact has been examined. That seems a self-evident truth, but like many other self-evident truths, it is constantly overlooked in practice. Take this present case. When I left Caldwell's house this morning the facts in my possession were these: (1) The man who murdered Caldwell was directly or indirectly connected with the Finger-print Department. (2) He was almost certainly a skilled photographer. (3) He probably committed the Winchmore Hill and the other burglaries. (4) He was known to Caldwell, had had professional dealings with him, and was probably being blackmailed. This was all, a very vague clue, as you see.

"There was the handkerchief, planted – as I had no doubt, but could not prove. The name stamped on it was Belfield's, but anyone can get a rubber stamp made. Then it was stained with blood, as handkerchiefs often are. That blood might or might not be human blood. It did not seem to matter a straw whether it was or not. Nevertheless, I said to myself: If it is human, or at least mammalian blood, that is a fact, and if it is *not* human blood, that is also a fact. I will have that fact, and then I shall know what its value is. I examined the stain when I reached home, and behold! It was camel's blood, and immediately this insignificant fact swelled up into evidence of primary importance. The rest was obvious. I had seen Woodthorpe's name on the form, and I knew several other officials. My business was to visit all places in London where there were camels, to get the names of all persons connected with them and to ascertain if any among them was a photographer. Naturally I went first to the Zoo, and at the very first cast hooked Joseph Woodthorpe. Wherefore I say again: Never call any fact irrelevant until you have examined it."

The remarkable evidence given above was not heard at the trial, nor did Thorndyke's name appear among the witnesses, for when the police searched Woodthorpe's rooms, so many incriminating articles were found (including a pair of fingerprint stamps which exactly answered to Thorndyke's description of them, and a number of photographs of finger-print forms) that his guilt was put beyond all doubt, and society was shortly after relieved of a very undesirable member.

R. AUSTIN FREEMAN'S
Detective Stories

The Great Portrait Mystery

By
R. AUSTIN FREEMAN
AUTHOR OF
John Thorndyke's Cases etc.

1918 Hodder & Stoughton Cover

Editor's Note

The Great Portrait Mystery *(1918)* *contained seven short stories,* *although only two, "Percival Bland's Proxy" and "The Missing* *Mortgagee", are about Dr. Thorndyke.*

The other five stories do not fall under the scope of this book, and are *therefore not included in this volume. For the curious, these stories are:*

- The Great Portrait Mystery
- The Bronze Parrot
- Powder Blue and Hawthorn
- The Attorney's Conscience
- The Luck of Barnabus Mudge

Percival Bland's Proxy
Part I

Mr. Percival Bland was a somewhat uncommon type of criminal. In the first place, he really had an appreciable amount of common-sense. If he had only had a little more, he would not have been a criminal at all. As it was, he had just sufficient judgment to perceive that the consequences of unlawful acts accumulate as the acts are repeated, to realise that the criminal's position must, at length, become untenable, and to take what he considered fair precautions against the inevitable catastrophe.

But in spite of these estimable traits of character and the precautions aforesaid, Mr. Bland found himself in rather a tight place and with a prospect of increasing tightness. The causes of this uncomfortable tension do not concern us, and may be dismissed with the remark that, if one perseveringly distributes flash Bank of England notes among the money-changers of the Continent, there will come a day of reckoning when those notes are tendered to the exceedingly knowing old lady who lives in Threadneedle Street.

Mr. Bland considered uneasily the approaching storm-cloud as he raked over the "miscellaneous property" in the Sale-rooms of Messrs. Plimpton. He was a confirmed frequenter of auctions, as was not unnatural, for the criminal is essentially a gambler. And criminal and gambler have one quality in common: Each hopes to get something of value without paying the market price for it.

So Percival turned over the dusty oddments and his own difficulties at one and the same time. The vital questions were: When would the storm burst? And would it pass by the harbour of refuge that he had been at such pains to construct? Let us inspect that harbour of refuge.

A quiet flat in the pleasant neighbourhood of Battersea bore a name-plate inscribed *Mr. Robert Lindsay*, and the tenant was known to the porter and the char woman who attended to the flat as a fair-haired gentleman who was engaged in the book trade as a travelling agent, and was consequently a good deal away from home. Now Mr. Robert Lindsay bore a distinct resemblance to Percival Bland, which was not surprising seeing that they were first cousins (or, at any rate, they said they were, and we may presume that they knew). But they were not very much alike. Mr. Lindsay had flaxen, or rather sandy, hair. Mr. Bland's hair was black. Mr. Bland had a mole under his left eye. Mr. Lindsay had no mole under his eye – but carried one in a small box in his waistcoat pocket.

At somewhat rare intervals the Cousins called on one another, but they had the very worst of luck, for neither of them ever seemed to find the other at home. And what was even more odd was that whenever Mr. Bland spent an evening at home in his lodgings over the oil shop in Bloomsbury, Mr. Lindsay's flat was empty, and as sure as Mr. Lindsay was at home in his flat so surely were Mr. Bland's lodgings vacant for the time being. It was a queer coincidence, if anyone had noticed it – but nobody ever did.

However, if Percival saw little of his cousin, it was not a case of "out of sight, out of mind". On the contrary – so great was his solicitude for the latter's welfare that he not only had made a will constituting him his executor and sole legatee, but he had actually insured his life for no less a sum than three-thousand pounds, and this will, together with the insurance policy, investment securities, and other necessary documents, he had placed in the custody of a highly respectable solicitor. All of which did him great credit. It isn't every man who is willing to take so much trouble for a mere cousin.

Mr. Bland continued his perambulations, pawing over the miscellaneous raffle from sheer force of habit, reflecting on the coming crisis in his own affairs, and on the provisions that he had made for his cousin Robert. As for the latter, they were excellent as far as they went, but they lacked definiteness and perfect completeness. There was the contingency of a "stretch", for instance – say fourteen years' penal servitude. The insurance policy did not cover that. And, meanwhile, what was to become of the estimable Robert?

He had bruised his thumb somewhat severely in a screw-cutting lathe, and had abstractedly turned the handle of a bird-organ until politely requested by an attendant to desist, when he came upon a series of boxes containing, according to the catalogue, *"a collection of surgical instruments the property of a lately deceased practitioner"*. To judge by the appearance of the instruments, the practitioner must have commenced practice in his early youth and died at a very advanced age. They were an uncouth set of tools, of no value whatever excepting as testimonials to the amazing tenacity of life of our ancestors, but Percival fingered them over according to his wont, working the handle of a complicated brass syringe and ejecting a drop of greenish fluid on to the shirt of a dressy Hebrew (who requested him to "point the dam' thing at thomeone elth nectht time"), opening musty leather cases, clicking off spring scarifiers, and feeling the edges of strange, crooked, knives. Then he came upon a largish black box, which, when he raised the lid, breathed out an ancient and fish-like aroma and exhibited a collection of bones, yellow, greasy and spotted in places with mildew. The catalogue described them as *"a complete set of*

400

human osteology" but they were not an ordinary "student's set", for the bones of the hands and feet, instead of being strung together on cat-gut, were united by their original ligaments and were of an unsavoury brown colour.

"I thay, misther," expostulat the Hebrew, "shut that bocth. Thmellth like a blooming inquetht."

But the contents of the black box seemed to have a fascination for Percival. He looked in at those greasy remnants of mortality, at the brown and mouldy hands and feet and the skull that peeped forth eerily from the folds of a flannel wrapping, and they breathed out something more than that stale and musty odour. A suggestion – vague and general at first, but rapidly crystallising into distinct shape – seemed to steal out of the black box into his consciousness, a suggestion that somehow seemed to connect itself with his estimable cousin Robert.

For upwards of a minute he stood motionless, as one immersed in reverie, the lid poised in his hand and a dreamy eye fixed on the half skull. A stir in the room roused him. The sale was about to begin. The members of the knock-out and other habitués seated themselves on benches around a long, baize table. The attendants took possession of the first lots and opened their catalogues as if about to sing an introductory chorus, and a gentleman with a waxed moustache and a striking resemblance to his late Majesty, the third Napoleon, having ascended to the rostrum bespoke the attention of the assembly by a premonitory tap with his hammer.

How odd are some of the effects of a guilty conscience! With what absurd self-consciousness do we read into the minds of others our own undeclared intentions, when those intentions are unlawful! Had Percival Bland wanted a set of human bones for any legitimate purpose – such as anatomical study – he would have bought it openly and unembarrassed. Now, he found himself earnestly debating whether he should not bid for some of the surgical instruments, just for the sake of appearances, and there being little time in which to make up his mind – for the deceased practitioner's effects came first in the catalogue – he was already the richer by a set of cupping-glasses, a tooth-key, and an instrument of unknown use and diabolical aspect, before the fateful lot was called.

At length the black box was laid on the table, an object of obscene mirth to the knockers-out, and the auctioneer read the entry. "Lot Seventeen: A complete set of human osteology. A very useful and valuable set of specimens, gentlemen."

He looked round at the assembly majestically, oblivious of sundry inquiries as to the identity of the deceased and the verdict of the coroner's jury, and finally suggested five shillings.

"Six," said Percival.

An attendant held the box open, and, chanting the mystic word, "Loddlemen!" (which, being interpreted, meant "Lot, gentlemen"), thrust it under the rather bulbous nose of the smart Hebrew, who remarked that "they 'ummed a bit too much to thoot him", and pushed it away.

"Going at six shillings," said the auctioneer, reproachfully, and as nobody contradicted him, he smote the rostrum with his hammer and the box was delivered into the hands of Percival on the payment of that modest sum.

Having crammed the cupping-glasses, the tooth-key and the unknown instrument into the box, Percival obtained from one of the attendants a length of cord, with which he secured the lid. Then he carried his treasure out into the street and, chartering a four-wheeler, directed the driver to proceed to Charing Cross Station. At the station he booked the box in the cloak (in the name of Simpson) and left it for a couple of hours, at the expiration of which he returned and, employing a different porter, had it conveyed to a hansom, in which it was borne to his lodgings over the oil-shop in Bloomsbury. There he, himself, carried it, unobserved, up the stairs, and, depositing it in a large cupboard, locked the door, and pocketed the key.

And thus was the curtain rung down on the first act. The second act opened only a couple of days later, the office of call-boy – to pursue the metaphor to the bitter end – being discharged by a Belgian police official who emerged from the main entrance to the Bank of England. What should have led Percival Bland into so unsafe a neighbourhood it is difficult to imagine, unless it was that strange fascination that seems so frequently to lure the criminal to places associated with his crime. But there he was within a dozen paces of the entrance when the officer came forth, and mutual recognition was instant. Almost equally instantaneous was the self-possessed Percival's decision to cross the road.

It is not a nice road to cross. The old horse would condescend to shout a warning to the indiscreet wayfarer. Not so the modern chauffeur, who looks stonily before him and leaves you to get out of the way of Juggernaut. He knows his "exonerating" coroner's jury. At the moment, however, the procession of Juggernauts was at rest, but Percival had seen the presiding policeman turn to move away and he darted across the fronts of the vehicles even as they started. The foreign officer followed. But in that moment the whole procession had got in motion. A motor omnibus thundered past in front of him. Another was bearing down on him relentlessly. He hesitated, and sprang back, and then a taxi-cab, darting out from behind, butted him heavily, sending him sprawling in the road, whence he scrambled as best he could back on to the pavement.

402

Percival, meanwhile, had swung himself lightly on to the footboard of the first omnibus just as it was gathering speed. A few seconds saw him safely across at the Mansion House, and in a few more, he was whirling down Queen Victoria Street. The danger was practically over, though he took the precaution to alight at St. Paul's, and, crossing to Newgate Street, board another west-bound omnibus.

That night he sat in his lodgings turning over his late experience. It had been a narrow shave. That sort of thing mustn't happen again. In fact, seeing that the law was undoubtedly about to be set in motion, it was high time that certain little plans of his should be set in motion, too. Only there was a difficulty – a serious difficulty. And as Percival thought round and round that difficulty his brows wrinkled and he hummed a soft refrain:

> *Then is the time for disappearing,*
> *Take a header – down you go –*

A tap at the door cut his song short. It was his landlady, Mrs. Brattle – a civil woman, and particularly civil just now. For she had a little request to make.

"It was about Christmas Night, Mr. Bland," said Mrs. Brattle. "My husband and me thought of spending the evening with his brother at Hornsey, and we were going to let the maid go home to her mother's for the night, if it wouldn't put you out."

"Wouldn't put me out in the least, Mrs. Brattle," said Percival.

"You needn't sit up for us, you see," pursued Mrs. Brattle, "if you just leave the side door unbolted. We shan't be home before two or three, but we'll come in quiet not to disturb you."

"You won't disturb me," Percival replied with a genial laugh. "I'm a sober man in general, but 'Christmas comes but once a year'. When once I'm tucked up in bed, I shall take a bit of waking on Christmas Night."

Mrs. Brattle smiled indulgently. "And you won't feel lonely, all alone in the house?"

"Lonely!" exclaimed Percival. "Lonely! With a roaring fire, a jolly book, a box of good cigars, and a bottle of sound port – ah, and a second bottle if need be. Not I."

Mrs. Brattle shook her head. "Ah," said she, "you bachelors! Well, well. It's a good thing to be independent!" And with this profound reflection, she smiled herself out of the room and descended the stairs.

As her footsteps died away Percival sprang from his chair and began excitedly to pace the room. His eyes sparkled and his face was wreathed with smiles. Presently he halted before the fireplace and, gazing into the embers, laughed aloud.

403

"Damn funny!" said he. "Deuced rich! Neat! Very neat! Ha! Ha!" And here he resumed his interrupted song. *"When the sky above is clearing, When the sky above is clearing, Bob up serenely, bob up serenely, Bob up serenely from below!"*

Which may be regarded as closing the first scene, of the second act.

During the few days that intervened before Christmas, Percival went abroad but little, and yet he was a busy man. He did a little surreptitious shopping, venturing out as far as Charing Cross Road, and his purchases were decidedly miscellaneous. A porridge saucepan, a second-hand copy of *Gray's Anatomy*, a rabbit skin, a large supply of glue, and upwards of ten pounds of shin of beef seems a rather odd assortment, and it was a mercy that the weather was frosty, for otherwise Percival's bedroom, in which these delicacies were deposited under lock and key, would have yielded odorous traces of its wealth.

But it was in the long evenings that his industry was most conspicuous, and then it was that the big cupboard with the excellent lever lock, which he himself had fixed on, began to fill up with the fruits of his labours. In those evenings the porridge saucepan would simmer on the hob with a rich lading of good Scotch glue, the black box of the deceased practitioner would be hauled forth from its hiding-place, and the well-thumbed *Gray* laid open on the table.

It was an arduous business though, a stiffer task than he had bargained for. The right and left bones were so confoundedly alike, and the bones that joined were so difficult to fit together. However, the plates in *Gray* were large and very clear, so it was only a question of taking enough trouble.

His method of work was simple and practical. Having fished a bone out of the box, he would compare it with the illustrations in the book until he had identified it beyond all doubt, when he would tie on it a paper label with its name and side – right or left. Then he would search for the adjoining bone, and, having fitted the two together, would secure them with a good daub of glue and lay them in the fender to dry. It was a crude and horrible method of articulation that would have made a museum curator shudder. But it seemed to answer Percival's purpose – whatever that may have been – for gradually the loose "items" came together into recognisable members such as arms and legs, the vertebra – which were, fortunately, strung in their order on a thick cord – were joined up into a solid backbone, and even the ribs, which were the toughest job of all, fixed on in some semblance of a thorax. It was a wretched performance. The bones were plastered with gouts of glue, and yet would have broken apart

404

at a touch. But, as we have said, Percival seemed satisfied, and as he was the only person concerned, there was no more to be said.

In due course, Christmas Day arrived. Percival dined with the Brattles at two, dozed after dinner, woke up for tea, and then, as Mrs. Brattle, in purple and fine raiment, came in to remove the tea-tray, he spread out on the table the materials for the night's carouse. A quarter-of-an-hour later, the side slammed, and, peering out of the window, he saw the shopkeeper and his wife hurrying away up the gas-lit street towards the nearest omnibus route.

Then Mr. Percival Bland began his evening's entertainment, and a most remarkable entertainment it was, even for a solitary bachelor, left alone in a house on Christmas Night. First, he took off his clothing and dressed himself in a fresh suit. Then, from the cupboard he brought forth the reconstituted "set of osteology" and, laying the various members on the table, returned to the bedroom, whence he presently reappeared with a large, savoury parcel which he had disinterred from a trunk. The parcel being opened revealed his accumulated purchases in the matter of shin of beef.

With a large knife, providently sharpened beforehand, he cut the beef into large, thin slices which he proceed to wrap around the various bones that formed the "complete set", whereby their nakedness was certainly mitigated though their attractiveness was by no means increased. Having thus "clothed the dry bones", he gathered up the scraps of offal that were left, to be placed presently inside the trunk. It was an extraordinary proceeding, but the next was more extraordinary still.

Taking up the newly clothed members one by one, he began very carefully to insinuate them into the garments that he had recently shed. It was a ticklish business, for the glued joints were as brittle as glass. Very cautiously the legs were separately inducted, first into underclothing and then into trousers, the skeleton feet were fitted with the cast-off socks and delicately persuaded into the boots. The arms, in like manner, were gingerly pressed into their various sleeves and through the arm-holes of the waistcoat, and then came the most difficult task of all – to fit the garments on the trunk. For the skull and ribs, secured to the back-bone with mere spots of glue, were ready to drop off at a shake, and yet the garments had to be drawn over them with the arms enclosed in the sleeves. But Percival managed it at last by resting his "restoration" in the big, padded arm-chair and easing the garments on inch by inch.

It now remained only to give the finishing touch, which was done by cutting the rabbit-skin to the requisite shape and affixing it to the skull with a thin coat of stiff glue, and when the skull had thus been finished with a sort of crude, makeshift wig, its appearance was so appalling as

405

even to disturb the nerves of the matter-of-fact Percival. However, this was no occasion for cherishing sentiment. A skull in an extemporised wig or false scalp might be, and in fact was, a highly unpleasant object – but so was a Belgian police officer.

Having finished the "restoration", Percival fetched the water-jug from his bedroom, and, descending to the shop, the door of which had been left unlocked, tried the taps of the various drums and barrels until he came to the one which contained methylated spirit, and from this he filled his jug and returned to the bedroom. Pouring the spirit out into the basin, he tucked a towel round his neck and filling his sponge with spirit proceeded very vigorously to wash his hair and eyebrows, and as, by degrees, the spirit in the basin grew dark and turbid, so did his hair and eyebrows grow lighter in colour until, after a final energetic rub with a towel, they had acquired a golden or sandy hue indistinguishable from that of the hair of his cousin Robert. Even the mole under his eye was susceptible to the changing conditions, for when he had wetted it thoroughly with spirit, he was able, with the blade of a penknife to peel it off as neatly as if it had been stuck on with spirit-gum. Having done which, he deposited it in a tiny box which he carried in his waistcoat pocket.

The proceedings which followed were unmistakable as to their object. First he carried the basin of spirit through into the sitting-room and deliberately poured its contents on to the floor by the arm-chair. Then, having returned the basin to the bedroom, he again went down to the shop, where he selected a couple of galvanised buckets from the stock, filled them with paraffin oil from one of the great drums, and carried them upstairs. The oil from one bucket he poured over the armchair and its repulsive occupant, the other bucket he simply emptied on the carpet, and then went down to the shop for a fresh supply.

When this proceeding had been repeated once or twice, the entire floor and all the furniture were saturated, and such a reek of paraffin filled the air of the room that Percival thought it wise to turn out the gas. Returning to the shop, be poured a bucketful of oil over the stack of bundles of firewood, another over the counter and floor, and a third over the loose articles on the walls and hanging from the ceiling. Looking up at the latter, he now perceived a number of greasy patches where the oil had soaked through from the floor above, and some of these were beginning to drip on to the shop floor.

He now made his final preparations. Taking a bundle of "Wheel" firelighters, he made a small pile against the stack of firewood. In the midst of the firelighters he placed a ball of string saturated in paraffin, and in the central hole of the ball he stuck a half-dozen diminutive Christmas candles. This mine was now ready. Providing himself with a stock of

406

firelighters, a few balls of paraffined string, and a dozen or so of the little candles, he went upstairs to the sitting-room, which was immediately above the shop. Here, by the glow of the fire, he built up one or two piles of firelighters around and partly under the arm-chair, placed the balls of string on the piles, and stuck two or three bundles in each ball. Everything was now ready. Stepping into the bedroom, he took from the cupboard a spare overcoat, a new hat, and a new umbrella – for he must leave his old hats, coat and umbrella in the hall. He put on the coat and hat, and, with the umbrella in his hand, returned to the sitting-room.

Opposite the arm-chair he stood awhile, irresolute, and a pang of horror shot through him. It was a terrible thing that he was going to do, a thing the consequences of which no one could foresee. He glanced furtively at the awful shape that sat huddled in the chair, its horrible head all awry and its rigid limbs sprawling in hideous grotesque deformity. It was but a dummy, a mere scarecrow – but yet, in the dim firelight, the grisly face under that horrid wig seemed to leer intelligently, to watch him with secret malice out of its shadowy eye-sockets, until he looked away with clammy skin and a shiver of half-superstitious terror.

But this would never do. The evening had run out, consumed by these engrossing labours. It was nearly eleven o'clock, and high time for him to be gone. For if the Brattles should return prematurely, he was lost. Pulling himself together with an effort, he struck a match and lit the little candles one after the other. In a quarter-of-an-hour or so, they would have burned down to the balls of string, and then –

He walked quickly out of the room, but, at the door, he paused for a moment to look back at the ghastly figure, seated rigidly in the chair with the lighted candles at its feet, like some foul fiend appeased by votive fires. The unsteady flames threw flickering shadows on its face that made it seem to mow and gibber and grin in mockery of all his care and caution. So he turned and tremblingly ran down the stairs – opening the staircase window as he went. Running into the shop, he lit the candles there and ran out again, shutting the door after him.

Secretly and guiltily he crept down the hall, and opening the door a few inches peered out. A blast of icy wind poured in with a light powdering of dry snow. He opened his umbrella, flung open the door, looked up and down the empty street, stepped out, closed the door softly, and strode away over the whitening pavement.

Part II
(Related by Christopher Jervis, M.D.)

It was one of the axioms of medico-legal practice laid down by my colleague, John Thorndyke, that the investigator should be constantly on his guard against the effect of suggestion. Not only must all prejudices and preconceptions be avoided, but when information is received from outside, the actual, undeniable facts must be carefully sifted from the inferences which usually accompany them. Of the necessity for this precaution our insurance practice furnished an excellent instance in the case of the fire at Mr. Brattle's oil-shop.

The case was brought to our notice by Mr. Stalker of the Griffin Fire and Life Insurance Society a few days after Christmas. He dropped in, ostensibly to wish us a Happy New Year, but a discreet pause in the conversation on Thorndyke's part elicited a further purpose.

"Did you see the account of that fire in Bloomsbury?" Mr. Stalker asked.

"The oil-shop? Yes. But I didn't note any details, excepting that a man was apparently burnt to death and that the affair happened on the twenty-fifth of December."

"Yes, I know," said Mr. Stalker. "It seems uncharitable, but one can't help looking a little askance at these quarter-day fires. And the date isn't the only doubtful feature in this one. The Divisional Officer of the Fire Brigade, who has looked over the ruins, tells me that there are some appearances suggesting that the fire broke out in two different places – the shop and the first-floor room over it. Mind you, he doesn't say that it actually did. The place is so thoroughly gutted that very little is to be learned from it, but that is his impression, and it occurred to me that if you were to take a look at the ruins, your radiographic eye might detect something that he had overlooked."

"It isn't very likely," said Thorndyke. "Every man to his trade. The Divisional Officer looks at a burnt house with an expert eye, which I do not. My evidence would not carry much weight if you were contesting the claim."

"Perhaps not," replied Mr. Stalker, "and we are not anxious to contest the claim unless there is manifest fraud. Arson is a serious matter."

"It is wilful murder in this case," remarked Thorndyke.

"I know," said Stalker. "And that reminds me that the man who was burnt happens to have been insured in our office, too. So we stand a double loss."

408

"How much?" asked Thorndyke.

"The dead man, Percival Bland, had insured his life for three-thousand pounds."

Thorndyke became thoughtful. The last statement had apparently made more impression on him than the former ones.

"If you want me to look into the case for you," said he, "you had better let me have all the papers connected with it, including the proposal forms."

Mr. Stalker smiled. "I thought you would say that – I know you of old, you see – so I slipped the papers in my pocket before coming here."

He laid the documents on the table and asked, "Is there anything that you want to know about the case?"

"Yes," replied Thorndyke. "I want to know all that you can tell me."

"Which is mighty little," said Stalker, "but such as it is, you shall have it.

"The oil-shop man's name is Brattle and the dead man, Bland, was his lodger. Bland appears to have been a perfectly steady, sober man in general, but it seems that he had announced his intention of spending a jovial Christmas Night and giving himself a little extra indulgence. He was last seen by Mrs. Brattle at about half-past six, sitting by a blazing fire, with a couple of unopened bottles of port on the table and a box of cigars. He had a book in his hand and two or three newspapers lay on the floor by his chair. Shortly after this, Mr. and Mrs. Brattle went out on a visit to Hornsey, leaving him alone in the house."

"Was there no servant?" asked Thorndyke.

"The servant had the day and night off duty to go to her mother's. That, by the way, looks a trifle fishy. However, to return to the Brattles. They spent the evening at Hornsey and did not get home until past three in the morning, by which time their house was a heap of smoking ruins. Mrs. Brattle's idea is that Bland must have drunk himself sleepy, and dropped one of the newspapers into the fender, where a chance cinder may have started the blaze. Which may or may not be the true explanation. Of course, an habitually sober man can get pretty mimsey on two bottles of port."

"What time did the fire break out?" asked Thorndyke.

"It was noticed about half-past eleven that flames were issuing from one of the chimneys, and the alarm was given at once. The first engine arrived ten minutes later, but, by that time, the place was roaring like a furnace. Then the water-plugs were found to be frozen hard, which caused some delay. In fact, before the engines were able to get to work the roof had fallen in, and the place was a mere shell. You know what an oil-shop is, when once it gets a fair start."

"And Mr. Bland's body was found in the ruins, I suppose?"

"Body!" exclaimed Mr. Stalker. "There wasn't much body! Just a few charred bones, which they dug out of the ashes next day."

"And the question of identity?"

"We shall leave that to the coroner. But there really isn't any question. To begin with, there was no one else in the house, and then the remains were found mixed up with the springs and castors of the chair that Bland was sitting in when he was last seen. Moreover, there were found, with the bones, a pocket knife, a bunch of keys and a set of steel waistcoat buttons, all identified by Mrs. Brattle as belonging to Bland. She noticed the cut steel buttons on his waistcoat when she wished him 'good-night'."

"By the way," said Thorndyke, "was Bland reading by the light of an oil lamp?"

"No," replied Stalker. "There was a two-branch gasalier with a porcelain shade to one burner, and he had that burner alight when Mrs. Brattle left."

Thorndyke reflectively picked up the proposal form, and, having glanced through it, remarked, "I see that Bland is described as unmarried. Do you know why he insured his life for this large amount?"

"No. We assumed that it was probably in connection with some loan that he had raised. I learn from the solicitor who notified us of the death, that the whole of Bland's property is left to a cousin – a Mr. Lindsay, I think. So the probability is that this cousin had lent him money. But it is not the life claim that is interesting us. We must pay that in any case. It is the fire claim that we want you to look into."

"Very well," said Thorndyke. "I will go round presently and look over the ruins, and see if I can detect any substantial evidence of fraud."

"If you would," said Mr. Stalker, rising to take his departure, "we should be very much obliged. Not that we shall probably contest the claim in any case."

When he had gone, my colleague and I glanced through the papers, and I ventured to remark, "It seems to me that Stalker doesn't quite appreciate the possibilities of this case."

"No," Thorndyke agreed. "But, of course, it is an insurance company's business to pay, and not to boggle at anything short of glaring fraud. And we specialists too," he added with a smile, "must beware of seeing too much. I suppose that, to a rhinologist, there is hardly such a thing as a healthy nose – unless it is his own – and the uric acid specialist is very apt to find the firmament studded with dumb-bell crystals. We mustn't forget that normal cases do exist, after all."

410

"That is true," said I. "But, on the other hand, the rhinologist's business is with the unhealthy nose, and our concern is with abnormal cases."

Thorndyke laughed. "'*A Daniel come to judgement*,'" said he. "But my learned friend is quite right. Our function is to pick holes. So let us pocket the documents and wend Bloomsbury way. We can talk the case over as we go."

We walked at an easy pace, for there was no hurry, and a little preliminary thought was useful. After a while, as Thorndyke made no remark, I reopened the subject.

"How does the case present itself to you?" I asked.

"Much as it does to you, I expect," he replied. "The circumstances invite inquiry, and I do not find myself connecting them with the shopkeeper. It is true that the fire occurred on quarter-day, but there is nothing to show that the insurance will do more than cover the loss of stock, chattels, and the profits of trade. The other circumstances are much more suggestive. Here is a house burned down and a man killed. That man was insured for three-thousand pounds, and, consequently, some person stands to gain by his death to that amount. The whole set of circumstances is highly favourable to the idea of homicide. The man was alone in the house when he died, and the total destruction of both the body and its surroundings seems to render investigation impossible. The cause of death can only be inferred, it cannot be proved, and the most glaring evidence of a crime will have vanished utterly. I think that there is a quite strong *prima facie* suggestion of murder. Under the known conditions, the perpetration of a murder would have been easy, it would have been safe from detection, and there is an adequate motive.

"On the other hand, suicide is not impossible. The man might have set fire to the house and then killed himself by poison or otherwise. But it is intrinsically less probable that a man should kill him self for another person's benefit than that he should kill another man for his own benefit.

"Finally, there is the possibility that the fire and the man's death were the result of accident, against which is the official opinion that the fire started in two places. If this opinion is correct, it establishes, in my opinion, a strong presumption of murder against some person who may have obtained access to the house."

This point in the discussion brought us to the ruined house, which stood at the corner of two small streets. One of the firemen in charge admitted us, when we had shown our credentials, through a temporary door and down a ladder into the basement, where we found a number of men treading gingerly, ankle deep in white ash, among a litter of charred

411

wood-work, fused glass, warped and broken china, and more or less recognisable metal objects.

"The coroner and the jury," the fireman explained, "come to view the scene of the disaster." He introduced us to the former, who bowed stiffly and continued his investigations.

"These," said the other fireman, "are the springs of the chair that the deceased was sitting in. We found the body – or rather the bones – lying among them under a heap of hot ashes, and we found the buttons of his clothes and the things from his pockets among the ashes, too. You'll see them in the mortuary with the remains."

"It must have been a terrific blaze," one of the jurymen remarked. "Just look at this, sir," and he handed to Thorndyke what looked like part of a gas-fitting, of which the greater part was melted into shapeless lumps and the remainder encrusted into fused porcelain.

"That," said the fireman, "was the gasalier of the first-floor room, where Mr. Bland was sitting. Ah! You won't turn that tap, sir. Nobody'll ever turn that tap again."

Thorndyke held the twisted mass of brass towards me in silence, and, glancing up the blackened walls, remarked, "I think we shall have to come here again with the Divisional Officer, but meanwhile, we had better see the remains of the body. It is just possible that we may learn something from them."

He applied to the coroner for the necessary authority to make the inspection and, having obtained a rather ungracious and grudging permission to examine the remains when the jury had "viewed" them, began to ascend the ladder.

"Our friend would have liked to refuse permission," he remarked when we had emerged into the street, "but he knew that I could and should have insisted."

"So I gathered from his manner," said I. "But what is he doing here? This isn't his district."

"No. He is acting for Bettsford, who is laid up just now, and a very poor substitute he is. A non-medical coroner is an absurdity in any case, and a coroner who is hostile to the medical profession is a public scandal. By the way, that gas-tap offers a curious problem. You noticed that it was turned off?"

"Yes."

"And consequently that the deceased was sitting in the dark when the fire broke out. I don't see the bearing of the fact, but it is certainly rather odd. Here is the mortuary. We had better wait and let the jury go in first."

We had not long to wait. In a couple of minutes or so the "twelve good men and true" made their appearance with a small attendant crowd

412

of ragamuffins. We let them enter first, and then we followed. The mortuary was a good-sized room, well-lighted by a glass roof, and having at its centre a long table on which lay the shell containing the remains. There was also a sheet of paper on which had been laid out a set of blackened steel waistcoat buttons, a bunch of keys, a steel-handled pocket-knife, a steel-cased watch on a partly-fused rolled-gold chain, and a pocket corkscrew. The coroner drew the attention of the jury to these objects, and then took possession of them, that they might be identified by witnesses. And meanwhile the jurymen gathered round the shell and stared shudderingly at its gruesome contents.

"I am sorry, gentlemen," said the coroner, "to have to subject you to this painful ordeal. But duty is duty. We must hope, as I think we may, that this poor creature met a painless if in some respects a rather terrible death."

At this point, Thorndyke, who had drawn near to the table, cast a long and steady glance down into the shell, and immediately his ordinarily rather impassive face seemed to congeal, all expression faded from it, leaving it as immovable and uncommunicative as the granite face of an Egyptian statue. I knew the symptom of old and began to speculate on its present significance.

"Are you taking any medical evidence?" he asked.

"Medical evidence!" the coroner repeated, scornfully. "Certainly not, sir! I do not waste the public money by employing so-called experts to tell the jury what each of them can see quite plainly for himself. I imagine," he added, turning to the foreman, "that you will not require a learned doctor to explain to you how that poor fellow mortal met his death?"

And the foreman, glancing askance at the skull, replied, with a pallid and sickly smile, that "he thought not."

"Do you, sir," the coroner continued, with a dramatic wave of the hand towards the plain coffin, "suppose that we shall find any difficulty in determining how that man came by his death?"

"I imagine," replied Thorndyke, without moving a muscle, or, indeed, appearing to have any muscles to move, "I imagine you will find no difficulty what ever."

"So do I," said the coroner.

"Then," retorted Thorndyke, with a faint, inscrutable smile, "we are, for once, in complete agreement."

As the coroner and jury retired, leaving my colleague and me alone in the mortuary, Thorndyke remarked, "I suppose this kind of farce will be repeated periodically so long as these highly technical medical inquiries continue to be conducted by lay persons."

413

I made no reply, for I had taken a long look into the shell, and was lost in astonishment.

"But my dear Thorndyke!" I exclaimed. "What on earth does it mean? Are we to suppose that a woman can have palmed herself off as a man on the examining medical officer of a London Life Assurance Society?"

Thorndyke shook his head. "I think not," said he. "Our friend, Mr. Bland, may conceivably have been a woman in disguise, but he certainly was not a negress."

"A negress!" I gasped. "By Jove! So it is! I hadn't looked at the skull. But that only makes the mystery more mysterious. Because, you remember, the body was certainly dressed in Bland's clothes."

"Yes, there seems to be no doubt about that. And you may have noticed, as I did," Thorndyke continued dryly, "the remarkably fire-proof character of the waistcoat buttons, watch-case, knife-handle, and other identifiable objects."

"But what a horrible affair!" I exclaimed. "The brute must have gone out and enticed some poor devil of a negress into the house, have murdered her in cold blood, and then deliberately dressed the corpse in his own clothes! It is perfectly frightful!"

Again Thorndyke shook his head. "It wasn't as bad as that, Jervis," said he, "though I must confess that I feel strongly tempted to let your hypothesis stand. It would be quite amusing to put Mr. Bland on trial for the murder of an unknown negress, and let him explain the facts himself. But our reputation is at stake. Look at the bones again and a little more critically. You very probably looked for the sex first. Then you looked for racial characters. Now carry your investigations a step farther."

"There is the stature," said I. "But that is of no importance, as these are not Bland's bones. The only other point that I notice is that the fire seems to have acted very unequally on the different parts of the body."

"Yes," agreed Thorndyke, "and that is the point. Some parts are more burnt than others, and the parts which are burnt most are the wrong parts. Look at the back-bone, for instance. The vertebrae are as white as chalk. They are mere masses of bone ash. But, of all parts of the skeleton, there is none so completely protected from fire as the back-bone, with the great dorsal muscles behind, and the whole mass of the viscera in front. Then look at the skull. Its appearance is quite inconsistent with the suggested facts. The bones of the face are bare and calcined and the orbits contain not a trace of the eyes or other structures, and yet there is a charred mass of what may or may not be scalp adhering to the crown. But the scalp, as the most exposed and the thinnest covering, would be the first to be destroyed, while the last to be consumed would be the structures about the jaws and the base, of which, you see, not a vestige is left."

Here he lifted the skull carefully from the shell, and, peering in through the great foramen at the base, handed it to me.

"Look in," he said, "through the *Foramen Magnum* – you will see better if you hold the orbits towards the skylight – and notice an even more extreme inconsistency with the supposed conditions. The brain and membranes have vanished without leaving a trace. The inside of the skull is as clean as if it had been macerated. But this is impossible. The brain is not only protected from the fire – it is also protected from contact with the air. But without access of oxygen, although it might become carbonised, it could not be consumed. No, Jervis, it won't do."

I replaced the skull in the coffin and looked at him in surprise. "What is it that you are suggesting?" I asked.

"I suggest that this was not a body at all, but merely a dry skeleton."

"But," I objected, "what about those masses of what looks like charred muscle adhering to the bones?"

"Yes," he replied, "I have been noticing them. They do, as you say, look like masses of charred muscle. But they are quite shapeless and structureless. I cannot identify a single muscle or muscular group, and there is not a vestige of any of the tendons. Moreover, the distribution is false. For instance, will you tell me what muscle you think that is?"

He pointed to a thick, charred mass on the inner surface of the left tibia or shin-bone. "Now this portion of the bone – as many a hockey-player has had reason to realise – has no muscular covering at all. It lies immediately under the skin."

"I think you are right, Thorndyke," said I. "That lump of muscle in the wrong place gives the whole fraud away. But it was really a rather smart dodge. This fellow Bland must be an ingenious rascal."

"Yes," agreed Thorndyke, "but an unscrupulous villain too. He might have burned down half the street and killed a score of people. He'll have to pay the piper for this little frolic."

"What shall you do now? Are you going to notify the coroner?"

"No, that is not my business. I think we will verify our conclusions and then inform our clients and the police. We must measure the skull as well as we can without callipers, but it is, fortunately, quite typical. The short, broad, flat nasal bones, with the 'Simian groove,' and those large, strong teeth, worn flat by hard and gritty food, are highly characteristic." He once more lifted out the skull, and, with a spring tape, made a few measurements, while I noted the lengths of the principal long bones and the width across the hips

"I make the Cranial Nasal Index 55," said he, as he replaced the skull, "and the Cranial Index about 72, which are quite representative numbers, and, as I see that your notes show the usual disproportionate length of arm

415

and the characteristic curve of the tibia, we may be satisfied. But it is fortunate that the specimen is so typical. To the experienced eye, racial types have a physiognomy which is unmistakable on mere inspection. But you cannot transfer the experienced eye. You can only express personal conviction and back it up with measurements.

"And now we will go and look in on Stalker, and inform him that his office has saved three-thousand pounds by employing us. After which it will be *Westward Ho!* for Scotland Yard, to prepare an unpleasant little surprise for Mr. Percival Bland."

There was joy among the journalists on the following day. Each of the morning papers devoted an entire column to an unusually detailed account of the inquest on the late Percival Bland – who, it appeared, met his death by misadventure – and a verbatim report of the coroner's eloquent remarks on the danger of solitary, fireside tippling, and the stupefying effects of port wine. An adjacent column contained an equally detailed account of the appearance of the deceased at Bow Street Police Court to answer complicated charges of arson, fraud and forgery, while a third collated the two accounts with gleeful commentaries.

Mr. Percival Bland, alias Robert Lindsay, now resides on the breezy uplands of Dartmoor, where, in his abundant leisure, he, no doubt, regrets his misdirected ingenuity. But he has not laboured in vain. To the Lord Chancellor he has furnished an admirable illustration of the danger of appointing lay coroners, and to me an unforgettable warning against the effects of suggestion.

The Missing Mortgagee
Part I

Early in the afternoon of a warm, humid November day, Thomas Elton sauntered dejectedly along the Margate esplanade, casting an eye now on the slate-coloured sea with its pall of slate-coloured sky, and now on the harbour, where the ebb tide was just beginning to expose the mud. It was a dreary prospect, and Elton varied it by observing the few fishermen and fewer promenaders who walked foot-to-foot with their distorted reflections in the wet pavement, and thus it was that his eye fell on a smartly-dressed man who had just stepped into a shelter to light a cigar.

A contemporary joker has classified the Scotsmen who abound in South Africa into two groups: Those, namely, who hail from Scotland, and those who hail from Palestine. Now, something in the aspect of the broad back that was presented to his view, in that of the curly, black hair, and the exuberant raiment, suggested to Elton a Scotsman of the latter type. In fact, there was a suspicion of disagreeable familiarity in the figure which caused him to watch it and slacken his pace. The man backed out of the shelter, diffusing azure clouds, and, drawing an envelope from his pocket, read something that was written on it. Then he turned quickly – and so did Elton, but not quickly enough. For he was a solitary figure on that bald and empty expanse, and the other had seen him at the first glance. Elton walked away slowly, but he had not gone a dozen paces when he felt the anticipated slap on the shoulder and heard the too well-remembered voice.

"Blow me, if I don't believe you were trying to cut me, Tom," it said.

Elton looked round with ill-assumed surprise. "Hallo, Gordon! Who the deuce would have thought of seeing you here?"

Gordon laughed thickly. "Not you, apparently, and you don't look as pleased as you might now you have seen me. Whereas I'm delighted to see you, and especially to see that things are going so well with you."

"What do you mean?" asked Elton.

"Taking your winter holiday by the sea, like a blooming duke."

"I'm not taking a holiday," said Elton. "I was so worn out that I had to have some sort of change, but I've brought my work down with me, and I put in a full seven hours every day."

"That's right," said Gordon. "'Consider the ant.' Nothing like steady industry! I've brought my work down with me too – a little slip of paper with a stamp on it. You know the article, Tom."

"I know. But it isn't due till to-morrow, is it?"

417

"Isn't it, by gum! It's due this very day, the twentieth of the month. That's why I'm here. Knowing your little weakness in the matter of dates, and having a small item to collect in Canterbury, I thought I'd just come on, and save you the useless expense that results from forgetfulness."

Elton understood the hint, and his face grew rigid.

"I can't do it, Gordon. I can't really. Haven't got it, and shan't have it until I'm paid for the batch of drawings that I'm working on now."

"Oh, but what a pity!" exclaimed Gordon, taking the cigar from his thick, pouting lips to utter the exclamation. "Here you are, blowing your capital on seaside jaunts and reducing your income at a stroke by a clear four pounds a year."

"How do you make that out?" demanded Elton.

"Tut, tut," protested Gordon, "what an unbusinesslike chap you are! Here's a little matter of twenty pounds quarter's interest. If it's paid now, it's twenty. If it isn't, it goes on to the principal and there's another four pounds a year to be paid. Why don't you try to be more economical, dear boy?"

Elton looked askance at the vampire by his side, at the plump blue-shaven cheeks, the thick black eyebrows, the drooping nose, and the full, red lips that embraced the cigar, and though he was a mild-tempered man, he felt that he could have battered that sensual, complacent face out of all human likeness with something uncommonly like enjoyment. But of these thoughts nothing appeared in his reply, for a man cannot afford to say all he would wish to a creditor who could ruin him with a word.

"You mustn't be too hard on me, Gordon," said he. "Give me a little time. I'm doing all I can, you know. I earn every penny that I am able, and I have kept my insurance paid up regularly. I shall be paid for this work in a week or two and then we can settle up."

Gordon made no immediate reply, and the two men walked slowly eastward, a curiously ill-assorted pair: The one prosperous, jaunty, overdressed; the other pale and dejected, and, with his well-brushed but napless clothes, his patched boots and shiny-brimmed hat, the very type of decent, struggling poverty.

They had just passed the pier, and were coming to the base of the jetty, when Gordon next spoke.

"Can't we get off this beastly wet pavement?" he asked, looking down at his dainty and highly-polished boots. "What's it like down on the sands?"

"Oh, it's very good walking," said Elton, "between here and Foreness, and probably drier than the pavement."

"Then," said Gordon, "I vote we go down," and accordingly they descended the sloping way beyond the jetty. The stretch of sand left by the

418

retiring tide was as smooth and firm as a sheet of asphalt, and far more pleasant to walk upon.

"We seem to have the place all to ourselves," remarked Gordon, "with the exception of some half-dozen dukes like yourself."

As he spoke, he cast a cunning black eye furtively at the dejected man by his side, considering how much further squeezing was possible, and what would be the probable product of a further squeeze, but he quickly averted his gaze as Elton turned on him a look eloquent of contempt and dislike. There was another pause, for Elton made no reply to the last observation. Then Gordon changed over from one arm to the other the heavy fur overcoat that he was carrying. "Needn't have brought this beastly thing," he remarked, "if I'd known it was going to be so warm."

"Shall I carry it for you a little way?" asked the naturally polite Elton.

"If you would, dear boy," replied Gordon. "It's difficult to manage an overcoat, an umbrella, and cigar all at once."

He handed over the coat with a sigh of relief, and having straightened himself and expanded his chest, remarked, "I suppose you're beginning to do quite well now, Tom?"

Elton shook his head gloomily. "No," he answered, "it's the same old grind."

"But surely they're beginning to recognise your talents by this time," said Gordon, with the persuasive air of a counsel.

"That's just the trouble," said Elton. "You see, I haven't any, and they recognised the fact long ago. I'm just a journeyman, and journeyman's work is what I get given to me."

"You mean to say that the editors don't appreciate talent when they see it."

"I don't know about that," said Elton, "but they're most infernally appreciative of the lack of it."

Gordon blew out a great cloud of smoke, and raised his eyebrows reflectively. "Do you think," he said after a brief pause, "you give 'em a fair chance? I've seen some of your stuff. It's blooming prim, you know. Why don't you try something more lively? More skittish, you know, old chap – something with legs, you know, and high shoes. See what I mean, old chap? High with good full calves and not too fat in the ankle. That ought to fetch 'em, don't you think so?"

Elton scowled. "You're thinking of the drawings in '*Hold Me Up*'," he said scornfully, "but you're mistaken. Any fool can draw a champagne bottle upside down with a French shoe at the end of it."

"No doubt, dear boy," said Gordon, "but I expect that sort of fool knows what pays."

419

"A good many fools seem to know that much," retorted Elton, and then he was sorry he had spoken, for Gordon was not really an amiable man, and the expression of his face suggested that he had read a personal application into the rejoinder. So, once more, the two men walked on in silence.

Presently their footsteps led them to the margin of the weed-covered rocks, and here, from under a high heap of bladder-wrack, a large green shorecrab rushed out and menaced them with uplifted claws. Gordon stopped and stared at the creature with Cockney surprise, prodding it with his umbrella, and speculating aloud as to whether it was good to eat. The crab, as if alarmed at the suggestion, suddenly darted away and began to scuttle over the green-clad rocks, finally plunging into a large, deep pool. Gordon pursued it, hobbling awkwardly over the slippery rocks, until he came to the edge of the pool, over which he stooped, raking inquisitively among the weedy fringe with his umbrella. He was so much interested in his quarry that he failed to allow for the slippery surface on which he stood. The result was disastrous. Of a sudden, one foot began to slide forward, and when he tried to recover his balance, was instantly followed by the other. For a moment he struggled frantically to regain his footing, executing a sort of splashing, stamping dance on the margin. Then, the circling sea birds were startled by a yell of terror, an ivory-handled umbrella flew across the rocks, and Mr. Solomon Gordon took a complete header into the deepest part of the pool. What the crab thought of it history does not relate. What Mr. Gordon thought of it is unsuitable for publication, but, as he rose, like an extremely up-to-date merman, he expressed his sentiments with a wealth of adjectives that brought Elton in the verge of hysteria.

"It's a good job you brought your overcoat, after all," Elton remarked for the sake of saying something, and thereby avoiding the risk of exploding into undeniable laughter. The Hebrew made no reply – at least, no reply that lends itself to verbatim report – but staggered towards the hospitable overcoat, holding out his dripping arms. Having inducted him into the garment and buttoned him up, Elton hurried off to recover the umbrella (and, incidentally, to indulge himself in a broad grin), and, having secured it, angled with it for the smart billycock which was floating across the pool.

It was surprising what a change the last minute or two had wrought. The positions of the two men were now quite reversed. Despite his shabby clothing, Elton seemed to walk quite jauntily as compared with his shuddering companion who trotted by his side with short miserable steps, shrinking into the uttermost depths of his enveloping coat, like an alarmed winkle into its shell, puffing out his cheeks and anathematising the Universe in general as well as his chattering teeth would let him.

For some time they hurried along towards the slope by the jetty without exchanging any further remarks. Then suddenly, Elton asked, "What are you going to do, Gordon? You can't travel like that."

"Can't you lend me a change?" asked Gordon. Elton reflected. He had another suit, his best suit, which he had been careful to preserve in good condition for use on those occasions when a decent appearance was indispensable. He looked askance at the man by his side and something told him that the treasured suit would probably receive less careful treatment than it was accustomed to. Still the man couldn't be allowed to go about in wet clothes.

"I've got a spare suit," he said. "It isn't quite up to your style, and may not be much of a fit, but I daresay you'll be able to put up with it for an hour or two."

"It'll be dry anyhow," mumbled Gordon, "so we won't trouble about the style. How far is it to your rooms?"

The plural number was superfluous. Elton's room was in a little ancient flint house at the bottom of a narrow close in the old quarter of the town. You reached it without any formal preliminaries of bell or knocker by simply letting yourself in by a street door, crossing a tiny room, opening the door of what looked like a narrow cupboard, and squeezing up a diminutive flight of stairs, which was unexpectedly exposed to view. By following this procedure, the two men reached a small bed-sitting-room – that is to say, it was a bed room, but by sitting down on the bed, you converted it into a sitting-room.

Gordon puffed out his cheeks and looked round distastefully.

"You might just ring for some hot water, old chappie," he said.

Elton laughed aloud. "Ring!" he exclaimed. "Ring what? Your clothes are the only things that are likely to get wrung."

"Well, then, sing out for the servant," said Gordon.

Elton laughed again. "My dear fellow," said he, "we don't go in for servants. There is only my landlady and she never comes up here. She's too fat to get up the stairs, and besides, she's got a game leg. I look after my room myself. You'll be all right if you have a good rub down."

Gordon groaned, and emerged reluctantly from the depths of his overcoat, while Elton brought forth from the chest of drawers the promised suit and the necessary undergarments. One of these latter Gordon held up with a sour smile, as he regarded it with extreme disfavour.

"I shouldn't think," said he, "you need have been at the trouble of marking them so plainly. No one's likely to want to run away with them."

421

The undergarments certainly contrasted very unfavourably with the delicate garments which he was peeling off, excepting in one respect: They were dry, and that had to console him for the ignominious change.

The clothes fitted quite fairly, notwithstanding the difference between the figures of the two men, for while Gordon was a slender man grown fat, Elton was a broad man grown thin, which, in a way, averaged their superficial area.

Elton watched the process of investment and noted the caution with which Gordon smuggled the various articles from his own pockets into those of the borrowed garments without exposing them to view, heard the jingle of money, saw the sumptuous gold watch and massive chain transplanted, and noted with interest the large leather wallet that came forth from the breast pocket of the wet coat. He got a better view of this from the fact that Gordon himself examined it narrowly, and even opened it to inspect its contents.

"Lucky that wasn't an ordinary pocketbook." he remarked. "If it had been, your receipt would have got wet, and so would one or two other little articles that wouldn't have been improved by salt water. And, talking of the receipt, Tom, shall I hand it over now?"

"You can if you like," said Elton, "but as I told you, I haven't got the money," on which Gordon muttered, "Pity, pity," and thrust the wallet into his, or rather, Elton's breast pocket.

A few minutes later, the two men came out together into the gathering darkness, and as they walked slowly up the close, Elton asked, "Are you going up to town to-night, Gordon?"

"How can I?" was the reply. "I can't go without my clothes. No, I shall run over to Broadstairs. A client of mine keeps a boarding-house there. He'll have to put me up for the night, and if you can get my clothes cleaned and dried I can come over for them to-morrow."

These arrangements having been settled, the two men adjourned, at Gordon's suggestion, for tea at one of the restaurants on the Front, and after that, again at Gordon's suggestion, they set forth together along the cliff path that leads to Broadstairs by way of Kingsgate.

"You may as well walk with me into Broadstairs," said Gordon. "I'll stand you the fare back by rail," and to this Elton had agreed, not because he was desirous of the other man's company, but because he still had some lingering hopes of being able to adjust the little difficulty respecting the instalment.

He did not, however, open the subject at once. Profoundly as he loathed and despised the human spider whom necessity made his associate for the moment, he exerted himself to keep up a current of amusing conversation. It was not easy, for Gordon, like most men whose attention is focussed on the mere acquirement of money, looked with a dull eye on the ordinary interests of life. His tastes in art he had already hinted at, and his other tastes lay much in the same direction. Money first, for its own sake, and then those coarser and more primitive gratifications that it was capable of purchasing. This was the horizon that bounded Mr. Solomon Gordon's field of vision.

Nevertheless, they were well on their way before Elton alluded to the subject that was uppermost in both their minds.

"Look here, Gordon," he said at length, "can't you manage to give me a bit more time to pay up this instalment? It doesn't seem quite fair to keep sending up the principal like this."

"Well, dear boy," replied Gordon, "it's your own fault, you know. If you would only bear the dates in mind, it wouldn't happen."

"But," pleaded Elton, "just consider what I'm paying you. I originally borrowed fifty pounds from you, and I'm now paying you eighty pounds a year in addition to the insurance premium. That's close on a hundred a year, just about half that I manage to earn by slaving. If you stick it up any farther you won't leave me enough to keep body and soul together, which really means that I shan't be able to pay you at all."

There was a brief pause, then Gordon said dryly, "You talk about not paying, dear boy, as if you had forgotten about that promissory note."

Elton set his teeth. His temper was rising rapidly. But he restrained himself.

"I should have a pretty poor memory if I had," he replied, "considering the number of reminders you've given me."

"You've needed them, Tom," said the other. "I've never met a slacker man in keeping to his engagements."

At this Elton lost his temper completely.

"That's a damned lie!" he exclaimed, "and you know it, you infernal, dirty, blood-sucking parasite."

Gordon stopped dead.

"Look here, my friend," said he. "None of that. If I've any of your damned sauce, I'll give you a sound good hammering."

"The deuce you will!" said Elton, whose fingers were itching, not for the first time, to take some recompense for all that he had suffered from the insatiable usurer. "Nothing's preventing you now, you know, but I fancy cent-per-cent is more in your line than fighting."

"Give me any more sauce and you'll see," said Gordon.

"Very well," was the quiet rejoinder. "I have great pleasure in informing you that you are a human maw-worm. How does that suit you?"

For reply, Gordon threw down his overcoat and umbrella on the grass at the side of the path, and deliberately slapped Elton on the cheek.

The reply followed instantly in the form of a smart left-hander, which took effect on the bridge of the Hebrew's rather prominent nose. Thus the battle was fairly started, and it proceeded with all the fury of accumulated hatred on the one side and sharp physical pain on the other. What little science there was appertained to Elton, in spite of which, however, he had to give way to his heavier, better nourished and more excitable opponent. Regardless of the punishment he received, the infuriated Jew rushed at him and, by sheer weight of onslaught, drove him backward across the little green.

Suddenly, Elton, who knew the place by daylight, called out in alarm. "Look out, Gordon! Get back, you fool!"

But Gordon, blind with fury, and taking this as attempt to escape, only pressed him harder. Elton's pugnacity died out instantly in mortal terror. He shouted out another warning and as Gordon still pressed him, battering furiously, he did the only thing that was possible: He dropped to the ground. And then, in the twinkling of an eye came the catastrophe. Borne forward by his own momentum, Gordon stumbled over Elton's prostrate body, staggered forward a few paces, and fell. Elton heard a muffled groan that faded quickly, and mingled with the sound of falling earth and stones. He sprang to his feet and looked round and saw that he was alone.

For some moments he was dazed by the suddenness of the awful thing that had happened. He crept timorously towards the unseen edge of the cliff, and listened.

There was no sound save the distant surge of the breakers, and the scream of an invisible sea-bird. It was useless to try to look over. Near as he was, he could not, even now, distinguish the edge of the cliff from the dark beach below. Suddenly he bethought him of a narrow cutting that led down from the cliff to the shore. Quickly crossing the green, and mechanically stooping to pick up Gordon's overcoat and umbrella, he made his way to the head of the cutting and ran down the rough chalk roadway. At the bottom he turned to the right and, striding hurriedly over the smooth sand, peered into the darkness at the foot of the cliff.

Soon there loomed up against the murky sky the shadowy form of the little headland on which he and Gordon had stood, and, almost at the same moment, there grew out of the darkness of the beach a darker spot amidst a constellation of smaller spots of white. As he drew nearer the dark spot took shape, a horrid shape with sprawling limbs and a head strangely awry. He stepped forward, trembling, and spoke the name that the thing had borne. He grasped the flabby hand, and laid his fingers on the wrist, but it only told him the same tale as did that strangely misplaced head. The body lay face downwards, and he had not the courage to turn it over, but that his enemy was dead he had not the faintest doubt. He stood up amidst the litter of fallen chalk and earth and looked down at the horrible, motionless thing, wondering numbly and vaguely what he should do. Should he go and seek assistance? The answer to that came in another question. How came that body to be lying on the beach? And what answer should he give to the inevitable questions? And swiftly there grew up in his mind, born of the horror of the thing that was, a yet greater horror of the thing that might be.

A minute later, a panic-stricken man stole with stealthy swiftness up the narrow cutting and set forth towards Margate, stopping anon to listen, and stealing away off the path into the darkness, to enter the town by the inland road.

Little sleep was there that night for Elton in his room in the old flint house. The dead man's clothes, which greeted him on his arrival, hanging limply on the towel-horse where he had left them, haunted him through the night. In the darkness, the sour smell of damp cloth assailed him with an endless reminder of their presence, and after each brief doze, he would start up in alarm and hastily light his candle, only to throw its flickering light on those dank, drowned-looking vestments. His thoughts, half-controlled, as night thoughts are, flitted erratically from the unhappy past to the unstable present, and thence to the incalculable future. Once he lighted the candle specially to look at his watch to see if the tide had yet crept up to that solitary figure on the beach, nor could he rest again until the time of high water was well past. And all through these wanderings of his thoughts there came, recurring like a horrible refrain, the question what would happen when the body was found? Could he be connected with it and, if so, would he be charged with murder? At last he fell asleep and slumbered on until the landlady thumped at the staircase door to announce that she had brought his breakfast.

As soon as he was dressed he went out. Not, however, until he had stuffed Gordon's still damp clothes and boots, the cumbrous overcoat and the smart billy-cock hat into his trunk, and put the umbrella into the darkest corner of the cupboard. Not that anyone ever came up to the room, but that, already, he was possessed with the uneasy secretiveness of the criminal. He went straight down to the beach, with what purpose he could hardly have said, but an irresistible impulse drove him thither to see if it was there. He went down by the jetty and struck out eastward over the smooth sand, looking about him with dreadful expectation for some small crowd or hurrying messenger. From the foot of the cliffs, over the rocks to the distant line of breakers, his eye roved with eager dread, and still he hurried eastward, always drawing nearer to the place that he feared to look on. As he left the town behind, so he left behind the one or two idlers on the beach, and when he turned Foreness Point he lost sight of the last of them and went forward alone. It was less than half-an-hour later that the fatal headland opened out beyond Whiteness.

Not a soul had he met along that solitary beach, and though, once or twice, he had started at the sight of some mass of drift wood or heap of seaweed, the dreadful thing that he was seeking had not yet appeared. He passed the opening of the cutting and approached the headland, breathing fast and looking about him fearfully. Already he could see the larger lumps of chalk that had fallen, and looking up, he saw a clean, white patch at the summit of the cliff. But still there was no sign of the corpse. He walked on more slowly now, considering whether it could have drifted out to sea, or whether he should find it in the next bay. And then, rounding the headland, he came in sight of a black hole at the cliff foot, the entrance to a deep cave. He approached yet more slowly, sweeping his eye round the little bay, and looking apprehensively at the cavity before him. Suppose the thing should have washed in there. It was quite possible. Many things did wash into that cave, for he had once visited it and had been astonished at the quantity of seaweed and jetsam that had accumulated within it. But it was an uncomfortable thought. It would be doubly horrible to meet the awful thing in the dim twilight of the cavern. And yet, the black archway seemed to draw him on, step by step, until he stood at the portal and looked in. It was an eerie place, chilly and damp, the clammy walls and roof stained green and purple and black with encrusting lichens. At one time, Elton had been told, it used to be haunted by smugglers, and then communicated with an underground passage, and the old smuggler's look-out still remained, a narrow tunnel, high up the cliff, looking out into Kingsgate Bay, and even some vestiges of the rude steps that led up to the look-out platform could still be traced, and were not impossible to climb. Indeed, Elton had, at his last visit, climbed to the platform and looked out through the spy-hole. He recalled the circumstance now, as he stood, peering nervously into the darkness, and straining his eyes to see what jetsam the ocean had brought since then.

At first he could see nothing but the smooth sand near the opening, then, as his eyes grew more accustomed to the gloom, he could make out the great heap of seaweed on the floor of the cave. Insensibly, he crept in, with his eyes riveted on the weedy mass and, as he left the daylight behind him, so did the twilight of the cave grow clearer. His feet left the firm sand and trod the springy mass of weed, and in the silence of the cave he could now hear plainly the rain-like patter of the leaping sand-hoppers. He stopped for a moment to listen to the unfamiliar sound, and still the gloom of the cave grew lighter to his more accustomed eyes.

And then, in an instant, he saw it. From a heap of weed, a few paces ahead, projected a boot – his own boot, he recognised the patch on the sole,

426

and at the sight, his heart seemed to stand still. Though he had somehow expected to find it here, its presence seemed to strike him with a greater shock of horror from that very circumstance.

He was standing stock still, gazing with fearful fascination at the boot and the swelling mound of weed, when, suddenly, there struck upon his ear the voice of a woman, singing.

He started violently. His first impulse was to run out of the cave. But a moment's reflection told him what madness this would be. And then the voice drew nearer, and there broke out the high, rippling laughter of a child. Elton looked in terror at the bright opening of the cavern's mouth, expecting every moment to see it frame a group of figures. If that happened, he was lost, for he would have been seen actually with the body. Suddenly he bethought him of the spy-hole and the platform, both of which were invisible from the entrance, and turning, he ran quickly over the sodden weed till he came to the remains of the steps. Climbing hurriedly up these, he reached the platform, which was enclosed in a large niche, just as the reverberating sound of voices told him that the strangers were within the mouth of the cave. He strained his ears to catch what they were saying and to make out if they were entering farther. It was a child's voice that he had first heard, and very weird were the hollow echoes of the thin treble that were flung back from the rugged walls. But he could not hear what the child had said. The woman's voice, however, was quite distinct, and the words seemed significant in more senses than one.

"No, dear," it said, "you had better not go in. It's cold and damp. Come out into the sunshine."

Elton breathed more freely. But the woman was more right than she knew. It was cold and damp, that thing under the black tangle of weed. Better far to be out in the sunshine. He himself was already longing to escape from the chill and gloom of the cavern. But he could not escape yet. Innocent as he actually was, his position was that of a murderer. He must wait until the coast was clear, and then steal out, to hurry away unobserved.

He crept up cautiously to the short tunnel and peered out through the opening across the bay. And then his heart sank. Below him, on the sunny beach, a small party of visitors had established themselves just within view of the mouth of the cave, and even as he looked, a man approached from the wooden stairway down the cliff, carrying a couple of deck chairs. So, for the present his escape was hopelessly cut off.

He went back to the platform and sat down to wait for his release, and, as he sat, his thoughts went back once more to the thing that lay under the weed. How long would it lie there undiscovered? And what would

427

happen when it was found? What was there to connect him with it? Of course, there was his name on the clothing, but there was nothing incriminating in that, if he had only had the courage to give information at once. But it was too late to think of that now. Besides, it suddenly flashed upon him, there was the receipt in the wallet. That receipt mentioned him by name and referred to a loan. Obviously, its suggestion was most sinister, coupled with his silence. It was a deadly item of evidence against him. But no sooner had he realised the appalling significance of this document than he also realised that it was still within his reach. Why should he leave it there to be brought in evidence – in false evidence, too – against him?

Slowly he rose and, creeping down the tunnel, once more looked out. The people were sitting quietly in their chairs, the man was reading, and the child was digging in the sand. Elton looked across the bay to make sure that no other person was approaching, and then, hastily climbing down the steps, walked across the great bed of weed, driving an army of sand-hoppers before him. He shuddered at the thought of what he was going to do, and the clammy chill of the cave seemed to settle on him in a cold sweat.

He came to the little mound from which the boot projected, and began, shudderingly and with faltering hand, to lift the slimy, tangled weed. As he drew aside the first bunch, be gave a gasp of horror and quickly replaced it. The body was lying on its back, and, as he lifted the weed he had uncovered – not the face, for the thing had no face. It had struck either the cliff or a stone upon the beach and – but there is no need to go into particulars. It had no face. When he had recovered a little, Elton groped shudderingly among the weed until he found the breast-pocket from which he quickly drew out the wallet, now clammy, sodden and loathsome. He was rising with it in his hand when an apparition, seen through the opening of the cave, arrested his movement as if he had been suddenly turned into stone. A man, apparently a fisherman or sailor, was sauntering past some thirty yards from the mouth of the cave, and at his heels trotted a mongrel dog. The dog stopped, and, lifting his nose, seemed to sniff the air, and then he began to walk slowly and suspiciously towards the cave. The man sauntered on and soon passed out of view, but the dog still came on towards the cave, stopping now and again with upraised nose.

The catastrophe seemed inevitable. But just at that moment the man's voice rose, loud and angry, evidently calling the dog. The animal hesitated, looking wistfully from his master to the cave, but when the summons was repeated, he turned reluctantly and trotted away.

Elton stood up and took a deep breath. The chilly sweat was running down his face, his heart was thumping and his knees trembled, so that he

428

could hardly get back to the platform. What hideous peril had he escaped and how narrowly! For there he had stood, and had the man entered, he would have been caught in the very act of stealing the incriminating document from the body. For that matter, he was little better off now, with the dead man's property on his person, and he resolved instantly to take out and destroy the receipt and put back the wallet. But this was easier thought of than done. The receipt was soaked with sea water, and refused utterly to light when he applied a match to it. In the end, he tore it up into little fragments and deliberately swallowed them, one by one.

But to restore the wallet was more than he was equal to just now. He would wait until the people had gone home to lunch, and then he would thrust it under the weed as he ran past. So he sat down again and once more took up the endless thread of his thoughts.

The receipt was gone now, and with it the immediate suggestion of motive. There remained only the clothes with their too legible markings. They certainly connected him with the body, but they offered no proof of his presence at the catastrophe. And then, suddenly, another most startling idea occurred to him. Who could identify the body – the body that had no face? There was the wallet, it was true, but he could take that away with him, and there was a ring on the finger and some articles in the pockets which might be identified. But – a voice seemed to whisper to him – these things were removable, too. And if he removed them, what then? Why, then, the body was that of Thomas Elton, a friendless, poverty-stricken artist, about whom no one would trouble to ask any questions.

He pondered on this new situation profoundly. It offered him a choice of alternatives. Either he might choose the imminent risk of being hanged for a murder that he had not committed, or he might surrender his identity for ever and move away to a new environment.

He smiled faintly. His identity! What might that be worth to barter against his life? Only yesterday he would gladly have surrendered it as the bare price of emancipation from the vampire who had fastened on to him.

He thrust the wallet into his pocket and buttoned his coat. Thomas Elton was dead, and that other man, as yet unnamed, should go forth, as the woman had said, into the sunshine.

Part II
(Related by Christopher Jervis, M.D.)

From various causes, the insurance business that passed through Thorndyke's hands had, of late, considerably increased. The number of societies which regularly employed him had grown larger, and, since the remarkable case of Percival Bland, the Griffin had made it a routine practice to send all inquest cases to us for report.

It was in reference to one of these latter that Mr. Stalker, a senior member of the staff of that office, called on us one afternoon in December, and when he had laid his bag on the table and settled himself comfortably before the fire, he opened the business without preamble.

"I've brought you another inquest case," said he, "a rather queer one, quite interesting from your point of view. As far as we can see, it has no particular interest for us excepting that it does rather look as if our examining medical officer had been a little casual."

"What is the special interest of the case from our point of view?" asked Thorndyke.

"I'll just give you a sketch of it," said Stalker, "and I think you will agree that it's a case after your own heart.

"On the 24th of last month, some men who were collecting seaweed, to use as manure, discovered in a cave at Kingsgate, in the Isle of Thanet, the body of a man, lying under a mass of accumulated weed. As the tide was rising, they put the body into their cart and conveyed it to Margate, where, of course, an inquest was held, and the following facts were elicited. The body was that of a man named Thomas Elton. It was identified by the name-marks on the clothing, by the visiting-cards and a couple of letters which were found in the pockets. From the address on the letters it was seen that Elton had been staying in Margate, and on inquiry at that address, it was learnt from the old woman who let the lodgings, that he had been missing about four days. The landlady was taken to the mortuary, and at once identified the body as that of her lodger. It remained only to decide how the body came into the cave, and this did not seem to present much difficulty, for the neck had been broken by a tremendous blow, which had practically destroyed the face, and there were distinct evidences of a breaking away of a portion of the top of the cliff, only a few yards from the position of the cave. There was apparently no doubt that Elton had fallen sheer from the top of the overhanging cliff on to the beach. Now, one would suppose with the evidence of this fall of about a hundred-and-fifty feet, the smashed face and broken neck, there was not much room

430

for doubt as to the cause of death. I think you will agree with me, Dr. Jervis?"

"Certainly," I replied, "it must be admitted that a broken neck is a condition that tends to shorten life."

"Quite so," agreed Stalker, "but our friend, the local coroner, is a gentleman who takes nothing for granted – a very Thomas Didymus, who apparently agrees with Dr. Thorndyke that if there is no *post-mortem*, there is no inquest. So he ordered a *post-mortem*, which would have appeared to me an absurdly unnecessary proceeding, and I think that even you will agree with me, Dr. Thorndyke."

But Thorndyke shook his head.

"Not at all," said he. "It might, for instance, be much more easy to push a drugged or poisoned man over a cliff than to put over the same man in his normal state. The appearance of violent accident is an excellent mask for the less obvious forms of murder."

"That's perfectly true," said Stalker, "and I suppose that is what the coroner thought. At any rate, he had the post-mortem made, and the result was most curious, for it was found, on opening the body, that the deceased had suffered from a smallish thoracic aneurism, which had burst. Now, as the aneurism must obviously have burst during life, it leaves the cause of death – so I understand – uncertain. At any rate, the medical witness was unable to say whether the deceased fell over the cliff in consequence of the bursting of the aneurism or burst the aneurism in consequence of falling over the cliff. Of course, it doesn't matter to us which way the thing happened. The only question which interests us is, whether a comparatively recently insured man ought to have had an aneurism at all."

"Have you paid the claim?" asked Thorndyke.

"No, certainly not. We never pay a claim until we have had your report. But, as a matter of fact, there is another circumstance that is causing delay. It seems that Elton had mortgaged his policy to a money lender, named Gordon, and it is by him that the claim has been made, or rather, by a clerk of his, named Hyams. Now, we have had a good many dealings with this man Gordon, and hitherto he has always acted in person, and as he is a somewhat slippery gentleman, we have thought it desirable to have the claim actually signed by him. And that is the difficulty. For it seems that Mr. Gordon is abroad, and his whereabouts unknown to Hyams, so, as we certainly couldn't take Hyams's receipt for payment, the matter is in abeyance until Hyams can communicate with his principal. And now, I must be running away. I have brought you, as you will see, all the papers, including the policy and the mortgage deed."

As soon as he was gone, Thorndyke gathered up the bundle of papers and sorted them out in what be apparently considered the order of their

431

importance. First he glanced quickly through the proposal form, and then took up the copy of the coroner's depositions.

"The medical evidence," he remarked, "is very full and complete. Both the coroner and the doctor seem to know their business."

"Seeing that the man apparently fell over a cliff," said I, "the medical evidence would not seem to be of first importance. It would seem to be more to the point to ascertain how he came to fall over."

"That's quite true," replied Thorndyke, "and yet, this report contains some rather curious matter. The deceased had an aneurism of the arch, that was probably rather recent. But he also had some slight, old-standing aortic disease, with full compensatory hypertrophy. He also had a nearly complete set of false teeth. Now, doesn't it strike you, Jervis, as rather odd that a man who was passed only five years ago as a first-class life should, in that short interval, have become actually uninsurable?"

"Yes, it certainly does look," said I, "as if the fellow had had rather bad luck. What does the proposal form say?"

I took the document up and ran my eyes over it. On Thorndyke's advice, medical examiners for the Griffin were instructed to make a somewhat fuller report than is usual in some companies. In this case, the ordinary answers to questions set forth that the heart was perfectly healthy and the teeth rather exceptionally good, and then, in the summary at the end, the examiner remarked, "the proposer seems to be a completely sound and healthy man, he presents no physical defects whatever, with the exception of a bony ankylosis of the first joint of the third finger of the left hand, which he states to have been due to an injury."

Thorndyke looked up quickly. "Which finger, did you say?" he asked.

"The third finger of the left hand," I replied.

Thorndyke looked thoughtfully at the paper that he was reading. "It's very singular," said he, "for I see that the Margate doctor states that the deceased wore a signet ring on the third finger of the left hand. Now, of course, you couldn't get a ring on to a finger with bony ankylosis of the joint."

"He must have mistaken the finger," said I, "or else the insurance examiner did."

"That is quite possible," Thorndyke replied, "but, doesn't it strike you as very singular that, whereas the insurance examiner mentions the ankylosis, which was of no importance from an insurance point of view, the very careful man who made the *post-mortem* should not have mentioned it, though, owing to the unrecognisable condition of the face, it was of vital importance for the purpose of identification?"

432

I admitted that it was very singular indeed, and we then resumed our study of the respective papers. But presently I noticed that Thorndyke had laid the report upon his knee, and was gazing speculatively into the fire.

"I gather," said I, "that my learned friend finds some matter of interest in this case."

For reply, he handed me the bundle of papers, recommending me to look through them.

"Thank you," said I, rejecting them firmly, "but I think I can trust you to have picked out all the plums."

Thorndyke smiled indulgently. "They're not plums, Jervis," said he. "They're only currants, but they make quite a substantial little heap."

I disposed myself in a receptive attitude (somewhat after the fashion of the juvenile pelican) and he continued, "If we take the small and unimpressive items and add them together, you will see that a quite considerable sum of discrepancy results, thus:

"In 1903, Thomas Elton, aged thirty-one, had a set of sound teeth. In 1908, at the age of thirty-six, he was more than half toothless. Again, at the age of thirty-one, his heart was perfectly healthy. At the age of thirty-six, he had old aortic disease, with fully established compensation, and an aneurism that was possibly due to it. When he was examined he had a noticeable incurable malformation, no such malformation is mentioned in connection with the body.

"He appears to have fallen over a cliff, and he had also burst an aneurism. Now, the bursting of the aneurism must obviously have occurred during life, but it would occasion practically instantaneous death. Therefore, if the fall was accidental, the rupture must have occurred either as he stood at the edge of the cliff, as he was in the act of falling, or on striking the beach.

"At the place where he apparently fell, the footpath is some thirty yards distant from the edge of the cliff.

"It is not known how he came to that spot, or whether he was alone at the time.

"Someone is claiming five-hundred pounds as the immediate result of his death.

"There, you see, Jervis, are seven propositions, none of them extremely striking, but rather suggestive when taken together."

"You seem," said I, "to suggest a doubt as to the identity of the body."

"I do," he replied. "The identity was not clearly established."

"You don't think the clothing and the visiting-cards conclusive."

"They're not parts of the body," he replied. "Of course, substitution is highly improbable. But it is not impossible."

"And the old woman – " I suggested, but he interrupted me.

433

"My dear Jervis," he exclaimed, "I'm surprised at you. How many times has it happened within our knowledge that women have identified the bodies of total strangers as those of their husbands, fathers, or brothers? The thing happens almost every year. As to this old woman, she saw a body with an unrecognisable face, dressed in the clothes of her missing lodger. Of course, it was the clothes that she identified."

"I suppose it was," I agreed, and then I said, "You seem to suggest the possibility of foul play."

"Well," he replied, "if you consider those seven points, you will agree with me that they present a cumulative discrepancy which it is impossible to ignore. The whole significance of the case turns on the question of identity, for, if this was not the body of Thomas Elton, it would appear to have been deliberately prepared to counterfeit that body. And such deliberate preparation would manifestly imply an attempt to conceal the identity of some other body.

"Then," he continued, after a pause, "there is this deed. It looks quite regular and is correctly stamped, but it seems to me that the surface of the paper is slightly altered in one or two places and if one holds the document up to the light, the paper looks a little more transparent in those places." He examined the document for a few seconds with his pocket lens, and then passing lens and document to me, said, "Have a look at it, Jervis, and tell me what you think."

I scrutinised the paper closely, taking it over to the window to get a better light, and to me, also, the paper appeared to be changed in certain places.

"Are we agreed as to the position of the altered places?" Thorndyke asked when I announced the fact.

"I only see three patches," I answered. "Two correspond to the name, Thomas Elton, and the third to one of the figures in the policy number."

"Exactly," said Thorndyke, "and the significance is obvious. If the paper has really been altered, it means that some other name has been erased and Elton's substituted, by which arrangement, of course, the correctly dated stamp would be secured. And this – the alteration of an old document – is the only form of forgery that is possible with a dated, impressed stamp."

"Wouldn't it be rather a stroke of luck," I asked, "for a forger to happen to have in his possession a document needing only these two alterations?"

"I see nothing remarkable in it," Thorndyke replied. "A moneylender would have a number of documents of this kind in hand, and you observe that he was not bound down to any particular date. Any date within a year

434

or so of the issue of the policy would answer his purpose. This document is, in fact, dated, as you see, about six months after the issue of the policy."

"I suppose," said I, "that you will draw Stalker's attention to this matter."

"He will have to be informed, of course," Thorndyke replied, "but I think it would be interesting in the first place to call on Mr. Hyams. You will have noticed that there are some rather mysterious features in this case, and Mr. Hyams's conduct, especially if this document should turn out to be really a forgery, suggests that he may have some special information on the subject." He glanced at his watch and, after a few moments' reflection, added, "I don't see why we shouldn't make our little ceremonial call at once. But it will be a delicate business, for we have mighty little to go upon. Are you coming with me?"

If I had had any doubts, Thorndyke's last remark disposed of them, for the interview promised to be quite a sporting event. Mr. Hyams was presumably not quite newly-hatched, and Thorndyke, who utterly despised bluff of any kind, and whose exact mind refused either to act or speak one hair's breadth beyond his knowledge, was admittedly in somewhat of a fog. The meeting promised to be really entertaining.

Mr. Hyams was "discovered", as the playwrights have it, in a small office at the top of a high building in Queen Victoria Street. He was a small gentleman, of sallow and greasy aspect, with heavy eyebrows and a still heavier nose.

"Are you Mr. Gordon?" Thorndyke suavely inquired as we entered.

Mr. Hyams seemed to experience a momentary doubt on the subject, but finally decided that he was not. "But perhaps," he added brightly, "I can do your business for you as well."

"I daresay you can," Thorndyke agreed significantly, on which we were conducted into an inner den, where I noticed Thorndyke's eye rest for an instant on a large iron safe.

"Now," said Mr. Hyams, shutting the door ostentatiously, "what can I do for you?"

"I want you," Thorndyke replied, "to answer one or two questions with reference to the claim made by you on the Griffin Office in respect of Thomas Elton."

Mr. Hyams's manner underwent a sudden change. He began rapidly to turn over papers, and opened and shut the drawers of his desk, with an air of restless preoccupation.

"Did the Griffin people send you here?" he demanded brusquely.

"They did not specially instruct me to call on you," replied Thorndyke.

"Then," said Hyams bouncing out of his chair, "I can't let you occupy my time. I'm not here to answer conundrums from Tom, Dick, or Harry."

Thorndyke rose from his chair. "Then I am to understand," he said, with unruffled suavity, "that you would prefer me to communicate with the Directors, and leave them to take any necessary action."

This gave Mr. Hyams pause. "What action do you refer to?" he asked. "And, who are you?"

Thorndyke produced a card and laid it on the table. Mr. Hyams had apparently seen the name before, for he suddenly grew rather pale and very serious.

"What is the nature of the questions that you wished to ask?" he inquired.

"They refer to this claim," replied Thorndyke. "The first question is, where is Mr. Gordon?"

"I don't know," said Hyams.

"Where do you think he is?" asked Thorndyke.

"I don't think at all," replied Hyams, turning a shade paler and looking everywhere but at Thorndyke.

"Very well," said the latter, "then the next question is, are you satisfied that this claim is really payable?"

"I shouldn't have made it if I hadn't been," replied Hyams.

"Quite so," said Thorndyke. "And the third question is, are you satisfied that the mortgage deed was executed as it purports to have been?"

"I can't say anything about that," replied Hyams, who was growing every moment paler and more fidgety. "It was done before my time."

"Thank you," said Thorndyke. "You will, of course, understand why I am making these inquiries."

"I don't," said Hyams.

"Then," said Thorndyke, "perhaps I had better explain. We are dealing, you observe, Mr. Hyams, with the case of a man who has met with a violent death under somewhat mysterious circumstances. We are dealing, also, with another man who has disappeared, leaving his affairs to take care of themselves, and with a claim, put forward by a third party, on behalf of the one man in respect of the other. When I say that the dead man has been imperfectly identified, and that the document supporting the claim presents certain peculiarities, you will see that the matter calls for further inquiry."

There was an appreciable interval of silence. Mr. Hyams had turned a tallowy white, and looked furtively about the room, as if anxious to avoid the stony gaze that my colleague had fixed on him.

"Can you give us no assistance?" Thorndyke inquired, at length.

Mr. Hyams chewed a pen-holder ravenously, as he considered the question. At length, he burst out in an agitated voice, "Look here, sir, if I tell you what I know, will you treat the information as confidential?

"I can't agree to that, Mr. Hyams," replied Thorndyke. "It might amount to compounding a felony. But you will be wiser to tell me what you know. The document is a side-issue, which my clients may never raise, and my own concern is with the death of this man."

Hyams looked distinctly relieved. "If that's so," said he, "I'll tell you all I know, which is precious little, and which just amounts to this: Two days after Elton was killed, someone came to this office in my absence and opened the safe. I discovered the fact the next morning. Someone had been to the safe and rummaged over all the papers. It wasn't Gordon, because he knew where to find everything, and it wasn't an ordinary thief, because no cash or valuables had been taken. In fact, the only thing that I missed was a promissory note, drawn by Elton."

"You didn't miss a mortgage deed?" suggested Thorndyke, and Hyams, having snatched a little further refreshment from the pen-holder, said he did not.

"And the policy," suggested Thorndyke, "was apparently not taken?"

"No," replied Hyams "but it was looked for. Three bundles of policies had been untied, but this one happened to be in a drawer of my desk and I had the only key."

"And what do you infer from this visit?" Thorndyke asked.

"Well," replied Hyams, "the safe was opened with keys, and they were Gordon's keys – or at any rate, they weren't mine – and the person who opened it wasn't Gordon, and the things that were taken – at least the thing, I mean – chiefly concerned Elton. Naturally I smelt a rat, and when I read of the finding of the body, I smelt a fox."

"And have you formed any opinion about the body that was found?"

"Yes, I have," he replied. "My opinion is that it was Gordon's body – that Gordon had been putting the screw on Elton, and Elton had just pitched him over the cliff and gone down and changed clothes with the body. Of course, that's only my opinion. I may be wrong, but I don't think I am."

As a matter of fact, Mr. Hyams was not wrong. An exhumation, consequent on Thorndyke's challenge of the identity of the deceased, showed that the body was that of Solomon Gordon. A hundred pounds reward was offered for information as to Elton's whereabouts. But no one ever earned it. A letter, bearing the post mark of Marseilles, and addressed by the missing man to Thorndyke, gave a plausible account of Gordon's death, which was represented as having occurred accidentally at the moment when Gordon chanced to be wearing a suit of Elton's clothes.

437

Of course, this account may have been correct, or again, it may have been false, but whether it was true or false, Elton, from that moment, vanished from our ken and has never since been heard of.

Apocryphal
Adventures

31 NEW INN

The Original 1905 Thorndyke Novella

Editor's Note

T*he novella* 31 New Inn *(1905) is the original Dr. Thorndyke story, predating the first Thorndyke novel* The Red Thumb Mark *(1907) by two years. It would later be expanded into the novel* The Mystery of 31 New Inn *(1912, included in Volume I of this series.)*

As in the expanded novel, the events of "31 New Inn" occur after The Red Thumb Mark. *Interestingly, even though* The Red Thumb Mark *would not be published for quite some time, it was clearly already planned in advance, as certain plot points from that book are discussed in this novella as having already occurred.*

I – The Mysterious Patient

The hour of nine was approaching – the blessed hour of release when the casual patient ceases from troubling (or is expected to do so) and the weary practitioner may put on his slippers and turn down the surgery gas.

The fact was set forth with needless emphasis by the little American clock on the mantel-shelf, which tick-tacked frantically, as though it were eager to get the day over and be done with it. Indeed, the approaching hour might have been ninety-nine from the to-do the little clock made about the matter.

The minute-hand was creeping up to the goal and the little clock had just given a kind of preliminary cough to announce its intention of striking the hour, when the bell on the door of the outer surgery rang to announce the arrival of a laggard visitor. A moment later the office-boy thrust his head in at my door and informed me that a gentleman wished to see me.

They were all gentlemen in Kennington Lane – unless they were ladies or children. Sweeps, milkmen, bricklayers, costermongers, all were impartially invested with rank and title by the democratic office-boy, and I was not, therefore, surprised or disappointed when the open door gave entrance to a man in the garb of a cabman or coachman.

As he closed the door behind him, he drew from his coat pocket a note, which he handed to me without remark. It was not addressed to me, but to my principal – to the doctor, that is to say, of whose practise I was taking charge in his absence.

"You understand, I suppose," I said, as I prepared to open the envelope, "that I am not Dr. Pike? He is out of town at present, and I am looking after his patients."

"It's of no consequence," the man replied. "You'll do just as well as him, I expect."

On this I opened the note and read the contents, which were quite brief and, at first sight, in no way remarkable.

Dear Sir:

Could you come at once and see my brother?
The bearer of this will give you further particulars and convey you to the house.

Yours truly,

J. Morgan

445

There was no address on the paper and no date, and the name of the writer was, of course, unknown to me.

"This note speaks of some further particulars," I said to the messenger. "What are the particulars referred to?"

"Why, sir, the fact is," he replied, "it's a most ridiculous affair altogether. The sick gentleman don't seem to me to be quite right in his head. At any rate, he's got some very peculiar ideas. He's been ailing now for some time, and the master, Mr. Morgan, has tried everything he knew to get him to see a doctor. But he wouldn't. However, at last it seems he gave way, but only on one condition. He said the doctor was to come from a distance and was not to be told who he was or where he lived or anything about him, and he made the master promise to keep to these conditions before he would let him send for advice. Do you think you could come and see him on them conditions, sir?"

I considered the question for a while before replying. We doctors all know the kind of idiot who is possessed with an insane dislike and distrust of the members of our profession and we like to have as little to do with him as possible. If this had been my own practise would have declined the case off-hand, but I could not lightly refuse work that would bring profit to my principal.

As I turned the matter over in my mind, I half-consciously scrutinized my visitor – rather to his embarrassment – and I liked his appearance as little as I liked his message. He kept his hat on, which I resented, and he stood near the door where the light was dim, for the illumination was concentrated on the table and the patient's chair, but I could see that he had a sly, unprepossessing face and a greasy red mustache that seemed out of character with his livery, though this was mere prejudice. Moreover, his voice was disagreeable, having that dull, snuffling quality that, to the medical ear, suggests a nasal polypus. Altogether I was unpleasantly impressed, but decided, nevertheless, to undertake the case.

"I suppose," I answered at length, "it is no affair of mine who the sick man is or where he lives. But how do you propose to manage the business? Am I to be blindfolded like the visitor to the bandits' cave?"

"No, sir," he replied with a forced smile and with evident relief at my agreement. "I have a carriage waiting to take you."

"Very well," I rejoined, opening the door to let him out, "I will be with you in a minute."

I slipped into a bag a small supply of emergency drugs and a few diagnostic instruments, turned down the gas, and passed out through the surgery. The carriage was standing by the curb and I viewed it with mingled curiosity and disfavor. It was a kind of large brougham, such as is used by some commercial travelers, the usual glass windows being

446

replaced by wooden shutters intended to conceal the piles of sample-boxes, and the doors capable of being locked from outside.

As I emerged, the coachman unlocked the door and held it open.

"How long will the journey take?" I asked, pausing with my foot on the step.

"Nigh upon half-an-hour." was the reply. I glanced at my watch and, reflecting gloomily that my brief hour of leisure would be entirely absorbed by this visit, stepped into the uninviting vehicle. Instantly the coachman slammed the door and turned the key, leaving me in total darkness.

As the carriage rattled along, now over the macadam of quiet side-streets and now over the granite of the larger thoroughfares, I meditated on the oddity of this experience and on the possible issues of the case. For one moment a suspicion arose in my mind that this might be a trick to lure me to some thieves' den where I might be robbed and possibly murdered, but I immediately dismissed this idea, reflecting that so elaborate a plan would not have been devised for so unremunerative a quarry as an impecunious general practitioner.

II – I Meet Mr. Morgan

My reflections were at length brought to an end by the carriage slowing down and passing under an archway – as I could tell by the hollow sound – where it presently stopped. Then I distinguished the clang of heavy wooden gates closed behind me, and a moment later the carriage door was unlocked and opened. I stepped out into a covered way that seemed to lead down to a stable, but it was all in darkness and I had no time to make any detailed observations, for the carriage had drawn up opposite a side door which was open, and in which stood an elderly woman holding a candle.

"Is that the doctor?" she inquired, shading the candle with her hand and peering at me with screwed-up eyes. Then, with evident relief, "I am glad you have come, sir. Will you please to step in?" I followed her across a dark passage into a large room almost destitute of furniture, where she set down the candle on a chest of drawers and turned to depart.

"The master will see you in a moment," she said. "I will go and tell him you are here."

With that she left me in the twilight of the solitary candle to gaze curiously at the bare and dismal apartment with its three rickety chairs, its unswept floor, its fast-closed shutters, and the dark drapery of cobwebs that hung from the ceiling to commemorate a long and illustrious dynasty of spiders.

Presently the door opened and a shadowy figure appeared, standing close by the thresh-old.

"Mr. Morgan, I presume?" said I, advancing toward the stranger as he remained standing by the doorway.

"Quite right, sir," he answered, and as he spoke I started, for his voice had the same thick, snuffling quality that I had already noticed in that of the coachman. The coincidence was certainly an odd one, and it caused me to look at the stranger narrowly. He appeared somewhat shorter than his servant, but then he had a pronounced stoop, whereas the coachman was stiff and upright in his carriage. Then the coachman had short hair of a light brown and a reddish mustache, whereas this man appeared, so far as I could see in the gloom, to have a shock head of black hair and a voluminous black beard. Moreover he wore spectacles. "Quite right, sir," said this individual, "and I thought I had better give you an outline of the case before you go up to the patient. My brother is, as my man has probably told you, very peculiar in some of his ideas, whence these rather foolish proceedings, for which I trust you will not hold me responsible, though I feel obliged to carry out his wishes. He returned a week or two

448

ago from New York and, being then in rather indifferent health, he asked me to put him up for a time, as he had no settled home of his own. From that time he has gradually become worse and has really caused me a good deal of anxiety, for until now I have been quite unable to prevail on him to seek medical advice. And even now he has only consented subject to the ridiculous conditions that my man has probably explained to you."

"What is the nature of his illness?" I asked. "Does he complain of any definite symptoms?"

"No," was the reply. "Indeed, he makes very few complaints of any kind, although he is obviously ill, but the fact is that he is hardly ever more than half-awake. He lies in a kind of dreamy stupor from morning to night."

This struck me as excessively odd and by no means in agreement with the patient's energetic refusal to see a doctor.

"But does he never rouse completely?" I asked.

"Oh, yes," Mr. Morgan answered quickly, "he rouses occasionally and is then quite rational and, as you may have gathered, rather obstinate. But perhaps you had better see for yourself what his condition is. Follow me, please. The stairs are rather dark."

The stairs were very dark and were, moreover, without any covering of carpet, so that our footsteps resounded on the bare boards as though we were in an empty house. I stumbled up after my guide, feeling my way by the handrail, and on the first floor followed him into a room similar in size to the one below and very barely furnished, though less squalid than the other. A single candle at the farther end threw its feeble light on a figure in the bed, leaving the rest of the room in a dim twilight.

"Here is the doctor, Henry," Mr. Morgan called out as we entered, and, receiving no answer, he added, "He seems to be dozing as usual."

I stepped forward to look at my patient while Mr. Morgan remained at the other end of the room, pacing noiselessly backward and forward in the semi-obscurity. By the light of the candle I saw an elderly man with good features and an intelligent and even attractive face, but dreadfully emaciated, bloodless, and yellow. He lay with half-closed eyes and seemed to be in a dreamy, somnolent state, although not actually asleep. I advanced to the bedside and addressed him somewhat loudly by name, but the only response was a slight lifting of the eyelids which, after a brief, drowsy glance at me, slowly subsided to their former position.

I now proceeded to feel his pulse, grasping his wrist with intentional bruskness in the hope of rousing him from his stupor. The beats were slow and feeble and slightly irregular, giving clear evidence, if any were wanted, of his generally lowered vitality. My attention was next directed to the patient's eyes, which I examined closely with the aid of the candle,

449

raising the lids somewhat roughly so as to expose the whole of the iris. He submitted without resistance to my rather ungentle handling, and showed no signs of discomfort even when I brought the flame of the candle to within a couple of inches of his eyes.

His extreme tolerance of light, however, was in no way surprising when one came to examine the pupils, for they were contracted to such a degree as to present only the minutest point of black upon the gray iris.

But the excessive contraction of the pupils was not the only singular feature in the sick man's eyes. As he lay on his back, the right iris sagged down slightly toward its center, showing a distinctly concave surface and, whenever any slight movement of the eyeball took place, a perceptible undulatory movement could be detected in it.

The patient had, in fact, what is known as a *tremulous iris*, a condition that is seen in cases where the crystalline lens has been extracted for the cure of cataract, or where it has become accidentally displaced, leaving the iris unsupported. Now, in the present case the complete condition of the iris made it clear that the ordinary extraction operation had not been performed – nor was I able, on the closest inspection with the aid of a lens, to find any signs of the less common "needle operation". The inference was that the patient had suffered from the accident known as dislocation of the lens, and this led to the further inference that he was almost or completely blind in the right eye.

This conclusion was, indeed, to some extent negatived by a deep indentation on the bridge of the nose, evidently produced by spectacles habitually worn, for if only one eye were useful, a monocle would answer the purpose. Yet this objection was of little weight, for many men, under the circumstances, would elect to wear spectacles rather than submit to the inconvenience and disfigurement of the single eyeglass.

As to the nature of the patient's illness, only one opinion seemed possible. It was a clear case of opium or morphia poisoning. To this conclusion all his symptoms seemed to point plainly enough. His coated tongue, which he protruded slowly and tremulously in response to a command bawled in his ear; his yellow skin and ghastly expression; his contracted pupils and the stupor from which he could be barely roused by the roughest handling, and which yet did not amount to actual insensibility – these formed a distinct and coherent group of symptoms, not only pointing plainly to the nature of the drug, but also suggesting a very formidable dose.

The only question that remained was: How and by whom that dose had been administered. The closest scrutiny of his arms and legs failed to reveal a single mark such as would be made by a hypodermic needle, and

450

there was, of course, nothing to show or suggest whether the drug had been taken voluntarily by the patient himself or administered by someone else.

And then there remained the possibility that I might, after all, be mistaken in my diagnosis – a reflection that, in view of the obviously serious condition of the patient, I found eminently disturbing. As I pocketed my stethoscope and took a last look at my patient, I realized that my position was one of extraordinary difficulty and perplexity. On the one hand my suspicions inclined me to extreme reticence, while, on the other, it was evidently my duty to give any information that might prove serviceable to the patient.

III – Foul Play?

"Well, Doctor, what do you think of my brother?" Mr. Morgan asked as I joined him at the darkened end of the room. His manner, in asking the question, struck me as anxious and eager, but of course there was nothing remarkable in this.

"I think rather badly of him, Mr. Morgan," I replied. "He is certainly in a very low state."

"But you are able to form an opinion as to the nature of the disease?" he asked, still in a tone of suppressed eagerness.

"I cannot give a very definite opinion at present," I replied guardedly. "The symptoms are decidedly obscure and might equally well indicate several different affections. They might be due to congestion of the brain and, in the absence of any other explanation, I am inclined to adopt that view. The most probable alternative is some narcotic drug such as opium, if it were possible for him to obtain access to it without your knowledge – but I suppose it is not?"

"I should say decidedly not," he replied. "You see, my brother is not very often left alone, and he never leaves the room, so I don't see how he could obtain anything. My housekeeper is absolutely trustworthy."

"Is he often as drowsy as he seems now?"

"Oh, very often. In fact, that is his usual condition. He rouses now and again and is quite lucid and natural for perhaps half-an-hour, and then he dozes off again and remains asleep for hours on end. You don't think this can be a case of sleeping-sickness, I suppose?"

"I think not," I answered, making a mental note, nevertheless, to look up the symptoms of this rare and curious disease as soon as I reached home. "Besides, he has not been in Africa, has he?"

"I can't say where he has been," was the reply. "He has just come from New York, but where he was before going there I have no idea."

"Well," I said, "we will give him some medicine and attend to his general condition, and I think I had better see him again very shortly. Meanwhile you must watch him closely, and perhaps you may have something to report to me at my next visit."

I then gave him some general directions as to the care of the patient, to which he listened attentively, and I once more suggested that I ought to see the sick man again quite soon.

"Very well, Doctor," Mr. Morgan replied, "I will send for you again in a day or two if he does not get better, and now if you will allow me to pay your fee, I will go and order the carriage while you write the prescription."

He handed me the fee and, having indicated some writing materials on a table near the bed, wished me good-evening and left the room.

As soon as I was left alone, I drew from my bag the hypodermic syringe with its little magazine of drugs that I always carried with me on my rounds. Charging the syringe with a full dose of atropin, I approached the patient once more, and, slipping up the sleeve of his night-shirt, injected the dose under the skin of his forearm. The prick of the needle roused him for a moment and he gazed at me with dull curiosity, mumbling some indistinguishable words. Then he relapsed once more into silence and apathy while I made haste to put the syringe back into its receptacle. I had just finished writing the prescription (a mixture of permanganate of potash to destroy any morphia that might yet remain in the patient's stomach) and was watching the motionless figure on the bed, when the housekeeper looked in at the door.

"The carriage is ready, doctor," said she, whereupon I rose and followed her down-stairs.

The vehicle was drawn up in the covered way, as I perceived by the glimmer of the housekeeper's candle, which also enabled me dimly to discern the coachman standing close by in the shadow. I entered the carriage, the door was banged to and locked, and I then heard the heavy bolts of the gates withdrawn and the loud creaking of hinges. Immediately after, the carriage passed out and started off at a brisk pace, which was never relaxed until we reached our destination.

My reflections during the return journey were the reverse of pleasant, for I could not rid myself of the conviction that I was being involved in some very suspicious proceedings. And yet it was possible that I might be entirely mistaken – that the case might in reality be one of some brain affection accompanied by compression such as slow hemorrhage, abscess, tumor. or simple congestion. Again, the patient might be a confirmed opium-eater, unknown to his brother. The cunning of these unfortunates is proverbial, and it would be quite possible for him to feign profound stupor so long as he was watched and then, when left alone for a few minutes, to nip out of bed and help himself from some secret store of the drug.

Still, I did not believe this to be the true explanation. In spite of all the various possibilities, my suspicions came back to Mr. Morgan and refused to be dispelled. All the circumstances of the case itself were suspicious. So was the strange and sinister resemblance between the coachman and his employer. and so, most of all, was the fact that Mr. Morgan had told me a deliberate lie.

For he had lied, beyond all doubt. His statement as to the almost continuous stupor was absolutely irreconcilable with his other statement as to his brother's wilfulness and obstinacy, and even more irreconcilable with the deep and comparatively fresh marks of the spectacles on the patient's nose. The man had certainly worn spectacles within twenty-four hours, which he would hardly have done if he had been in a state bordering on coma.

My reflections were, for the moment, interrupted by the stopping of the carriage. The door was unlocked and thrown open and I emerged from my dark and stuffy prison.

"You seem to have a good fresh horse," I remarked, as a pretext for having another look at the coachman.

"Ay," he answered, "he can go, he can. Good-night, sir."

He slammed the carriage door, mounted the box, and drove off as if to avoid further conversation, and as I again compared his voice with those of his master, and his features with those I had seen so imperfectly in the darkened rooms, I was still inclined to entertain my suspicion that the coachman and Mr. Morgan were one and the same person.

Over my frugal supper, I found myself taking up anew the thread of my meditations, and afterward, as I smoked my last pipe by the expiring surgery fire, the strange and sinister features of the case continued to obtrude themselves on my notice. Especially was I puzzled as to what course of action I ought to follow. Should I maintain the professional secrecy to which I was tacitly committed, or ought I to convey a hint to the police?

Suddenly, and with a singular feeling of relief, I bethought me of my old friend and fellow student, John Thorndyke, now an eminent authority on medical jurisprudence. Thorndyke was a barrister in extensive special practice, and so would be able to tell me at once what was my duty from a legal point of view, and, as he was also a doctor of medicine, he would understand the exigencies of medical practise. If I could only find time to call at the Temple and put the case before him, all my doubts and difficulties would be resolved.

Anxiously I opened my visiting-list to see what kind of day's work was in store for me on the morrow. It was not a heavy day, but I was doubtful whether it would allow of my going so far from my district, until my eye caught, near the foot of the page, the name of Burton. Now Mr. Burton lived in one of the old houses on the east side of Bouverie Street – less than five minutes' walk from Thorndyke's chambers in King's Bench Walk, and he was, moreover, a "chronic" who could safely be left for the last. When I had done with Mr. Burton, I could look in on my friend with a good chance of catching him on his return from the hospital.

Having thus arranged my program, I rose, in greatly improved spirits, and knocked out my pipe just as the little clock banged out the hour of midnight.

IV – I Consult Thorndyke

"And so," said Thorndyke, eyeing me critically as we dropped into our respective easy chairs by the fire with the little tea-table between us, "you are back once more on the old trail?"

"Yes," I answered, with a laugh, "'the old trail, the long trail, the trail that is always new.'"

"And leads nowhere," added Thorndyke grimly.

I laughed again – not very heartily, for there was an uncomfortable element of truth in my friend's remark, to which my own experience bore only too complete testimony. The medical practitioner whose lack of means forces him to subsist by taking temporary charge of other men's practises is likely to find that the passing years bring him little but gray hairs and a wealth of disagreeable experience.

"You will have to drop it, Jervis, you will, indeed," Thorndyke resumed after a pause. "This casual employment is preposterous for a man of your class and professional attainments. Besides, are you not engaged to be married, and to a most charming girl?"

"Juliet has just been exhorting me in similar terms – except as to the last particular," I replied. "She threatens to buy a practise and put me in at a small salary and batten on the proceeds. Moreover, she seems to imply that my internal charge of pride, vanity, and egotism is equal to about four-hundred-pounds-to-the-square-inch and is rapidly approaching bursting-point. I am not sure that she is not right, too."

"Her point of view is eminently reasonable, at any rate," said Thorndyke. "But as to buying a practice – before you commit yourself to any such thing I would ask you to consider the suggestion that I have made more than once – that you join me here as my junior. We worked together with excellent results in the 'Red Thumbmark' case, as the newspapers called it, and we could do as well in many another. Of course, if you prefer general practise, well and good. Only remember that I should be glad to have you as my junior, and that in that capacity and with your abilities you would have an opening for something like a career."

"My dear Thorndyke," I answered, not without emotion, "I am more rejoiced at your offer and more grateful than I can tell you, and I should like to go into the matter this very moment. But I must not, for I have only a very short time now before I must go back to my work, and I have not yet touched upon the main object of my visit."

"I supposed that you had come to see me," remarked Thorndyke.

"So I did. I came to consult you professionally. The fact is, I am in a dilemma, and I want you to tell me what you think I ought to do." Thorndyke paused in the act of refilling my cup and glanced at me anxiously.

"It is nothing that affects me personally at all," I continued. "But perhaps I had better give you an account of the whole affair from the beginning."

Accordingly I proceeded to relate in detail the circumstances connected with my visit to the mysterious patient of the preceding evening, to all of which Thorndyke listened with close attention and evident interest.

"A very remarkable story, Jervis," he said, as I concluded my narrative. "In fact, quite a fine mystery of the good, old-fashioned Adelphi drama type. I particularly like the locked carriage. You have obviously formed certain hypotheses on the subject?"

"Yes, but I have come to you to hear yours."

"Well," said Thorndyke, "I expect yours and mine are pretty much alike, for there are two obvious alternative explanations of the affair."

"As for instance – ?"

"That Mr. Morgan's account of his brother's illness may be perfectly true and straightforward. The patient may be an opium-eater or morphinomaniac hitherto unsuspected. The secrecy and reticence attributed to him are quite consistent with such a supposition. On the other hand, Mr. J. Morgan's story may be untrue – which is certainly more probable – and he may be administering morphia for his own ends.

"The objection to this view is that morphia is a very unusual and inconvenient poison, except in a single fatal dose, on account of the rapidity with which tolerance of the drug is established. Nevertheless, we must not forget that slow morphia poisoning might prove eminently suitable in certain cases. The prolonged use of morphia in large doses enfeebles the will, confuses the judgment, and debilitates the body, and so might be adopted by a poisoner whose aim was to get some instrument or document executed, such as a will or assignment, after which, death might, if necessary, be brought about by other means. Did it seem to you as if Mr. Morgan was sounding you as to your willingness to give a death-certificate?"

"He said nothing to that effect, but the matter was in my mind, which was one reason for my extreme reticence."

"Yes, you showed excellent judgment in circumstances of considerable difficulty," said Thorndyke, "and, if our friend is up to mischief, he has not made a happy selection in his doctor. Just consider what would have happened – assuming the man to be bent on murder – if some blundering, cocksure idiot had rushed in, jumped to a diagnosis, called the case, let us say, an erratic form of Addison's Disease, and predicted a fatal termination. Thenceforward the murderer's course would be clear: He could compass his victim's death at any moment, secure of getting a death-certificate. As it is, he will have to move cautiously for the present – always assuming that we are not doing him a deep injustice."

"Yes," I answered, "we may take it that nothing fatal will happen just at present, unless some more easy-going practitioner is called in. But the question that is agitating me is, 'What ought I to do?' Should I, for instance, report the case to the police?"

"I should say certainly not," replied Thorndyke. "In the first place, you can give no address, nor even the slightest clue to the whereabouts of the house, and, in the second, you have nothing definite to report. You certainly could not swear an information and, if you made any statement, you might find, after all,, that you had committed a gross and ridiculous breach of professional confidence. No, if you hear no more from Mr. J. Morgan, you must watch the reports of inquests carefully and attend if necessary. If Mr. Morgan sends for you again, you ought undoubtedly to fix the position of the house. That is your clear duty for many and obvious reasons, and especially in view of your finding it necessary to communicate with the coroner or the police."

"That is all very well," I exclaimed, "but will you kindly tell me, my dear Thorndyke, how a man, boxed up in a pitch-dark carriage, is going to locate any place to which he may be conveyed?"

"I don't think the task presents any difficulties," he replied. "You would be prepared to take a little trouble, I suppose?"

"Certainly," I rejoined. "I will do my utmost to carry out any plan you may suggest."

"Very well, then. Can you spare me a few minutes?"

"It must be only a few," I answered, "for I ought to be getting back to my work."

"I won't detain you more than five minutes," said Thorndyke. "I will just run up to the workshop and get Polton to prepare what you will want, and when I have shown you how to get to work I will let you go."

He hurried away, leaving the door open, and returned in less than a couple of minutes.

"Come into the office," said he, and I followed him into the adjoining room – a rather small but light apartment of which the walls were lined with labeled deed-boxes. A massive safe stood in one corner and, in another, close to a window, was a great roll-top table surmounted by a nest of over a hundred labeled drawers. From one of the latter he drew a paper-

458

covered pocket note-book and, sitting down at the table, began to rule the pages each into three columns, two quite narrow and one broad.

He was just finishing the last page when there came a very gentle tap at the door.

"Is that you, Polton? Come in," said my friend.

The dry, shrewd-looking, little elderly man entered and I was at once struck by the incongruity of his workman's apron and rolled-up sleeves with his refined and intellectual face.

"Will this do?" he asked, holding out a little thin board about seven-inches-by-five, to one corner of which a pocket compass had been fixed with shellac.

"The very thing, Polton, thank you."

"What a wonderful old fellow that is, Jervis!" my friend observed, as his assistant retired with a friendly smile at me. "He took in the idea instantly and he seems to have produced the finished article by magic, as the conjurors bring forth bowls of goldfish at a moment's notice. And now as to the use of this appliance. Can you read a compass?"

"Oh, yes," I replied. "I used to sail a small yacht at one time."

"Good, then you will have no difficulty, though I expect the compass needle will jig about a good deal in the carriage. Here is a pocket reading-lamp, which you can hook on to the carriage lining. This note-book can be fixed to the board with an India-rubber band – so. You observe that the thoughtful Polton has stuck a piece of thread on the glass of the compass to serve as a lubber's line. Now this is how you will proceed: As soon as you are locked in the carriage, light your lamp – better have a book with you in case the light is seen – get out your watch and put the board on your knee. Then enter in one narrow column of your note-book the time – in the other, the direction shown by the compass and, in the broad column, any particulars, including the number of steps the horse makes in a minute, Thus – "

He opened the note-book and made one or two sample entries in pencil as follows:

> *9:40 – S.E. Start from home.*
> *9:41 – S.W. Granite blocks.*
> *9:43 – S.W. Wood pavement. Hoofs 104.*
> *9:47 – W. by S. Granite crossing Macadam.*

"And so on. You follow the process, Jervis?"

"Perfectly," I answered. "It is quite clear and simple, though, I must say, highly ingenious. But I must really go now."

"Good-by, then," said Thorndyke, slipping a well-sharpened pencil through the rubber band that fixed the note-book to the board. "Let me know how you get on, and come and see me again as soon as you can, in any case."

He handed me the board and the lamp, and when I had slipped them into my pocket, we shook hands and I hurried away, a little uneasy at having left my charge so long.

V – The Mystery Deepens

A couple of days passed without my receiving any fresh summons from Mr. Morgan, a circumstance that occasioned me some little disappointment, for I was now eager to put into practise Thorndyke's ingenious plan for discovering the whereabouts of the house of mystery. When the evening of the third day was well advanced and Mr. Morgan still made no sign, I began to think that I had seen the last of my mysterious patient and that the elaborate preparations for tracking him to his hiding-place had been made in vain.

It was therefore with a certain sense of relief and gratification that I received, at about ten minutes to nine, the office-boy's laconic announcement of "Mr. Morgan's carriage," followed by the inevitable "Wants you to go and see him at once."

The two remaining patients were of the male sex – an important time-factor in medical practise – and, as they were both cases of simple and common ailments, I was able to dispatch their business in about ten minutes.

Then, bidding the boy close up the surgery, I put on my overcoat, slipped the little board and the lamp into the pocket, tucked a newspaper under my arm, and went out.

The coachman was standing by the horse's head and touched his hat as he came forward to open the door.

"I have fortified myself for the long drive, you see," I remarked, exhibiting the newspaper as I stepped into the carriage.

"But you can't read in the dark," said he.

"No, but I have a lamp," I replied, producing it and striking a match.

"Oh, I see," said the coachman, adding, as I hooked the lamp on to the back cushion, "I suppose you found it rather a dull ride last time?" Then, without waiting for a reply, he slammed and locked the door and mounted the box.

I laid the board on my knee, looked at my watch, and made the first entry.

9:05 – S.W. Start from home. Horse 13 hands.

As on the previous occasion, the carriage was driven at a smart and regular pace, but as I watched the compass I became more and more astonished at the extraordinarily indirect manner in which it proceeded. For the compass needle, though it oscillated continually with the vibration, yet remained steady enough to show the main direction quite plainly, and I was able to see that our course zigzagged in a way that was difficult to account for.

Once we must have passed close to the river, for I heard a steamer's whistle – apparently a tug's – quite near at hand, and several times we passed over bridges or archways. All these meanderings I entered carefully in my note-book, and mightily busy the occupation kept me, for I had hardly time to scribble down one entry before the compass needle would swing round sharply, showing that we had, once more, turned a corner.

At length the carriage slowed down and turned into the covered way, whereupon, having briefly noted the fact and the direction, I smuggled the board and the note-book – now nearly half-filled with hastily scrawled memoranda – into my pocket, and when the door was unlocked and thrown open, I was deep in the contents of the evening paper.

I was received, as before, by the housekeeper, who, in response to my inquiry as to the patient's condition, informed me that he had seemed somewhat better. "As, indeed, he ought to," she added, "with all the care and watching he gets from the master. But you'll see that for yourself, sir, and, if you will wait here, I will go and tell Mr. Morgan you have come."

An interval of about five minutes elapsed before she returned to usher me up the dark staircase to the sick-room, and, on entering, I perceived Mr. Morgan, stooping over the figure on the bed. He rose, on seeing me, and came to meet me with his hand extended.

"I had to send for you again, you see, Doctor," he said. "The fact is, he is not quite so well this evening, which is extremely disappointing, for he had begun to improve so much that I hoped recovery had fairly set in. He has been much brighter and more wakeful the last two days, but this afternoon he sank into one of his dozes and has seemed to be getting more and more heavy ever since."

"He has taken his medicine?" I asked.

"Quite regularly," replied Mr. Morgan, indicating with a gesture the half-empty bottle on the table by the bedside.

"And as to food?"

"Naturally he takes very little. And, of course, when these attacks of drowsiness come on, he is without food for rather long periods."

I stepped over to the bed, leaving Mr. Morgan in the shadow, as before, and looked down at the patient. His aspect was, if anything, more ghastly and corpse-like than before. He lay quite motionless and relaxed, the only sign of life being the slight rise and fall of his chest and the soft gurgling snore at each shallow breath. At the first glance I should have said that he was dying, and indeed, with my previous knowledge of the case, I viewed him with no little anxiety, even now.

462

He opened his eyes, however, when I shouted in his ear, and even put out his tongue when asked in similar stentorian tones, but I could get no answer to any of my questions – not even the half-articulate mumble I had managed to elicit on the previous occasion. His stupor was evidently more profound now than then and, whatever might be the cause of his symptoms, he was certainly in a condition of extreme danger. Of that I had no doubt.

"I am afraid you don't find him any better to-night," remarked Mr. Morgan as I joined him at the other end of the room.

"No," I answered. "His condition appears to me to be very critical. I should say it is very doubtful whether he will rouse at all."

"You don't mean that you think he is dying?" Mr. Morgan spoke in tones of very unmistakable anxiety – even of terror.

"I think he might die at any moment," I replied.

"Good God!" exclaimed Morgan. "You horrify me!"

He evidently spoke the truth, for his appearance and manner denoted the most extreme agitation.

"I really think," he continued, " – at least I hope that you take an unnecessarily serious view of his condition. He has been like this before, you know."

"Possibly," I answered. "But there comes a last time, and it may have come now."

"Have you been able to form any more definite opinion as to the nature of this dreadful complaint?" he asked.

I hesitated for a moment and he continued, "As to your suggestion that his symptoms might be due to drugs, I think we may consider that disposed of. He has been watched, practically without cessation, since you came last and, moreover, I have myself turned out the room and examined the bed, and not a trace of any drug was to be found. Have you considered the question of sleeping-sickness?"

I looked at the man narrowly before answering, and distrusted him more than ever. Still, my concern was with the patient and his present needs. I was, after all, a doctor, not a detective, and the circumstances called for straightforward speech and action on my part.

"His symptoms are not those of sleeping-sickness," I replied. "They are brain symptoms and are, in my opinion, due to morphia poisoning."

VI – Mr. Morgan's Spectacles

"**B**ut, my dear sir," he exclaimed, "the thing is impossible! Haven't I just told you that he has been watched continuously?"

"I can judge only by the appearances I find," I answered. Then, seeing that he was about to offer fresh objections, I continued, "Don't let us waste precious time in discussion, or your brother may be dead before we have reached a conclusion. If you will get some strong coffee made, I will take the other necessary measures, and perhaps we may manage to pull him round."

The decision of my manner cowed him, besides which he was manifestly alarmed. Replying stiffly that I "must do as I thought best," he hurried from the room, leaving me to carry out my part of the cure. And as soon as he was gone I set to work without further loss of time.

Having injected a full dose of atropin, I took down from the mantelshelf the bottle containing the mixture that I had prescribed – a solution of potassium permanganate. The patient's lethargic condition made me fear that he might be unable to swallow, so that I could not take the risk of pouring the medicine into his mouth for fear of suffocating him. A stomach-tube would have solved the difficulty, but of course I had none with me.

I had, however, a mouth-speculum, which also acted as a gag, and, having propped the patient's mouth open with this, I hastily slipped off one of the rubber tubes from my stethoscope and inserted into one end of it a vulcanite ear-speculum to act as a funnel. Then, introducing the other end of the tube into the gullet, I cautiously poured a small quantity of the medicine into the extemporized funnel.

To my great relief, a movement of the throat showed that the swallowing reflex still existed, and, thus encouraged, I poured down the tube as much of the fluid as I thought it wise to administer at one time.

I had just withdrawn the tube and was looking round for some means of cleansing it when Mr. Morgan returned and, contrary to his usual practise, came close up to the bed. He glanced anxiously from the prostrate figure to the tube that I was holding and then announced that the coffee was being prepared. As he spoke, I was able, for the first time, to look him fairly in the face by the light of the candle.

Now it is a curious fact – though one that most persons must have observed – that there sometimes occurs a considerable interval between the reception of a visual impression and its transfer to the consciousness. A thing may be seen, as it were, unconsciously, and the impression consigned, apparently, to instant oblivion, and yet the picture may be subsequently revived by memory with such completeness that its details can be studied as though the object were still actually visible. Something of that kind must have happened to me now, for, preoccupied as I was by the condition of the patient, the professional habit of rapid and close observation caused me to direct a searching glance at the man before me. It was only a brief glance, for Mr. Morgan, perhaps embarrassed by my intent regard of him, almost immediately withdrew into the shadow, but it revealed two facts of which I took no conscious note at the time, but which came back to me later and gave me much food for speculation.

One fact thus observed was that Mr. Morgan's eyes were of a bluish-gray, like those of his brother, and were surmounted by light-coloured eyebrows, entirely incongruous with his black hair and beard.

But the second fact was much more curious. As he stood, with his head slightly turned, I was able to look through one glass of his spectacles at the wall beyond. On the wall was a framed print, and the edge of the frame, seen through the spectacle-glass, appeared unaltered and free from distortion, as though seen through plain window-glass – and yet the reflections of the candle-flame in the spectacles showed the flame inverted, clearly proving that the glasses were concave on one surface at least.

These two apparently irreconcilable appearances, when I subsequently recalled them, puzzled me completely, and it was not until sometime afterward that the explanation of the mystery came to me.

For the moment, however, the sick man occupied my attention to the exclusion of all else. As the atropin took effect he became somewhat less lethargic, for when I spoke loudly in his ear and shook him gently by the arm he opened his eyes and looked dreamily into my face. But the instant he was left undisturbed, he relapsed into his former condition. Presently the housekeeper arrived with a jug of strong black coffee, which I proceeded to administer in spoonfuls, giving the patient a vigorous shake-up between whiles and talking loudly into his ear.

Under this treatment he revived considerably and began to mumble and mutter in reply to my questions, at which point Mr. Morgan suggested that he should continue the treatment while I wrote a prescription.

"It seems as if you were right, after all, Doctor," he conceded, as he took his place by the bedside, "but it is a complete mystery to me. I shall have to watch him more closely than ever, that is evident."

His relief at the improvement of his brother's condition was most manifest and, as the invalid continued to revive apace, I thought it now safe to take my departure.

"I am sorry to have kept you so long," he said, "but I think the patient will be all right now. If you will take charge of him for a moment, I will go and call the coachman. And perhaps, as it is getting late, you could make up the prescription yourself and send the medicine back with the carriage."

To this request I assented and, as he left the room, I renewed my assaults upon the unresisting invalid.

In about five minutes, the housekeeper made her appearance to tell me that the carriage was waiting and that she would stay with the patient until the master returned.

"If you take my candle, you will be able to find your way down, sir," she said.

To this I agreed and took my departure, candle in hand, leaving her shaking the patient's hand with pantomimic cordiality and squalling into his ear shrill exhortations to "wake up and pull himself together."

As soon as I was shut in the carriage, I lighted my lamp and drew forth the little board and note-book, but the notes that I jotted down on the return journey were must less complete than before, for the horse, excelling his previous performances, rattled along at a pace that rendered writing almost impossible, and indeed more than once he broke into a gallop.

The incidents of that evening made me resolve to seek the advice of Thorndyke on the morrow and place the note-book in his hands, if the thing could possibly be done, and with this comforting resolution I went to bed. But the best-laid schemes o' mice and men Gang aft a-gley, and my schemes, in this respect, went "a-gley" with a vengeance. In the course of the following morning a veritable avalanche of urgent messages descended on the surgery, piling up a visiting-list at which I stood aghast.

Later on, it appeared that a strike in the building trade had been followed immediately by a general failure of health on the part of the bricklayers who were members of the benefit clubs, accompanied by symptoms of the most alarming and unclassical character, ranging from "sciatica of the blade-bones", which consigned one horny-handed sufferer to an arm-chair by the kitchen fire, to "windy spavins", which reduced another to a like piteous plight. Moreover, the sufferings of these unfortunates were viewed with callous skepticism by their fellow members (not in the building trade) who called aloud for detailed reports from the medical officer.

And, as if this were not enough, a local milkman, having secretly indulged in an attack of scarlatina, proceeded to shed microbes into the milk-cans, with the result that a brisk epidemic swept over the neighborhood.

From these causes I was kept hard at work from early morning to late at night, with never an interval for repose or reflection. Not only was I unable to call upon Thorndyke, but the incessant round of visits, consultations, and reports kept my mind so preoccupied that the affairs of my mysterious patient almost faded from my recollection. Now and again, indeed, I would give a passing thought to the silent figure in the dingy house, and, as the days passed and the carriage came no more, I would wonder whether I ought not to communicate my deepening suspicions to the police. But, as I have said, my time was spent in an unceasing rush of work and the matter was allowed to lapse.

VII – Jeffrey Blackmore's Will

The hurry and turmoil continued without abatement during the three weeks that remained before my employer was due to return. Long harassing days spent in tramping the dingy streets of Kennington, or scrambling up and down narrow stairways, alternated with nights made hideous by the intolerable jangle of the night-bell, until I was worn out with fatigue. Nor was the labor made more grateful by the incessant rebuffs that fall to the lot of the "substitute," or by the reflection that for all this additional toil and anxiety I should reap not a farthing of profit.

As I trudged through the dreary thoroughfares of this superannuated suburb with its once rustic villas and its faded gardens, my thoughts would turn enviously to the chambers in King's Bench Walk and I would once again register a vow that this should be my last term of servitude.

From all of which it will be readily understood that when one morning there appeared opposite our house a four-wheeled cab laden with trunks and portmanteaux I hurried out with uncommon cordiality to greet my returning principal. He was not likely to grumble at the length of the visiting-list, for he was, as he once told me, a glutton for work, and a full day-book makes a full ledger. And, in fact, when he ran his eye down the crowded pages of my list he chuckled aloud and expressed himself as more than eager to get to work at once.

In this I was so far from thwarting him that by two o'clock I had fairly closed my connection with the practise, and half-an-hour later found myself strolling across Waterloo Bridge with the sensations of a newly-liberated convict and a check for twenty-five guineas in my pocket. My objective was the Temple, for I was now eager to hear more of Thorndyke's proposal, and wished, also, to consult him as to where in his neighborhood I might find lodgings in which I could put up for a few days.

The "oak" of my friend's chambers stood open and when I plied the knocker the inner door was opened by Polton.

"Why, it's Dr. Jervis," said he, peering up at me in his quick birdlike manner. "The Doctor is out just now, but I am sure he wouldn't like to miss you. Will you come in and wait? He will be in very shortly."

I entered and found two strangers seated by the fire, one an elderly professional-looking man – a lawyer as I guessed. The other a man of about twenty-five, fresh-faced, sunburnt, and decidedly prepossessing in appearance. As I entered, the latter rose and made a place for me by the fire, for the day was chilly, though it was late spring.

"You are one of Thorndyke's colleagues, I gather," said the elder man after we had exchanged a few remarks on the weather. "Since I have known him I have acquired a new interest in and respect for doctors. He is a most remarkable man, sir, a positive encyclopedia of out-of-the-way and unexpected knowledge."

"His acquirements certainly cover a very wide area," I agreed.

"Yes, and the way in which he brings his knowledge to bear on intricate cases is perfectly astonishing," my new acquaintance continued. "I seldom abandon an obscure case or let it go into court until I have taken his opinion. An ordinary counsel looks at things from the same point of view as I do myself and has the same kind of knowledge, if rather more of it, but Thorndyke views things from a radically different standpoint and brings a new and totally different kind of knowledge into the case. He is a lawyer and a scientific specialist in one, and the combination of the two types of culture in one mind, let me tell you emphatically, is an altogether different thing from the same two types in separate minds."

"I can well believe that," I said, and was about to illustrate my opinion when a key was heard in the latch and the subject of our discourse entered the room.

"Why, Jervis!" he exclaimed cheerily. "I thought you had given me the slip again. Where have you been?"

"Up to my eyes in work," I replied. "But I am free – my engagement is finished."

"Good!" said he. "And how are you, Mr. Marchmont?"

"Well, not so young as I was at your age," answered the solicitor with a smile. "I have brought a client of mine to see you," he continued. "Mr. Stephen Blackmore."

Thorndyke shook hands with the younger man and hoped that he might be of service to him.

"Shall 1 take a walk and look in a little later?" I suggested.

"Oh, no," answered Thorndyke. "We can talk over our business in the office."

"For my part," said Mr. Blackmore, "I see no necessity for Dr. Jervis to go away. We have nothing to tell that is not public property."

"If Mr. Marchmont agrees to that," said Thorndyke, "I shall have the advantage of being able to consult with my colleague if necessary."

"I leave the matter in your hands, Doctor," said the solicitor. "Your friend is no doubt used to keeping his own counsel."

"He is used to keeping mine, as a matter of fact," replied Thorndyke. "He was with me in the Hornby case, you may remember, Marchmont, and a most trusty colleague I found him. So, with your permission, we will consider your case with the aid of a cup of tea." He pressed an electric bell three times, in response to which signal Polton presently appeared with a teapot and, having set out the tea-service with great precision and gravity, retired silently to his lair on the floor above.

"Now," said Mr. Marchmont, "let me explain at the outset that ours is a forlorn hope. We have no expectations whatever."

"Blessed are they who expect nothing," murmured Thorndyke.

"Quite so – by the way, what delicious tea you brew in these chambers! Well, as to our little affair. Legally speaking, we have no case – not the ghost of one. Yet I have advised my client to take your opinion on the matter, on the chance that you may perceive some point that we have overlooked. The circumstances, briefly stated, are these: My client, who is an orphan, had two uncles, John Blackmore, and Jeffrey, his younger brother. Some two years ago – to be exact, on the twenty-third of July, 1898 – Jeffrey executed a will by which he made my client his executor and sole legatee. He had a pension from the Foreign Office, on which he lived, and he possessed personal property to the extent of about two thousand pounds.

"Early last year he left the rooms in Jermyn Street, where he had lived for some years, stored his furniture and went to Nice, where he remained until November. In that month, it appears, he returned to England and at once took chambers in New Inn, which he furnished with some of the things from his old rooms. He never communicated with any of his friends, so that the fact of his being in residence at the Inn only became known to them when he died.

"This was all very strange and different from his customary conduct, as was also the fact that he seems to have had no one to cook for him or look after his rooms.

"About a fortnight ago he was found dead in his chambers, under slightly peculiar circumstances, and a more recent will was then discovered, dated the ninth of December, 1899. Now no change had taken place in the circumstances of the testator to account for the new will, nor was there any material change in the disposition of the property. The entire personality, with the exception of fifty pounds, was bequeathed to my client, but the separate items were specified, and the testator's brother, John Blackmore, was named as the executor and residuary legatee."

"I see," said Thorndyke. "So that your client's interest in the will would appear to be practically unaffected by the change."

"There it is!" exclaimed the solicitor, slapping the table to add emphasis to his words. "Apparently his interest is unaffected, but actually the change in the form of the will affects him in the most vital manner."

"Indeed!"

"Yes. I have said that no change had taken place in the testator's circumstances at the time the new will was executed. But only two days before his death, his sister, Mrs. Edmund Wilson, died and, on her will being proved, it appears that she had bequeathed to him her entire personality, estimated at nearly thirty-thousand pounds." Thorndyke gave a low whistle.

"You see the point," continued Mr. Marchmont. "By the original will this great sum would have accrued to my client, whereas by the second will it goes to the residuary legatee, Mr. John Blackmore, and this, it appears to us, could not have been in accordance with the wishes and intentions of Mr. Jeffrey, who evidently desired his nephew to inherit his property."

"The will is perfectly regular?" inquired Thorndyke.

"Perfectly. Not a flaw in it."

"There seem to be some curious features in the case," said Thorndyke. "Perhaps we had better have a narrative of the whole affair from the beginning."

He fetched from the office a small note-book and a blotting-pad which he laid on his knee as he reseated himself.

"Now let us have the facts in their order," said he.

VIII – Thorndyke Takes Evidence

"Well," said Mr. Marchmont, "we will begin with the death of Mr. Jeffrey Blackmore. It seems that about eleven o'clock in the morning of the twenty-seventh of March, that is, about a fortnight ago, a builder's man was ascending a ladder to examine a gutter on one of the houses in New Inn when, on passing a window that was open at the top, he looked in and perceived a gentleman lying on the bed. The gentleman was fully dressed and had apparently lain down to rest, but, looking again, the workman was struck by the remarkable pallor of the face and by the entire absence of movement. On coming down, he reported the matter to the porter at the lodge.

"Now the porter had already that morning knocked at Mr. Blackmore's door to hand him the receipt for the rent and, receiving no answer, had concluded that the tenant was absent. When he received the workman's report, therefore, he went to the door of the chambers, which were on the second floor, and knocked loudly and repeatedly, but there was still no answer.

"Considering the circumstances highly suspicious, he sent for a constable, and when the latter arrived the workman was directed to enter the chambers by the window and open the door from the inside. This was done, and the porter and the constable, going into the bedroom, found Mr. Blackmore lying upon the bed, dressed in his ordinary clothes, and quite dead."

"How long had he been dead?" asked Thorndyke.

"Less than twenty-four hours, for the porter saw him on the previous day. He came to the Inn about half-past six in a four-wheeled cab."

"Was any one with him?"

"That the porter cannot say. The glass window of the cab was drawn up and he saw Mr. Blackmore's face through it only by the light of the lamp outside the lodge as the cab passed through the archway. There was a dense fog at the time – you may remember that very foggy day about a fortnight ago?"

"I do," replied Thorndyke. "Was that the last time the porter saw Mr. Blackmore?"

"No. The deceased came to the lodge at eight o'clock and paid the rent."

"By a check?" asked Thorndyke.

"Yes, a crossed check. That was the last time the porter saw him."

"You said, I think, that the circumstances of his death were suspicious."

"No, I said 'peculiar', not 'suspicious'. It was a clear case of suicide. The constable reported to his inspector, who came to the chambers at once and brought the divisional surgeon with him. On examining the body they found a hypodermic syringe grasped in the right hand, and at the post-mortem a puncture was found in the right thigh. The needle had evidently entered vertically and deeply instead of being merely passed through the skin, which was explained by the fact that it had been driven in through the clothing.

"The syringe contained a few drops of a concentrated solution of strophanthin, and there were found on the dressing-table two empty tubes labeled '*Hypodermic Tabloids, Strophanthin 1-500 grain*', and a tiny glass mortar-and-pestle containing crystals of strophanthin. It was concluded that the entire contents of both tubes, each of which was proved to have contained twenty tabloids, had been dissolved to charge the syringe. The postmortem showed, naturally, that death was due to poisoning by strophanthin.

"It was also proved that the deceased had been in the habit of taking morphia, which was confirmed by the finding in the chamber of a large bottle half-full of morphia pills, each containing half-a-grain."

"The verdict was suicide, of course?" said Thorndyke.

"Yes. The theory of the doctors was that the deceased had taken morphia habitually and that, in a fit of depression caused by reaction from the drug, he had taken his life by means of the more rapidly acting poison."

"A very reasonable explanation," agreed Thorndyke. "And now to return to the will. Had your Uncle Jeffrey any expectations from his sister, Mr. Blackmore?"

"I can't say with certainty," replied Blackmore. "I knew very little of my aunt's affairs, and I don't think my uncle knew much more, for he was under the impression that she had only a life interest in her late husband's property."

"Did she die suddenly?" asked Thorndyke.

"No," replied Blackmore. "She died of cancer."

Thorndyke made an entry on his note-book and, turning to the solicitor, said, "The will, you say, is perfectly regular. Has the signature been examined by an expert?"

"As a matter of form," replied Mr. Marchmont, "I got the head cashier of the deceased's bank to step round and compare the signatures of the two wills. There were, in fact, certain trifling differences, but these are probably to be explained by the drug habit, especially as a similar change was to be observed in the checks that have been paid in during the last few

473

months. In any case the matter is of no moment, owing to the circumstances under which the will was executed."

"Which were – ?"

"That on the morning of the ninth of December Mr. Jeffrey Blackmore came into the lodge and asked the porter and his son, a house-painter, who happened to be in the lodge at the time to witness his signature. 'This is my will,' said he, producing the document, 'and perhaps you had better glance through it, though that is not necessary.' The porter and his son accordingly read through the will and then witnessed the signature and so were able to swear to the document at the inquest."

"Ah, then that disposes of the will," said Thorndyke, "even of the question of undue influence. Now, as to your Uncle Jeffrey, Mr. Blackmore. What kind of man was he?"

"A quiet, studious, gentle-mannered man," answered Blackmore, "Very nervous, about fifty-five years of age, and not very robust. He was of medium height – about five-feet-seven – fair, slightly gray, clean-shaven, rather spare, had gray eyes, wore spectacles and stooped slightly as he walked."

"And is now deceased," added Mr. Marchmont dryly, as Thorndyke noted down these apparently irrelevant particulars.

"How came he to be a civil-service pensioner at fifty-five?" asked Thorndyke.

"He had a bad fall from a horse, which left him, for a time, a complete wreck. Moreover, his eyesight, which was never very good, became much worse. In fact, he practically lost the sight of one eye altogether – it was the right one, I think – and as this had been his good eye, he felt the loss very much."

"You mentioned that he was a studious man. Of what nature were the subjects that occupied him?"

"He was an Oriental scholar of some position, I believe. He had been attached to the legations at Bagdad and Tokyo and had given a good deal of attention to Oriental languages and literature. He was also much interested in Babylonian and Assyrian archeology and assisted, for a time, in the excavations at Birs Nimroud."

"I see," said Thorndyke. "A man of considerable attainments. And now as to your Uncle John?"

"I can't tell you much about him," answered Blackmore. "Until I saw him at the inquest, I had not met him since I was a boy, but he is as great a contrast to Uncle Jeffrey in character as in appearance."

"The two brothers were very unlike in exterior, then?"

"Well, perhaps I am exaggerating the difference. They were of much the same height, though John was a shade taller, and their features were, I

474

suppose, not unlike, and their coloring was similar. But, you see, John is a healthy man with good eyesight and a brisk, upright carriage and he wears a large beard and mustache. He is rather stout, too, as I noticed when I met him at the inquest. As to his character, I am afraid he has not been a great credit to his family. He started in life as a manufacturing chemist, but of late years he has been connected with what they call, I think, a bucket-shop, though he describes himself as a stockbroker."

"I see – an outside broker. Was he on good terms with his brother?"

"Not very, I think. At any rate, they saw very little of each other."

"And what were his relations with your aunt?"

"Not friendly at all. I think Uncle John had done something shady – let Mr. Wilson in, in some way, over a bogus investment – but I don't know the details."

"Would you like a description of the lady, Thorndyke?" asked Mr. Marchmont with genial sarcasm.

"Not just now, thanks," answered Thorndyke with a quiet smile, "but I will note down her full name."

"Julia Elizabeth Wilson."

"Thank you. There is just one more point. What were your uncle's habits and manner of life at New Inn?"

"According to the porter's evidence at the inquest," said Mr. Blackmore, "he lived in a very secluded manner. He had no one to look after his rooms, but did everything for himself, and no one is known to have visited the chambers. He was seldom seen about the Inn, and the porter thinks that he must have spent most of his time indoors or else he must have been away a good deal – he cannot say which."

"By the way, what has happened to the chambers since your uncle's death?"

"I understand that the porter has been instructed by the executor to let them."

"Thank you, Mr. Blackmore. I think that is all I have to ask at present. If anything fresh occurs to me, I will communicate with you through Mr. Marchmont."

The two men rose and prepared to depart.

"I am afraid there is little to hope for," said the solicitor as he shook my friend's hand, "but I thought it worthwhile to give you a chance of working a miracle."

"You would like to set aside the second will, of course?" said Thorndyke.

"Naturally – and a more unlikely case I never met with."

"It is not promising, I must admit. However, I will digest the material and let you have my views after due reflection."

475

The lawyer and his client took their departure, and Thorndyke, with a thoughtful and abstracted air, separated the written sheets from his note-book, made two perforations in the margins by means of a punch, and inserted them into a small Stolzenburg file, on the outside of which he wrote, "*Jeffrey Blackmore's Will*".

"There," said he, depositing the little folio in a drawer labeled "*B*" – "there is the nucleus of the body of data on which our investigations must be based – and I am afraid it will not receive any great additions, though there are some very singular features in the case, as you doubtless observed."

"I observed that the will seemed as simple and secure as a will could be made," I answered, "and I should suppose the setting of it aside to be a wild impossibility."

"Perhaps you are right," rejoined Thorndyke, "but time will show. Meanwhile I understand that you are a gentleman at large now. What are your plans?"

"My immediate purpose is to find lodgings for a week or so, and I came to you for guidance as to their selection."

"You had better let me put you up for the night, at any rate. Your old bedroom is at your service and you can pursue your quest in the morning, if you wish to. Give me a note and I will send Polton with it to bring up your things in a cab."

"It is exceedingly good of you, Thorndyke, but I hardly like – "

"Now don't raise obstacles, my dear fellow," urged Thorndyke. "Say yes, and let us have a long chat to-night over old times."

I was glad enough to be persuaded to so pleasant an arrangement, so I wrote a few lines on one of my cards, which was forthwith dispatched by the faithful Polton.

IX – The Cuneiform Inscription

"**W**e have an hour-and-a-half to dispose of before dinner," said Thorndyke, looking at his watch. "What say you, my dear Jervis – shall we wander over the breezy uplands of Fleet Street or shall we seek the leafy shades of New Inn? I incline to New Inn, if that sylvan retreat commends itself to you."

"Very well," said I, "let it be New Inn. I suppose you want to nose around the scene of the tragedy, though what you expect to find is a mystery to me."

"A man of science," replied Thorndyke, "expects nothing. He collects facts and keeps an open mind. As for me, I am a mere legal snapper-up of unconsidered trifles of evidence. When I have accumulated a few facts, I arrange them and reason from them. It is a capital error to decide beforehand what data are to be sought for."

"But surely," said I, as we emerged from the doorway and turned up toward Mitre Court, "you cannot see any possible grounds for disputing that will?"

"I don't," he answered, "or I should have said so. But I am engaged to look into the case and I shall do so, as I said just now, with an open mind. Moreover, the circumstances of the case are so singular, so full of strange coincidences and improbabilities, that they call for the closest and most searching examination."

"I hadn't observed anything so very abnormal in the case," I said. "Of course, I can see that the second will was unnecessary – that a codicil would have answered all purposes – that, as things have turned out, it does not seem to carry out the wishes of the testator. But then, if he had lived, Jeffrey Blackmore would probably have made a new will."

"Which would not have suited Brother John. But have you considered the significance of the order in which the events occurred and the strange coincidences in the dates?'

"I am afraid I missed that point," I replied. "How do the dates run?"

"The second will," replied Thorndyke, "was made on the ninth of December 1899. Mrs. Wilson died of cancer on the twenty-fourth of March, 1900. Jeffrey Blackmore was seen alive on the twenty-sixth of March, thus establishing the fact that he survived Mrs. Wilson, and his body was found on the twenty-seventh of March. Does that group of dates suggest nothing to you?"

I reflected for a while and then had to confess that it suggested nothing at all.

"Then make a note of it and consider it at your leisure," said Thorndyke, "or I will write out the dates for you later, for here we are at our destination."

It was a chilly day, and a cold wind blew through the archway leading into New Inn. Halting at the half-door of the lodge, we perceived a stout, purple-faced man crouching over the fire, coughing violently. He held up his hand to intimate that he was fully occupied for the moment, so we waited for his paroxysm to subside.

"Dear, dear!" exclaimed Thorndyke sympathetically, "you ought not to be sitting in this drafty lodge with your delicate chest. You should make them fit a glass door with a pigeonhole."

"Bless you," said the porter, wiping his eyes, "I daren't make any complaints. There's plenty of younger men ready to take the job. But it's terrible work for me in the winter, especially when the fogs are about."

"It must be," rejoined Thorndyke, and then, rather to my surprise, he proceeded to inquire with deep interest into the sufferer's symptoms and the history of the attack, receiving in reply a wealth of detail and discursive reminiscence delivered with the utmost gusto. To all of this I listened a little impatiently, for chronic bronchitis is not, medically speaking, an entertaining complaint, and consultations out of business hours are an abomination to doctors. Something of this perhaps appeared in my manner, for the man broke off suddenly with an apology.

"But I mustn't detain you gentlemen talking about my health. It can't interest you, though it's serious enough for me."

"I am sure it is," said Thorndyke, "and I hope we may be able to do something for you. I am a medical man and so is my friend. We came to ask if you had any chambers to let."

"Yes, we've got three sets empty."

"Not furnished, I suppose?"

"Yes, one set is furnished. It is the one," he added, lowering his voice, "that the gentleman committed suicide in – but you wouldn't mind that, being a doctor?"

"Oh, no," laughed Thorndyke. "The disease is not catching. What is the rent?"

"Twenty-three pounds, but the furniture would have to be taken at a valuation. There isn't much of it."

"May I see the rooms?"

"Certainly. Here's the key. I've only just had it back from the police. There's no need for me to come with gentlemen like you. It's such a drag up all those stairs. The gas hasn't been cut off because the tenancy has not expired. It's Number 31, second floor."

478

We made our way across the Inn to the doorway of Number 31, the ground floor of which was occupied by solicitors' offices. The dusk was just closing in and a man was lighting a lamp on the first-floor landing as we came up the stairs.

"Who occupies the chambers on the third floor?" Thorndyke asked him as we turned on to the next flight.

"The third floor has been empty for about three months," was the reply.

"We are looking at the chambers on the second floor," said Thorndyke. "Are they pretty quiet?"

"Quiet!" exclaimed the man. "Lord bless you! The place is like a deaf-and-dumb cemetery. There's the solicitors on the ground floor and the architects on the first floor. They both clear out at about six, and then the 'ouse is as empty as a blown hegg. I don't wonder poor Mr. Blackmore made away with hisself, he must 'ave found it awful dull."

"So," said Thorndyke, as the man's footsteps echoed down the stairs, "when Jeffrey Blackmore came home that last evening the house was empty."

He inserted the key into the door, above which was painted in white letters the deceased man's name, and we entered, my companion striking a wax vesta and lighting the gas in the sitting-room. "Spare and simple," remarked Thorndyke, looking round critically, "but well enough for a solitary bachelor. A cupboard of a kitchen – never used, apparently – and a small bedroom opening out of the sitting-room. Why, the bed hasn't been made since the catastrophe! There is the impression of the body! Rather gruesome for a new tenant, eh?"

He wandered round the sitting-room, looking at the various objects it contained as though he would question them as to what they had witnessed. The apartment was bare and rather comfortless, and its appointments were all old and worn. A small glass-fronted bookcase held a number of solid-looking volumes – proceedings of the Asiatic Society and works on Oriental literature for the most part – and a half-dozen framed photographs of buildings and objects of archeological interest formed the only attempts at wall decoration.

Before one of these latter Thorndyke halted and, having regarded it for a few moments with close attention, uttered an exclamation. "Here is a very strange thing, Jervis," said he.

I stepped across the room and looked over his shoulder at an oblong frame enclosing a photograph of an inscription in the weird and cabalistic arrow-head character.

"Yes," I agreed, "the cuneiform writing is surely the most uncanny-looking script that was ever invented. I wonder if poor Blackmore was able to read this stuff. I suppose he was, or it wouldn't be here."

"I should say there is no doubt that he was able to read the cuneiform character, and that is just what constitutes the strangeness of this," and Thorndyke pointed, as he spoke, to the framed photograph on the wall.

"I don't follow you at all," I said. "It would seem to me much more odd if a man were to hang upon his wall an inscription that he could not read."

"No doubt," replied Thorndyke. "But you will agree with me that it would be still more odd if a man should hang upon his wall an inscription that he could read – and hang it upside-down!"

"You don't mean to say that this is up side-down!" I exclaimed.

"I do indeed," he replied.

"But how can you tell that? I didn't know that Oriental scholarship was included in your long list of accomplishments."

Thorndyke chuckled. "It isn't," he replied, "but I have read with very keen interest the wonderful history of the decipherment of the cuneiform characters, and I happen to remember one or two of the main facts. This particular inscription is in the Persian cuneiform, a much more simple form of the script than the Babylonian or Assyrian. In fact, I suspect that this is the famous inscription from the gateway at Persepolis – the first to be deciphered, which would account for its presence here in a frame.

"Now this script reads, like our own writing, from left to right, and the rule is that all the wedge-shaped characters point to the right or downward, while the arrow-head forms are open toward the right. But if you examine this inscription you will see that the wedges point upward and to the left, and that the arrow-head characters are open toward the left. Obviously the photograph is upside down."

"But this is really mysterious!" I exclaimed. "What do you suppose can be the explanation? Do you think poor Blackmore's eyesight was failing him, or were his mental faculties decaying?"

"I think," replied Thorndyke, "we may perhaps get a suggestion from the back of the frame. Let us see." He disengaged the frame from the two nails on which it hung and, turning it round, glanced for a moment at the back, which he then presented toward me with a quaint, half-quizzical smile. A label on the backing-paper bore the words: "*J. Budge, Frame-maker and Gilder, Gt. Anne St., W.C.*"

"Well?" I said, when I had read the label without gathering from it anything fresh.

"The label, you observe, is the right way up."

"So it is," I rejoined hastily, a little annoyed that I had not been quicker to observe so obvious a fact. "I see your point. You mean that the frame-maker hung the thing upside-down and Blackmore never noticed the mistake."

"No, I don't think that is the explanation," replied Thorndyke. "You will notice that the label is an old one. It must have been on some years, to judge by its dingy appearance, whereas the two mirror-plates look to me comparatively new. But we can soon put that matter to the test, for the label was evidently stuck on when the frame was new, and if the plates were screwed on at the same time, the wood which they cover will be clean and new-looking." He drew from his pocket a "combination" knife containing, among other implements, a screw-driver, with which he carefully extracted the screws from one of the little brass plates by which the frame had been suspended from the nails.

"You see," he said, when he had removed the plate and carried the photograph over to the gas-jet, "the wood covered by the plate is as dirty and time-stained as the rest of the frame. The plates have been put on recently."

"And what are we to infer from that?"

"Well, since there are no other marks of plates or rings upon the frame, we may safely infer that the photograph was never hung up until it came to these rooms."

"Yes, I suppose we may. But what is the suggestion that this photograph makes to you? I know you have something in mind that bears upon the case you are investigating. What is it?"

"Come, come, Jervis," said Thorndyke, playfully, "I am not going to wet-nurse you in thus fashion! You are a man of ingenuity and far from lacking in the scientific imagination. You must work out the rest of the train of deduction by yourself."

"That is how you always tantalize me!" I complained. "You take out the stopper from your bottle of wisdom and present the mouth to my nose, and then, when I have taken a hearty sniff and gat my appetite fairly whetted, you clap in the stopper again and leave me, metaphorically speaking, with my tongue hanging out."

Thorndyke chuckled as he replaced the little brass plate and inserted the screws.

"You must learn to take out the stopper for yourself," said he. "Then you will be able to slake your divine thirst to your satisfaction. Shall we take a look round the bedroom?"

X – We Rent 31 New Inn

He hung the photograph upon its nails and we passed on to the little chamber, glancing once more at the depression on the narrow bed, which seemed to make the tragedy so real.

"The syringe and the rest of the lethal appliances and material have been removed, I see," remarked Thorndyke. "I suppose the police or the coroner's officers have kept them."

He looked keenly about the bare, comfortless apartment, taking mental notes, apparently, of its general aspect and the few details it presented.

"Jeffrey Blackmore would seem to have been a man of few needs," he observed presently. "I have never seen a bedroom in which less attention seemed to be given to the comfort of the occupant." He pulled at the drawer of the dressing-table, disclosing a solitary hair-brush, peeped into a cupboard, where an overcoat surmounted by a felt hat hung from a peg like an attenuated suicide. He even picked up and examined the cracked and shrunken cake of soap on the washstand, and he was just replacing this in its dish when his attention was apparently attracted by something in the dark corner close by. As he knelt on the floor to make a close scrutiny, I came over and stooped beside him. I found the object of his regard to be a number of tiny fragments of glass, which had the appearance of having been trodden upon and then scattered by a kick of the foot. "What have you found?" I asked.

"That is what I am asking myself," he replied. "As far as I can judge from the appearance of these fragments, they appear to be the remains of a small watch-glass. But we can examine them more thoroughly at our leisure."

He gathered up the little splintered pieces with infinite care and bestowed them in the envelope of a letter which he drew from his pocket.

"And now," he said as he rose and dusted his knees, "we had better go back to the lodge, or the porter will begin to think that there has been another tragedy in New Inn."

We passed out into the sitting-room, where Thorndyke once more halted before the inverted photograph.

"Yes," he said, surveying it thoughtfully, "we have picked up a trifle of fact which may mean nothing, or, on the other hand, may be of critical importance."

He paused for a few moments and then said suddenly, "Jervis, how should you like to be the new tenant of these rooms?"

"It is the one thing necessary for my complete happiness," I replied with a grin.

"I am not joking," said he. "Seriously, these chambers might be very convenient for you, especially in some new circumstances that I, and I hope you also, have in contemplation. But in any case, I should like to examine the premises at my leisure, and I suppose you would not mind appearing as the tenant if I undertake all liabilities?"

"Certainly not," I answered.

"Then let us go down and see what arrangements we can make." He turned out the gas and we made our way back to the lodge.

"What do you think of the rooms, sir?" asked the porter as I handed him back the key.

"I think they would suit me," I replied, "if the furniture could be had on reasonable terms."

"Oh, that will be all right," said the porter. "The executor – deceased's brother – has written to me saying that the things are to be got rid of for what they will fetch, but as quickly as possible. He wants those chambers off his hands, so, as I am his agent, I shall instruct the valuer to price them low."

"Can my friend have immediate possession?" asked Thorndyke.

"You can have possession as soon as the valuer has seen the effects," said the porter. "The man from the broker's shop down Wych Street will look them over for us."

"I would suggest that we fetch him up at once," said Thorndyke. "Then you can pay over the price agreed on and move your things in without delay – that is, if our friend here has no objection."

"Oh, I have no objection," said the porter. 'If you like to pay the purchase-money for the furniture and give me a letter agreeing to take on the tenancy, and a reference, you can have the key at once and sign the regular agreement later."

In a very short time this easy-going arrangement was carried out. The furniture broker was decoyed to the Inn and, having received his instructions from the porter, accompanied us to the vacant chambers.

"Now, gentlemen," said he, looking round disparagingly at the barely furnished rooms, "you tell me what things you are going to take and I will make my estimate."

"We are going to take everything – stock, lock and barrel," said Thorndyke.

"What! Clothes and all?" exclaimed the man, grinning.

"Clothes, hats, boots – everything. We can throw out what we don't want afterward, but my friend wishes to have immediate possession of the rooms."

483

"I understand," said the broker, and without more ado he produced a couple of sheets of foolscap and fell to work on the inventory.

"This gentleman didn't waste much money on clothes," he remarked presently after examining the contents of a cupboard and a chest of drawers. "Why, there's only two suits all told!"

"He doesn't seem to have embarrassed himself with an excessive number of hats or boots either," said Thorndyke. "But I believe he spent most of his time indoors."

"That might account for it," rejoined the broker, and he proceeded to add to his list the meager account of clothing.

The inventory was soon completed and the prices affixed to the items, when it appeared that the value of the entire contents of the rooms amounted to no more than eighteen pounds, twelve shillings. This sum, at Thorndyke's request, I paid to the porter, handing him my recently-acquired check for twenty-five guineas and directing him to drop the change into the letter-box of the chambers.

"That is a good thing done," remarked Thorndyke, as we took our way back toward the Strand. "I will give you a check this evening and you might let me have the key for the present. I will send Polton down with a trunk this evening, to keep up appearances. And now we will go and have some dinner."

"To come back," said Thorndyke, when Polton had set before us our simple meal, with a bottle of sound claret, "to the new arrangement I proposed the other day: You know that Polton gives me a great deal of help in my work, especially by making appliances and photographs and carrying out chemical processes under my directions. But still, clever as he is and wonderfully well-informed, he is not a scientific man, properly speaking, and of course his education and social training do not allow of his taking my place excepting in a quite subordinate capacity. Now there are times when I am greatly pushed for the want of a colleague of my own class, and it occurred to me that you might like to join me as my junior or assistant. We know that we can rub along together in a friendly way, and I know enough of your abilities and accomplishments to feel sure that your help would be of value to me. What do you think of the proposal?"

To exchange the precarious, disagreeable, and uninteresting life of a regular *locum* with its miserable pay and utter lack of future prospects, for the freedom and interest of the life thus held out to me with its chances of advancement and success, was to rise at a bound out of the abyss into which misfortune had plunged me, and to cut myself free from the millstone of poverty which had held me down so long. Moreover, with the salary that Thorndyke offered and the position that I should occupy as

484

junior to a famous expert, I could marry without the need of becoming pecuniarily indebted to my wife – a circumstance which I was sure she would regard with as much satisfaction as I did. Hence I accepted joyfully, much to Thorndyke's gratification, and, the few details of our engagement being settled, we filled our glasses and drank to our joint success.

XI – The Empty House

"By the way, Jervis," said my new principal – or colleague, as he preferred to style himself – when, our dinner over and our chairs drawn up to the fire, we were filling our pipes in preparation for a gossip, "you never told me the end of that odd adventure of yours."

"I went to the house once again," I answered, "and followed your directions to the letter, though how much skill and intelligence I displayed in following them you will be able to judge when you have seen the note-book. It is in my trunk up-stairs with your lamp and compass."

"And what became of the patient?"

"Ah," I replied, "that is what I have often wondered. I don't like to think about it."

"Tell me what happened at the second visit," said Thorndyke.

I gave him a circumstantial description of all that I had seen and all that had happened on that occasion, recalling every detail that I could remember, even to the momentary glimpse I had of Mr. J. Morgan, as he stood in the light of the candle. To all of this my friend listened with rapt attention and asked me so many questions about my first visit that I practically gave him the whole story over again from the beginning.

"It was a fishy business," commented Thorndyke as I concluded, "but of course you could do nothing. You had not enough facts to swear an information on. But it would be interesting to plot the route and see where this extremely cautious gentleman resides. I suggest that we do so forthwith."

To this I assented with enthusiasm and, having fetched the note-book from my room, we soon had it spread before us on the table. Thorndyke ran his eye over the various entries, noting the details with an approving smile.

"You seem to the manner born, Jervis," said he with a chuckle, as he came to the end of the first route. "That is quite an artistic touch – '*Passenger station to left*'. How did you know there was a station?"

"I heard the guard's whistle and the starting of a train – evidently a long and heavy one, for the engine skidded badly."

"Good!" said Thorndyke. "Have you looked these notes over?"

"No," I answered. "I put the book away when I came in and have never looked at it since."

"It is a quaint document. You seem to be rich in railway bridges in those parts, and the route was certainly none of the most direct. However, we will plot it out and see whither it leads us."

He retired to the laboratory and presently returned with a T-square, a military protractor, a pair of dividers, and a large drawing-board, upon which was pinned a sheet of paper.

"I see," said he, "that the horse kept up a remarkably even pace, so we can take the time as representing distance. Let us say that one inch equals one minute – that will give us a fair scale. Now you read out the notes and I will plot the route."

I read out the entries from the note-book – a specimen page of which I present for the reader's inspection – and Thorndyke laid off the lines of direction with the protractor, taking out the distance with the dividers from a scale of equal parts on the back of the instrument.

9:05	S.W.	Start from house. Horse 13 hands
9:05:30	S.E. by E.	Macadam. Hoofs 110
9:06	N.E. by N.	Granite
9:06:25	S.E.	Macadam
9:07:20	N.	Macadam
9:08	N.E.	Under bridge. Hoofs 120
9:08:30	N.E.	Cross granite road. Tram-lines
9:09:35	N. N.W.	Still macadam. Hoofs 120
9:10:30	W. by S.	Still macadam. Hoofs 120
9:11:30	W. by S.	Cross granite road. Tram-lines. Then under bridge
9:12	S.S.E.	Macadam
9:12:15	E.N.E.	Macadam
9:12:30	E.N.E.	Under bridge. Hoofs 116
9:12:45	S.S.E.	Granite road. Tram-lines
9:14	E.N.E.	Macadam

As the work proceeded, a smile of quiet amazement spread over his keen, attentive face, and at each new reference to a railway bridge he chuckled softly.

"What! Again?" he laughed, as I recorded the passage of the eighth bridge. "Why, it's like a game of croquet! Ah, here we are at last! '9:38 – Slow down. Enter arched gateway to left. Stop. Wooden gates closed.' Just look at your route, Jervis."

He held up the board with a quizzical smile, when I perceived with astonishment that the middle of the paper was occupied by a single line that zigzagged, crossed and recrossed in the most intricate manner, and terminated at no great distance from its commencement.

"Now," said Thorndyke, "let us get the map and see if we can give to each of these marvelous and erratic lines 'a local habitation and a name'. You started from Lower Kennington Lane, I think?"

"Yes, from this point," indicating the spot with a pencil.

"Then," said Thorndyke, after a careful comparison of the map with the plotted route, "I think we may take it that your gateway was on the north side of Upper Kennington Lane, some three hundred yards from Vauxhall Station. The heavy train that you heard starting was no doubt one of the Southwestern expresses. You see that, rough as was the method of tracing the route, it is quite enough to enable us to identify all the places on the map. The tram-lines and railway bridges are invaluable."

He wrote by the side of the strange crooked lines the names of the streets that its different parts represented and, on comparing the amended sketch with the ordnance map, I saw that the correspondence was near enough to preclude all doubt.

"Tomorrow morning," observed Thorndyke, "I shall have an hour or two to spare, and I propose that we take a stroll through Upper Kennington Lane and gaze upon this abode of mystery. This chart has fairly aroused the trailing instinct – although, of course, the affair is no business of mine."

The following morning, after an early breakfast, we pocketed the chart and the note-book and, issuing forth into the Strand, chartered a passing hansom to convey us to Vauxhall Station.

"There should be no difficulty in locating the house," remarked Thorndyke presently, as we bowled along the Albert Embankment. "It is evidently about three-hundred yards from the station, and I see you have noted a patch of newly laid macadam about halfway."

"That new macadam will be pretty well smoothed down by now," I objected.

"Not so very completely," answered Thorndyke. "It is only three weeks, and there has been no wet weather lately."

A few minutes later the cab drew up at the station and, having alighted and paid the driver, we made our way to the bridge that spans the junction of Harleyfard Road and Upper Kennington Lane.

"From here to the house," said Thorndyke, "is three-hundred yards – say four-hundred-and-twenty-paces, and at about two-hundred paces we ought to pass a patch of new road-meld. Now, are you ready? If we keep step we shall average our stride."

We started together at a good pace, stepping out with military regularity, and counting aloud as we went. As we told out the hundred-and-ninety-fourth pace, I observed Thorndyke nod toward the roadway a little ahead and, looking at it attentively as we approached, it was easy to

488

see, by the regularity of the surface and lighter color, that it had recently been remetaled.

Having counted out the four-hundred-and-twenty paces, we halted, and Thorndyke turned to me with a smile of triumph.

"Not a bad estimate, Jervis," said he. "That will be your house if I am not much mistaken." He pointed to a narrow turning a dozen yards ahead, apparently the entrance to a yard and closed by a pair of massive wooden gates.

"Yes," I answered, "there is no doubt that this is the place. But, by Jove!" I added, as we drew nearer. "The nest is empty. Do you see?" I pointed to a small bill that was stuck on the gate announcing, *"These premises, including stabling and workshops, to be let"*, and giving the name and address of an auctioneer in Upper Kennington Lane as the agent.

"Here is a new and startling development," said Thorndyke, "which leads one to wonder still more what has happened to your patient. Now the question is, should we make a few inquiries of the auctioneer, or should we get the keys and have a look at the inside of the house? I think we will do both, and the latter first, if Messrs Ryman Brothers will trust us with the keys."

We made our way to the auctioneer's office, and were, without demur, given permission to inspect the premises.

"You will find the place in a very dirty and neglected condition," said the clerk, as he handed us a couple of keys with a wooden label attached. "The house has not been cleaned yet, but is just as it was left when we took out the furniture."

"Was Mr. Morgan sold up then?" inquired Thorndyke.

"Oh, no. But he had to leave rather unexpectedly, and he asked us to dispose of his effects for him."

"He had not been in the house very long, had he?"

"No. Less than six months, I should say."

"Do you know where he has moved to?"

"I don't. He said he should be travelling for a time and he paid us a half-year's rent in advance to be quit. The larger key is that of the wicket in the front gate."

Thorndyke took the keys and we returned together to the house which, with its closed window-shutters, had a very gloomy and desolate aspect. We let ourselves in at the wicket, when I perceived, half-way down the entry, the side door at which I had been admitted by the unknown woman.

"We will look at the bedroom first," said Thorndyke, as we stood in the dark and musty-smelling hall. "That is, if you can remember which room it was."

"It was on the first floor," said I, "and the door was just at the head of the stairs." We ascended the two flights and as we reached the landing I halted. "This was the door," I said, and was about to turn the handle when Thorndyke caught me by the arm.

"One moment, Jervis," said he. "What do you make of this?" He pointed to four screw-holes, neatly filled with putty, near the bottom of the door, and two others on the jamb opposite them.

"Evidently," I answered, "there has been a bolt there, though it seems a queer place to fix one."

"Not at all," rejoined Thorndyke. "If you look up you will see that there was another at the top of the door and, as the lock is in the middle, they must have been highly effective. But there are one or two other things that strike one. First, you will notice that the bolts have been fixed on pretty recently, for the paint that they covered is of the same grimy tint as that on the rest of the door. Next, they have been taken off, which, seeing that they could hardly have been worth the trouble of removal, seems to suggest that the person who fixed them considered that their presence might appear remarkable, while the screw-holes would be less conspicuous.

"They are on the outside of the door – an unusual situation for bolts – and if you look closely you can see a slight indentation in the wood of the jamb, made by the sharp edges of the socket-plate, as though at some time a forcible attempt has been made to drag the door open when it was bolted."

"There was a second door, I remember," said I. "Let us see if that was guarded in a similar manner."

We strode through the empty room, awakening dismal echoes as we trod the bar boards, and flung open the other door. At top and bottom, similar groups of screw-holes showed that this also had been made secure, the bolts in all cases being of a very substantial size.

"I am afraid these fastenings have a very sinister significance," said Thorndyke gravely, "for I suppose we can have no doubt as to their object or by whom they were fixed."

"No, I suppose not," I answered, "but if the man was really imprisoned, could he not have smashed the window and called for help?"

"The window looks out on the yard, as you see. And I expect it was secured, too."

He drew the massive old-fashioned shutters out of their recess and closed them.

"Yes, here we are!" He pointed to four groups of screw holes at the corners of the shutters and, lighting a match, narrowly examined the insides of the recesses into which the shutters folded.

"The nature of the fastening is quite evident," said he. "An iron bar passed right across at the top and bottom and was secured by a staple and padlock. You can see the mark the bar made in the recess when the shutters were folded. By heaven, Jervis!" he exclaimed as he flung the shutters open again. "This was a diabolical affair, and I would give a good round sum to lay my hand on Mr. J. Morgan!"

XII – In a Little Heap of Rubbish

"It is a thousand pities we were unable to look round before they moved out the furniture," I remarked. "We might then have found some clue to the scoundrel's identity."

"Yes," replied Thorndyke, gazing round ruefully at the bare walls, "there isn't much information to be gathered here, I am afraid. I see they have swept up the litter under the grate. We may as well turn it over, though it is not likely that we shall find anything of much interest."

He raked out the little heap of rubbish with the crook of his stick and spread it out on the hearth. It certainly looked unpromising enough, being just such a rubbish-heap as may be swept up in any untidy room during a move. But Thorndyke went through it systematically, examining each item attentively, even to the local tradesmen's bills and empty paper bags, before laying them aside. One of the latter he folded up neatly and laid on the mantel-shelf before resuming his investigations.

"Here is something that may give us a hint," said he presently. He held up a battered pair of spectacles of which only one hooked side-bar remained, while both the glasses were badly cracked.

"Left eye a concave cylindrical lens," he continued, peering through the glasses at the window "Right eye plain glass – these must have belonged to your patient, Jervis. You said the tremulous iris was in the right eye, I think?"

"Yes," I replied, "these are his spectacles, no doubt."

"The frames, you notice, are peculiar," he continued. "The shape was invented by Stopford of Moorfields and is made, I believe, by only one optician – Cuxton and Parry of New Bond Street."

"What should you say that is?" I asked, picking up a small object from the rubbish. It was a tiny stick of bamboo furnished with a sheath formed of a shorter length of the same material, which fitted it closely, yet slid easily up and down the little cane.

"Ha!" exclaimed Thorndyke, taking the object eagerly from my hand. "This is really interesting. Have you never seen one of these before? It is a Japanese pocket brush or pencil, and very beautiful little instruments they are, with the most exquisitely delicate and flexible points. They are used principally for writing or drawing with Chinese or, as it is usually called, Indian ink. The bamboo in this one is cracked at the end and the hair has fallen out, but the sliding sheath, which protected the point, remains to show what it has been."

492

He laid the brush-stick on the mantel-shelf and once more turned to the rubbish-heap.

"Now here is a very suggestive thing," he said presently, holding out to me a small wide-mouthed bottle. "Observe the flies sticking to the inside, and the name on the label – '*Fox, Russell Street, Covent Garden*'. You were right, Jervis, in your surmise. Mr. Morgan and the coachman were one and the same person."

"I don't see how you arrive at that, all the same," I remarked.

"This," said Thorndyke, tapping the bottle with his finger, "contained – and still contains a small quantity of – a kind of cement. Mr. Fox is a dealer in the materials for making-up, theatrical or otherwise. Now your really artistic make-up does not put on an oakum wig, nor does he tie on a false beard with strings as if it were a baby's feeder. If he dons a false mustache or beard, the thing is properly made and securely fixed on, and then the ends are finished with ends of loose hair, which are cemented to the skin and afterward trimmed with scissors. This is the kind of cement that is used for that purpose."

He laid the bottle beside his other treasure-trove and returned to his search. But, with the exception of a screw and a trouser-button, he met with no further reward for his industry. At length he rose and, kicking the discarded rubbish back under the grate, gathered up his gleanings and wrapped them in his handkerchief, having first tried the screw in one of the holes in the door, from which he had picked out the putty, and found that it fitted perfectly.

"A poor collection," was his comment, as he pocketed the small parcel of miscellaneous rubbish, "and yet not so poor as I had feared. Perhaps, if we question them closely enough, these unconsidered trifles may be made to tell us something worth hearing, after all. We may as well look through the house and yard before we go."

We did so, but met with nothing that even Thorndyke's inquisitive eye could view with interest and, having returned the keys to the agent, betook ourselves back to the Temple.

XIII – A Change in Signature

On our return to Thorndyke's chambers I was inducted forthwith into my new duties, for an inquest of some importance was pending and my friend had been commissioned to examine the body and make a full report upon certain suspected matters.

I entered on the work with a pleasure and revived enthusiasm that tended to drive my recent experiences from my mind. Now and again, indeed, I gave a passing thought to the house in Kennington Lane and its mysterious occupants, but even then it was only the recollection of a strange experience that was past and done with.

Thorndyke, too, I supposed to have dismissed the subject from his mind, in spite of the strong feeling that he had shown and his implied determination to unravel the mystery. But on this point I was mistaken, as was proved to me by an incident that occurred on the fourth day of my residence and which I found, at the time, not a little startling.

We were sitting at breakfast, each of us glancing over the morning's letters, when Thorndyke said rather suddenly, "Have you a good memory for faces, Jervis?"

"Yes," I answered, "I think I have, rather. Why do you ask?"

"Because I have a photograph here of a man whom I think you may have met, Just look at it and tell me if you remember the face." He drew a cabinet-size photograph from an envelope that had come by the morning's post and passed it to me,

"I have certainly seen this face somewhere," said I, taking the portrait over to the window to examine it more thoroughly, "but I cannot at the moment remember where,"

"Try," said Thorndyke. "If you have seen the face before, you should be able to recall the person."

I looked intently at the photograph, and the more I looked, the more familiar did the face appear. Suddenly, the identity of the man flashed into my mind and I exclaimed in a tone of astonishment, "By heaven, Thorndyke! It is the mysterious patient of Kennington Lane!"

"I believe you are right," was the quiet reply, "and I am glad you were able to recognize him. The identification may be of value."

I need not say that the production of this photograph filled me with amazement and that I was seething with curiosity as to how Thorndyke had obtained it, but, as he replaced it impassively in its envelope without volunteering any explanation, I judged it best to ask no questions.

Nevertheless, I pondered upon the matter with undiminished wonder and once again realized that my friend was a man whose powers, alike of observation and inference, were of no ordinary kind, I had myself seen all that he had seen and, indeed, much more. I had examined the little handful of rubbish that he had gathered up so carefully and I would have flung it back under the grate without a qualm. Not a single glimmer of light had I perceived in the cloud of mystery, nor even a hint of the direction in which to seek enlightenment.

And yet Thorndyke had, in some incomprehensible manner, contrived to piece together facts that I had not even observed, and that very completely, for it was evident that he had already, in these few days, narrowed the field of inquiry down to a very small area and must be in possession of the leading facts of the case.

As to the other case – that of Jeffrey Blackmore's will – I had had occasional proofs that he was still engaged upon it, though with what object I could not imagine, for the will seemed to me as incontestable as a will could be. My astonishment may therefore be imagined when, on the very evening of the day on which he had shown me the photograph of my patient, Thorndyke remarked coolly, as we rose from the dinner-table.

"I have nearly finished with the Blackmore case. In fact, I shall write to Marchmont this evening and advise him to enter a *caveat* at once."

"Why," I exclaimed, "you don't mean to say that you have found a flaw in the second will, after all!"

"A flaw!" repeated Thorndyke. "My dear Jervis, that will is a forgery from beginning to end! Of that I have no doubt whatever. I am only waiting for the final, conclusive verification to institute criminal proceedings."

"You amaze me!" I declared. "I had imagined that your investigations were – well – "

"A demonstration of activity to justify the fee, eh?" suggested Thorndyke, with a mischievous smile.

I laughed a little shamefacedly, for my astute friend had, as usual, shot his bolt very near the mark.

"I haven't shown you the signatures, have I?" he continued. "They are rather interesting and suggestive. I persuaded the bank people to let me photograph the last year's checks in a consecutive series, so as to exhibit the change which was admitted to have occurred in the character of the signature. We pinned the checks to a board in batches, each check overlapping the one below so as to show the signature only and to save space, and the dates were written on a slip of paper at the side. I photographed them full size, a batch at a time, with a tele-photo lens."

"Why a tele-photo?" I asked.

"To enable me to get a full-sized image without bringing the checks close up to the camera," he replied. "If I had used an ordinary lens, the checks could hardly have been much more than a foot from the camera and then the signatures on the margin of the plate would certainly have undergone some distortion from the effects of perspective – even if the lens itself were free from all optical defects. As it is, the photographs are quite reliable, and the enlargements that Polton has made – magnified three diameters – show the characters perfectly."

He brought out from a drawer a number of whole-plate photographs which he laid on the table end to end. Each one contained four of the enlarged signatures and, thus exhibited in series in the order of their dates, it was easy to compare their characters. Further to facilitate the comparison, the signatures of the two wills – also enlarged – had each a card to itself and could thus be laid by the side of any one of the series.

"You will remember," said Thorndyke, "Marchmont referred to a change in the character of Jeffrey Blackmore's signature?"

I nodded.

"It was a very slight change and, though noticed at the bank, it was not considered to be of any moment. Now if you will cast your eye over the series, you will be able to distinguish the differences. They are very small indeed. The later signatures are a little stiffer, a little more shaky, and the *B* and the *K* are both appreciably different from those in the earlier signatures. But there is another fact which emerges when the whole series is seen together, and it is so striking and significant a fact that I am astonished at its having occasioned no inquiry."

"Indeed!" said I, stooping to examine the photographs with increased interest. "What is that?"

"It is a very simple matter and very obvious, but yet, as I have said, very significant. It is this: The change in the characters of the signatures is not a gradual or insidious change, nor is it progressive. It occurs at a certain definite point and then continues without increase or variation. Look carefully at the check dated twenty-ninth of September and you will see that the signature is in what we may call the 'old manner', whereas the next check, dated the eighteenth of October, is in the 'new manner'.

"Now if you will run your eye through the signatures previous to the twenty-ninth of September, you will observe that none of them shows any sign of change whatever. They are all in the 'old manner', while the signatures subsequent to the twenty-ninth of September, from the eighteenth of October onwards, are, without exception, in the 'new manner'.

"The alteration, slight and trivial as it is, is to be seen in every one of them, and you will also notice that it does not increase as time goes on. Tt is not a progressive change. The signature on the last check – the one that was drawn on the twenty-sixth of March to pay the rent – does not differ from the 'old manner' any more than that dated the eighteenth of October. A rather striking and important fact."

"Yes. And the signatures of the two wills?"

"The first will is signed in the 'old manner', as you can see for yourself, while the signature of the second will has the characters of what we have called the 'new manner'. It is identical in style with the signatures subsequent to the twenty-ninth of September."

"Yes, I see that it is as you say," I agreed, when I had carefully made the comparison, "and it is certainly very curious and interesting. But what I do not see is the bearing of all this. The second will was signed in the presence of witnesses and that seems to dispose of the whole matter."

"It does," Thorndyke admitted, "but we must not let our data overlap. It is wise always to consider each separate fact on its own merits and work it out to a finish without allowing ourselves to be disturbed or our attention diverted by any seeming incompatibilities with other facts. Then, when we have each datum as complete as we can get it, we may put them all together and consider their relations to one another. It is surprising to see how the incompatibilities become eliminated if we work in this way – how the most (apparently) irreconcilable facts fall into agreement with one another."

"As an academic rule for conducting investigations," I replied, "your principle is, no doubt, entirely excellent. But when you seek to prove by indirect and collateral evidence that Jeffrey Blackmore did not sign a will which two respectable men have sworn they saw him sign, why, I am inclined to think that – "

"That, in the words of the late Captain Bunsby, 'the bearing of these observations lies in their application.'"

"Precisely," I agreed, and we both laughed.

XIV – Some Bits of Glass

"However," I resumed presently, "as you are advising Marchmont to dispute the will, I presume you have some substantial grounds for action, though I cannot conceive what they may be."

"You have all the facts that I had to start with and on which I formed the opinion that the will was probably a forgery. Of course I have more data now, for, as 'money makes money', so knowledge begets knowledge, and I put my original capital out to interest. Shall we tabulate the facts that are in our joint possession and see what they suggest?"

"Yes, do," I replied, "for I am hopelessly in the dark." Thorndyke produced a note-book from a drawer and, uncapping his fountain pen, wrote down the leading facts, reading each aloud as soon as it was written.

1. *The second will was unnecessary, since a codicil would have answered the purpose.*
2. *The evident intention of the testator was to leave the bulk of his property to Stephen Blackmore.*
3. *The second will did not, under existing circumstances, give effect to this intention, while the first will did.*
4. *The signature of the second will differs slightly from that of the first and also from the testator's ordinary signature.*

"And as to the very curious group of dates –

5. *Mrs. Wilson made her will at the end of 1897, without acquainting Jeffrey Blackmore, who seems to have been unaware of the existence of this will.*
6. *His own second will was dated the ninth of December, 1899.*
7. *Mrs. Wilson died of cancer on the twenty-fourth of March, 1900.*
8. *Jeffrey Blackmore was last seen alive on the twenty-sixth of March, 1900, i.e., two days after Mrs. Wilson's death.*
9. *His body was discovered on the twenty-seventh of March, three days after Mrs. Wilson's death.*
10. *The change in the character of his signature occurred abruptly between the twenty-ninth of September and the eighteenth of October.*

"You will find that collection of facts repays careful study, Jervis, especially when considered in relation to the last of our data, which is:

> 11.   *We found, in Blackmore's chambers, a framed inscription hung on the wall upside down."*

He passed the book to me and I pored over it intently, focusing my attention upon the various items with all the power of my will. But, struggle as I would, no general conclusion could be made to emerge from the mass of apparently disconnected facts.

"Well," said Thorndyke presently, after watching with grave interest my unavailing efforts, "what do you make of it?"

"Nothing!" I exclaimed desperately, slapping the book down upon the table. "Of course I can see that there are some queer features in the case, but you say the will is a forgery. Now I can find nothing in these facts to give the slightest color to such a supposition. You will think me an unmitigated donkey, I have no doubt, but I can't help that,"

My failure, it will be observed, had put me somewhat out of humor, and, observing this, Thorndyke hastened to reply, "Not in the least my dear fellow. You merely lack experience. Wait until you have seen the trained legal intelligence brought to bear on these facts – which you will do, I feel little doubt, very soon after Marchmont gets my letter. You will have a better opinion of yourself then. By the way, here is another little problem for you. What was the object of which these are parts?"

He pushed across the table a little cardboard box, having first removed the lid. In it were a number of very small pieces of broken glass, some of which had been cemented together by their edges.

"These, I suppose, are the pieces of glass that you picked up in poor Blackmore's bed-room," I said, looking at them with consider able curiosity.

"Yes," replied Thorndyke. "You see that Polton has been endeavoring to reconstitute the object, whatever it was, but he has not been very successful, for the fragments were too small and irregular and the collection too incomplete. However, here is a specimen, built up of six small pieces, which exhibits the general character of the object fairly well."

He picked out the little irregular-shaped object and handed it to me, and I could not but admire the neatness with which Polton had joined the little fragments together.

"It was not a lens," I pronounced, holding it up before my eyes and moving it to and fro as I looked through it.

"No, it was not a lens," Thorndyke agreed.

"And so cannot have been a spectacle glass. But the surface was curved – one side convex and the other concave – and the little piece that remains of the original edge seems to have been ground to fit a bezel or frame. I should say that these are portions of a small watch-glass."

"That is Polton's opinion," said Thorndyke. "And I think you are both wrong."

"What do you think it is?" I asked.

"I am submitting the problem for solution by my learned brother," he replied with an exasperating smile.

"You had better be careful!" I exclaimed, clapping the lid on to the box and pushing it across to him. "If I am tried beyond endurance I may be tempted to set a booby-trap to catch a medical jurist. And where will your reputation be then?"

Thorndyke's smile broadened, and he broke into an appreciative chuckle.

"Your suggestion has certainly extensive possibilities in the way of farce," he admitted "and I tremble at your threat. But I must write my letter to Marchmont and we will go out and lay the mine in the Fleet Street post-box. I should like to be in his office when it explodes."

"I expect, for that matter," said I, "the explosion will soon be felt pretty distinctly in these chambers."

"I expect so, too," replied Thorndyke. "And that reminds me that I shall be out all day to-morrow, so, if Marchmont calls and seems at all urgent, you might invite him to look in after dinner and talk the case over."

I promised to do so and hoped sincerely that the solicitor would accept the invitation, for I, at any rate, was on tenterhooks of curiosity to hear my colleague's views on Jeffrey Blackmore's will.

XV – A Call From the Lawyers

My friend's expectations in respect to Mr. Marchmont were fully realized, for on the following morning, within an hour of his departure from the chambers, the knocker was plied with more than usual emphasis and, on my opening the door, I discovered the solicitor in company with a somewhat older gentleman. Mr. Marchmont appeared rather out of humor, while his companion was obviously in a state of extreme irritation.

"Howdy-do, Dr. Jervis?" said Marchmont, as he entered at my invitation. "Your colleague, I suppose, is not in just now?"

"No, and he will not be returning until the evening."

"Hmm. I'm sorry. We wished to see him rather particularly. This is my partner, Mr. Winwood."

The latter gentleman bowed stiffly, and Marchmont continued, "We have had a letter from Mr. Thorndyke, and it is, I may say, a rather curious letter – in fact, a very singular letter indeed?'

"It is the letter of a madman!" burst in Mr. Winwood.

"No, no, Winwood, don't say that. But it is really rather incomprehensible. It relates to the will of the late Jeffrey Blackmore – you know the main facts of the case – and we cannot reconcile it with those facts."

"This is the letter," exclaimed Mr. Winwood, dragging the document from his wallet and slapping it down on the table. "If you are acquainted with the case, sir, just read that and let us hear what you think."

I took up the letter and read:

> *Dear Mr. Marchmont,*
>
> *Jeffrey Blackmore, decd: I have gone into this case with some care and have now no doubt that the second will is a forgery. I therefore suggest that, pending the commencement of criminal proceedings, you lose no time in entering a* caveat, *and I will furnish you with particulars in due course.*
>
> *Yours truly,*
> *John Thorndyke*

"Well!" exclaimed Mr. Winwood, glaring ferociously at me, "what do you think of the learned counsel's opinion?"

"I knew that Thorndyke was writing to you to this effect," I replied "but I must frankly confess that I can make nothing of it. Have you acted on his advice?"

"Certainly not!' shouted the irascible lawyer. "Do you suppose we wish to make ourselves the laughing-stock of the courts? The thing is impossible – ridiculously impossible!"

"It can't be that, you know," said I a little stiffly, for I was somewhat nettled by Mr. Winwood's manner, "or Thorndyke would not have written this letter. You had better see him and let him give you the particulars, as he suggests. Could you look in this evening after dinner – say at eight o'clock?"

"It is very inconvenient," grumbled Mr. Winwood. "We should have to dine in town."

"Yes, but it will be the best plan," said Marchmont. "We can bring Mr. Stephen Blackmore with us and hear what Dr. Thorndyke has done. Of course, if what he says is correct, Mr. Stephen's position is totally changed."

"Bah!" exclaimed Winwood, "he has found a mare's-nest, I tell you. However, I suppose we must come, and we will bring Mr. Stephen by all means. The oracle's explanation should be worth hearing – to a man of leisure, at any rate."

With this the two lawyers took their departure, leaving me to meditate upon my colleague's astonishing statement, which I did, considerably to the prejudice of other employment. That Thorndyke would be able to justify the opinion he had given I had no doubt whatever. Yet there was no denying that the thing was, upon the face of it, as Mr. Winwood had said, "ridiculously impossible."

When Thorndyke returned, I acquainted him with the visit of the two lawyers, and also with the sentiments they had expressed, whereat he smiled with quiet amusement.

"I thought that letter would bring Marchmont to our door before long," said he. "As to Winwood, I have never met him, so he promises to give us what the variety artists would call an 'extra turn'. And what do you think of the affair yourself?"

"I have given it up," I answered, "and feel as if I had taken an overdose of *Cannabis Indica*."

Thorndyke laughed. "Come and dine," said he, "and let us crack a bottle, that our hearts may not turn to water under the frown of the disdainful Winwood."

He rang the bell for Polton, and when that ingenious person made his appearance, said, "I expect that a man named Walker will call presently,

Polton. If he does, take him to your room and detain him till I send for him."

We now betook ourselves to a certain old-world tavern in Fleet Street at which it was our custom occasionally to dine and where on the present occasion certain little extra touches gave a more than unusually festive character to our repast. Thorndyke was in excellent spirits, under the influence of which – and a bottle – he discoursed brilliantly on the evidence of the persistence of ancient racial types in modern populations, until the clock of the Law Courts, chiming three-quarters, warned us to return home.

XVI – Some Singular Facts

We had not been back in the chambers more than a few minutes when the little brass knocker announced the arrival of our visitors. Thorndyke himself admitted them and then closed the oak.

"We felt that we must come round and hear a few particulars from you," said Mr. Marchmont, whose manner was now somewhat flurried and uneasy. "We could not quite understand your letter."

"Quite so," said Thorndyke. "The conclusion was a rather unexpected one."

"I should say, rather," exclaimed Mr. Winwood with some heat, "that the conclusion was a palpably ridiculous one."

"That," replied Thorndyke suavely, "can perhaps be better determined after examining all the facts that led up to it."

"No doubt, sir," retorted Mr. Winwood, growing suddenly red and wrathful, "but I speak as a solicitor who was practising in the law when you were an infant in arms! You say that this will is a forgery. I would remind you, sir, that it was executed in broad daylight in the presence of two unimpeachable witnesses, who have not only sworn to their signatures but, one of whom – the house-painter – obligingly left four greasy finger-prints on the document, for subsequent identification, if necessary!"

"After the excellent custom of the Chinese," observed Thorndyke. "Have you verified those finger-prints?"

"No, sir, I have not," replied Mr. Winwood. "Have you?"

"No. The fact is they are of no interest to me, as I am not disputing the witnesses' signatures."

At this, Mr. Winwood fairly danced with irritation. "Marchmont," he exclaimed fiercely, "this is a mere hoax! This gentleman has brought us here to make fools of us

"Pray, my dear Winwood," said Marchmont, "control your temper. No doubt he – "

"But, confound it!" roared Winwood. "You yourself have heard him say that the will is a forgery, but that he doesn't dispute the signatures, which," concluded Winwood, banging his fist down upon the table, "is nonsense!"

"May I suggest," interposed Stephen Blackmore, "that we came here to listen to Dr. Thorndyke's explanation of his letter? Perhaps it would be better to postpone any comments until we have heard it."

"Undoubtedly, undoubtedly," said Marchmont. "Let me beg you, Winwood, to listen patiently and refrain from interruption until we have our learned friend's exposition of his opinion."

"Oh, very well," replied Winwood sulkily. "I'll say no more." He sank into a chair with the manner of a man who shuts himself up and turns the key, and so remained throughout most of the subsequent proceedings, stony and impassive like a seated effigy at the portal of some Egyptian tomb. The other men also seated themselves, as did I, too, and Thorndyke, having laid on the table a small heap of documents, began without preamble.

"There are two ways in which I might lay the case before you," said he. "I might state my theory of the sequence of events and furnish the verification afterward, or I might retrace the actual course of my investigations and give you the facts in the order in which I obtained them myself, with the inferences from them. Which will you have first – the theory or the investigation?"

"Oh, – the theory!" growled Mr. Winwood, and shut himself up again with a snap.

"Perhaps it would be better," said Marchmont, "if we heard the whole argument from the beginning."

"I think," agreed Thorndyke, "that that method will enable you to grasp the evidence more easily. Now, when you and Mr. Stephen placed the outline of the case before me, there were certain curious features in it which attracted my attention, as they had, no doubt, attracted yours. In the first place, there was the strange circumstance that the second will should have been made at all, its provisions being, under the conditions then existing, practically identical with the first, so that the trifling alteration could have been met easily by a codicil. There was also the fact that the second will – making John Blackmore the residuary legatee – was obviously less in accordance with the intentions of the testator, so far as they may be judged, than the first one.

"The next thing that arrested my attention was the mode of death of Mrs. Wilson. She died of cancer. Now cancer is one of the few diseases of which the fatal termination can be predicted with certainty months before its occurrence, and its date fixed, in suitable cases, with considerable accuracy.

"And now observe the remarkable series of coincidences that are brought into light when we consider this peculiarity of the disease. Mrs. Wilson died on the twenty-fourth of March, 1900, having made her will two years previously. Mr. Jeffrey's second will was signed on the ninth of December, 1899 – at a time, that is to say, when the existence of cancer must have been known to Mrs. Wilson's doctor, and might have been

505

known to Mr. Jeffrey himself or any person interested. Yet it is practically certain that Mr. Jeffrey had no intention of bequeathing the bulk of his property to his brother John, as he did by executing this second will.

"Next, you will observe that the remarkable change in Mr. Jeffrey's habits coincides with the same events, for he came over from Nice, where he had been residing for a year – having stored his furniture meanwhile – and took up his residence at New Inn in

September 1899, at a time when the nature of Mrs. Wilson's complaint must almost certainly have been known. At the same time, as I shall presently demonstrate to you, a distinct and quite sudden change took place in the character of his signature.

"I would next draw your attention to the singularly opportune date of his death, in reference to this will. Mrs. Wilson died upon the twenty-fourth of March. Mr. Jeffrey was found dead upon the twenty-seventh of March, and he was seen alive upon the twenty-sixth. If he had died only four days sooner, Mrs. Wilson's property would not have devolved upon him at all. If he had lived a few days longer, it is probable that he would have made a new will in his nephew's favor. Circumstances, therefore, conspired in the most singular manner in favor of Mr. John Blackmore.

"But there is yet another coincidence that you will probably have noticed.

"Mr. Jeffrey's body was found on the twenty-seventh of March, and then by the merest chance. It might have remained undiscovered for weeks – or even months, and if this had happened, it is certain that Mrs. Wilson's next of kin would have disputed John Blackmore's claim – most probably with successes – on the grounds that Mr. Jeffrey died before Mrs. Wilson. But all this uncertainty and difficulty was prevented by the circumstance that Mr. Jeffrey paid his rent personally to the porter on the twenty-sixth, so establishing the fact beyond question that he was alive on that date.

"Thus, by a series of coincidences, John Blackmore is enabled to inherit the fortune of a man who, almost certainly, had no intention of bequeathing it to him."

Thorndyke paused, and Mr. Marchmont, who had listened with close attention, nodded as he glanced at his silent partner.

"You have stated the case with remarkable lucidity," he said, "and I am free to confess that some of the points you have raised had escaped my notice."

"Well, then," resumed Thorndyke, "to continue: The facts with which you furnished me, when thus collated, made it evident that the case was a very singular one, and it appeared to me that a case presenting such a series of coincidences in favor of one of the parties should be viewed with some suspicion and subjected to very close examination. But these facts yielded no further conclusion, and it was clear that no progress could be made until we had obtained some fresh data.

"In what direction, however, these new facts were to be looked for did not for the moment appear. Indeed, it seemed as if the inquiry had come to a full stop.

"But there is one rule which I follow religiously in all my investigations, and that is to collect facts of all kinds in any way related to the case in hand, no matter how trivial they may be or how apparently irrelevant."

XVII – The Man in New Inn

"Now, in pursuance of this rule, I took an opportunity, which offered, of looking over the chambers in New Inn, which had been left untouched since the death of their occupant, and I had hardly entered the rooms when I made a very curious discovery. On the wall hung a framed photograph of an ancient Persian inscription in cuneiform characters."

The expectant look which had appeared on Mr. Marchmont's face changed suddenly to one of disappointment, as he remarked, "Curious, perhaps, but not of much importance to us, I am afraid."

"My uncle was greatly interested in cuneiform texts, as I think I mentioned," said Stephen Blackmore. "I seem to remember this photograph, too – it used to stand on the mantelpiece in his old rooms, I believe."

"Very probably," replied Thorndyke. "Well, it hung on the wall at New Inn, and it was hung upside-down."

"Upside-down!" exclaimed Blackmore. "That is really very odd."

"Very odd indeed," agreed Thorndyke. "The inscription, I find, was one of the first to be deciphered. From it Grotefend, with incredible patience and skill, managed to construct a number of the hitherto unknown signs. Now is it not an astonishing thing that an Oriental scholar, setting so much store by this monument of human ingenuity that he has a photograph of it framed, should then hang that photograph upon his wall upside-down?"

"I see your point," said Marchmont, "and I certainly agree with you that the circumstance is strongly suggestive of the decay of the mental faculties."

Thorndyke smiled almost imperceptibly as he continued, "The way in which it came to be inverted is pretty obvious. The photograph had evidently been in the frame some years, but had never been hung up until lately, for the plates by which it was suspended were new, and when I unscrewed one, I found the wood underneath as dark and time-stained as elsewhere, and there were no other marks of plates or rings.

"The frame-maker had, however, pasted his label on the back of the frame, and as this label hung the right way up, it appeared as if the person who fixed on the plates had adopted it as a guide."

"Possibly," said Mr. Marchmont somewhat impatiently. "But these facts, though doubtless very curious and interesting, do not seem to have much bearing upon the genuineness of the late Mr. Blackmore's will."

"On the contrary," replied Thorndyke, "they appeared to me to be full of significance. However, I will return to the chambers presently, and I will now demonstrate to you that the alteration, which you have told me had been noticed at the bank, in the character of Mr. Jeffrey's signature, occurred at the time that I mentioned and was quite an abrupt change."

He drew from his little pile of documents the photographs of the checks and handed them to our visitors, by whom they were examined with varying degrees of interest.

"You will see," said he, "that the change took place between the twenty-ninth of September and the eighteenth of October and was, therefore, coincident in time with the other remarkable changes in the habits of the deceased."

"Yes, I see that," replied Mr. Marchmont, "and no doubt the fact would be of some importance if there were any question as to the genuineness of the testator's signature. But there is not. The signature of the will was witnessed, and the witnesses have been produced."

"Whence it follows," added Mr. Winwood, "that all this hairsplitting is entirely irrelevant and, in fact, so much waste of time."

"If you will note the facts that I am presenting to you," said Thorndyke, "and postpone your conclusions and comments until I have finished, you will have a better chance of grasping the case as a whole. I will now relate to you a very strange adventure which befell Dr. Jervis."

He then proceeded to recount the incidents connected with my visits to the mysterious patient in Kennington Lane, including the construction of the chart, presenting the latter for the inspection of his hearers. To this recital our three visitors listened in utter bewilderment, as, indeed, did I also, for I could not conceive in what way my adventures could be related to the affairs of the late Mr. Blackmore. This was manifestly the view taken by Mr. Marchmont, for during a pause, in which the chart was handed to him, he remarked somewhat stiffly, "I am assuming, Dr. Thorndyke, that the curious story you are telling us has some relevance to the matter in which we are interested."

"You are quite correct in your assumption," replied Thorndyke. "The story is very relevant indeed, as you will presently be convinced."

"Thank you," said Marchmont, sinking back once more into his chair with a sigh of resignation.

"A few days ago," pursued Thorndyke, "Dr. Jervis and I located, with the aid of this chart, the house to which he had been called. We found that it was to let, the recent tenant having left hurriedly, so, when we had obtained the keys, we entered and explored in accordance with the rule that I mentioned just now."

Here he gave a brief account of our visit and the conditions that we observed, and was proceeding to furnish a list of the articles that he had found, when Mr. Winwood started from his chair.

"Good heavens, sir!" he exclaimed, "have I come here, at great personal inconvenience, to hear you read the inventory of a dust-heap?"

"You came by your own wish," replied Thorndyke, "and I may add that you are not being forcibly detained."

At this hint, Mr. Winwood sat down and shut himself up once more.

"We will now," pursued Thorndyke with unmoved serenity, "consider the significance of these relics and we will begin with this pair of spectacles. They belonged to a person who was near-sighted and astigmatic in the left eye and almost certainly blind in the right. Such a description agrees entirely with Dr. Jervis's account of the sick man."

He paused for a moment, and then, as no one made any comment, proceeded, "We next come to this little bamboo stick. It is part of a Japanese brush, such as is used for writing in Chinese ink or for making small drawings."

Again he paused as though expecting some remark from his listeners, but no one spoke, and he continued. "Then there is this bottle with the theatrical wig-maker's label on it, which once contained cement. Its presence suggests some person who was accustomed to 'make up' with a false mustache or beard. You have heard Dr. Jervis's account of Mr. Morgan and his coachman, and will agree with me that the circumstances bear out this suggestion."

He paused once more and looked round expectantly at his audience, none of whom, however, volunteered any remark.

"Do none of these objects that I have described seem to have any suggestion for us?" he asked in a tone of some surprise.

"They convey nothing to me," said Mr. Marchmont, glancing at his partner, who shook his head like a restive horse.

"Nor to you, Mr. Blackmore?"

"No," replied Stephen, "unless you mean to suggest that the sick man was my Uncle Jeffrey."

"That is precisely what I do mean to suggest," rejoined Thorndyke. "I had formed that opinion, indeed, before I saw them and I need not say how much they strengthened it."

"My uncle was certainly blind in the right eye," said Blackmore.

"And," interrupted Thorndyke, "from the same cause – dislocation of the crystalline lens."

"Possibly. And he probably used such a brush as you found, since I know that he corresponded in Japanese with his native friends in Tokyo. But this is surely very slender evidence."

510

"It is no evidence at all," replied Thorndyke. "It is merely a suggestion."

"Moreover," said Marchmont, "there is the insuperable objection that Mr. Jeffrey was living at New Inn at this time."

"What evidence is there of that?" asked Thorndyke.

"Evidence!" exclaimed Marchmont impatiently. "Why, my dear sir – " he paused suddenly and, leaning forward, regarded Thorndyke with a new and rather startled expression, " – you mean to suggest – " he began.

"I suggest to you what that inverted inscription suggested to me – that the person who occupied those chambers in New Inn was not Jeffrey Blackmore!"

XVIII – Thorndyke Explains

The lawyer appeared thunderstruck. "This is an amazing proposition!" he exclaimed. "Yet the thing is certainly not impossible, for, now that you recall the fact, no one who had known him previously ever saw him at the Inn! The question of identity was never raised!"

"Excepting," said Mr. Winwood, "in regard to the body, which was certainly that of Jeffrey Blackmore."

"Yes, of course," said Marchmont. "I had forgotten that for the moment. The body was identified beyond doubt. You don't dispute the identity of the body, do you?"

"Certainly not," replied Thorndyke.

"Then for heaven's sake, tell us what you do mean, for I must confess that I am completely bewildered in this tangle of mysteries and contradictions!"

"It is certainly an intricate case," said Thorndyke, "but I think that you will find it comes together very completely. I have described to you my preliminary observations in the order in which I made them and have given you a hint of the nature of my inferences. Now I will lay before you the hypothesis that I have formed as to what were the actual occurrences in this mysterious case.

"It appeared to me probable that John Blackmore must have come to know, in some way, of the will that Mrs. Wilson had made in his brother's favor and that he kept himself informed as to the state of her health. When it became known to him that she was suffering from cancer, and that her death was likely to take place within a certain number of months, I think that he conceived the scheme that he subsequently carried out with such remarkable success.

"In September of 1899, Jeffrey Blackmore returned from Nice, and I think that John must have met him and either drugged him then and there and carried him to Kennington Lane, or induced him to go voluntarily. Once in the house and shut up in that dungeonlike bedroom, it would be easy to administer morphia – in small quantities at first and in larger doses afterward, as toleration of the drug became established."

"But could this be done against the victim's will?" asked Marchmont.

"Certainly. Small doses could be conveyed in food and drink, or administered during sleep, and then, you know, the morphia habit is quickly formed and, once it was established, the unfortunate man would probably take the drug voluntarily. Moreover this drug-habit weakens the will and paralyzes the mental faculties to an extraordinary degree – which was probably the principal object in using it.

"John Blackmore's intention, on this hypothesis, would be to keep his brother in a state of continual torpor and mental enfeeblement as long as Mrs. Wilson remained alive, so that the woman, his accomplice, could manage the prisoner, leaving him, John, free to play his part elsewhere.

"As soon he had thus secured his unfortunate brother, I suggest that this ingenious villain engaged the chambers at New Inn. In order to personate his brother, he must have shaved off his mustache and beard and worn spectacles, and these spectacles introduce a very curious and interesting feature into the case.

"To the majority of people the wearing of spectacles, for the purpose of disguise or personation, seems a perfectly simple and easy proceeding. But to a person of normal eyesight it is nothing of the kind, for if he wears spectacles suited for long sight, he is unable to see distinctly through them at all, while if he wears even weak concave or near-sight glasses, the effort to see through them soon produces such strain and fatigue that his eyes become disabled altogether. On the stage, of course, the difficulty is got over quite simply by using spectacles of plain window-glass, but in ordinary life this would hardly do – the 'property' spectacles would probably be noticed and give rise to suspicion.

"The personator would, therefore, be in this dilemma: If he wore actual spectacles he would not be able to see through them, while if he wore sham spectacles of plain glass his disguise might be detected. There is only one way out of the difficulty, and that not a very satisfactory one, but Mr. J. Morgan seems to have adopted it in lieu of a better.

"We have learned from Dr. Jervis that this gentleman wore spectacles and that these spectacles seemed to have had very peculiar optical properties. For while the image of the candle-flame reflected in them was inverted, showing that one surface at least was concave, my colleague observed that objects seen through them appeared quite free from distortion or change of size, as if seen through plain glass. But there is only one kind of glass which could possess these optical properties, and that is a plain glass with curved surfaces like an ordinary watch-glass."

I started when Thorndyke reached this point, and thought of the contents of the card-board box, which I now saw was among the objects on the table.

"Do you follow the argument?" my colleague inquired.

"Yes," replied Mr. Marchmont, "I think I follow you, though I do not see the application of all this."

"That will appear presently. For the present we may take it that Mr. J. Morgan wore spectacles of this peculiar character, presumably for the purposes of disguise, and I am assuming, for the purposes of the argument, that Mr. J. Morgan and Mr. John Blackmore are one and the same."

"It is assuming a great deal," grunted Mr. Winwood.

"And now," continued Thorndyke, disregarding the last remark, "to return from this digression to John Blackmore's proceedings. I imagine that he spent very little time at the Inn – for the porter saw him only occasionally and believed him to be frequently absent – and when he was at Kennington Lane or at his office in the city, or elsewhere, he would replace his beard with a false one of the same appearance, which would require to be fixed on securely and finished round the edges with short hairs cemented to the skin – for an ordinary theatrical beard would be detected instantly in daylight.

"He would now commence experiments in forging his brother's handwriting, which he must have practised previously to have obtained Jeffrey's furniture from the repository where it was stored. The difference was observed at the bank, as Mr. Marchmont has told us, but the imitation was close enough not to arouse suspicion.

"The next thing was to make the fresh will and get it witnessed, and this was managed with such adroitness that, although neither of the witnesses had ever seen Jeffrey Blackmore, their identification has been accepted without question. It is evident that, when shaved, John Blackmore must have resembled his brother pretty closely or he would never have attempted to carry out this scheme, and he will have calculated, with much acuteness, that the porter, when called in to identify the body, would observe only the resemblance and would disregard any apparent difference in appearance.

"The position in which John Blackmore was now placed was one of extraordinary difficulty. His brother was immured in Kennington Lane, but, owing to the insecurity of his prison and the frequent absence of his jailer, this confinement could be maintained with safety only by keeping the imprisoned man continuously under the influence of full doses of morphia.

"This constant drugging must have been highly injurious to the health of a delicate man like Jeffery and, as time went on, there must have loomed up the ever-increasing danger that he might die before the appointed time, in which event John would be involved in a double catastrophe, for, on the one hand, the will would now be useless, and, on the other, the crime would be almost inevitably discovered.

"It was, no doubt, with this danger in view, that John called in Dr. Jervis – making, as it turned out, a very unsuitable choice. My colleague's assistance was invoked, no doubt, partly to keep the victim alive and partly in the hope that if that were impossible, he might be prepared to cover the crime with a death-certificate.

"We are now approaching the end of the tragedy. Mrs. Wilson died on the twenty-fourth of March. Circumstances point to the conclusion that the murder took place on the evening of the twenty-sixth. Now on that day, about half-past six in the evening, the supposed Jeffrey Blackmore entered New Inn in a four-wheeled cab, as you are aware, his face being seen at the window by the porter as the vehicle passed the lodge under the archway. There was a dense fog at the time, so the cab would be lost to sight as soon as it entered the Square. At this time the offices at No. 31 would be empty and not a soul present in the house to witness the arrival.

"From the first time that my suspicions took definite shape that cab seemed to me to hold the key to the mystery. There can be no doubt that it contained two people – one of them was John Blackmore, whose face was seen at the window, and the other, his victim, the unfortunate Jeffrey.

"As to what happened in that silent house there is no need to speculate. The peculiar vertical manner in which the needle of the syringe was introduced is naturally explained by the fact of its being thrust through the clothing, and we cannot but admire the cool calculation with which the appliances of murder were left to give color to the idea of suicide.

"Having committed the crime, the murderer presently walked out and showed himself at the lodge, under the pretext of paying the rent, thus furnishing proof of survival in respect to Mrs. Wilson. After this he returned to the Inn, but not to the chambers, for there is a postern-gate, as you know, opening into Houghton Street. Through this, no doubt, the murderer left the Inn, and vanished, to reappear at the inquest unrecognizable in his beard, his padded clothing and eyes uncovered by spectacles.

"With regard to the identification of the body by the porter there is, as I have said, no mystery. There must have been a considerable resemblance between the two brothers, and the porter, taking it for granted that the body was that of his tenant, would naturally recognize it as such, for even if he had noticed any departure from the usual appearance, he would attribute the difference to changes produced by death.

"Such, gentlemen, is my theory of the circumstances that surrounded the death of Jeffrey Blackmore, and I shall be glad to hear any comments that you may have to make."

XIX – Step by Step

There was an interval of silence after Thorndyke had finished which was at last broken by Mr. Winwood.

"I must admit, sir," said he, "that you have displayed extraordinary ingenuity in the construction of the astonishing story you have told us, and that this story, if it were true, would dispose satisfactorily of every difficulty and obscure point in the case. But is it true? It seems to me to be a matter of pure conjecture, woven most ingeniously around a few slightly suggestive facts. And, seeing that it involves a charge of murder of a most diabolical character against Mr. John Blackmore, nothing but the most conclusive proof would justify us in entertaining it."

"It is not conjecture," said Thorndyke, "although it was so at first. But when I had formed a hypothesis which fitted the facts known to me, I proceeded to test it and have now no doubt that it is correct."

"Would you mind laying before us any new facts that you have discovered which tend to confirm your theory?" said Mr. Marchmont.

"I will place the entire mass of evidence before you," said Thorndyke, "and then I think you will have no more doubts than I have.

"You will observe that there are four points which require to be proved: The first is the identity of Jeffrey with the sick man of Kennington Lane; the second is the identity of Mr. J. Morgan with John Blackmore; the third is the identity of John Blackmore with the tenant of 31 New Inn; and the fourth is the presence together of John and Jeffrey Blackmore at the chambers on the night of the latter gentleman's death.

"We will take the first point. Here are the spectacles I found in the empty house. I tested them optically with great care and measured them minutely and wrote down on this piece of paper their description. I will read it to you:

> "*Spectacles for distance, curl sides, steel frames, Stopford's pattern, with gold plate under bridge. Distance between centers, 6.2 cm. Right eye plain glass. Left eye-3D spherical-2D cylindrical, axis 35°.*

"Now spectacles of this pattern are, I believe, made only by Cuxton and Parry of New Bond Street. I therefore wrote to Mr. Cuxton, who knows me, and asked if he had supplied spectacles to the late Jeffrey Blackmore, Esq., and, if so, whether he would send me a description of them, together with the name of the oculist who prescribed them.

516

"He replied, in this letter here, that he had supplied spectacles to the late Jeffrey Black-more and described them thus:

> "*The spectacles were for distance and had steel frames of Stopford's pattern, with curl sides and a gold plate under the bridge. The formula, which was from Mr. Hindley's prescription, was 'R. E. plain glass. L.E.-3D sph. – 2D cyl., axis 35°*.

"You see the descriptions are identical. I then wrote to Mr. Hindley, asking certain questions, to which he replied thus:

> "'*You are quite right. Mr. Jeffrey Blackmore had a tremulous iris in his right eye (which was practically blind) due to dislocation of the lens. The pupils were rather large, certainly not contracted.*'

"Thus, you see, the description of the deceased tallies with that of the sick man as given by Dr. Jervis, excepting that there was then no sign of his being addicted to taking morphia. One more item of evidence I have on this point, and it is one that will appeal to the legal mind.

"A few days ago, I wrote to Mr. Stephen, asking him whether he possessed a recent photograph of his Uncle Jeffrey. He had one and sent it to me by return. This portrait I showed to Dr. Jervis, asking him if he recognised the person. After examining it attentively, without any hint from me, he identified it as a portrait of the sick man of Kennington Lane."

"Indeed!" exclaimed Mr. Marchmont. "This is most important. Are you prepared to swear to the resemblance, Dr. Jervis?"

"Perfectly. I have not the slightest doubt," I replied.

"Excellent!" said Mr. Marchmont. "Pray go on, Dr. Thorndyke."

"Well, that is all the evidence I have on the first point," said Thorndyke, "but, to my mind, it constitutes practically conclusive proof of identity."

"It is undoubtedly very weighty evidence," Mr. Marchmont agreed. "Now, as to the second point – the identity of John Blackmore with Mr. J. Morgan of Kennington Lane. To begin with the *prima facie* probabilities, in relation to certain assumed data. If we assume:

> "1.   That the sick man was Jeffrey Blackmore;
> "2.   That his symptoms were due to the administration of a slow poison.

517

"That the poison was being administered by J. Morgan, as suggested by his manifest disguise and the strange secrecy of his conduct. And if we then ask ourselves who could have a motive for causing the death of Mr. Jeffrey in this manner and at this time, the answer is John Blackmore, the principal beneficiary under the very unstable second will. The most obvious hypothesis, then, is that Mr. J. Morgan and John Blackmore were one and the same person."

"But this is mere surmise," objected Mr. Marchmont.

"Exactly, as every hypothesis must be until it has been tested and verified. And now for the facts that tend to support this hypothesis. The first item – a very small one – I picked up when I called on the doctor who had attended Mrs. Wilson. My object was to obtain particulars as to her illness and death, but, incidentally, I discovered that he was well acquainted with John Blackmore and had treated him – without operation and, therefore, without cure – for a nasal polypus. You will remember that Mr. J. Morgan appeared to have a nasal polypus. I may mention, by the way, that John Blackmore had been aware of Mrs. Wilson's state of health from the onset of her symptoms and kept himself informed as to her progress. Moreover, at his request a telegram was sent to his office in Copthall Avenue, announcing her death.

"The next item of evidence is more important. I made a second visit to the house-agent at Kennington for the purpose of obtaining, if possible, the names and addresses of the persons who had been mentioned as references when Mr. Morgan took the house. I ascertained that only one reference had been given – the intending tenant's stockbroker – and the name of that stockbroker was John Blackmore of Copthall Avenue."

"That is a significant fact," remarked Mr. Marchmont.

"Yes," answered Thorndyke, "and it would be interesting to confront John Blackmore with this house-agent, who would have seen him with his beard on. Well, that is all the evidence that I have on this point. It is far from conclusive by itself, but, such as it is, it tends to support the hypothesis that J. Morgan and John Blackmore were one and the same.

"I will now pass on to the evidence of the third point – the identity of John Blackmore with the tenant of New Inn.

"With reference to the inverted inscription, that furnishes indirect evidence only. It suggests that the tenant was not Jeffrey. But if not Jeffrey, it was someone who was personating him, and that someone must have resembled him closely enough for the personation to remain undetected even on the production of Jeffrey's body. But the only person known to us who answers this description is John Blackmore.

"Again, the individual who personated Jeffrey must have had some strong motive for doing do. But the only person known to us who could have had any such motive is John Blackmore.

"The next item of evidence on this point is also merely suggestive and indirect, though to me it was of the greatest value, since it furnished the first link in the chain of evidence connecting Jeffrey Blackmore with the sick man of Kennington. On the floor of the bedroom in New Inn I found the shattered remains of a small glass object which had been trodden on. Here are some of the fragments in this box, and you will see that we have joined a few of them together to help us in our investigations.

"My assistant, who was formerly a watchmaker, judged them to be fragments of the thin crystal glass of a lady's watch, and that, I think, was also Dr. Jervis's opinion. But the small part which remains of the original edge furnishes proof in two respects that this was not a watch-glass. In the first place, on taking a careful tracing of this piece of the edge, I found that its curve was part of an ellipse, but watch-glasses, nowadays, are invariably circular. In the second place, watch-glasses are ground on the edge to a single bevel to snap into the bezel or frame, but the edge of this is ground to a double bevel, like the edge of a spectacle-glass which fits into a groove and is held in position by a screw.

"The unavoidable inference is that this was a spectacle-glass – but since it had the optical properties of plain glass, it could *not* have been used to assist vision and was there-fore presumably intended for the purpose of disguise. Now you will remember that Mr. J. Morgan wore spectacles having precisely the optical properties of a crystal watch-glass, and it was this fact that first suggested to me a possible connection between New Inn and Kennington Lane."

"By the way," said Stephen Blackmore, "you said that my uncle had plain glass in one side of his spectacles?"

"Yes," replied Thorndyke, "over his blind eye. But that was actually plain glass with flat surfaces, not curved like this one. I should like to observe, with reference to this spectacle-glass, that its importance as a clue is much greater than might, at first sight, appear. The spectacles worn by Mr. Morgan were not merely peculiar or remarkable. They were probably unique. It is exceedingly likely that there is not, in the whole world, another similar pair of spectacles. Hence, the finding of this broken glass does really establish a considerable probability that J. Morgan was, at some time, in the chambers in New Inn. But we have seen that it is highly probable that J. Morgan was, in fact, John Blackmore, wherefore the presence of this glass is evidence suggesting that John Blackmore is the man who personated Jeffrey at New Inn.

"You will have observed, no doubt, that the evidence on the second and third points is by no means conclusive when taken separately, but I think you will agree that the whole body of circumstantial evidence is very strong and might easily be strengthened by further investigation."

"Yes," said Marchmont, "I think we may admit that there is enough evidence to make your theory a possible and even a probable one, and if you can show that there are any good grounds for believing that John and Jeffrey Blackmore were together in the chambers on the evening of the twenty-sixth of March, I should say that you had made out a *prima face* case. What say you, Winwood?"

"Let us hear the evidence," replied Mr. Winwood gruffly.

"Very well," said Thorndyke, "you shall. And, what is more, you shall have it firsthand."

XX – The Enemy Decides

He pressed the button of the electric bell three times and, after a short interval, Polton let himself in with his latch-key and beckoned to someone on the landing.

"Here is Walker, sir," said he, and he then retired, shutting the oak after him and leaving a seedy-looking stranger standing near the door and gazing at the assembled company with a mixture of embarrassment and defiance.

"Sit down, Walker," said Thorndyke, placing a chair for him. "I want you to answer a few questions for the information of these gentlemen."

"I know," said Walker with an oracular nod. "You can ask me anything you like."

"Your name, I believe, is James Walker?"

"That's me, sir."

"And your occupation?"

"My occupation, sir, don't agree with my name at all, because I drives a cab – a four-wheeled cab is what I drives – and an uncommon dry job it is, let me tell you."

Acting on this delicate hint, Thorndyke mixed a stiff whisky and soda and passed it across to the cabman, who consumed half at a single gulp and then peered thoughtfully into the tumbler.

"Rum stuff, this soda-water," he remarked. "Makes it taste as if there wasn't no whisky in it."

This hint Thorndyke ventured to ignore and continued his inquiries. "Do you remember a very foggy day about three weeks ago?"

"Rather. It was the twenty-sixth of March. I remember it because my benefit society came down on me for arrears that morning."

"Will you tell us now what happened to you between six and seven in the evening of that day?"

"I will," replied the cabman, emptying his tumbler by way of bracing himself up for the effort. "I drove a fare to Vauxhall Station and got there a little before six. As I didn't pick up no one there, I drove away and was just turning down Upper Kennington Lane when I see two gentlemen standing at the corner by Harleyford Road, and one of 'em hails me, so I pulls up by the curb. One of 'em seemed to be drunk, for the other one was holding him up, but he might have been feeling queer – it wasn't no affair of mine.

"But the rum thing about 'em was that they was as like as two peas. Their faces was alike, their clothes was alike, they wore the same kind of hats and they both had spectacles. 'Wot!' says I to myself, "'ere's the Siamese Twins out on the jamboree!' Well, the gent what wasn't drunk he opens the door and shoves in the other one what was, and he says to me, he says, 'Do you know New Inn?' he says. Now there was a silly question to ask a man what was born and brought up in White Horse Alley, Drury Lane. 'Do I know my grandmother?' says I.

"'Well,' says he, 'you drive in through the gate in Wych Street,' he says.

"'Of course I shall,' I says. 'Did you think I was going to drive in the back way down the steps?' I says.

"'And then,' he says, 'you drive down the Square nearly to the end and you'll see a house with a large brass plate at the corner of the doorway. That's where we want to be set down,' he says. With that, he nips in and pulls up the windows and off we goes.

"It took us nigh upon half-an-hour to get to New Inn through the fog, and as I drove in under the archway I saw it was half-past six by the clock in the porter's lodge. I drove down nearly to the end of the square and drew up opposite a house where there was a large brass plate by the doorway. Then the gent what was sober jumps out and begins hauling out the other one. I was just getting down off the box to help him when he says, rather short-like, "'All right, cabman,' he says, 'I can manage,' and he hands me five bob.

"The other gent seemed to have gone to sleep, and a rare job he had hauling him across the pavement. I see them, by the gas-lamps on the staircase, going upstairs – regular Pilgrim's Progress it was, I tell you – but they got up at last, for I saw 'em light the gas in a room on the second floor. Then I drove off."

"Could you identify the house?" asked Thorndyke.

"I done it, this morning. You saw me. It was No. 31."

"How was it," said Marchmont, "that you did not come forward at the inquest?"

"What inquest?" inquired the cabman. "I don't know nothing about any inquest. The first I heard of the business was when one of our men told me yesterday about a notice what was stuck up in a shelter offering a reward for information concerning a four-wheel cab what drove to New Inn at six-thirty on the day of the fog at the end of last month. Then I came here and left a message, and this morning this gentleman came to me on the rank and paid up like a gentleman."

The latter ceremony was now repeated, and the cabman, having remarked that his services were at the disposal of the present company to an unlimited extent on the same terms, departed, beaming with satisfaction.

When he had gone, our three visitors sat for a while looking at one another in silence. At length Stephen Blackmore rose with a stern expression on his pale face and said to Thorndyke. "The police must be informed of this at once. I shall never be able to rest until I know that justice has been dealt out to this coldhearted, merciless villain!"

"The police have already been informed," said Thorndyke. "I completed the case this morning and at once communicated with Superintendent Miller of Scotland Yard. A warrant was obtained immediately and I had expected to hear that the arrest had been made long before this, for Mr. Miller is usually most punctilious in keeping me informed of the progress of cases which I introduce to him. We shall hear to-morrow, no doubt."

"And for the present, the case seems to have passed out of our hands," observed Mr. Marchmont.

"I shall enter a *caveat*, all the same," said Mr. Winwood.

"Why, that doesn't seem very necessary," said Marchmont. "The evidence that we have heard is enough to secure a conviction, and there will be plenty more when the police go into the case. And a conviction would, of course, put an end to the second will."

"I shall enter *a caveat*, all the same," said Mr. Winwood.

As the two partners showed a disposition to become heated over this question, Thorndyke suggested that they might discuss it at leisure by the light of subsequent events.

Taking this as a hint, for it was now close upon midnight, our visitors prepared to depart and were, in fact, making their way towards the door, when the bell rang.

Thorndyke hastily flung open the door and, as he recognized his visitor, uttered an exclamation of satisfaction.

"Ha! Mr. Miller, we were just speaking of you. This is Mr. Stephen Blackmore, and these gentlemen are Messrs. Marchmont and Winwood, his solicitors, and my colleague, Dr. Jervis."

"Well, Doctor, I have just dropped in to give you the news, which will interest these gentlemen as well as yourself."

"Have you arrested the man?"

"No. He has arrested himself. He is dead!"

"Dead!" we all exclaimed together.

"Yes. It happened this way. We went down to his place at Surbiton early this morning, but it seemed lie had just left for town, so we took the next train and went straight to his office. But they must have smoked us and sent him a wire, for, just as we were approaching the office, a man answering the description ran out, jumped into a hansom and drove off like the devil.

523

"We chanced its being the right man and followed at a run, hailing the first hansom that we met, but he had a good start and his cabby had a good horse, so that we had all our work cut out to keep him in sight. We followed him over Blackfriars Bridge and down Stamford Street to Waterloo, but as we drove up the slope to the station we met a cab coming down and, as the cabby kissed his hand and smiled at us, we concluded it was the one we had been following.

"I remembered that the Southampton Express was due to start about this time, so we made for the platform and, just as the guard was about to blow his whistle, we saw a man bolt through the barrier and run up the platform. We dashed through a few seconds later and just managed to get on the train as it was moving off. But he had seen us, for his head was out of the window when we jumped in, and we kept a sharp lookout on both sides in case he should hop out again before the train got up speed.

"However, he didn't, and nothing more happened until we stopped at Southampton. You may be sure we lost no time in getting out and we ran up the platform, expecting to see him make a rush for the barrier. But there was no sign of him anywhere, and we began to think that he had given us the slip.

"Then, while my inspector watched the barrier, I went down the train until I came to the compartment that I had seen him enter. And there he was, lying back in the off corner, apparently fast asleep. But he wasn't asleep. He was dead. I found this on the floor of the carriage."

He held up a tiny glass tube, labeled *Aconitin Nitrate gr. 1-640*".

"Ha!" exclaimed Thorndyke. "This fellow was well up in poisons, it seems! This tube contained twenty tabloids, a thirty-second of a grain altogether, so if he swallowed them all he took about twelve times the medical dose. Well, perhaps he has done the best thing, after all."

"The best thing for you, gentlemen," said Mr. Miller, "for there is no need to raise any questions in detail at the inquest, and publicity would be very unpleasant for Mr. Blackmore. It is a thousand pities that you or Dr. Jervis hadn't put us on the scent in time to prevent the crime – though, of course, we couldn't have entered the premises without a warrant. But it is easy to be wise after the event. Well, good-night, gentlemen. I suppose this accident disposes of your business as far as the will is concerned?"

"I suppose it does," said Mr. Winwood, "but I shall enter a *caveat*, all the same."

The Dead Hand

A 1912 Thorndyke Novella
Later expanded into the novel
The Shadow of the Wolf *(1925)*

I – How It Happened

About half-past eight on a fine, sunny June morning, a small yacht crept out of Sennen Cove, near the Land's End, and headed for the open sea. On the shelving beach of the cove two women and a man, evidently visitors (or "foreigners", to use the local term), stood watching her departure with valedictory waving of cap or handkerchief, and the boatman who had put the crew on board, aided by two of his comrades, was hauling his boat up above the tide-mark.

A light, northerly breeze filled the yacht's sails and drew her gradually seaward. The figures of her crew dwindled to the size of dolls, shrank with the increasing distance to the magnitude of insects, and at last, losing all individuality, became mere specks merged in the form of the fabric that bore them.

On board the receding craft two men sat in the little cockpit. They formed the entire crew, for the *Sandhopper* was only a ship's lifeboat, timbered and decked, of light draught and, in the matter of spars and canvas, what the art critics. would call "reticent".

Both men, despite the fineness of the weather, wore yellow oilskins and sou'westers, and that was about all they had in common. In other respects they made a curious contrast – the one small, slender, sharp-featured, dark almost to swarthiness, and restless and quick in his movements, the other large, massive, red-faced, blue-eyed, with the rounded outlines suggestive of ponderous strength – a great ox of a man, heavy, stolid, but much less unwieldy than he looked.

The conversation incidental to getting the yacht under way had ceased, and silence had fallen on the occupants of the cockpit. The big man grasped the tiller and looked sulky, which was probably his usual aspect, and the small man watched him furtively.

The land was nearly two miles distant when the latter broke the silence.

"Joan Haygarth has come on wonderfully the last few months. Getting quite a fine-looking girl. Don't you think so, Purcell?"

"Yes," answered Purcell, "and so does Phil Rodney."

"You're right," agreed the other. "She isn't a patch on her sister, though, and never will be. I was looking at Maggie as we came dawn the beach this morning and thinking what a handsome girl she is. Don't you agree with me?"

Purcell stooped to look under the boom, and answered without turning his head. "Yes, she's all right."

"All right!" exclaimed the other. "Is that the way – "

"Look here, Varney," interrupted Purcell. "I don't want to discuss my wife's looks with you or any other man. She'll do for me or I shouldn't have married her."

A deep, coppery flush stole into Varney's cheeks. But he had brought the rather brutal snub on himself and apparently had the fairness to recognise the fact, for he mumbled an apology and relapsed into silence.

When next he spoke, he did so with a manner diffident and uneasy, as though approaching a disagreeable or difficult subject.

"There's a little matter, Dan, that I've been wanting to speak to you about when we got a chance of a private talk."

He glanced rather anxiously at his stolid companion, who grunted, and then, without removing his gaze from the horizon ahead, replied. 'You've a pretty fair chance now, seeing that we shall be bottled up together for another five or six hours. And it's fairly private unless you bawl loud enough to be heard at the Longships."

It was not a gracious invitation. But if Varney resented the rebuff he showed no sign of annoyance, for reasons which appeared when he opened his subject.

"What I wanted to say," he resumed, "was this. We're both doing pretty well now on the square. You must be positively piling up the shekels, and I can earn a decent living, which is all I want. Why shouldn't we drop this flash note business?"

Purcell kept his blue eye fixed on the horizon and appeared to ignore the question, but after an interval and without moving a muscle he said gruffly. "Go on," and Varney continued.

"The lay isn't what it was, you know. At first it was all plain sailing. The notes were first-class copies, and not a soul suspected anything until they were presented at the bank. Then the murder was out, and the next little trip that I made was a very different affair. Two or three of the notes were queried quite soon after I had changed them, and I had to be precious fly, I can tell you, to avoid complications. And now that the second batch has come in to the Bank, the planting of fresh specimens is going to be harder still. There isn't a money-changer on the Continent of Europe that isn't keeping his weather eyeball peeled, to say nothing of the detectives that the Bank people have sent abroad."

He paused and looked appealingly at his companion, but Purcell, still minding his helm, only growled "Well?"

"Well, I want to chuck it, Dan. When you've had a run of luck and pocketed your winnings, it is time to stop play."

"You've come into some money, then, I take it?" said Purcell.

"No, I haven't. But I can make a living now by safe and respectable means, and I'm sick of all this scheming and dodging with the gaol everlastingly under my lee."

"The reason I asked," said Purcell, "is that there is a trifle outstanding. You hadn't forgotten that, I suppose?"

"No, I hadn't forgotten it, but I thought that perhaps you might be willing to let me down a bit easily."

The other man pursed up his thick lips and continued to gaze stonily over the bow.

"Oh, that's what you thought?" he said, and then, after a pause, "I fancy you must have lost sight of some of the facts when you thought that. Let me just remind you how the case stands. To begin with, you start your career with a little playful embezzlement, you blue the proceeds and you are mug enough to be found out. Then I come in. I compound the affair with old Marston for a couple of thousand, and practically clean myself out of every penny I possess, and he consents to regard your temporary absence in the light of a holiday.

"Now, why do I do this? Am I a philanthropist? Devil a bit. I'm a man of business. Before I ladle out that two-thousand, I make a business contract with you. I have discovered how to make a passable imitation of the Bank of England paper. You are a skilled engraver and a plausible scamp. I am to supply you with paper blanks. You are to engrave plates, print the notes, and get them changed. I am to take two-thirds of the proceeds, and, although I have done the most difficult part of the work, I agree to regard my share of the profits as constituting repayment of the loan.

"Our contract amounts to this: I lend you two-thousand without security – with an infernal amount of insecurity, in fact. You 'promise, covenant, and agree,' as the lawyers say, to hand me back ten-thousand in instalments, being the products of our joint industry. It is a verbal contract which I have no means of enforcing, but I trust you to keep your word, and up to the present you have kept it. You have paid me a little over four-thousand. Now you want to cry off and leave the balance unpaid. Isn't that the position?"

"Not exactly," said Varney. "I'm not crying off the debt. I only want time. Look here, Dan. I'm making about three-fifty-a-year now. That isn't much, but I'll manage to let you have a hundred-a-year out of it. What do you say to that?"

Purcell laughed scornfully. "A hundred a year to pay off six thousand! That'll take just sixty years, and as I'm now forty-three, I shall be exactly a hundred-and-three years of age when the last instalment is paid. I think,

Varney, you'll admit that a man of a hundred-and-three is getting past his prime."

"Well, I'll pay you something down to start. I've saved about eighteen-hundred pounds out of the note business. You can have that now, and I'll payoff as much I can at a time until I'm clear. Remember, that if I should happen to get clapped in chokee for twenty years or so, you won't get anything. And, I tell you, it's getting a risky business."

"I'm willing to take the risk," said Purcell.

"I daresay you are," Varney retorted passionately, "because it's *my* risk. If I am grabbed, it's my racket. You sit out. It's I who passed the notes, and I'm known to be a skilled engraver. That'll be good enough for them. They won't trouble about who made the paper."

"I hope not," said Purcell.

"Of course they wouldn't, and you know I shouldn't give you away."

"Naturally. Why should you? Wouldn't do you any good."

"Well, give me a chance, Dan," Varney pleaded. "This business is getting on my nerves. I want to be quit of it. You've had four-thousand. That's a hundred percent. You haven't done so badly."

"I didn't expect to do badly. I took a big risk. I gambled two thousand for ten."

"Yes, and you got me out of the way while you put the screw on poor old Haygarth to make his daughter marry you."

It was an indiscreet thing to say, but Purcell's stolid indifference to his danger and distress had ruffled Varney's temper.

Purcell, however, was unmoved. "I don't know," he said, "what you mean by getting you out of the way. You were never in the way. You were always hankering after Maggie, but I could never see that she wanted you."

"Well, she certainly didn't want you," Varney retorted. "And, for that matter, I don't much think she wants you now."

For the first time Purcell withdrew his eye from the horizon to turn it on his companion. And an evil eye it was, set in the great, sensual face, now purple with anger.

"What the devil do you mean?" he exclaimed furiously. "You infernal, sallow-faced, little whipper-snapper! If you mention my wife's name again, I'll knock you on the head and pitch you overboard."

Varney's face flushed darkly, and for a moment he was inclined to try the wager a battle. But the odds were impossible, and if Varney was not a coward, neither was he a fool. But the discussion was at an end. Nothing was to be hoped for now. These indiscreet words had rendered further pleading impossible.

The silence that settled down in the yacht and the aloofness that encompassed the two men were conducive to reflection. Each ignored the presence of the other. When the course was altered southerly, Purcell slacked out the sheets with his own hand as he put up the helm. He might have been sailing single-handed. And Varney watched him askance, but made no move, sitting hunched up on the locker, nursing a slowly-matured hatred and thinking his thoughts.

Very queer thoughts they were. He was following out the train of events that might have happened, pursuing them to their possible consequences. Supposing Purcell had carried out his threat? Well, there would have been a pretty tough struggle, for Varney was no weakling. But a struggle with that solid fifteen stone of flesh could end only one way. No, there was no doubt – he would have gone overboard.

And what then? Would Purcell have gone back to Sennen Cove, or sailed alone into Penzance? In either case, he would have had to make up some sort of story, and no one could have contradicted him, whether the story was believed or not. But it would have been awkward for Purcell.

Then there was the body. That would have been washed up sooner or later, as much of it as the lobsters had left. Well, lobsters don't eat clothes or bones, and a dent in the skull might take some accounting for. Very awkward this – for Purcell. He would probably have had to clear out – to make a bolt for it, in short.

The mental picture of this great bully fleeing in terror from the vengeance of the law gave Varney appreciable pleasure. Most of his life he had been borne down by the moral and physical weight of this domineering brute. At school, Purcell had fagged him. He had even bullied him up at Cambridge, and now he had fastened on forever, like the Old Man of the Sea. And Purcell always got the best of it. When he, Varney, had come back from Italy after that unfortunate little affair, behold! The girl whom they had both wanted (and who had wanted neither of them) had changed from Maggie Haygarth into Maggie Purcell. And so it was even unto this day. Purcell, a prosperous stockjobber now, spent a part of his secret leisure making, in absolute safety, these accursed paper blanks, which he, Varney, must risk his liberty to change into money. Yes, it was quite pleasant to think of Purcell sneaking from town to town, from country to country, with the police at his heels.

But in these days of telegraphs and extradition there isn't much chance for a fugitive. Purcell would have been caught to a certainty, and he would have been hanged. No doubt of it. The imagined picture of the execution gave him quite a lengthy entertainment. Then his errant thoughts began to spread out in search of other possibilities. For, after all, it was not an absolute certainty that Purcell could have got him overboard. There was just the chance that Purcell might have gone overboard himself. That would have been a very different affair.

Varney settled himself composedly to consider the new and interesting train of consequences that would thus have been set going. They were more agreeable to contemplate than the others, because they did not include his own demise. The execution scene made no appearance in this version. The salient fact was that his oppressor would have vanished, that the intolerable burden of his servitude would have been lifted forever, that he would have been free.

It was mere idle speculation to while away a dull hour with an uncongenial companion, and he let his thoughts ramble at large. One moment he was dreamily wondering whether Maggie would ever have listened to him, ever have come to care for him. The next, he was back in the yacht's cabin, where hung from a hook on the bulkhead the revolver that the Rodneys used to practise at floating bottles. It was usually loaded, he knew, but, if not, there was a canvas bag full of cartridges in the starboard locker. Again, he found himself dreaming of the home that he would have had, a home very different from the cheerless lodgings in which he moped at present, and then his thoughts had flitted back to the yacht's hold, and were busying themselves with the row of half-hundredweights that rested on the timbers on either side of the kelson.

When Varney had thus brought his mental picture, so to speak, to a finish, its completeness surprised him. It was so simple, so secure. He had actually planned out the scheme of a murder, and he found himself wondering whether many murders passed undetected. They well might if murders were as easy and as safe as this – a dangerous reflection for an injured and angry man. And at this critical point his meditations were interrupted by Purcell, continuing the conversation as if there had been no pause.

"So you can take it from me, Varney, that I expect you to stick to your bargain. I paid down my money, and I'm going to have my pound of flesh."

It was a brutal thing to say, and it was brutally said. But more than that, it was in-opportune – or opportune, as you will, for it came as a sort of infernal doxology to the devil's anthem that had been, all unknown, ringing in Varney's soul.

Purcell had spoken without looking round. That was his unpleasant habit. Had he looked at his companion, he might have been startled. A change in Varney's face might have given him pause: A warm flush, a sparkle of the eye, a look of elation, of settled purpose, deadly, inexorable – the look of a man who has made a fateful resolution.

It was so simple, so secure! That was the burden of the song that echoed in Varney's brain.

He glanced over the sea. They had opened the south coast now, and he could see, afar off, a fleet of black-sailed luggers heading east. They wouldn't be in his way. Nor would the big four-master that was creeping away to the west, for she was hull down already, and other ships there were none.

There was one hindrance, though. Dead ahead the Wolf Rock Lighthouse rose from the blue water, its red-and-white ringed tower looking like some gaudily painted toy. The keepers of lonely lighthouses have a natural habit of watching the passing shipping through their glasses, and it was possible that one of their telescopes might be pointed at the yacht at this very moment. That was a complication.

Suddenly there came down the wind a sharp report like the firing of a gun, quickly followed by a second. It was the explosive signal from the Longships Lighthouse – but when they looked round there was no lighthouse to be seen – the dark-blue, heaving water faded away at the foot of an advancing wall of vapour.

Purcell cursed fluently. A pretty place, this, to be caught in, in a fog! And then, as his eye lighted on his companion, he demanded angrily, "What the devil are you griming at?"

For Varney, drunk with suppressed excitement, snapped his fingers at rocks and shoals. He was thinking only of the lighthouse keeper's telescope and of the revolver that hung on the bulkhead. He must make some excuse presently to go below and secure that revolver.

But no excuse was necessary. The opportunity came of itself. After a hasty glance at the vanishing land and another at the compass, Purcell put up the helm to gybe the yacht round on to an easterly course.

As she came round, the single headsail that she carried in place of jib and foresail shivered for a few seconds, and then filled suddenly on the opposite tack. And at this moment the halyards parted with a loud snap. The end of the rope flew through the blocks, and, in an instant, the sail was down and its upper half trailing in the water alongside.

Purcell swore volubly, but kept an eye to business. "Run below, Varney," said he, "and fetch up that coil of new rope out of the starboard locker while I had the sail on board. And look alive. We don't want to drift down on to the Wolf."

Varney obeyed with silent alacrity and a curious feeling of elation. It was going to be even easier and safer than he had thought. He slipped through the hatch into the cabin, quietly took the revolver from its hook, and examined the chambers.

Finding them all loaded, he cocked Ike hammer and slipped the weapon carefully into the inside breast pocket of his oilskin coat. Then he took the coil of rope from the locker and went on deck.

As he emerged from the hatch, he perceived that the yacht was already enveloped in fog, which drifted past in steamy clouds, and that she had come up head to wind. Purcell was kneeling on the forecastle, tugging at the sail, which had caught under the forefoot, and punctuating his efforts with deep-voiced curses.

Varney stole silently along the deck, steadying himself by mast and shroud, softly laid down the coil of rope, and approached. Purcell was quite engrossed with his task. His back was towards Varney, his face over the side, intent on the entangled sail. It was a chance in a thousand.

With scarcely a moment's hesitation, Varney stooped forward, steadying himself with a hand on the little windlass, and softly drawing forth the revolver, pointed it at the back of Purcell's head at the spot where the back seam of his sou'wester met the brim.

The report rang out but weak and flat in that open space, and a cloud of smoke mingled with the fog, but it blew away immediately, and showed Purcell almost unchanged in posture, crouching on the sail, with his chin resting on the little rim of bulwark, while behind him his murderer, as if turned into bronze, still stood stooping forward, one hand grasping the windlass, the other still pointing the revolver.

Thus the two figures remained for some seconds motionless like some horrible waxworks, until the little yacht, lifting to the swell, gave a more than usually lively curvet, when Purcell rolled over on to his back, and Varney relaxed the rigidity of his posture like a golf-player who has watched his ball drop.

Purcell was dead. That was the salient fact. The head wagged to and fro as the yacht pitched and rolled, the limp arms and legs seemed to twitch, the limp body to writhe uneasily. But Varney was not disturbed. Lifeless things will move on an unsteady deck. He was only interested to notice how the passive movements produced the illusion of life. But it was only illusion. Purcell was dead. There was no doubt of that.

The double report from the Longships came down the wind, and then, as if in answer, a prolonged, deep bellow. That was the fog-horn of the lighthouse on the Wolf Rock, and it sounded surprisingly neat. But, of course, these signals were meant to be heard at a distance. Then a stream of hot sunshine, pouring down on deck, startled him, and made him hurry. The body must be got overboard before the fog lifted.

With an uneasy glance at the clear sky overhead, he hastily cast off the broken halyard from its cleat and cut off a couple of fathoms. Then he hurried below, and, lifting the trap in the cabin floor, hoisted out one of the iron half-hundredweights with which the yacht was ballasted.

536

As he stepped on deck with the weight in his hand, the sun was shining overhead, but the fog was still thick below, and the horn sounded once more from the Wolf. And again it struck him as surprisingly neat.

He passed the length of rope that he had cut off twice round Purcell's body, hauled it tight, and secured it with a knot. Then he made the ends fast to the handle of the iron weight.

Not much fear of Purcell drifting ashore now. That weight would hold him as long as there was anything to hold. But it had taken some time to do, and the warning bellow from the Wolf seemed to draw nearer and nearer. He was about to heave the body over when his eye fell on the dead man's sou'wester, which had fallen off when the body rolled over.

That hat must be got rid of, for Purcell's name was worked in silk on the lining and there was an unmistakable bullet-hole through the back. It must be destroyed, or, which would be simpler and quicker, lashed securely on the dead man's head.

Hurriedly, Varney ran aft and descended to the cabin. He had noticed a new ball of spun-yarn in the locker when he had fetched the rope. This would be the very thing.

He was back again in a few moments with the ball in his hand, unwinding it as he came, and without wasting time he knelt down by the body and fell to work.

And every half-minute the deep-voiced growl of the Wolf came to him out of the fog, and each time it sounded nearer and yet nearer.

By the time he had made the sou'wester secure, the dead man's face and chin were encased in a web of spun-yarn that made him look like some old-time, grotesque-vizored Samurai warrior.

Varney rose to his feet. But his task was not finished yet. There was Purcell's suitcase. That must be sunk, too, and there was something in it that had figured in the detailed picture that his imagination had drawn. He ran to the cockpit where the suit-case lay, and having tried its fastenings and found it unlocked, he opened it and took out a letter that lay on top of the other contents. This he tossed through the hatch into the cabin, and, having closed and fastened the suit-case, he carried it forward and made it fast to the iron weight with half a dozen turns of spun-yarn.

That was really all, and indeed it was time. As he rose once more to his feet the growl of the foghorn burst out, as it seemed, right over the stern of the yacht, and she was drifting stern foremost, who could say how fast. Now, too, he caught a more ominous sound, which he might have heard sooner had he listened – the wash of water, the boom of breakers bursting on a rock.

A sudden revulsion came over him. He burst into a wild, sardonic laugh. And had it come to this, after all? Had he schemed and laboured only to leave himself alone on an unmanageable craft drifting down to shipwreck and certain death? Had he taken all this thought and care to secure Purcell's body, when his own might be resting beside it on the sea-bottom within an hour?

But the reverie was brief. Suddenly, from the white void over his very head, as it seemed, there issued a stunning, thunderous roar that shook the deck under his feet. The water around him boiled into a foamy chaos, the din of bursting waves was in his ears, the yacht plunged and wallowed amidst clouds of spray, and for an instant a dim, gigantic shadow loomed through the fog and was gone. In that moment his nerve had come back. Holding on with one hand to the windlass he dragged the body to the edge of the forecastle, hoisted the weight outboard, and then, taking advantage of a heavy lurch, gave the corpse a vigorous shove. There was a rattle and a hollow splash, and corpse and weight and suitcase had vanished into the seething water.

He clung to the swinging mast and waited. Breathlessly he told out the allotted seconds until once again the invisible Titan belched forth his thunderous warning. But this time the roar came over the yacht's bow. She had drifted past the rock then. The danger was over, and Purcell would have to go down to Davy Jones' locker companionless after all.

Very soon the water around ceased to boil and tumble, and as the yacht's wild plunging settled down once more into the normal rise and fall on the long swell, Varney turned his attention to the refitting of the halyard. But what was this on the creamy, duck sail? A pool of blood and two gory imprints of his own left hand! That wouldn't do at all. He would have to clear that away before he could hoist the sail, which was annoying, as the yacht was helpless without her headsail, and was evidently drifting out to sea.

He fetched a bucket, a swab, and a scrubbing-brush, and set to work. The bulk of the large bloodstain cleared off pretty completely after he had drenched the sail with a bucket-full or two and given it a good scrubbing. But the edge of the stain where the heat of the deck had dried it remained like a painted boundary on a map, and the two handprints – which had also dried, though they faded to a pale buff – continued clearly visible.

Varney began to grow uneasy. If those stains would not come out – especially the hand-prints – it would be very awkward, they would take so much explaining. He decided to try the effect of marine soap, and fetched a cake from the cabin, but even this did not obliterate the stains completely, though it turned them a faint, greenish brown, very unlike the colour of blood. So he scrubbed on until at last the hand-prints faded away entirely, and the large stain was reduced to a faint green, wavy line, and that was the best he could do – and quite good enough, for if that faint line should ever be noticed no one would suspect its origin.

He put away the bucket and proceeded with the refitting. The sea had disengaged the sail from the forefoot, and he hauled it on board without difficulty. Then there was the reeving of the new halyard, a troublesome business involving the necessity of his going aloft, where his weight – small man as he was – made the yacht roll most infernally, and set him swinging to-and-fro like the bob of a metronome. But he was a smart yachtsman and active, though not powerful, and a few minutes' strenuous exertion ended in his sliding down the shrouds with the new halyard running fairly through the upper block. A vigorous haul or two at the new, hairy rope sent the head of the dripping sail aloft, and the yacht was once more under control.

The rig of the *Sandhopper* was not smart, but it was handy. She carried a short bow-sprit to accommodate the single headsail and a relatively large mizzen, of which the advantage was, that by judicious management of the mizzen-sheet, the yacht would sail with very little attention to the helm. Of this advantage Varney was keenly appreciative just now, for he had several things to do before entering port. He wanted refreshment, he wanted a wash, and the various traces of recent events had to be removed. Also, there was that letter to be attended to. So that it was convenient to be able to leave the helm in charge of a lashing for a minute now and again.

When he had washed, he put the kettle on the spirit stove, and while it was heating busied himself in cleaning the revolver, flinging the empty cartridge-case overboard, and replacing it with a cartridge from the bag in the locker. Then he picked up the letter that he had taken from Purcell's suit-case and examined it. It was addressed to "*Joseph Penfield, Esq., George Yard, Lombard Street*", and was unstamped, though the envelope was fastened up. He affixed a stamp from his pocket-book, and when the kettle began to boil, he held the envelope in the steam that issued from the spout. Very soon the flap of the envelope loosened and curled back, when he laid it aside to mix himself a mug of hot grog, which, together with the letter and a biscuit-tin, he took out into the cockpit. The fog was still dense, and the hoot of a steamer's whistle from somewhere to the westward caused him to reach the foghorn out of the locker, and blow a long blast on it. As if in answer to his treble squeak came the deep bass note from the Wolf, and unconsciously he looked round. He turned automatically, as one does towards a sudden noise, not expecting to see anything but fog, and what he did see startled him not a little.

For there was the lighthouse – or half of it, rather – standing up above the fog-bank, clear, distinct, and hardly a mile away. The gilded vane, the sparkling lantern, the gallery, and the upper half of the red-and-white ringed tower, stood sharp against the pallid sky. But the lower half was invisible. It was a strange apparition – like half a lighthouse suspended in mid-air – and uncommonly disturbing, too. It raised a very awkward question. If he could see the lantern, the light-keepers could see him. But how long had the lantern been clear of the fog?

Thus he meditated as, with one hand on the tiller, he munched his biscuit and sipped his grog. Presently he picked up the stamped envelope and drew from it a letter and a folded document, both of which he tore into fragments and dropped overboard. Then, from his pocket-book, he took a similar but unaddressed envelope from which he drew out the contents, and very curious those contents were.

There was a letter, brief and laconic, which he read over thoughtfully. *"These"* it ran, *"are all I have by me, but they will do for the present, and when you have planted them I will let you have a fresh supply."* There was no date and no signature, but the rather peculiar hand-writing was similar to that on the envelope addressed to Joseph Penfield, Esq.

The other contents consisted of a dozen sheets of blank paper, each of the size of a Bank of England note. But they were not quite blank, for each bore an elaborate water-mark, identical with that of a twenty-pound bank note. They were, in fact, the "paper blanks" of which Purcell had spoken. The envelope with its contents had been slipped into his hand by Purcell, without remark, only three days ago.

Varney refolded the "blanks", enclosed them within the letter, and slipped letter and "blanks" together into the stamped envelope, the flap of which he licked and reclosed.

"I should like to see old Penfield's face when he opens that envelope," was his reflection as, with a grim smile, he put it away in his pocket-book. "And I wonder what he will do," he added, mentally. "However, I shall see before many days are over."

Varney looked at his watch. He was to meet Jack Rodney on Penzance Pier at a quarter-to-three. He would never do it at this rate, for when he opened Mount's Bay, Penzance would be right in the wind's eye. That would mean a long beat to windward. Then Rodney would be there first, waiting for him. Deuced awkward, this. He would have to account for his being alone on board – would have to invent some lie about having put Purcell ashore at Mousehole or Newlyn. But a lie is a very pernicious thing. Its effects are cumulative. You never know when you have done with it. Now, if he had reached Penzance before Rodney, he need have said nothing about Purcell – for the present, at any rate, and that would have been so much safer.

When the yacht was about abreast of Lamorna Cove, though some seven miles to the south, the breeze began to draw ahead and the fog cleared off quite suddenly. The change of wind was unfavourable for the moment, but when it veered round yet a little more until it blew from east-north-east, Varney brightened up considerably. There was still a chance of reaching Penzance before Rodney arrived, for now, as soon as he had fairly opened Mount's Bay, he could head straight for his destination and make it on a single board.

Between two and three hours later the *Sandhopper* entered Penzance Harbour and, threading her way among an assemblage of luggers and small coasters, brought up alongside the Albert Pier at the foot of a vacant ladder. Having made the yacht fast to a couple of rings, Varney divested himself of his oilskins, locked the cabin scuttle, and climbed the ladder. The change of wind had saved him after all and, as he strode away along the pier, he glanced complacently at his watch. He still had nearly half-an-hour to the good.

He seemed to know the place well and to have a definite objective, for he struck out briskly from the foot of the pier into Market Jew Street, and from thence by a somewhat zig-zag route to a road which eventually brought him out about the middle of the Esplanade. Continuing westward, he entered the Newlyn Road along which he walked rapidly for about a third-of-a-mile, when he drew up opposite a small letter-box which was let into a wall. Here he stepped to read the tablet on which was printed the hours of collection, and then, having glanced at his watch, he walked on again, but at a less rapid pace.

When he reached the outskirts of Newlyn, he turned and began slowly to retrace his steps, looking at his watch from time to time with a certain air of impatience. Presently a quick step behind him caused him to look round. The newcomer was a postman, striding along, bag on shoulder, with the noisy tread of a heavily-shod man, and evidently collecting letters. Varney let him pass, watched him halt at the little letterbox, unlock the door, gather up the letters and stow them in his bag, heard the clang of the iron door, and finally saw the man set forth again on his pilgrimage. Then he brought forth his pocket-book and, drawing from it the letter addressed to Joseph Penfield, Esq., stepped up to the letter-box. The tablet now announced that the next collection would be at 8:30 p.m. Varney read the announcement with a faint smile, glanced again at his watch, which indicated two-minutes-past-four, and dropped the letter into the box.

As he walked up the pier, with a large paper bag under his arm, he became aware of a tall man, who was doing sentry-go before a Gladstone bag, that stood on the coping opposite the ladder, and who, observing his approach, came forward to meet him.

541

"Here you are, then, Rodney," was Varney's rather unoriginal greeting.

"Yes," replied Rodney, "and here I've been for nearly half-an-hour. Purcell gone?"

"Bless you, yes, long ago," answered Varney.

"I didn't see him at the station. What train was he going by?"

"I don't know. He said something about taking Falmouth on the way – had some business or other there. But I expect he's gone to have a feed at one of the hotels. We got hung up in a fog – that's why I'm so late. I've been up to buy some prog."

"Well," said Rodney, "bring it on board. It's time we were under way. As soon as we are outside, I'll take charge and you can go below and stoke up at your ease."

The two men descended the ladder and proceeded at once to hoist the sails and cast off the shore-ropes. A few strokes of an oar sent them clear of the lee of the pier, and in five minutes the yacht *Sandhopper* was once more outside, heading south with a steady breeze from east-north-east.

II – The Unraveling
of the Mystery
(Related by Christopher Jervis, M.D.)

Romance lurks in unsuspected places. We walk abroad amidst scenes made dull by familiarity, and let our thoughts ramble far away beyond the commonplace. In fancy we thread the ghostly aisles of some tropical forest; we linger on the white beach of some lonely coral island, where the cocoa-nut palms, shivering in the sea-breeze, patter a refrain to the song of the surf; we wander by moonlight through the narrow streets of some southern city, and hear the thrum of the guitar rise to the shrouded balcony; and behold! All the time Romance is at our very doors.

It was on a bright afternoon early in March, that I sat beside my friend Thorndyke on one of the lower benches of the lecture theatre of the Royal College of Surgeons. Not a likely place this to encounter Romance, and yet there it was, if we had only known it, lying unnoticed at present on the green baize cover of the lecturer's table. But, for the moment, we were thinking of nothing but the lecture.

The theatre was nearly full. It usually was when Professor D'Arcy lectured, for that genial savant had the magnetic gift of infusing his own enthusiasm into the lecture, and so into his audience, even when, as on this occasion, his subject lay on the outside edge of medical science. To-day he was lecturing on marine worms, standing before the great blackboard with a bunch of coloured chalks in either hand, talking with easy eloquence – mostly over his shoulder – while he covered the black surface with those delightful drawings that added so much to the charm of his lectures.

I watched his flying fingers with fascination, dividing my attention between him and a young man on the bench below me, who was frantically copying the diagrams in a large note-book, assisted by an older friend, who sat by him and handed him the coloured pencils as he needed them.

The latter part of the lecture dealt with those beautiful sea-worms that build themselves tubes to live in, worms like the *Serpula*, that make their shelly or stony tubes by secretion from their own bodies, or, like the *Sabella* or *Terebella*, build them up with sand-grains, little stones, or fragments of shell.

When the lecture came to an end, we trooped down into the arena to look at the exhibits and exchange a few words with the genial professor. Thorndyke knew him very well, and was welcomed with a warm handshake and a facetious question.

543

"What are you doing here, Thorndyke?" asked Professor D'Arcy. "Is it possible that there are medico-legal possibilities even in a marine worm?"

"Oh, come!" protested Thorndyke. "Don't make me such a hidebound specialist. May I have no rational interest in life? Must I live forever in the witness-box, like a marine worm in its tube?"

"I suspect you don't get very far out of your tube," said the professor, with a smile at my colleague. "And that reminds me that I have something in your line. What do you make of this? Let us hear you extract its history."

Here, with a mischievous twinkle, he handed Thorndyke a small, round object, which my friend inspected curiously as it lay in the palm of his hand.

"In the first place," said he, "it is a cork. The cork of a small jar."

"Right," said the professor, " – full marks. What else?"

"The cork has been saturated with paraffin wax."

"Right again."

"Then some Robinson Crusoe seems to have used it as a button, judging by the two holes in it, and an end of what looks like catgut."

"Yes."

"Finally, a marine worm of some kind – a *Terebella*, I think – has built a tube on it."

"Quite right. And now tell us the history of the cork or button."

"I should like to know something more about the worm first," said Thorndyke.

"The worm," said Professor D'Arcy, "is *Terebella Rufescens*. It lives, unlike most other species, on a rocky bottom, and in a depth of water of not less than ten fathoms."

It was at this point that Romance stepped in. The young man whom I had noticed working so strenuously at his notes had edged up alongside, and was staring at the object in Thorndyke's hand, not with mere interest or curiosity, but with the utmost amazement and horror. His expression was so remarkable that we all, with one accord, dropped our conversation to look at him.

"Might I be allowed to examine that specimen?" he asked, and when Thorndyke handed it to him, he held it close to his eyes, scrutinising it with frowning astonishment, turned it over and over, and felt the frayed ends of catgut between his fingers, Finally, he beckoned to his friend, and the two whispered together for a while, and watching them I saw the second man's eyebrows lift, and the same expression of horrified surprise appear on his face. Then the younger man addressed the professor.

"Would you mind telling me where you got this specimen, sir?"

The professor was quite interested. "It was sent to me," he said, "by a friend, who picked it up on the beach at Morte Hoe, on the coast of North Cornwall."

The two young men looked significantly at one another, and, after a brief pause, the older one asked, "Is this specimen of much value, sir?"

"No," replied the professor, "it is only a curiosity. There are several specimens of the worm in our collection. But why do you ask?"

"Because I should like to acquire it. I can't give you particulars – I am a lawyer, I may explain – but, from what my brother tells me it appears that this object has a bearing on – er – on a case in which we are both interested. A very important bearing, I may add, on a very important case."

The professor was delighted. "There, now, Thorndyke," he chuckled. "What did I tell you? The medico-legal worm has arrived. I told you in was something in your line, and now you've been forestalled. Of course," he added, turning to the lawyer, "you are very welcome to this specimen. I'll give you a box to carry it in, with some cotton wool." The specimen was duly packed in its box, and the latter deposited in the lawyer's pocket, but the two brothers did not immediately leave the theatre. They stood apart, talking earnestly together, until Thorndyke and I had taken our leave of the professor, when the lawyer advanced and addressed my colleague.

"I don't suppose you remember me, Dr. Thorndyke," he began, but my friend interrupted him.

"Yes, I do. You are Mr. Rodney. You were junior to Brooke in *Jelks v. Partington*. Can I be of any assistance to you?"

"If you would be so kind," replied Rodney. "My brother and I have been talking this over, and we think we should like to have your opinion on the case. The fact is, we both jumped to a conclusion at once, and now we've got what the Yankees call 'cold feet'. We think that we may have jumped too soon. Let me introduce my brother, Dr. Philip Rodney."

We shook hands, and, making our way out of the theatre, presently emerged from the big portico into Lincoln's Inn Fields

"If you will come and take a cup of tea at my chambers in Old Buildings," said Rodney, "we can give you the necessary particulars. There isn't so very much to tell, after all. My brother identifies the cork or button, and that seems to be the only plain fact that we have. Tell Dr. Thorndyke how you identified it, Phil."

"It is a simple matter," said Philip Rodney. "I went out in a boat to do some dredging with a friend named Purcell. We both wore our oilskins as the sea was choppy and there was a good deal of spray blowing about, but Purcell had lost the top button of his, so that the collar kept blowing open and letting the spray down his neck. We had no spare buttons or needles or thread on board, but it occurred to me that I could rig up a jury button with a cork from one of my little collecting jars, so I took one out, bored a couple of holes through it with a pipe-cleaner, and threaded a piece of cat-gut through the holes."

"Why cat-gut?" asked Thorndyke.

"Because I happened to have it. I play the fiddle, and I generally have a bit of a broken string in my pocket – usually an *E* string – the *E* strings are always breaking, you know. Well, I had the end of an *E* string in my pocket then, so I fastened the button on with it. I bored two holes in the coat, passed the ends of the string through, and tied a reef-knot. It was as strong as a house."

"You have no doubt that it's the same cork?"

"None at all. First there is the size, which I know from having ordered the corks separately from the jars. Then I paraffined them myself after sticking on the blank labels. The label is there still, protected by the wax. And lastly there is the cat-gut – the bit that is left is obviously part of an *E* string."

"Yes," said Thorndyke, "the identification seems to be unimpeachable. Now let us have the story."

"We'll have some tea first," said Rodney. "This is my burrow." As he spoke, he dived into the dark entry of one of the ancient buildings on the south side of the little square, and we followed him up the crabbed, timeworn stairs, so different from our own lordly staircase in King's Bench Walk. He let us into his chambers and, having offered us each an armchair, said, "My brother will spin you the yarn while I make the tea. When you have heard him you can begin the examination-in-chief. You understand that this is a confidential matter and that we are dealing with it professionally?"

"Certainly," replied Thorndyke, "we quite understand that." And thereupon Philip Rodney began his story.

"One morning last June, two men started from Sennen Cove, on the west coast of Cornwall, to sail to Penzance in a little yacht that belongs to my brother and me. One of them was Purcell, of whom I spoke just now, and the other was a man named Varney. When they started, Purcell was wearing the oilskin coat with this button on it. The yacht arrived at Penzance at about four in the afternoon. Purcell went ashore alone to take the train to London or Falmouth, and was never seen again dead or alive. The following day Purcell's solicitor, a Mr. Penfield, received a letter from him bearing the Penzance postmark and the hour 8:45 p.m. The letter was evidently sent by mistake – put into the wrong envelope – and it appears to have been a highly compromising document. Penfield refuses to give any particulars, but thinks that the letter fully accounts for Purcell's disappearance – thinks, in fact, that Purcell has bolted.

546

"It was understood that Purcell was going to London from Penzance, but he seems to have told Varney that he intended to call in at Falmouth. Whether or not he went to Falmouth we don't know. Varney saw him go up the ladder on to the pier, and there all traces of him vanished. Varney thinks he may have discovered the mistake about the letter and got on board some outward-bound ship at Falmouth, but that is only surmise. Still, it is highly probable, and when my brother and I saw that button at the museum, we remembered the suggestion and instantly jumped to the conclusion that poor Purcell had gone overboard."

"And then," said Rodney, handing us our tea-cups, "when we came to talk it over we rather tended to revise our conclusion."

"Why?" asked Thorndyke.

"Well, there are several other possibilities. Purcell may have found a proper button on the yacht and cut off the cork and thrown it overboard – we must ask Varney if he did – or the coat itself may have gone over or been lost or given away, and so on."

On this Thorndyke made no comment, stirring his tea slowly with an air of deep preoccupation. Presently he looked up and asked, "Who saw the yacht start?"

"I did," said Philip. "I and Mrs. Purcell and her sister and some fishermen on the beach. Purcell was steering, and he took the yacht right out to sea, outside the Longships. A sea fog came down soon after, and we were rather anxious, because the Wolf Rock lay right to leeward of the yacht."

"Did anyone besides Varney see Purcell at Penzance?"

"Apparently not. But we haven't asked. Varney's statement seemed to settle that question. He couldn't very well have been mistaken, you know," Philip added with a smile.

"Besides," said Rodney, "if there were any doubt, there is the letter. It was posted in Penzance after eight o'clock at night. Now I met Varney on the pier at a quarter-past four, and we sailed out of Penzance a few minutes later to return to Sennen."

"Had Varney been ashore?" asked Thorndyke.

"Yes, he had been up to the town buying some provisions."

"But you said Purcell went ashore alone."

"Yes, but there's nothing in that. Purcell was not a genial man. It was the sort of thing he would do."

"And that is all that you know of the matter?" Thorndyke asked, after a few moments' reflection.

"Yes. But we might see if Varney can remember anything more, and we might try if we can squeeze any more information out of old Penfield."

'You won't," said Thorndyke. "I know Penfield and I never trouble to ask him questions. Besides, there is nothing to ask at present. We have an item of evidence that we have not fully examined. I suggest that we exhaust that, and meanwhile keep our own counsel most completely."

Rodney looked dissatisfied. "If," said he, "the item of evidence that you refer to is the button, it seems to me that we have got all that we are likely to get out of it. We have identified it, and we know that it has been thrown up on the beach at Morte Hoe. What more can we learn from it?"

"That remains to be seen," replied Thorndyke. "We may learn nothing, but, on the other hand, we may be able to trace the course of its travels and learn its recent history. It may give us a hint as to where to start a fresh inquiry."

Rodney laughed sceptically. "You talk like a clairvoyant, as if you had the power to make this bit of cork break out into fluent discourse. Of course, you can look at the thing and speculate and guess, but surely the common sense of the matter is to ask a plain question of the man who probably knows. If it turns out that Varney saw Purcell throw the button over-board, or can tell us how it got into the sea, all your speculations will have been useless. I say, let us ask Varney first, and if he knows nothing, it will be time to start guessing."

But Thorndyke was calmly obdurate. "We are not going to guess, Rodney. We are going to investigate. Let me have the button for a couple of days. If I learn nothing from it, I will return it to you, and you can then refresh your legal soul with verbal testimony. But give scientific methods a chance first."

With evident reluctance Rodney handed him the little box. "I have asked your advice," he said rather ungraciously, "so I suppose I must take it, but your methods appeal more to the sporting than the business instincts."

"We shall see," said Thorndyke, rising with a satisfied air. "But, meanwhile, I stipulate that you make no communication to anybody."

"Very well," said Rodney, and we took leave of the two brothers.

As we walked down Chancery Lane, I looked at Thorndyke, and detected in him an air of purpose for which I could not quite account. Clearly, he had something in view.

"It seems to me," I said tentatively, "that there was something in what Rodney said. Why shouldn't the button just have been thrown overboard?"

He stopped and looked at me with humorous reproach. "Jervis!" he exclaimed, "I am ashamed of you. You are as bad as Rodney. You have utterly lost sight of the main fact, which is a most impressive one. Here is a cork button. Now an ordinary cork, if immersed long enough, will soak up water until it is waterlogged, and then sink to the bottom. But this one is impregnated with paraffin wax. It can't get water-logged, and it can't sink. It would float forever."

"Well?"

"But it *has* sunk. It has been lying at the bottom of the sea for months, long enough for a *Terebella* to build a tube on it. And we have D'Arcy's statement that it has been lying in not less than ten fathoms of water. Then, at last, it has broken loose and risen to the surface and drifted ashore. Now, I ask you, what has held it down at the bottom of the sea? Of course, it may have been only the coat, weighted by something in the pocket, but there is a much more probable suggestion."

"Yes, I see," said I.

"I suspect you don't – altogether," he rejoined, with a malicious smile. And in the end it turned out that he was right.

The air of purpose that I noted was not deceptive. No sooner had we reached our chambers then he fell to work as if with a definite object. Standing by the window, he scrutinised the button, first with the naked eye, and then with a lens, and finally laying it on the stage of the microscope, examined the worm-tube by the light of a condenser with a two-inch objective. And the result seemed to please him amazingly.

His next proceeding was to detach, with a fine pair of forceps, the largest of the tiny fragments of stone of which the worm-tube was built. This fragment he cemented on a slide with Canada balsam and, fetching from the laboratory a slip of Turkey stone, he proceeded to grind the little fragment to a flat surface. Then he melted the balsam, turned the fragment over, and repeated the grinding process until the little fragment was ground down flat. Then he applied fresh balsam and a cover-glass. The specimen was now ready for examination, and it was at this point that I suddenly remembered I had an appointment at six o'clock.

It had struck half-past seven when I returned, and a glance round the room told me that the battle was over – and won. The table was littered with trays of mineralogical sections and open books of reference relating to geology and petrology, and one end was occupied by an outspread geological chart of the British Isles. Thorndyke sat in his armchair, smiling with a bland contentment, and smoking a Trichinopoly cheroot.

"Well," I said cheerfully, "what's the news?"

He removed the cheroot, blew out a cloud of smoke, and replied in a single word: "*Phonolite.*"

"Thank you," I said. "Brevity is the soul of wit. But would you mind amplifying the joke to the dimensions of intelligibility?"

"Certainly," he replied gravely. "I will endeavour to temper the wind to the shorn lamb. You noticed, I suppose, that the fragments of rock of which that worm-tube was built are all alike?"

"All the same kind of rock? No, I did not."

"Well, they are, and I have spent a strenuous hour identifying that rock. It is the peculiar, resonant, volcanic rock known as phonolite, or clink-stone."

"That is very interesting," said I. "And now I see the object of your researches. You hope to get a hint as to the locality where the button has been lying."

"I hoped, as you say, to get a hint, but I have succeeded beyond my expectations. I have been able to fix the locality exactly."

"Have you really?" I exclaimed. "How on earth did you manage that?"

"By a very singular chance," he replied. "It happens that phonolite occurs in two places only in the neighbourhood of the British Isles. One is inland and may be disregarded. The other is the Wolf Rock."

"The rock of which Philip Rodney was speaking?"

"Yes. He said, you remember, that he was afraid that the yacht might drift down on it in the fog. Well, this Wolf Rock is a very remarkable structure. It is what is called a 'volcanic neck,' that is, it is a mass of altered lava that once filled the funnel of a volcano. The volcano has disappeared, but this cast of the funnel remains standing up from the bottom of the sea like a great column. It is a single mass of phonolite, and thus entirely different in composition from the seabed around or anywhere near these islands. But, of course, immediately at its base, the sea-bottom must be covered with decomposed fragments which have fallen from its sides, and it is from these fragments that our *Terebella* has built its tube. So, you see, we can fix the exact locality in which that button has been lying all the months that the tube was building, and we now have a point of departure for fresh investigations."

"But," I said, "this is a very significant discovery, Thorndyke. Shall you tell Rodney?"

"Certainly I shall. But there are one or two questions that I shall ask him first. I have sent him a note inviting him to drop in to-night with his brother, so we had better run round to the club and get some dinner. I said nine o'clock."

It was a quarter-to-nine when we had finished dinner, and ten minutes later we were back in our chambers. Thorndyke made up the fire, placed the chairs hospitably round the hearth, and laid on the table the notes that he had taken at the late interview. Then the Treasury clock struck nine, and within less than a minute our two guests arrived.

"I should apologise," said Thorndyke, as we shook hands, "for my rather peremptory message, but I thought it best to waste no time."

"You certainly have wasted no time," said Rodney, "if you have already extracted its history from the button. Do you keep a tame medium on the premises, or are you a clairvoyant yourself?"

"There is our medium," replied Thorndyke, indicating the microscope standing on a side-table under its bell glass. "The man who uses it becomes to some extent a clairvoyant. But I should like to ask you one or two questions if I may."

Rodney made no secret of his disappointment. "We had hoped," said he, "to hear answers rather than questions. However, as you please."

"Then," said Thorndyke, quite unmoved by Rodney's manner, "I will proceed, and I will begin with the yacht in which Purcell and Varney travelled from Sennen to Penzance. I understand that the yacht belongs to you and was lent by you to these two men?"

Rodney nodded, and Thorndyke then asked, "Has the yacht ever been out of your custody on any other occasion?"

"No," replied Rodney, "excepting on this occasion, one or both of us have always been on board."

Thorndyke made a note of the answer and proceeded. "When you resumed possession of the yacht, did you find her in all respects as you had left her?"

"My dear sir," Rodney exclaimed impatiently, "may I remind you that we are inquiring – if we are inquiring about anything – into the disappearance of a man who was seen to go ashore from this yacht and who certainly never came on board again? The yacht is out of it altogether."

"Nevertheless," said Thorndyke, "I should be glad if you would answer my question."

"Oh, very well," Rodney replied irritably. "Then we found her substantially as we had left her."

"Meaning by 'substantially' – ?"

"Well, they had had to rig a new jib halyard. The old one had parted."

"Did you find the old one on board?"

"Yes, in two pieces, of course."

"Was the whole of it there?"

"I suppose so. We never measured the pieces. But really, sir, these questions seem extraordinarily irrelevant."

"They are not," said Thorndyke. "You will see that presently. I want to know if you missed any rope, cordage, or chain."

Here Philip interposed. "There was some spun-yarn missing. They opened a new ball and used up several yards. I meant to ask Varney what they used it for."

Thorndyke jotted down a note and asked, "Was there any of the ironwork missing? Any anchor, chain, or any other heavy object?"

Rodney shook his head impatiently. but again Philip broke in.

"You are forgetting the ballast-weight, Jack. You see," he continued, addressing Thorndyke, "the yacht is ballasted with half-hundred-weights, and, when we came to take out the ballast to lay her up for the winter, we found one of the weights missing. I have no idea when it disappeared, but there was certainly one short, and neither of us had taken it out."

"Can you," asked Thorndyke, "fix any date on which all the ballast-weights were in place?"

"Yes, I think I can. A few days before Purcell went to Penzance we beached the yacht – she is only a little boat – to give her a scrape. Of course, we had to take out the ballast, and when we launched her again I helped to put it back. I am certain all the weights were there then." Here Jack Rodney, who had been listening with ill-concealed impatience, remarked, "This is all very interesting, sir, but I cannot conceive what bearing it has on the movements of Purcell after he left the yacht."

"It has a most direct and important bearing," said Thorndyke. "Perhaps I had better explain before we go any further. Let me begin by pointing out that this button has been lying for many months at the bottom of the sea at a depth of not less than ten fathoms. That is proved by the worm-tube which has been built on it. Now, as this button is a waterproofed cork, it could not have sunk by itself – it has been sunk by some body to which it was attached, and there is evidence that that body was a very heavy one."

"What evidence is there of that?" asked Rodney.

"There is the fact that it has been lying continuously in one place. A body of moderate weight, as you know, moves about the sea-bottom impelled by currents and tide-streams, but this button has been lying unmoved in one place."

"Indeed," said Rodney with manifest scepticism. "Perhaps you can point out the spot where it has been lying."

"I can," Thorndyke replied. "That button, Mr. Rodney, has been lying all these months at the base of the Wolf Rock."

The two brothers started very perceptibly. They stared at Thorndyke, they looked at one another, and then the lawyer challenged the statement.

"You make this assertion very confidently," he said. "Can you give us any evidence to support it?"

Thorndyke's reply was to produce the button, the section, the test-specimens, the microscope, and the geological chart. In great detail, and with his incomparable lucidity, he assembled the facts, and explained their connection, evolving the unavoidable conclusion.

The different effect of the demonstration on the two men interested me greatly. To the lawyer, accustomed to dealing with verbal and documentary evidence, it manifestly appeared as a far-fetched, rather fantastic argument. Ingenious, amusing, and entirely unconvincing. On Philip, the doctor, it made a profound impression. Accustomed to acting on inferences from facts of his own observing, he gave full weight to each item of evidence, and I could see that his mind was already stretching out to the, as yet unstated, corollaries.

The lawyer was the first to speak. "What inference," he asked, "do you wish us to draw from this very ingenious theory of yours?"

"The inference," Thorndyke replied impassively, "I leave to you, but perhaps it would help you if I recapitulate the facts."

"Perhaps it would," said Rodney.

"Then," said Thorndyke, "I will take them in order. This is the case of a man who was seen to start on a voyage for a given destination in company with one other person. His start out to sea was witnessed by a number of persons. From that moment he was never seen again by any person excepting his one companion. He is said to have reached his destination, but his arrival there rests upon the unsupported verbal testimony of one person, the said companion. Thereafter he vanished utterly, and since then has made no sign of being alive, although there are several persons with whom he could have safely communicated.

"Some eight months later a portion of this man's clothing is found. It bears evidence of having been lying at the bottom of the sea for many months, so that it must have sunk to its resting place within a very short time of the man's disappearance. The place where it has been lying is one over, or near, which the man must have sailed in the yacht. It has been moored to the bottom by some very heavy object, and a very heavy object has disappeared from the yacht. That heavy object had apparently not disappeared when the yacht started, and was not seen on the yacht afterwards. The evidence goes to show that the disappearance of that object coincided in time with the disappearance of the man, and a quantity of cordage disappeared, certainly, on that day. Those are the facts in our possession at present, Mr. Rodney, and I think the inference emerges automatically."

There was a brief silence, during which the two brothers cogitated profoundly and with very disturbed expressions. Then Rodney spoke.

"I am bound to admit, Dr. Thorndyke, that, as a scheme of circumstantial evidence, this is extremely ingenious and complete. It is impossible to mistake your meaning. But you would hardly expect us to charge a highly respectable gentleman of our acquaintance with having murdered his friend and made away with the body on a – well – a rather farfetched theory."

"Certainly not," replied Thorndyke. "But, on the other hand, with this body of circumstantial evidence before us, it is clearly imperative that some further investigations should be made before we speak of the matter to any human soul."

Rodney agreed somewhat grudgingly. "What do you suggest?" he asked.

"I suggest that we thoroughly overhaul the yacht in the first place. Where is she now?"

"Under a tarpaulin in a yard at Battersea. The gear and stores are in a disused workshop in the yard."

"When could we look over her?"

"To-morrow morning, if you like," said Rodney.

"Very well," said Thorndyke. "We will call for you at nine, if that will suit."

It suited perfectly, and the arrangement was accordingly made. A few minutes later the two brothers took their leave, but as they were shaking hands, Philip said suddenly, "There is one little matter that occurs to me. I have only just remembered it, and I don't suppose it is of any consequence, but it is as well to mention everything. You remember my brother saying that one of the jib halyards broke that day?"

"Yes."

"Well, of course, the jib came down and went partly overboard. Now, the next time I hoisted the sail, I noticed a small stain on it, a greenish stain like that of mud, only it wouldn't washout, and it is there still. I meant to ask Varney about it. Stains of that kind on the jib usually come from a bit of mud on the fluke of the anchor, but the anchor was quite clean when I examined it, and besides, it hadn't been down on that day. I thought I'd better tell you about it."

"I'm glad you did," said Thorndyke. "We will have a look at that stain to-morrow. Good-night." Once more he shook hands, and then, reentering the room, stood for quite a long time with his back to the fire, thoughtfully examining the toes of his boots.

We started forth next morning for our rendezvous considerably earlier than seemed necessary. But I made no comment, for Thorndyke was in that state of extreme taciturnity which characterised him whenever he was engaged on an absorbing case with an insufficiency of evidence. I knew that he was turning over and over the facts that he had, and searching for new openings, but I had no clue to the trend of his thoughts until, passing the gateway of Lincoln's Inn, he walked briskly up Chancery Lane into Holborn, and finally halted outside a wholesale druggist's.

"I shan't be more than a few minutes," said he. "Are you coming in?" I was, most emphatically. Questions were forbidden at this stage, but there was no harm in keeping one's ears open, and when I heard his order I was the richer by a distinct clue to his next movements. Tincture of Guaiacum and Ozonic Ether formed a familiar combination, and the size of the bottles indicated the field of investigation.

We found the brothers waiting for us at Lincoln's Inn. They both looked rather hard at the parcel that I was now carrying, and especially at Thorndyke's green canvas-covered research case, but they made no comment, and we set forth at once on the rather awkward cross-country journey to Battersea. Very little was said on the way, but I noticed that both men took our quest more seriously than I had expected, and I judged that they had been talking the case over.

Our journey terminated at a large wooden gate on which Rodney knocked loudly with his stick, whereupon a wicket was opened, and, after a few words of explanation, we passed through into a large yard. Crossing this, we came to a wharf, beyond which was a small stretch of unreclaimed shore, and here, drawn well above high-water mark, a small, double-ended yacht stood on chocks under a tarpaulin cover.

"This is the yacht," said Rodney. "The gear and loose fittings are stored in the workshop behind us. Which will you see first?"

"Let us look at the gear," said Thorndyke, and we turned to the disused workshop into which Rodney admitted us with a key from his pocket. I looked curiously about the long, narrow interior with its prosaic contents, so little suggestive of tragedy or romance. Overhead the yacht's spars rested on the tie-beams, from which hung bunches of blocks. On the floor a long row of neatly-painted half-hundredweights, a pile of chain-cable, two anchors, a stove, and other oddments such as water breakers, buckets, mops, etcetera., and on the long benches at the side, folded sails, locker cushions, side-light lanterns, the binnacle, the cabin lamp, and other more delicate fittings. Thorndyke, too, glanced round inquisitively, and, depositing his case on the bench, asked, "Have you still got the broken jib halyard of which you were telling me?"

"Yes," said Rodney, "it is here under the bench." He drew out a coil of rope and, flinging it on the floor, began to uncoil it, when it separated into two lengths.

"Which are the broken ends?" Thorndyke asked.

"It broke near the middle," said Rodney, "where it chafed on the cleat when the sail was hoisted. This is the one end, you see, frayed out like a brush in breaking, and the other – " He picked up the second half and, passing it rapidly through his hands, held up the end. He did not finish the sentence, but stood with a frown of surprise staring at the rope in his hands.

"This is queer," he said, after a pause. "The broken end has been cut off. Did you cut it off, Phil?"

"No," replied Philip. "It is just as I took it from the locker, where, I suppose, you or Varney stowed it."

"The question is," said Thorndyke, "how much has it been cut off? Do you know the original length of the rope?"

"Yes. Forty-two feet. It is not down in the inventory, but I remember working it out. Let us see how much there is here."

He laid the two lengths of rope along the floor and we measured them with Thorndyke's spring tape. The combined length was exactly thirty-one feet.

"So," said Thorndyke, "there are eleven feet missing, without allowing for the lengthening of the rope by stretching. That is a very important fact."

"What made you suspect that part of the halyard might be missing, as well as the spun-yarn?" Philip asked.

"I did not think," replied Thorndyke, "that a yachtsman would use spun-yarn to lash a half-hundredweight to a corpse. I suspected that the spun-yarn was used for something else. By the way, I see you have a revolver there. Was that on board at the time?"

"Yes," said Rodney. "It was hanging on the cabin bulkhead. Be careful. I don't think it has been unloaded."

Thorndyke opened the breech of the revolver, and dropping the cartridges into his hand, peered down the barrel and into each chamber separately.

"It is quite clean inside," he remarked. Then, glancing at the ammunition in his hand, "I notice," said he, "that these cartridges are not all alike. There is one Curtis and Harvey, and five Eleys."

Philip looked with a distinctly startled expression at the little heap of cartridges in Thorndyke's hand, and picking out the odd one, examined it with knitted brows.

"When did you fire the revolver last, Jack?" he asked, looking up at his brother.

"On the day when we potted at those champagne bottles," was the reply.

Philip raised his eyebrows. "Then," said he, "this is a very remarkable affair. I distinctly remember on that occasion, when we had sunk all the bottles, reloading the revolver with Eleys, and that there were then three cartridges left over in the bag. When I had loaded I opened the new box of Curtis and Harvey's, upped them into the bag and threw the box overboard."

"Did you clean the revolver?" asked Thorndyke.

"No, I didn't. I mean to do it later, but forgot to."

"But," said Thorndyke, "it has undoubtedly been cleaned, and very thoroughly. Shall we check the cartridges in the bag? There ought to be forty-nine Curtis and Harvey's and three Eleys if what you tell us is correct."

Philip searched among the raffle on the bench and produced a small linen bag. Untying the string, he shot out on the bench a heap of cartridges which he counted one by one. There were fifty-two in all, and three of them were Eleys.

"Then," said Thorndyke, "it comes to this: Since you used that revolver, it has been used by someone else. That someone fired only a single shot, after which he carefully cleaned the barrel and reloaded. Incidentally, he seems to have known where the cartridge bag was kept, but did not know about the change in the make of the cartridges. You notice," he added, looking at Rodney, "that the circumstantial evidence accumulates."

"I do, indeed," Rodney replied gloomily.

"Is there anything else that you wish to examine?"

"Yes. There is the sail. You spoke of a stain on the jib. Shall we see if we can make anything of that?"

"I don't think you will make much of it," said Philip. "It is very faint. However, you shall see it." He picked out one of the bundles of white duck and, while he was unfolding it, Thorndyke dragged an empty bench into the middle of the floor under the skylight. Over this the sail was spread so that the mysterious mark was in the middle of the bench. It was very inconspicuous, just a faint, grey-green, wavy line like the representation of an island on a map. We all looked at it attentively for a few moments, and then Thorndyke said, "Would you mind if I made a further stain on the sail? I should like to apply some re-agents."

"Of course, you must do what is necessary," said Rodney. "The evidence is more important than the sail."

Accordingly Thorndyke unpacked our parcel, and as the two bottles emerged, Philip read the labels with evident surprise, remarking, "I shouldn't have thought the Guaiacum Test would have been of any use after all these months."

"It will act, I think, if the pigment is there," said Thorndyke, and as he spoke he poured a quantity of the tincture – which he had ordered diluted to our usual working strength – on the middle of the stained area. The pool of liquid rapidly spread considerably beyond the limits of the stain, growing paler as it extended. Then Thorndyke cautiously dropped small quantities of the Ether at various points around the stained area and watched closely as the two liquids mingled in the fabric of the sail.

557

Gradually the Ether spread towards the stain, and, first at one point and then at another, approached and finally crossed the wavy grey line, and at each point the same change occurred: First, the faint grey line turned into a strong blue line, and then the colour extended to the enclosed space, until the entire area of the stain stood out, a conspicuous blue patch.

Philip and Thorndyke looked at one another significantly, and the latter said, "You understand the meaning of this reaction, Mr. Rodney. This is a bloodstain, and a very care-fully washed bloodstain."

"So I supposed," Rodney replied, and for a while we were all silent. There was something very dramatic and solemn in the sudden appearance of this staring blue patch on the sail, with the sinister message that it brought. But what followed was more dramatic still. As we stood silently regarding the blue stain, the mingled liquids continued to spread, and suddenly, at the extreme edge of the wet area, we became aware of a new spot of blue. At first a mere speck, it grew slowly as the liquid spread over the canvas into a small oval, and then a second Spot appeared by its side,

At this point Thorndyke poured out a fresh charge of the tincture, and when it had soaked into the cloth, cautiously applied a sprinkling of Ether. Instantly the blue spots began to elongate, fresh spots and patches appeared, and as they ran together there sprang out of the blank surface the clear impression of a hand – a left hand, complete in all its details excepting the third finger, which was represented by an oval spot at some two-thirds of its length.

The dreaded significance of this apparition and the uncanny and mysterious manner of its emergence from the white surface impressed us so that for a while none of us spoke. At length I ventured to remark on the absence of the impression of the third finger.

"I think," said Thorndyke, "that the impression is there. That spot looks like the mark of a finger-tip, and its position rather suggests a finger with a stiff joint."

As he made this statement, both brothers simultaneously uttered a smothered exclamation.

Thorndyke looked up at them sharply. "What is it?" he asked.

The two men looked at one another with an expression of awe. Then Rodney said in a hushed voice, hardly above a whisper, "Varney, the man who was with Purcell on the yacht – he has a stiff joint on the third finger of his left hand."

There was nothing more to say. The case was complete. The keystone had been laid in the edifice of circumstantial evidence. The investigation was at an end.

After an interval of silence, during which Thorndyke was busily writing up his notes, Rodney asked, "What is to be done now? Shall I swear an information?"

Thorndyke shook his head. No man was more expert in accumulating circumstantial evidence – none was more loth to rely on it.

"A murder charge," said he, "should be supported by proof of death and, if possible, by production of the body."

"But the body is at the bottom of the sea!"

"True. But we know its whereabouts. It is a small area, with the lighthouse as a landmark. If that area were systematically worked over with a trawl or dredge, or better still, with a creeper, there should be a very good chance of recovering the body, or, at least, the clothing and the weight."

Rodney reflected for a few moments. "I think you are right," he said at length. "The thing is practicable, and it is our duty to do it. I suppose you couldn't come down and help us?"

"Not now. But in a few days the spring vacation will commence, and then Jervis and I could join you, if the weather were suitable."

"Thank you both," replied Rodney. "We will make the arrangements, and let you know when we are ready."

It was quite early on a bright April morning when the two Rodneys, Thorndyke, and I steamed out of Penzance Harbour in a small open launch. The sea was very calm for the time of year, the sky was of a warm blue, and a gentle breeze stole out of the north-east. Over the launch's side hung a long spar, secured to a tow-rope by a bridle, and to the spar were attached a number of creepers – lengths of chain fitted with rows of hooks. The outfit further included a spirit compass, provided with sights, a sextant, and a hand-lead.

"It's lucky we didn't run up against Varney in the town," Philip remarked as the harbour dwindled in the distance.

"Varney!" exclaimed Thorndyke. "Do you mean that he lives at Penzance?"

"He keeps rooms there, and spends most of his spare time down in this part. He was always keen on sea-fishing, and he's keener than ever now. He keeps a boat of his own, too. It's queer, isn't it, if what we think is true?"

"Very," said Thorndyke, and by his meditative manner I judge that circumstances afforded him matter for curious speculation.

As we passed abreast of the Land's End, and the solitary lighthouse rose ahead on the verge of the horizon, we began to overtake the scattered members of a fleet of luggers, home with lowered mainsails and hand-lines down, others with their black sails set, heading for a more distant fishing-ground. Threading our way among them, we suddenly became aware that one of the smaller luggers was heading so as to close in on us. Rodney, observing this, was putting over the helm to avoid her when a seafaring voice from the little craft hailed us.

"Launch ahoy there! Gentleman aboard wants to speak to you."

We looked at one another significantly and in some confusion, and meanwhile our solitary "hand" – seaman, engineer, and fireman combined – without waiting for orders, shut off steam. The lugger closed in rapidly and of a sudden there appeared, holding on by the mainstay, a small dark fellow who hailed us cheerfully. "Hullo, you fellows! Whither away? What's your game?"

"God!" exclaimed Philip. "It's Varney. Sheer off, Jack! Don't let him come alongside."

But it was too late. The launch had lost way and failed to answer the helm. The lugger sheered in, sweeping abreast of us within a foot and, as she crept past, Varney sprang lightly from her gunwale and dropped neatly on the side bench in our stern sheets.

"Where are you off to?" he asked. "You can't be going out to fish in this baked-potato can?"

"No," faltered Rodney, "we're not. We're going to do some dredging – or rather – "

Here Thorndyke came to his assistance. "Marine worms," said he, "are the occasion of this little voyage. There seem to be some very uncommon ones on the bottom at the base of the Wolf Rock. I have seen some in a collection, and I want to get a few more if I can."

It was a skillfully-worded explanation, and I could see that, for the time, Varney accepted it. But from the moment when the Wolf Rock was mentioned all his vivacity of manner died out. In an instant he had become grave, thoughtful, and a trifle uneasy.

The introductions over, he reverted to the subject. He questioned us closely, especially as to our proposed methods. And it was impossible to evade his questions. There were the creepers in full view, there was the compass and the sextant, and presently these appliances would have to be put in use. Gradually, as the nature of our operations dawned on him, his manner changed more and more. A horrible pallor overspread his face, and a terrible restlessness took possession of him.

Rodney, who was navigating, brought the launch to within a quarter-of-a-mile of the rock, and then, taking cross-bearings on the lighthouse and a point of land, directed us to lower the creepers.

It was a most disagreeable experience for us all. Varney, pale and clammy, fidgeted about the boat, now silent and moody, now almost hysterically boisterous. Thorndyke watched him furtively and, I think, judged by his manner how near we were to the object of our search.

Calm as the day was, the sea was breaking heavily over the rock, and as we worked in closer the water around boiled and eddied in an unpleasant and even dangerous manner. The three keepers in the gallery of the lighthouse watched us through their glasses, and one of them bellowed to us through a megaphone to keep further away.

"What do you say?" asked Rodney. "It's a bit risky here, with the rock right under our lee. Shall we try another side?"

"Better try one more cast this side," said Thorndyke, and he spoke so definitely that we all, including Varney, looked at him curiously. But no one answered, and the creepers were dropped for a fresh cast still nearer the rock. We were then north of the lighthouse, and headed south so as to pass the rock on its east side. As we approached, the man with the megaphone bawled out fresh warnings, and continued to roar at us until we were abreast of the rock in a wild tumble of confused waves.

At this moment Philip, who held the towline with a single turn round a cleat, said that he felt a pull, but that it seemed as if the creepers had broken away. As soon, therefore, as we were out of the backwash into smooth water, we hauled in the linen to examine the creepers.

I looked over the side eagerly, for something new in Thorndyke's manner impressed me. Varney, too, who had hitherto taken little notice of the creepers, now knelt on the side bench, gazing earnestly into the clear water, when the tow-rope was rising.

At length the beam came in sight, and below it, on one of the creepers, a yellowish object, dimly seen through the wavering water.

"There's somethin' on this time," said the engineer, craning over the side. He shut off steam and, with the rest of us, watched the incoming creeper. I looked at Varney, kneeling on the bench apart from us, not fidgeting now, but still rigid, pale as wax, and staring with dreadful fascination at the slowly-rising object.

Suddenly the engineer uttered an exclamation. "Why, 'tis a sou'wester, and all laced about wi' spuny'n. Surely 'tis – Hi! Steady, sir! My God!"

There was a heavy splash, and as Rodney rushed forward for the boat-hook I saw Varney rapidly sinking head first through the clear, blue-green water, dragged down by the hand-lead that he had hitched to his waist. By the time Rodney was back he was far out of reach, but for a long time, as it seemed, we could see him sinking, sinking, growing paler, more shadowy, more shapeless, but always steadily following the lead sinker, until at last he faded from our sight into the darkness of the ocean.

561

Not until he had vanished did we haul on board the creeper with its dreadful burden. Indeed, we never hauled it on board, for as Philip, with an unsteady hand, unhooked the sou'wester hat from the creeper, the encircling coils of spun-yarn slipped, and from inside the hat a skull dropped into the water and sank. We watched it grow green and pallid and small, until it vanished, as Varney had vanished. Then Philip turned and flung the hat down in the bottom of the boat. Thorndyke picked it up and unwound the spun-yarn.

"Do you identify it?" he asked, and then, as he turned it over, he added, "But I see it identifies itself." He held it towards me, and I read in embroidered letters on the silk lining, "*Dan Purcell*".

The Art of the
Detective Story
by R. Austin Freeman

The status in the world of letters of that type of fiction which find its principal motive in the unravelment of crimes or similar intricate mysteries presents certain anomalies. By the critic and the professedly literary person the detective story – to adopt the unprepossessing name by which this class of fiction is now universally known – is apt to be dismissed contemptuously as outside the pale of literature, to be conceived of as a type of work produced by half-educated and wholly incompetent writers for consumption by office boys, factory girls, and other persons devoid of culture and literary taste.

That such works are produced by such writers for such readers is an undeniable truth, but in mere badness of quality the detective story holds no monopoly. By similar writers and for similar readers there are produced love stories, romances, and even historical tales of no better quality. But there is this difference: That, whereas the place in literature of the love story or the romance has been determined by the consideration of the masterpieces of each type, the detective story appears to have been judged by its failures. The status of the whole class has been fixed by an estimate formed from inferior samples.

What is the explanation of this discrepancy? Why is it that, whereas a bad love story or romance is condemned merely on its merits as a defective specimen of a respectable class, a detective story is apt to be condemned without trial in virtue of some sort of assumed original sin? The assumption as to the class of reader is manifestly untrue. There is no type of fiction that is more universally popular than the detective story. It is a familiar fact that many famous men have found in this kind of reading their favourite recreation, and that it is consumed with pleasure, and even with enthusiasm, by many learned and intellectual men, not infrequently in preference to any other form of fiction.

This being the case, I again ask for an explanation of the contempt in which the whole genus of detective fiction is held by the professedly literary. Clearly, a form of literature which arouses the enthusiasm of men of intellect and culture can be affected by no inherently base quality. It cannot be foolish, and is unlikely to be immoral. As a matter of fact, it is neither. The explanation is probably to be found in the great proportion of failures, in the tendency of the tyro and the amateur perversely to adopt this difficult and intricate form for their 'prentice efforts, in the crude literary technique often associated with otherwise satisfactory productions, and perhaps in the falling off in quality of the work of regular novelists when they experiment in this department of fiction, to which they may be adapted neither by temperament nor by training.

Thus critical judgment has been formed, not on what the detective story can be and should be, but on what it too frequently was in the past when crudely and incompetently done. Unfortunately, this type of work is still prevalent, but it is not representative. In late years there has arisen a new school of writers who, taking the detective story seriously, have set a more exacting standard, and whose work, admirable alike in construction and execution, probably accounts for the recent growth in popularity of this class of fiction. But, though representative, they are a minority, and it is still true that a detective story which fully develops the distinctive qualities proper to its genus, and is, in addition, satisfactory in diction, in background treatment, in characterization, and in general literary workmanship is probably the rarest of all forms of fiction.

The rarity of good detective fiction is to be explained by a fact which appears to be little recognized either by critics or by authors, the fact, namely, that a completely executed detective story is a very difficult and highly technical work, a work demanding in its creator the union of qualities which, if not mutually antagonistic, are at least seldom met with united in a single individual. On the one hand, it is a work of imagination, demanding the creative, artistic faculty. On the other, it is a work of ratiocination, demanding the power of logical analysis and subtle and acute reasoning, and, added to these inherent qualities, there must be a somewhat extensive outfit of special knowledge. Evidence alike of the difficulty of the work and the failure to realize it is furnished by those occasional experiments of novelists of the orthodox kind which have been referred to, experiments which commonly fail by reason of a complete misunderstanding of the nature of the work and the qualities that it should possess.

A widely prevailing error is that a detective story needs to be highly sensational. It tends to be confused with the mere crime story, in which the incidents – tragic, horrible, even repulsive – form the actual theme, and the quality aimed at is horror – crude and pungent sensationalism. Here the writer's object is to make the reader's flesh creep, and since that reader has probably, by a course of similar reading, acquired a somewhat extreme degree of obtuseness, the violence of the means has to be progressively increased in proportion to the insensitiveness of the subject. The sportsman in the juvenile verse sings:

I shoot the hippopotamus with bullets made of platinum
Because if I use leaden ones his hide is sure to flatten 'em.

. . . and that, in effect, is the position of the purveyor of gross sensationalism. His purpose is, at all costs, to penetrate his reader's mental epidermis, to the density of which he must needs adjust the weight and velocity of his literary projectile.

Now no serious author will complain of the critic's antipathy to mere sensationalism. It is a quality that is attainable by the least gifted writer and acceptable to the least critical reader, and, unlike the higher qualities of literature, which beget in the reader an increased receptiveness and more subtle appreciation, it creates, as do drugs and stimulants, a tolerance which has to be met by an increase of the dose. The entertainments of the cinema have to be conducted on a scale of continually increasing sensationalism. The wonders that thrilled at first become commonplace, and must be reinforced by marvels yet more astonishing. Incident must be piled on incident, climax on climax, until any kind of construction becomes impossible. So, too, in literature. In the newspaper serial of the conventional type, each instalment of a couple-of-thousand words, or less, must wind up with a thrilling climax, blandly ignored at the opening of the next instalment, while that *ne plus ultra* of wild sensationalism, the film novel, in its extreme form is no more than a string of astonishing incidents, unconnected by any intelligible scheme, each incident an independent "thrill", unexplained, unprepared for, devoid alike of antecedents and consequences.

Some productions of the latter type are put forth in the guise of detective stories, with which they apparently tend to be confused by some critics. They are then characterized by the presentation of a crime – often in impossible circumstances which are never accounted for – followed by a vast amount of rushing to-and-fro of detectives or unofficial investigators in motor cars, aeroplanes, or motor boats, with a liberal display of revolvers or automatic pistols and a succession of hair-raising adventures. If any conclusion is reached, it is quite unconvincing, and the interest of the story to its appropriate reader is in the incidental matter, and not in the plot. But the application of the term "detective story" to works of this kind is misleading, for in the essential qualities of the type of fiction properly so designated they are entirely deficient. Let us now consider what those qualities are.

The distinctive quality of a detective story, in which it differs from all other types of fiction, is that the satisfaction that it offers to the reader is primarily an intellectual satisfaction. This is not to say that it need be deficient in the other qualities appertaining to good fiction: In grace of

565

diction, in humour, in interesting characterization, in picturesqueness of setting or in emotional presentation. On the contrary, it should possess all these qualities. It should be an interesting story, well and vivaciously told. But whereas in other fiction these are the primary, paramount qualities, in detective fiction they are secondary and subordinate to the intellectual interest, to which they must be, if necessary, sacrificed. The entertainment that the connoisseur looks for is an exhibition of mental gymnastics in which he is invited to take part, and the excellence of the entertainment must be judged by the completeness with which it satisfies the expectations of the type of reader to whom it is addressed.

Thus, assuming that good detective fiction must be good fiction in general terms, we may dismiss those qualities which it should possess in common with all other works of imagination and give our attention to those qualities in which it differs from them and which give to it its special character. I have said that the satisfaction which it is designed to yield to the reader is primarily intellectual, and we may now consider in somewhat more detail the exact nature of the satisfaction demanded and the way in which it can best be supplied. And first we may ask: What are the characteristics of the representative reader? To what kind of person is a carefully constructed detective story especially addressed?

We have seen that detective fiction has a wide popularity. The general reader, however, is apt to be uncritical. He reads impartially the bad and the good, with no very clear perception of the difference, at least in the technical construction. The real connoisseurs, who avowedly prefer this type of fiction to all others, and who read it with close and critical attention, are to be found among men of the definitely intellectual class: Theologians, scholars, lawyers, and to a less extent, perhaps, doctors and men of science. Judging by the letters which I have received from time to time, the enthusiast par excellence is the clergyman of a studious and scholarly habit.

Now the theologian, the scholar, and the lawyer have a common characteristic: They are all men of a subtle type of mind. They find a pleasure in intricate arguments, in dialectical contests, in which the matter to be proved is usually of less consideration than the method of proving it. The pleasure is yielded by the argument itself and tends to be proportionate to the intricacy of the proof. The disputant enjoys the mental exercise, just as a muscular man enjoys particular kinds of physical exertion. But the satisfaction yielded by an argument is dependent upon a strict conformity with logical methods, upon freedom from fallacies of reasoning, and especially upon freedom from any ambiguities as to the data.

By schoolboys, street-corner debaters, and other persons who are ignorant of the principles of discussion, debates are commonly conducted by means of what we may call "argument by assertion". Each disputant seeks to overwhelm his opponent by pelting him with statements of alleged fact, each of which the other disputes, and replies by discharging a volley of counterstatements, the truth of which is promptly denied. Thus the argument collapses in a chaos of conflicting assertions. The method of the skilled dialectician is exactly the opposite of this. He begins by making sure of the matter in dispute and by establishing agreement with his adversary on the fundamental data. Theological arguments are usually based upon propositions admitted as true by both parties, and the arguments of counsel are commonly concerned, not with questions of fact, but with the consequences deducible from evidence admitted equally by both sides.

Thus the intellectual satisfaction of an argument is conditional on the complete establishment of the data. Disputes on questions of fact are of little, if any, intellectual interest, but in any case an argument – an orderly train of reasoning – cannot begin until the data have been clearly set forth and agreed upon by both parties. This very obvious truth is continually lost sight of by authors. Plots, *i.e.*, arguments, are frequently based upon alleged "facts" – physical, chemical, and other – which the educated reader knows to be untrue, and of which the untruth totally invalidates conclusions drawn from them and thus destroys the intellectual interest of the argument.

The other indispensable factor is freedom from fallacies of reasoning. The conclusion must emerge truly and inevitably from the premises, it must be the only possible conclusion, and must leave the competent reader in no doubt as to its unimpeachable truth.

It is here that detective stories most commonly fail. They tend to be pervaded by logical fallacies, and especially by the fallacy of the undistributed middle term. The conclusion reached by the gifted investigator, and offered by him as inevitable, is seen by the reader to be merely one of a number of possible alternatives. The effect when the author's "must have been" has to be corrected by the reader into "might have been" is one of anti-climax. The promised and anticipated demonstration peters out into a mere suggestion, the argument is left in the air and the reader is balked of the intellectual satisfaction which he was seeking.

Having glanced at the nature of the satisfaction sought by the reader, we may now examine the structure of a detective story and observe the means employed to furnish that satisfaction. On the general fictional qualities of such a story we need not enlarge excepting to contest the prevalent belief that detective fiction possesses no such qualities. Apart from a sustained love interest – for which there is usually no room – a detective novel need not, and should not, be inferior in narrative interest or literary workmanship to any other work of fiction. Interests which conflict with the main theme and hinder its clear exposition are evidently inadmissible, but humour, picturesque setting, vivid characterization and even emotional episodes are not only desirable on aesthetic grounds, but, if skilfully used, may be employed to distract the reader's attention at critical moments in place of the nonsensical "false clues" and other exasperating devices by which writers too often seek to confuse the issues. *The Mystery of Edwin Drood* shows us the superb fictional quality that is possible in a detective story from the hand of a master.

Turning now to the technical side, we note that the plot of a detective novel is, in effect, an argument conducted under the guise of fiction. But it is a peculiar form of argument. The problem having been stated, the data for its solution are presented inconspicuously and in a sequence purposely dislocated so as to conceal their connexion, and the reader's task is to collect the data, to rearrange them in their correct logical sequence, and ascertain their relations, when the solution of the problem should at once become obvious. The construction thus tends to fall into four stages: (1) Statement of the problem; (2) Production of the data for its solution ("clues"); (3) The discovery, *i.e.*, completion of the inquiry by the investigator and declaration by him of the solution; (4) Proof of the solution by an exposition of the evidence.

1.   The problem is usually concerned with a crime, not because a crime is an attractive subject, but because it forms the most natural occasion for an investigation of the kind required. For the same reason – suitability – crime against the person is more commonly adopted than crime against property, and murder – actual, attempted or suspected – is usually the most suitable of all. For the villain is *the player on the other side*, and since we want him to be a desperate player, the stakes must be appropriately high. A capital crime gives us an adversary who is playing for his life, and who consequently furnishes the best subject for dramatic treatment.

2.   The body of the work should be occupied with the telling of the story, in the course of which the data, or "clues", should be produced as inconspicuously as possible, but clearly and without ambiguity in regard to their essentials. The author should be scrupulously fair in his conduct of the game. Each card as it is played should be set down squarely, face

upwards, in full view of the reader. Under no circumstances should there be any deception as to the facts. The reader should be quite clear as to what he may expect as true. In stories of the older type, the middle action is filled out with a succession of false clues and with the fixing of suspicion first on one character, then on another, and again on a third, and so on. The clues are patiently followed, one after another, and found to lead nowhere. There is feverish activity, but no result. All this is wearisome to the reader and is, in my opinion, bad technique.

My practice is to avoid false clues entirely and to depend on keeping the reader occupied with the narrative. If the ice should become uncomfortably thin, a dramatic episode will distract the reader's attention and carry him safely over the perilous spot. Devices to confuse and mislead the reader are bad practice. They deaden the interest, and they are quite unnecessary. The reader can always be trusted to mislead himself, no matter how plainly the data are given.

Some years ago I devised, as an experiment, an inverted detective story in two parts ["The Case of Oscar Brodski"]. The first part was a minute and detailed description of a crime, setting forth the antecedents, motives, and all attendant circumstances. The reader had seen the crime committed, knew all about the criminal, and was in possession of all the facts. It would have seemed that there was nothing left to tell. But I calculated that the reader would be so occupied with the crime that he would overlook the evidence. And so it turned out. The second part, which described the investigation of the crime, had to most readers the effect of new matter. All the facts were known, but their evidential quality had not been recognized.

This failure of the reader to perceive the evidential value of facts is the foundation on which detective fiction is built. It may generally be taken that the author may exhibit his facts fearlessly provided only that he exhibits them separately and unconnected. And the more boldly he displays the data, the greater will be the intellectual interest of the story. For the tacit understanding of the author with the reader is that the problem is susceptible of solution by the latter by reasoning from the facts given, and such solution should be actually possible. Then the data should be produced as early in the story as is practicable. The reader should have a body of evidence to consider while the tale is telling. The production of a leading fact near the end of the book is unfair to the reader, while the introduction of capital evidence – such as that of an eye-witness – at the extreme end is radically bad technique, amounting to a breach of the implied covenant with the reader.

3.   The "discovery", *i.e.*, the announcement by the investigator of the conclusion reached by him, brings the inquiry formally to an end. It is totally inadmissible thereafter to introduce any new matter. The reader is given to understand that he now has before him the evidence and the conclusion, and that the latter is contained in the former. If it is not, the construction has failed, and the reader has been cheated. The "discovery" will usually come as a surprise to the reader and will thus form the dramatic climax of the story, but it is to be noted that the dramatic quality of the climax is strictly dependent on the intellectual conviction which accompanies it. This is frequently overlooked, especially by general novelists who experiment in detective fiction. In their eagerness to surprise the reader, they forget that he has also to be convinced. A literary friend of mine, commenting on a particularly conclusive detective story, declared that "the rigid demonstration destroyed the artistic effect." But the rigid demonstration was the artistic effect. The entire dramatic effect of the climax of a detective story is due to the sudden recognition by the reader of the significance of a number of hitherto uncomprehended facts, or if such recognition should not immediately occur, the effect of the climax becomes suspended until it is completed in the final stage.

4.   Proof of the solution. This is peculiar to "detective" construction. In all ordinary novels, the climax, or denouement, finishes the story, and any continuation is anti-climax. But a detective story has a dual character. There is the story, with its dramatic interest, and enclosed in it, so to speak, is the logical problem, and the climax of the former may leave the latter apparently unsolved. It is then the duty

of the author, through the medium of the investigator, to prove the solution by an analysis and exposition of the evidence. He has to demonstrate to the reader that the conclusion emerged naturally and reasonably from the facts known to him, and that no other conclusion was possible.

If it is satisfactorily done, this is to the critical reader usually the most interesting part of the book, and it is the part by which he – very properly – judges the quality of the whole work. Too often it yields nothing but disappointment and a sense of anticlimax. The author is unable to solve his own problem. Acting on the pernicious advice of the pilot in the old song to "*Fear not, but trust in Providence,*" he has piled up his mysteries in the hope of being able to find a plausible explanation, and now, when he comes to settle his account with the reader, his logical assets are nil. What claims to be a demonstration turns out to be a mere specious attempt to persuade the reader that the inexplicable has been explained, that the fortunate guesses of an inspired investigator are examples of genuine reasoning.

A typical instance of this kind of anti-climax occurs in Poe's "Murders in the Rue Morgue" when Dupin follows the unspoken thoughts of his companion and joins in at the appropriate moment. The reader is astonished and marvels how such an apparently impossible feat could have been performed. Then Dupin explains, but his explanation is totally unconvincing, and the impossibility remains. The reader has had his astonishment for nothing. It cannot be too much emphasized that to the critical reader the quality in a detective story which takes precedence of all others is conclusiveness. It is the quality which, above all others, yields that intellectual satisfaction that the reader seeks, and it is the quality which is the most difficult to attain, and which costs more than any other in care and labour to the author.

About the Author

Richard Austin Freeman was born on April 11th, 1862 in the Soho district of London. He was the son of a skilled tailor and the youngest of five children. As he grew, it was expected that he would become a tailor as well, but instead he had an interest in natural history and medicine, and so he obtained employment in a pharmacist's shop. While there, he qualified as an apothecary and could have gone on to manage the shop, but instead he began to study medicine at Middlesex Hospital.

Austin Freeman qualified as a physician in 1887, and in that same year he married. Faced with the twin facts of his new marital responsibilities and his very limited resources as a young doctor, he made the unusual decision to join the Colonial Service, spending the next seven years in Africa as an Assistant Colonial Surgeon. This continued until the early 1890's, when he contracted Blackwater Fever, an illness that eventually forced him to leave the service and return permanently to England.

For several years, he served as a *locum tenens* for various physicians, a bleak time in his life as he moved from job to job, his income low, and his health never quite recovered. However, he supplemented his meager income and exercised his creativity during these years by beginning to write. His early publications included *Travels and Live in Ashanti and Jaman* (1898), recounting some of his African sojourns.

In 1900, Freeman obtained work as an assistant to Dr. John James Pitcairn (1860-1936) at Holloway Prison. Although he wasn't there for very long, the association between the two men was enough to turn Freeman's attention toward writing mysteries. Over the next few years, they co-wrote several under the pseudonym *Clifford Ashdown*, including *The Adventures of Romney Pringle* (1902), *The Further Adventures of Romney Pringle* (1903), *From a Surgeon's Diary* (1904-1905), and *The Queen's Treasure* (written around 1905-1906, and published posthumously in 1975.)

In approximately 1904, Freeman began developing a mystery novella based on a short job that he had held at the Western Ophthalmic Hospital. This effort, "31 New Inn", was published in 1905, and it is the true first Dr. Thorndyke story. In 1907, the first Thorndyke novel, *The Red Thumb Mark*, was published.

From Thorndyke's creation until 1914, Freeman wrote four novels and two volumes of short stories. Then, with the commencement of the First World War, he entered military service. In February 1915, at the age of fifty-two, he joined the Royal Army Medical Corps. Due to his health, which had never entirely recovered from his time in Africa, he spent the duration of the war involved with various aspects of the ambulance corps, having been promoted very early to the rank of Captain. He wrote nothing about Thorndyke during this period, but he did publish one book concerning the adventures of a scoundrel, *The Exploits of Danby Croker* (1916).

Following the war, he resumed his previous life, writing approximately one Thorndyke novel per year, as well as three more volumes of Thorndyke short stories and a number of other unrelated items, until his death on September 28th, 1943 – likely related to Parkinson's Disease, which had plagued him in later years. He is buried in Gravesend.

The MX Book of New Sherlock Holmes Stories
Edited by David Marcum
(MX Publishing, 2015-   )

Also From MX Publishing

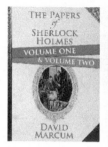 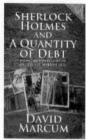 

Sherlock Holmes in Montague Street
by Arthur Morrison
Edited, Holmes-ed, and with Original Material
by David Marcum

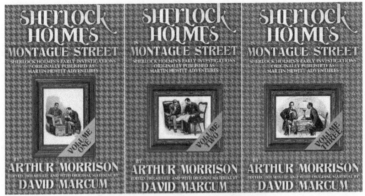

Separate Paperback Editions

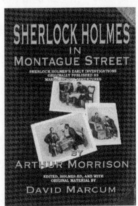

Combined Hardcover Edition

"It's been suggested that Hewitt was the young Mycroft Holmes,
but David Marcum has a more plausible and attractive theory
– that he was Sherlock, early in his career as an investigator
. . . these are remarkably convincing in their new guise."
– Roger Johnson, Editor, *The Sherlock Holmes Journal,*
The Sherlock Holmes Society of London

Thanks to all the Kickstarter backers,
especially
The Mysterious Debra Werth
for their support.

579

MX Publishing

MX Publishing is the world's largest specialist Sherlock Holmes publisher, with several hundred titles and over a hundred authors creating the latest in Sherlock Holmes fiction and non-fiction.

From traditional short stories and novels to travel guides and quiz books, MX Publishing caters to all Holmes fans.

The collection includes leading titles such as *Benedict Cumberbatch In Transition* and *The Norwood Author*, which won the 2011 *Tony Howlett Award* (Sherlock Holmes Book of the Year).

MX Publishing also has one of the largest communities of Holmes fans on *Facebook*, with regular contributions from dozens of authors.

www.mxpublishing.co.uk (UK) and *www.mxpublishing.com* (USA)